D0323343

The Color of Summer

Also by Reinaldo Arenas

~

SINGING FROM THE WELL

THE PALACE OF THE WHITE SKUNKS

FAREWELL TO THE SEA

THE ASSAULT

THE ILL-FATED PEREGRINATIONS OF
FRAY SERVANDO

BEFORE NIGHT FALLS: A MEMOIR

Reinaldo Arenas

THE COLOR OF SUMMER

~ *or* ~

The New Garden of Earthly Delights

Translated from the Spanish
by Andrew Hurley

VIKING

VIKING
Published by the Penguin Group
Penguin Putnam Inc., 375 Hudson Street,
New York, New York 10014, U.S.A.
Penguin Books Ltd, 27 Wrights Lane, London W8 5TZ, England
Penguin Books Australia Ltd, Ringwood, Victoria, Australia
Penguin Books Canada Ltd, 10 Alcorn Avenue,
Toronto, Ontario, Canada M4V 3B2
Penguin Books (N.Z.) Ltd, 182–190 Wairau Road,
Auckland 10, New Zealand

Penguin Books Ltd, Registered Offices:
Harmondsworth, Middlesex, England

First published in 2000 by Viking Penguin,
a member of Penguin Putnam Inc.

1 3 5 7 9 10 8 6 4 2

Originally published in Spanish as *El color del verano* by
Ediciones Universal, Miami, Florida.

PUBLISHER'S NOTE

This is a work of fiction. Names, characters, places, and incidents either are the product of the author's imagination or are used fictitiously, and any resemblance to actual persons, living or dead, business establishments, events, or locales is entirely coincidental.

LIBRARY OF CONGRESS CATALOGING-IN-PUBLICATION DATA
Arenas, Reinaldo, 1943–1990.
[Color del verano. English]
The color of summer, or, The new garden of earthly delights / Reinaldo Arenas;
translated from the Spanish by Andrew Hurley.
p. cm.
ISBN 0-670-84065-3
1. Cuba—Politics and government—Fiction. I. Title : Color of summer.
II. Title : New garden of earthly delights. III. Hurley, Andrew. IV. Title.

PQ7390.A72 C5513 2000
863—dc21 99-055698

This book is printed on acid-free paper.

Printed in the United States of America
Set in Granjon
Designed by Kathryn Parise

Because I'll tell you, anywhere there are this many whores,
you can't make a single one of 'em follow orders.

Carajicomedia

Notice

~

The author of this work is solely responsible, both in life and in death, for the ideas and opinions contained herein, and expressly relieves his publisher, estate, translator, and literary agent of any liability that might arise out of the publication of this volume.

To the Judge

~

Whoa, girl, just hold it right there. Before you start going through these pages looking for things to have me thrown in jail for, I want you to try to remember that you're reading a work of fiction here, so the characters in it are made up—they're concoctions, denizens of the world of imagination (literary figures, parodies, metaphors—*you* know), not real-life people. And another thing, my dear, while we're at it—I wrote this novel in 1990 and set it in 1999. I mean think about it—how fair would it be to haul me into court for a bunch of fictitious stuff that when it was written down hadn't even happened yet?

The Author

CONTENTS

THE COLOR OF SUMMER

Notice to the Audience

Extremely important. Please read.

Before the play begins, we are obliged by law to advise all persons wishing to attend the play that the rules of the drama require that one spectator be chosen from the audience to be shot and killed during the performance. Neither management nor author assumes any resposibility for this voluntary death.

All persons are hereby notified that entering the theater may result in their death by gunshot.

For insurance purposes, upon purchase of a ticket of admission each spectator is required to sign in the space below, attesting that he or she understands these conditions and agrees to abide by them.

I have read the paragraphs above and understand them. I am aware that attending this play may result in the loss of my life by gunshot during the performance, and by signing below I agree to accept that condition of my attendance.

____

Name of audience member, date

____

Address

The Flight of Gertrudis Gómez de Avellaneda

A light comedy in one act

(of repudiation)

SETTINGS: The Antilles and their surrounding waters (the Atlantic Ocean and the Caribbean Sea)
Key West
The Malecón in Havana.

TIME: July 1999.

DRAMATIS PERSONAE:

On the sea: Gertrudis Gómez de Avellaneda
José Martí

On the Malecón:
(In order of appearance)

Halisia Jalonzo
Virgilio Piñera
Fifo (played by a double)
Delfín Proust (also in Key West)
Nicolás Guillotina
Dulce María Leynaz
Tina Parecía Mirruz
Karilda Olivar Lubricious
H. Puntilla (also on the sea and in Key West)
José Zacarias Talet
A chorus of rehabilitated prostitutes
Rita Tonga
Paula Amanda, a.k.a. Luisa Fernanda
Odiseo Ruego (also in Key West)
Endinio Valliegas
José Lezama Lima
Julián del Casal

Chorus on the Malecón in Havana:
Made up of minor poets such as Cynthio Métier, Retamal, José Martínez Mata, Pablo Amando, Miguel Barniz, and a hundred or so others; also including members of the Comité para la Defensa de la Revolución (a.k.a. the Watchdog Committee), midgets,

high-ranking military officers, and anybody else that's on the Malecón at the time.

In Key West:

(In order of appearance)

José María Heredia
Raúl Kastro (also on the Malecón)
Fernando González Esteva
Zebro Sardoya
An announcer
Primigenio Florido
A chorus of children
Bastón Dacuero

Chorus of poetesses:

Angel Gastaluz (This character possesses, by papal bull, the gift of omnipresence, so throughout the work s/he is able to be in several places at the same time if s/he so desires.)
The Mayor of Miami
The President of the United States
A leading politician
The female editor of a fashion magazine
Kilo Abierto Montamier
A prizewinning poetess
A congressman from the state of Ohio
The Attorney General
The Bishop of Miami
Ye-Ye, a.k.a. PornoPop, The Only Remaining Go-Go Fairy Queen in Cuba (who also possesses the gift of omnipresence, bestowed by St. Nelly)
Mariano Brull
A society lady from Miami
An old woman
A priest
A nun
A female professor of literature
Another poetess (who's awarded herself her own prize)
An astrologer
Alta Grave de Peralta
A woman wearing a great deal of jewelry
A university type
The director of a Cuban museum (in exile)
Andrés Reynaldo

Chorus in Key West:

Three thousand poetesses, professors of Latin, hundreds of aspirants to the office of the presidency of Cuba, and other notable politicians; sometimes includes the entire population of Key West, sometimes subdivided into small choruses.

CREDITS, HAVANA LOCATION:

Director: Fifo

Makeup and Choreography:
Raúl Kastro

Resurrections:
Oscar Horcayés

Music: Cuban National Symphony Orchestra, under the direction of Manuel Gracia Markoff, a.k.a. Yechface and the Marquesa de Macondo.

KEY WEST LOCATION:

Director: Moscoso

Makeup and choreography:
Kilo Abierto Montamier

Resurrections:
Alta Grave de Peralta

Music: The Guadalajara Symphony Orchestra, under the direction of Octavio Plá, a.k.a. (according to lies told by Tomás Borge) Fray Nobel.

The action begins in Havana, and as the curtain rises Gertrudis Gómez de Avellaneda, who has been brought back to life on Fifo's orders so that she will be able to take part in the festivities honoring Fifo's fiftieth year in power, escapes in a little fishing boat and heads for Florida. Learning instantly about the escape, Fifo sends out orders for her arrest, but realizing almost in the same breath that an arrest would cause an international scandal, he orders the people of Cuba to stage an act of repudiation against the poetess, while secretly ordering his trained sharks and diligent midgets to do everything in their power to block her flight. The act of repudiation begins with the appearance of a group of eminent poets who are still on the Island, some of whom have been brought back to life especially for this event. The idea is that all these poets will be able to persuade Avellaneda not to leave the country. On Fifo's orders, they will throw at the fleeing poetess large quantities of rotten eggs, which thousands of midgets have piled along the edge of the ocean. Meanwhile, although at first it isn't clear where Avellaneda is headed (the part about "headed for Florida" was a taunt flung by Radio Aguado), the Cuban poets in exile, including some brought back to life for this event, decide to have a huge demonstration on the southernmost tip of the United States (i.e., Key West) in order to encourage Avellaneda and show their moral support for her. In addition to reciting a great number of poems dedicated to her, they shower her with candy bars, California apples, bonbons, and even fake pearls.

AVELLANEDA: *(On the Malecón in Havana, throwing a small, frail boat into the water)*

Pearl of the ocean! Star of the West!
Once glorious isle,

now pain in the ass!
I've had it up to here with you! Farewell!
I mean, *Adios!*
And a thousand times adios,
for tell me, how is one supposed
to put up with this mess?
See these big ugly bags under my eyes?
I haven't slept for days, because
this brilliant sky of yours, no longer does
Night cover with her sable veil—and so I'm off!
Don't try to stop me! *The ubiquitous mob*
has forced me to flee my native land.
Adios, once happy homeland, beloved Eden
where even Numero Uno, the head hoodlum,
has to keep one eye on his behind.
No more of this for me; I've made up my mind!
(Plus—however far and wide I searched, however hard I tried
I never found the man to make me bride.)
Into the boat! Hope swells my ample breast!
Florida awaits. Next stop—Key West!

She clambers into the dinghy and begins to row quickly away. Avellaneda is a heavyset woman swathed in a long black nineteenth-century gown and wearing an equally black veil that covers her face. Upon seeing this bizarre figure, all the sharks swim away, howling piteously. The midgets also recoil in fright, and then whirl around and head back toward the coast. Fifo has no choice but to trust that the act of repudiation, which he orders to begin at once, will work.

Halisia Jalonzo, entering STAGE LEFT, *inaugurates the act of repudiation. She is carrying a huge ostrich egg. The truth is, Jalonzo ought not to be in the part of the ceremony devoted to poets, but once she gets something in her head, honey, nobody can do a* thing *with her—plus, we mustn't forget that she just had her hundredth birthday, or so they say. Still, it's not right—and we'll be sure René Tavernier (R.I.P.), the president of the PEN Club, hears about this.*

HALISIA JALONZO:
Go then, witch! Good riddance to bad rubbish!
And don't come back, ingrate Gertrudis!
(No way this flight is her idea.
Behind it all, I know, is Plizescaya—
my nemesis, the cunning Plizescaya.)
Go—we'll all be better off without ya!

She raises the huge ostrich egg and throws it into the sea, making an enormous splash (for the first time in years, honey!) and raising columns of water that drench Avellaneda.

AVELLANEDA: *(dripping wet, but still rowing; to* HALISIA)
The show you make makes crystal clear
that you're in Fifo's pay, my dear—

whoring, as always, for that "art" of yours.
Some art! You haven't really danced in years.
Farewell, I leave you in Fifo's keeping,
in lands of misery and weeping,
while I depart to seek my freedom.
Before I go, though, I just want to say:
it breaks my heart to see you sell yourself this way—
(though at your age, and in the shape you're in, you kind of *have* to stay . . .)
but good luck, Halisia, anyway—
and as they say in show biz, sweetie, break a leg!
Oh, and thank you for the egg.

Halisia Jalonzo, an expression of defeat on her face, takes out a huge magnifying glass and peers through it at Avellaneda's bosom, which swells to ENORMOUS proportions. Unable to control herself, but to herself alone, she speaks these lines:

HALISIA JALONZO:

Go on—paddle off, you decrepit old hag,
leave me here to hold the bag,
an old, blind, crippled, washed-up prima ballerina
that can't work up the nerve to say what's really in her. . . .

Just then, one of the muscular midgets gives Virgilio Piñera a nudge (a shove) so he'll get on with his part of the act of repudiation. The poet, trembling miserably, climbs up on the wall on the Malecón and, looking seaward, quietly muses:

VIRGILIO PIÑERA:

The dratted circumstance of water, water everywhere
exhorts you, dear friend, to flee, to fly—get out of here.
Oh, I wish that I could join you! But this double-crossing queer
(Miss Coco Salas) has been assigned to keep an eye on me, for fear
that I might try it.
So woe is me! I cannot fly! I cannot flee!
And to top it off, they say tonight
Fifo's thugs are going to take my life.
The order's out, the die is cast, the time is ripe.
And so—
spied upon, spat upon, and hooted,
malnourished, impoverished, barefooted,
watching you sail into the west
while I wait to greet my death,
I raise my glass in tribute to you—
We who are about to die salute you.

(Avellaneda looks back in concern, hesitates.)

No, Gertrudis, don't look back. Forget I said that, dear—
Don't let the dratted circumstance of water, water everywhere
get to you. Be you, be free, be all that you can be—
Flee this horrid Island! Flee!—Godspeed!

FIFO: *(enraged)*

What's that old faggot that I'm going to screw tonight muttering?

VIRGILIO PIÑERA: *(desperately raising his voice to a shout, and changing his tune)*

Don't go, Avellaneda—take my advice.
You're better off here by far.
If you go North you'll pay the price:
here, at least you're a star.
I beg you—reconsider, dear;
the Island's awfully nice.
Turn back now—there'll be no harm to you;
These dwarves will open their arms to you.

(To himself)

God, how could I write such awful lines!
I can't believe they're really mine!
But if I don't try as hard as I can
to lure Avellaneda back again
I'll never see tomorrow.
But hold on!
—Didn't Fifo put out a contract on yours truly?
That's what I was told, so surely
I'm damned if I do and damned if I don't!
And then when I'm dead and they've buried me,
that horrid Olga Andreu will pray for me
and Arrufat will grab my dictionary
and who knows *what* they'll say about me—
but screw 'em all—
I'll be vindicated by History, they'll see!

Virgilio halfheartedly throws a little-bitty kestrel egg, but as luck would have it, it hits Avellaneda right in the eye. Avellaneda, enraged, turns like the basilisk whose glance is fatal and picks up the anchor out of the bottom of her boat and throws it at the crowd on the Malecón, killing a midget—some say a hundred-headed one.

FIFO: *(more enraged yet)*

No more delay! Do what I say—
torpedo Avellaneda!
Brought back from the grave for this special day,
this is how she repays us!
No more mercy, no more pleas—
blast her out of the waves!
The broadest spot is the best spot to aim—
do it! Bombs away!
Be sure to shoot for the backside, boys! Death to every traitor!

AVELLANEDA:

No, not the backside, seat of inspiration!
Take aim at the fore!

All who read me know my slogan:
I wish all to enter through the front door.

All the participants in the act of repudiation throw rotten eggs at Avellaneda.

CHORUS:

No more mercy, no more pleas—
blast her out of the waves!
The backside's the best spot to aim,
so do it! Bombs away!

AVELLANEDA:

If that's the way it's going to be,
if that's the way they're going to treat me,
then I'm glad I decided not to stay.
Clearly, here there's no home for me,
so I'll make my getaway . . .
But if I ever get my hands on that Horcayés
that brought me back from the dead,
when I get through with him he'll need
the finest seamstress in Key West,
to sew back on his head.
Meanwhile, on my rowing let me concentrate—
I think I'm going to have to paddle with both arms and both feet!

VIRGILIO PIÑERA: *(moving away)*

Well done! Bravo! Bravo!
You've got ***bi-i-ig*** *feet*
and one heel's crooked on your shoe . . .
Go—there's nothing for you here.

Suddenly, seeing that Coco Salas is right behind him with a tape recorder, he turns toward the sea and shouts at the top of his lungs:

VIRGILIO PIÑERA:

Where are you going, you ingrate!
Come back—we'll forgive you! It's not too late!

AVELLANEDA: *(growing farther and farther away from the Malecón and the harbor)*

Ingrate! Ungrateful for *what?*
That parting shot
to my vulnerable backside?
No thanks, you snot—
I'll take my chances
in New York or Florida or Kansas.

CHORUS: *(standing on the wall of the Malecón)*

No more mercy, no more pleas—
blast her out of the waves!
The backside's the best spot to aim,
so do it! Bombs away!

A new barrage of rotten eggs is launched.

AVELLANEDA: *(now pulling into the open sea in a hail of rotten eggs)*

What ineffable light, what strange happiness!
Night's mourning is banished from the skies.
The hour's come round, the artillery thunders;
fire, fire, fire, you murderers,
fire at this trembling bosom!

Meanwhile, back on shore, Delfín Proust arrives. After first making a quick check of himself in a portable mirror that opens like a huge fan, he makes a grand pirouette and leaps up onto the Malecón. He whirls about several times, hops like a frog, opens and closes his arms. Prancing about, he begins his poetic discourse:

DELFÍN PROUST:

Where it should be you that grows
a mahogany tree spreads its wide boughs . . .
I grow old . . .
No longer am I the master of my fear and of the city;
I do as I am told.
Conquered are we all; a baleful light claims victory.
And we all grow old.
Of course, to console me there's always this:
all that you are giving up, I can enjoy on the Hill of the Cross
where it should be you that grows.
Come back, and I'll take you personally to Tina Parecía Mirruz.

Delfín Proust tosses a mahogany-tree seed to Avellaneda, and it falls between her breasts. Avellaneda picks out the seed, gazes upon it sadly, and throws it into the sea. Immediately she becomes animated again.

AVELLANEDA:

From Betis harbor
along the shore
my little ship
sails free.
Rotten eggs
and mahogany seeds
shall never, ever
deflect me
from my chosen course.
So row, row, kindly oars-
man, for the morn-
ing sun doth rise.
And I hie me to other shores.

The sound of barking is heard. A bulldog appears, walking on its two hind legs with the aid of a huge walking stick. This is the famous Nicolás Guillotina, poet laureate of Cuba, who flaps his enormous ears and shakes his walking stick threateningly at the fleeing poetess.

NICOLÁS GUILLOTINA: *(to a tune from Gilbert and Sullivan)*

Flee this Island thou shalt not!

The Party, Miss Smarty, calls the shots,
and the Party has decided
that here with us thou shalt abide!
    Ta-ra-ra, thou shalt not!
    For the Party calls the shots.
    Flee this land thou surely shalt not.

Here with us thou must remain.
Thou'rt a woman old and vain
and death on the high seas surely fear,
so let me whisper in thy ear:
        Ta-ra-ra, thou shalt not!
        For the Party calls the shots.
        Flee this land thou surely shalt not.

If *I* must bide here and flee not
because the Party calls the shots,
what makes you think that you're so grand, eh?
What's sauce for the goose is sauce for the gander!
            Ta-ra-ra, thou shalt not!
            For the Party calls the shots!
            Flee this land thou most surely, most su-u-u-re-*ly*—shalt *NOT!*

But then, while the symphony orchestra, in great confusion, plays El son entero, *Guillotina, belying his own words, throws down his walking stick and dives into the ocean, trying to overtake the boat in which Gertrudis Gómez de Avellaneda is fleeing. His ears row like huge outlandish paddle wheels.*

CHORUS: *(giving the alarm)*
    Sensemayá the serpent—he's getting away!

Fifo orders Guillotina pulled from the ocean. IMMEDIATELY. The poet laureate of Cuba, dripping water, is led into Fifo's presence.

FIFO *(sarcastic, to Guillotina)*
    Sometimes I think that you've forgotten
    Just exactly who I am.
    You know, Guillotina, you need a lesson.
    Midgets—cut off that man's gams!

The diligent midgets pull out a saw and perform the operation. The poet bleeds all over the Malecón and dies of gangrene. The symphony orchestra plays taps and then a death knell. By order of Fifo, the crowd observes a moment of silence in honor of the deceased poet laureate. Then the orchestra plays a few typically Cuban dances while, on a stage near the Malecón, Halisia dances The Death of the Black Swan.

RAÚL KASTRO: *(while a hundred diligent midgets bear away Guillotina's mortal remains)*
    What hullabaloo!
    What a racket!

I'll tell you, with all this whoop-de-doo,
I'll never find a man to *string my racket!*
(Winks lasciviously.)

The whole army, thinking perhaps that this is a farewell lament for Nicolás Guillotina, repeats, over and over, the lines that Raúl has just spoken—until Fifo orders silence by pulling his finger slowly across his throat. Everyone gets the idea.

FIFO:

That'll be enough of that, you nance.
No more of this campy fairy shit.
This is a repudiation, not a dance.
The Carnival hasn't even started yet!
Besides, they're watching us live on satellite in France—
so cut out the horseplay—quit, I tell you, quit!
Hey, speaking of France, I wish we still had Sartre
to turn our firing squads into art.
But we'll make do the best we can—
Let's get this started—Lights, camera, *achtung!*
Bring on Dulce María Leynaz,
bring on Tina Parecía Mirruz—
this is gonna be delicious!
Oh, and don't forget Karilda Olivar Lubricious.

Enter Dulce María Leynaz. She climbs the improvised steps that lead up onto the Malecón. She is wearing a long silk gown, white gloves, and a wide-brimmed straw hat to which she has tied a live vulture—the last one on the entire island.

DULCE MARÍA LEYNAZ:

Oh, how the water sparkles in the moonlight!
If I could squeeze it into a fountain streaming,
and toss a little strychnine in—
that'd teach Avellaneda to take flight!
Remember that I am of the aristocracy,
so I *love* Fifo's bureaucracy
and consider royal purple very dressy—
appearances, my dear, do truly matter;
why, I even serve my guests cocaine on a lovely silver platter.

Leynaz offers a bag of cocaine to Tina Parecía Mirruz, who steps up onto the Malecón on the arm of Cynthio Métier, who's steadying her. Tina, with the exquisite humility of a campesina, starts to take the cocaine, but Cynthio stops her.

CYNTHIO MÉTIER:

Stop! You gotta be loca,
girl—that stuff is coca!
Haven't you learned to just say no?

TINA:

Sure, I know how to say no,
and I knew that it was coca,

but I wasn't taking it for *moi*—
it was for Paquito Métier, papá . . .

Now standing on top of the Malecón, Tina begins her poem:

TINA PARECÍA MIRRUZ:

If you don't mind my saying so, sweet girl of mine,
you *are* somewhat past your prime
in making love and making rhyme—
I saw you, in Lenin Park, watching the men come and go,
Wishing for one more hunky gigolo.
I, too, have somewhat lost my touch.
Now the old poetry doesn't seem to flow as much
as once it did.
We're sisters, you and I, under the skin—
come back, and I will take you in,
comfort you in my thatched cottage,
warm you, make you a lovely pottage
(whatever the hell that is),
and we'll grow old together,
through fair and stormy weather,
like two aging twins!
Once you had soft, silky clothes, my pet—
although at the moment I see they're soaking wet;
if you return you shall have them again,
clothes sewn for you by fairy hands—
for there are *lots* of fairies on this island.
Come back—you can live with me,
and we'll have cookies with our tea!

Karilda Olivar Lubricious sweeps upon the scene. She is wearing a red evening gown—very décolleté. In her mouth, a rose as red as her dress. Once she has wriggled up onto the Malecón, she makes a grand gesture with one of her long arms and tosses the rose to Fifo.

KARILDA OLIVAR LUBRICIOUS:

It's not love that that Miss Country Mouse,
Miss Prissy Hausfrau's talking about.
Real love makes you want to twist and shout.
Love is *a kiss of flesh, a taste of the hereafter,*
and *that,* my dear, is the kind of love I'm after—
and it's that kind of love that Tula's after, too, I vow.

Tula, you *professional fire-starter,* now sputtered out,
I know for you it's been three strikes at love, and you've struck out.
That's why I'm here today, to call you to my side—
come on, Gertrudis, come back, and *I'll* make you my bride—
for when I see your heaving, swelling bosom

I fear I'll lose my senses, lose my reason.
I feel my pulse race, feel my breathing quicken,
feel my blood and vaginal secretions thicken—
Oh, I am about to swo-o-o-oooon!

Tell me—how many men have you slept with?
  How many soldiers have you bivouacked with?
  How many innocents have you corrupted?
  And how many of those coituses have been interrupted?
You don't need a man, you need a *woman!*
And tell the truth—the idea kind of turns you on . . .
You know that I have always yearned to give you pleasure—
yearned to probe between your thighs for buried treasure.
My oft-tilled flesh awaits your tickling plow—
come, and plant your mahogany seed in me *now!*
Don't deprive me, dear Gertrudis, of that bliss.
Bestow on me—if only once—a netherlabial French kiss.

You who once struck fire to matchless fuses,
come—engage *me* in sweet sexual abuses.
Turn your boat around, come back, come back,
and you and I will embark on another tack;
we may be getting on in years—
(taken a good look in the mirror lately, dear?)—
but there's still time to make a little hay—
"gather ye rosebuds," Tula, "while ye may!"

Oh, *slay me with spittle,* kill me with sweet pain—
"whatever turns you on" is my favorite saying!
My arms yearn to wrap themselves about your body,
my tongue longs to lick you and talk dirty—
and if you *cannot* break that bourgeois habit
of having a man in bed, then we'll cohabit
with a man, or centaur, or, like the President, a rabbit.
Though I myself prefer a centaur, hung like a horse—
oh, turn around, Tula, change your course,
and paddle your dinghy back to me—
I fall upon the thorns of life, I bleed!

Toss me a line, and I'll even haul you in.
Come, live with me, wallow with me in sin—
  but come back now, or I promise you—Fifo will have your skin!

When she has completed her declamation, Karilda checks to see what effect her plea has had on Avellaneda. Seeing that the old poetess is not turning back, Karilda walks over to one of the cannons that the diligent midgets have set on the wall of the

Malecón, pulls out (as tight as that dress is, honey, lord knows from where!) a huge papaya, rolls it like a cannonball into the mouth of the cannon, and lights the fuse. The huge papaya shoots out of the cannon and explodes smack in the middle of Avellaneda's chest, knocking her over—her black dress is RUINED. The boat tips, bobbles, and begins to fill with water. Avellaneda eats a few handfuls of the fruit and tosses the rest of it back to her enemies. Then, with her hands and a mantilla, she starts bailing out the boat.

Fifo gives H. Puntilla a kick in the rear to signal him to get on with his poetical declamation. H. Puntilla rubs his bruised backside gingerly and, still staggering forward from the kick, stumbles up onto the Malecón.

H. PUNTILLA:

There she goes, like a wounded seagull
wallowing in the waves.
There she goes, like some ominous seafowl
clouding our sunny days.

Avast, begone! foul albatross—
augury of misery and horror.
Avast, begone! foul albatross,
besmirching our island's honor.

(Softly)

There I go, the heavy again!
I *hate* this role they make me play,
I'm sick of being the villain—
When do I get to just be *me?*
Baka! Grab those wings that Coco's got on—
I'm going to fly away!

While the Chorus dances in a ring to El condor pasa, *sung by Miriam Acebedo, H. Puntilla pulls on a huge pair of owl's wings and, in the midst of the confusion, flies off.*

He disappears into the distant sky. Spotlights are trained on Avellaneda, who is still being pelted by rotten eggs as she attempts to keep her boat afloat. Now, bailing with the aid of a veil, she looks up at the sky and fans herself with a lotus flower.

AVELLANEDA

No ties any longer hold me, all are rent.
Heaven wills it thus, and so—amen!
This frail bark, I fear, is going under;
this tidal wave is ripping it asunder.
And yet—
the bitter cup I gladly quaff, my self expires,
my soul finds peace at last, and naught more desires.

When she finishes speaking these lines, Avellaneda begins to masturbate frenziedly with the lotus flower. Reaching orgasm, she falls in a faint into the boat, which continues drifting, threatening at any moment to sink.

Suddenly lights come up on the other side of the stage, on KEY WEST. *In a large pool of light, José María Heredia appears. He is dressed in the clothing characteristic of the early nineteenth century. Kilo Abierto Montamier approaches him with a makeup brush and paints great bags under the poet's eyes. Heredia now stands alone in the spotlight. He turns away photographers and journalists, but he can't keep an enormous electric fan behind him from ruffling his hair. With the fan always trained on him, Heredia climbs up onto the stage that has been set up in Key West for this event.*

HEREDIA: *(trying to make Avellaneda hear him)*

Soft rules the sun the peaceful waves
as the proud ship cuts through the deep.
A broad track of white it leaves in its wake,
bright foam in the endless sea.

Anxiously we scan the horizon,
eagerly we wait to spread the welcome!
Be courageous, Gertrudis, and stay the course.
A golden destiny awaits you on this shore.

Come—life in America has its perks.
Girl, they're republishing your Collected Works!

The lights of KEY WEST *go down. We see Avellaneda in the middle of the ocean. Heredia's little white lies give new spirit to the poetess, who, filled with enthusiasm, begins to clean all the trash out of her boat while she declaims:*

AVELLANEDA:

How much more thrilling to me is that virile voice
than some vulgar (no doubt pirated) new edition.
Fear not, Heredia, I have made my choice
to join you and my compatriots—that is my mission.

For you, old poet, I would brave
winds, tempests, rotten eggs, the waves,
and more—if beside you I might stand
and share a second *belovèd Eden, happy homeland.*

Who gives a fig about Key West, Florída?
We will journey on to Iberia,
and when our traveling days are done,
stroll together under the palms.

Darkness. We hear the rumble of the ocean and then the Guadalajara Symphony Orchestra, under the direction of Octavio Plá, playing La Bayamesa. *The lights come up once more. In the sky appears H. Puntilla. Beating his huge wings, he hovers over Avellaneda's boat. He pulls out a thick manuscript. It is titled* Herod Is Grazing in My Garden.

H. PUNTILLA:

Tula, I can't take it anymore. Nobody can stand living there, not even

Chelo, who works for State Security. I'll just leave this with you if you don't mind—would you see that J. J. Armas Maquiavelo gets it? Tell him that's half of it. They say that Ufano's supposed to come soon, but I can't wait any longer . . .

H. Puntilla continues his flight, arrives in KEY WEST, *and approaches José Martí, who is among the crowd, but incognito; he has come back to life of his own volition. H. Puntilla embraces him familiarly and then from his jacket he pulls out a bottle of gin, which he immediately drinks down. Martí walks away disgusted, to a spot beside the ocean.*

We now see a huge crowd of people in KEY WEST. *In an act of welcome they are throwing chocolate bars, pieces of fruit, and all sorts of trinkets and gewgaws at Avellaneda. All this stuff splashes water on her, and anything that falls outside the boat is devoured by the sharks. Avellaneda, making a desperate effort, struggles to lift H. Puntilla's heavy manuscript. Finally she lifts it enough to tumble it overboard. A shark passes by (Pedro Ramón Lapa) and swallows it in one gulp, then gives a death-leap in the water and expires. Avellaneda now paddles at full speed.*

KEY WEST CHORUS:

Row faster, faster! as fast as you can!
Come, be with your friends—
Oh, how we want you here beside us,
Here where the streets are invariably golden
and the Welcome Wagon's open
serving milk and honey, fruits and *nuts!*

Countless poetesses, carrying their books dedicated to "La Franca India," "La Peregrina," "Tula," and other pseudonyms used at one time or another by Avellaneda, continue to arrive in Key West. Standing on a huge stage, Martha Pérez sings the zarzuela *"Cecilia Valdés." Buses full of senators, mayors, and notables from the world of religion arrive on the key. Somebody announces that in a few moments the presidential helicopter will be making its arrival. Now the poetesses, approaching the water, toss (hurl, pitch, etc.) their books to Avellaneda. Under the avalanche of paper falling into her boat, she almost capsizes. But "La Franca India" dumps their cargo into the sea and continues onward. The sharks swim away, whining piteously. . . .*

Amid the confusion that reigns in Key West, Raúl Kastro, sent as a spy, is swishing around disguised as Olga Guillot.

RAÚL KASTRO: *(looking hungrily at the American sailors)*

What hullabaloo!
What a racket!
I'll tell you, with all this whoop-de-doo,
I'll never find a man to *string my racket!*

Raúl Kastro strips off the Olga Guillot drag, asks to borrow the wings from H. Puntilla (who is delighted to hand them over), and flies off toward the Malecón in Havana. But he doesn't find his longed-for buttstuffer there, either. Enraged, he calls Abrantes, the Minister of the Interior, and sentences him to death for dereliction of duty. "You let the man of my dreams escape!" he shouts as he pummels the minister. Abrantes, along with other high-ranking military officers, is led away by an escort of midgets. We hear a volley of shots off to one side of La Cabaña Prison.

FIFO: *(enraged)*

What are you doing, you halfwit pansy!
Did you forget the silencer?!

RAÚL:

Don't worry, the Carnival has started—
People will think it's a skyrocket.

FIFO: *(irate)*

I told you there'll be no Carnival, you twit,
till we bring back that Avellaneda bitch.
So out with it—tell me what you spotted, eh?
up there in Key West, Florid-ay.

RAÚL:

Oh, it was terrible—my stomach almost turned!
The island is covered with filthy Cuban worms,
all waiting to welcome her with open arms—
like she was some kind of heroine! The gall!
I'll tell you, bro, it was enough to make your skin crawl.

FIFO:

We mustn't allow her to reach Key West!
Did you see my other spies, by any chance?

RAÚL:

Sure. I even saw the president.
Now, if you'll excuse me . . . (winks lasciviously again)

FIFO:

Hold on. I'm working on a plan.

At a gesture from Fifo, the "spontaneous" demonstrations against Avellaneda continue. The orchestra, conducted by Manuel Gracia Markoff, plays a guaracha. *While everyone dances, Silvo Rodríguez sings "They're Even Being Killed for Love."*

FIFO:

Strangle that man this instant!
Shut him up any way you can—
I have to get my thoughts together,
and besides, I prefer "Stormy Weather."

(To Raúl)

Is it true that Puntilla swiped those wings of yours
and headed north?

RAÚL:

'Fraid so. Although for what it's worth
I don't think he'll stay.

FIFO:

Oh, he'll be back—and this time he'll *really* pay!

Suddenly a huge zeppelin, sent by the BBC in London, appears above the ocean. A voice from the blimp announces that it is over international waters and that its purpose is to broadcast impartially to the world at large. The Cuban community in exile has invoked the "equal time" doctrine, and so there is to be a mano-a-mano *between the poets of* KEY WEST *and those on the* MALECÓN *in* HAVANA.

The spotlights in KEY WEST *come on with a boom. The poet Fernando González Esteva appears, wearing a guayabera and carrying a pair of maracas. (From this point on, the program can be seen on television, so I challenge you to keep reading.)*

GONZÁLEZ ESTEVA:

She threw herself
on the mercy of the seas
in a leaky ship;
as old as she is,
and frail as can be,
it's a wonder she didn't break her hip!
But with Gertrudis' grand arrival
Poetry incarnate will grace our proud nation
I've come all the way from Calle Ocho
to express to the poetess our deep admiration.

KEY WEST CHORUS:

Come, Avellaneda, come on, dear—
there are *ever* so many nice things here,
things you've never seen before,
like traffic jams, and Disneyworld,
mamey milkshakes, the Internet,
and thousands of kick-boxing poets.

Acting out the words of the Chorus, thousands of poets (and poetesses, naturally) begin to kick at each other. While this is going on, Olga Guillot sings "I've got you under my skin." KEY WEST *goes dark. Now it's the* MALECÓN*'s turn. From the zeppelin, a voice announces: "Now we will hear from an old horse thief and chameleon—can anybody guess who that might be? It's none other than—José Zacarias Talet!" José Zacarias Talet, who has just turned a hundred and one, climbs laboriously up onto the Malecón wall. The cheery voice of the color announcer is heard: "This old fellow, who's still so full of spirit, has just received the José Martí Order of Merit." The lights in* KEY WEST *come up. José Martí is waving his hand, trying to say Oh, please—leave my name out of it!* KEY WEST *goes dark and the* MALECÓN *comes up.*

JOSÉ ZACARIAS TALET:

Heavens, Tula, is this some kind of joke?
Turn your boat around and come back home!
You big overgrown goateed old biddy,
can't you just once show some pity?
Don't turn a deaf ear, or pretend you're blind—
have you no feeling for us who've stayed behind?
Why, for you I feel nothing but tremendous love
(though not unmixed with lingering remorse)—

I wish I'd shown you *this* before—
Look at this prick,
look how it's still kickin'.
I might be a hundred and seven,
but *this* takes a licking and keeps on ticking!

When he finishes his speech, Talet stumbles and falls flat on his back on the Malecón, allowing us to see that he is sporting a monster erection. We hear his raspy voice shouting "Nobody can take it all!" But two militia recruits carry him off on a stretcher.

CHORUS OF REHABILITATED PROSTITUTES: *(wriggling and writhing as they look out at the sea)*

Avellaneda, go away,
and don't come back another day.
If you do, we'll make your pay—
sticks and stones your bones will break.

Nyah! Nyah! And what's more—
you're a dirty fat old whore!

As the dance continues, Elena Burke (with that potbelly and outsized head of hers!) sings "Sentimental Me." Her bellowing and honking ends in a long moo-oo-oo. Now the light in the lighthouse of EL MORRO *comes on. We see Avellaneda, whose boat is still being swamped by the rotten eggs thrown at her from Cuba and the chocolate bars from Key West. It has started to get dark, and night is coming on, but the spotlights of the helicopter and the lighthouse at El Morro make the glimmering ocean as bright as day. Even so, as Avellaneda rows, she begins to recite her famous poem "Night of sleeplessness and the light of morning."*

AVELLANEDA: *(tossing eggs and chocolate bars overboard)*

Dark
night
now attired
in air
sky
ocean
land . . .

Suddenly a huge screen is lowered at the back of the stage. On it we see a fat transvestite with long fake eyelashes and long curls, like Avellaneda's. S/he is wearing a crown of laurel. This is Zebro Sardoya (a.k.a. Chelo), who, wriggling her backside laboriously, begins to address the audience. While in the foreground we see Zebro Sardoya's face, behind it, on the ocean, we see Avellaneda's lips moving, but the sound has been cut off.

ZEBRO SARDOYA: *(looking quickly back at Avellaneda, then addressing the audience)*

We're very sorry, but neither the BBC in London nor France-Radio nor any other news organization in the world can *possibly* carry that whole poem. I mean, it would totally spoil the show and turn it into a long lyrical *bore!* Oh, Gertrudis hon, forgive me, but I'm from Camagüey, and we have an old saying—"time is not poetry, it's golden." (And speaking of gold, that's what that sable-skinned hunk I was with last night was worth his weight in!) But anyway, folks—before returning to the escape that has us all sitting on the edge of our seats—look at me, I'm so tense I'm about to have a spasm, but they tell me there's not room for another single fairy in the hospitals!—let's pause for some very appealing commercials, which I understand have some information that is *extremely* important for your delicate health. . . . So-o-o-o, pay attention, everyone, please!

Zebro Sardoya fades out and the screen is filled by a well-known Miami announcer. He has long sideburns and a huge moustache.

ANNOUNCER: *(his voice hysterical and his eyes bugging out of their sockets)* Ladies and gentlemen, tonight for the first time we are proud to introduce *Avellanela*—a new milk shake that'll make your taste buds *shake it!* This all-natural product is made with (and I know you Cuban-American friends of mine out there will know what I'm talking about) avena, avellana, canela, and *Vanilla!*—Sure to become a habit! A taste-treat for your palate! Poetry for the taste buds! And *lots* tastier than Milwaukee suds!—So drink Avellanela! Made from the pure pulp and squeezing of that peerless poetess, our own Gertrudis! Don't make your stomach grovel for this gruel, this dietary poetry—give it Avellanela! And don't forget—it's got avena, avellana, canela, and *Vanilla!* Made by Goya for goys and gays and guys and dolls, for young pissers and old farts alike! And Avellanela comes in plastic or glass bottles—whichever you prefer. Goya—good foi ya!

The announcer raises his arm, milk shake in hand. He takes a big swig and falls over dead. The movie screen is immediately lifted away and KEY WEST *lights up. Aerial shot of the key, from which the white shafts of arc lights, as though at a big movie premiere, swing back and forth across the sky. Hollywood stars begin to arrive, and they immediately try to steal the show or at least promote their latest pictures. Among the stars are Elizabeth Taylor (who says she supports Avellaneda's escape), Jane Fonda (who's opposed), and Joan Fontaine (neutral). There are also sports stars and an entire basketball team, which spontaneously begins to play a pickup game with some of the crowd. Among the sports figures is José Canseco, who declares that he's going to give a demonstration, right there, of his power as a home-run hitter. And sure enough, Canseco hits one so hard that the ball sails out of Key West and heads out to sea, where it hits Avellaneda in the chest, knocking her unconscious for a few seconds. While rumors fly that the presidential helicopter is about to land at any moment, there arrive, to the sound of snare drums, a delegation of radical feminist lesbians. On a broad lawn alongside the harbor of Key West, they give a demonstration of self-defense techniques, while the Guadalajara Symphony Orchestra accompanies them. When they complete their demonstration of martial arts (perfectly executed), the great poet Primigenio Florido steps up onto the stage.*

Florido is wearing a huge pair of earphones, an attempt to improve his hearing. They look like big earmuffs, or the big ears of a donkey, and they stick up high above his head.

PRIMIGENIO FLORIDO: *(gazing out at the sea where, in the distance, we can begin to see Avellaneda's little boat)*

Oh, there she is! There—on the far horizon!
A figure like a tiny island in the ocean,
like a bobbing buoy on the waves' crest,
and far in the van, her peerless breast!

Oh, would that I might fly to save her,
would that these old arms could cradle her,
but we must wait—I'll just wave at her . . .
Oh, that one day that grand, grand heart
beating beneath that bosom divine
might—it's never too late for love to start—
beat, here, alongside mine!

That swelling breast—
I could gaze upon it without halt
as though I'd turned to a pillar of salt
or a colossus plunked down on the beach.
But the colossus (of poetry, of course) is she—
sailing toward us, but still just out of reach.

(In the stiff wind, Florido's enormous earmuffs sometimes lift the poet several feet up off the stage and set him down again in the same spot, where, unfazed, he continues reciting his poem.)

Yes, white statue, goddess of alabaster, row,
row! Flee fearsome Fifo Kaster-o.
For how well I know you know,
my dear peerless geographer,
that fiery is the air
and sulfurous the dew
anywhere
you can't even say Boo.
O kiss of paella,
toothsome heartthrob,
how glad we all are
that you
(as we do)
detest *the ubiquitous mob.*

Come to us, my steel-willed pigeon!
Come, fly that horrid dungeon!

Row, Gertrudis, seize that gusty wind
that's giving me so much trouble! (Shoot!
I can't keep my feet on the pavement!)
Come, for to you we've built a monument—
a bright statue, our kisses mute,
And mumble, mumble, mumble, mumble . . .

Florido's words are lost as the wind lifts him up to a tremendous height. When he's almost at the same height as the clouds, though, his earmuffs, I mean earphones, come off, and they fall straight into Avellaneda's boat. She snatches them up and uses them for sails. They're so efficient that the boat skims the water at tremendous speed before the wind.

AVELLANEDA: *(full speed over the waves)*

Anchors aweigh!
Cut through the spray!
On through the foam,
the whitecapped waves!

Far from home,
sailing on—
as we pull on the oars
we sing out our song!

Florido falls back onto the stage in KEY WEST *and picks up the poem where he left off, not hearing the screaming of the crowd or the yelling of the Organizing Committee, who try to tell him his time is up. Finally, several people pick him up (still reciting) and carry him off the stage.*

Meanwhile, the mayor of Hialeah is addressing the crowd, suggesting that they should take Florido's words literally *and erect a monument to Avellaneda in Key West Harbor, where they are all standing, awaiting her arrival. At the mayor's words, an angry argument breaks out, and fierce competition arises among those who want to carve her statue. Hundreds of sculptors present their projects to the mayor of Hialeah. It is decided that each sculptor will make a statue and submit it to a jury, which will make the decision. Immediately they all start to carve away at statues of Avellaneda, because there's very little time. Key West becomes filled with hundreds of gigantic statues—Avellaneda nude, Avellaneda with a long dress and a shield on her head, Avellaneda with a dove on one shoulder and a torch in her hand . . . From out of the hundreds of sample statues, the jury gives the award to the one by Tony López, portraying Avellaneda in a long dress, dripping wet with sea water, sailing through a grove of palm trees. Stars twinkle among the palm fronds, and in the top of one of the palm trees sits a naked black man playing a trumpet. A banner reading WELCOME TULA! runs from one side of the grove of palm trees to the other. A crane deposits this magnificent statue at the entrance to Key West Harbor. But the losers protest so bitterly that the jury declares that all the statues are finalists, and therefore should also be exhibited. Now Key West is one huge mob of statues and people, among whom the Guadalajara Symphony Orchestra continues to play. On each statue, a child with long curly locks is sitting.*

CHORUS OF CHILDREN: *(perched on the statues)*

Look! Look!
She's coming! She's coming!
Another nail
In that pig Fifo's coffin!

(The lights on the Malecón come up. Raúl is standing next to Fifo.)

RAÚL:

Well, I never! Dear me! Did you hear that!
That stubborn Gertrudis just won't quit!
And adding insult to injury,
those brats are calling you a pig!
I tell you, Fifo—
Why not just cut the old bag loose,
and let *me* get dressed and go out to cruise?

FIFO:

That woman is paddling like a speedboat,
and all you can think of is your libido!

RAÚL:

Well, it's *you* and your stupid ideology
that's made her this heroic prodigy.
(Looking through a spyglass)
My god—somebody's even erected her a statue—
though *it's got big feet*
and one heel's crooked on its shoe.

FIFO:

Enough of this chitchat, you fool—
we've got to think of something to do.
I know, *we'll* do a statue, too, Raúl!
And not just some silly statuette—
I want the biggest statue yet!
A statue of ignominy!
A statue of infamy!
A statue of repudiation!

RAÚL:

Hey, that's not a bad solution
but who's supposed to do the labor?

FIFO:

Rita Tonga—if she's available.

RAÚL:

Available!
Why, your every wish is her command.
I'll get her right on it.

FIFO:

Good man.

While Rita Tonga carves out the statue at full speed, Halisia and her corps de ballet perform the "dance of repudiation." This is a series of enraged leaps, kicks, spits, and the motions of squashing lice and cockroaches and throwing them into the sea.

RITA TONGA: *(completing the statue and bowing to Fifo)*

Here's the statue of Avellaneda.
Look how *hideous* I made 'er!

FIFO:

Yes! What an eyesore!
This is priceless!
Rita—this may be your masterpiece!

RAÚL:

Boy, is that statue ugly! Uff!
The spitting image of Gorbachev!

FIFO:

How dare you mention that name in my presence!
He's the one that got us in this mess.

RAÚL:

Yeah, but Raisa's got a contract out on him, I hear.

FIFO:

Hush! Do you want the KGB to hear?

RAÚL:

Are you kidding? The KGB *and* the CIA,
have—both of them—seen better days;
no *way* there're any agents around here—
and besides—you think they'd listen to some silly queer?

(Puts hands on hips.)

FIFO:

Yeah, but still . . . you know about loose lips . . .
Anyway—let's have a closer look at this.

(He walks over to the statue of Avellaneda.)

Oh, no! What a disappointment!
It's got feet instead of stumps,
and tits instead of scorpions—
and I wanted it to be short and squat.
This isn't what I had in mind at all,
this is not what I meant, at all—
That mouth, that figure, that haunting smile . . .
Shit! I wanted a crocodile!
We cannot idealize the enemy!
Gimme that chisel—I'll show you what I mean!
And you midgets over there—

get this woman out of here!
She may call this statue awful,
but to *me* it's way WAY *WAY* too beautiful.

While Rita Tonga is being tied up and kicked to a patrol car, Fifo, furious, signs a report denouncing Rita—"the traitor!"—and defaces the statue so that it's even more hideous than it was before.

Halisia and her troupe dance among the ruins of what was once the statue. At one point, Halisia, peeking through a hole in the statue, inspires such terror that even Fifo cringes in the arms of Raúl.

FIFO:

Yikes! Where'd *that* ugly thing come from?

RAÚL:

Oh, it's just mad Halisia, hon,
and her Dance of Repudiation.
Not to worry, she's one of the faithful—
while she dances she sings *Fidel! Fidel!*

FIFO:

There's nothing more faithful than a statue,
the *only* thing that you can trust a secret to.
(You know, Raúl, I don't even trust you!)
So since Halisia's one of the elite
let's give her a special Fifaronian treat—
a quick dip in a tubful of concrete!

There follows a fierce attempt to catch Halisia, who, in a series of blinding jetés, kicks Raúl in the belly. Then she leaps, in one bound, into the sea. In the water, she begins to dance the second act from Swan Lake. *Under the pretext of saving Halisia, almost all her dancers throw themselves into the sea, but transformed suddenly into veritable swans themselves, they swim away at full speed, leaping like dolphins over the head of Avellaneda (further threatening the stability of her little boat) and arriving in* KEY WEST, *where they are met with cheers and huzzahs. Halisia, still dancing near the coast, is caught by Coco Salas and brought back.*

FIFO: *(to Raúl)*

Wait—she's no use to us petrified.
We need her to testify
against those speedboating vermin.

HALISIA: *(irate, defending her dancers)*

Speedboats, nothing! They were swimmin'!

FIFO:

I know that, you ditzy dame,
but to save face we've got to claim
at the least that they were paddling!
(Jesus, I can feel my poor brains addling
from dealing with this crazy old hag—
not to mention my brother the fag.)

CHORUS: *(singing one of Fifo's anthems)*

Our victory shall never be forgotten.
Onward marches the Revolution.
Give me a C, give me a U, give me a B, give me an A!
Cuba, Cuba—forever and a day!

While the hymn is sung over and over, the lights go up on Avellaneda, still sailing onward, and then turn slowly on KEY WEST. *The giant movie screen is rolled down again, and on it appears Zebro Sardoya.*

ZEBRO SARDOYA: *(on screen)*

And now, ladies and gentlemen, let me introduce the poet Bastón Dacuero . . . And you know, folks, I think the old fellow's in love—but it's apparently unrequited. He keeps threatening to "die because he does not die."

The screen goes dark and we see Bastón Dacuero on the stage in KEY WEST.

BASTÓN DACUERO:

I am a homeless wanderer
come to the seaside
to greet you when you arrive . . .

(The screen lights up again and Zebro Sardoya interrupts Bastón Dacuero:)

ZEBRO SARDOYA:

And *I'm* here to see you sixty-nine,
you miserable panhandler.

(The screen goes dark behind Dacuero, who glares at it furiously but continues with his poem:)

BASTÓN DACUERO:

I am a homeless wanderer
wandering from park to park
to find a place to sleep . . .

(The screen lights up again.)

ZEBRO SARDOYA:

A homeless wanderer, indeed, mister!
I know about all those checks
you used to get from Batista!

(The screen goes dark.)

BASTÓN DACUERO: *(angrier and angrier, but trying to control himself)*

Ay, Carolina, let's
go to the country
to sate ourselves on delicacies . . .

ZEBRO SARDOYA: *(on the screen)*

Delicacies! Oh, please!
You know you eat like a horse!
You can down fifteen chickens in the first course!

BASTÓN DACUERO: *(trying to ignore Sardoya)*

I shall wait for you on every corner—

radiant as an amapola—
there, where in robes of glory
you beach your little boat—*olé!*

ZEBRO SARDOYA: *(on the screen)*
Jesus Christ, give me a break!
Enough of this coochie-coochie, artsy-fartsy
stuff—come on, get it over with and let's party!

BASTÓN DACUERO: *(in a voice of thunder)*
I am here to sing a welcoming anthem
to the undying Rose of Villalba
not to have a *mano-a-mano*
with some bald foul-mouthed queen . . . ahem!

And at that, Bastón Dacuero leaps headfirst at the movie screen on which Zebro Sardoya appeared. But he crashes through the screen and tumbles out on the other side. For a second the only thing we see is the screen in tatters, and on it, the shattered image of Zebro Sardoya, swaying gently.

CHORUS OF POETESSES: *(jumping up and down around the torn movie screen)*
What on earth's gotten into you two?
Stop that nonsense right this instant!
Don't you know we're not here for you,
we're here for our beloved Gertrudis.
So behave yourselves—say a novena
for that poor dear Avellaneda.
While you're at it, make a sign of the cross,
and let's get Father Gastaluz to give her a pep talk.

The poet Angel Gastaluz steps up onto the stage in KEY WEST. *He is wearing his priest's habit and around his neck there hangs a gigantic scapular that ends in a sterling-silver cross that keeps getting all tangled up between his legs. In one hand he is carrying a smoking incense-burner with which he seems to be exorcising the ocean and the huge crowd gathered in Key West, applauding him madly. Standing on the stage, the priest untangles himself from the long scapular, whose cross, still on its chain, is hanging down into the water.*

ANGEL GASTALUZ:
Liberare me O Deus: quoniam intraverunt aquae usque ad animam meae . . .

Suddenly a shark, apparently still loyal to Fifo, takes the huge silver cross in its mouth and, pulling on the scapular, drags the priest into the ocean.

ANGEL GASTALUZ: *(in the ocean, being towed by the shark)*
Save me, O my God!—for thy waters have penetrated to my very soul . . .

The poet disappears into the water. Immediately a spontaneous demonstration breaks out in Key West. The demonstrators are carrying big posters insulting Fifo and asking for clemency and freedom for Padre Angel Gastaluz. Now the gigantic movie screen descends, and on it an announcer is saying that the president of the United States is about to arrive at any moment in Key West, and that to support the demonstration and steal a little publicity from Fifo, he'll be making love, in public, to his beloved rabbit. Tremendous air of expectancy. And now, on the screen, we see Air Force One landing. The door to the plane opens and the president begins to descend the steps, cradling a white rabbit in his arms. The screen goes dark. We see the poet Angel Gastaluz being towed along by the shark. The poet passes alongside Avellaneda's dinghy, and he desperately makes a grab at it. Miraculously, he snares it, but that turns Avellaneda's boat around and heads it toward Cuba at full speed. Avellaneda picks up an oar and starts beating at the priest's hands. He falls back into the water.

AVELLANEDA:

Turn loose, turn loose, what are you doing?
You're going to drag me back to Cuba!
Please, Angel, accept your fate—
make peace with your God, it's not too late.
Besides, you know *this worldly mire* is filed with hate;
you're going to a far better place.
Be brave—that shark is the ferry of Acheron;
it'll take you to the Great Beyond.

Shark and priest disappear in the middle of the ocean, while the lights on the MALECÓN *come up.*

PAULA AMANDA, A.K.A. LUISA FERNANDA: *(to Fifo)*

Quick, the Orígenes gang has launched a counterattack!

FIFO:

Stop them, you idiots! Push them back—
Grab a stake and drive it through their heart.

PAULA AMANDA:

I've got a better idea. Call in the official bard—
the *sacred cow,* of course, I mean—
so he can recite his favorite paean
and *bore* them all to death!

FIFO:

Well, whatever you do, you'd better make it fast!
There's no time to lose, I fear;
I know that when the President's plane lands,
he'll upstage us for sure.

PAULA AMANDA:

Not to worry. This old goat
is guaranteed to sink their boat.

FIFO:

I don't see any old goat—where'd he go?

PAULA AMANDA:

Here he is. Odiseo Ruego!

We see the poet Odiseo Ruego, goateed, making his way along laboriously with the aid of a walking stick and then climbing up on the Malecón. While he recites his poem, on the movie screen we see the President making love to the rabbit.

ODISEO RUEGO: *(addressing his words to Avellaneda, who's drawing farther and farther away)*

I ask you, lady of exalted lute,
sailing like an owl in your pea-green boat,
what it is you're expecting to do?
And will your peapod stay afloat?
Here you can blissfully contemplate
the poplar trees of Paula Avenue
through the iron bars of the grate
in the prison cell that's waiting for you.

As Odiseo is reciting his poem, we see behind him, on the screen, the president of the United States and his rabbit in a wild erotic wrestling match—an encounter that grows more and more frenzied. The president has removed all his clothes; the rabbit has its entire head rammed up the president's ass. The president gives a shriek of pleasure. The rabbit gnaws and burrows at the presidential rectum with its teeth and claws, as though trying to tunnel in. The president's heavy breathing mixes with the rabbit's squealing.

ODISEO RUEGO:

O lady of fruit and other pleasures,
reach out—here for you are untold treasures.
Save yourself, lady of the oars,
don't sail into that land of whores!

On the screen we now see the rabbit even more furiously digging and burrowing between the presidential cheeks. Finally, with a little popping sound, the rabbit climbs all the way into the president's anus. The president gives an ear-piercing shriek of pleasure, and begins to leap and hop about the screen with the rabbit up his ass. Finally, he takes off running, hopping form key to key and giving howls of pleasure—all the way to the White House, where he spatters the white columns with blood.

ODISEO RUEGO:

For once up north, how keenly you will yearn
for the sea's soft mist
and the waves' whisper,
how hotly, fiercely you will burn
for the ocean's warm caress
of your ample keester . . .

FIFO:

What the *hell* is that idiot babbling about? He's just stolen the whole show and now he's going on about sea mist and caresses and who knows *what* nonsense!

PAULA AMANDA:

It's what's called poetic license.

FIFO:

As far as I'm concerned that's no defense.

PAULA AMANDA:

But Comandante, it's really excellent.

FIFO:

Bullshit! I've had enough of this!
Poet or not, he can kiss my royal arse!
I'm gonna feed him to the sharks!

Fifo runs over to the Malecón and with a single dropkick launches Odiseo into the bay.

ODISEO RUEGO: *(as he sinks)*

O corruption, O witch with hardly any rear,
your ass is grass,
your end is near—
prepare to meet your maker!

FIFO:

I think *you're* the one that better prepare yourself, you faker!

As Ruego sinks, Padre Angel Gastaluz appears, now riding the shark that had been pulling him.

GASTALUZ:

Get up on this beast I've converted to Christianity,
and let's make a run for it.

The two poets, riding the shark, speed away. The priest guides the shark by pulling this way and that on his long scapular, which he is now using as reins.

FIFO: *(sneering)*

What do I care about those small fry?
They're nothing to me—
let 'em think they're getting away,
they're bound to die at sea.

(To Paula Amanda)

Now then—after that presidential hanky-panky
we're going to need something X-rated.
I want to see people spank their monkey
till they can't see straight!

PAULA AMANDA:

Spanking monkeys!
Ooooh—I love it!
It sounds so wonderfully depraved!

FIFO:

(I give up!)—It's just a saying.
I want people to *masturbate!*
The idea's to get back in the spotlight,
to get all eyes on us tonight,
and to do that we need some sex appeal.

PAULA AMANDA:

If you want to make sure people squirm and squeal

and engage in a little pre-Carnival whoopee,
I can call in Endinio Valliegas—
he's the best, I guarantee;
he's even played Las Vegas.
Of course first you'll have to get him fed—
he's just been brought back from the dead
and I'm sure he's ravenous.

FIFO:

No problem there—
just get him, please,
and I'll send out for Chinese.

Before Valliegas begins his poem, the lights come up on KEY WEST. *We see several executives, mayors, presidents of museums, and press agents sitting around a table.*

THE MAYOR OF MIAMI:

After that screw of the President's,
I think it's pretty safe to say
we won the ratings battle today,
which, as we know, is what really counts.
Because whether Tula comes ashore or drowns,
the more people watch, the more the sponsors pay.

A POLITICAL LEADER:

Yes, but don't forget—Fifo's on the other channel,
so we've gotta make sure that people stay tuned in.
I say we put on a special panel,
I know, a shouting match!—like they do on CNN.

THE EDITOR OF A FASHION MAGAZINE:

What I have learned, and I'll pass this on to you,
is that without TV, there'd be no ads,
and without ads, there'd be no dough,
and without dough, you might as well be dead!—
'cause money, as we all, I'm sure, have found,
is what makes the little wheels go round.

KILO ABIERTO MONTAMIER:

There's also power, too, of course . . .

THE ATTORNEY GENERAL:

Girl, I couldn't agree with you more!

A POETESS LAUREATE:

You know, now that everyone's
into this resurrection thing,
somebody ought to do an ad campaign,
with designs
by Kelvin Klein—
Resurrection—
it would sell a million!

A CONGRESSMAN:

And it's not important who gets selected
to be the next celebrity
that's resurrected;
what counts is the publicity.

THE BISHOP OF MIAMI:

By the way, who *is* going to be the next candidate
for resuscitation from the dead?
Because I think it would be *very* cool
to borrow a tutu made of tulle
from my dear friend (and sometime office-mate)
the Cardinal.

A NUN:

Perfect! It's scheduled to be Mariano Brull!

CHORUS OF POETESSES:

Brull! Brull! Brull! Brull!

BISHOP:

Mariano Brull! No! He'll be *divine* in tulle!

CHORUS OF POETESSES:

Tulle! Tulle! Tulle! Tulle!

Suddenly all the people in Key West—including children, old folks, and statues—are wearing long tulle dresses. Swaying, they all begin to dance the Dance of the Resurrection of Mariano Brull. From out of the dancers emerges Alta Grave de Peralta with a gigantic egg that she constantly, rhythmically waves about. The egg appears to be quite light; sometimes it floats high, high up and then suddenly plumps back down again—it gets knocked down by the chopper blades. All raise their hands to heaven. We see Ye-Ye, the Only Remaining Go-Go Queen in Cuba (undoubtedly an infiltrator) reciting one of her PornoPop poems.

THE ONLY REMAINING GO-GO QUEEN: *(as she dances)*

A fairy queen in her elegant tutu,
A fairy queen, in tulle of baby blue!

The egg floats up so high that it's almost out of sight and it looks like it's not ever coming back down again. Then Alta Grave de Peralta pulls out a pistol from under her tulle skirt and shoots at it. The egg bursts open and out of it emerges, like a butterfly from a chrysalis, Mariano Brull, dressed head to foot in tulle. Swaddled and wrapped in yards and yards of vaporous fabric, he drifts down slowly, gently, as though descending on a parachute. The poet lands on the stage at KEY WEST *and begins to recite:*

MARIANO BRULL: *(absolutely head to foot in tulle, my dear, with a long skirt, leg-o-mutton sleeves, the whole nine yards)*

I am a prisoner of the rhythm of the ocean,
and that, dear boy, is precisely the reason
that *I am bound for the sea of June,*
for, dear boy, the sea of June,
in my tulle and ermine.

On scores of Mondays, under scores of suns
on scores of sunlight-dappled beaches
I have scored with surfer-hunks,
and with hunks agricultural
in the middle of the cane field.

And when comes 'round the big blue new moon,
in the hot green month of June
I'll cruise again (in gowns of tulle)
the lovely fields of Purial—
cruise the sweet green greenery, the sugary green scenery
 of the itchy fields of prurient Purial!
Grr-grr-grr-grr-grrrrowl!

Then through the sweet green scenery I'll steal,
steal through the hothouse scenery of the fields,
in pink flesh gloriously incarnate I will come,
come the queen omnicuntipotent,
come—on Monday or on Friday come,
come, cunning queen omnicuntiferous,
roly-poly feline pussiferous—
mrr-mrr-mrr-mrr-meoow!

Sea-greeniferous, omnimellifluous,
polymorphous perversiferous,
but not a *trace* of syphilis,
will come the tool-seeking, tulle-dripping Brull—
grr-grr-grr-grrroowl!

Through the green all lemony and limey—
but watch out! they might take a bite out of your heinie!—
through the sea-green, pea-green verdor,
will come the cuntiferous, lickerous whore!
(This queen sucks dick
and pays for it!)
But then through the green green green green greenery
the humected wet-dream long-live-the-queenly-queen green
the wet sweet and eminently eatable purslane—
I fade
(how it pains me to relinquish it)
once more away—
 prisoner of the rhythm of the sea,
 prisoner of the rhythm of the ocean.
"—Hey! you forgot
to get *me* off!"

We see Zebro Sardoya, accompanied by the Guadalajara Symphony Orchestra, singing "I'm a Prisoner of the Rhythm of the Ocean."

A MIAMI SOCIETY LADY: *(all in tulle, dancing)*

So that's Cuba's national poet?
If you ask me, he's a pervert.

AN OLD WOMAN: *(in a wheelchair)*

Not national—*municipal.*

A PRIEST:

National, municipal, I don't care if he's pontifical,
if you ask me, he's not—um—you know, normal.

ZEBRO SARDOYA: *(laboriously swaying his hips through the crowd and pausing beside some people who are having a perfectly nice conversation)*

I am a prisoner of the rhythm of the ocean . . .

A NUN:

I am *utterly* repulsed
by those disgusting verses
which, I agree, are totally perverse
and to which, like you, I am utterly averse.
They are totally detestable,
  virtually indigestible,
  and radically homosexual—
  a sin against our nature
  and an offense against the Church.

A FEMALE PROFESSOR OF LITERATURE:

And to think that once upon a time
his poetry was so sublime . . .

ANOTHER POETESS LAUREATE (SELF-ANOINTED):

The one to blame for it—eh?—
is surely Avellaneda.
She was, after all, his inspiration.

THE NUN:

And therefore his perdition!

THE OLD WOMAN:

No, *that* would be Cepeda.

A HIGHLY RESPECTED ASTROLOGER NOW LIVING IN MIAMI:

O dearly beloved,
the planets and stars above us
tell me that Gertrudis,
being a Sagittarius,
will be caught committing incest
in the year 2001
in a whorehouse in Tijuana.

THE ATTORNEY GENERAL:

Good lord! Alert immigration!
She's a menace to the nation—

we do not want people like her
in our neighborhoods.

THE NUN:
And another thing that I've heard tell
is that she's illiterate—can't even *spell!*

A HOUSEWIFE:
But you know, I bet that's Cuban propaganda—
they do that sort of thing a lot, down in Havana.

THE ASTROLOGER:
It's not propaganda—it's a fact!
She couldn't spell her way out of a paper sack.

THE OLD WOMAN:
And they also say that she's a glutton.

THE FEMALE PROFESSOR OF LITERATURE:
Just look at her—she's busting her buttons!
I ask you: Could anyone as fat as that
be a decent poet?

MARIANO BRULL: *(still dressed in tulle)*
How can you people mention me in the same sentence
as that big fat thing (and so-so poet) Gertrudis!?
She and I are *nothing* alike—not even close!
She's never written poems to a rose
and I've never lived a life as scandalous as hers.
Plus—I *live* to wear the latest clothes
while she's *completely* out of fashion!
Did I mention my poems to the rose?
You'll love them, just have a listen:
Rosa rosarum, rosisimus amorisimus!
That buzzardous comatose (and very obese) poetess
has *never* hymned the rose!
She's nothing but a posthumous poetizing *poseuse!*

CHORUS: *(pointing out to sea where Avellaneda has almost capsized)*
A comatose posthumous poetizing *poseuse!*

Key West darkens and the Malecón lights come up.

DELFÍN PROUST:
Now again, ladies and gentlemen, here comes that john of all trades—
Endinio Valliegas!

ENDINIO VALLIEGAS: *(standing on the wall of the Malecón)*
Barefoot I walk the golden beach,
naked I swim in the green sea,
for I am a pink cockleshell
and any boy (I mean *anybody)* can pick up *me!*

DELFÍN PROUST: *(interrupting)*
You're not a cockleshell, you're a sea urchin!
A sea-cucumber at the bottom of the ocean!

ENDINIO VALLIEGAS:

I am a tree, the needle's prick . . .

DELFÍN PROUST:

A queen who lives to turn a trick.

VALLIEGAS:

I am not one to overreach,
to visit the salon or palace
of some new social leech.

DELFÍN PROUST:

The leech is Coco Salas.

VALLIEGAS: *(furious, to Delfín)*

Your grandmother Alice
is the leech, you bloodsucker!

(now calmer)

I do not betray the turtledove
(or, like Delfín, charge for my love).
I am the swallow with spread wings,
the flight of the owl,
the startled little squirrel . . .

DELFÍN:

A frog that tries to sing . . .

VALLIEGAS:

I am all things, save that dreariness
portrayed in graveyards and whorehouses . . .

DELFÍN:

A faggot famous for his fatuousness.

VALLIEGAS:

I am whatever you make of me,
whatever you invent for me,
to turn my tears to morning mist.

DELFÍN:

An imbecile babbling pure nonsense.

VALLIEGAS:

I am a green voice, a lover forsaken,
innocently seeking,
with the sweet panpipe tweeting
of a wounded shepherd.

DELFÍN:

You're a drag queen—no, make that *screaming* queen—
that screws German shepherds.

VALLIEGAS:

I am all things, save that which hides,
with a mask covering its face.

DELFÍN:

I'm a fairy shrieking, "I'm leaving this place!!"

VALLIEGAS: *(to Delfín)*

Shut up, asshole—for that, there's a reason!

(Now addressing the ocean, speaking in a voice breaking with emotion:)

A buried life, blind obedience—

it's better to leave than serve out a life sentence.

DELFÍN:

My advice to you, Mary, is patience.

VALLIEGAS:

I try, I try,

but I cannot acclimatize.

DELFÍN: *(imitating Valliegas' tone of voice)*

"Here are the hustlers come to slay me—

but when I dead and bloody be,

weep no more, dolphins of the deep,

I didn't give them blow jobs till I'd lost all of my teeth."

VALLIEGAS:

Shut *up,* you insolent curmudgeon.

I'll have no more aspersions

cast on my poetry.

DELFÍN:

You shut up, you pitiful old queen.

VALLIEGAS: *(trying to ignore Delfín)*

In golden gambolings I disport,

in poesy's airy curvets I cavort.

DELFÍN:

It sounds to me like a horse fart!

VALLIEGAS: *(waving a razor blade)*

Shut your mouth or I'll cut out your heart!

FIFO:

I've had enough of these two faggots, by god.

Take them both to the firing squad.

DELFÍN AND VALLIEGAS: *(in unison, and leaping into the ocean)*

I am a silent fish— a cod!

(Suddenly transformed into codfish, the two men swim off into the sunset.)

FIFO:

Goddammit, two *more* sons of bitches that got away from me!

Oh, well, that means there's that much more to go around, he-he.

Plus, what contempt for the proprieties,

for the *comme il faut!*

RAÚL:

Fifo, Fifo, Fifo,

please, forget it,

don't fret your old gray head about it;

for the next appearance we're going to resurrect

a poet of such great genius (however epicene),
and such renown, and such respect,
that people will forget that obscene scene.

FIFO:

Who can you mean, eh?

RAÚL:

José Lezama Lima!

The MALECÓN *darkens and the lights come up on* KEY WEST. *Delfín Proust and Endinio Valliegas swim in to shore. Immediately, everyone abandons Odiseo Ruego and Angel Gastaluz and runs over to see the new arrivals.*

A JOURNALIST:

These two, you know, are the real thing, you betcha.
Not like those two *Orígenes* poets that were dragged in on a stretcher.

DELFÍN:

What?! I thought they rode in on sharks' backs.
That's why I braved this old queen's attacks.
A shark's the only man or animal that brings me to climax.

THE JOURNALIST:

Yeah, you're right, sharks' backs, you betcha.
Which of course brought them under our suspicion.
But they collapsed from malnutrition,
and *that* explains the stretcher.

A LADY IN JEWELS:

That arrival *does* lend itself to suspicion—
we all know the sharks are Fifo's agents,
so they should have come in on sea serpents
if they expected us to trust them.

DELFÍN:

And Avellaneda—what will be *her* reception?
Will *she* be under suspicion?

THE BEJEWELED LADY:

Oh, you know, we'll do the usual—
We'll make the standard fuss.
The problem is, we don't know anything about her,
whether she's one of Fifo's spies or one of *us.*

A POLITICAL LEADER:

She'll definitely be looked into. And we'll thoroughly search her purse.
You can never be too careful. She might be carrying a bomb!

DELFÍN:

Heavens, before I subject my person *or* my purse
to these idiotic (and very rude!) inspections,
I'm going back where I came from!

Delfín jumps into the ocean and swims back to the Malecón, though not without first butting Avellaneda's boat with his head—the boat bobbles uncontrollably.

With the arrival of Delfín, the lights come up on the MALECÓN. *Just then, the arrival of the poet José Lezama Lima is announced. Great air of expectancy. A squad of midgets comes on stage, bearing a huge stretcher on which there is a gigantic ball of a thing with what looks like a tablecloth draped over it. They set the enormous stretcher down on the wall of the Malecón. María Luisa Bautista gently tugs at the cloth, and from under it appears the poet Lezama Lima, who is dressed in a Greek toga-contraption. The poet gets to his feet with some difficulty and, still standing on the stretcher, begins his speech.*

JOSÉ LEZAMA LIMA:

Oh, I fervently pray that you escape, since I could not, for dark Atropos, aided by the gondolier of watery footsteps who plied his pole to pull away from me before I could halt him by uttering his name, cut her skein and cut off my retreat.

Myriads of horrid Lestrigons, flesh-eating savages, swooped down upon me *from a darkling plain—antelopes, serpents, pink fenestrations,* phallic cornets, tiny elves making erotic signs, enchanted palanquins from Tibet—a monstrous dog (perhaps a whippet) swimming backward through the blood—and the tiara of the Helot zealot.

FIFO:

What the *hell* is he talking about? Who on earth *is* this idiot!?

LEZAMA: *(unfazed)*

I suckle, errant marshy mallow,
blind, thy nectarous drops in clots.
Marmots, marmots, marmots, marmots
marmots from far Tibet, oh-ho.
I shall not hunt the heron, nor the thrush,
nor even the magnificent wild boar
whose carnal plow
assails me with an anal rush
and makes me yearn for more.
Cats upon cats—both he and she—
and gold-plated toenail clippers,
all of that I see,
plus Old Rosa's slippers—
that goat-herding hag with carbuncles,
the witch of Perronales,
a place where, when Persephone
returns from underground,
septentrional storms beat down.
A magic spell, the wind plants a lighthouse upon the beach.
A trick employed by cunning Euridice
to snare succulent mameys.
Canines of accursèd flames.

Aberrant contortions.
The lemon tree, the almond tree,
and swarms and swarms of hornets.

O faun of poultry farms, slip nude I beg
into my marmoreal bed
with stealthy *night-snail tread.*
The rings of Uranus—or is it Saturn?—
for your sweet arrival burn,
for you shall cunningly dive, ah-ha!,
into the repertoire of my saliva.

O glorious grace-filled secular world,
O faun that plays upon my toconcma curled
making it stir and rise at thy embrace—
O bed-meadow infused with sacred grace!

The deeper the digging, the more treasure,
the deeper the hole, the greater the pleasure,
O buried Pharaoh of blind eye.

The slippery attack,
like a mule's kick,
fitting rings to finger—
ring after ring, kick after kick—
this is a humdinger!

FIFO:

Somebody shut up that prick!
And in the ocean fling him!

Soldiers and midgets, carrying long sticks, roll Lezama along the Malecón down to the seaside, to the sound of tremendous noise and shouting.

LEZAMA: *(as he rolls down to the sea)*

This plunge into the depths shall be my epiphany;
I greet my descent like proud Antigone.
But wait a moment—tell me, can ya?—
is it true that my friend Rodrigo de Triana
has given up on sodomy?

He falls into the water, causing the tide to rise so high that it floats the Malecón—and swamps Avellaneda's boat.

AVELLANEDA: *(bobbing about in the waves)*

Sea—
for the world,

profound
consolation.
I think I'll fly.
Perhaps in the sky
I shall find
liberation.

FIFO: *(to Paula Amanda)*
So you recommended this clown, huh?
And then he practically drowns us!
This time, Paula, you've *really* fucked up!

RAÚL:
And with all these expenses, we're going to be bankrupt!

FIFO:
You'd better think of something fast!

PAULA AMANDA: *(desperate)*
I promise I'll get someone more suitable,
someone who'll be truly memorable
and utterly without parallel.

FIFO:
Such as?

PAULA AMANDA:
I know! Julián del Casal!

Paula Amanda and other police officers compel Horcayés to immediately bring Casal back to life. The poet rises on the wall of the Malecón in a worn and faded nineteenth-century suit.

JULIÁN DEL CASAL: *(looking out to sea where Avellaneda is in full flight)*
I am filled with a longing to commit suicide,
and therefore I applaud your own suicidal flight.
I, too, sigh *for those distant realms*
whose skies are filled with halcyons,
gliding over the blue ocean.
A paradise—that is what I want to live in;
a paradise of centurions
beckoning
me to blow jobs.

FIFO: *(enraged)*
What! Call out the firing squads!
No—better make it cannons!

While the artillery prepares its cannons, Casal goes on with his poem.

CASAL:
To see a different sky, a different sun a-rising,
a different beach, and different horizons
where, singing like a mockingbird,
before a squad of men with vibrating erections

I can hover like a hummingbird
and sip at their sweet nectar.

FIFO:

Ready, aim—and *fa-a-ahr!*

CASAL: *(with the cannons trained on him)*

Oh, if I, like you, should seek exile
far from this isle of crocodiles,
no place would make me cheerier
than exotic, warm Algeria,
where a hundred—no, a thousand—studly men
would await me in their palaces
(all ruddy and golden)
with their phalluses
emboldened.

FIFO:

Not another word, d'you hear!

CASAL: *(as fast as he can talk)*

Yes—Algiers!
That would be my intention.
Where every man's bisexual or queer
and his prick's at attention.

Fifo's troops open fire, killing Casal and seriously damaging Avellaneda's dinghy—she loses her oars.

AVELLANEDA:

Oh, dear, my boat is shipping water! Help!
O Cepeda, O Fonseca, O dear Gabriel,
O Quintana, O Zorrilla,
O Camilo José Cela,
quick—launch the Coast Guard's best flotilla!
Sound the alarm! Two-whee! Too-whoo!
Hurry, my brothers! To the rescue!

While Avellaneda barely manages to stay afloat, in KEY WEST *a heated argument breaks out about the numbers in a survey that a big U.S. company has taken in an attempt to assess Fifo's popularity, which scholars claim is on the rise.*

A MAYOR:

The press, on good authority, has said
that Fifo's brought back from the dead
all sorts of famous men and women—
Julián del Casal, José Lezama Lima—
all sorts of poets and poetesses
for his big event.
Which means, damn it, it's been a huge success.

CHORUS:

Yes! Yes! Yes! Yes!

A POETESS:

It's really sinister, the press.
Infiltrated by evil Fifo's spies,
and always ready to print lies—
    It's just not right!

CHORUS:

Yes! Yes! Yes! Yes!

THE PRESIDENT OF A CUBAN MUSEUM:

And who bears the burden of this plight?
We do—and I say we ought to fight!

CHORUS:

Right! Right! Right! Right!

A SCHOLAR:

Yes, it's a deplorable situation,
so let's give them some of their own medicine.
Let's have our *own* resurrection,
bring back somebody that'll get people's attention.
I know—we'll call Alta Grave de Peralta, see?
and resurrect José Martí.

CHORUS:

Sí! Sí! Sí! Sí!

Tremendous tension in Key West. Alta Grave de Peralta appears with her gigantic plastic egg that she is still throwing up in the air, spotlights trained on it. The egg keeps rising, higher and higher. The giant movie screen drops down and on it we see Zebro Sardoya.

ZEBRO SARDOYA:

In just a few seconds, ladies and gentlemen,
from that egg up there you are going to see
Cuba's greatest poet descend—
    The one, the only—José Martí!

The egg keeps rising.

ZEBRO SARDOYA: *(on the screen)*

It looks like it's not coming down . . .

ALTA GRAVE DE PERALTA:

Drat! You'll have to shoot it down!

The sheriff of Key West pulls out a .45 and fires at the egg, which splits into two halves. It's empty. Meanwhile, out of the crowd (where he was lurking) comes José Martí, riding a stick horse and carrying an odd sort of suitcase or briefcase of some kind.

A POETESS LAUREATE:

There he is! Over there! José Martí!

CHORUS:

Sí! Sí! Sí! Sí!

Martí rides his stick horse through the crowd, which falls silent, and throws himself into the sea. He rides out to Avellaneda.

AVELLANEDA: *(to Martí)*

O dear god, help me!
I am sinking into the sea!
Perhaps if we work together
we can save each other.

MARTÍ:

No way!
For my fate
is to ride on horseback.

AVELLANEDA:

Then woe is me,
for then *my* fate
is to die a shipwreck.

MARTÍ:

No doubt—your boat is very rickety.

AVELLANEDA:

Have mercy! Give me a hand.
Don't leave me—I need a man,
and I am not persnickety.

(Martí makes no effort to help.)

You will not help?
That is very bad!
Are you truly such a cad?
I beg you, tell me what your name is
so I may discover whose the blame is
for my eminent—I mean imminent—demise.

MARTÍ:

My name is José Martí.

AVELLANEDA:

Oh, so you're José Martí.
I have read your poetry,
and I confess
I am impressed.
But I cannot pardon you
for preferring Zambrana
to me.

MARTÍ:

You and I are two ships passing in the night;
I will not tarry for some trivial, purely literary fight.
You embarked to flee—or search for—power,
while I am on a journey to a star.

AVELLANEDA:

A star? Some tacky star? Who is she?
What's her name, Martí?
I confess to pangs of jealousy.

MARTÍ:

Her name, Avellaneda, is liberty—
Miss Liberty.
And she's no woman, she is destiny
 and every honorable person's duty.

AVELLANEDA:

But you would abandon a land of liberty
 to go in search of abstract Liberty?
I think your arguments are thin.
I'm not convinced; I say *cherchez la femme.*

MARTÍ:

You certainly know how to exasperate a man . . .
Look, I'm leaving because I don't feel right here,
because I hate how people live their lives here.
Money is all anybody cares about,
and that is not what I think life's about.
Here, all's filthy lucre, mercantilism.
I long for something higher—idealism.
I want things that money cannot buy.

I'm leaving because I miss the Island's sun and sky;
I want to lie under a guásima tree,
let the boughs of a jubabán rock me—
I want to be, or at least try to be,
what I truly *am*—a Cuban,
 a man of the Caribbean.

Look—up here for months you almost freeze to death
and *I'm dying of loneliness, dying of homesickness.*
I want to fight for that thing that is *mine.*
For me, no more the exile's bitter bread,
 no more sleepless nights in exile's bed.
I do not know if you can understand me.
Only the flowers of one's native land smell sweet.
Here, joys do not bloom, they do not flower,
people's eyes don't simply look, they wound me,
the sun possesses no healing power—
 it burns, it stings, it glowers.

AVELLANEDA:

About the U.S.A. you are such a skeptic,
while I'm an incurable romantic.

MARTÍ:

Tula, my dear, you're living in the past—
and when I say past I do mean *past.*

Here, it's a terrible existence
ruled by the laws of planned obsolescence.

AVELLANEDA:

Does that apply to poetry, too, by chance?
No more Zambrana, no Lezama Lima,
No more villanelles, no terza rima?
I have a sonnet I wrote for Washington—
now, I guess, a sonnet's out of fashion.

MARTÍ:

I read it—and it is one
of my favorite poems of yours.
It may be a bit overdone
but you're right to take it on tour.

AVELLANEDA:

I'm glad you at least half approve—
It's just a silly old thing
I've had for such a long time.
But I read it to a friend,
and she loved the rhyme.

MARTÍ:

You're the best at rhyme of all of us.

AVELLANEDA:

Oh, you're too kind, you make me blush!
Of course there also has to be meaning—
I'll read it to you again, so you'll see what I mean.

MARTÍ:

No, I don't have time, I'm late to a party meeting!
I have a small band of the faithful that I lead.

AVELLANEDA:

Oh, but politics aside one moment, stay
and listen to the lay
I wrote for Washington.
Tonight, I beg, your trip delay;
you and I'll have so much fun—
here, rest upon my breast till break of day.

(Martí remains unmoved)

Do my pleas and tears no longer persuade?
Have you no pity on this poor maid?

MARTÍ:

Pity? Who dares speak of pity?!
My life's the one that's shitty!
And it always has been . . .

AVELLANEDA:

Each one of us our burden's giv'n . . .

MARTÍ:

Oh, but the burden that you've chosen
is to be feted at *hommages*
and in salons
to wear couturier gowns,
to have men kiss your hand—
and be the showpiece of a tyrant!

AVELLANEDA:

How dare you! I am eagle, foe of tyrants!
Of course I have my weaknesses.
All of us are human.
You, for instance,
betrayed a friend:
you slept with the wife
of a man who saved your life.

MARTÍ:

Friend? Oh, please!
Look—I'm leaving because I want to die in peace.
I am not the man I was—and not the man I want to be.

AVELLANEDA:

But there is still your poetry.
It is for the ages; it is undying verse.
You still possess the entire universe!

MARTÍ:

Which I will never see.

AVELLANEDA:

How can that be?

MARTÍ:

Don't you realize
that if I am to be immortal
I first have to die?
I am no longer a man of this world,
and the cause of liberty needs martyrs—
I'm returning to Cuba to be crucified.

AVELLANEDA:

But in Cuba you can't be crucified;
now there's only crucifuckingfixion.

MARTÍ: *(under his breath)*

Damn! I'm going to have to rethink my mission . . .

AVELLANEDA:

What if you lived for many years yet?

MARTÍ:

I'd die of disappointment,
of weariness and disillusion.

So I'm off.
Really, I've had enough.

AVELLANEDA:

Enough of what, Martí?
What, I wonder, are your true reasons,
  your real complaints,
that lead you to set out to sea
in the season of hurricanes?

MARTÍ:

My true reasons? Did I not make them plain?
Besides having to deal with rogues and rapscallions,
my reasons
are autumn's yellow leaves, winter's bare trees and freezing rain,
living in a borrowed house and a foreign tongue—
bitter winters, itchy long johns.
I am out of here—I'm gone!
I am naught but the fruit's bitter rind.
Does that answer your question?

AVELLANEDA:

Have you, then, nothing here to live for?

MARTÍ:

Life here is a wound there is no cure for.

AVELLANEDA:

Listen to what I'm going to tell you.
All of that is very well for you,
but it's also a little overly romantic,
not to say melodramatic—
and if you land in Cuba, they'll definitely kill you.

MARTÍ:

So? Remember, it is good to die
when it is horrible to live a lie.

AVELLANEDA:

Die *here.* Cuba is a desert island,
  an infinite, infernal prison.

MARTÍ:

My blood will be the water for a garden.

AVELLANEDA:

You know that what I say is true.
You know that they will use you,
  betray you,
  and make mincemeat out of you,
  and that there you'll find no rest.

MARTÍ:

And what about those people in Key West?

Do you think their heartlessness is any less?

AVELLANEDA:

Of course it's not my first choice, it's not the best,
but for the time being it will do.

MARTÍ:

So they've brainwashed you, too?

AVELLANEDA:

Not at all—I am perfectly lucid, as you'll see:
I have a plan,
and I think that it will work:
I'm going to publish my Collected Works,
find a nice place to settle down,
and live on the royalties.
If you came with me, we could work together.
We could help each other,
and be one another's inspiration.

MARTÍ:

Woman, what an imagination!
What I'm looking for is a gun,
and a map, and a flashlight—
I want to start a fight,
a second Cuban Revolution!

AVELLANEDA:

That means I won't be seeing you again?

MARTÍ:

Oh, you'll see me again, I'm sure—
when they put up my statue
as they keep threatening to do.
But I warn you in advance,
I've seen the plaster cast
and there's not much resemblance,
especially the head—which is immense!

AVELLANEDA:

Noble, no doubt, is what you meant.

MARTÍ:

No, I mean it's a *gigantic* head.
And as for the forehead,
it's broader and nakeder than a dry river bed.

AVELLANEDA:

A broad forehead is a sign of great intelligence.

MARTÍ:

It's a sign of a receding hairline, in my case.

AVELLANEDA:

But really, one must often pardon

artists who portray the human form.
Look at me—a veritable sylph,
and they always give me huge tits.

MARTÍ: *(looking more closely at Avellaneda's bosom)*
I had no idea that you wore falsies.

AVELLANEDA:
Falsies?! How dare you! What an indignity!
These breasts, I'll have you know, belong to me.
Here—I'll show you . . .

MARTÍ:
Whoa . . .
Let's not go overboard.
(It's just a figure of speech!)
Anyway, as I was saying, when you reach the beach,
you'll see a monstrous statue of me,
"The Apostle of Liberty,"
which is another reason I'm off to Cuba to do battle—
I've got to live up to my title . . .

AVELLANEDA:
Wait, hold on—
just one last question:
What's in that suitcase that you're carrying?

MARTÍ:
A flamethrower,
to win the war.

AVELLANEDA:
Have I missed something, or is that a contradiction?
I mean, it seems bizarre—
you know you're going to sure perdition,
yet you plan to win the war.

MARTÍ:
When a man dies for a cause,
when he dies for right and duty,
his death is victory,
even when his life is lost.

AVELLANEDA:
But you also thirst for glory.

MARTÍ:
No, but I do have an ideal.

AVELLANEDA:
Oh, dear, oh, dear—
how can you leave a woman
who loves you?
I love you.

And you have no one . . .

MARTÍ:

I have my flamethrower.

Martí pulls out the flamethrower and brings it up to his waist. Avellaneda looks in rapture toward the long, heavy, thick piece of armament.

AVELLANEDA: *(stroking the barrel of the powerful weapon)*

Ah, the flamethrower! Mighty weapon!
My pulse throbs, my breast heaves—oh, heaven!
Can I have a demonstration?

As Martí prepares to give a demonstration, Avellaneda can't keep her hands off it.

It is so potent-looking, so long, so grand!

MARTÍ:

It is a powerful new invention,
a most ingenious sort of weapon,
and the patent is held by an American.

AVELLANEDA: *(embracing Martí while she squeezes the end of the flamethrower)*

Shoot! And let the fire consume us both!

Though Martí fires toward the ocean, Avellaneda's boat is raked by the flames.

MARTÍ:

And now I must be off—Adios!

AVELLANEDA:

You would leave me here abandoned and alone,
while you go off trailing glory's flames—oh!—
and cloudy warlike smoke
like a proud volcano?

MARTÍ:

War is serious business, not a game,
and you will not be long alone.
People will soon be standing in line, shouting your name,
waiting to hear you recite your poems.

AVELLANEDA:

Wait, wait—will you not heed my lamentations?

MARTÍ:

Avellaneda, I have no more patience.
I long to be in the jungle, a guerrilla,
or in the middle of a cane field.
I long to hear a mockingbird again,
the palm trees whispering in the wind,
my native tongue spoken by a real Cuban,
not those hyphenates in Miami.
I want to kill the tyrant, see?
and if I must, to fall a casualty
in the color of the summer I was born in.

AVELLANEDA:

The heat, the infernal heat,
of the Cuban summer, I'm sure you mean.

MARTÍ:

You may be right, my dear,
but I want to die *there.*

AVELLANEDA:

You *will* leave me, then?

MARTÍ:

I leave you to the waves and wind.

AVELLANEDA:

Don't listen to this poor maid's beseeching, then,
but think at least of the acclamation
that you are throwing away.

MARTÍ:

My *idée fixe* takes me another way—
to Cuba. But in Key West
you will be an honored guest.
You will be treated like royalty,
as you deserve, Tula, for your poetry.

AVELLANEDA:

You go off on this wild-goose chase, this quest
for a will-o'-the-wisp, a chimera at best—
at worst, a nightmare in a nightmarish land;
you disdain my hand
and all that I might give
because you no longer want to live.
Is there no other choice, no other path?

MARTÍ:

No, only this one. I will not turn back.

AVELLANEDA:

Oh, dear, oh, dear—
it is so sad to watch you disappear
into the color of that tropical summer.
As people say now—it's a real bummer.

MARTÍ:

Nonetheless, it's what I've come for.
Summer is my favorite color . . .

AVELLANEDA:

José! José!
Where are you going on that stick horse?

MARTÍ:

To die for my cause.

Martí starts to ride away on his stick horse, on the surface of the water, the flamethrower held before him.)

AVELLANEDA:

Indeed, I know . . .
And I am proud to see you go.
Oh, had I the courage of your convictions!
But I have only my fictions.

MARTÍ:

Indeed, that's so . . .

AVELLANEDA: *(to herself)*

Despite my pleas that he not go,
he's gone, gone with his flamethrower . . .
And now I hear the sound of gunfire!
Oh, what is happening to him?
Jesus! They've murdered him!
And me with my boat on fire.
Help me! I can't swim!

We hear shots, then a single loud report, much closer: a member of the audience is killed, and the person's body must be taken out of the theater immediately. Avellaneda tries desperately to put out the flames in the boat, but they only grow worse. She calls out for help. But the only reply she receives is a hail of rotten eggs from the people on the MALECÓN *in* HAVANA *and another rain of chocolate bars from the people in* KEY WEST. *And as the hail of missiles continues, the two groups now begin to shout insults at one another.*

CHORUS ON THE MALECÓN:

Traitors! Maggots!

CHORUS IN KEY WEST:

Pigs! Faggots!

AVELLANEDA:

Help me! This boat will not last!

CHORUS ON THE MALECÓN:

Capitalist-imperialist apostles!

CHORUS IN KEY WEST:

Commie Marxist fossils!

AVELLANEDA:

Oh, I'm sinking fast!

CHORUS IN KEY WEST:

You socialist slugs!

CHORUS ON THE MALECÓN:

You multinational thugs!

AVELLANEDA:

Oh, glug glug glug glug glug . . .

As the trading of insults continues, Avellaneda slowly sinks into the ocean. Silence. The gigantic movie screen descends. On it, we see only waves on the high seas. Then immediately we cut to a deserted park, and two statues pitted and worn by time—one of Martí and one of Avellaneda. From behind these statues appears the poet Andrés Reynaldo.

ANDRÉS REYNALDO:

Gertrudis Gómez de Avellaneda wrote that a man is great only if he contributes to his country's greatness, and that a man is free only when he is ruled by free men. José Martí wrote—or rather cried out in silence—that the beaches of exile are beautiful only when we bid them farewell. For the love of God—oh, Néstor Almendros!—get their photographs!

A blinding radiance illuminates the audience, as a flashbulb goes off. The audience has been photographed. Darkness. Curtain.

A Tongue Twister (1)

Such shit that crazy Zebro scribbles! I mean that crazy queen Zebro scribbles *shit!* The gall of that cockamamie cocksucker!—D'you suppose that skag of a scabrous Zebro doesn't know we know his scribbling sucks? 'Course not! Zebro's never sober, so no *way* she'd know. Just keeps rescripting other scriveners' scribblings, hits other guitar-pickers' licks, and expects us not to kick! Prick! *Kobra* was the last time that cocky queen's abracadabra works with *this* sucker.

(For Zebro Sardoya)

"HM, TOP, SEEKING SAME . . ."

The old bull macho laboriously raised himself from his Barcalounger® and shuffled through his enormous house, a mansion now in ruins and almost empty that had been a gift from Fifo many years ago, in the days when they'd gone out hustling together. The old butch made his way through the grand empty living room and on back through the house, and finally he stood before the mirror that covered one wall of his bedroom—the mirror in which he had relished most of his butch-on-butch conquests for these last sixty years. The old man contemplated his dried-out face, the pendulous rooster-wattle of his throat, the furrows of his forehead, the terrible bags that hung under his eyes like two black lizards. Of what had been rows of sparkling teeth there were but two fangs left, and his body was nothing now but atrophied veins, bony joints, and loose dangling folds of chicken skin. His once proud, firm legs had gone knock-kneed, and on top of his head, out of the middle of the desert of his bald pate, there grew a ridiculous, insulting little bud—not even a grassy tuft—of snow-white hair. *And to think,* he said to himself, looking at that image of himself in the mirror, *that I was once Bull Macho Numero Uno in all of Cuba, the only man ever to have screwed Mella, Grau San Martín, and Batista, all celebrated bull tops in their own right, and even*—how his sunken chest swelled with the thought of it!—*even Fifo, who's celebrating a half century in power today. Fifty years . . . although it's really only forty, which Fifo adds the extra ten to because he's always loved red-letter anniversaries, not to mention publicity. . . .* And that human rag doll that looked at itself in the mirror still not only had the gall to be alive; more tragic even than that (which was tragic enough), he still craved an ass to screw. And not just any ass, mind you—it had to be an ass-fucker's ass. *Because make no mistake about me, you people out there—as a macho's macho, a true top, which is what I've always been (and therein lies my tragedy), I've never been able to screw some pansy faggot.* Yes, Mary, our old bull macho's tragedy was this: his prick would come to attention only when it was saluting another top. *Díos mío!* Yes, my dear, I kid you not. . . . But little by little, after years of trolling for catches and reeling them in, the glorious bull macho (who wasn't an old man back then) realized that he was the only top, the only *real man,* the only *nonfaggot,* left on earth. In all his long erotic wanderings through the world, he, the supermacho top, had always thought he was screwing another top. But imagine his surprise to realize that all those supposed tops were really just a bunch of pansy faggots, because they would allow their butts to be stuffed by other tops—tops, in turn, who weren't really tops because they would allow their butts to be stuffed by other tops, and so on, *ad infinitum*. In fact, *ad nauseam*. Because to his horror, the old bull macho had finally realized that the world had contained no *men* at all—there was nothing but pansy faggots. Faggots of all kinds—some, of course, passing themselves off as tops, but others totally and absolutely in the closet (those were the worst), married men with wives, mistresses, children and grandchildren, closet queens who got off by screwing each other or, in the majority of cases, not even that—sunk in a bovine and beatific state of denial, wasting their lives sitting in front of the TV secretly fantasizing about the baskets on the black basketball players, spending their lives in one long stupor of eyes-only faggotry. The old bull macho made his halting way to the large framed image of the Sacred Heart of Jesus that stood upon an altar in one corner of his bedroom. *Lord,* he said, *tell me—where can I find a real butt-stuffer that I can screw?* Nowhere, replied the Lord, turning the other asscheek. *That's what I figured,* the old butch macho said to himself with a sigh, and he recalled the disillusionment that had been the last straw for him. At the time he was personal bull macho butt-stuffer to Fifo, who made himself out to be a supermacho top and swore that he played bottom to the not-yet-quite-so-old bull macho's top only as an act of sacrifice and even love. One day, intending to have himself another piece of Fifo's ass, our supertop had climbed the stairs to the top floor of the Piti Fajardo Hospital, which Fifo had turned into a "male room." There the old bull macho found Fifo, on all fours, receiving a package in the rear cargo compartment from Ché Guevara, with Ché accepting a delivery through the back door from Camilo Cienfuegos, and Camilo one from . . . At the memory of that betrayal, the old bull macho lost it—all his old rage returned. He went and picked up his massive Barcalounger®, staggered with it all the way through the mansion, and heaved it into the huge portrait of Fifo that hung above the fireplace (yes, Miss Thing, a *fireplace*—the height of luxury, my dear, like anything that's totally useless). The portrait (painted by Raúl Martínez) hung in tatters. Then the old bull macho stuffed a wad of ancient bills into his pocket and walked resolutely out of that mansion to which, on Fifo's personal orders, he was now supposedly confined under house arrest. He was taking to the streets. . . .

A throng of people were coming down Quinta Avenida—it was the entourage accompanying the president of Argentina, who had just arrived in Cuba for the party being hosted at that very moment by Fifo. The old bull macho saw the president and his escorts all feeling up each other's asses; sickened, he kept walking. From the seawall on the Malecón, teenagers with golden-tanned backsides were diving into the waves, braving sharks and dodging surveillance for the pleasure of playing grab-ass under the water. *I am the last true top in the world,* the old bull macho said tragically to himself, shaking his head. And as he was standing there on the wall, a police van pulled up and a dozen police officers, with the butch voices and gestures of make-no-mistake-about-it straights, rounded up all the teenagers skinny-dipping in the surf and with the butts of their rifles herded them into the van. Once the skinny-dippers were all in the van, the cops started sucking the young faggots' cocks.

I am the last true top in the world, the old bull macho said again, this time even more tragically. And he turned and started walking toward Coco Solo. He came to the house of José Antonio Portuonto, who was said to have once been a famous hustler, and went in. Portuonto was just putting the finishing touches on a hurdy-gurdy organ. "I'm going to play it at the Carnival, when Fifo makes his entrance," he proudly explained. "After a tribute like that, Fifo will surely rehabilitate me and name me ambassador to the Vatican." And Portuonto began to turn the crank on the hurdy-gurdy, which played the tune to "The cayman's crawling off, crawling off to Barranquilla." And in spite of his ninety years, as he turned the crank Portuonto writhed and wriggled in lascivious abandon. The old bull macho said good-bye to Portuonto, who didn't hear a word, and headed for the house of an old friend of his—a black man named Cuquejo. *Even if Cuquejo's retired and way past his prime,* thought the old bull macho, *he was a good top once; I never saw him give his ass to anybody.* "Cuquejo! Cuquejo!" called the old bull macho at the old black man's door, and when nobody answered it, he turned the knob and stepped inside. The house looked like a cave that'd just had a cave-in. And only then did the old bull macho hear deep sighs and heavy breathing. He peeked around a corner and saw old black Cuquejo lying naked on his back, his legs in the air, trying to stuff a huge black rubber dildo up his butt. The dildo finally slipped in, but not satisfied with that, Cuquejo crammed the two synthetic balls up inside him too. The old bull macho sighed and turned and left, closing the door quietly behind him. In one of the out-of-the-way corners of Parque Central he saw Skunk in a Funk; he was rewriting his lost novel *The Color of Summer* yet again. He was working on a chapter titled "HM, top, seeking same." *What can that poor queen know about tops?* thought the old top, and he crept away through the huge bandstands and stages erected for the upcoming Carnival. *No faggot has ever known a true butch macho top, because a true butch macho top never screws a faggot. In my book, any butch macho that screws a pansy faggot is just another pansy faggot. . . .* Disconsolate, the old bull macho decided to go visit his grandfather, an old gentleman named Esteban Montejo who was more than 130 years old. When the old bull macho was a boy, his grandfather had raped him. Obviously, thought the old bull macho, my granddad was a natural-born butt-stuffer like me. *Child!* the grandfather said when he saw his grandson, *I can't believe how old and decrepit you've let yourself start looking! But come on in, honey, I'm gettin' myself up for the party.* And the old bull macho saw that his grandfather was dressed from head to toe in drag. *Come on in here and tell me what you think about this new getup I've put together to wear to Carnival.* But the old bull macho didn't go in; he headed off along the coastline. In a cane field near the ocean, several volunteer cane cutters were sucking each other off while they were still whacking away at the cane stalks. In a dug-out trench, dozens of soldiers in fatigues were tirelessly screwing each other. In a park, the so-called men were leaving their wives sitting on benches while they went off to a latrine to get their butts stuffed by other faggots. *I am the last true bull macho top, the last one in the world,* the old bull macho sobbed in what was almost a cry of despair, remembering those golden days of his youth as a soldier, when he would break a masculine young black man's cherry and the black guy would go off and hang himself—those days when, on a secret mission, he had screwed a Colombian guerrilla fighter and the head of the KGB in Panama. *There are no more real men anymore,* the old bull macho said to himself; *all the real butt-stuffers, the machos that don't play drop-the-soap for anybody, have been wiped out—or were always just a fiction. Everything's just appearances, playacting, a mask they never take off. And behind that mask, pansy faggots can delude themselves that they're being screwed by a Real Man Bull Macho Butt-Stuffing Top, and pansy butt-stuffers can be fucked by other pansy faggots without any pangs of conscience because yesterday they played the part of the top. Good upstanding husbands can screw their wives and put their kids to bed and then because they've met their masculine obligations they can go off and pay some purported butt-stuffing hustler to fuck 'em. And they can even think they're happy. But not me—burdened by this one-way butt-fucking taste of mine, I wander the earth alone, bearing my cock, I mean my cross, of iron. . . .* The old bull macho saw Raúl Kastro chase down a white mare and cut off her tail with a machete, then steal a huge mosquito net from Vilma Espina. (It was the mosquito net that covered the whole floor of the dormitory that the woman giants slept in.) He watched him jump the high wall of the Colón Cemetery and snatch from the tomb of Luisa Pérez de Zambrana the crown of golden laurel leaves that Avellaneda had returned, though grudgingly, at Fifo's request. And with that motley collection stuffed in a green duffel bag, the Fairy General climbed in an armored Toyota and drove off in the direction of Fifo's palace. Because that very night, at the Grand Fiferonian Fiesta, if his brother (who'd been discovered to have cancer of the rear) didn't appoint him his sole and absolute heir—especially after he'd had him take fifty of his favorite generals (part of whose duties it had been to screw the two brothers) to the firing squad and shoot 'em—then he, Raúl Kastro, head of the country's armed forces, would throw himself into the ocean in the middle of Carnival wearing a horse's tail, the crown of laurels, and the huge mosquito net wrapped around him as a shroud. . . . *Well, I better get a move on,* the old butch macho suddenly said to himself as he watched Raúl rush off at full steam. *I'm gonna show that faggot Fifo—I'm gonna poop on his party.*

Calling upon almost his last ounce of strength, the old bull macho hobbled as fast as he could to the huge door of the catacomb-like palace.

"Fifo!" he yelled in a voice that could be heard all the way to the poles. "You pansy faggot! You tricked me—passing yourself off as a top while other people, not just me, were ramming it up your butt! But you listen to me,

Fifo—I am the first and last butt-stuffer who'll ever commit suicide over you!"

And at that, the old bull macho pulled out a pistol that dated from those days in the Revolution when he'd fought alongside Mella, and he shot himself in the head. Mortally wounded, the old bull macho toppled onto the body of the president of the Spanish Royal Academy, who as the reader may or may not recall had succumbed on that spot only hours earlier when the iron gate of the palace had dropped on him like a guillotine. *Jesus Christ! I might have known!* thought the old bull macho as he lay dying—*some miserable son of a bitch beat me to it, so I can't even be the first person to commit suicide on the doorstep of Fifo's palace.* And at that, in his last agony the old bull macho rolled over, perhaps out of instinct, onto the backside of the recently deceased president of the Royal Academy. And at *that* indignity—which the president of the Royal Academy, even in death, considered a mortal insult—the venerable academician returned to life, and with a vengeance! *How dare you touch my ass!* he yelled at the old bull macho, grabbing him by the neck. *I don't care if I* am *dead, I will not allow such an atrocity against my person! The only one that plays grab-ass around here is* me! And as the old bull macho bled and was simultaneously strangled to death, he howled with laughter—at the end of his life he'd finally found a top he could have some respect for. And as the two men wrestled fiercely to see which one would bugger the other's ass, they both expired before the palace gate.

Surely the noise of our struggle has been heard inside, thought the old bull macho as his eyes closed for the last time. But I'll tell you, girl, there was so much noise from all the high heels—that clickety-clackety, tickety-tickety sound they make, you know?—and the cackling of the palace groupies and floozies and queens, that nobody could hear a sound from the outside world, at least not right then. Of course the guards posted outside and the security forces all around the palace had witnessed the battle, but they didn't think it was anything worth reporting to Fifo. And anyway, they were all screwing each other at the time. The only people who'd followed that amazing postmortem battle with any degree of attention at all were the huge crowd of peeved (and I mean pissed-*off*) citizens who hadn't been invited to the party but insisted that they should've been. "Oh dear, I don't think we ought to stand too close to those dead bodies," said Padre Gastaluz, who made the sign of the cross over them and slipped away on the steadying arms of Valentina Terescova and Deaconess Marina. The Pissed-Off Disinvited followed those personages and took up positions near the coast—not too far from the palace, but at a prudent distance from the huge palace door.

In the Monster Men's Room

Omigod! What time is it?! Two o'clock in the afternoon, three o'clock in the afternoon, three fifteen. —If she kept looking at the clock it'd soon be midnight. And all that in less than five minutes! Obviously Skunk in a Funk, her enemy number one, had driven her clock crazy so it would run six times as fast as it ought to and there'd be no way poor Eachurbod could get *anywhere* on time, much less to that encounter that she'd been dying to get to. Because it was an *encounter* that awaited her—she had a *date,* an *appointment with destiny,* a rendezvous with a veritable *army* of men, a throng of big strong hunks, thousands—almost a million—hot and horny beauties. Oh, no doubt about it, that masculine multitude was waiting for her out there in all that ass-shaking and backside-wiggling and drum-beating—waiting to (at last!) impale her. Run, run!—and she was already beginning to see in the distance, dancing to the driving rhythm of the drums, the sex-frenzied crowd. Weigh that anchor, lift off!—you know this is your last chance, because tonight the Carnival begins and ends, never to return. That's what Fifo announced in that last twelve-hour speech of his. *After this Carnival,* he intoned, *the party's over. We will have to work at least a hundred years to meet our glorious goals!* . . . Oh, but my goal needs meeting *now,* thought Eachurbod. And so my hope lies in reaching that crowd and getting laid. Hurry, hurry!—so you can get there before all those other fairies beat you to it and take possession of those zippered treasures. And so Eachurbod clutched to his breast Volume XXVII of the *Complete Works of Lenin,* with a foreword by Juan Marillo—a book Eachurbod used as an ideological shield—and with the thick volume as a kind of coat of arms, she took off running, to get there in time. But oh dear! his clock, knocked out of whack by Skunk in a Funk, was running so fast it made your head spin. Four o'clock in the afternoon, five on the dot, six in the evening, and Eachurbod had gone no more than two or three blocks. And there, in the distance, those bright colors, that happy confusion, all those blacks and mulattoes shimmying, swaying, shaking their asses, those wide-legged pants they wore displaying the divine treasure of their godheads. What if she should be too late for that magnificent gathering? What if all he found when he arrived was a pile of empty paper cups, trampled and pissed-on signs and posters, tattered streamers? She could begin to see a big, bright open-air stage that a thousand half-naked whores were dancing on. Oh, wait, pleasegodwaitforme, remember that I am the man-eater, the superdiabolic, the never-say-die vamp, that I am *Eachurbod!*

And no sooner had she uttered those words than her watch jumped ahead two hours in a single minute. If things kept going that way, the party would be over before he got to the center of the swirling mass where surely everyone was waiting for her. Eachurbod quickly pulled out her pistol—the pistol she had secretly hoarded away (along with the bottle of kerosene) so she could blow her brains out if she turned out to really be condemned for all eternity to virginity—and fired a shot in the air as a signal that she was almost there, that they should *wait* for her. The drums, indifferent to the poor queen's anguish and distress, went on drumming out that horrid, inflaming rhythm, while a line of *stunning* men, squeezing their bodies against one another in the frenzy of a conga line, began to snake down the Avenida del Puerto. Eachurbod, desperate, running at full tilt with her red-bound book, yet barely making any headway—sometimes, even, unknowingly losing ground—looked up at the sky, at the lowering summer sky, and saw that the clouds, too, were flying toward the Grand Carnival, and that they were being blown by the wind into the shapes of swollen testicles and enormous erect phalluses. And down below, pushing its way through the massive parade, Eachurbod saw, or (such were the cruel tricks of Skunk in a Funk) *thought* she saw, the huge red ball that Fifo rode inside, high above the dancers' heads. And an itch came over the queen that she absolutely *had* to scratch. Really, Mary, put yourself in her place—dancing in the middle of a huge crowd of drunk and *very* horny men. There's no way—*no way!*—that she could miss this; they had to wait for her. So Eachurbod, in spite of the risk she ran for "illegal use of firearms," fired off another round or two into the air, and then, almost in desperation, flung the pistol to the wind. Ah, but right over there, almost right beside her, and clearly in a hurry, there was a man. And what a man! A creature of golden curls, nimble legs, and harmoniously rounded dimensions. That love god possessed the most beautiful hands that human eyes had ever seen, and one of those hands was straying to the fly of the dream-man's pants and giving a squeeze at the groin, as though beckoning toward the gates of paradise. And then that wondrous apparition turned toward Eachurbod and asked what time it was. *What time is it?! What time is it?!* But the hands of Eachurbod's watch started whirling around even more deliriously than the queen herself. Desperately she tried to pin down the time. She stooped over the watch, she tried to follow the dizzying, whirling hands, and suddenly she was nothing but a round blur—a queen chasing her tail (right there on the sidewalk!) to keep up with the flying hands of time. *What time is it?! Yes, yes, the time!* she shrieked, over and over, as she whirled in an ever-tightening circle. But the young man, who apparently had no time to lose (even to find out what time it was), took off walking, faster and faster—the truth is, he was practically running—so Eachurbod stopped whirling and took off after him. And anyway, where could that marvelous creature be going if not to that place over there where all those bodies were winking and sparkling almost like flashes of lightning. Over there, over there, where the ocean roared and reared up lustfully, where men danced for one last time around a conga drum. And now the young man was rushing ever faster, clutching at his bulging fly; and the queen flew along behind him, still clutching at her own bulging Volume XXVII of the *Complete Works of Lenin.* The pansy felt as though she were riding a wheelchair on a sea of broken glass on her very own tongue, moving forward, endlessly, until the end. Suddenly, the young man stopped in front of a large wooden door at the entrance to a *glorious* colonial mansion—the most magnificent one on the whole street, perhaps in the whole city. The young man pushed open the door, and then he slammed it in Eachurbod's eager face. As if by magic, the well-built (and apparently horny) love god had vanished—*poof!* Eachurbod, unable to move, like a doe caught in the headlights, stood there frozen (though still not stuffed) before the colonial mansion's imposing door. And there she was still standing when another divine (and *very* manly) man, a mulatto in a white polo shirt and blue velveteen pants, and this one also pawing at his divine privates, pushed open the door and then—same song, second verse—slammed it in Eachurbod's face again. Then, within seconds, a teenager (and omigod *what* a teenager) went through the door, followed by a young sailor boy with quite a duffel bag. Dear heavens, and now there was a black man in a pair of mechanic's overalls, clutching at his toolbox. Behind the black man came several fresh army recruits and a respectable-looking gentleman dressed in white from head to toe, and sporting a Máximo Gomez moustache. What *was* this? How many dazzling men had been invited to this house? Who lived here? Do you suppose Fifo himself was holding one of his secret orgies in there? Stepping in front of the self-interrogating Eachurbod, three fresh-scrubbed farmworkers, several students in their ironed school uniforms, and several high-ranking military types pushed through the door, all of them clutching at their crotches when they arrived as though that were the password that gained them admittance. Jesus! and now a still-pubescent bright-skinned mulatto (with eyes of amber) entered, holding his crotch, his unparalleled crotch, a crotch that could have been painted by Hieronymus Bosch and that was threatening to burst from its bonds. And then another mulatto of fiery skin and eyes, but with a sweet sword shaft between his legs, penetrated that sanctum—and he was already unzipping his fly (a fly which whispered a command that neither Eachurbod nor you either, Mary, could have disobeyed). And so the fluttering queen, shaking off his dejection and jumping up and down in the puddle of his own nervous perspiration, started toward the door. He was almost certain that if he went inside he could be arrested, tortured, sentenced to death as a terrorist, or maybe under suspicion of espionage—because the odds were that this house was the reception or training center for all the secret police who were keeping an eye on the ideological direction the Carnival took—but the order *(Follow me . . .)* given by that body, by all the bodies that had just gone in there, was stronger than all the fear and terror of the risk. Using the red-bound volume (so as not to leave any fingerprints), Eachurbod pushed open the enormous colonial door, which still proudly sported a brass knocker with the face of a dragon and several copper nails, and stepped into the mansion. Instantly, he discovered that that noble two-hundred-year-old villa, the birthplace of the Condesa de Merlín, was now furnished with long troughs hung on the walls of every room, and before those long troughs hundreds of men, staffs of virility in hand, were urinating—the mansion was now a huge fountain fed by the most beautiful human springs ever imagined. *The Condesa de Merlín,* whispered Eachurbod, inhaling a fragrance that intoxicated him, *could never have imagined that her home would be dedicated to such a noble cause.* And so it was—by order of Urban Renewal (and therefore by order of Fifo himself, who hated colonial architecture—any architecture, in fact, that was not of his own design), that historical residence, that national monument, had been turned into a gigantic latrine.

A TONGUE TWISTER (2)

Gotta watch that puta Puntilla—she'd sell you for twenty pieces of pewter, stool-pigeon you for a tin pizza plate, turn turncoat on you for a tiddlywink—she doesn't give two poots. Yep, to take care of her own sweet patooty, Puntilla the pie-eyed prostitute turns tricks for whoever's got the biggest dick. Puntilla the potbellied poetaster—*ptui!*

For H. Puntilla, whose real name is Leopoldo Avila

PAINTING

I will paint plants with their roots upside down, seeking their nutrients in the sky. I will paint leaves that move about the canvas and ask impossible questions when one looks at them. I will paint a heap of bones—me—rotting in a field overrun with weeds. I will paint the suffering face of the moon looking down on me. I will paint not-children tucked among the newly budding leaves, all those fetuses that could not manage to be born because there's no room in this place of mine for another canvas, not to mention the bed and the four chairs in which I politely seat those visitors who come to get information out of me, and on whose visits I have to file my own reports. I will paint Tomasito the Goya-girl denouncing herself to the computers because he doesn't have anybody else to denounce. I will paint the blazing rock-strewn wastes and stinking puddles where young people gather, dreaming that they're at the beach. I will paint demons that flee in terror, and a huge spotlight, manned by other terrified demons, shining on them. I will paint my beloved Calle Muralla crumbling down, crumbling down, and along that street Skunk in a Funk dragging a trunk full of empty bottles. I will paint the cracked and peeling walls of my body. Strange birds and clouds, and rats playing musical instruments riding atop them. I will paint a huge crowd of people dancing around a gigantic red object that resembles some sort of fruit, and on top, a naked black man commanding them all to skip in a circle around it, threatening them if they don't. I will paint Eachurbod's desperate tongue unrolling through the whole city. I will paint the city with its calamitous sky, and in that sky, Gabriel and Lazarito trying to sail away in a balloon. I will paint Reinaldo's desolation at not being able to write the novel that justifies the life that's about to be taken from him. I will paint Odoriferous Gunk's dying mother as she lies in an improvised tent near here, in Havana Park. I will paint the police rounding up all those young men who are sent off to a forced-labor camp. Armed storm troopers—*Hands up!*—a spotlight, and the bull macho, roaring. Shaved heads, hair floating up into the sky, a gigantic plate of spaghetti that is that hair, and Fifo wolfing it down in front of the starving, bulging eyes of the crowd waiting in line below, ration books in hand, for the bread that will never come. The painting I will paint will also be the huge moan of the tropics, the deafening crash of that moaning as it collapses in a heap. I will paint armies of sex-hungry sharks under Fifo's command, prowling the dark blue band of water where the open seas begin. I will paint a palace with a sinister aquarium in which Bloodthirsty Shark performs his executions. I will paint Miss Mayoya standing in ecstasy on the beach, gazing at the gleaming, supple shark. I will paint Oscar flying over the city, endlessly searching for the teenager of his dreams, and the whole city shall also be laid out there, and my fallen breasts, and all the consequences thereof. And the entire Island shall be painted, too, and the walls of the city also—blood-spattered walls shall be painted (or repainted); and the foundation that upholds the Island shall also be painted, the foundation gnawed at by the teeth of all those who want to tear the Island from its mooring and escape, sail away on it like some gigantic boat—to anywhere. I will paint a bench under a tree, and on the bench two lovebirds kissing and caressing one another, and in the branches of the tree Rubén Valentín Díaz Marzo, the Areopagite, masturbating. Now through the park where that tree grows, thousands of young men and women thronging toward lord only knows what hideout, basement, or embassy that somebody says has opened its doors and is swallowing people like some black hole and spitting them out again in another world, and pursuing that crowd, a furious stampede—mobs with picks and shovels, machine guns, flags, a sinister-looking hag on a white horse—bloody hammers, corollas, and pistils. I will paint the most loyal rages, angers, and wraths of all young people. I will paint Teodoro Tampon, my husband, gazing at a piece of wood and thinking: I could make some platform heels out of this that'd be higher than the ones Mahoma makes, and *that* would turn me from a dwarf into a giant. . . . The last part of the painting will be very dark, almost black. In it, all those who have been expelled will huddle together—that is, all those who tried to live and were therefore sentenced to death by the sinister god that rules all human destinies, and viewers will see a sky lit by a strange light, and if they come closer they'll be able to hear explosions and screams and the muted sound of the city collapsing. They will see the panicked flight and the final disaster. My painting will splatter the entire Island with horror, and on that canvas, the viewer will see, crouched down among the leaves and thorns, or behind a crumbling column, me—myself or my double—the whore in hiding, looking at my six-year-old son begging a quarter from a sailor and making signs to him that he knows a woman (me) that the sailor can sleep with, and it'll only cost him five pesos. Oh, yes, let him learn to pimp while he's still young, let him learn to ingratiate himself, especially with the Greek sailors, so one day he'll be able to slip into a barrel on some boat and not come out till he gets to Mykonos, or even China—everything else is fiction. I am painting the barrel now, and the boat, and my son wriggling around in the barrel. I will paint the immense ocean and thousands of birds flying above it, rescuing my son and carrying him far, far away—so far that the journey will never end, because if he ever gets anywhere, finally arrives, there's no doubt he'll find the same shit, the same horror (more or less disguised but horror all the same) no matter where. And above it all, Oscar fluttering desperately above the place the Island used to be, but where all that will be left now is a vortex of turbulent water, swallowing everything that floats by. . . . I will paint all that and much more, because I will also paint the Carnival, the last Carnival of this century, and me at that Carnival wearing my big falsies and flaunting my forbidden Carnival costumes. There will not be a homo alive who escapes me, beginning with my husband; there will not be a snitch or a pay-for-play snatch that escapes me, beginning with myself; there will not be a bawling baby, or a desperate mother, or an entire people shoved up against the wall, any calamity at all that I will not portray. Cat shit and suns of fire, unflushable toilets and full buses—swindles, shouting, darned and mended rags, mauled and ravaged bodies, high government muckety-mucks and misery-beset beggars, all dancing in a circle around the big red ball, the gigantic and apparently, from a distance, delicious piece of fruit, every one of them wanting to wolf down an apple, a banana, a cluster of grapes, a prick, a thing that will wind up turning against us, against our greedy innocence, our endless solitude, and blowing us all to hell. *Boom!* Death will play its fiddle for even the most persistent, brave, or stubborn lovers. The stink of sweaty feet and toothless old women, screaming queens, and men who, when they screw me—it's just a manner of speaking, really, it never happens anymore—will die of disappointment because they wanted to be the ones getting screwed. God on all fours sucking off a black man, and the black man furious, wishing he could find a cock for himself. Midgets up in the trees, mares on two feet dancing the minuet, herds of swine masturbating with their mouths, the Condesa de Merlín sodomizing a mouse. Oh, yes, oh, yes, don't you worry, I'll put Avellaneda in it, too, swimming along on her tits like water wings . . . Flimflams and ass-wiggling, terror and stupidity, fear and self-assurance—all of it, among the leaves, plagues, hypocrisies, bones, and sharks' teeth. You will see the moon set in a urinal, kettledrums that bellow like a bull, bodies that shake themselves out of joint. Nothing will escape me. And in the third section of the triptych, the final explosion, you will see everyone, myself included, bursting—and to think, after we'd lived through all those horrors! Bursting into a million pieces—that's the thanks God gives His children who have wanted nothing more than to enjoy His work. Swollen bodies out of which flow streams of blood, and pus, and shit—streams that bubble up like geysers, or shoot up like the plumes of some enormous fountain, up to where my son, towed by birds, is trying futilely to escape. Damnation for every soul, without explanation and without end—it must be *perfect, all-encompassing* damnation. That will be my painting. I will paint all that, and right now, right this minute, I am going to start. In an ecstasy of rage and fury I will paint it, all of it, before the Carnival begins. I will paint the Carnival even before I go out and see it. Those people that thought my painting days were done, thought my masterpieces were all behind me, had better think again. I will paint my greatest work *right now*. . . . Omigod, I just realized—I don't have another single canvas, or rag, or tube of paint. I'll have to pay a visit to Saúl Martínez or Peña or that Miss Medive thing or some other faggot official painter (the ones that've got everything because they spend their lives painting olive-green portraits of Ché and Fifo), and while I give them a little piece of useful information, maybe denounce my butt-stuffing great-grandfather, I can steal some brushes and paint and a big canvas. And maybe first I ought to run by Padre Gastaluz's ossuary so I can take the painters a bone so they can make a nice thick soup out of it. My work—my work, that's what's important. Teodoro! *Teodoro!* Wake up! Wake up, girl, and get yourself dressed, and scratch some of this dirty crust off these legs of mine and dig the earwax out of my ears. For God's sake, open your eyes and turn over—get a wiggle on, man! And put on your highest platform pumps—because right this minute we're going to pay a little visit to Saúl Martínez. Oh, and bring the tape recorder the lieutenant gave us, in case the pansy faggot decides to tell one of his little counterrevolutionary jokes. . . .

The Seven Major Categories of Queenhood

"The seven major categories of queenhood, distinguished ladies and gentlemen, are the following. And I will not tolerate any interruptions during this brief but smashing presentation," said the AntiChelo as she stood up and took the podium in the rapidly flooding auditorium. This particular queen, Chelo's antithesis, was a pansy of profound thought and a slender figure you could die for, and he spoke as follows:

First major category: SUBLIMITY. It is this species of queenhood that engenders heroes, martyrs, and true geniuses. Examples: Jesus Christ, Leonardo da Vinci, Cervantes.

Second major category: BEAUTY. This type of queenhood produces great artists and impassioned, insane suicides. It can also lead to lustfulness. Examples: Dostoyevsky, Virginia Woolf, Marcel Proust . . .

Third major category: INTUITION. This type of queen may craft works of some quality, but they are always subject to the accidents of time. Examples: almost all the writers who have won the Nobel Prize in Literature, from Sartre to Hermann Hesse, and in general almost all "writers of some talent."

Fourth major category: INTELLIGENCE. This queenhood does not produce works of art, but those who are possessed by it know how to negotiate the world the artist inhabits and thus may be academics, literary agents, outstanding journalists. Examples of this type are innumerable; we will cite but one case: Karmen Valcete.

Fifth major category: COMMON SENSE. This type of queenhood despises art and almost all the other beautiful things of life. Persons in this category are, in general, moderately self-effacing, hardworking bureaucrats but may also be great but obscure traitors; they are also often engaged in business. Example: John D. Rockefeller, Armand Hammer, et al.

Sixth major category: NORMALITY. This terrible type of queenhood is the least normal of all, and the closest to Common Sense. It can beset almost any member of the human race and has a permanent mediocritizing effect. The victims within this category may live for as long as a hundred years. Sometimes they suffer from delusions of superiority, or even think they belong to other categories of queenship. One example among thousands: Rafael Alberti.

Seventh major category: GROTESQUENESS. Diametric opposite of

Sublimity. Those who suffer under this queenhood occupy presidencies of countries, or become great dictators, or turn into vagabonds and homeless persons. They are much given to playing putatively historic roles. Examples: Hitler, Stalin, and our own adored Fifo.

All these things were said by the AntiChelo on behalf of Albert Jünger, who as a person that was still alive had refused in no uncertain terms to participate in this event, though he did send in his paper with the Condesa de Merlín. The Condesa, of course, modified the paper to suit her own ends and commissioned one of her beautiful robots (the AntiChelo) to read it.

Fairies on the Beach

"Oh, I love that one that just came out of the water," said La Reine des Araignées.

"A noble specimen, indeed," nodded the Duchess.

"Oh, girls, look at that black one that's getting out of the car over there! He's the best-looking man on all of La Concha," shrieked Uglíssima.

"They say he's one of Skunk in a Funk's husbands, so he's got gonorrhea," remarked the Duchess.

"I hear he's got a prick almost as big as the Key to the Gulf's. And that basket of his would certainly make one think so," purred SuperSatanic.

"On the subject of pricks the definitive word has not yet been written," said La Reine in her most pedantic manner. "Appearances can often be deceiving to a poor girl."

"Well, anyway, he charges ten pesos. So we can forget about him, darlings," said the Duchess.

"This beach has always been famous for having the *most* magnificent hustlers. Why, a hundred years ago Marlon Brando and Tennessee Williams would come here directly from Key West to find their muscle muffins," SuperSatanic solemnly informed them.

"Oh, look, girls—look who just got here! Golden Boy!" exclaimed Uglíssima, pointing toward the entrance-gate to the beach.

"I have never been one to corrupt the morals of a minor . . ." said La Reine. "Give me a real man, like the ones Voris Palovoi preferred."

"Tonight, in all the confusion at the Carnival," said SuperSatanic, lowering her voice, "maybe you'll be able to find one. Right along here is where things will start to break up."

"And," said the Duchess in her most insinuating voice, "after a fellow has three beers and steps into the latrine, *anybody* can pick him up . . ."

"Uh-huh, if it weren't that for every man who steps into the latrine there are ten thousand fairies waiting for him," moaned Uglíssima.

"And ten thousand cops standing around watching," added the Duchess.

"Sometimes the cops let their hair down a little themselves," winked La Reine.

"Yeah, but if you look at 'em cross-eyed you could land in the clinker," replied the Duchess.

"Sometimes they screw you and then take you in precisely because you let 'em do it," SuperSatanic told them.

"These days, you can't even trust a natural-born butt-stuffer anymore," said La Reine, shaking her head.

"Lots of them become cops just so they can screw other cops," said Uglíssima, pursing her lips in pique.

"Yeah, and in time they turn into fairies," said SuperSatanic.

"That's often the way it goes, all right," said La Reine, nodding, in a voice of tragedy.

Then suddenly, looking out toward the ocean, they all fell silent. Near the coast, a pack of glorious stud-muffins were jogging through the surf, churning it into foam. It was an imploring, yearning surf that tried to reach the young men's thighs, splash their bathing trunks. The waves, shattered, emitted little moans and whines of pain at not being able to reach the sought-after goal. But the pack of stud-muffins jogged on impassively, while everyone on the beach sat as though petrified, gazing at that vision.

At last, emerging from her trance, Uglíssima spoke.

"They must belong to Fifo's secret service—he always gets the best ones."

"They say that after he sleeps with a man he has him shot," remarked SuperSatanic.

"That's not Fifo, that's Ramiro Valdés," said the Duchess.

"For heaven's sake, girls, if every time Fifo slept with a man he had him shot, there wouldn't be a man left on this whole godforsaken island," put in La Reine.

"So exactly how many do you think are left?" Uglíssima asked politely. "Between the men that Fifo shoots and the ones that get eaten by the sharks, this place is getting so low on meat that pretty soon we'll have to join a convent."

"Which would not require any great adjustment on *your* part, darling," said SuperSatanic.

"Here comes Mayoya!" announced the Duchess. "They say she's fallen in love with Bloodthirsty Shark."

"Not a word about Fifo or the sharks, now, girls," whispered La Reine. "Mayoya is bad news—she's a snitch, I'm sure of it. I've seen her swim way out to sea without getting even a nibble from the sharks."

"What we ought to do is take advantage of all the confusion at the Carnival to carve her face up a little bit," suggested SuperSatanic.

"And her tits. 'Cause the faggot has taken to thinking he's got tits," added Uglíssima.

"Hush now! Here she comes!" commanded La Reine.

And all the queens with their faded bathing suits made out of scraps of burlap and cast-off pants lay down on the beach to sun, though they had to cover their ears—the screams of the waves that couldn't reach the thighs of the young men jogging through the surf were deafening.

A Prayer

What new rhythm will I discover today? What word that I was beginning to think I would never be able to remember will give me back my childhood? What colors will surprise my eyes? What trilling will I hear among the pines, and with all my heart desire to imitate? What flower, or mushroom, or seashell found beside a rotting tree trunk will fill my cup of happiness to overflowing? What roar, what clamor will the waves greet me with? When I dive into the water, what new underwater landscapes will I discover there? What fragrances will the sea perfume me with? What peerless leaf will I find in the grass? What splendid teenager will turn me to worshipful stone when I round the corner? What ruffle in the air, what zephyr, what soft breeze will the evening offer me? What distant song will I hear, reminding me of another distant song and commanding me to sing *another* distant song? What tiny stone that I bend to pick up and put in my pocket will attract my attention? What happy voice will call out somewhere behind me and infuse me with its happiness? What mass of clouds that I have never seen before will I see today? What sunset will transfix me until it fades away? What piece of branch will I bring to my nose, its perfume a unique adventure? What gigantic black man will beckon me with a sign that I will not, and would never, ignore? What pane of glass will take fire in my honor with a sudden blaze of light? What sudden calm will fall over the sea and bestow upon me knowledge of the All? What crunching of tree limbs will rend my soul? What book, opened at random, will restore my faith in words? What housefly, dressed for the party, will buzz past my head? What intimations of inner peace will the darkness sigh, drawing me into complicity? What inexpungible splendor will the sky display? What secret susurrations will fill the night? What lovely image in my memory will I fall asleep to? What distant whistle will make me dream that I am still that man and that I am still alive? . . . Oh, God, of all those miracles, grant me at least one, even if the most insignificant of them.

A Letter

Dear Reinaldo,

I don't know whether this letter will reach you either, but I'm going to write to you anyway. Naturally, the first thing I did when I got here, even before washing off the dust of the road, was go into a bookstore and try to find a copy of that book you so terribly wanted me to get for you, to replace the one you lost on the beach while you were trying to get away from that hustler who was threatening to murder you, remember?—The Magic Mirror? But Spanish, French, even Chinese—I haven't been able to find a single copy of it. So I guess you'll have to do your novel without quoting it like you did in the ones before. Either that or just use the same quotations. Anyway, at this point, my dear, people don't read anything anymore. And if they do, they misread it.

I have met some writers over here, and I've talked to them about you, about your far-from-coddled captivity. They're all very circumspect, in spite of all that's happened in the world recently—they don't want to get into a "thing" with Fifo's government, since his beaches (which of course you aren't allowed to set foot on) are beautiful, his agents are very accommodating (in every sense of the word) to foreign writers, and then there are the literary prizes and other "awards" that Fifo hands out. A lot of them still think that attacking Fifo is in bad taste—not to mention the "relationships" that have developed over a period of forty years. When they finally do come out and criticize Fifo, they do so in a very roundabout and guarded way—they wouldn't want to offend, you know. And as for the sacred cows here in exile, they're just that—cows. They all think they're geniuses, and they're hypersensitive about their purported talent. None of them think even for one instant that they're any less great than the great Cervantes himself.

They all seem to think their shit smells like ice cream, as people here say—a nice expression, don't you think?

But since I know you're not interested in gossip about writers, let me move on. I want to tell you about a bridge.

I had no sooner got to Paris than I saw a bridge, far off in the distance. It was a beautiful bridge, of black, finespun antique railings that looked like the tendrils of some wonderful climbing vine. And not a car crossing that bridge. Just people. As soon as I could, I went out and tried to locate the bridge, but by the time I could catch even the slightest glimpse, it suddenly started raining—one of those icy, pouring rains that cut you to the bone (not to mention the soul)—and I had to turn back. I took the Metro back for fear of catching pneumonia. But the next week I armed myself with an umbrella and headed for that bridge again. But just my luck, my dear—before I could get there, another downpour. This one was a real storm, with wind that turned the umbrella inside out and stripped the nice black nylon right off the ribs and almost blew yours truly into the Seine. So I turned what was left of the umbrella loose (gone with the wind, indeed) and started toward the Metro entrance, for fear of that damned pneumonia again, since those of us who have the AIDS virus (which I do, of course) are especially susceptible. I figure at least my umbrella made it to the bridge. . . . I've tried a couple of other times to reach it (always in the rain—a rain like diarrhea, which is what the rain is like here, and which _always_ falls that way even when there's another kind of rain at the same time), but every time I leave the house, everything looks so gray and wet that I'm not sure, really, whether it's worth it for me to walk all the way there. Although sooner or later, of course, I _will_ see it close up, and I'll send you a photo, too, if I don't turn green from mildew or freeze to death or die of depression first. Because here, _spring is slow in coming,_ as "The Magic Mirror" says, _though the grass of grief grows green in every season._ No, my dear, don't come—melt in the sun down there, die of fury within your _own_ solitude. Don't come to Paris to experience this cold that isn't yours and calamities that are foreign to you but that you'll have to bow to. My saints have all dried up, my orishas have lost all their feathers, and even their chicken skin. And as though that weren't bad enough, there's the Plague. We can't even screw anymore, sugar. We've all turned into holy virgin martyrs, but waiting for a horrible slow death instead of canonization or immediate destruction. Who'd've thought that our sufferings would never end and on top of that be so totally unpredictable? What do you think of the grin the She-Devil has grinned at us? Because if Hell does exist, and it's the <u>only</u> thing that exists, it's not even ruled over by the Devil—it's a She-Devil that runs the show! It's cruel to write all this to you of all people, especially since you still have hopes for life on the other side of the wall. But it might be crueler yet to keep it to myself.

As for the French—most of them have no chin and a turned-up nose that looks like they were smelling a rat held up about twelve feet off the floor. By the expression on their faces, the rat's not particularly fresh, either. Of course, the whole city smells like cunt.

I'm off to New York. I'll write when I get there, like I always do, wherever I am. But why don't <u>you</u> write <u>me?</u> I've sent you <u>hundreds</u> of letters and haven't received even <u>one</u> reply. I've sent letters to every pseudonym and by every route imaginable, even by mail. I've visited Maoist tourists that have <u>promised</u> to drop the letter in a Cuban mailbox, because I lied and said I was an <u>intimate</u> friend of Chelo's. Some of them have told me that they even slipped the letter under your door at the Hotel Monserrate. So I mean you <u>have</u> to have gotten a note from me. Don't tell me you joined the Party and are using my letters as a proof of your loyalty, turning them in to the lieutenant who's your contact. Or tell me that you <u>are,</u> so I can write you more often and continue to be a help to you. But either way, for goodness' sake, <u>write.</u> Take pity on one who lives in this sopping-wet desert. And to top it off, even the Arabs have given up butt-fucking and the pansies have all gotten married and started having kids.

A big smooch from yours in deepest mourning—
Skunk in a (very blue) Funk

A Walking Tour Through Old Havana in the Company of Alejo Sholekhov

The door of the catacomb-like palace opened and the procession, led by Fifo, emerged. Although on solar time it was almost ten o'clock at night, to all appearances the sun was blazing in the sky—because in order to prolong the hours of daylight during this once-in-a-lifetime event the Island had changed over to Fiferonian Time, and cannons, lasers, floating light rigs, huge mirrors, and an immense flamethrower that Fifo's agents claimed to have confiscated from an agent of the CIA were pressed into service, substantial modifications were made to the natural course of things, and a blazing noon (which might suddenly become the darkest night) assailed the entire Island.

The Program of Activities indicated that before Fifo inaugurated the Grand Carnival, there was to be a walking tour through Old Havana guided by Alejo Sholekhov, who had also been brought back to life especially for that event. It was hoped that in compliance with a request made by Fifo himself, Sholekhov would be brief. But heavens, who had the heart to shut up an old man with a nineteenth-century speaking style (meaning you couldn't get a word in edgewise, the old thing just went on and on) and who on top of that had spent the last twenty years or so in silence under a gravestone? So that reading-room baroque of his just bubbled out like an old fountain, and in a voice like the croaking of a French frog with rheumatism. Followed closely on his right hand by Alfredo Lam (who had also been resurrected for this event and who handled his wheelchair with a skill that would have been admirable even in the finest horseman of the Arthurian Round Table), Sholekhov began his tour not with Old Havana, as might have been expected, but instead (at a pace amazing for a man of his age) down the Calzada de Jesús del Monte, then (lecturing all the way) up the Calzada del Cerro, then (still talking) down the Calzada de Luyanó, the Avenida Carlos III, and the Paseo de la Infanta. Then, not even stopping to catch his breath, the old man climbed Galiano and walked the whole length of the Calle de la Reina, lecturing not only in Spanish but in French as well on the beauties of iron pickets, brass door knockers, and spur stones. From time to time he would suddenly halt at the head of the exhausted procession, tick off (with upraised cane) the advantages of Le Corbusier's *brise-soleil* or declare that throughout Havana one could see wonderful examples of an architecture *dans le style parisien au fin de siècle*—even including those improvised wooden sleeping lofts (built by Skunk in a Funk in so many Havana rooms) that held up to a hundred people. . . . The people who'd been roped into the tour couldn't take much more of this. They could feel the rhythms of the Carnival's infectious revelry beginning to get to them, while like some strange procession of the faithful they had to follow this old man dressed in black who was now going on and on about majestic carved-mahogany screens, stained-glass lunettes, and other things you never saw anywhere anymore. No doubt to the *épatement* even of Lezama Lima's capacious memory, Sholekhov made associations between ogives and snippets from Racine and declared (always in that deep-throated croak like some Gallic frog) that the architecture of Havana was much closer to that of Segovia and Cádiz than Cholula's, or even El Morro Fortress', was. . . . Festooned doublets fraternized (for reasons that are no doubt as clear to you as they were to anybody else, darling) with Louis Juvet's legs, the theories of Robert Desnos, and a few paragraphs of André Breton. At last (at last!), steadying himself on his cane as he smartly clicked his heels, Sholekhov turned down Calle Obispo in Old Havana. And there he launched into a grand theory of the Cuban baroque, which in his view could be defined by accumulation, collection, multiplication, division, and addition. And so, using arithmetical explanations, he leapt from Calle Obispo to the French Revolution and from the French Revolution to Versailles and the palace's wrought-iron bars with rosettes shaped like peacocks' tails, intertwining arabesques, and prodigious rows of lances. . . . While the writer spoke of the orders of wrought-iron bars—severe, votive, Gothic, and a style he himself called "tortured"—his tortured audience had reached the limit of their patience. As had Fifo, who ordered one of his midgets to strangle (and I quote) "that old son of a bitch." (Lam volunteered to run over him with his wheelchair.) But before Sholekhov's execution could be carried out, the Minister of Culture whispered in Fifo's ear that among the audience there was a powerful delegation from UNASCO (made up entirely of Frenchmen, of course), which was going to make a large contribution toward the supposed restoration of Old Havana—which meant that Sholekhov's lecture was of vital importance. So there was nothing for it but to keep listening to the long-dead author, who was now declaring that the wrought-iron grillwork of Cuba was an imitation of the goat motif (the cabrioles) used in the ironwork of the house of El Greco, and that Cuba possessesd Alcázars in the Moorish style and medieval castles with modernized facades and some quite unexpected allusions to Blois de Chambord. And then, hardly stopping for breath, the elderly gentleman sprang (on his cane) to the center of the Plaza Vieja, where he launched into what we might call the "heart of his lecture": "As I was saying, Havana, the gateway to the New World, is the proud possessor of more columns than any other city of the continent." And here the renowned author, followed by the procession of the faithful, began to march through colonnade after colonnade (most of them shored up by two-by-fours and piles of rubble), naming over, and sometimes tapping with his cane, every single column. . . . "Here we have a half-length Doric column; then a Corinthian; and this one here is a stunted or 'dwarf' column; and this one, with its concrete caryatids, is an extraordinary example of a nineteenth-century *vignoble.* It is by virtue of all these columns that we Cubans, for so I still consider myself, have been able to brave the sun and even time. This is, dear friends, truly the City of Columns. Columns, colonnades, columnists, columniasts—we have lived so long among these columns that we have *forgotten* about columns, and about the fact that they must be saved, for not only do they protect us from the heat of summer, they sustain our roofs and rooftop aeries and accompany even Ferdinand VII with his emblematic lions. . . . Columns, the trunks of the trees of imaginary jungles and unimaginable forums—infinite coliseums. Columns, columns, the magical columns of Havana, which sensibly remind us of those lines of Baudelaire:

Temple où de vivants piliers
Laissent parfois sortir de confuses paroles . . . ."

And here the reborn author, about to take a breath and continue with his recitation of the poem (for we must not forget that the members of the UNASCO delegation were all French), leaned against one of his beloved columns—an act that was to cost him his new life, for this column, like all the columns in Old Havana, was held up by little more than the grace of the Holy Spirit and a few rusty iron reinforcing rods. There was no way in the world the column could support the old man's weight, and so it collapsed—and with it the entire roof, and then, like a row of dominoes, one by one, every column on the street. The last words (in French, for the record) that Sholekhov spoke were drowned in the noise of the falling columns that entombed him.

But perhaps the most astonishing thing about this disaster was not the toppling of the columns—which was going to happen sooner or later, anyway—but rather the fact that along with the columns and roofs there collapsed into the street a field of corn, a stand of plantains, a tomato garden, and a little plot of cassava. You see, the inhabitants of Old Havana had their own aerial truck farm, where they grew what food they could to mitigate the hunger produced by forty years of rationing. So a jungle that was not only architectural, but vegetable as well, entombed the author of *El saco de las lozas* for all eternity. But this last detail—the collapse of the vegetable gardens—apparently went unnoticed by the members of the UNASCO delegation as well as the procession in general, who looked with a sigh of relief upon the mound of rubble under which the author lay buried. So relieved were they, in fact, that they broke into applause for the "brilliant" lecture and the "heroic" end of the writer who sacrificed himself for his city. On the spot, the cave-in was declared a national disaster and the members of the UNASCO delegation pledged aid of not only the ten million dollars they had already promised, but fifty million more.

"Let's get that humanitarian agreement signed at once!" ordered Fifo.

And on the instant, among the ruined columns, the uprooted tubers of the cassava, and the stalks of corn, the contract was signed and it was agreed by all the signatories that Old Havana would for all eternity thereafter be called *The City of Columns* (it occurred to no one that it could also be called *Men of Corn*)—and that on that spot there would be erected a column taller than that in Barcelona upon which stands the statue of Columbus. Crowning the column would be a likeness of Sholekhov, who would hold in his hand a tiny Ionic column.

"And now," shouted a happy Fifo, "let's *party!* The hour for the Carnival has come round at last!"

And the official procession, led by Fifo riding inside a huge red balloon, turned down the Avenida del Puerto. Behind it there came the gigantic parade, and then the floats and all the bands. And thus it was that the Great Havana Carnival—which in fact had begun several hours earlier—officially began.

Buses or Turtles?

The Duchess, Sanjuro, Le Seigneur des Camélias, SuperSatanic, the Clandestine Clairvoyant, Uglíssima, La Reine, SuperChelo, the Eggsucking Dog, and a couple of other screaming queens, after frying themselves to a crisp all morning cruising La Concha beach, had skipped and trudged, sometimes trying to thumb a ride and sometimes being sideswiped by the mudflaps on a Number 62 bus, to the beach at El Mégano, always in quest of their El Dorado—i.e., a golden-bronze man.

After three hours of cruising *that* hellishly hot beach, the only man they'd seen had been a policeman (a policeman who actually told them what time it was) dressed in civilian clothes, who'd asked for their ID cards. And after checking the obligatory identification, he told the fairies that that beach was posted as a tourist zone and was off limits to Cuban citizens, so they'd better move along.

The Duchess argued that her grandparents (or somebody) were Italians, and that she was descended from the noble house of Piamontes.

"Look," impatiently said the policeman, a round and firm and fully-packed specimen of love-godhood who looked to be about twenty, "you can pee on Monty if he lets you, I really don't much care one way or the other, but you'll have to do it somewhere else, because you people make the country look bad to the tourists. So pick up your things and beat it," concluded the stunning instrument of repression "—now!"

I'll tell you, girl . . . *Enough of that "girl" stuff; I'm fifty years old and've got more hair than a grizzly bear.* Ungrateful thing, I was just trying to be nice. *Well, OK then . . .* So as I was saying, you fat old queen with that chicken-skin neck of yours: The poor pansies had to take the Villadiego road and march—and I do mean march, eyes front and everything, because that hunk of a policeman escorted them every step of the way—all the way to the bus stop where they could catch the bus that would take them to the Guanabo bus terminal where they'd have to stand in a line about half a mile long so they could finally get their defeated and feather-bedraggled asses back to Havana. The policeman, thighs and crotch about to burst out of those foreign-made mechanic's overalls of his, stood there, right by the bus stop (although not too close to the fairies), waiting for the hags to catch their bus and beat it. He knew if he turned his back on them for a second, they'd go back to the beach.

The sun inflicted such martyrdom on the poor queens (specifically on them, for some reason) that they hopped up and down on one foot on the shimmering pavement.

Suddenly, the queens saw the figure of a skinny, ungainly-looking fairy with a wet backpack slung over his shoulder walk barefoot out of the stand of pines down near the shore and head straight for the magnificent cop-dressed-as-a-teenybop. It was Skunk in a Funk, whose swim fins had been stolen by Tatica on Patricio Lumumba Beach and who for days (or maybe it was just for hours, but *hours and hours)* had been *so* unable to contain her rage—and her desire for revenge—that she had stalked every beach, every inch of Havana's coastline on the trail of that gorgeous but cruel thief Tatica. Hot with a double fury—moral and rectal—Skunk in a Funk had finally reached Guanabo—searching every wave, every pine tree, every cubic inch of sand along the way, and sidling up suggestively to all the young hunks on the beach, too, whispering sweet nothings in their ears, but all of them had frowned at her and spit. Finally, swimming underwater, he had yanked on the pricks of about a hundred of the kids, who swam after her through the ocean (ready to kill her) even at the risk of being eaten by the sharks. Finally, the outraged twinks had threatened to slit Skunk in a Funk's throat if she ever set foot on land again, but expert swimmer that she was (even without her swim fins), she dived underwater and swam along the bottom of the ocean (sea urchins and sand dollars fleeing in terror) and emerged down the coast—emerged, in fact, almost right beside the magnificent hunk of a cop who was keeping an eye on the banished fairies.

"Don't tell 'er he's a cop. Don't even say hello, so he'll arrest her," said SuperSatanic.

"Ooh, what a wonderful idea! Let's watch them put the handcuffs on her, and maybe even beat her," shivered the Duchess. "Because if they're going to run me—*me,* who am descended from royal blood—away, imagine the tortures in store for that *peasant."*

"Would you look at the gall that crazy suicide's got, the way she cozies up to that trick and just starts chatting," said La Reine, feigning regal unconcern.

"And the trick, like the upstanding cop he is, leads her on so she'll show her true colors," remarked Uglíssima.

"Which she's already doing, if you'll notice," said Sanjuro. "Look, she's flaunting that little bubble-butt of hers."

"Now she'd done for, they'll be coming to take her away," predicted the Clandestine Clairvoyant.

"They might just shoot her in the head," wished SuperSatanic.

"Omigod!" exclaimed La Reine, "that my noble eyes should have to see a murder perpetrated virtually under my royal eyelashes . . ."

"Listen, you nelly faggot," shot back the SuperChelo, "don't play the saint with us—we know you're *dying* to see the queen get her brains blown out."

"Well I never! My sentiments are as pure as Odoriferous Gunk's herself's," La Reine replied.

"Can you believe that Funky-girl's balls!" shrieked Eggsucking Dog.

"Look how she's just leading that cop right off under that guava tree, still talking a mile a minute."

"And that cop! What's he waiting for?! He's supposed to arrest her!" whined SuperSatanic.

"Don't look, girls—they might arrest us too, as accomplices," counseled the Clandestine Clairvoyant.

"Oooh, how stupid we were! We should have stood under that guava tree so we wouldn't be out here broiling our pansy asses in this sun," Sanjuro complained.

"Look! Look! That Skunk's got her hands all over the cop's crotch!" softly shrieked the Duchess.

"Look! Look! The cop's crotch looks like it's about to explode."

"My *God!* What sights must these noble eyes be forced to look upon!"

"Calm down, girls, calm down . . . This is when he takes out his gun and shoots her in the head. He's probably got it hidden right there under his balls. . . ."

"Look! Look! Skunk in a Funk is on her knees and . . . *she's sucking that cop off!*"

"Omigod, I can't stand it! Call the police!"

"You idiot, that *is* the police!"

"Look Look! Skunk in a Funk has slipped off her jeans and her underwear and she's still sucking! Look at the way that glutton stuffs the whole thing in her mouth . . ."

"Calm down, now, girls, this is where he's bound to shoot her, with her mouth at the cookie jar."

"Cookie jar! And what I wouldn't give for some of that cookie! He'll kill her, all right, but with that prick."

"My *God!* Right out where anybody can watch! And to think that I, La Reine, the queen of queens, should have to witness such a sight. Why, a child could walk by and see it. I insist that we call the police."

"Girlfriend, the police has his hands full at the moment, as you can see."

"Look! Look! Skunk in a Funk has pulled off the cop's pants and *the cop is screwing her!*"

"Oh. My. God. I think I'm going to faint. . . ."

The queens, more flustered and envious by the minute, went on with their off-color commentary, their play-by-play broadcast of Skunk in a Funk's score. And the truth was, the sexual square-off between Skunk in a Funk and the young cop had no parallel in the sexual history of the public thoroughfares of Guanabo. The Skunk, pants around her ankles, had thrown her arms around the trunk of the guava tree as the cop had his way with her, and the force of their coupling was shaking the guava tree with such fury that their naked bodies were being pelted with falling fruit. The young cop snorted with pleasure, while Skunk in a Funk emitted howls that echoed throughout the pine grove and the guava tree shook, shimmied, and dropped its hail of guavas. Finally, the two bodies stripped off *all* their clothes and fell to the ground. Skunk in a Funk, on all fours, was taking the entire length of the policeman's member (which was, I'll tell you honey, *huge)*. Under the tropical sun, you'd watch that big black nightstick of his going in and out and in and out of the Skunk's arched body. Skunk herself was going crazy with pleasure, pulling up grass with her teeth and throwing guavas up in the air. In a wink, the policeman slipped off his olive-green underwear and pistol and went back to humping Skunk in a Funk, who, possessed by delirium as well as by the cop, grabbed the gun and threw it way off into the undergrowth and followed it up with her own backpack, out of which dropped the wet manuscript of the novel, *The Color of Summer,* that she was working on. . . . Boots, olive-green socks, olive-green underwear, grass, leaves, seeds, a cartridge belt filled with bullets, ripe guavas—it all sailed through the air as though by magic from those naked bodies locked in a sexual combat more powerful than politics or geography. Finally, Skunk sprawled out on the grass face down and was drilled wildly by the policeman, who now seemed to be screwing not a human body but rather the entire planet.

Just then, to the delight of the openmouthed (and drooling) fairies who were contemplating that outrageous coupling, a Number 162 bus appeared on the horizon.

"Flag it down," ordered La Reine. "Make it stop right here and take those two depraved perverts prisoner."

"Right on!" shouted SuperSatanic. "Let 'em rot in jail for contempt of court, making a public nuisance, sodomy in the public thoroughfare . . ."

"And high treason," put in the SuperChelo. "Don't forget, there's a soldier involved."

"And damage to state property," added the Clandestine Clairvoyant. "Look what they've done to that guava tree—not a guava left on it. Com*plete*ly destroyed."

"What an outrage!" exclaimed La Reine. "And for the firing squad—because most assuredly they shall face the firing squad—I believe I'll wear my diadem."

"Well, I'm going to wear a loincloth made out of guava leaves," said Uglíssima.

"I'll be stunning. Black right up to my chin. It is a solemn act . . ."

"I . . ."

"Hush, now, all of you. Here comes the bus."

A Number 162 full of people came to a stop beside the queens, who were jumping up and down and pointing off to where the impassioned coupling was going on. And that bus went *wild,* honey! Hundreds of heads started sticking out the windows (or as much as they could—those windows are pretty narrow). One woman died of a heart attack. The uproar was so uproarious that the driver had to honk three or four times before he could make himself heard.

"Ladies and gentlemen!" he shouted. "You all just pull your hands out of your pockets or wherever you've got them and listen up. If you all agree, then instead of going on to the bus stop in Guanabo, we'll go straight to the nearest police station, which is just five minutes from here. We'll send a patrol car and have 'em arrested."

"Why don't you arrest them yourself?" asked La Reine des Araignées.

"Do I look like a cop?" replied the driver (who was, however, starting to show a very coplike woody about now). And having nothing else to stomp on, he stomped on the accelerator and sped off toward the police station.

"Queers!" shouted the passengers in unison at the naked bodies, which were still totally oblivious to everything but their own lust.

So now the envious queens were riding along with big smiles on their faces, headed toward the police station. They were hanging on to the door of the bus, since not another speck of fairy dust would fit inside. They would be the main witnesses in the case—although of course so would the other passengers, all those people who despite feeling more than a little itchy, a little antsy, if you know what I mean, wrapped themselves in a mantle of morality. Never have I seen such piety, girl. . . .

I told you to stop calling me girl!

Such piety, you old queen—I mean even the old queens (like yourself) and the crazy, desperate, broken-down old biddies (like yourself) that couldn't take their eyes off the spectacle ten minutes ago, not to mention taking their hand off the bulging fly of that young man standing there beside them in that bus, all suddenly turned nuns. Miss Erick, the Carmelite nun; Miss Osuna, a Dominican nun; even Miss Horrid Marmot, who was traveling in military drag and who'd sucked off a militia boy right there in the bus—she'd turned into a cloister queen. Nuns, I tell you!—even the queens that were hanging on the doors of the bus would sometimes, risking their lives, hold on with just one hand while they piously made the sign of the cross over themselves. . . . But oh, sugar, as in the age-old division between spirit and flesh, the traveler may think one thing, but the vehicle thinks another—and by "vehicle" I mean the bus that all those justice-craving nuns were riding in. Because I can tell you, you old she-donkey . . .

Your mother's *the she-donkey!*

I can tell you, you little she-mule you, that the above-mentioned bus (a female member of the species) was first cousin to that Pandarus Leyland (now a poor old battered, beaten-up shadow of himself who'd been sent off to pasture on the Number 10 line) who'd given succor to so many guys getting sucked off on the municipal and interprovincial routes that it once ran. Anyway, what I'm saying is that the sex gene seems to've run in the family, because in her early days, this Number 162 number that we've just met had been a secret *and intimate* friend of Margot Thayert. Their friendship blossomed (burst forth, more like it) at first sight the day the Prime Minister went to visit the Leyland bus factory. The Prime Minister was enchanted by that shining, powerful specimen of a *real lady bus,* and as she ran her hand over her admiringly she whispered a place and time for a tryst—she would be in a certain place, she promised, that very night, dressed as a transport worker. And on that night of love, the lustful words spoken by the Prime Minister, her sexual potency (in fact, that night the Iron Lady discovered that her sexual passion could be matched only by that of an English omnibus) awoke in all the female members of the noble Leyland clan a lesbian militancy that was indestructible and supremely powerful.

That is why when the long-suffering old Leyland girl (Celestina by name), sent to Cuba to become a Number 162, saw those naked bodies rolling around in the grass, she felt her chassis, her flywheels, her tires, and especially her engine getting hotter and hotter. The erotic charge that those bodies inspired in her was so irresistible that she took off like a *much* younger machine, in search not of the Guanabo police station but of another Leyland bus that she could get it on with.

The speed at which that old bus was now traveling was truly dizzying (more than two hundred miles an hour), and all the passengers were screaming for it to slow down; but the driver, who was yelling a little himself, couldn't do a thing. The bus, gushing Russian oil and gasoline, was roaring, growling, mooing, and clattering along in search of another bus that she could screw—and the sooner the better, hon—and totally oblivious to both the driver's desperate attempts to control her and the passengers'screams of terror—among which, one, a *H-E-E-E-E-E-LP!* in C-sharp major held for a record-breaking time by the SuperChelo, is particularly worth noting, though I must say in all honesty that it was accompanied by an entire chorus of screaming queens suddenly turned streaking meteors.

When Celestina, in a fury of lust, came to the wooden bridge at Bocaciega, she met an old Number 62 huffing and puffing toward Havana. Without so much as a howdy-do, the sexually aroused Celestina threw herself on the other bus and began to rub up against her so violently that her springs, tires, seats, lightbulbs—everything—started falling off. The passengers, terrified (and having not the slightest clue as to what was really going on), yelled and screamed to open the doors so they could escape the collision. The driver tried time and time again—he pushed, pulled, and squeezed every button and lever that could be pushed, pulled, or squeezed—but the doors would not open. The two buses were oblivious to anything but their mutual *frottage.* Turned sideways in the middle of the wooden bridge (which creaked piteously throughout all this), they rubbed their metal bellies against each other with such force that soon the two iron lesbians turned cherry-red. And then, in the paroxysm of their lust, a spark ignited both engines and both gas tanks. Suddenly there was a terrible—*a deafening*—explosion, and the two buses, now inflamed for real, and locked in a burning embrace, rose several yards into the sky, culminating their rite of love in a grand and final fireball—which was taken by the entire population of Havana to be the official kickoff of the grand celebration of Fifo's fifty years in power, the fireworks that were getting the show started. But within a few minutes, Radio Rebel scotched that rumor. To a rather premature drumroll, a stern-voiced announcer reported that "a drunken, depraved, and counterrevolutionary bus driver has driven his bus, which the Party had entrusted him to drive, into another bus, which was also in public service, causing the death of three hundred twenty-five comrades."

The only survivors of this catastrophe were the Duchess, Sanjuro, SuperSatanic, the Clandestine Clairvoyant, Uglíssima, La Reine des Araignées, the SuperChelo, and Eggsucking Dog, plus three other screaming queens who had been hanging onto the outside of the bus and so were flung free of the explosion before they could be incinerated. In fact, once they were in the air, like the good fairy queens they were, they just kept flying along until they landed (a little singed, but otherwise just fine) on the Malecón, where the floats and bands were beginning their final rehearsals.

When Skunk in a Funk heard the explosion, she thought it was the young cop who'd finally (finally!) cum inside her—deserving as she was of such a tribute (the conceited thing). So she pu-u-u-ulled her still-quivering body out from under him, threw on her clothes as fast as she could, gathered up her belongings (plus three ripe guavas), and took off.

"Stop right there, you faggot, you're under arrest!" shouted the gorgeous policeman (who'd cum inside the fugitive some twelve times, which meant that he'd managed to recover his revolutionary morality—and his pistol). "Stop right there, you *rodent,* or I'll shoot!"

But Skunk in a Funk, who was always prepared for this sort of eventuality (and even worse), disappeared as though by magic among the mangroves while behind her, she heard a shot.

Oscar Flies by Night

Oscar is a queen with huge teeth, a round bald head, and a bent, knotty body like a bat's. But a very hip old queen (Papayi Toloka? Miss Julio Natilla?) had once given him a very hip piece of advice: *In the dark, man,* the old queen crooned, *all cats are gay.* So Oscar did his flying by night.

—*Oscar! Oscar!* The fairy hears someone calling his name—and ooh, it's those hunky young men gathered under the big trees at the Copelia ice-cream parlor. But as he descends, as he lights on one of the branches, Oscar sees a group of screaming, limp-wristed, fluttering queens (just like her) futilely trying to pick up a man. . . . So Oscar spreads his big wings and once more, eyes peeled, mounts into the sky. . . . *Oscar! Oscar! Oscar!* Once more he hears his name—hears thousands of young men calling out her name. And the big queer bat descends. A thousand desperate fairies, perched on the branches of the trees, are cackling, pecking at each other, flinging insults back and forth, tearing at each other's flesh—and making the most *awful* racket. Oscar flaps his wings again and lifts off into the night sky. . . . —*Oscar! Oscar! Oscar!* His name is being called again, this time by what sounds like the most virile men in the world. And Oscar flaps his big bat wings, peels his big red bug-eyes, and lowers his outsized head. Thousands of faggots of the *worst* sort are flooding the Paseo del Prado, and so many feathers, so much twinkle-dust gets raised by their milling about that for a moment Oscar can't even see what's happening down there. Finally the air clears, and, once more disillusioned, he rises into the sky again. . . . Now, from up above, Oscar contemplates the jam-packed, hysterical city, the infinite lines for an ice-cream cone or a pizza, the superinfinite lines to see a movie you've already seen a hundred times, the sea wall on the Malecón that thousands of people approach very cautiously, because Fifo's sharks are sometimes lurking just at the edge of the water. Oscar now flies even higher into the clouds, and he dreams. . . . *If only. . .*, he thought, *if only there existed someplace . . . someplace where a poor fairy of supreme ugliness could be accepted.* But Oscar knows that if for him there's the slightest chance of getting screwed, then that chance lies here, on this island festering with madness, desperation, and chaos. Anywhere else, they'd throw her in a cage and exhibit her in some circus. Not here—here there's no need to, because horror is so familiar here. And besides—everybody is already in a cage. —*Oscar! Oscar!* He once more hears the cries of an army calling out her name, wanting to possess her. And so Oscar descends, and she almost hits the ground before she swiftly flies up again—he's witnessing the biggest round-up of queers ever recorded in the history of humanity and faggotry. Thousands of queens, fairies, faggots, and even just bi-curious young men are arrested and kicked into buses, iron cages, and patrol cars, and from there transferred to forced-labor camps. Oscar takes off like a rocket, and now, now he's in the clouds again—the moon shrinks back in horror—hearing the voices of the thousands of young men that call out to him.

A Journey to Holguín

Gabriel was going back to Holguín to visit his mother, as he did every year. Each time he came back to the place where he once lived, in that (perversely named) neighborhood of Vista Alegre, his mother would be outside, sweeping the street. His mother swept so lightly that the broom would barely brush the ground, much less sweep away the dirt. To Gabriel's eyes, the way his mother swept had something stubbornly resigned about it, yet in a sense something poetic, too. For it really wasn't the sweeping itself that was important, it was what his mother *said* by sweeping—she said (or showed) that she would never give in to so much dust and dirt, so much litter, even though she knew she could never sweep it all away, would never be able to sweep (much less keep) the whole street clean. But there was another symbolism in it, too, thought Gabriel: Since he always wrote to announce that he was coming, he sensed that his mother was always there, waiting for him, broom in hand, in order to show him, the son who had abandoned her, how painful, how filled with suffering and hard work her life was, how many defeats (still not swept away) her memory still held. For in that face there was, deeper than resignation, a tremendous sadness, a quiet grief, as she went on, endlessly, with her pointless labor, sweeping tattered pieces of paper from one place to another, sweeping leaves into a pile, struggling almost spiritlessly (yet unable to stop) against the crumbling rocks and cement, the omnipresent grime. Sometimes she would talk to herself, but so softly that only the broom could hear her. Sometimes it may have been, in fact, a real conversation between her and the broom, which had been her most faithful friend for more than sixty years.

The mother had once had a husband, but he abandoned her with a son who, hardly more than a teenager, had also fled the little town. But she still had her broom. Still had, that is, what she had always had. When she was a girl, hadn't she danced with the broom? And the way she endlessly swept the street and softly talked—wasn't that her way of taking a little walk with her most faithful friend, the broom? It was only logical that she'd talk to the broom, the only thing that hadn't run off and left her.

Gabriel came up to his mother, and his mother, never turning loose of the broom, hugged and kissed him. They went inside the house, which seemed feverish from its fiber-cement roof. Before the mother gave her son her full attention, she gave a few swipes of the broom at the living room. Then she set her instrument, her tool, her equipment, beside the door. And there the broom sat, as though watching over the conversation between the mother and the son, a conversation which was always the same. MOTHER: How has your health been, how has your work been, how have your wife and son been, why don't you come to see me, Havana is so noisy, why don't you move to Holguín? SON: I've been fine, my work isn't bad, the baby is very healthy and my wife is too, you know how it is, we've gotten used to Havana, it's so hard to move. . . . And the mother would adopt an expression of patient resignation with the son—the same expression she wore with the broom. And the son would feel tremendous pity for her, tremendous love, a tremendous desire to go to her and hug her and beg her not to make that sad, grieving face like that, because after all, she didn't have so much to complain about. He would even feel like telling her that if he'd left the town he grew up in, it was so she wouldn't have to hear the rumors of his private life, and that if he'd gotten married and even had a son it was so she could tell her friends about it (and no doubt her broom too), and put to rest all those suspicions about his sexual life—the sexual life of *her son.* Listen, I've gotten married, I have a child, I've done all of that for *you.* I've made other people unhappy for you, I've brought a baby into the world that didn't have to come into this hell and suffer, and it was for you. And above all—listen, listen—I have not betrayed myself. I'm not a person, I'm two or three people at the same time. For you, I'm still Gabriel, for those who read what I write but can hardly ever publish, I'm Reinaldo, for the rest of my friends, with whom I escape from time to time in order to be totally myself, I'm Skunk in a Funk. You have your broom; all I have is desperation. Understand me! Accept me as I am! I have sacrificed almost everything for you. Forgive the fact that once in a while I'm Skunk in a Funk and run out to chase after some man, or thousands of men. Because—listen to me—maybe I like men so much because you couldn't hold on to the one you had, and somehow that cycle interrupted in you has to be completed. That man, or the *men,* that you desired and never had—that man is me (by some mysterious law), who has to seek them out in weedy fields, or anywhere, at the risk of my own life. I am the guilty one. Although really, nobody is guilty for any of this. . . .

"I suppose the baby's already crawling?"

"Uh-huh. He's even walking a little bit," lied Gabriel.

"I suppose your wife's gone back to work now?"

"Uh-huh. Months ago," lied Reinaldo.

"Tell me the truth—are you two happy, do you get along?"

"Yes! Oh, yes!" enthusiastically lied Skunk in a Funk. "I'm very happy."

"And what about her?" the mother asked, now beginning to sweep the hall.

"She's very happy too. Why shouldn't she be?" asked Gabriel.

"I don't know," said the mother. "The last time I saw her there seemed to be something in her . . . something she didn't want to tell me. Something very sad."

"I told you she's as happy as I am," Reinaldo assured her.

Happy—what a stupid word, thought Skunk in a Funk. *Happy,* and it was all he could do not to burst out laughing behind his mother, who was still sweeping. Not a happy burst of laughter, either. How could a queer who was married with a child, officially "integrated" into the system, be happy? How could a person be happy when his true existence was a secret one, when he almost always had to wear a mask—perform, play a part, pretend that he believed, that he loved, that he fully trusted in the regime that he despised yet apparently was a militant in yet timidly conspired against? . . . *Happy?*—don't make me laugh! Oh, there were times, whenever he could escape from his role as husband and father, that he would be transformed, become another person, and have those adventures with some man (or somebody that at least looked like one). Before he got married, Skunk in a Funk had lived with an evil aunt—a sinister person who would steal the little that his ration card permitted him to have. But he had had a room in that house, which the real owners had abandoned when they fled to Miami; into that room, Skunk in a Funk (sneaking—or thinking she was sneaking—past the aunt's lookout) would smuggle some man. Then, in spite of the danger, while somebody (some *body*) possessed her, Skunk in a Funk was truly happy, or thought she was, maybe because she was young. But the danger loomed more certain every day, the aunt reported her to the authorities, she spent a year in the prison at El Morro. Oh, the face of his mother walking into El Morro with her shopping bag. . . . At that point, Skunk in a Funk decided to "cure herself," get married, forget about her sexual preferences, her own life, and think instead of the life of that lonely old woman whose only possession, only consolation, was her broom. Yes, he got married (the mother went to the wedding), had a son (the mother attended the almost clandestine christening). Gabriel came to feel real affection for his wife and tremendous love for his son. But nobody can betray himself for his entire life. And when a young man walked by, when a man looked at him, Gabriel would turn into Skunk in a Funk disguised as a man and, child in his arms, wife beside him, would feel a pull more inexorable than all others. And he would realize that for him, there was no deliverance but going to bed with one of those men that he furtively gazed at. It was impossible for Reinaldo, even when most immersed in literature, to disobey that call, which was more powerful than any danger—and Gabriel would once more become Skunk in a Funk, once more return to that room that he had managed (employing every subterfuge he could invent) to get for himself in the Hotel Monserrate shortly after he'd been released from jail, once more become a queen, though now even more desperate than the queen he'd been before—because now he was older, and the time left him for bedding down some body was growing shorter by the day. The fact was, months would now go by without his seeing his wife and son—both of whom he had killed off, anyway, along with himself, the husband, in one of his unpublishable novels.

"I don't like Havana," said the mother, turning to deposit the broom behind the front door. "There are so many bad people there, so many immoral people. So much envy. Remember what they did to *you.* You wound up in jail. That almost killed me."

"Please, mother, let's not start in on that again. That was a long time ago. I know what I'm doing."

But the mother started in on that again. That same old song—how much she'd suffered on his account: If you'd only stayed here in Holguín, those lowlifes that claimed to be your friends wouldn't have gotten you into political trouble (that was the story that Skunk in a Funk told her mother about why she was sent to prison), you'd never have wound up in jail, and I'd never have been destroyed. *Destroyed*—that was the word she used. And since there was no other word that could paint the tragedy of her life in any blacker terms, the mother gave several swipes of the broom at the front porch and then went off to start dinner.

"Since I knew you were coming I got some things on the underground market—a piece of steak and some yautías. When you were a little boy you used to love yautías. I'd boil them and mash them up for you. . . . You used to love yautías."

They spent the rest of the day talking about how bad things were these days, all the shortages. "We only get water every other day now," the mother noted. As night began to fall, they were still talking, and the subject of rationing and other present-day calamities had not yet been exhausted. Reinaldo asked the mother to bring him the box with the family photographs. That way, at least, he could take a trip into the past and forget the present hell. But the mother told him that one of his cousins (that cousin again)—*She's* always *asking about you*—had taken the photos home with her to paste them in an album.

Gabriel knew that that particular cousin, like many of his relatives, was now a member of the secret police, or at least an informant. She'd taken the photographs away with her for some political reason, and now he, Reinaldo, would never again be able to contemplate himself when he was a child. While the mother went on talking, Skunk in a Funk spent the rest of the evening brooding on how mean, how utterly *despicable,* the system was that would make family members spy on each other, demand to see even their childhood snapshots. Right this minute, he'd bet, some psychiatrist was analyzing his most boyish gestures. He'd bet those photographs were now the contents of some thick and dangerous file. Not only did these reflections add to the eternal and ever-present terror in which Gabriel lived, they plunged him into a depression so dark, so dreary, that his countenance grew even more glum than it had been before. He began to have that air of tragedy that would sometimes come over him in the middle of the beach, in the middle of a men's room, in the middle of a crowd—the look that had earned him the nickname Skunk in a Funk. The mother stopped talking, and before night fell completely they sat down to eat, in silence. "Now we just get electricity every other day," remarked the mother, lighting a candle as they were finishing dinner. And Skunk in a Funk's expression turned even funkier. But before night fell completely, the mother stood up and started digging around in a box full of odds and ends of rusty, jumbled things. The old woman made so much racket that Skunk in a Funk, emerging from his funk, asked her what she was looking for.

"I'm looking for the flathead. I've got a nail sticking up in my shoe and I want to fix it."

Flathead! Suddenly Skunk in a Funk's expression changed, his face lit up, and he almost even smiled. *Flathead, flathead,* he repeated aloud as he went toward his mother. What a word. What a word. And the word transported him back to his childhood, back to his grandfather's house where there was an anvil with a hornlike projection on each end, not like the other anvils with just one horn, that his grandfather always called a flathead. Gabriel would use it for repairing his shoes. And now, clinging to that word, Skunk in a Funk became a child again, a country boy in his element. And once more he was running through the shade of the trees, splashing in the creek, playing in the dirt out in the yard, throwing leaves up into the air.

"Flathead! Flathead! Flathead!" he exclaimed as he hugged his mother.

"You've gone crazy too," said the mother, "like everybody in this country."

But finally she allowed herself to be infected with the son's happiness, and the two of them were soon laughing uproariously.

The flathead (which never turned up) had broken the ice between the mother and the son. And, more importantly, it had shattered that sense of despair that Gabriel had been possessed by for some time now.

That night, the mother and the son sat out on the porch and talked about the family, and there was even a moment when the mother told a funny story and the two of them laughed again. Gabriel went to bed that night feeling that he had returned to his childhood. And he fell asleep to the lullaby of a no longer existent myriad of invisible crickets.

The next morning, Reinaldo said good-bye to his mother on the porch. I wish I could stay longer, Gabriel told his mother, but my work, my responsibilities. . . The mother told him she understood, and she gave him a hug.

"Next time, come with your wife and the baby—or babies, because maybe by then you'll have another one."

"We're planning to have a dozen," Skunk in a Funk said, rolling her eyes, and kissed his mother again. "Oh, and thanks for the flathead . . ."

"What! You're not taking your grandfather's flathead!"

"I'm taking the *word,* mother," Reinaldo said, shrugging on the backpack that his mother had loaded down with food she'd made for him, the sweetened wheat-powder that passed for candy that he'd always liked, and even a bottle of rendered pork fat. *You don't know the sacrifices I've had to make to find those things for you.*

At the corner, on his way to the train station, Gabriel turned and saw his mother sweeping the street with that same old air of resignation in her face and body, and with that same light stroke—so light this time that the broom didn't even touch the ground. The glow of happiness that the word *flathead* had kindled in his face faded away.

A Journey to the Moon

Long before Skunk in a Funk wound up in the prison at El Morro, he had been caught in a dragnet in Havana—I think on the corner where Copelia is, or maybe at the Capri where everybody went for coffee, but it may have been on the beach at La Concha. They sent him, along with seven or eight thousand other fairies—I don't remember exactly how many because I was just a little girl at the time—to a concentration camp in Camagüey. There, he spent three years pulling up weeds by hand. That was where he really got that funky, sulky, unsociable attitude of his. Once something happened that deeply moved him: One day a young queen took off running, trying to get out of the camp, and she was so desperate to escape that she threw herself on the electrified fence. She was electrocuted—"fried chicken" as the camp humor put it. Knowing that so far as the rest of the world was concerned neither she nor any of the other thousands of fairies locked up in that camp were of the slightest interest—at the time, the whole world was singing the praises of the Socialist Revolution and its New Man, the way people sing the praises of that witch doctor in Uganda today—Skunk in a Funk put her own troubles aside, pushed her sexual desires out of the picture totally, and wrote whenever she could—and pulled weeds when she couldn't. Then one day one of the queens, a fairy who held Skunk in a Funk in some esteem (from a distance), came up to her and gave her the following news: *Man has just landed on the moon.* Skunk in a Funk didn't say a word, she just looked at the raggedy faggots pulling weeds, and then turned her eyes on the terrible electrified fence. Then she went on with her work. But that night there was a full moon, and all the inmates were able to witness the spectacle of Skunk in a Funk, standing on a rock in the center of the field in which they assembled for work every day, in the throes of some strange, ritual, ceremonial lunacy, ripping off her clothes, tearing out her hair, and digging her fingernails into her face—and then, naked, bleeding, turning toward the moon.

Tell me it isn't true! Tell me it isn't true! she screamed, leaping up and down under that huge satellite, supplicating, in despair.

A Tongue Twister (3)

In a chain gang in a cane field in the rain, in-your-face gay tale-teller Reinaldo Arenas is constrained by hyenas to raise cane. Unswayingly praying to Ares to pave the way to his release from this chained travail, escapist Arenas entertains himself by telling himself tales he's spun of penises seen in urinals and train terminals until, flayed by the hyenas' maces, he's returned to the traces.

But one day Reinaldo Arenas's prayers to Ares are answered—not by Ares or by Venus but by Hera, Zeus's chosen, who, irate, hears Arenas's keening pleas for release and unchains him posthaste from the chain gang.

Escaping the chasing hyenas, escapist escape-artist Reinaldo Arenas hastily hails a plane for Spain, where his daydreams of unpersecuted penises seen in urinals and train terminals are realized.

For Reinaldo Arenas

Before Undertaking a Long Journey

Gabriel was going back to Holguín to visit his mother, as he did every year. Each time he came back to the place where he once lived, in that (perversely named) neighborhood of Vista Alegre, his mother would be outside sweeping the street. His mother swept so lightly that the broom would barely brush the ground, much less sweep away the dirt.

Sitting on a bench in the train terminal, Reinaldo reread the paragraph he'd just written, the first paragraph of a new chapter in his novel. Immediately, he added *The truth was, the mother wasn't sweeping up dirt and leaves and scraps of paper, she was sweeping up her entire past and present. The mother was trying to sweep up everything she had suffered and was still suffering, a man who had abandoned her, an only son who had turned out to be a queer and therefore wound up in jail. Because her son couldn't fool her—although she* pretended *she was fooled, she knew everything. Because motherhood—that state, that* nature *told her who her son was and what he was doing. The mother was sweeping up solitude, discontent and dissatisfaction, humiliation of every kind. And she did it in the way she did it—lightly, constantly, and futilely—because she knew that sweeping up so many sorrows was impossible; those sorrows were her life.*

Gabriel stopped writing; it struck him that this writing of his was not going to help his mother's suffering, either. Quite the contrary—if she read this manuscript, it would make her even sadder. During the night he'd spent in Holguín he'd wanted to be very careful not to let his mother discover the novel, so he'd tucked it into the false lining of his backpack. Like all the true, authentic things he'd done in his life, the novel had to be hidden from his mother.

The truth was, this novel (which he almost never let out of his sight) was a kind of curse that had been dogging him now for more than twenty years. He knew the risks he ran if the police discovered the manuscript again, which was why every time he had to go off somewhere for "volunteer labor" (which obviously meant going someplace he couldn't take this particular text), Reinaldo would stuff all its pages and scraps of paper into a huge bag (a fifty-pound cement bag, in fact) and haul it from house to house, trying to find a friend he could entrust his treasure to. Eva Felipe, an old friend of Gabriel's, kept the novel for him the whole of one summer—until she started reading it. Shocked, she ran to Reinaldo with the manuscript—more precisely, with the cement bag slung over her shoulder. *My husband is a first lieutenant,* she explained to Skunk in a Funk; *if he discovers these papers he'll have me arrested. . . .* Then Eachurbod promised to keep "those papers of yours," but when he discovered that he himself was in it, and portrayed as one of the ugliest and most desperate queens on the planet, she visited Reinaldo and said: *I have just done you a big favor. Rather than doing my duty and turning your novel over to the police, I've burned it.* Skunk in a Funk moved Eachurbod up to the top of his enemies list (a *long* list), and sat down that minute to rewrite *The Color of Summer,* the manuscript of which disappeared yet again when Tatica stole his swim fins off the bridge at Patrice Lumumba Beach. So Reinaldo rewrote the novel *again.* It was about that time that Aurélico Cortés' resurrection occurred. In his novel, Reinaldo gave Cortés the name "St. Nelly," since Cortés was the only queen in the entire world who had died a virgin, and therefore in a state of grace. When Cortés was reborn and learned that he had been canonized, and that in addition she had supposedly performed a number of miracles (not to speak of being resurrected!), she ran (without shaking off the dust of the tomb) all the way to where Skunk in a Funk lived, seized the evil manuscript, and consigned it to the flames on the instant. So Reinaldo rewrote the novel yet again, put it in some black plastic bags he had swiped while he was planting coffee seedlings in the Havana Cordon, and hid it under the roof tiles of his Aunt Orfelina's house, in which he was then living. A few months later, Skunk in a Funk and Coco Salas were arrested when they were caught *in flagrante delicto* with two professional baseball players *(enormous!)* out in the middle of a weedy playing field at the Palace of Sports. (Skunk in a Funk was found guilty; Coco, being an informant for G-2, was found innocent.) Imprisoned in El Morro, Reinaldo, having learned that his novel had (according to the Three Weird Sisters) been turned over to the police by his Aunt Orfelina, began to write his novel again. But once smuggled out of prison, the work wound up in the hands of the political police yet again. When he had served his sentence and was released, Gabriel went back to his old room in his aunt's house, but his aunt, who'd had a new lock installed, told him never to darken her door again. So for days Skunk in a Funk wandered the streets, trying to think of a way to recover his novel—because the truth was, he could no longer be sure that the story the Weird Sisters had told him was true. (In fact, he was almost convinced that the novel was still up on the roof of his Aunt Orfelina's house, hidden under those roof tiles.) One night, while the Brontë Sisters stood watch, Reinaldo climbed up on the roof, lifted up the roof tiles, and saw with his own eyes that the manuscript had disappeared. Who had committed this militant and most highly patriotic deed? Coco Salas? The lieutenant that was Skunk in a Funk's contact? His Aunt Orfelina, as the Weird Sisters had said? The Weird Sisters (those bitches!) themselves? Eachurbod? The Ogress, a.k.a. Ramón Sernada? Whoever it was, *somebody* had made away with that manuscript and was holding it over him, waiting (threatening) to send him to jail when the time was right. There were so many mean, nasty, *horrid* informants, envious faggots ready to stab him in the back.

. . . While Reinaldo wandered the streets, marking time and pretending to undergo rehabilitation by cutting weeds all the way to Lenin Park (where Coco strolled about on the arm of Celia Sánchez), he once more began to write *The Color of Summer.* Gabriel was quickly "rehabilitated," married in the space of a minute, had a son in five, buried his married life in three more, and wrote (or meditated on) a book about the tragedy of a married faggot and his passion for a teenage boy—a task that took some twelve hours. And all of this he performed while feigning (and suffering) a double, or triple, life, and working without a moment's rest on the sixth (or was it seventh?) version of his novel—which now, with furtive pleasure, while he was waiting for the train, he was rereading and adding bits and pieces to.

To touch those pages was to touch an authenticity, a rightness, that the world denied him. And yet (Reinaldo, suddenly disconsolate, asked himself as he caressed the yellowing pages) what sense did any of this make? Who would ever read this text? Where in the world would he ever publish it? How long would he be able to carry these pages around without being discovered? And as he contemplated the yautías and the bottle of rendered pork fat alongside the novel that he had now stuffed into his backpack again, he thought again of his mother—he saw her desolately sweeping, sweeping, sweeping the street, and he began to wonder whether the possible happiness of that woman mightn't be more important than the fate, or the very existence, of these pages hen-scratched in anxiety and fear. He had to choose between the novel that was his very life and the happiness of others. He had to choose between his own beloved, forbidden life and the life of his loved ones. In the world he lived in (maybe in any world) there was no space in which he could live a happy man without making life miserable for the people he loved most. The price he had to pay in order to be himself was so high that the best thing might be to give up on being himself once and for all and offer himself to those other people the way they wanted him. The best thing might be to forget about this manuscript that hounded and haunted him and at the same time constantly eluded and escaped him, and to forget too about hounding and haunting men, whom he also lived for yet who constantly eluded and escaped him. Forget about his life—his whole life—and start a new one. Just like that, as tacky and clichéd and impossible as it sounded: *a new life.* Yes. Devote himself to his wife and son (whom he'd now have to bring back to life, the two of them) and his mother. Because really, if he made that renunciation, what would he be losing? Had living the life he lived brought him any particular happiness? Wasn't the price he had to pay for a furtive minute of (almost always unachievable) pleasure altogether too high? *Renounce, renounce.* Choose between the bottle of rendered pork fat and that manuscript. Throw that manuscript away right now and keep the bottle of pork fat. Look at your mother—she is that green bottle of rendered pork fat looking up at you (from the bottom of the backpack) with eyes made sad and sorrowful by all the grief you've caused her. And so deep was the sadness that Skunk in a Funk felt upon seeing her mother turned into a bottle of rendered pork fat that the expression on her face became gloomier and gloomier, funkier and funkier—so sunk-in-a-funk-looking, in fact, that the people sitting around her began sliding and scooting away, as though she were actually some old skunk beginning to exude her unbearable stink. . . . Gabriel might become a macho, a good father and husband, a beloved son. Had others not been able to pull that off? Nicolaiv Dorrt, for instance, formerly the queenliest of queens—did he not walk now with a manly gait and manner, speak in a rich baritone, and have three (three!) children? My dear! (he was suddenly interrupted by that other fairy who lived inside him) remember that Nicolaiv Dorrt had to be taken to the Emergency Room of Calixto García Hospital with a lightbulb up his ass. . . . *But it won't be that way with me,* Skunk in a Funk, now become a New Gabriel, promised himself. This trip to Holguín had been a revelation. It had revealed to him the futility of his empty, dangerous, and desperate life lived far from the warmth of a true home. Peace!—that was what he needed, yet had never had. If everything had a price, and in his case the price was renouncing Fairyland, then he would renounce.

But just at that moment there walked past a recruit whose uniform sat upon him like a royal mantle. The recruit sat down on the same bench Gabriel was sitting on—and Gabriel, now suddenly become once more the Skunk in a Funk, asked the young man what time it was, his eyes coyly eyeing the area between the young thing's legs. The young man looked her up and down, and replied in the following way:

"This watch doesn't give the time of day to faggots—it's a *man*'s watch."

And at that, the soldier went off to sit on another bench, next to a real man.

A man! A man! That's what Skunk in a Funk had to become. The humiliation she'd just been subjected to confirmed it. What's more, she was sure that what had just happened happened so that she, Skunk in a Funk, would be encouraged to recover her most macho manliness. God Himself had sent that young recruit to convince Skunk in a Funk that she had to change her life, once and for all. Yes. There was no alternative. She chose the bottle of pork fat. Skunk in a Funk uncrossed her legs (which had been practically wound around each other), spread 'em, and laid her elbows across the back of the bench. Now, at last, all man, Gabriel sat back to wait for the train.

Hell Hath No Fury Like a Fairy Spurned

Down by the ocean, off to one side of the Fifingian Palace in which the Fifofest was now fully under way, a large group of angry, milling people had gathered—all those who felt that they'd been humiliated (and thus *insulted)* by not having been invited to the reception. Among the celebrities who found themselves on Fifo's blacklist were (and don't get the wrong idea—even if we don't list all of them now, that doesn't mean we won't include them later on) the Deaconess Marina and her husband the Pope of the Russian Orthodox Church, the Polish ambassador to Cuba, the Queen of Carnival in Rio de Janeiro, the head of the Italian Communist Party, Sakuntala la Mala, Clara Mortera and her husband Teodoro Tampon, the president of the Spanish Royal Academy (who, unable to bear the affront, committed suicide by smashing his head against the great door of the Fiferonian Palace—any other version of the incident is false), Padre Angel Gastaluz with his silver aspergillum, Corazón Aquino, Tiki-Tiki, Bishop O'Condom, Odoriferous Gunk and his dying mother (in her pup tent), SuperSatanic, the eleven wives of the dictator of Libya, Peerless Gorialdo, and the promoter of the anti-Pinochet plebiscite, who was pacing furiously back and forth along the rocks on the coastline, unable to understand the brazenness of this snub, especially since Pinochet was enjoying the hospitality of the palace as its guest of honor. (And indeed it *was* hard to understand—not only this exclusion but others, as well, which may perhaps be mentioned at a later time.) But as we were saying, this heterogeneous group of spurned (and decidedly irate) dignitaries, a virtual army (which had just been joined by General Noriega, an escapee from Sing Sing, and the King of Romania), decided to stay, come hell or high water, in their place alongside the Fiferonian Palace, awaiting the coveted, but so far withheld, invitation.

A Journey by Train

"Why, you old queen, imagine running into you *here!*"

It was La Reine des Araignées (the Spider Queen to you, Mary), teetering along the platform, come upon the manly Gabriel. She was wearing a shirt dyed with gentian violet and adorned with tropical landscapes painted by Clara Mortera, a pair of pants made out of a flour sack she'd stolen from a neighbor of hers and dyed red, and huge clogs carved by hand by the cunning Mahoma, and on this costume the fairy had stuck all kinds of metal buttons and pins made of beer caps and pieces of cans scavenged out of dumps. The four hairs that she still had on her head were dyed a bright yellow that made the queen look like some exotic firebird.

The firebird—I mean La Reine—dropped two cardboard suitcases, a trunk, some lumpy roped-together bundles masquerading as luggage, several shopping bags, and a backpack to the floor, and with wide looping motions of her butterfly wings—I mean arms—descended upon Gabriel, who in the almost luminescent presence of this queenly apparition was immediately transformed into Skunk in a Funk. The two fairies hugged, and then, in a riot of reciprocal cackling, took seats.

"So, girl, what's new with you?" Skunk in a Funk asked La Reine.

"What does it look like, you goose? I'm going on a trip. I've made up my mind—I'm leaving. And this time it's for good, too. To quote Madame Bovary and Coco Salas, I *abhor* the countryside, and country living. I mean, get me *out* of here! Look at me—are *these* the clothes of a milkmaid?"

He stood and, leaping atop her bags, gave two or three turns that she knew were *smashing.*

"Fabulous," lied Skunk in a Funk through her teeth.

"And *you!* You look *marvelous* yourself, though I must say you don't have those wonderful things on that I see you wearing in *Havana."*

"I'm on my way back from my mother's house. . . ."

While the two fairies continued their affectionate effusions, let me tell you, you thousands or millions of gay men reading me out there (and if you're not reading me, you'd better get a move on, 'cause time flies, hon), that La Reine des Araignées, like Skunk in a Funk, was from the town of Holguín, or the outskirts of the town of Holguín, and, like Skunk in a Funk, bore three names, almost four. Her real name was Hiram Prats; her literary and social name was Delfín Proust (to which she would sometimes, in cases of emergency, add her matronymic: Stalisnasky), and her *nomme de guerre* was, of course, La Reine des Araignées. That was the method by which a fairy might protect his (or her) various identities, depending on the circle in which s/he found her/himself at any given moment. And it did keep her safe—not even Coco Salas (who like all the most in-your-face faggots on the face of the earth was *also* from Holguín) had been able to jail this particular queen, since legally, she didn't even exist. With her matronymic, she could pass herself off as a foreigner, and it was also good for scaring off pro-Soviet cops. Plus it was known for a fact that Hiram, or Delfín, or La Reine des Araignées, or whatever the hell she called herself, had really truly been in the former Stepmotherland, and she was rumored to chatter giddily in Russian and even to file long reports in that dead language with the KGB.

The truth of the story was that when she was just a little boy, this bucolic nymph had been sent off by Fifo to the former U.S.S.R., where she studied Russian under Popov at the University of Lomonosov. Da, da, darling, this Holguín queen wound up in Lomonosov when he was no more than a tykette, but soon after (s)he'd arrived in that supersacred Stepmotherland (s)he began to give signs of superswishing. One day, in fact, all of Moscow (well, *almost* all) was rocked by the unprecedented spectacle afforded by this rural femme. As a Cuban scholarship student, you see, Hiram had had the honor of being invited to the Bolshoi to see *Swan Lake.* To this day, no one is certain what ruses were employed by the cunning creature to excite the high-ranking military cadet sitting beside her—it may even be that the naive Russian lad thought Hiram was a woman. Whatever—during an intermission, Hiram dragged the hunk of a soon to-be soldier (a peach of a country boy from Georgia, with a bushel basketful between his legs, my dear) off behind the "drapes" up on the stage. And behind those heavy velvet curtains, the queen curtsied and went down. The orchestra boomed forth, Maya Plisezcaya appeared onstage as the White Swan, the curtains began to part. And as they completed their glide into the wings, those lovely wine-colored drapes revealed to the entire astonished audience Hiram, on his worshipful knees before the enormous joint of the young Georgia cadet, while Plisezcaya fluttered her double-jointed arms and the *corps de ballet* swooped onto the boards. So immersed in their ecstatic union were the soldier and the fairy that they hadn't noticed that the curtain had risen on the ballet and they were now on stage before more than ten thousand people (among them Nikita Khrushchev and his wife, Anastasia Mikoyana). Iron hands swept the insolent interlopers from the stage; the cadet was shot by firing squad on the instant; the Cuban faggot was deported so that Fifo could *personally* have her executed. On the Russian ship (which took more than six months to reach Cuba), the femme changed her name, voice, and way of walking, falsified seventy official documents, plucked his eyebrows (which never *ever* grew back), and with his new face (as bald as a boa's backside) arrived in Cuba as (ta *dum!)* Delfín Proust Stalisnasky. The version that she herself gave the world, and that both Fifo and the KGB chivalrously accepted, was that Hiram Prats, filled with revolutionary repentance and self-repugnance, had thrown himself overboard into the Black Sea. La Reine des Araignées would recount, with tears in her reptilian eyes, how she had seen the fairy fling himself, to the chords of *L'Internationale,* into the sea. . . .

In her guise of Delfín Proust, the queen would attend the soirées hosted by Olga Andreu at which Virgilio Piñera reigned supreme. She was "La Reine des Araignées" to almost everyone at Copelia, from Mayra the Mare to Uglíssima. Mischief-maker, spinner of a web of lies, cunning, horrid, always leaping up and down and waggling feet and hands at the same time, she not only reminded one of a spider, but when she was being screwed she wiggled and turned and contorted herself so fiercely that she *became* a virtual tarantula. And as though that weren't enough, the fact of having been discovered sucking the cock of a high-ranking Soviet cadet behind a curtain was proof that this fairy, the terrible Spider Queen, wove a web that was capable of entangling even a Hero of the Former Stepmotherland. My god, and from Stalin's own province. . . . Oh, the fag was a Stalinist, all right, as we shall see further on. . . . And also (this is strictly between you and me, darling) a snitch—not to mention a gossip, a troublemaker, a nasty piece of work, and a spinner of confidence schemes. No one knew where the sticky threads of her web might reach. —You better beware of that one, honey. If you see her, make the sign of the cross and *run.*

But Skunk in a Funk, the silly cunt, did *not* run when she saw La Reine des Araignées coming. On the contrary, they got on the train together and Skunk in a Funk even helped her with her bags. Once on the train, the two femmes, to shoves and bumps and much fluttering of wings, pushed their way through the exhausting crush. At last they found an empty seat and there, in a great scattering of feathers and fairy dust in the air, they plumped. Then, after trying to open the window (which naturally wouldn't budge), they looked around.

"How utterly depressing!" remarked La Reine des Araignées.

And the truth was, the terrible queen was right. The nineteenth-century railroad cars were crammed full of people who were all obscenely deformed. There were extended families in which every family member had what appeared to be a huge, distended belly (because between them, they were smuggling a whole cow into Havana); there were women with outrageous boobs (because they'd stuffed bags and bags of black-market rice into their brassieres). One man was wearing an enormous hat under which he was carrying a live hen for his great-grandmother, who was dying and sorely needed some broth made from this avian species now on the verge of extinction in Cuba. Other men seemed to be wearing not hats but some sort of Byzantine domes on their heads; under this headgear they were carrying hogs, turkeys, goats, sheep, and other animals stolen from farms around town—animals which, because their mouths were tied shut, could only give off pathetic bleats and moans deep in their throats, which the smugglers, lip-synching, pretended came from themselves. But it was the children, perhaps because their parents trusted in the immunity of tender years, who bore the heaviest cargoes. Nor were they exactly children—they were more like huge balls in which all you could see were eyes, stuffed as the kids' clothes were with quarts of milk, bags of dried beans, brown paper bags of old bread, big tin cans of crackers, packages of sugar, spools of thread . . . Ay! Every one of those dear children was a walking general store—or a rolling one, rather, as their mothers would roll them down the aisle until they found a seat. And above all that, there floated an inescapable smell of fart, dirty cunt, collective sweat, cat piss, dead dog, rutting goat, gaping asshole, hog's balls, just-burst tumor, feet that had never yet seen water, and other unclassifiable emanations.

In observing the tricks and ruses the travelers employed to smuggle their foodstuffs so the Fifarian Police wouldn't catch them—and on a trip that might, in addition, be almost infinite—Reinaldo remembered with terror that he was carrying several pounds of yautía and a bottle of rendered pork fat in his backpack. My god, his entire life trying to keep from being arrested on account of his novel, and to wind up in jail for a bottle of pork fat!

"And what *is* all this?" Skunk in a Funk asked, gesturing toward La Reine's bags and parcels. "—The whole Hill of the Cross from back in Holguín?"

"No, *my dear,* all I'm carrying are some *divine* costumes, a few things I bought centuries ago in the Soviet Union. I never carry anything illegal, much less food. I barely eat. Can't you see my splendid figure, you thing?"

Skunk in a Funk looked at Hiram Prats and saw only a horrific bald queen with knobby arms in constant motion.

"You look *marvelous,*" she said.

"I intend to make quite a splash at Carnival."

"They say it's the last one, that Fifo won't hear of another one."

"All the more reason to make my splash! Listen—and you have to promise not to breathe a word of this to *anyone*—I'm invited to the party that Fifo is giving in his underground palace before the real Carnival starts."

"My god, the only people that go to *that* are officers from the Ministry of the Interior . . ."

"Uh-huh, which is why *you,* my dear, are invited, *too.* Because everybody that's *anybody,* anybody at *all,* goes. Didn't you know that Fifo was a fairy, just like us?"

"Mary!—we may have to wash that mouth full of false teeth out with soap! *How do you know?*"

"The same way you do, my dear, so don't act so innocent. Plus, Coco Salas told me that he'd jerked him off himself, and he commissioned me to find *men* for Fifo . . ."

"*Ave María purísima!* But honestly, I haven't told a *soul!* . . . By the way, you know people say Coco Salas is not a queen, he's really a *woman,* which is why every bull macho in Cuba wants to kill her—she's tricked every dick, tom, and harry. I couldn't testify to that *myself,* of course . . . but I can tell you that she is one mean son of a bitch. Did you know I went to jail because of that cunt?"

". . . and it looks like this train is never going to move," remarked La Reine des Araignées in reply. The sweat (for perspiration it was not) was beginning to make streambeds down her face. It was yellowish, greenish, reddish sweat which, when it mixed with the violet-colored sweat that bathed her shirt, became an indescribable shade of . . . but it was indescribable. "There goes my makeup," wailed La Reine tragically.

"We must make do," said Skunk in a Funk.

"Yes, we must make do," agreed La Reine des Araignées.

And the two fairies, stupefied by the terrible heat, the terrible ugliness, and the terrible smell, made themselves as comfortable as they could in their terribly uncomfortable seats and tried to sleep, in spite of the human and animal cackling, bleating, lowing, moaning, and lamenting going on all about them. Oh, dear, but just at that moment, and now the train was burping and bellowing in sign of departure, a creature of light appeared in the car. It was like a golden fish in a sea populated only by deformed sharks; it was like a radiant comet in a sky filled with broad-assed stars. It was, not to put too fine a point on it, the splendid recruit whom Skunk in a Funk had asked the time of and who had kicked her, emotionally, in the ass. Ay, an inaccessible love god. Even the hogs and all the other animals, suffocating under the crowns of their various pieces of headgear, peeked out through the chinks in the woven palm fronds and fell silent. My God, and the hunk, looking nowhere at all, as though he were making his way down the carpet that led directly to his throne, walked on, finally found an empty seat, threw down his olive-green duffel bag, and spread wide his thighs, stretching out in the seat like the long and impressive specimen that he was. Nor need I tell *you,* you clever old thing, that Skunk in a Funk and La Reine des Araignées were keenly observing this imperial (and unparalleled) young man, although the Skunk, who knew that the recruit was unassailable, feigned indifference.

"Did you see that *god* that has shown us the grace to travel on our very train?" exclaimed La Reine.

"Of course I *saw* him," replied Skunk in a Funk. "Am I blind? But he's not my type." And assuming an air of importance, she looked uninterestedly out the window, past which a jumble of squat, shored-up houses were beginning to glide.

"This is *me* you're talkin' to, my dear," La Reine replied. "You're drooling so hard you can't even talk. I can hear that little heart of yours go pitty-pat from all the way over here. In fact, I think you're about to have a seizure."

"Twit, what you hear is this stupid train. I've had the best men in Havana and all of Oriente, not counting the other provinces."

"I doubt it, but that's not the point. That was then and this is *now,* honey. Which is what interests *me—the present.* What we've got here in the present, in case you haven't noticed, is a greatbighuge hunk of a thing with his legs spread just a few feet from where I'm sitting."

"He's all yours."

"Thank you, my dear, but I doubt that he's yours to give away. I shall work for him. As soon as the lights go out, I'll spring. You can watch my things for me."

"They don't turn out the lights on trains anymore, you know. Since that terrible scandal when Miguel Barniz was discovered on the Matanzas-Havana train being fucked by three black men while Karilda Olivar Lubricious was masturbating under an open umbrella, Fifo has given orders that all trains will be lighted, or at least partially lighted, at night."

"Dark, lighted, or semilighted, that soldier is *mine*. I think he even looked this way."

"Uh-huh, he did," said Skunk in a Funk, hoping to see the queen get in over her head, because Skunk in a Funk knew firsthand that the recruit wanted nothing to do with faggots.

The train had been jogging along for several hours now, and La Reine des Araignées hadn't taken her eyes off the young recruit, who for his part had fallen asleep and started snoring the second the train began moving.

"He's just playing, pretending to snore," La Reine des Araignées whispered to Skunk in a Funk. "He's doing it so he can get a blow job and not have any moral responsibility for it, no pangs of conscience—you know, *it all happened while I was asleep*. Thousands of men have gotten blow jobs that way, my dear, on trains and buses and planes and boats. They pretend they're snoring, and while they're sawing logs they come all over you!"

At midnight, the light grew dimmer, and only a single bulb toward the center of the car remained lit—to save precious fuel. Fifo's order was apparently honored in the breach. And speaking of breeches, in the light of that one dim light, the recruit's treasures looked even more alluring. In the dimness, his body relaxed even further, his legs spread wider; all of Glory culminated at the intersection of those olive-green thighs.

"I can't take it any longer. I'm off to war," said La Reine des Araignées.

"Attack! Attack! I'll watch your things," the wicked Skunk in a Funk softly encouraged.

In a single leap, La Reine des Araignées landed beside the still-snoring hunk.

The fairy's thigh approached the young soldier's thigh. La Reine des Araignées allowed her diminutive thigh to brush the muscular other one. And then she began to rub that diminutive thigh of hers up against the greatbighuge other one. The owner of those muscular other thighs went on snoring, legs akimbo. Hiram, as though hypnotized by the power of those spread thighs, her eyes sparkling wildly, allowed her diminutive hand to fall onto the greatbighuge thigh. Through the dimness, Skunk in a Funk, surrounded by suitcases and shopping bags and packages-tied-with-string and backpacks and stench, looked on. Hiram's hand had daringly moved to the still-snoring recruit's fly. Oh, god, what if Skunk in a Funk were just a disgusting old queen that nobody wanted anymore, a faggot ready for the old folks' home, a wreck, and that knock-your-eyes-out recruit had spurned her not because he didn't like fags but because he didn't like old, decrepit, *over-the-hill* fags. Oh, look, she thought she'd die: La Reine des Araignées had unzipped the hunk's fly and was sticking her hand down into the cave where the fabulous treasure was buried. My God, my God, what Skunk in a Funk was now seeing was Hiram, handling the job in the *most* skillful way, completely opening the recruit's pants—first unbuckling his belt, then pulling his underwear all the way down, and then, without further ado, going down on him. And all the while, the recruit went on snoring. And all the while, Skunk in a Funk had to watch La Reine des Araignées's things. What *gall* that Hiram's got, thought Skunk in a Funk, watching him on his knees before the recruit, burying the soldier's gigantic cock (and even, at one point, both testicles!) in his throat. La Reine des Araignées, her mouth stuffed, directed a look of triumph at Skunk in a Funk, who was *moribund* with envy. In ecstasy over his triumph, Hiram put a hand on each of the recruit's thighs and began to knead and caress them, while his mouth went on devouring the divine member, giving it little love nips, wetting it with saliva, and uttering soft and lascivious moans. At last, this slurping and moaning began to penetrate the recruit's sleeping brain, and he began to stir. He stopped snoring, opened his eyes. And then (omigod!) he was awake (because he really had been asleep). And what he saw made his eyes almost pop out of his head: His pants were down around his ankles and some kind of fairy hummingbird was sucking the nectar from the flower of his manhood.

"WHAT ARE YOU DOING, YOU FAGGOT!" boomed the voice of the recruit—so loudly that everyone on the train, including the moaning animals, fell silent.

And instantly the recruit, pulling up his pants, grabbed Hiram by the neck and started strangling him. But just as the queen was about to expire, her spider nature returned to her, and she began to spin, hands and feet flailing, till she unscrewed her neck, like a bolt from a nut, from the infuriated recruit's grip. And before the eyes of the passengers, who sat paralyzed at this scene of lust and mayhem, La Reine des Araignées vaulted over to where a smiling Skunk in a Funk sat, picked up all her bags and baggage, and took off down the aisle, scattering beans and rice and every other kind of grain to the four winds and setting free all the domestic animals, which now were also running along behind the queen, no doubt looking (as she was) for the exit. A little way behind her came the gigantic, enraged recruit and Skunk in a Funk, who didn't want to miss the end of this epic chase. . . . Never again, my dear, in the national or international history of the railroad will a page such as this be written: Carrying his cardboard suitcases, a trunk, five briefcases, several shopping bags, and a backpack, the queen ran through the entire length of the train, smashing ankles and inspiring screams of pain and cries of *"Kill 'er!"* And still running, still carrying all her bags and baggage, like Halley's Comet but with a *much* longer tail, she ran the length of the train, keeping a car-length lead on her pursuers. But the train, unfortunately, was not infinitely long, and so finally, in the last car, La Reine des Araignées had to stop. In seconds, the enraged recruit, Skunk in a Funk, a crowd of people who'd been bruised and stepped on by the fleeing queen, and lord knows how many animals—the whole train caught up with her.

"You son of a bitch faggot!" the recruit screamed as he pummeled La Reine des Araignées. "You won't get away with this! You sucked my cock—while I'm still under investigation! Do you hear that—under investigation?"

"Under investigation for what?" asked La Reine as she tried to shield herself with some of her baggage.

"Under investigation for admission to the Young Communists! This could go on my record, it could ruin my career! You know what I ought to do to you? I ought to kill you. You've done a terrible thing, God will never forgive you. That's what I ought to do—I ought to kill you," the delicious recruit screamed in fury as Skunk in a Funk looked on high-mindedly and approvingly. "But no," the young soldier stopped himself, looking down scornfully at the queen he had thrown to the floor. "No . . . I won't dirty my hands with a filthy faggot. That could go on my record, too, and get me blackballed. I'm not going to kill you, but I'm not going to keep traveling on a train with a sick, perverted faggot. That could go on my record too. So I'll tell you what, faggot—if you don't want me to throttle you, you jump off this train."

Hiram realized that it was an order that was not negotiable—that if he didn't throw himself off the moving train he'd die at the hands of the enraged giant. With desperate eyes he looked over toward Skunk in a Funk.

"I've got to jump," he said. "Be a dear and throw my things off after me—*all* my things. *All.*" And without further ado the queen opened the back door of the train and leaped into the void—and she was followed by almost all the animals that had been brought on the train.

"Throw it all to me—all my bundles, all my bags, all the packages—don't leave anything on board," La Reine des Araignées called out to Skunk in a Funk as he rolled over and over along the tracks.

Skunk in a Funk began throwing off the suitcases, bundles, briefcases, shopping bags . . .

"All of it, *all* of it," shouted Hiram. "Throw everything you've got there." And Skunk in a Funk threw out all the boxes and bags and bundles and backpacks that lay about her.

Hiram was now a distant spot between the rails. Unable to contain her hilarity, Skunk in a Funk returned to her seat. The recruit was once more snoring stentoriously, legs akimbo. *I've got to write this story,* Reinaldo said to himself, reaching down for the thick manuscript of his novel eternally in progress. But where was his backpack? It was then that he realized that along with all of Hiram's belongings he had thrown his own backpack (with the yautías, the bottle of rendered pork fat, and the manuscript of his novel) off the train. *Oh, my god!* he cried, *and now I'll have to rewrite the story of my novel for a* seventh *time!*

The Story

This is the story of an island ruled over by an absolute tyrant named Fifo. The tyrant had been in power for forty years, and naturally he exercised absolute control over every inhabitant of the island. People might be starving to death but night and day they were required to praise the abundance in which they lived, an abundance made possible by techniques of production introduced by the tyrant. Nobody was allowed to leave the island or make even the slightest remark against the tyrant; instead, night and day they were obliged to sing anthems to the marvelous freedom and shining future that the tyrant had given them. On the island of this story, all the inhabitants lived at least a double life: publicly there was not a moment they did not praise and laud the tyrant, while secretly they loathed him and prayed in desperation for him to die—preferably a horrible death. But the tyrant had an enormous army and a wonderful intelligence machine, so that destroying him was virtually impossible. The dream of the entire population of the island was no longer to be free, but rather that someday they be able to escape from the island, which was a perfect prison. But how was one to escape from a perfect prison? By air, escape was impossible; only the tyrant had planes and helicopters, and even balloons were under his control. Escape by land was not even to be considered, since *the island was an island.* That left the sea, and the truth was, in the beginning a lot of people had escaped that way—in boats, on inner tubes, on a couple of floating planks lashed together, once even in a number 2 washtub. But the tyrant tripled the coast guard, patrolled the coast with superfast speedboats, salted the ocean with supersensitive mines, until it was almost impossible to escape by sea. So great was their desperation that people finally decided that the only way of escape was by using the island itself. Once the island could move about, it would run aground near some continent, some free terra firma. So tacitly (they obviously could not speak of this) they decided to gnaw away at the platform that bound the island to the seabed until they had separated the island from its base, and then, when the island was free-floating, entrust their fate to wind and waves. . . . Of course separating the island from its base was no easy task; the base was (as bases have to be) of hardest rock. The conspirators also had to be able to go down to considerable depth underwater in order to chip away at it, and since all tools were under the control of the tyrant the only tool the people had to work with was their teeth. And so, constantly, endlessly diving deep into the sea, the people of Cuba began to gnaw away at the base of their island with their teeth, and in time, they evolved lungs that allowed them to remain underwater for almost an hour and huge buck teeth, like those of Aurélico Cortés and Tomasito the Goya-Girl.

Of course that constant gnawing at the base of the island meant that the island experienced frequent earthquakes, geysers, temblors, landslides, cave-ins, and even the occasional reddish-colored eruption of a volcano, when hundreds or thousands of the island's big-toothed inhabitants would be spewed forth, their bodies turned into a huge, purple, flaming plume of smoke. Naturally, all these geological changes attracted the tyrant's attention, and soon his most trusted national and international agents discovered "a terrible act of communal treason: Vile citizens, become bucktoothed *rodents,"* read the report, "are attempting to steal the island and deliver it to an imperialist power." The word *rodent,* hardly honorific in itself, became the worst insult one could fling at a human being. It goes without saying that immediate attempts would be made to eliminate any person so categorized. And yet these *rodents* continued to gnaw away without mercy at the base of the island; now, when the seas were very heavy, one began to feel the island sway. The dictator hired thousands of divers and experts in underwater hunting and charged them with eliminating the rodents, but they failed. In fact, sometimes the antirodent forces would even gnaw a bit themselves. Ay, sometimes a general, a comandante, a government minister, or even a bishop of the Catholic Church would dive down in his official uniform (or vestments, as the case might be) and start gnawing. The tyrant could no longer trust even his most trusted troops.

But there was a more fundamental problem even than that: no soldier, however trustworthy he might be, could remain underwater twenty-four hours a day exterminating rodents. What was needed was a force of rodent-repressors whose natural element was the ocean. After much official meditation, the Ministress of Hunting and Fishing, Rolandina Rodríguez, submitted a most thoughtful proposal: "Sea-based antirodentary material," it said, "exists in abundance along our coasts; we have only to train it. The waters of the Caribbean are the most shark-infested waters in the world. We should, therefore, employ sharks against the rodents. We must create a force of unsleeping and unwearying sharks to devour them. . . ." The tyrant thought this idea so brilliant that he immediately gave orders that the Ministress of Hunting and Fishing be shot by firing squad (since it was inconceivable that anyone except the tyrant could have such a brilliant idea) and stole the idea for himself. Aided by virtually every scientist in the world and the governments of virtually every nation, the tyrant created a huge shark farm where the young denizens of the deep could be trained. The classes would consist of not feeding the beasts, and then when their hunger was unbearable, showing them a rodent, which the shark would instantly devour.

To this end, the tyrant constructed a miniature island and populated it with volunteer rodents (lured with promises of all the food they could eat, so when the time came they'd be well fed), who went out swimming and were instantly scarfed down by the ravenous sharks. Thus, in only a few months a huge army of antirodent sharks had been created, and these troops, after the playing of the national anthem and a longish speech by the tyrant, were duly deployed into the ocean. The tyrant had had the foresight to appoint a shark over all the other sharks: the strongest, ablest, and most bloodthirsty of the race, whose responsibilities were to command and lead the others, and the Übershark's name was Bloodthirsty Shark. And indeed Bloodthirsty Shark was a glorious example of the species: an athletic, muscular, gleaming creature possessed of fourteen rows of perfect teeth and a formidable member which the beast employed in the most sadistic way, for sometimes as it devoured its victim it would ejaculate within it. The tyrant would personally feed that gleaming and to a certain point—one must be fair—beautiful creature. From his presidential gunboat or his helicopter, Fifo would toss Bloodthirsty Shark the tastiest of the rodents, and in response Bloodthirsty Shark would make graceful pirouettes in the sea, leaping above the waves, diving and surfacing again, its shining belly upward, exhibiting its ranks of glistening teeth, its fearsome sex. The tyrant would shudder rapturously at the sight. Finally he had found an ally—an excellent leader, a good soldier who, to make it all the more perfect, could not talk, and who would help him to exterminate the rodents—every last one of them. In order to be in closer contact with the shark, the tyrant had had a huge underground palace built, just at the edge of the sea. There, he installed an aquarium with an immense glass window behind which he would spend long hours transfixed, contemplating the graceful motions of Bloodthirsty Shark, who would sometimes bring a rodent to the glass in its jaws and there, before the tyrant's eyes, kill it, rape it, tear it to pieces, and swallow it, while he, the tyrant, would leap about in glee.

Yet the incredible thing about all this was that in spite of that terrible, incredibly disciplined underwater army and the absolutely trustworthy voracity of Bloodthirsty Shark, the people of the island continued to gnaw away at the island's mooring.

A Tongue Twister (4)

Bibulous Barniz, like some burlesque burgher, stood imbibing beer in a bar in Borneo (or perhaps Batavia) when a bearded Bedouin (or perhaps Berber), putting back bourbon after bourbon, tipped his biretta and proffered him his prominent protuberance. Barniz, bedazzled by the Bedouin (or perhaps Berber), put by his beer and imbibed the bubbly brew produced by the barbarian's protuberance. Oh, what a bubbly brew the bibulous Barniz imbibed!

For Miguel Barniz

Virgilio Piñera Reads His Evanescent Poems

It was a red-letter night at Olga Andreu's house—Virgilio Piñera was going to read his poems. From the *crème de la crème* of Havana society—composed of (among others) La Arrufada, Miss Starling-Bird, Skunk in a Funk (in her role as Reinaldo), the cunning Mahoma, Miguel Barniz, and Paula Amanda, a.k.a. Luisa Fernanda—Olga Andreu had invited all those queens who in her view (1) could be trusted and (2) adored Virgilio Piñera. The living room of the small apartment was wall-to-wall with queens of all ages, from Harolda Gratmatges (ninety-eight years old and blind) to Miss Mayoya, an illiterate queen with a truly sculptural body who according to rumors spread by Virgilio himself was still a virgin, since she was saving herself for none other than Bloodthirsty Shark, whom she'd fallen madly in love with. And "wall to wall" is not just a manner of speaking, my dear: People were sitting on the floor, so crowded together they were practically on top of one another—and the heat was *stifling*. Among the other guests were the Brontë Sisters, the Three Weird Sisters, Miss Oscar, Chug-a-Lug (not named for his beer-drinking skills), Tomasito the Goya-Girl, the Ogress, the Horrible Marmot, Miss Pricked by Thorns Amid the Roses, and almost a hundred more. The screeching and racket those queens made was like something out of Pantagruel. Sakuntala La Mala was saying that she predicted that a new comet, much larger than Halley's, was approaching, and heralding no end of horrors; Miss Mayoya, an incorrigible exhibitionist, was dancing to the rhythm of her own clapping hands, trying out a special wiggle she was planning to debut at the Carnival; La Arrufada was exchanging viperous sussurations with Miss Starling-Bird. La Reine des Araignées was telling Reinaldo how she'd managed to make it back to Havana after fifteen days of dreadfully perilous adventures and every imaginable sort of exploit on sugarcane trucks, tractor-trailers, pickups, and mules. She claimed (who knew?) to have been screwed by more than two thousand men on that hallucinogenic journey; the most memorable, she said, was when she'd gotten into the back of a pickup in Matanzas and discovered a runaway black man, completely naked so his prison uniform wouldn't give him away. La Reine *said* she'd crossed the entire province of Matanzas sucking on the black man's cock. The pickup had sped through the countryside, she said, leaving thousands of campesinos and the entire population of Matanzas (including the Dowager Duchess de Valero) openmouthed in incredulity, though they were witnessing the blow job with their own eyes. "It was a *mar-*

velous trip," sighed Delfín Proust at last. Then Skunk in a Funk asked her what had happened to all the bags. "Gone! Utterly lost! Lost forever!" exclaimed Delfín, fluttering her spidery arms and (*perhaps* unintentionally) scratching the cunning Mahoma's gigantic face. Mahoma gave a shriek and hurled herself at the other queen with every intention of murdering her. An earsplitting cat fight broke out, ten times louder and shriller than the normal shrieking and cackling of a moment before. Miss Mayoya, the Weird Sisters, Miss Not Out Yet, and several other fairies (apparently friends of Hiram) tried to stop Mahoma, but Skunk in a Funk was yelling "Kill her! Kill her!" in the pre-murderess's ear, hoping that if La Reine were dead, she wouldn't be able to turn the manuscript of *The Color of Summer* over to Fifo—because Skunk in a Funk was *certain* that Hiram hadn't lost it. So anyway—there was Mahoma, standing in the middle of the room shrieking, her two monstrous hands around La Reine des Araignées's neck, lifting her off the floor with every intention of smashing her head against one of the walls of Olga Andreu's apartment. But just at that moment, Olga announced that Virgilio Piñera was about to begin his reading—his reading of his evanescent poems.

Total silence fell upon the room. Gingerly, Mahoma deposited the near-dead La Reine on the floor, and everyone settled down to listen to the poet, who for hours had been locked up in Olga Andreu's bedroom, waiting to make his appearance until all the guests had arrived. So now, barefoot and dressed only in a guayabera so long that it reached all the way to his ankles, Virgilio made his entrance.

"Maestro! Maestro! Welcome!" shouted the queens almost in unison.

"Bring in the brazier," was the poet's only greeting.

Olga Andreu, Mahoma, and Skunk in a Funk hurried out to the kitchen and returned with a hibachi filled with charcoal. They placed it beside the small table that the poet was sitting at, and immediately Virgilio began. He began with a poem he had written the night before—and his listeners immediately knew they were in the presence of greatness. It was a perfect poem, containing all the most secret, hidden sadness of every person individually and the pain of humanity in general. While the poet read, a magical hush, a sort of spell, a wondrous enchantment, fell over all those terrified and grotesque figures. The guests' expressions became peaceful, their eyes filled with sweet tears, their bodies took on a serenity, a repose that terror had prevented them from feeling for many years. All were enveloped in a sort of ecstasy of beauty. Even Uglíssima, the most horrific queen on earth, took on an undefinable but visible loveliness that sensibly contrasted with her formerly bloodcurdling features. Olga Andreu had turned off the living room lights (leaving Virgilio illuminated only by the glow of the hibachi) and now as she stepped forward to find a seat on the floor, she was a beautiful sylphlike teenage girl. Everyone was enthralled. Poetry had taken the listeners to another realm, a place that no longer existed almost anywhere, much less there, on that island accursed and at the mercy of Fifo's insane and often cruel caprices. And so while the poet read, the guests, now transported to a place far from all those horrors, found themselves led deeper and deeper into magical gardens where music played, where an unearthly, beautiful song was heard, where time, its implacable horrors in abeyance, molded realms that were actually habitable, paths that wandered off into misty promises, wondrously life-affirming anthems, soft blue peaks, and fields of sunflowers. . . . But then, alas, Virgilio's reading of the poem ended, and before the applause broke out, before the spell was broken, he had tossed it into the flames of the hibachi.

A gasp of horror escaped all those who had heard the poem.

"Maestro, what are you *doing?"* cried Sakuntala La Mala, tearing at her wig, while Antón Arrufada stuck his hands in the flames to try to rescue the poem.

But Mahoma and Skunk in a Funk, obeying a sign from Virgilio, stopped the queen, and even slapped her a couple of times. Virgilio then spoke.

"Yes—cry, shout, kick, pull your hair or your toupees. But heed me, my friends—these poems are the originals, not copies. And tonight, as I read them, I shall burn them."

"Maestro, for heaven's sake, think of us! How can you deprive us of this beauty?" exclaimed Uglíssima.

And cries of approval seconded Uglíssima, who suddenly looked more horrific than ever. But Virgilio, ignoring the voices of protest, went on talking.

"I shall burn them *all.* But first I shall give *you* the opportunity to enjoy them, *myself* the opportunity to read them. One writes for others, there is no doubt of that. And all writing is revenge—to that rule, there can be no exception. Thus, I write my revenge and then am obliged to read it; if I didn't, it would be as though it had never existed. But immediately afterward, I must burn what I have read. I can leave no proof of my revenge, for if I did, then a greater revenge, *Fifo's* revenge, would swoop down upon me and annihilate me. Resign yourselves to hearing these poems one time and one time only, as I have resigned myself to my own fate, which is yet more terrible—the fate of having to write them, read them but once, and consign them forever to the flames."

And at that, the poet put on his thick glasses, picked up another sheet of paper, and began to read another brilliant poem. Instantly, his audience was once again transformed. This time, the room was filled with angels, slender nymphs, teenagers with the faces and bodies of demigods, and all in thrall to the music of a true God.

When he had finished reading, Virgilio raised the poem and addressed his audience curtly:

"I repeat—there are no copies, this is the original. Once I fling it into the flames it will be gone forever."

And so saying, the poet flung that manuscript into the flames.

A wail of horror filled the apartment. Tomasito the Goya-Girl writhed in grief on the floor, Chug-a-Lug gave a cavernous moan, Arrufada wept, Coco Salas removed his glasses, and Paula Amanda stifled a scream with a kitchen towel that she was planning to steal from Olga Andreu. And yes, even the fairies who would inform on Virgilio the next day could not contain their emotions.

But by then the poet was already beginning to read his third great poem of the night. This was a poem that embodied the sound of rhythmic drumming and the echo of great hymns, and it celebrated the length and breadth of the Island. Its listeners did not simply listen, they *became* the poem—leaves, fruit, flowers, cool burbling water that ran among the rocks and through the plains, lakes, a tree filled with birds, furiously satisfied desires, clamor, and revenge. Suddenly, they were all heroes; suddenly, they were all giants; suddenly, they were all children. Suddenly, they were all sitting under a green palm tree listening to a sweet melody. Rain pattered on the leaves. They listened to the music of the rain as it fell on the leaves. They were transported into the center of low clouds, came out onto a wide field where thousands of people were working in the hellish sun, and after that horrible vision they returned to the primordial tree where, returned to beauty and innocence, they fell asleep to the thought that that last, horrible, *other* vision was but a nightmare which made the reality the poet had showed them all the more beautiful.

"Another ephemeral poem that shall be fuel for the flames," resounded the voice of the poet as he ended his reading and dropped the poem onto the brazier.

This time the listeners expressed their dismay with wails of shock. So loud were the protests of disbelief and pain that Olga Andreu turned on the lights and begged them to control their grief, since otherwise the Watchdog Committee for her block might hear them, and then, in the face of the possibility of a search, Virgilio would have to burn his poems *before* he read them.

"What we might do is gag those who can't control themselves," suggested Virgilio, who was terrified that the Watchdog Committee might knock at the door. "Raise your hand if you want to be gagged."

And everyone, including Skunk in a Funk, Mahoma, Sakuntala La Mala, and even Olga Andreu herself, raised a hand. The hostess decided to sacrifice one of the few bedsheets she had left, and she, Skunk in a Funk, Mahoma, and La Reine des Araignées tied a gag on everyone in the living room. Then, after they had also gagged themselves, Virgilio continued his reading.

Now they were seeing thousands of Indians massacred (some burned alive) and other thousands who turned, armed with sticks and stones, to confront their persecutors. They saw millions of black men and women enslaved, and thousands of runaways hunted down with dogs, but sometimes instead of being devoured by the howling pack the runaways would turn the tables and devour the hounds that pursued them. They saw thousands of guajiros, simple country people, machetes upraised, advancing against an oppressor's army that exterminated them by the hundreds with every cannon blast, yet the survivors continued advancing. And now they saw millions of people of *all* races enslaved and constantly monitored, but somehow managing to elude the surveillance and throw themselves into the sea, to gnaw away at the base of the island. And they saw themselves, under the ocean, gnawing desperately, while armies of sharks (led by one huge and particularly bloodthirsty specimen) bore down on them to devour them. And then, at last, they saw the country and the countercountry—because every country, like all things in this world, has its contrary, and that contrary-to-a-country is its countercountry, the forces of darkness that work to ensure that only superficiality and horror endure, that all things noble, beautiful, brave, and life-enhancing—the *true* country—disappear. The countercountry (the poem somehow revealed this) is monolithic, rigid vulgarity; the country is all that is diverse, luminous, mysterious—and *festive.* And this revelation, more than the images of all the beautiful things that they had seen, invested the listeners with an identity and a faith. And they realized that they were not alone, because beyond all the horror—including that horror that they themselves exuded—there existed the sheltering presence of a tradition formed of beauty and rebelliousness: *a true country.*

When Virgilio burned the poem, whines, moans, whimpers, bleats, muted and desperate sounds of weeping were heard, in spite of the muzzles and gags. (Perhaps the sounds came from deeper inside.) Some of the guests, prevented from verbalizing their shock and dismay at the loss of all that beauty, scourged themselves; others banged their heads against the wall; many scratched their faces with their fingernails; some pulled out an eye or inflicted some other terrible pain upon themselves. Miguel Barniz, for example, pulled out all his hair and hit himself so hard in the face that ever since then he has been a bald, puffy fag.

"You can put out the fire now," said Virgilio, ending the reading. He had read eighty brilliant poems.

The guests took off their gags, and when they fully realized that the poems they had heard were irrevocably lost, that those heartrending verses now lay among the ashes of the hibachi that Mahoma and Skunk in a Funk were carrying back into the kitchen, they could not stifle a unanimous howl.

"The Watchdogs *must* have heard *that* wail," said Olga Andreu, terrified. "It's five A.M."

"Get me out of here, then!" Virgilio cried. "They may think we're plotting something!"

Instantly, countless fairies leaped to transport the poet back to his apartment. Since he was barefoot, and Fifo's troops might consider such a thing a "public spectacle" or evidence of "extravagant behavior," they surrounded him. And so, almost as though on a litter, and hiding his bare feet, Virgilio was accompanied back to his two-room apartment in El Vedado.

Once home again in his little apartment, Virgilio, unable to sleep, and possessed by the rage to create, began to work on a new collection of brilliant poems, which would be burned next week at Olga Andreu's house.

For Bosch, She Noshes

But gosh, even if she could steal paint and a couple of canvases from Saúl Martínez, how was she supposed to paint that apocalyptic painting she intended to paint, if she'd never seen a masterpiece in real life? And especially if she'd never seen *The Garden of Earthly Delights* by Hieronymus Bosch—if all she had was a vague idea that she'd gotten from those dreadful reproductions that she'd seen, and that didn't even belong to her. She *had* to go to the Prado! See the masterpieces firsthand. See *Guernica*—see, above all, Bosch's great triptych, the great apocalypse that she would use as a model for the horrors she was suffering, for all the things that she saw around her. There was no other solution. She had to visit the Prado. And with that decision, Clara Mortera also became a rodent.

Some Unsettling Questions

Before going any further with this story, I want to make it clear that I have never been able to discover why Fifo refused to admit a substantial group of VIPs—people who were photogenic, impressive, and sometimes even faithful to him—into the Fifo-fest at his palace. My guess is that personal intrigues, old grudges, chicanery, Machiavellian ruses, professional jealousies, and political strategies, in addition to compelling reports that I have had no access to, must have influenced this defiant posture—a posture which caused (among other things) a desperate open letter to be written (using a boulder for a writing desk) and thrown, after being tied to a big rock, through the castle door. I cannot understand, for instance, why Odoriferous Gunk and the Anglo-Campesina weren't invited while Mayoya and Skunk in a Funk, among other notorious queens, were. Why had an invitation been extended to Karilda Olivar Lubricious and not to the Duchess of Alba and Clara Mortera? Why had an invitation been sent to the president of the French Neo-Nazi Party while the King of Morocco hadn't even been allowed to land his plane? Why was the head of Alfaguara Publishers there, while the CEO of Siglo XXI had been locked out? It was even more astounding to find that the Shah of Iran's son was in the palace while the eleven wives of the dictator of Libya had been turned away. Why, for example, was Jane Fonda in attendance while a fine Scottish mare sent by the Queen of England had been denied admittance? Nor is it easy to understand why a hunter of poisonous arachnids in Nepal would be feted while the foremost lobster-fisherman in Nipe Bay wouldn't even be allowed to approach the building. Or why a world-renowned advocate of the right of women to enter the Catholic priesthood should be turned away while an invitation had been extended to the chairwoman of a group for the conservation and training of lesbian whales in northern Greenland. And what about the fact that honors were paid to the head executioner in Iran while the chief executioner of Albania had been overlooked? What was Coco Salas doing there, sitting in the chair reserved for the president of the Spanish Royal Academy? Why had the president of the French Communist Party been invited and not the most famous bull macho in all of Outer Mongolia? What was the leader of the Galapagos Island guerrilla movement doing there when the wild-dog catcher in Puerto Rico had been left out? Why was the head of the North Korean secret police admitted when the self-invitation that

Chelo, a super Mata Hari (among other things), sent herself had not been honored?

I believe the most likely explanation is that there'd been some confusion when the guests were chosen.

For example, around a table covered with exquisite delicacies and surrounded with waiters even more exquisite sat Swiss bankers, Catalonian terrorists, raggedy men and bag ladies chosen from the ranks of the homeless in New York City, Soviet cosmonauts, Greek royalty, prostitutes from Madrid's Calle Ballesta, Tibetan monks, international Mafiosi, Hollywood stars, Mother Teresa, the President-for-Life of Ulaanbaatar, Mayra the Mare, the president of the Swedish Academy, Bokassa, Peerless Gorialdo, the Key to the Gulf, Uglíssima, the president of the PEN Club of South Korea, the inventor of the neutron bomb, three Iraqi assassins, the secretary of the World Peace Movement, the creator of AIDS, the Secretary-General of the United Nations, the mother superior of the monastery of Clarist nuns in Manila, the chief executioner of Senegal, Nena Sarragoitía, five winners of the Cervantes Prize, the Chief Rabbi of Miami Beach, Soviet Academy-member What's-His-Name Popov, Papayi Toloka, the commander-in-chief of the Red Army of China, the madam of the largest brothel in Kyoto, the president of Afghanistan, several farmers from the southern United States, a worker from Baku, a Finnish labor leader, Günter Greasy, the primíssima ballerina of Nova Zembla, several Olympic athletes, Mao's widow's daughter, the last bull macho butt-stuffer in Riga, the lady director of the National Endowment for Democracy, a professor of South American indigenous languages, the spokeswoman for the World Nudist Society, the bishop of Tucumán, the leading bull macho butt-stuffer in Baghdad, a sharpshooter from South Yemen, the head of the Extreme Left Party of the Marianas Islands, Stalin's daughter's granddaughter, the tallest black man in Zaïre, the king of Saudi Arabia, Sydney Australia's leading drag queen, two winners of the Nobel Prize for Chemistry and one for Literature, the inventor of concentration camps controlled by lasers (who had also been given a Nobel Prize) . . . But the bottom line is, there's no way my poor brain can understand these anomalies (which may not even *be* anomalies), much less explain them to anybody else—I've got enough to do just telling what I saw.

A Tongue Twister (5)

On what bleak barbican or bulwark, what brigantine beached in Barbados, what veranda in Baltimore, or in what base brothel in Bordeaux did Virgilio banish his virginity?

'Twas on neither barbican nor brigantine nor veranda, nor in one of Bordeaux's brothels, that Virgilio's virginity was banished.

Instead, one bright morning around breakfast, the embattled bard invited a dog, a Saint Bernard, to partake of his vittles. But the Saint Bernard, deaf, badly misunderstood, and drilled him with his vermilion rod.

Had the Saint Bernard but gobbled the vittles, Virgilio's virginity would never have been plucked, and undoubtedly to this day be intact instead of banished.

For Virgilio Piñera

In the Monster Men's Room

One after another, men were entering the monster men's room. They would pull out their imposing tools and urinate in the most imposing way. Eachurbod studied these maneuvers—that manly, *captivating* way they did it, that defiant move they made as they *threw* open the doors to the mansion and strode in and undid their flies. Oh, my dear, that indifference yet concentration with which they pulled out their tools and looked up toward the ceiling or at the walls covered with erotic drawings and graffiti—outings of closet queens cheek by jowl with cartoons of certain individuals closely linked to the country's power structure — and therefore to Fifo himself. Some brazen (i.e., suicidal) queers had posted on that public wall the hours during which they could be found at the Copelia ice-cream parlor or in a certain corner of the park; others boasted of their talent for blow jobs or their skill at making even the most dormant phallus stand again. And then there were the hustlers and trade who advertised their merchandise: thickness, length in inches, and, of course, price per inch.

But that was all just words, toilet literature, thought Eachurbod. Those queers weren't looking for blow jobs, they were blowhards. They didn't have the balls to be in the places they said they'd be in, and those hustlers didn't exist. O divine St. Nelly, tell me—is it true, as some have said, that the top is an extinct species, which disappeared with the advance of civilization? Are there no longer Men upon the earth willing to get it on with a youthful, ethereal, and elastic girl-queen such as I? Eachurbod, receiving no reply from St. Nelly, looked again at the army of pissers standing at serious attention before the urinals, immersed in their pissing. But she, the devouress, knew that secretly *they* knew that they were in a special place, a place where there were only men exhibiting their pricks, and that this somehow compromised them, and made them either tops or topped. And gazing at that divine collection of hoses in all colors, and the seriousness of expression that formed itself upon the faces of their (apparently guilt-ridden) owners, Eachurbod composed one of his most profound sayings of the day: "Every man that walks into a men's room where there are only men peeing becomes a citizen, voluntarily or not, of Fairyland." Oh, yes, under the influence of Skunk in a Funk, who was a friend of the great poet José Lezama Lima (whose poem "The Death of Narcissus" she sometimes recited to Eachurbod *sotto voce*), the unhappy and misshapen queen had suddenly turned poet-queen-philosopher herself. . . . But it was not Narcissus who was about to die this time, it was Eachurbod himself, if he didn't scratch his itch, didn't find a Man among all these Men. Oh, if only one of those menacing mulattoes, one of those hunky chocolate dreams, would make her a sign of complicity. How could this desperate queen have lived (have *stood*) so many years of abstinence, how could she never have been skewered, if she lived *only* to be skewered? How could no man have possessed her, even by mistake, if her entire life she had done nothing but run after men? What curse hung over her now dried-out ass? What Stygian lightning bolt had condemned her tongue to drool in solitude? And yet—in spite of her unending failures—Eachurbod was not giving up. Quite the contrary: every man she saw yet could not conquer was a goad that spurred her on to further seeking. So desperate was her desperation that many was the time (unable to bear it a moment longer) that the poor wallflower had thrown herself at the groin of some big giant of a man who she thought had signed her dance-card. And what had she gotten in return for such girlish forwardness? A fist, a horrid insult, jail, and sometimes death itself. Yes, my dear, death itself—because Eachurbod had been murdered several times, though her rectal fire was so powerful that even after death it goaded her to get up, rise from the grave or the sea, and throw herself into the chase once more. There was, for Eachurbod, no hope even for the consolation of a lasting peace after death. For this warrior-queen, there was no rest. There was even the famous story, anthologized by Agustín Plá and the lovely Doctor Lapique, in which Eachurbod, about to be buried (for the fifth time, or the ninth?), broke through the casket and threw herself at the zipper of a once-in-a-lifetime black gravedigger. Of course the truth was, as everybody including Agustín Plá admitted, that black gravedigger *could* raise the dead. . . . But now my dear Paquita, I mean Eachurbod, you're alive and kicking once again, in one of the most magnificent men's rooms in the world, surrounded by exquisite thugs with golden skin, pissing with the roar of a cataract before rejoining the conga line. But none of those phalluses swings even an inch in your direction. *Vei e mori.*

Her red eyes surveyed the field. She began over in the corner, at the mighty colonial door hewn from two blocks of finest cedar wood. Turning slowly back through ninety degrees, she scanned the entire room. One by one she inspected the bodies of those men, their stony faces, and (naturally) their members, until her retroceding gaze fell upon one of her own claws or grappling irons ("lily-whites," the innocent creature called them) and she saw—horrors!—that in one of them she was carrying Volume XXVII of the *Complete Works of Lenin.* Ay, that dratted book given her for protection by her intimate friend Nicolás Guillotina (for whom she often danced naked, to the music of *Sóngoro cosongo,* upon the glass top of his dressing table). *Always carry this book, Eachurbod, wherever you go,* he had told her. *It will save you from any suspicion of heresy; it will be like carrying a Bible when you walk down the street in Ireland, or a copy of the Koran in Teheran, or a novel by Corín Tellado in Miami.* And the queen, out of respect for her protector (who was that to her, my dear, and nothing more), now lugged that heavy red-bound tome around with her wherever she went. . . . *Now* she realized why men ran away from her. What man was going to fall for any girl's sparkling smiles, or winks, or coquettish come-ons if she was going to be carrying around Volume XXVI (*Didn't you say it was XXVII?*) of the *Complete Works of Vladimir Ilyich Lenin?* That book, that name, were practically synonymous with the Communist Party and consequently with Fifo and consequently with the implacable army that hunted down and punished all "sexual deviation." Anyone carrying that book—and flashing it around like that, so openly—*had* to be a political commissar at the very least; i.e., somebody you had to hide every life-affirming (and consequently phallic) manifestation from. Dratted book—where on earth, here, so publicly, could the poor queen get rid of it? Dumping it into a public toilet would be considered treason so foul that it would cost her her life. Could she eat it? No way. Not only was it awfully thick; everybody knew that if you so much as nibbled at one corner of one of its pages, you'd lose not just your mind but also your life. So as quick as a vaudeville magician, Eachurbod sucked in his tummy, swept the book under his shirt, tucked the volume into his pants, and then, transformed into a refrigerator-shaped queen (the book was almost as tall as she was), returned with much greater confidence to her cruising.

And she'd been right—within minutes she proved beyond a shadow of a doubt that the red-bound book was an albatross about her neck. The second she'd tucked it away, a splendid sailor from the Gulf Fishing Fleet stood alongside her, planted his stunning legs wide apart, unzipped his bulging fly, and fished out a lovely rosy-pink eel that Eachurbod couldn't take her eyes off of. And for greater comfort, the young sailor (was it the same one that had killed Cernuda?) took out not only his pink phallus but his two pinkíssimo testicles as well. *Enormous quantities of pink,* Eachurbod recited to himself (in honor of Lezama) as he gazed upon those divine dimensions—two enormous Dominican mameys, and sprouting from between them the king of fruits, a burnished, splendid banana. And the monarch of the sea began to spout a stream of piss that flowed to the farthest horizon. Ay, such was the potency of that young sailor, who had perhaps just stepped off his ship after months of abstinence, that his piss did not fall into the streambed of the urinal, but splashed against the prick-graffiti'd wall. Oh, if I were only one of those drawings! sighed Eachurbod as he watched that hose that washed them down. When the young sailor—broad shoulders, brush-cut hair, red-cheeked face, manly legs and bubble butt almost bursting from his tight pants—had finished, he stood there, beside the devouress, shook his magnificent bell-clapper, and, never losing his sailor-boy (and therefore absolutely otherworldly) composure, looked out of the corner of his eye at Eachurbod. I'll ring those sweet bells for you, Eachurbod thought as he looked at the pendulous roundness of the testicles and the lovely phallus which, rather than being tucked away into the uniform, was still out—standing so gracefully pert and unconcerned that it might have been riding the waves. And like the waves, the lovely phallus throbbed and swelled and almost gamboled before the astonished eyes of the devouress. There was no time to lose—experience had shown, beatings had shown (and Guillotina had drummed into her) that when one stood in the presence of such a phenomenon, a phenomenon as rare as the appearance of Halley's Comet, one couldn't waste a second. Eachurbod put out a hand and caressed that regal campanile, and at her touch the great bell-clapper swung so high that it clapped against the young sailor's chest, emitting a heavenly peal. At last! After a hundred (perhaps even a thousand) years! The queen had found her yearned-for love god! Now all she had to do was kneel before him. Eachurbod took out Volume XXVIII (*Now hold it — I'm* sure *you said it was Volume XXVII!*) of the *Complete Works of Lenin* and knelt upon it as though it were a silken cushion—which brought her mouth just to the level of that glorious mouthful. Eachurbod opened her worshipful mouth, stuck out her tongue of fire, and moved toward the place where the staff of life stood erect.

And at that moment, a mezzo-soprano voice, so potent that it paralyzed every pisser in the place, burst forth in the monster men's room. All the pissers whirled around (including the young sailor), and what to their wondering eyes should appear but a skeletally thin lady of mature years, dressed head to foot in the style of mid-nineteenth-century France, standing in the center of the men's room, singing. It was María Mercedes de Santa Cruz, the Condesa de Merlín, who a hundred and fifty years later, driven by homesickness and rage, was returning for a second time to her residence in Havana, where she intended to sing once more, within those beloved walls, the opera *Norma* that Bellini had composed in 1831.

A Tour of Inspection

Fifo emerged from his underground palace surrounded by his personal escort—imposing specimens able to bring Satan himself to his knees by merely cupping their balls—and made his way to the presidential helicopter on the palace roof, which had been turned into a huge helipad scrubbed down night and day by three hundred diligent midgets. Followed by several government ministers, the Lady of the Veil (a personage who was traveling incognito, and about whom it was known only that she—or he?—was a prominent figure in the Arab world), a group of technical advisers, two physicians, the escort, and the pilot and copilot, the Supreme Leader boarded his helicopter. "Take us around the whole island," he instructed the pilot, and instantly the helicopter rose aloft. Armed with an antique spyglass, binoculars, a telescope, several pairs of magnifying glasses, and other artifacts for seeing at a distance, Fifo leaned back in his presidential seat, lit a cigar, and ordered the pilot to fly over the island *slowly,* so he could inspect everything before the Carnival. "First of all," he said, "find Bloodthirsty Shark for me. I want to see how he's doing." The gigantic helicopter descended almost to the surface of the ocean, where the great shark had called all the other sharks together for an inspection and an antirodent exhortation, while he himself remained forever vigilant. When Fifo saw Bloodthirsty Shark, his jowly face filled with tenderness and he softly caressed his long white prickly beard. And when Bloodthirsty Shark saw the presidential helicopter, he emerged and did fantastic pirouettes on the surface of the waves, exhibiting the flexibility, vigor, and virility of his powerful body.

"Throw him a piece of human flesh," Fifo ordered the Prime Minister. "His appetite must be kept keen."

It was the Prime Minister's habit, and also his duty, to always bring along a sack of human flesh on these inspection junkets, pieces of which he would throw down to Bloodthirsty Shark as a gift from Fifo, who would sometimes pull on a pair of rubber gloves and personally toss the tasty morsels to his pet. When the Prime Minister heard Fifo's order this time, though, he blanched. Fifo hadn't announced this junket beforehand, and everything had come together so suddenly (as was almost always the case with Fifo's whims) that the Prime Minister hadn't had time to send off one of the household midgets to kill one of the prisoners and throw him into a sack.

"What's the matter?" cried Fifo. "Where's the sack?"

"Comandante, w-w-we left so fast I forgot it."

"What!?" roared Fifo, livid, while Bloodthirsty Shark continued leaping about in the water, jaws agape in expectation of the usual tasty tidbit. "I have never heard of such dereliction of duty! I ought to have you shot by the firing squad this minute, for high treason!"

"I apologize, Comandante," whined the Prime Minister. "I've been so busy with the preparations for the Carnival and the palace festivities—it just slipped my mind. I promise it'll never happen again."

"All right, I will spare your life this time," Fifo relented. "So we'll just cut off one of your arms and throw it to him."

At a signal from Fifo, the two physicians amputated one of the Prime Minister's arms, and the Prime Minister, using the only hand he had left, tossed his amputated limb straight into the shark's maw. The immense fish showed its thanks by leaping out of the water almost as high as the helicopter itself, then plunging torpedo-like once more into the sea, showering the aircraft with spray.

"The arm of a prime minister must be quite a delicacy," remarked Fifo, now in a much better humor, while the helicopter increased its altitude. Then turning again to the pilot, he said, "Let's fly over Guanabo. I want to see how many faggots are on the beach today. It's a workday, so everybody *ought* to be at work."

But there were people swimming and sunning among the rocks. This made Fifo furious again, and with his walkie-talkie he ordered the Minister of the Interior to round up everybody on the beach.

"It is not moral for persons to swim without the veil," remarked the Lady of the Veil. "And doing so in that way, half naked and in the sight of everyone, is indeed a mortal sin. May Allah protect us . . ."

But Fifo ignored the Lady of the Veil—he was still looking out the window of the helicopter.

"What are all those holes that somebody's made down there along the coast?" he asked the Prime Minister, who was softly moaning as he bled to death.

"Those are the trenches that you ordered dug last week, Comandante . . ."

"Fill 'em in and have an oil well drilled where every one of 'em used to be! I'm sure there's oil down there; I can almost *smell* it."

"But Comandante . . ." one of the technical advisors screwed up his courage to stammer, "ten years ago we drilled test wells, and there's no oil here."

"What!?" Fifo roared again. "Ten years!? You're telling me that nature can't change in ten years?! You're telling me that nature is more powerful than we are?! You're telling me you don't believe in dialectical materialism?! Oil! *Oil!* I'm sure there's a river of oil down there. Oh, yes, I can smell it. And you, traitor, what you want is for us to remain in a state of underdevelopment forever, and for lack of fuel not to be able to go to war with our enemies. Which is a greater danger than ever now, I remind you, when the czar of Russia has cut off our oil supplies."

"Oil is basic for the life of a nation," affirmed the Lady of the Veil.

"Of course it's basic!" brayed Fifo. "But this son of a bitch doesn't want us to have any!" And pointing at the adviser, he cried to his escort, "Shoot him!"

"We'll have to stab him," replied the squad leader. "It's too dangerous to the passengers to have a firing squad on a helicopter in midair."

"All right, if there's no other way, stab him," conceded Fifo grudgingly.

And within seconds the guards had riddled the adviser's body with the bayonets affixed to their rifles and thrown the corpse into the sea—to the further delight of Bloodthirsty Shark, who was swimming along at full speed just under the presidential helicopter.

Now calmer, Fifo spoke to the pilot: "See if you can find Skunk in a Funk somewhere around here. I want to use this spyglass to see what he's up to. He thinks I've swallowed that bullshit about his 'rehabilitation,' but I'm nobody's fool. The only reason I've spared his life is to see how this story turns out, but when it's over I'm eliminating him. We wouldn't advise him to kid himself. . . ."

"Comandante, Skunk in a Funk isn't in Guanabo today."

"All right, then, let's move on. One faggot more, one faggot less—big deal. There are plenty to go around, lord knows."

They were now flying over the province of Matanzas, directly above its tallest prominence.

"Will you get a load of that mountain!"

"Comandante, sir, that's the Matanzas Breadloaf."

"Breadloaf my sweet ass! There's no bread in Cuba! Bread is a Christian bourgeois prejudice! I want that mountain of bread leveled this instant, and yautías planted in its place."

"Comandante," said the Minister of Agriculture, who was along for the ride, "it isn't easy to level that mountain. And besides, yautías won't grow in limestone soils."

"What do *you* know about yautías or soils!?" Fifo shouted, a veritable ball of rage. "Yautías! Yautías! I want yautías, and I want them *there!* You want to deprive me of my yautías, and deprive this country of what I promised it more than forty years ago and haven't been able to give it yet? Now I see the cause of all this: we don't have yautías because you've sabotaged the plans. You're a swine, and an agent of the CIA, and a son of a bitch. Stab him!" he ordered his escorts, who instantly and professionally obeyed. "The minute the Carnival is over, that mountain is coming down," Fifo said, and then he turned once more to the pilot: "Now take me to Zapata Swamp. I want to see how my crocodiles are doing."

They flew at full speed to the swamp. Fifo began counting the crocodiles.

"Since the last time I was here, twenty-seven males and eleven females have died," he calculated. "Obviously this unhealthy climate in the swamp is bad for my little crocs. I want all the crocodiles moved out of this swamp to the Bay of Matanzas! They can breathe pure air there!"

Instantly the dying Prime Minister got on his shortwave radio and put out a call to the Army of Matanzas, the Territorial Militia, and the Provincial

Navy, and in less than half an hour, more than a million crocodiles invaded the Bay of Matanzas.

Beaming at this quick action, Fifo ordered the inspection trip to continue.

"What're all those plants down there?" he asked as they flew over the Yumurí Valley.

"A stand of palm trees, sir," answered the pilot.

"Cut 'em down and plant lentils." Then turning to his guest of honor, the Lady of the Veil, he cooed: "Lentils have a tremendous amount of iron."

"Iron is *also* very important," the Lady of the Veil replied, looking down to see a huge bulldozer razing all the palms in the lovely valley.

They were now passing over the province of Las Villas, directly above the dam that supplied water to the city of Santa Clara.

"What's that?" asked Fifo.

"It's the Camilo Cienfuegos Dam that you ordered me to build, which I did, sir, in less than a year, surpassing all our goals," Fifo's chief of waterworks answered with pride.

"Well, tear it down and build an army training field. The enemy is more important than water!"

"But Comandante. . . ," the adviser hesitantly suggested, "it's the largest dam in the country, it cost millions of dollars to build, plus doing away with Hanabanilla Falls; it supplies water not only to Santa Clara but to all the fields and even to the Niña Bonita fish hatchery that you yourself founded. . . ."

"Oh, where do these advisers of mine come from?" sighed Fifo dramatically. "Not one of them is a true revolutionary. We're at war, and you're thinking about water instead of the enemy. That dam should never have been built in that spot in the first place, right in the center of the country, at our very geographical heart. Surely it's the first location the enemy will attack. Now I see it all very clearly—*very* clearly—you built that dam there so that when the enemy invaded we'd be wiped out!'

"No! No! I built it there because that's where the river . . ."

"River my ass! You think I don't see through you? The only one that knows where the rivers run is me! The only one that makes the plans around here is me! The only one that's trying to save the country is me! I want you to order that dam torn down RIGHT NOW!"

With tears in his eyes, the adviser gave the order to dynamite the dam.

"Now, slit his throat," Fifo ordered the guards.

The adviser, as his throat was being slit, saw the enormous dam, his great masterpiece, blown to bits with dynamite, and saw the city of Santa Clara flooded. His body, hurled from the helicopter, was swept away in the rushing waters.

"Water is not a necessity," said the Lady of the Veil, "but without oil one cannot live."

"And what's that thing down there that looks like a snake?" asked Fifo, looking out the window.

"It's the Río Máximo, Comandante," said one of the members of his escort, who was from the province of Camagüey.

"The Río Máximo? The *Río Máximo?!* Is that what you said? How dare you insult me in that way! The only *Máximo* around here is me! How can you say that there's a river that's the Máximo when *I'm* the Máximo, when *I'm* the eternal spring to which all the peoples of the world make pilgrimages to drink? And *nothing,* do you hear—*nothing!*—can be more Máximo than me, because there's no word that means greater than the *greatest!* So, you weasly son of a bitch, you've insulted me and mocked me—you want to give the title of Máximo to a river, a teeny-tiny creek, and make *me* some tinkly piece of shit! I'll teach you to minimize *me!* To *think* that a man with those ideas, a traitor of such proportions, should be a member of my escort! Execute this man immediately! . . . Oh, and about that Río Máximo—pave it over, build a highway on top of it."

The bayonet-riddled body of the guard fell onto the newly built roadway.

They were now flying along above the almost infinite plains of Camagüey.

"Why hasn't anything been planted down there? Why is all that land going to waste? Answer me!"

"Comandante," replied a livestock specialist, "those are the plains. No crops grow there. It's a pastureland. That's why at your own suggestion we planted pangola grass."

"Forget pangola. That's a perfect place for California apples."

"The climate isn't right for apples, Comandante," the agricultural adviser hazarded.

"So our climate isn't right for growing California apples, but California is? It's very obvious what you people are saying—you're saying that imperialism is more powerful than we are. *They* can plant apples in California wherever they want to, but *we* can't plant an apple tree if our life depends on it. It's a crime, planting all that land down there in pangola grass when Cuba could be the world's leading exporter of California apples. Why, we could sell our apples to California itself. But *no-o-o,* with imperialist agents like you people occupying key positions, we'll *never* get out of this state of underdevelopment, or out of a single-crop economy either. Execute those two men immediately!"

Two bayonet-riddled bodies fell into a stubbly brown field planted in withered California apple trees.

"American imperialism is the Great Satan," said the Lady of the Veil. "*Of course* you can grow California apples."

But Fifo, rather than answering the Lady of the Veil, sat gazing out the window, lost in thought. Sometimes he would use his spyglass, sometimes his large spectacles, sometimes the telescope—still others, he would bring sophisticated binoculars to his eyes.

"What's the meaning of all those naked men down there?" he suddenly asked his whole entourage.

"Comandante," said the Minister of Education unctuously, "that's the concentration camp for homosexuals that you yourself designed and that I built on the instant. We have fifteen thousand fairies locked up in there."

"What?! What are you saying!? A concentration camp!? What will our honored guest think of us? That we're a bunch of Fascist barbarians, that I'm some sort of Hitler, running concentration camps? Are you saying that in this nation where there is *nothing* but liberty and freedom we have concentration camps?"

"Comandante, you yourself gave the order to build them."

The Lady of the Veil, fascinated, peered out the window.

"It's a rehabilitation camp for criminals," Fifo explained to her.

"Rehabilitation is most necessary," the Lady of the Veil replied.

"Yes indeed," Fifo agreed, and turning to the Minister of Education, he said, "*Rehabilitation,* but never, ever, 'concentration camps.' What we do is educate or reeducate; we never hold anyone by force. Those young men are in that camp voluntarily because they want to be reeducated," he continued, meanwhile using his spyglass to be sure that the electrified fences around the concentration camp were all in good working order and there weren't any breaks in them. "If you think that's a concentration camp down there, that means that you yourself are not sufficiently rehabilitated. Guards! Throw this man out the window! Throw him into that reeducation center so he can start his reeducation as soon as possible!"

"Should we bayonet him first?"

"From this height it won't be necessary," Fifo replied, and he lit one of his huge cigars.

That day the fairies in the concentration camp had a celebration: the Minister of Education, the terrible Gallego Fernández, who had designed the camp, suddenly fell to earth in their midst. To everyone's glee, body parts went flying.

"By the way," said Fifo, turning to the leader of his escort as the minister splattered below, "why did you ask me whether the Minister of Education should be bayoneted? I want it very clear that we tossed him into the reeducation center so that he could be reeducated. Or do you think that reeducating a person and killing him are the same thing?"

And before the escort leader could defend himself, Fifo ordered the rest of the escort to tie his hands, bayonet him, and throw him out the window of the helicopter.

"You really can't trust a man that stupid," Fifo said as he exhaled a cloud of smoke. "He could be an enemy. How could I never have realized it, how could I have such a man as one of my escorts? Uff."

And on the spot, he appointed one of the remaining guards squad leader.

The helicopter flew out of that region into the former province of Oriente, so after exchanging a few words with the Lady of the Veil, Fifo, showing great interest, began to peer out the window.

"What are all those boxes down there?" he asked as they flew over a city.

"That's the city of Holguín, Comandante. It has a population of three million people and it's the capital of the province of the same name," replied the copilot, who was from Holguín and proud of it.

"Well, that city is very badly located," Fifo observed. "It looks like down there in all that flatland there ought to be a bullfrog farm. I want the whole population moved out of there, all those boxes torn down, and a big lake full of bullfrogs put in."

"Comandante," offered the copilot, who loved his hometown with all his heart and would do anything to save it, "it's hard to put a lake in the middle of a flat field, but Bayamo and Santiago de Cuba are just a little farther on, and they're surrounded by mountains and have lots of good big rivers. It's the perfect place to build a bullfrog farm."

"Sure," said Fifo sarcastically, "and destroy two national monuments and two national shrines—Bayamo, the Cradle of Independence; and Santiago de Cuba, the Cradle of the Revolution. You swine! You counterrevolutionary swine! Holguín has always been a shitty little town that's produced little shits like you! And you want to sacrifice two heroic cities in exchange for *shit!* Execute this man immediately!"

"Could I make one last request?" the copilot pleaded.

"Speak."

"I want my corpse thrown out over the city of Holguín."

"Request granted," said Fifo.

But by the time the bayoneted body of the copilot hit the ground, in place of the city of Holguín there was an enormous bullfrog-populated lake, into which the body fell—inspiring a deafening protest from the bullfrogs.

The helicopter was now flying over a swiftly flowing river.

"What's that?" asked an irritated and suspicious Fifo.

"Comandante, that's the Río Cauto, which despite its name, which is 'Cautious,' is the swiftest and most powerful river in the country," one of the few ministers still alive had the courage to respond, thinking that such a basic answer could hardly get him into much trouble.

Oh, but the comandante looked down in rage upon those swiftly flowing waters, and then more furiously yet at the minister.

"*Cautious!* So in this country, where everything should be crystal-clear, where no one should be afraid of anything, we have a *cautious* river—a fearful, circumspect river, and river that's a little *wary,* and therefore a river that isn't fully convinced of the Revolution's truth. I'll bet that's where the armies of rodents that are undermining the nation come from! And naturally, since it's a freshwater river, Bloodthirsty Shark can't swim up it, traitors use it as their hideout, and the river, the very *cautious* river, very cautiously and circumspectly protects them. I want that river dried up *NOW!* This instant! And *you!*" he said, turning to the minister and boxing his ears, "you should have been more *cautious* and not had such nice things to say about a traitorous river, much less in front of a foreign visitor to our nation. Do you think wartime secrets and the strategies and strengths of an enemy ought to be divulged to a foreign power? Does nobody around here know the rules for national security and international protocol? But that's all right, there's no need for you to know those rules, because you're going headfirst into the Río Cauto, and you'll disappear along with it."

At a sign from Fifo, the minister was executed and tossed into the river, where his body fell into the now dried-up riverbed.

"Comandante! Comandante! We're coming to the Cradle of the Revolution!" exclaimed in unison the last two ministers still alive (including the dying Prime Minister), knowing that Fifo was always happy when he came to the city in which he had proclaimed his victory.

The pilot circled the city so that Fifo could take in the view. He knew that Fifo always liked to show it off to foreign visitors. But this time, Fifo looked down pensively at Santiago de Cuba.

"It resembles a great amphitheater," said the Lady of the Veil.

"You're right! You're right! A huge amphitheater!" cried Fifo. "That's exactly the image I was searching for and couldn't put my finger on! An amphitheater! All those mountains rising in ever higher tiers and circling the city that way—why, it makes a perfect amphitheater! Who needs another city—what we need in this country is an amphitheater. Imagine," he cried jubilantly, turning to the Lady of the Veil, "imagine what grand and glorious political celebrations we could have in an amphitheater like that—an amphitheater with acoustics magnified by those magnificent mountains. What an echo it would have! Why, I could talk for eight or ten hours and my voice would echo for a year. . . . We've got to build an amphitheater. Tear down that city and start today."

"But Comandante, it's the Cradle of the Revolution, it's a heroic city," said the two ministers, almost in unison.

"Execute those two men—they're deviationists! Around here the cradle, the babe, the Revolution, and the hero, all in one, is *me!*"

When the last two ministers had been thrown out of the helicopter into the amphitheater, Fifo looked out over the great stage and with a note of nostalgia gave his next order.

"Right there, in the center of the amphitheater, I want a gigantic statue of White Udder, the cow I have loved more than any other cow in my entire life."

For a few moments, Fifo was oblivious to everything around him; his every thought lay with that dear departed cow. . . . In life he had loved this noble creature so deeply, and she had given him such delight, that when she died he had covered the island with larger-than-life-size statues to her memory. . . . All the other people on the helicopter, including the pilot, also fell into a reverie, trying (as they always did) to imitate Fifo's every pose and gesture. This caused the helicopter to miss by inches crashing into a gigantic mound of rock that rose into the clouds.

"Shit! What's that?" cried Fifo, coming out of his meditations.

"It's the Baracoa Anvil, Comandante," said the new commander of the guards. "We almost crashed into it."

"You mean I was about to die in a helicopter crash and you, commander of the guard, who should have been watching out for me, didn't even notice? That's the way you guard my life? Your duty is to watch over me day and night! I want this man executed as an object lesson to the other guards! Bayonets!" he commanded, signalling to the other guards.

And instantly the few guards who were left alive bayoneted their leader.

"Throw him down on that Baracoa Anvil," Fifo ordered, "and let's head back to Havana. I've got a million things to do before the Carnival starts. Oh, and about that anvil there—melt it down. It's an obscurantist medieval symbol or something—anyway, it's got nothing to do with our new society. Melt it down and put up a giant hammer and sickle."

And instantly Fifo fell asleep, but as the aircraft passed over the huge lake where the city of Holguín had formerly stood, the deafening croaking of the bullfrogs woke him.

"What in hell is *that!?* Have the Americans landed?" asked Fifo groggily.

"Comandante," replied one of the few surviving technical advisors, "it's the bullfrog farm you ordered built."

"Bullfrogs!? *Bullfrogs!?* Are you nuts!? Whose idea was that?"

And since no one dared answer *that* question, Fifo got even angrier.

"Do you mean to tell me you've destroyed a city full of hardworking people so you could raise bullfrogs!? Which one of you idiot sons of bitches did such a thing? Whose idea was it?"

No one answered. Fifo ordered the escort to torture the technical advisers until they talked. Finally, one of the three advisers who were left said that the idea had come from Fifo himself. Fifo turned black with rage. So they thought he was a madman capable of such imbecility? And the adviser was instantly sentenced to death and thrown into the lake. The two other advisers, who refused to talk, died from their tortures and their bodies were thrown into the lake too. Several members of the guard began to be interrogated and tortured by other members. And so, one by one, they were killed and their bodies thrown out over various provinces. When the aircraft arrived in Havana, all that remained (with the exception of Fifo, of course) were two members of his private escort, the Lady of the Veil, and the pilot.

"I want that pilot shot," Fifo said to his minuscule guard as soon as the Lady of the Veil had retired to her quarters. "Because of his dereliction of duty we were all almost killed at the Baracoa Anvil."

The two escorts immediately shot the pilot, then snappily saluted. But no sooner had they saluted than Fifo called up his special forces and more than five hundred of his loyal midgets and ordered them to shoot the two surviving members of his former private escort.

"They know too much," he told the midgets. "And as for the Lady of the Veil, I want her stabbed in the cunt and killed during the Carnival. It should look like a crime of passion. I don't want any political trouble with the Arab world."

Rosa's Little Pink Slippers, the Magic Ring, and the Seven-League Swim Fins

How gaily Tomasito the Goya-Girl tripped along in her pink platform shoes. They were really *marvelous* shoes, and they'd been made especially for her out of genuine red crocodile hide. Uh-huh, *red,* because all the crocodiles, after they'd been moved on Fifo's orders to the Bay of Matanzas, got so mad they turned absolutely *livid,* and they stayed that way.... Oh, but how gaily, how perfectly cheerily, the queen tripped along in those attention-getting red shoes. To think that she had spent more than ten years writing some aunt of hers who lived in Miami (although she had to admit it wasn't her real aunt, it was just her aunt by marriage), begging her to send her a pair of platform shoes just like these. (One of her most sacred treasures was the picture of a pair of platform shoes she'd snipped out of a foreign fashion magazine that she'd bought on the black market.) And all of a sudden, at one of Virgilio's get-togethers (and poetry readings), she'd met the cunning Mahoma. There that great whalelike thing sat, wearing a pair of platform shoes *just like* the ones whose photograph she gazed at longingly, lovingly, rapturously, day and night. And when she'd asked Mahoma where she'd found such a treasure, the fat thing had told her that she manufactured them herself, and that they cost three hundred pesos. Tomasito the Goya-Girl couldn't believe her ears: three hundred pesos was three months' salary! Tomasito pleaded with Mahoma for a discount, even a teeny one, but the cruel queen told her to forget it, she had an *infinite* list of clients ready to pay whatever she asked for her creations, but what she *could* do was put Tomasito's name on the bottom of the list and give her a chance to start saving up. And you better save fast, hon, because if Fifo finds out about my little business he'll take it away from me—he might even have me stoned to death with platforms.

And so poor Tomasito the Goya-Girl followed the advice of the cunning Mahoma and after work at the Tire Collective, she put in ten hours extra every day for three months (alongside Olga Andreu) picking up cigarette butts at bus stops and selling them wholesale in the Plaza de la Catedral. Finally, carrying the three hundred pesos, she climbed up to the loft (built in an architectural style known universally in Havana as "the barbecue grill") where Mahoma lived. And there sat the great flabby thing surrounded with gigantic half-finished clogs. God, how beautiful! Some of those platforms must have been a foot and a half tall! With platforms like that, Tomasito the Goya-Girl said to herself, I'll be the slenderest girl-queen in the world.

"Now these are just samples, in case some thieving bull macho top (which they all are—thieving, I mean) gets the idea to steal them," Mahoma winked conspiratorially at Tomasito. "I've got the real stuff hidden." And at that, the shoe queen opened a gigantic closet that no one would have ever suspected existed, since it was behind a wall covered with an immense oil portrait of Mahoma himself signed by Clara Mortera. And there, before Tomasito the Goya-Girl's eyes, lay a treasure trove of platform shoes, the most dazzling sight she'd ever seen. They were made out of precious woods pulled through the hole in Clara's wall and covered with canvas that Mahoma dyed so skillfully that no one would ever have imagined that it wasn't genuine alligator. Although for very special clients—such as Tomasito the Goya-Girl—the shoe queen had *real* crocodile skin, taken from crocs hunted down and skinned by the Dowager Duchess de Valero and Karilda Olivar Lubricious' husband Teodor Tampon, who happened to possess a razor-sharp saber. The shoe queen chose from among the ones with real crocodile-hide the tallest, loudest, *reddest* pair of platforms she had to offer. "These, darling, are *you,"* she said to Tomasito. "If the problem is attracting attention, then these are perfect. And they're made of the real stuff." Tomasito paid the three hundred pesos and started down the steep steps from the barbecue grill so fast that she lost her footing and slid halfway down headfirst. "You need to practice walking with those platforms, honey!" shouted Mahoma. "Or else you might break something!" But Tomasito picked herself up and flew like lightning out the door, her glorious red platform shoes making such a clickety-clack that she even gave a fright to the Weird Sisters, who were on their way to a special reading with Lagunas, the Clandestine Clairvoyant.

Although she hadn't eaten in three months (she'd been saving her money, girl, remember?), those red platform shoes filled Tomasito the Goya-Girl with uncontrollable energy. "I won't be Tomasito the Goya-Girl anymore," she told herself, "I'll be a Queen; I'll stand so tall that this stupid nickname that Skunk in a Funk hung on me won't make any sense anymore." And yet somehow it did still fit her, because now, rather than being one of those monstrous court dwarves in Goya's paintings, she was one of the figures on stilts. But utterly unconscious of this sad fact, Tomasito clickety-clacked from one end of Havana to another. And when, like Hector in the *Iliad,* she had made three circuits of the city, she heard a whistle from one of the little nooks along the Malecón. Ay, somebody was whistling at her, the former Goya-Girl—and it was a black man so huge and so well-equipped that he obviously had to be one of the members of the national pole-vault team—a team that Fifo himself selected and took personal charge of. The towering fairy stopped dead in her clickety-clacks; there came the whistle again. This time the gigantic black man motioned for her to come over. And a conversation was struck up that grew more and more . . . shall we say *intimate.* While he talked, the ebony love god from time to time would delicately (as though he had a secret itch that was just the slightest bit embarrassing) scratch and reaccommodate his balls. The towering fairy would give a little clickety-clack, step back, and then clickety-clack just a *little* closer to the sweet Ethiop. Why don't we take a little walk along the Malecón? he finally said, sweeping her from head to foot with a look so lustful and so lecherous that Tomasito thought she'd faint dead away on the spot. And so they came to the Castle of Running Waters, a colonial fortress converted on Fifo's orders into a public toilet. The teetering fairy looked at the *very* impressive black man, who was already disappearing into the blackness of the interior of the building, and she gave a few short, nervous, doubtful little click-clacks. But the gigantic hunk called out to her from the darkness within: "Come on, I'm gonna screw you till it comes out your tonsils." Heavens, who could resist such an exquisite offer? And so like a flash the teetering-towering fairy rushed into the blackness of the Castle of Power. She felt herself grasped by her nonexistent waist, felt her gigantic lover raise her into the air, felt the burning breath of that body that was about to fill her with meaty happiness. The black man raised her, higher and higher, gave her a little toss, and in midair ripped the platform shoes off Tomasito, just as she felt she was about to be *truly* levitated. But when she fell to the floor what she saw was the gigantic black man standing above her with the gorgeous platform shoes in his hands, and the words of love he was speaking were these: "You better make a run for it, faggot, unless you want that ugly head of yours smashed in with these platforms." And when she made a gesture of protest, the black man gave her such a whack in the head with the platform shoes that Tomasito the Goya-Girl finally realized that she was about to be killed by a professional assassin. The fairy, no longer towering, dragged herself, trembling and barefooted, from the Castle of Power, and barefooted she continued on through the city, until she came to her own hovel, another barbecue grill made by Skunk in a Funk out of wood pulled through the hole in Clara's wall.

Lying on her stomach on the wooden bridge at Patrice Lumumba Beach, Skunk in a Funk finished writing the story of Tomasito's adventure (or misadventure) and she smiled in delight, not only because he was happy with the story he'd just finished writing, but also because she was sure that this tragic but absolutely true story would never happen to *her.* That sort of thing only happened to silly queens who threw caution to the wind and followed any old good-looking thug into some dark place—nobody had ever stolen as much as a safety pin from *her.* Not for nothing was she a friend of the cunning Mahoma, not for nothing did she distrust *everybody,* and especially Men. There she lay, Skunk in a Funk, next to the ocean with her gleaming rubber swim fins under the manuscript of her novel. How many princely black men, how many glorious teenagers, how many *hunks,* had come up to her and asked to borrow her swim fins? But *no-o-o,* she was too wise to ever lend anybody her swim fins. *If they come, let it be for my beauty—never for my swim fins,* she told herself. Not to mention that those brand-spanking-new swim fins, made in *France,* my dear, were the only material treasure that Skunk in a Funk possessed. She had been dreaming of these swim fins for more than ten years, and finally one day a Frenchwoman (a visiting professor brought to the University of Havana by Fifo, and who could reach orgasm only when made love to by a gay man) took a liking to Skunk in a Funk and on one of her trips to Paris brought the treasure back with her. Of course Skunk in a Funk had to squeeze her eyes tight, take a deep breath, swallow her pride, and make love to the professor to get them, but in the end she even got her pregnant, thanks to the erotic inspiration (prodding) of a daisy chain they were in at the time. Nine months later, the Frenchwoman gave birth to a baby boy that was totally white on one side and totally black on the other. In terror she abandoned her son and her husband, Captain Miguel Figueroa (who also screwed women using the daisy-chain method), and took refuge for the rest of her days in a cave in the Pyrenees. . . .

Uh-huh, that was all true (and tragic) enough, but what counted was that Skunk in a Funk now had her swim fins, and *that* more than offset the guilt she felt for betraying her sex by screwing a woman. Pulling on those gleaming black rubber swim fins, Skunk in a Funk would dive into the waters off Patrice Lumumba Beach, La Concha, Cubanaleco, or anywhere in Guanabo, and glide along the seabed more gracefully than any fish. She would glide between the legs of the men who stood waist- or neck-deep in the warm water, conversing with their wives and children, and as that family conversation followed its conventional course (chicken pox, smallpox, the French pox), the glorious hunk's sexual temperature, as he felt the underwater nibblings and gropings of the artful Skunk, would begin to rise (as would something else, too). Then all Skunk in a Funk would have to do would be pull down the hunk's bathing suit and suck, while on the surface the noble domestic chat continued—the atomic bomb, the hydrogen bomb, the neutron bomb. The hunk would cum with a deep sigh and sometimes even a stirring *Ah!* that would surprise the people he was talking to, while Skunk in a Funk, always below the water, would swim off to the next luscious mouthful. . . . What's wrong? the wife or sweetheart would ask when one of those gorgeous hunks emitted his *Ah* of delight. Oh, nothing, the glorious hunk whose member had just been sucked would reply, I thought I stepped on a sea urchin or a jellyfish. And the Divine Ms. Skunk in a Funk, with her wonderful swim fins, would work her way along the shoreline, wreaking domestic and aquatic devastation. By now a school of brightly-colored fish that had learned to like the taste of cum (an *exotic* species, certainly) would follow along, knowing that near whatever legs the agile swimmer hovered, a celestial liquor soon would flow. But one must say, in all good conscience, that sometimes Skunk in a Funk would leave off her oral pleasure-giving (and -taking), dive straight down near the shoreline, and begin to gnaw furiously at the base of the island. Because in spite of that wondrous sea that brought her such marvelous men, Skunk in a Funk was another one of those who wanted to flee the island. That was why he gnawed away at the island's foundation, although she also dreamed of using her swim fins to make it at least to Key West.

Yes, she would leave the island, but not without taking her swim fins with her and not before her novel, *The Color of Summer,* was completed. And thinking about that novel she picked up the pen that she'd slipped in her pocket not long ago at a reception for Carlitos Olivares, the Most In-Your-Face Queen in Cuba, and started writing again.

Coco Salas' dream had come true at last! He owned a leather belt a good eighteen inches wide with a buckle that was *more* than a buckle—it was two enormous, gleaming harness rings. It was a *wonderful* belt. Halisia Jalonzo had brought it back with her from one of her trips to Europe. Coco cinched the belt around his waist and contemplated herself in the mirror at the foot of her bed in the Hotel Monserrate. Squealing with delight, she clinked the buckle-rings together two or three times and as she paraded all about the room she practically *crowed.*

One had to admit that the change the belt made on the old queen was amazing. Coco Salas was one of those cases that are totally thin and bony yet have a huge potbelly. Right in the middle of that ironing-board figure there bulged a *big round mound*—she looked like a boa constrictor that had swallowed a whole chicken. And what that potbelly blooming so unexpectedly out of that sack of bones did was, it made Coco's ugliness even uglier. But *now!*—now that marvelous belt did away with the bulge, or at least held it in a bit. Coco Salas still looked like a boa constrictor (a bald, skinny boa constrictor standing on its tail, "the garter snake from Holguín," as Delfín Proust had called her), but now a ringed one, without that disfiguring bulge. But it wasn't just that the belt favored her physically; it also did her a world of good emotionally, and it *had* to help in the pecking order. After all, it had been a gift from Halisia Jalonzo, the world's primeríssima prima ballerina (that was what the island newspapers said) and intimate friend of Fifo. Oh, what a terrible blow it would be to Coco's friends and foes alike (and in the life of a queen they were almost *always* alike) when she showed up in public with that wonderful belt. And as for the men—how would they ever be able to resist her? How could she not be the center of attention with those brightly gleaming harness rings? *I bought it right across the street from the cathedral in Segovia,* Halisia had told her; *between you and me, I think it has magical powers, my dear, because the same day I bought it, La Pasionaria keeled over and died. Put it on, Coco darling—you'll knock 'em dead.*

And that same night, Coco Salas cinched the belt tight around his waist and (almost unable to breathe) headed for Coney Island. When she made her entrance at the Coney Island Amusement Park in Mariano, even Ye-Ye (Miss PornoPop to you, Mary), who in her own special way was the most sophisticated queen in the world, had to put her cruising on autopilot for a minute and inspect that belt; even the Flower Boys, who were there to be looked at, not to look, looked. Hiram, La Reine des Araignées, who was up on a dais choosing the prettiest of the teenagers, those who would take part in Fifo's private party for all the high muckety-mucks in the government, paused for a moment in her probing, testing, and speechmaking to gaze upon the luminescent apparition. And she, Coco Salas, walked regally down the rank of gorgeous boys picked out by Delfín Proust and elbowed her way into the crowd where even Eachurbod, indefatigably searching for a man, halted for a moment in her eyelash-fluttering to contemplate the leather-queen bound by that *devastatingly* butch belt. Even the hustlers from Sandy Creek made a mute but unmistakable (and *very* masculine) gesture. Peerless Gorialdo cupped his balls when the queen passed by. But Coco Salas continued onward, rigidly at attention (the belt kept her from walking any other way), through the multitude that parted as it gazed in wonder at her wonderfulness. The Dowager Duchess de Valero, La Reine, Divinely Malign, and SuperSatanic put their chicanery and machinations on hold to stand in petrified amazement as Coco martially marched past in her marvelous belt. Heavens, and when Mayoya, unable to contain her curiosity, asked Coco where *on earth* she'd found such a belt, and Coco told her it was a gift from Halisia, a thousand fairies and assorted queens, including La Reine des Araignées and the Dowager Duchess de Valero, bowed in reverent respect before the boa constrictor honored by the witch. But the boa constrictor honored by the dancing hag continued her progress through all of Coney Island without a moment's pause at any compliment, wink, or whistle, or even the obvious erotic gestures made by the most *stunning* pistol-packers. One could only assume that she felt there was no one at Coney Island worthy of screwing a queen who possessed such a glamorous girdle. *My grandeur prevents me from fraternizing with anyone who is not of the stature of my belt,* Coco said to herself (though she was unable to swell with pride as she'd have wished, since the belt was fairly strangling her). And she continued walking through the crowd of inferior creatures clad in their rustic clothes and plastic belts. It was only toward midnight, in one of the most out-of-the-way places in the park, that the regal personage discovered a love god worthy of her light-emitting harness rings. But the love god, precisely because he was God, didn't so much as look at her. The queen, making the belt clank even more and rubbing the rings to make them shine all the brighter (in fact, they now seemed to emit bolts of lightning), circled the apparently unimpressed love god several times, but to no avail. He just kept looking off toward the Ferris wheel, whose revolutions traced rings of light in the dark sky. *This cannot be,* said the queen to herself, *that I, the protegée of Halisia Jalonzo, with this wonderful belt on, should be ignored.* And at that, all asparkle, she approached the love god. The love god was one of those sophisticated, breathtaking, *irresistible* street thugs, a child of sixteen with a body, face, and hair that would have made Antinous himself turn green with envy. Yet no one in the multitudinous world of Pansyland had ever known that delicious boy to have anything to do with fairies. The sweet young hunk's reputation was such that he became known as the White Angel of Marianao. But a queen wearing that marvelous belt was not some mere mortal queen, she was a love goddess in her own right, and there was no way she was going to be intimidated by an angel. And so, my dear, without preamble, she planted herself before that angel and spoke these wingèd words: "You can follow me if you want to. I'm going into that stand of palm trees over there." It was the command of a crown princess whose sweet loins were set off by a sparkling girdle. And without looking back, Coco Salas walked with poise and serenity into the stand of palm trees. She stopped beside a tree and turned. In the light of the powerfully gleaming harness rings that cinched the girdle to her waist, she saw the Angel of Marianao approaching. Few were the words spoken. *The gods have ways of understanding one another,* said the love goddess to herself. And swiftly she began unbuttoning the God's shirt (since she had already capitalized Him), unbuckled his plastic belt (bought with an H-190 ration coupon), and weighed his celestial attributes in her cupped hand. Coco started to bow down before those divine dimensions to bestow a kiss upon them, but her glamorous girdle would not allow it. And taking off her belt was like asking Elizabeth Regina to remove her crown. Coco, loco, imprisoned by her belt, continued to caress the angel's divine prepuce, which swelled ever larger by the moment. *Turn around, I want to stick it to you,* the angel said to the love goddess, who twinkled within the palm grove like some huge lightning bug. And the queen turned, and the angel began to embrace her from behind. *You turn me on, bitch,* said the angel, and the love goddess thought she was going to melt. *Come on, let me stick it to you,* the angel insisted as he fumbled at that glorious belt and tried to push her pants down. *No,* said the love goddess, making a supreme effort, *I don't want you to take my belt off. . . . Well, I can't do anything with it on,* the angel said, his celestial member pointing straight as an arrow at her heart. *And besides, with all that sparkling, somebody'll see us.* And the love goddess, swayed by such persuasive suasion, allowed the angel to unbuckle the magnificent belt and pull down her pants. *Get down on your hands and knees,* the angel begged her, a tremulous hitch in his voice, and the queen of queens could not refuse a request so sublime. And so on all fours under the palm trees, she knelt in readiness for the angelic benediction (with a capital Dick). But then, across her naked buttocks waiting expectantly, tremblingly, for the scepter of the love god, there exploded *a horrible pain!* What's happening!? shrieked Coco, and she saw the angel holding her wondrous belt by one end and raising it to deliver yet another mortal blow. The angel was thrashing the queen of queens with the gleaming buckle of her glorious belt. Coco Salas tried to run away, but with her pants around her ankles it was hard to do—the only thing she could manage was to scurry away on all fours. And so hoist, as it were, by her own petard, she desperately (agonizingly slowly) scrambled toward Coney Island while the two huge luminescent harness rings pummeled her pained and reddened buttocks. With ever-increasing fury, the angel, a.k.a. Lisa's Tatica, lashed her—until the four-legged love goddess could finally manage to reach the lights. And then the gorgeous boy put on the belt and walked away. The bloody, bowed, and belted (though disbelted) love goddess, once more sporting an enormous round potbelly, pulled herself to her feet on a fence—the fence that surrounded the Ferris wheel, which was still making radiant circles in the sky.

❀

Reinaldo put the finishing touches on the story of Coco Salas' belt and smiled; then he lay back once more, his head on the manuscript that lay atop his swim fins. Skunk in a Funk gave a quick look down the wooden bridge she was sunning on, writing on, resting on, and cruising on, and took an inventory of the more than a hundred fairies that had gaggled together on it. Over there were the Three Weird Sisters knitting endless pullovers, underwear, and bathing suits with which they attempted to seduce the beachgoers. And a little farther on were Miguel Barniz showing off his misshapen body and César Lapa, the Mulatto of Fire, making those grotesque gestures that she thought were *divine.* Making up the predictable coven over that way were the Duchess, Sanjuro, La Reine des Araignées, Uglíssima, and SuperSatanic talking about Carita Montiel's last movie, which they'd just seen. Poor creatures, thought Skunk in a Funk, they think that old movie from the seventies is *le dernier cri*—why, I bet they don't even know that Carita's dead, I think at the age of a hundred and twelve. In a little corner of the bridge the Dowager Duchess de Valero was chatting with Teodoro Tampon, Clara Mortera, SuperChelo, and Carlitos Olivares, the Most In-Your-Face Queen in Cuba (a title he wore on his wing, I mean sleeve). In another nook, somewhat removed from the rest—oh dear!—the Ogress was exposing her scabs and bulges to the sun. And way over there were Tomasito the Goya-Girl, the Brontë Sisters, the cunning Mahoma, and the Siamísima Twins Brielíssima and Singadíssima, joined at the navel. At that horrid sight, Skunk in a Funk (who wanted to go on thinking about her novel, not get involved in stupid chatter) hid her face in her arms and rested, her head on the manuscript of her novel and her beloved swim fins. The fierce sun of summer made her drowsy. When she awoke, an angel was hovering before her eyes. It was a *gorgeous* boy, of harmonious hunklike proportions, with curly yellow hair and sweet nostalgic eyes and a towel over his shoulder. It was (dare I say it?) Lisa's Tatica, the White Angel of Marianao. So lovely was this teenage creature that no one could tell by looking at him, not even those few people who *knew* him, that he was a common (and *common,* my dear) thief. That's how such a chaste and angelic myth had been able to grow up around him—he didn't look like the thug he was. The dreamboat gazed at Skunk in a Funk so tenderly that she simply *had* to sit up on the edge of the bridge and say hello. *How's it going,* Skunk in a Funk said to him, trying to control her nervousness at being in the presence of such a vision of delight. *Kinda boring,* said Cinderella's Prince, *the only interesting kid around here is you, the rest of 'em just chatter away.* Omigod! The Fair-Haired Child had called Skunk in a Funk, that hunchbacked old thing, a *kid!* And Skunk in a Funk fell for it. Oh yes, she was a kid, a guy, a young hunk who could still run up the Mount of the Cross without getting winded, the way she'd done thirty years ago. But Gabriel, out of the past, rushed to Skunk in a Funk's rescue. He made her see herself the way she was now—an old queen lying spread-eagled on a bridge at Patrice Lumumba Beach, looking glassy-eyed and openmouthed at the beckoning bulge that bulged *for what seemed like miles* in the almost transparent bathing suit of a common criminal. Oh, but the common criminal had scooted a little closer to Skunk in a Funk, and while he stretched his lovely legs, brushing Skunk in a Funk's legs as he did so, his voice grew ever more intimate. *Nobody knows how lonely I feel,* the thieving angel murmured, *it's so hard to find anybody you feel like you can talk to. . . . I wish I had a friend, a real friend, somebody that didn't just want to go to bed with me. . . .* Don't pay any attention! Reinaldo shouted at Skunk in a Funk from somewhere deep inside Skunk in a Funk herself. Don't be an idiot, just keep working on our novel! . . . But the diabolical angel, with his increasingly angelic smile, asked Skunk in a Funk if he could stay there a while, next to her. *No!* shouted Gabriel from Holguín. *Tell him you're not buying any of this bullshit,* Reinaldo whispered from down inside. Of course you can stay here, Skunk in a Funk replied. It's a free country. Thanks, answered the angel, who stretched out facedown (the whole hunky length of him) alongside Skunk in a Funk. Look at him there, all gold and honey, life force radiating forth from him like a beacon, bubbling forth like a fountain of youth before your bulging eyes. He's dozed off. He's closed his eyes and dozed off, safe in the assurance that you will watch over his sleep and guard his lovely white towel. His lo-o-ong eyelashes have fluttered closed like the wings of some fantastic bird. And the queen watches over the sleep of the Golden Prince, and naturally she makes sure nobody runs off with his towel, she protects him from the thuggish looks and vulgar pawings of Peerless Gorialdo and the notorious chickenhawks of Arroyo Naranjo, who pass dangerously close to the towel several times. Oh, she is the Fairy Guardmother watching over the Angel's sleep, property, and life—that snow-white angel who had so innocently trusted in her, the monstrous Skunk in a Funk. She saw it now—reality contradicted what she herself had written about this man-child. How could such a sweet teenager be bad—he was Goodness itself, that's what he was, a poor misunderstood kid, a jewel in the rough, perhaps a great poet in a mud puddle. The angel slept for more than an hour under Skunk in a Funk's watchful eye. By the time he woke up, Skunk in a Funk had already planned how she would invite him up to her room, over there, near the beach; they would talk like real friends, none of that wanna-do-it stuff. She and the Golden Boy would traverse the trash heap of life together; they would do battle together against the world. She would defend her Prince against the terrible chickenhawks that wanted to rape him, against the queens that wanted to swallow him whole. No one would harm her Angel; she would take care of him. Maybe—why not?—in a gesture of brotherhood she would kiss his balls once in a while. Uh-huh, but that was all, that was all, and then she would rock him to sleep. Oh, maybe, if the man-child absolutely *insisted,* she would kiss his prick. Uh-huh, but that was all, that was all. All right, maybe, when the poor creature couldn't bear the suffering of the world any longer, she would lie down beside him, kiss him ever so delicately, and allow herself to be ravaged by the Boy-Prince, to prove to him that he was not alone in the world. Uh-huh, she might do that, but that was all, that was all. Other times, giving in to the constant pleadings of the Princely Hunk, she would rear back, rock back against him as fast as she could and be skewered by the child, and they would live that way, forming a single harmony of coupling, for year after year. Uh-huh, but that was all. . . . Adaze in these erotico-domestic meditations was Skunk in a Funk when the Golden Boy, springing up so fast she couldn't figure out what was happening, pulled on her brand-new swim fins and dived into the water, vanishing as if by magic. Skunk in a Funk, unable to *conceive* that the Child of Glory, whom she had just been so tenderly watching over, was capable of such a thing, looked out at the ocean expecting to see the young man leap out of the water and return to her side. But Tatica, swimming underwater, was not coming back; he was swimming away (with the swim fins) as fast as he could swim. When Skunk in a Funk came to her senses, she realized that she was sitting all by herself on the wooden bridge at Patrice Lumumba Beach beside the only thing the Golden Boy had left her to remember him by—an old, holey, shit-covered towel. Skunk in a Funk looked around and saw all the fairies and queens that she knew so well—her natural enemies—making sarcastic remarks; some were falling on the ground, they found it all so hilarious. All of them were laughing at the queen who had just been made a fool of. . . . But even if it was too late to save the swim fins, it wasn't too late to save some face. And so Skunk in a Funk stood up on the bridge and called out to Tatica as though he were swimming along underwater right there underneath the bridge—*Tatica, honey, I'm tired, I'll wait for you in my room. I'll take your towel so these thieves all over the place won't steal it. . . .* And with the graceful and self-assured air of a true lady, and carrying the shit-stained towel as though it were the scepter of a real-life queen, Skunk in a Funk made her way through the cackling and camping and retired from the beach. But oh, my dear, when she stepped off Patrice Lumumba Beach, she realized that she had forgotten the manuscript of her novel—she'd left it on the bridge. Reinaldo ran like the wind back to the beach. There were the other faggots, laughing like hyenas, but the manuscript was nowhere to be seen. How could he question those pansies, it would be so humiliating. Besides—if they had taken the novel it was only logical to think that they wouldn't give it back to him. Gabriel looked desperately down into the water under the bridge, expecting to see pages of the manuscript floating there, because there hadn't been time for it to sink entirely. But not the slightest sign of it. So Skunk in a Funk arrived at the unfair conclusion that that evil Tatica himself, out of sheer innate malignity, had stolen her novel, too, just to spite her. . . . But she couldn't show her dejection in front of this pack of cackling fairies that were watching her consternation from the bridge, fluttering their wings and feathers. Even Oscar was frenziedly beating his huge beat-up wings, like some great vampire bat. And so, screwing up her courage, and putting her best face forward, and smiling like the trouper that she was, Skunk in a Funk walked over to the railing and called out to Tatica once more as though the Golden Boy were right there, swimming among the piles of the bridge: *Oh, and thanks for remembering to throw out the paper I was writing on, the way I asked you to. I was telling the story of all my friends, and it could have done a good deal of damage. Thanks for being so understanding, sweetheart. . . .* And even more regally than before, Skunk in a Funk walked off the bridge and off the beach.

But when she came to her room, a former maid's room that she rented from her Aunt Orfelina (the She-Devil), Reinaldo couldn't stand it any more, and giving a terrible cry of pain he began to bang his head against the wall. He banged the wall so hard that his Aunt Orfelina (the She-Devil), thinking that her nephew was having another one of his orgies, dialed the special number that Fifo had given her and was promoted on the spot to Stool Pigeon First Class.

In the end, Reinaldo grew more quiet. He sat down at the typewriter that he'd screwed to the table so that nobody could steal it, and he began to write, once more, the story of his novel.

The Story

This is the story of an island trapped within a sinister tradition, the victim of every conceivable political catastrophe, every kind of blackmail, every sort of bribery, every grandiloquent speech, every false promise ever made, and hunger that seems to have no end. This is the story of an island wearied and worn away by confidence games, the noise of bluster and braggadocio, five hundred years of violence and crimes. This is the story of a people that has always lived for grand illusions, glorious dreams, and has always suffered the most cruel disappointments—a people that has had to learn to humble itself, humiliate itself, betray itself in order to survive. This is the story of a people that intones anthems in praise of the tyrant by day and mutters prayers of rage and hatred of him by night—a people that bends over and scrabbles at the earth by day, planting yautías, pangola grass, nettles, California apples, ersatz coffee, and anything else the tyrant can think of, and by night gnaws away at the undersea rock that holds up the island ruled singlehandedly by that tyrant. This is the story of an island that has never known peace; that was discovered by a boatload of thieves, adventurers, ex-prisoners, and murderers; that was colonized by a gang of thieves and murderers; that was governed by a pack of thieves and murderers—and that finally (after so many *petty* thieves and murderers) fell into the hands of Fifo, the supreme thief, the Summa of our most glorious murderous tradition. This is the story of an island turned first into a huge colonial plantation, then into the world's whorehouse, and now into a perfect and unanimous prison—an island in which the authorities talk about prosperity while they deposit in offshore banks all the treasure that they've stolen, an island in which the people are stabbed to death as they dance. This is the story of an island whose discoverer, while declaring it the most beautiful island in the world, at the same time was making plans to destroy it. This is the story of an island where only the most servile and mediocre have succeeded—an island subjected to infinite summer heat, infinite tyranny, and the unanimous flight of its inhabitants, who while applauding the wonders of the island think only of ways to flee it. This is the story of an island which is spangled in the tinsel of official rhetoric while, underneath, it tears at its own skin and lays its hopes in the final holocaust.

A Tongue Twister (6)

Man and woman, once warp and woof woven into human weft, oft warred. One half of weft, womb, woman, was worn by work of giving birth, oft to words, however wondrous sprung, and wanted rest; one half, worthy though oft wordless, was restless, wept for unspoken yearnings, would wound.

Woolf, wishing to give words to work of birth, to wounds, to man-woman war, but adrift in words unable to be sung, one day finds harbor.

Woolf moored, war won, words sung, wondrous armistice engendered, Woolfian splendor: Orlando.

For Virginia Woolf

A LETTER

New York, May 20, 1996

My dear Reinaldo,

This, my friend, is my seventh letter to you from New York. Since I haven't received any reply, I thought I'd try again. It wasn't easy to get here. I'm only semi-legal, as lots of people are. I told you that New York is like a huge factory, full of tall crates with people running in and out of them. I can tell you now that in the months I've been here, I've seen the twinkliest of fairies and the queenliest of queens on earth, but the list is _way_ too long to send you. Odoriferous Gunk is here. Don't make the mistake of thinking the old queen is still down there—she came up here and left a double in charge of her dying mother. She's definitely here, running around writing poems that are _so bad_ that she's already made a great reputation for herself in Miami (a town whose name I do not wish to remember). Up here, every Cuban queen considers herself a queen (if you get my drift) just because she's alive, and a lot have made themselves into painters—such as Carlota María Luis and Brielíssima and Singadíssima (who, like so many of our queer compatriots, have escaped the island and left doubles behind, or double-doubles in the case of the Siamísimas). Just yesterday, while I was walking through Central Park, I ran into Brielíssima and Singadíssima, joined at the navel, cruising in the "badlands," you know, but Brielíssima held her head so high and was walking so stiffly that she kept whacking her head against the tree limbs—so there she was, her bald head bleeding like crazy, but she would _not_ bow her head. Apparently that jungle queen hasn't realized that Noo Yawk is a jungle.

Naturally, I've tried to promote some interest in your work up here, dear brother, but as you know, here in the United States there are no intellectuals, no artists, no politicians. All there are are businessmen, and all they're interested in is the short run—and that includes the president himself (who by law has to be mentally retarded). Up here, memory has been replaced by an unbelievable sense of rapacity. Why, Fifo herself could buy this country if she wanted to, and if she had the money—although you know, come to think of it the U.S. banks might give the poor old thing a loan if she'd pay a high enough interest rate. She might already be looking into that, who knows, or something along those lines. Anyway, the supposed U.S. "intelligentsia" (which of course doesn't exist) calls itself "progressive," "leftist," etc., and in order to continue to be "liberal" (what a word), it opposes everything that the government might try to do—and, naturally, never does.

The beaches here are cold and dirty, and there are no men. The black men up here are the most beautiful things on earth, but as with all good things here, you have to content yourself with looking but not touching. There's even a word for it here—window-shopping. Which doesn't mean you go out buying windows, darling. And then, of course, with The Plague we've returned to the Middle Ages. Tell me—should we continue "onward"? And just what might that word "onward" mean? . . . "Gays" (that's what they call themselves up here) are organized into unions, and they screw only among themselves. Some kid themselves that they've been screwed by a man. Not me. Down there, I was at least *real,* even though what you might call Painfully Real. Up here, I'm a shadow. Who the hell is going to care about my pain when all anybody is interested in up here is what's called the Quick and Dirty? The Show. No Complications. And yet, my friend, this is the only place in the world where one can survive—I say that with all my heart, because I say it without illusions.

Some fairies, such as Miguel Correderas, have given themselves up to *la vie bohème.* With the adventures Miguel has had, he could write a book. Poor queen, always running after some nonexistent (i.e., extinct) man. On a beach one day he ran into a leather boy who handcuffed him, started whipping him, and forced him to lick his boots for *hours.* Then, practically beating him to death, he forced him to fuck him. All this on a public beach, mind you. After screwing this American specimen, Correderas had to pay him. Another time, he was jogging through the Village (an area where these gays dress in lavender and spend their lives working out in gyms so they'll have big tits) and this gay called out to him from a window (so he says). It was New Year's Eve and the poor old queen thought he was going to see out the year in the *most* exciting way. But it turns out that this supposed man throws Miguel into a cage he's got in his living room and keeps him there for eight *days*, giving him vodka enemas and insulting him day and night. . . . Along with Correderas, Julieta Blanca, and several other screaming queens, I've explored the porno neighborhood on 42nd Street. There are some *real hunks* that hang out around there. Of course they're hustlers, so they have their price, or prices. For ten dollars you can suck them off, for example; for fifteen, they'll suck *you* off; and for twenty they'll bend over for you. And they'll tell you all this without batting an eye, as if they're reading a contract.

A lot of us have died of The Plague, which is *raging*, my dear. So those of us who are left are the survivors of an afterlife that we pay for with our very lives—lives we are literally about to lose. Only the remotest twist of fate can offer even the *possibility* of increasing our life span—an increase that would in fact be a betrayal of life, because any homosexual man who lives more than fifty years in these times ought to die of shame.

However, even though I've arrived at the Big Five-Oh (how we used to laugh at that expression, not to mention that the birthday seemed so far away at the time) and, naturally, have been caught by The Plague (it's not that *you* catch *it*, love—*it* catches *you*), I haven't given up—in fact, I've gone out looking for a ceiba tree. Uh-huh, a ceiba tree—a famous *curandera* out in Queens (we *were* speaking of queens, weren't we?) said it was the only thing that could save me. She gave me a *bilongo*—which is this little-bitty package with chicken claws and feathers and stuff in it, wrapped in a piece of cloth and tied with string—and told me to find a ceiba tree, walk around it three times with this bilongo in my pocket, stab the tree trunk three times, gently, kiss its trunk, throw the bilongo down, and without looking back, take off running. But don't think it's easy to find a ceiba tree in New York City, and don't think this is Equatorial Africa or Brotherhood Park in lovely downtown Havana. I spent the whole winter dreaming of a ceiba tree. Finally I found out that there's one in the Zoo over in the Bronx. So there I went, in the snow, with Salermo and Julieta Blanca. It was a huge tree, and it stood under an enormous vault and was surrounded with a tall iron fence. It was in a greenhouse, of course, with its name in Latin and everything, like something from another planet, and it wasn't easy for me to get to the trunk. But I jumped the fence, stabbed it three times, kissed it, and threw down the bilongo. And just then, a security guard shows up (the other queens take off running), makes me pick up the bilongo (No littering, the sign says), and gives me a ticket. So now I have to go to court for assaulting a tree or jaywalking or something. Ñica told me that with that on my record I'd never become a U.S. citizen, but I never planned to, anyway.

I went to Prida again for a consultation, and she told me that if I hadn't been able to throw the bilongo down at the foot of the ceiba tree, I should leave it behind the altar of a church. So I went to the fanciest church in New York City—St. Patrick's—and there I witnessed a scene that I'm going to tell you about so that if this letter reaches you, you can put it in your novel.

Before I went into the church, I saw this gigantic black man—naked as the day he was born—walking back and forth in front of it in the snow. This is right on Fifth Avenue. But me, who can't think of anything but my bilongo, I go into the church, and I've already totally forgotten about this naked black man. If you can imagine me forgetting about a naked black man. But the black man went into the church too, where there was a mass going on with organ music and everything. Full, full, full. The black man walks down the central aisle, picks up this huge candelabra that's up near the altar, and starts swinging it around. He kills the bishop that was officiating at the mass with one swing and then starts hitting other priests and stuff that were trying to subdue him, and I think he killed a sacristan. Then the police came and killed him.

The next day I read in the paper that this black guy was a Cuban—OK?—that he'd come on the Mariel boatlift in 1980, and that he was crazy.

But in the church I had realized immediately that that black man was Christ, which is why in the confusion I threw my bilongo on top of his body (which was full of bullet holes) and turned and without looking back ran out the door. . . . Now I don't know what'll happen to me, but I also don't think I ought to give it too much thought. Imagine how cold that black man must've been before he went into that church. Of course, you can't believe how hot it is now. I don't think there's a nice middle ground anywhere.

Americans walk very very fast and if you don't keep up with them, they'll knock you down. You'd think they had important matters to attend to—and in fact, they do work like crazy. But the rush is over something else—they're rushing to get home, take off their shoes, and lie on the couch and watch TV, which is awful.

Remember—don't come up here. Or you'll wind up walking into a church and killing a bishop and getting killed. You'll wind up that way _if you're lucky._

Love and kisses—
Gabriel

P.S. Yesterday I went to the public library on 42nd Street. They didn't have _The Magic Mirror._ But I'll keep looking.

Medicinal Immersions

Water cures everything, says the Ogress. And she leaps from the bridge at Patrice Lumumba Beach into the sea. When the water comes in contact with that sick and misshapen body (whose owner's real name is Ramón Sernada), it begins to bubble, smoke, and even give off little flames. A terrible smell of sulfur emerges from that area of the ocean in which the Ogress is submerged. All the fish that are swimming in the area die of pollution. Thanks to that strange immunity (the immunity of AIDS) that prevents even Bloodthirsty Shark from eating her, the Ogress can swim out into the open sea and float along the line of the horizon. *Water cures everything,* the queen repeats in fervent hopefulness, recalling the words of Clara Mortera. Water, lots of water—that was also the suggestion (the prescription) that the Three Weird Sisters gave the Ogress when she consulted them in their room next to the hole in Clara's wall in Old Havana. But even the terrible Weird Sisters refused to examine the Ogress's sick body up close. The Eldest Fate poked at it from a distance with a trident and the Baby Sister Fate scooped up (in a spoon with a handle three feet long) the icky fluids that oozed out of it. The Weird Sisters pulled on huge goggles, plastic shower caps, aluminum aprons, and rubber gloves and they examined those fluids, looked at each other in bewildered terror, and threw the three-foot-long spoon though the hole in Clara's wall (instantly killing a member of the Party who was making off with three chalices). Then, looking at the Ogress, they declared: Water cures everything—go jump in the ocean. . . . And ever since then, the Ogress has been taking dips in the ocean. But tumors, chancres, running sores have continued to spread over her body. *Life has been too cruel with me,* thought the Ogress. In her youth he'd done no more than any other fairy did—chase after men—but the immense majority of fairies did the same thing, and they all seemed to be in good health, or at least they weren't erupting or melting down before your eyes, the way the Ogress was. Yes, what fate had done to her was a clear injustice. Even the nickname the other fairies had given her was so *unfair.* And in that she was right, for Ramón Sernada was not a bad person. The title Ogress had been bestowed on her because of her deformity, and also—the truth, the whole sad truth—because of the bad humors that filled the queen's body and changed her personality. But how could her personality not suffer, how could she not have bad moods, with all the calamities that had befallen her? And so it was that the innocuous fairy who had once been a sweet thing with long straight hair was transformed little by little into a swollen, yellow, bald-headed, red-eyed horror. Other fairies were impaled every day on the prick of some petty thief, ex-felon, or common hustler who carried the fatal virus, and to all appearances, nothing happened to them—but all the Ogress had to do was touch a cock through a pair of jeans and she broke out with pustules all over. Other queens would suck any cock that swung in front of their lips, but all the Ogress had to do was stick out her tongue a yard away from the nearest prick and her face would turn totally black and blue. Other femmes could go into men's rooms and get screwed any number of times, but all the noble Ogress had to do was stand at the door and she'd be doubled over with the colic before you could blink an eye, her legs would break out in a nasty rash, and her belly would swell up something terrible. Ever since she was a filly she'd caught every infectious disease there was, from measles to chicken pox, from whooping cough to hepatitis—diseases she'd caught, she said, from just *looking* at some kid in the neighborhood—and now came *this,* on top of all those other calamities. But Ramón Sernada had decided that if it came down to a choice between being a not-person, a not-thing, and being dead, he'd choose death. (Because the only way that she, as a born fairy, could *be* was by being screwed.) Made up by every brush and color in Clara Mortera's arsenal, she threw herself into the street, ready to die, but first to live—even if only for one night, one night of pleasure. But the Ogress was not to have even that one night. The first man she ran into, a sailor who was splendid-looking and knew it, no sooner screwed her than he transmitted to the poor queen every infectious disease known to humankind. Suddenly the sailor was having his way not with a fairy painted up by Clara Mortera, but with a ball of pus. Enraged, the sailor pulled his prick out of Ramón Sernada's ass and Ramón Sernada's ass emitted a sulfurous stench. From that time on, the poor faggot's life had been one long calvary, a chase from one *curandero* to the next, and very secretly so, since if Fifo found out about her illness he'd have her thrown in a concentration camp. But after paying a visit to the Three Weird Sisters, and then getting the same advice from Clara Mortera as she'd gotten from them, the Ogress would now go to the beach and float for hours on the surface of the ocean, filled with the distant hope that the waves would wash away all her diseases. *Water cures everything,* the Ogress says aloud as she floats on her back on the ocean. Clara Mortera and the Three Weird Sisters couldn't be wrong about that, she thinks. *Every*body goes to them for advice. Even the Marquesa de Macondo. Why, the Holy Father himself hinted that he planned to return to Cuba to consult those expert oracles of medicine—for his hemorrhoids, they say. . . . *I will be cured. I will be cured,* said the Ogress, filled with hope, as she exposed her terrible excrescences to sea and sky. And it was in that trance of almost mystical ecstasy that she was floating when suddenly something terribly violent, emerging like a missile from underneath the sea, hit her, and blew her to smithereens. The perpetrator of this deed was none other than Tatica, the

Angel from Marianao, who had leaped out of the sea, far offshore, with the aid of Skunk in a Funk's swim fins. The Golden Child kept swimming, fleeing Skunk in a Funk, and he didn't stop till he reached the beach at Santa Fe.

On the beach at Santa Fe, perched on a boulder in the sun, sat Chug-a-Lug. Tired of not finding anything at Patrice Lumumba Beach, she had flown (yes, flown—on Oscar's wings, my dear, if you must know) down here, and as she sat there she saw the White Angel emerge from the water and strike a pose that she thought unbearably statuesque. She beckoned. The Angelic Creature, pulling off the swim fins, walked over to the queen, and on his face there was still the smile of satisfaction at recalling that he had blown the Ogress to bits. In fact, the Ogress's explosion, scattering bloody bits of her across the surface of the ocean, spread the dreaded AIDS virus—the most terrible disease yet known to humankind—throughout the world. But the only person who doesn't appear on the list of victims of this dread disease is Ramón Sernada himself. Obviously, not even after death could the poor Ogress manage to be anything.

A TONGUE TWISTER (7)

That cute kid, not yet come to puberty, cavorting with that goatherd, is actually a chick (or chicken) that collects for coupling. The goatherd approaches, she collects, then they copulate—him covering her, her not caring a hoot. A couple of cavorts a week, and she's set.

How many goatherds would a kid cavort with if a kid cavorted with every Cuban goatherd?

Couldn't care less—considers herself another Cabrera Infante.

For Hilarión Cabrisas, a.k.a. the Anglo-Campesina

The Party Begins

The huge armored-steel gate of the grand ceremonial hall rolled upward and behind it stood Fifo in all his magnificence. He was dressed from head to foot in olive-green: gigantic olive-green boots, olive-green military jacket, olive-green uniform pants bloused at the knee, olive-green tie, and olive-green cap. Near him, but in red, was his brother Raúl, and some distance away, all the ministers and the new presidential guard, made up of a thousand hunky men in camouflage fatigues. At a signal from Fifo, the guests began to file in to the elite reception (to be followed by the Carnival) held to celebrate Fifo's purported fifty years in absolute power.

Among the thousands of personalities who filed through the massive door (each one bowing reverently) were the ambassadors of all Communist, formerly Communist, capitalist, and neutral countries; the papal nuncio Monsignor Sacchi, who told Fifo that the Holy Father might very possibly make an appearance at the last minute; the Marquesa de Macondo, who, not content to shake the dictator's hand, shook his testicles; the Lady of the Veil; England's Princess Dinorah, who arrived completely nude and followed by her enormous retinue and a swarm of photographers (who were denied entrance); the King and Queen of Castile; the King and Queen of Switzerland; the executioner of Cambodia; the Prime Minister of India with the mummy of his mother (whom he himself had murdered); the emperor of Belgium; Mother Teresa; the head of the Medellín cartel; the Satrap of Verania; the most important members of the Cuban exile community, all of whom were, it now turned out, agents in the pay of Fifo; the presidents of all Latin American republics and dictatorships with their respective spouses (who served as Prime Ministers); Papayi Taloka, the famous Japanese transvestite who had been jerking off Emperor Hirohito for eighty years; the Prime Minister of Ceylon; Outer Mongolia's greatest terrorist followed by 1,326 lesser terrorists who headed up international terrorist organizations; and Raisa Gorbachev on the arm of the First Lady of the United States, who told Fifo that the President was sorry not to be able to come but he was making love to his rabbit. Fifo nodded understandingly and, breaking the rules of protocol that he himself had set, embraced the American First Lady and Madame Gorbachev. And the parade of dignitaries continued—African kings, Arab dictators, former presidents now in exile, Norwegian princes, millionaires who owned whole islands and sometimes whole countries, Deng Xiaoping on a stretcher, an

Eskimo filmmaker, the Turkish High Bugger, the latest Miss Universe, a eunuch from Madagascar, the leader of the South African Workers Union, five hundred cloistered nuns, the doorman of Sing Sing Prison, all the members of the Swedish Academy (who were planning to give Fifo the Nobel Peace Prize), six Argentine cows, a Canadian zebu, five hundred or so monkeys in their cages, the president of the OAS, Fr. Bettino, the administrator of the London necropolis, the inventor of AIDS, the president of the World Federation of Women, seven hundred renowned writers, an expert in bacteriological weapons, the world high-diving champion, Yasir Arafat with twenty-five Panamanian hunks, the head of the French Communist Party, the Empress of Yugoslavia, the director of the Bronx Zoo, the Electric Venus, the head of Amnesty International, the mummies of Andre Ceauşescu and his wife Elena on a gurney pushed by Vanessa Redgrave, the Queen of Vietnam on the arm of the inventor of the hydrogen bomb, actors, senators, three thousand trained and licensed whores, male ballet dancers, the editors of the world's most important newspapers, a hundred or so Totomoya Indians, and thousands of men and women of imposing physical grace and bearing, wearing the most outlandish costumes or completely nude. . . . After these came the local guests—among them, Halisia Jalonzo on the arm of Coco Salas, Alfredo Güevavara on the arm of Miss Pereyrra, the executioner of La Cabaña Prison, Manetta, Paula Amanda (a.k.a. Luisa Fernanda), Miss Mayoya, Skunk in a Funk, H. Puntilla, Nicolás Guillotina, La Reine des Araignées with her company of gorgeous teenage boys (among whom the resplendent Key to the Gulf would play a central role in tonight's festivities), Silbo Rodríguez, Dulce María Leynaz, Eee-u-u-ugh Desnoës, Miguel Barniz, Miss Divinely Malign, SuperSatanic, and AntiChelo, the SuperChelo, and thousands more queens, fairies, and femme leather boys preceded by impressive specimens of Cuban butchhood and other outstanding figures in the island's political, agricultural, naval, and literary worlds. The heterogeneity of the guest list will perhaps be less puzzling if we bear in mind—and this might be one response to the chapter "Some Unsettling Questions"—that Fifo had invited not only close friends and allies but also persons under suspicion of various crimes and acts of treason, several *personae non gratae,* and even a few outright enemies whose noses he took great pleasure in rubbing in this coup that had swept the world.

Dressed in his olive-green uniform and flanked by his gorgeous security forces, Fifo triumphantly gave the order for the party to begin. At that, the Armed Forces Orchestra played the Fifonian National Anthem, which all stood to hear, hands over hearts as the midgets had instructed, and then the national anthems of every country of the world. Fifo wanted to be sure to please all his honored guests—who would be enjoying not only the fabulous dinner and the exquisite wines and other liquors that not even kings and queens could taste any longer, but also (as the invitation had promised) "rare and edifying spectacles." Among the events announced for that night was a superskewering, one canonization and two decanonizations, a crucifuckingfixion, a self-decapitation, five hundred strangulations performed by five hundred expert midgets, twenty-seven resurrections of famous people, a striptease performed by the chief executioner of Teheran, a Russian-roulette duel between the mayor of Boston and Tomasito the Goya-Girl, *Giselle* danced by Halisia Jalonzo, a Grand Oneirical Theological Political Philosophical Satirical Conference whose subjects were god, the devil, madness, dreams, paradise, hell, Florentine art, the steam engine, and the categories of queenhood, among other fascinating topics. The speakers were to be Delfín Proust, the Archbishop of Canterbury, José Lezama Lima, the Divinely Malign, André Breton, Salman Rushdie, Skunk in a Funk, the Queen of Holland, the AntiChelo, SuperSatanic, and several winners of the Nobel Prize (among others). The program was then to continue with a second retractation by H. Puntilla, the official introduction of Bloodthirsty Shark, an excursion to the Garden of Computers, and a walking tour through Old Havana under the guidance of Alejo Sholekhov. . . . It was a *fascinating* program. And in the middle of the opening ceremonies, his ears deafened by the acclamations of his guests and the noise of the orchestra, stood Fifo, olive-greener and more beaming by the minute, personally seeing that the evening's activities went off without a hitch. Only the Marquesa de Macondo dared interrupt him; unable to contain herself, she fell to her knees before the high commander and fleetingly brushed his ball-sack with her lips. Many, including Arturo Lumski, feared that this irreverence would cost the Marquesa her life, but Fifo, smiling, slapped her head away and continued his hostess-with-the-mostest duties without missing a beat.

The Lock Queen

That fish is *dinner,* said Chug-a-Lug to herself when she saw the Angel of Marianao emerge from the ocean. And with great self-possession, poise, and aplomb she signaled the golden young carp to come over. Chug-a-Lug knew that after a young thug had perpetrated a few offenses, he needed to show his noble side; she also knew (since she knew almost everything) that if that young thug had been mugging queens, and had even taken the poor Ogress's life, what he needed now was a queen with whom to expiate his crimes. And that queen was she, Chug-a-Lug. That was why, without further ado, she told Tatica that she had a room in Miramar and would be *delighted* if he'd spend a little time there with her; maybe they could even listen to a few Beatles albums. Tatica said OK, and his bathing suit immediately stood up a little, giving *very* promising signs.

Here, we pause for a background break: Chug-a-Lug was a fairy who was very accomplished at picking up young thieves, hoodlums, that sort of trade, and bringing them home to her room. And since she knew that all fairies were constantly exposed to the risk of being robbed, even by their most faithful lover-boy, she had taken the precaution of safeguarding all her belongings behind three, four, or as many as ten locks. Her refrigerator (a gift from Fernández Mell) was built into the wall and locked behind a double iron gate secured with three Yale locks (the gift of Ramiro Valdéz); her television set (a gift from Joaquín Ordoqui back when he was flush) was also chained and locked and built into the wall and protected by shatterproof glass (a gift from Papito Serguera); her Tiffany lamps (gifts from Raúl Roa) were enclosed in metal cages, and each cage was protected by seven locks. Even the toilet seat was under lock and key inside a metal cage, as was the record-player. As for the bed and the rocking chair (cunningly placed just at the foot of the bed), they were completely encircled by a thick chain which in turn was chained and padlocked by countless unpickable padlocks to a thick iron bar set into the wall. All of this gave Chug-a-Lug a certain sense of security—for a while. Because after hearing about the robberies committed against Tomasito the Goya-Girl, Coco Salas, and thousands of other fairies exactly like herself, Chug-a-Lug centupled the locks in her room and put a dozen new locks on the door to the stairwell, another dozen on the door at the bottom of the stairs, and more than two dozen on the door to the hall that led (on the other side of an interior patio) to the street door (on which she put a hundred locks)—and that whole hallway, between the patio and the street, she filled with iron gates, and on every gate she put at least twenty locks. . . .

And now we return to our story:

Staggering under the key ring weighing more than fifty pounds that she had to carry around with her in her backpack night and day, Chug-a-Lug was leading Tatica toward her top-security love nest. But it wasn't easy to get from Santa Fe to her room in La Puntilla. Not easy *at all.* First, fairy and golden boy took a number 91 bus that had a blowout; then the fairy, figuring what the hell, hailed a cab, whose engine exploded—either from the heat of the tropics or from the heat that came all over the pansy Chug-a-Lug when she contemplated the enormous bulge that continued to grow in Tatica's bathing suit. So then they thumbed a ride on a truck loaded with volunteer workers, but when Chug-a-Lug climbed on board with that hundred-pound key ring, the truck lost its balance, zigzagged all over the highway, and finally crashed into a telephone pole, killing six female workers-emerita. So chickenhawk and chicken started walking, but Chug-a-Lug soon felt her strength flagging—there was no way she could walk so many miles with that many keys in her backpack. At that, Golden Boy suggested that they swim; he'd tow her with those *excellent* swim fins he'd stolen from Skunk in a Funk. And so Chug-a-Lug threw her thousand-pound backpack over her shoulder again—yes, a thousand pounds, or wait a minute, I mean a thousand keys. *No way—it was a thousand and seven, I counted them myself, every one.* . . . All right, Mary, have it your way, a thousand and seven. . . . Anyway, she threw the backpack with the thousand and seven keys in it over her back and was towed by the Golden Child (who swam at *fantastic* speed) to the beach of La Puntilla. What a trip, my dear, riding the sweet golden dream king who was later going to impale her on his sweet golden scepter. I must confess that even Bloodthirsty Shark, who was observing all this from afar, felt a certain envy—we aren't sure whether envy of the Golden Boy or Chug-a-Lug, who was not much past the twink stage herself.

At last, Fairy and Marianao Angel reached their destination. Tatica was exhibiting signs of an urgency that was not to be denied, much less postponed. Indeed, as Antón Arrufada had written more than sixty years ago, "all appeared to feign hopefulness." That delicious piece of chicken with that big delicious piece of white meat begged only to be eaten; his only desire seemed to be to get to that bed and have his way with Chug-a-Lug. Ay, but when, after their odyssey, they came to the door of Chug-a-Lug's room, it wasn't so easy to get in. The fairy took out her gigantic key ring and began to open and close locks. *Very slowly* open and close locks, because she got more nervous and desperate by the minute and Tatica was getting hotter by the second. Every time she looked over at that fabulous bulge she got the wrong key in the wrong lock, and sometimes it took her half an hour to unlock a single lock. Finally, by the time she'd opened and closed those thousand (sorry, thousand and seven) locks, fifteen years had gone by. Chug-a-Lug was no longer a young fairy, she was an old, slack-skinned, bald, bony *queen,* and Tatica, who honestly wanted to screw the youthful Chug-a-Lug (not rob her), seeing that old *thing* standing before him, inviting him into her room, stepped back, vaulted all the gates and locks in a single bound, and ran full speed away. Chug-a-Lug, seeing herself in the mirror (which was cemented into the wall in her room), decided to take her own life. She would commit suicide by swallowing every key on her gigantic key ring. As she swallowed the keys one by one, she said a prayer of desperation to the patron saint and fairy godmother of all fairies, St. Nelly, asking her to find her a nice cool place in hell—or at least one that wasn't *too* hot. But St. Nelly, who couldn't *bear* to be around this particular pansy—much less in the other world, where she was living like a queen, thank you very much—decided to perform a miracle. At one swoop of her wing-claws she made time run backward, and suddenly the old queen Chug-a-Lug, looking at herself in the mirror cemented into her wall as she swallowed key number 328, saw that she was once more young and beautiful, so she leaped up and ran after Tatica, who had just left (if you remember), hornier than ever. But heavens, how was she going to get out of that cage she was in if most of the keys were in her stomach? The old queen with the keys inside her vaulted all the gates and locks, too. But by now the Golden Boy had been picked up by a high government muckety-muck type that lived in the house across the street—Leopoldo Avila, no less, the number one trade queen on the entire island. And so by the time the desperate Chug-a-Lug had reached the street, Lt. Avila was already guiding Golden Rod by his ever more prominent rod into his magnificent muckety-muck mansion. Chug-a-Lug gave a scream of fury and vomited up all the keys she still had in her stomach, all over the street.

While a hail of keys fell across the asphalt, from the mansion came the unmistakable sounds of the lieutenant's cries of pleasure and Tatica's moans of satisfaction.

A Tongue Twister (8)

Committing himself to conceding a consignment consisting of a cornucopia chockful of commodities—condoms and condiments, a considerable quantity of cuticle cutters, a crate of Cocoa Pops, a carload of khakis, a tube of Colgate anticavity, and a cardboard box containing captured mosquitoes—cock-crazed Coco talked a cocky ex-con into a quickie.

Coco's quickies cost him carloads of commodities.

What quantities of commodities do Coco's quickies cost him?

For Coco Salas

Nouveaux Pensées de Pascal, ou Pensées d'Enfer

If you don't want your son to be unhappy, kill him at birth.

If you don't want to be responsible for your son's unhappiness, kill yourself. You *are* the one to blame.

Avoid at all costs dying with your conscience burdened by the fact that you never killed anyone: You will not enter the kingdom of heaven or any other kingdom.

Suffering degrades us; pleasure corrupts us. Poverty makes us criminals; money makes us murderers.

A man may pardon another man almost anything except greatness.

The greatest honor to which a hero should aspire is that his country detest him. It is an honor that he *will* attain.

The coward will allow no man to defend him; the wretched man will forgive no man who defends him.

Society condemns a man not for his defects but for his virtues.

Men should not buy but rent.

Never ask that people love you; ask that they please you. That is much harder, and the only thing that's worth asking for.

It is much easier to love men than to please them; that's why there are more prophets and fewer pimps every day.

Friends are more dangerous than enemies because they can get closer to you.

When you see your neighbor's beard on fire, pour on more fuel.

It's an ill wind that blows nobody ill. In front of every silver lining there's a cloud. No good deed goes unpunished.

Always remember that your best friend may be the most accomplished snitch.

The only great public encounters occur (or used to occur) in public men's rooms.

There have never been any guardian angels, just guards.

Eyes are the mirror not of the soul but of the liver.

The soul dies before the body.

And he said, "I'm going to be good," and he felt great fear.

A person who loves life too greatly cannot live long.

Speak well of your enemy, so that you may do him the greatest harm possible.

Do evil—and let it not matter to whom—because whomever you do evil to, you are doing *someone* a favor.

Why spend so much energy trying to prove the existence of God if God has never taken the trouble to do so?

Don't fight an enemy with his own weapons; use weapons that are even more terrible.

A macho has such a high opinion of masculinity that his greatest pleasure would be taking it up the ass from another man.

From our inhibitions arise repressive law, communism, Christian morality, and bourgeois customs.

True intellectuals are too intelligent to believe, too intelligent to doubt, but wise enough to deny. That is why great intelligence comes at last not to power but to prison.

By this late date in our history, being right-wing or left-wing is just a strategy.

The only way to be free is to be left alone—but even that is not enough; one must *be* alone.

Only great disasters make us feel that we belong to a community. The brotherhood of men is grounded upon catastrophe.

Every day we learn something new, but we never put it into practice.

Men live only to feed their vanity; that is why they are used so easily, especially by the powerful and the cunning.

Modern man is not even faithful to one evil; he needs to take part in several so as to betray all.

The first person a dictator should keep his eye on is the hangman.

A concert is a pretext for every tubercular old woman in the city to come to the concert hall to cough.

Nothing is as perverse as freedom; those who have it can't stand it, and those who don't have it kill each other for it.

A good dictator extols freedom while destroying it, but democrats destroy it without extolling it.

Only slaves know the value of freedom; that's why the first thing they do when they achieve it is set up the stocks.

There is only one strength: the strength of desperation.

Note: When you wish to *really* say something terrible about someone, you should always begin with the following words: "He is the vilest person on earth after Gabriel García Markoff."

Cervantes was the only Spaniard who didn't crawl on all fours; he is said to have had only one arm.

Nothing lasts, not even destiny. That's why we shouldn't become too fond of any familiar habit.

Man's essence is sinister. Of course, there are exceptions: good men are necessary so that evil can manifest itself in all its glory. Being sinister against something or someone sinister would be, to a certain point, justifiable. Good, then, is a necessary instrument so that evil may reach true fullness of being.

God is the most irrefutable proof of the existence and power of the devil.

God, therefore, came to earth to aid the devil.

Light came in order to blind us, or to make us see that we are blind.

Good is an instrument of evil, allowing evil to stand out as though against its most becoming background. Ergo, God is the devil's most perfect creation.

All great murderers are—and must be—fanatically religious.

The only thing we never lose is dissatisfaction.

Every person is a bad person, although some people don't want to admit it. That is because there are two kinds of bad people: the consciously bad and the unconsciously bad.

Hell is not other people (as a resentful toad once said); it is ourselves.

For every moment of true pleasure, we must endure at least twenty years of horror. So a person who lasts for eight years will have lived four minutes.

It is obvious that we are not from this planet; that is why we want to go to heaven after we're dead. And to prevent that, we're buried or cremated when we die. Cemeteries are posthumous prisons.

Eternity belongs only to the man who has contempt for life.

The only thing that redeems a man's life is suicide. Every great work of mankind, therefore, stems from a suicidal inspiration.

Sex is a source of bitterness. Life and death are two viruses that are transmitted by sexual contact.

The Super-Skewer

Olga Figuerova had journeyed to Cuba with the full intention of being screwed by every fairy on the Island. Although she was a ravishingly beautiful woman, she didn't like men—or women either, for that matter—she wanted nothing but the most femme fairies. And when she found out that Cuba was full of them—so full that faggots would be thrown out of the country by the million and there'd still be just as many as there had been before—Figuerova packed her bags. On the strength of her Russian-sounding surname she got a visa (issued by Fifo himself), and within a few weeks she had arrived at the shores of Cuba and seen with her own eyes that the Island was, indeed, one gigantic *cage aux folles.* "Ooh," she cooed, "I've found paradise." And she was off to realize her dream. The first thing she did was marry a fairy, who agreed to tie the knot in exchange for a cuticle cutter that he'd promised Coco Salas in exchange for a ticket to the ballet. Olga (fag-hag *extraordinaire*) persuaded her fag-husband to fill the house with fags, promising him nail clippers and cuticle cutters by the thousand, not to mention lipstick, powder, sheer underwear, and even portable radios. At that, the fag started looking for fags to screw his wife. And he performed this task with great efficiency, especially since he himself was unable to carry out his own husbandly duties to the degree that his wife's erotic needs required—imagine the poor queen's sacrifice: having to screw a *woman* day and night! Anyway, there he was, looking for fairies day and night, when he came upon Skunk in a Funk.

We ourselves don't fully understand why it was that Olga Figuerova took such a liking to Skunk in a Funk. But she did, and *such* a liking that she kicked her faggot-husband out of the house and brought Skunk in a Funk in. Skunk in a Funk, for her part, after more than a month of constant come-ons, gave in; he agreed to sleep with Olga in exchange for a pair of swim fins. Olga flew to France and returned with the most wonderful swim fins to be found on the market anywhere in the world. "Now you've got to keep your end of the bargain," she said in perfect Spanish to Skunk in a Funk. "Since the day I met you, I've made love to no other faggot—I mean man. I have been waiting just for you. . . . "

"Tonight," promised Skunk in a Funk.

Skunk in a Funk knew he was going to have some trouble being turned on by a woman (and those who doubt it should read *Farewell to the Sea*), so that night she hired a big, muscular black man who worked as a stevedore down on the docks, and who happened to be Daniel Sakuntala's husband of the moment. Skunk in a Funk hid the black man in the closet and when he turned off the lights and was about to mount Olga, the black guy came out of the closet (but I mean literally, honey, not figuratively—figuratively he'd been out for *years*) and began to have his way with Skunk in a Funk, whose pecker immediately stood at attention so he could begin to penetrate Olga. At that, the black man, excited at seeing a real woman, and one sighing and panting frenziedly, in bed with himself and Skunk in a Funk, got even more turned on. His member grew to fearsome proportions—so fearsome, in fact, that it went almost all the way through Skunk in a Funk and ejaculated *inside* the queen's balls. Skunk in a Funk, feeling that supreme pleasure, ejaculated inside Olga, who thus was inseminated by Skunk in a Funk and the black man at the same time. This phenomenon, practiced on the Island by almost all respectable married couples, is what is known as the Super-Skewer. Sometimes a woman will be impregnated by from five to as many as fifteen men, who all (with the exception of the poor guy who's last in line) are possessed in turn by other men, with respectively longer dongs. The Super-Skewer has given rise (so to speak) to an incredible mixture of races in a single baby. The case of Olga Figuerova, who had a part-black, part-white baby, is a case of *simple* Super-Skewer. but how about the case of Clara Mortera, my dear, who had a baby with one blue eye and one green one, one Malaysian ear and the other Ranquel Indian, hair that was straight, curly, and woolly and white, blond, and blue-black at the same time? This baby's skin (Nasser was the little boy's name, by the way) was black, white, copper, transparent, red, yellow, smooth, creamy, oily, and hairy, all once. There is no doubt that the child was the result of one of the most gigantic Super-Skewers ever to occur in the erotic history of the Island. Clara Mortera was possessed by (I hope I get this right) her husband, who was possessed by a Chinaman, who was possessed by an Indian, who was possessed by a Malaysian, who was possessed by a German, who was possessed by a Swede, who was possessed by a Spaniard, who was possessed by an Eskimo, who was possessed by an Arab, who was possessed by a mulatto, who was possessed by a black man, who was possessed by a monumental Irish guy. Clara thus received, at one and the same time, and through the *vas deferens* of her husband, that entire gamut of sperm, and thereby conceived one of the most curious examples in the history of genetics.

This same type of Super-Skewer, or something even Superior, was what Fifo had planned that night for his celebrity guests. It was not just that he was fascinated by races' cumming together (because of the genetic "stirring of the pot," so to speak, that resulted); he also wanted to show his guests, and therefore the entire world, that his Island was the birthplace of the Super-Skewer and therefore the indisputable homeland of the New Man, that creature who required collective energies and efforts to be born, a true offspring of Humanity. It was with that patriotic purpose that he had composed a song—titled "It Takes a Village."

As for Olga Figuerova, when she found that she'd given birth to a child that was half white and half black, and not knowing the cause of this phenomenon (a "phenomenon" that Skunk in a Funk took advantage of to repudiate her), she gave it up to a foster home, sewed up her cunt, became a world-class judo expert, and dedicated her life to seducing queers. When she got them into her room she gave them a choice: screw her or she'd strangle them. The other version—don't interrupt me!—the version that says that Olga retired to a cave in the Pyrenees, is absolutely false.

THE THREE WEIRD SISTERS, PLUS ONE

Atropos, Lachesis, and Chloe, I mean Clotho, a.k.a. the Fickle Fates, a.k.a. the Three Weird Sisters, were getting ready for their evening walk. Every evening it was their job to knit Skunk in a Funk's fate, so they always carried gigantic knitting needles and huge skeins of yarn of all different colors with them on their stroll. And as they walked, they knitted. Hiram, La Reine des Araignées, would lead the Three Weird Sisters through the crowds of people on the street—we couldn't have them bumping into people or breaking their venerable heads against some wall, could we, as they concentrated on their knitting? But then the truth was, somebody *always* had to go with the Ladies of Luck when they went out on their afternoon strolls, just to protect them, because otherwise hordes of housewives, desperate to have that yarn for themselves (so they could knit their respective husbands nice new pullovers) would mug the poor girls for their knitting. I mean you know how it is, girl—on our dear Island even yarn is rationed, so the Weird Sisters, being who they are, are the only people who can get any, and then only with the special ration card that Fifo personally issued to them and that they have to present every month at the headquarters of the Ministry of Interior Trade.

Anyway . . .

The Weird Sisters, seeing-eyed by Delfín/Hiram/La Reine des Araignées (because in addition to all their other problems finding raw materials and all, they were pretty blind), would knit and knit, and then they would unknit it all again—because they could never agree on Skunk in a Funk's fate. Clotho wanted the poor thing to undergo every known calamity; Lachesis said Skunk in a Funk ought to suffer, no problem with that, but before they crushed her once and for all they ought to at least give her the chance to finish her novel; and Atropos, more charitably still, wanted to extend Skunk in a Funk's life until she'd *published* the novel, along with a long explanatory introduction written by the Dowager Duchess de Valero. And there, as you can see, things got even *more* complicated, because then they had to stretch out not only Skunk in a Funk's life, but the life of the Dowager Duchess de Valero, too, who was already *well* over a hundred. . . . So the Weird Sisters, knitting and unknitting, would get all entangled in that wrangling of theirs, which (like the knitting) never seemed to end. I mean, even the name that Skunk in a Funk would be known by was problematic. Clotho thought he ought to be called Skunk in a Funk—"period," she added, making two or three nervous backstitches. Lachesis said the name that Skunk in a Funk ought to have was Reinaldo, which was how he signed his novels. But Atropos, holding her knitting needle aloft in an imperious gesture, declared that Skunk in a Funk's real name was the name his mother had given him at birth—Gabriel—and was therefore the name he ought to die with.

This particular day, as the argument grew more and more heated, La Reine des Araignées was spreading her arms wide in every direction, skipping about, whirling a hundred and eighty degrees, cocking her head and bestowing a watchful smile on the three weird old sisters, and then springing ahead of them once more, her arms always flinging open expansively—a tic that never left her for a moment but that fortunately helped to make a way for the old girls. And so, with the way open, Moira I, Moira II, and Moira III (as they were also known) could go on knitting and unknitting the fate of Skunk in a Funk. "Every conceivable disaster," shouted Clotho, "that's what that horrid Skunk deserves." "I think seventy percent is about right," replied Lachesis, holding up the piece she'd just knitted. "There's no need to be so hard on the poor queen," clucked Atropos, holding up her own handiwork and unknitting Clotho's piece, Clotho meanwhile tugging on Atropos' and spoiling all her hard work. And when Lachesis started to intervene in the dispute, the other two sisters yanked on her ball of thread and ruined all *her* work, too.

And so they walked along, knitting and unraveling and squabbling incessantly. When they came to the corner of Prado and San Rafael, Hiram opened her arms with such force that one of his hands smacked into the groin of a gigantic black man who was standing on the corner waiting for the light to change. This *monster* of a man (none other than the chairman of the Communist Party of Matanzas Province) glared at the four queens (and even more furiously because of the liberty taken with his person in precisely the most sacred region of his body) and jumped on them like a black tornado. Delfín Proust, seeing that gigantic black cloud advancing on him, managed to get out of the way, but the Three Weird Sisters (and they were *really* weird that day), who went on knitting, oblivious to everything but the unrolling fate of Skunk in a Funk, received such a pummeling from the Black Avenger that they fell to the asphalt completely unstrung, and tangled inextricably in their many-colored skeins. The black man, evidencing great satisfaction at the moral lesson he'd delivered (which all the passers-by—including Delfín, the rat—applauded), went on his way. So then La Reine des Araignées went over to the Weird Sisters and helped them to their feet (not without some huffing and puffing) and on the march again. But the Three Weird Sisters, infuriated by that totally undeserved assault, had come to an agreement on Skunk in a Funk's fate: it would, they all agreed, be the *worst.* And immediately they started to knit it. Delfín, a.k.a. La Reine des Araignées, smiling with satisfaction at that decision that they'd made in large part thanks to him, continued down the street, opening his arms expansively and repeating under his breath: *They may be the big bad Fates, but I am definitely the baddest fate around.*

The Guest in Distress

After burning Mayoya at the stake, the immense crowd of Disinvited Nobodies continued to mill about at the edge of the ocean, not far from the entrance of Fifo's palace. From time to time several of the Dissed & Pissed, as they had begun to call themselves, would dive down into the water, gnaw at the Island's platform for a while, and reemerge, tanned by the ocean breezes and the beams of the artificial-tropical sun.

There they were, forming a large human landfill beside the sea (a king, several bishops, former Miss Universes, internationally renowned landscape artists, prizewinning actors and actresses, the leaders of peace movements, generals, well-known celebrities from all walks of life, and thousands of whores—all university graduates—plus the usual bunch of S&M queens, among them Odoriferous Gunk), when they saw Karilda Olivar Lubricious running toward them along the beach, pursued pell-mell by her husband, who was brandishing a sword in the *most* alarming way and screaming that he was going to cut off her head. Hot on the heels of Karilda came the Dowager Duchess de Valero, with a huge pair of binoculars hanging around her naked, wrinkled neck. And as though all that weren't enough, the fleeing women were accompanied by an army of she-cats, mewling fiercely.

Faced with that astounding spectacle (which was now passing directly before them, leaving a wake of sea foam, flying sand, and pulverized stones and sea urchins), the Dissed & Miffed rose to their feet as one and stood upon the rocks.

"What, Oh Lord, is the cause of this latest commotion?" asked Bishop O'Condom, raising his hands and rosary toward heaven.

Well, Miss Pisshog, I mean bishop, If you'll just keep your pants on I will tell you.

Ahem. For many years, too many to mention, Karilda Olivar Lubricious, followed around by her she-cats and the Dowager Duchess de Valero, had spent her days wandering through the parks of the province of Matanzas, shaking the coconut trees in the hope that a black man would fall out of one of them and screw her and her entourage—including, naturally, the she-cats. When one or another black man, terrified at that visitation, would hang on for dear life to the reeling and quaking palm fronds, Karilda's sweet she-cats would climb up the coconut tree and bite, scratch, and meow at the poor man until he finally gave up and shinnied down.

Naturally, this flight of every black man in Matanzas to the treetops had occurred in the first place because of the ever more demanding come-ons to which they were subjected by Karilda and the Dowager Duchess. But they could not find shelter even in the highest branches of the coconut trees, because no matter how they tried to hide, the Dowager Duchess de Valero and her binoculars could ferret them out, and the black men had no choice but to fall (legs and arms akimbo) from the treetops and service those merciless creatures.

And of course word of these events got around. Throughout Matanzas, all you could see was coconut trees (shaken by Karilda and the Dowager Duchess de Valero) raining down coconuts and black men who had to turn sexual athlete on the spot. The news of all this finally reached Karilda's young husband, a man who was completely bonkers and therefore madly in love with his senile, lecherous poetess. Karilda's husband was an opera singer, and therefore an expert sword fighter—that was why he always wore an enormous nineteenth-century sword as part of his daily (though outlandish) costume. On hearing the news of his wife's promiscuity, the great sword fighter and opera singer ran (with his sword) to Central Park in Matanzas, where he caught her *in flagrante delicto*—his beloved wife and the Dowager Duchess de Valero were busily shaking a coconut tree, hoping that a heavenly black stud would fall out. The aggrieved husband, giving a war cry more typical of a samurai than a baritone, charged—saber aloft—at the grove of coconut trees. All the black men ran for the trees again, but Karilda and the Dowager Duchess had no choice but to run for it, period, and so, followed by their faithful retinue of she-cats and that enraged, bloodthirsty man, they hightailed it along the coast—Karilda, the Dowager Duchess, the she-cats, and the young but crazed husband, down the Havana shoreline, passing the crowd that now called itself the Dissed & Miffed, or Dissed & Pissed, I'm not sure which. . . . Anyway, before she got to the huge armored-steel Fifonian gate, Karilda started screaming so loudly that her screams penetrated the huge salons of the palace and even reached the ears of Fifo himself. (Karilda was one of the official invitees.)

"Open the gate and then close it immediately!" came Fifo's orders.

The huge gate rose, and Karilda rushed through the opening like a streak of lightning followed by the Dowager Duchess and the she-cats. Skunk in a Funk, Mahoma, Hiram, and SuperSatanic also took the opportunity to return to the reception after attending the burning of Mayoya. But when the great sword fighter and karate star (I forgot to say he was a black belt in karate, too) tried to get in, the gate fell in his face like a guillotine. The desperate (and desperately jealous) husband sang his (baritone) song of woe to the Dissed & Pissed, and then he joined them, waiting for the huge armored-steel gate to open again at the inauguration of the Carnival.

"Then I'll kill her," he said.

And Bishop O'Condom once more raised his hands to heaven.

The Death of Lezama

Reinaldo was out on the balcony of the apartment that belonged to Aristotle Pumariega, who was trying everything he could think of to persuade his wife to become a lesbian, because Pumariega could experience orgasm only when he watched two women making love. Pumariega's wife, who was seventeen years old (he was in his sixties), absolutely refused to engage in that sort of sexual behavior. The argument had gone on for hours. Gabriel, bored, was looking out over the stalled traffic on the Rampa. Just then PornoPop, The Only Remaining Go-Go Fairy Queen in Cuba, arrived in an absolute *delirium* of delight, because she'd been invited to Fifo's big party. She was going to read her Pornopoems at the Grand Oneirical Theological Political Philosophical Satirical Conference! And without further ado—more or less as a rehearsal, but in the most Aristophanic way (since she was, after all, in Aristotle's house)—she began to recite several of her brilliant poems. When she finished, she went over to Reinaldo and sat down beside him on the balcony.

"Can you believe Joseito died!" she sighed.

"Joseito? Who's Joseito?" Gabriel asked.

"José Lezama Lima, silly. They buried him this morning."

"Oh, yeah, terrible," Reinaldo said, looking back out toward the Rampa without another word.

"Oh, *darling!* I almost forgot to tell you—the section of the congress on dreams—*Impossible* Dreams it's called, isn't that precious!—is going to be chaired by André Breton, who's coming back from the dead just for this event!"

But Gabriel just looked out over the Rampa.

That night Reinaldo (Gabriel forgotten, now Skunk in a Funk) went with Hiram to Lenin Park. They were going to steal all the mariposa jasmine (Cuba's symbolic flower, since as everyone knows, *mariposa* means fairy in Spanish) they could, to sell it on the black market so they could buy some cream cheese and soda crackers for their poor empty stomachs. At nightfall, staggering under a load of white flowers, they stopped at the bridge over the reservoir in the park, which had been built by Celia Sánchez herself. There, Skunk in a Funk told Delfín Proust about Lezama's death, and as he spoke he began to sob. Delfín tried to console Reinaldo, but Skunk in a Funk's crying got louder and louder. Finally, dropping the huge load of flowers, Gabriel leaned out over the water and began to howl. At that, La Reine des Araignées picked up some of the long branches of jasmine and began flagellating the weeping queen, who ran back and forth on the bridge, shrieking and wailing. Soon the white petals of the flowers covered the queen's bruised and welted body. But Delfín, not satisfied with that, ran back to the vast field of mariposa flowers, picked every one of them, and returned to the bridge, where she went on flagellating (now harder than ever) the face and body of Skunk in a Funk, who was bleeding and crying out *Lezama! Lezama! Lezama!* Finally, giving one last enormous howl, the queen, covered in blood and white flower petals, jumped feet first into the waters of the reservoir.

After that act of homage and exorcism, Skunk in a Funk emerged as fresh and moist as a daisy, and Delfín helped her out of the water.

Off to one side of the bridge, more than two dozen teenagers had witnessed this spectacle. The two queens, redolent of jasmine flower, approached the delicious bouquet of multicolored adolescence, and in less than three minutes' time they had all retired to an abandoned picnic pavilion where the teenagers, driven to a frenzy by the fragrance of the flowers and Skunk in a Funk's tears, made mad love to them till midnight.

Along toward dawn, the two queens (fragrant, flushed, and ethereal) left Lenin Park. Each of them carried a long stalk that ended in a splendid-looking jasmine flower. Swiftly they swished toward the Cementerio Colón, where they laid the flowers on Lezama's still-fresh grave.

A Tongue Twister (9)

That Miche is quite an accomplished muchacha, whether cha-cha-ing a cha-cha or chomping pork chops or launching a coffee shop or just shopping for the cheapest shipping charges to Chicago. But secretly, she's a chippy—she's got the itchiest britches in the Michigan vicinity. When the itch hits her, she scratches her snatch, unlatches the back hatch of her hatchback, and with a catch in her voice yells Pancho! Pancho! And Pancho chows down.

But the last time Pancho and Miche matched passions in the back of her hatchback—ouch! Secret chippy Miche *loves* to get her snatch's itch scratched, but the last time she latched onto Pancho to scratch it, she got a nasty rash.

For E. Michelson

St. Nelly

Aurélico Cortés (a.k.a. Cornelius Cortés) had died at the age of eighty-two never having been laid by a man. Not that he didn't go for men—Aurélico Cortés was one of the screamingest queens on the face of the earth. It was just that for seventy years he had lived with his mother and father and had been brought up with a horror of sin and an idea of the shame of it all if the world should learn that he was queer. "Before I have a queer for a son, I'll commit suicide," said his mother when Cortés was only seven (she lived to be ninety-nine), and the poor little queen, who was already feeling an indescribable attraction for men, made a vow that *she* was never going to be the cause of her mother's death (much less by suicide). "A fag for a son, and I'll set myself afire!" swore the mother on Cortés' twelfth birthday. And at that, the poor little prepubescent fairy realized once and for all that she'd never be able to enjoy the pleasure of sleeping with a man—which was, on the other hand, the only thing that might give her life meaning.

Cortés renounced even the pleasure of looking at men, let alone speaking to them. He devoted himself to his studies and was first in his class at the National School of Dental Prosthetics. Dressed all in white, like a nun, she spent her days pulling rotten teeth out of mouths without ever once looking at the groins of her clients, some of whom were really quite impressive. On Sundays and her other days off she made pious pilgrimages to the Cinémathèque to see *The Battleship Potemkin,* much to the joy of her father, who had been one of the founders of the Popular Socialist Party. Every month she turned her salary over to her mother, who counted it methodically and gave little Aurélico back exactly enough to go to the Cinémathèque to see *The Battleship Potemkin.* Sometimes his father would suggest that Cortés also see "A True Man," but Cortés would shiver with emotion and terror just at hearing the title.

Since she had read somewhere that salt and spices could act as aphrodisiacs, her diet was frugal and her food lacked any savor whatsoever. When her mother and father died—Cortés being seventy-something at the time—his skinny figure was all hunchbacked from leaning over all those open mouths for so many years; his head was almost bald, with only a few curly wisps emerging from the middle of his scalp; and his teeth, which he had always taken such pains to keep looking nice, were gigantic, almost horselike. It was too late to be starting a new life. And so Cortés plodded on with his monklike existence. And besides—what man was going to screw such a horrid old bag as herself? An additional consideration was that her father, and especially her mother, still exerted an enormous influence on Cortés' behavior. The most tragic part of the whole thing was that as she grew older, her virginity became ever more unbearable—but the fear of sinning was stronger than all her homoerotic yearnings.

The queen sublimated her faggotry by offering her help to other queens—putting in false teeth without charging a penny, giving them her own ration of meat (out of fear that any protein she consumed might bring on concupiscence), even passing out her salary among the indigent queens such as Delfín Proust and thousands of others who lined up in front of the Ministry of Public Health on the day Cortés collected his wages. And so, as the years went by (and the queen became an increasingly horrendous old thing), she never ceased doing good deeds for queens. But always, always, *always,* under the condition that none of them *dare* say that she, Aurélico Cortés, was a queen too. Oh, if his mother's memory should be sullied by such an indignity! She would die a virgin, and no one would ever be able even to hint that she was a . . . you know. She had never even *mentioned* the subject of faggotry to any other fag. My god! How that poor queen suffered, seeing all the other queens swishing around as openly as you please, fluttering their wings around in all directions, making jokes about themselves and their men, and talking constantly about their conquests (which they always exaggerated, of course). So terrible were her sufferings that although she was in perfect health, she died one night as she lay atop the ironing board that she always slept on (head downward, for greater mortification). She died a virgin (not like that slut of a daughter of Bernarda Alba's) and with the knowledge that no one could prove (at least beyond a reasonable doubt) that she had been a queen.

But when Cortés died, her friends (all queens) realized that a *saint* had died, and they rushed (at the urging of Skunk in a Funk, for whom Aurélico had made a perfect partial plate and installed it free of charge) to begin the process of her canonization as St. Nelly. A huge committee, the Committee for the Canonization of Aurélico Cortés, was formed by Skunk in a Funk, and its members—Tomasito the Goya-Girl, Antón Arrufada, the cunning Mahoma, Mayoya, La Reine des Araignées, the Dowager Duchess de Valero, Uglíssima, and Carlitos Olivares (the Most In-Your-Face Queen in Cuba), among others—worked day and night at the job, while ten thousand others sent a hundred letters a day to the Pope requesting (sometimes demanding, sometimes pleading) that Aurélico Cortés be canonized. At last the old pope, who felt an extraordinary attraction for men (so great an attraction, in fact, that he did not allow women to be priests), took up the request to beatify the Cuban queen. In St. Peter's Basilica, as his eye fell upon a young man in shorts who was asking for the papal blessing, the Supreme Pontiff meditated: *A saint for faggots is good political strategy for the Catholic Church. The world is full of fairies who have fallen away from the Church because of our tradition of discrimination; with this canonization, all those queers—which is to say half the population of the world—will return to the fold. And besides—poor old queen, how she must have suffered, never to have felt the pleasure of the male member. Yes, that's it, I'll have her canonized.*

The canonization, announced in Rome, took place the next week in the Cathedral in Havana at a ceremony that is unlikely to be outshone in the long history of Catholic liturgies. There, upon the altar, lay the mummified corpse of the deceased and soon-to-be canonized queen. Two thousand cardinals knelt before the body while Monsignor Carlos Manuel de Céspedes read the homily and the apologia. Then Monsignor Sacchi, in the name of the Supreme Pontiff, also pronounced a panegyric. Last, taking even Fifo by surprise, His Holiness the Pope himself burst into the nave—he had decided at the last minute that he couldn't let the opportunity to appear before the television cameras of the world (which were following the ceremony's every detail) go to waste. The Pope confirmed, authorized, and pronounced a special encyclical by which Aurélico Cortés was canonized, under the name St. Nelly. More than a million queens, filling the sanctuary and crowding into the plaza outside the Cathedral, fell to their knees at the Holy Father's words, and then in unison intoned a *Te Deum Laudamus.*

The canonization had been a triumph. Even Fifo, who at first resented all the pomp and show (after all, he was still in the closet, so he hated and *despised* maricones), finally saw that the Pope's visit to the Island was a propaganda triumph for his regime. *And anyway,* he thought as he knelt, *with or without St. Nelly these faggots here had better watch out. I'm tired of them screwing even my handpicked private guards—men I've reserved for myself—and making me have to kill them for high treason.*

The body of the canonized queen inside its magnificent coffin and the Pope in his Popemobile led a procession almost fourteen miles long through the streets of Havana to the Cementerio Colón, where the remains of St. Nelly were to be laid to rest. The huge tomb, with its papal seals and coats of arms, was surmounted by a gigantic white statue that portrayed the saint as a smiling young queen, her outspread wings bigger even than Oscar Horcayés'. All the fairies in the procession touched the image, crossed themselves, and, sure that they now had a patroness to protect them, went off cruising, filled with optimism and faith.... St. Nelly would perform miracles, St. Nelly would find *hunks* for them, St. Nelly would free them from those awful thugs and every infectious disease.

And indeed, within days the miracles of St. Nelly were the talk of Havana. She had saved Skunk in a Funk's life when Skunk was caught *in flagrante delicto* in a tent, being buggered by a lifeguard: the Skunk, chased down the beach by a platoon of soldiers shooting at her wildly, threw herself into the waves, her death apparently imminent. But just as that moment St. Nelly unleashed a ferocious thunderstorm, and such fierce rain fell all along La Concha beach that the poor queen was soon invisible, so she was able to swim (with her clothes on top of her head) to her room in Miramar.... Another well-publicized miracle was that of the rain of tickets for free meals at This Little Piggy, The White Rabbit, and other fine restaurants in Havana that St.

Nelly showered over Coney Island (on the beach at Marianao) when she saved the life of Eachurbod, and although Eachurbod did perish, St. Nelly was later instrumental in her resurrection. . . . And then there was the miracle she performed with Ñica, darling—that hundred-year-old invalid of a queen who suddenly stood up and *ran,* not walked, to the water's edge, threw herself into the sea, and, eluding all of her pursuers, which was an army of *at least* a million sharks, swam till she reached Key West. Uh-huh, I'll tell you—within a few days St. Nelly, the miracle-working fairy godmother, was the toast of Fairyland.

But as you know, my dear, you can't please everybody all the time, much less if we're talking about queens—and so pretty soon there were thousands of faggots, led by that Miguel Barniz creature, that were beginning to question St. Nelly's alleged virginity. A faggot dying virgin at the age of eighty-two? Get outta here. Who ever *heard* of such a thing? . . . Rumors, protests, whispering campaigns, fistfights, catfights—in a word, controversy—followed. Even Fifo himself heard the rumor that St. Nelly was no saint; she was just a lowlife faggot that had played around with Fifo's handpicked escorts. Enraged, Fifo gave permission to a group of high-ranking queens to go to Rome and ask the Pope to formally decanonize St. Nelly. Immediately the group took off (in one of Fifo's private planes) for the Vatican; among them were Paula Amanda (a.k.a. Luisa Fernanda), that Miss Barniz, Chug-a-Lug, Miss César Lapa, María Félix, Coco Salas, Nicolás Guillotina, the Divinely Malign, and a hundred or so other high-ranking fairies, who managed to at least plant doubt in the Holy Father's mind about the virginity of St. Nelly, and certainly to convince His High Holiness that Fifo *really wanted* the Church's newest saint decanonized. The Holy Father, contemplating the long document that Fifo had sent (along with a million dollars for the Poor Box), thought: *A faggot turned saint is really not such a good thing for the Church, because although everybody is queer, almost everyone denies it, and therefore everyone will turn away from St. Nelly and the Church won't receive any offerings in her name. And besides, these are increasingly reactionary times. In fact, at the request of the College of Bishops, I'm planning to start up the Inquisition again, which also means burning people at the stake* ad majorem Dei gloriam; *fairies will be going to the bonfire. So how am I going to have a fairy saint? So that's it—St. Nelly's got to be defrocked.* And standing on one of the basilica's many balconies in order to look down on a procession of delicious Polish altar boys who'd come to ask for the Holy Father's blessing, the Pope spoke these holy words to the Cuban delegation: "Look, guys, I have no problem with fucking over this faggot and decanonizing him, but first you've got to prove that she was really not a virgin. It's a rule. You've got to exhume the body, and if it's not a virgin, I'll have his sainthood on the spot. Let's go to Cuba—no time to dillydally. I want to get this over with."

The energetic Pope arrived in Cuba once more, and once more the immense crowd, following the Popemobile, came to the Cementerio Colón. Beside the tomb of St. Nelly stood once more all the queens in the country (and not a few from foreign lands), plus Fifo and his entire staff. The tension was palpable. The Pope ordered the mummified body of Aurélico Cortés taken from the tomb. The body was laid at his feet. And then the Supreme Pontiff, raising his pontifical scepter, spoke to the multitude, and these were his words: *Beloved brothers and sisters, the only way to prove that St. Nelly died a virgin is to inspect his backside. The test will be performed with this holy crozier. If it enters the deceased's anus without encountering any obstacle, that will be* prima facie *proof that he was not a virgin.* And at once the Holy Father fitted the scepter to the dead queen's rear. But that anus which had never taken delight in any type of penetration was as tight as a drum. So the Holy Father (who was determined to prove that Aurélico Cortés was not a virgin) pu-u-ushed the scepter with all his might. And so great was the pleasure that that thick staff sliding up his rear end brought to the dead queen that she immediately came to life again. Because the queen really *had* been a virgin, and she returned to life the first time she was penetrated. And so, with the papal staff (the staff of life) rammed halfway up her ass, Aurélico Cortés looked out upon that astonished multitude that had fallen to its knees before her; saw the Holy Father giving her his blessing (and trying to upstage her, the bitch!); heard the shouts of the millions of queens, unable to contain their joy, who were shouting *vivas* to St. Nelly; and, finally, consulting a nearby fairy, discovered what had happened: She, Aurélico Cortés, who had kept her homosexuality hidden for eighty-two years, had been canonized as St. Nelly. So all her years of abstinence and chastity had been for nothing, and after she was dead her "perversion" had been published to the world. *I can't believe this,* she said to herself, *I've been outed by the Pope!* Livid with rage (and in spite of the fact that she'd been in the tomb for *weeks and weeks*), the resurrected queen ripped the staff out of her ass and started cracking it over the head and shoulders of the Pope and all the other dignitaries. As she distributed drubbings right and left, the queen found out not only that the news of her canonization had been broadcast throughout the world, but also that there was a novel, written by Skunk in a Funk, which contained all the details. Still clutching the staff (the Pope meanwhile shrieking *Excommunication! Anathema! Excommunication!*), St. Nelly rushed off to Skunk in a Funk's room, gave her four whacks with the stick, and before the writer's astonished eyes snatched up the manuscript of the novel *The Color of Summer* and reduced it to shreds with his big horsy buckteeth.

Aurélico Cortés, deeply embarrassed at the brouhaha that had proclaimed him a fairy to the entire world, fled the city and found refuge in the mountainous region of the former province of Oriente—Mayarí Arriba, to be exact. There, disguised as a campesino, he settled down, joined a forestry project, and, employing the papal staff as a walking stick, gathered seeds from pine trees day and night, hoping that in time his canonization would be forgotten. But the fame of St. Nelly did not die; rather, it grew more widespread day by day. If St. Nelly had been able to resurrect herself, the world mused, could she not perform even greater miracles for others? . . . And out in the wilderness among the dense pine forests, almost every day Aurélico Cortés, disguised as a campesino, would come upon some new altar erected in homage to St. Nelly. Cortés would descend upon the altar in a rage, smash it to smithereens with the papal staff, and exclaim that it was shameful that in a socialist country people still believed in such nonsense. But whether she wanted to or not, St. Nelly was still performing miracles, because faith is stronger than reality, and the number of her worshipers grew larger every day.

As for Skunk in a Funk, having suffered the destruction of her manuscript, she began in the most disciplined way to write the story once again.

THE STORY

This is the story of an island on which a very big man had been born. The man was so big that he didn't fit on the island, because he made all the other people who lived on the island feel very, very small. So the dictator of the island sent the big man to a smaller island, the island where the dictator sent *all* the men that were not of small spiritual stature. There, as the big man broke rocks in a quarry, he started talking about how big his island was and how big those who lived on that island were. The man spoke with a remarkable voice—a voice noble, and grand, and *big*—so big that it carried all the way from that little island he was living on, to the ears of the men on the big island. And the people who were living on that big island couldn't stand that enormous voice that they didn't have. So the dictator of the island deported the big man to a place far, far away, beyond the ocean, where his voice couldn't be heard on the island. But the man kept talking—constantly—giving speeches that were so beautiful and so filled with light that they caused him to be bigger and bigger, so big, in fact, that even the people who had been deported from the island because they were big, or because they *wanted* to be big, were envious of that big man. So not only was the big man attacked by the dictator of the island and the biggest part (numerically speaking) of the people who lived there; he was also attacked by the dictator's *enemies,* who didn't live on that island but wanted to liberate it, yet who couldn't bear the presence of a man so big that he'd surely prevent them from becoming dictators in their own right when they finally *did* liberate it. Living in exile, a man without a country, the big man became the target of all sorts of plots, insults, and slanders—millions of them. He was called a coward, "Captain Spider," a pervert, an elitist, a drunk, a drug addict, and even a friend of the dictator of the island. And the dictator of the island echoed those insults and slanders, and added a few more of his own. Sometimes it was the dictator himself who invented and spread nasty rumors about the big man—nasty rumors that were gratefully respread even by the dictator's enemies, who couldn't bear the existence of that man who was so big. But despite the war that was being fought against him—against him *personally*—the man kept growing; he just kept getting bigger and bigger, and he continued to fight against the dictator. And the bigger he got, the more he realized—the clearer it all became—that none of that bigness made any sense if he couldn't die on his beloved island, where, on the other hand, there was no place for bigness like his. And so, while he was insulted and verbally abused not only by all the people who wanted to keep the island under absolute tyranny but also by all the people who wanted to free it, the big man sneaked off to the island. When he got there, all the armies—the friendly forces as well as the unfriendly ones—conspired together, and they killed him. So then the big man dissolved into the island and nourished its soil. And when he was dust and nobody could even remember where he'd fallen or where his grave was, the natives of the island, friend and foe alike, were proud to have had such a big man. And they started to put up statues to him. And now there are so many statues that there's not a single corner of the island where you can't contemplate the thoughtful visage of that big man.

A Tongue Twister (10)

Cloistered, locked in quarantine, behind the thick bulwarks and hard iron bars of the ancestral bastion-prison of El Morro, where, locked up lacking air conditioning, he's turned into a yicky despicable slob gobbed with gunk and perspiration, the crafty captive languishes. But one day the crafty captive encounters a compassionate fellow convict carrying a crowbar, and, speculating quickly, he conceives an escape and convinces his fellow captive to entrust the crowbar to him. Cleverly concealing the crowbar by day, he uses the conveniently encountered crowbar to excavate, and in a week the gunk-covered cloistered and confined convict tricks his captors by scrabbling his way to victory.

For Odoriferous Gunk,
whose real name is Bishop Toca

THE FOUR MAJOR CATEGORIES OF TOPS

When the apparent Chelo, disguised as Delfín Proust (or the other way around), finished putting her life on the line to enumerate the categories of queenhood, SuperChelo (whose job it was to put the other Chelo in the shade) leaped over the retreating rafts and tumbled, eyes bulging, onto the table where the Grand Oneirical Theological Political Philosophical Satirical Conference had just taken place. She turned her blazing eyes on the alleged Chelo (who was planning to flee to Paris and keep working for both the French and the Cuban police), and addressing an audience which wasn't listening because it was following Fifo to the Garden of Computers, she spoke the following words:

"This decrepit old mulatto rumba-dancing hag, who was born in Camagüey during the time of Agramonte and was the mistress of an old mummy in Paris, has overlooked the system of classifying bull macho butt-stuffers which is employed throughout the world. We all know that without bull machos there are no queens, and vice versa. So if we fail to make known to this jury the system for classifying bull machos that has recently been approved by the Security Council of the United Nations, her dissertation on the subject of queenliness will be incomplete. . . . Ladies and gentlemen, distinguished guests, stop for a moment and listen: bull macho butt-stuffers may be classified in four major categories of tops, to wit: . . ."

And while the attendees were rushing for the exits, SuperChelo began the list.

"First: THE OCCASIONAL, OR SLEEPING, TOP. This type of top generally lives a normal life, not seeking out fairies to screw in any systematic way yet once in a while, in obedience to some unknown secret impulse, some mysterious and uncontrollable urge, feeling the need for a piece of fairy ass. The occasional butt-stuffer may love women and have many children, but one day in a men's room, in a tunnel, or out in the middle of some field, a butterfly will flutter by, he will be dusted with fairy-dust, and he who on other occasions has been offended by a faggot and may even have busted a queen's nose will at that fairy touch feel a certain stirring in the loins (the sleeping bull macho awakes), and he will ram it up the fairy's butt. Then, zipping his fly, he recovers his manhood and his dignity and retreats to the bosom of his family or continues standing guard at his work center. As an example of the occasional bull macho butt-stuffer, we might cite any man."

The water rose higher and higher in the room, the rafts were now being paddled ever more swiftly, but the queen continued her discourse:

"Second major category: THE TOP WITH A COMPLEX. This type of top is crippled by a curious sense of guilt at desiring another man's ass, and his face reflects his terrible inner pain. He has tried everything he can think of to put his 'perverse' urges aside, and in practice is a good family man. Oh, but sometimes, when one of his small children climbs up on his lap, the suffering butt-stuffer feels a thrill. At that point, he wants to kill himself, but instead of putting a rope around his neck, he rushes into the street and puts a knot of flesh around his prick. After screwing some fairy—any fairy, actually, that comes along—he recovers his lost manhood and returns home, filled with remorse and a terrible sense of guilt but still turned on by the pleasure he felt as he rammed it up a fairy's ass. As an example of the bull macho butt-stuffer with a complex we might cite Ramón Stivenson and almost all boxers, karatecas, and judokas. In ancient times, we might point to Christ, who loved all men."

The huge conference room was now empty, the waters were rising, but the queen went on with her dissertation:

"Third major category: THE NATURAL-BORN TOP. The natural-born bull macho butt-stuffer is the kind of top that's interested not in women, but only in faggots, and it's faggots and only faggots that he aims his divine male dart at. The natural-born bull macho can screw up to thirty fairies in one day; he can also be married to one, though that doesn't keep him from screwing every queen on the block, and all the 'real men,' too. Sometimes wars will break out between him and another natural-born butt-stuffer over some fairy they both have their eyes on. He may have a scar on his face as a mark of those bull macho butt-stuffer battles. He is tough, always ready for a fight, and extremely masculine. He's a loud talker, and every five minutes he's almost unconsciously cupping his balls or adjusting his cock, even when he's talking to another natural-born butt-stuffer. As an example of this type of top we might cite Peerless Gorialdo, Lance Yardlong, or Maltheatus. In antiquity, we might mention the names of King Arsurbanipal and Alexander of Macedonia."

The waters continued to rise. Out in the lobby one could see thousands of midgets diligently swimming for their lives, knives in their teeth, toward the Garden of Computers. But SuperChelo continued with her presentation:

"Fourth the last major category: THE SUPERBUGGER. This rare type, now nearing extinction if not already extinct, is a man who is interested in screwing only another man—that is, another Superbugger like himself. The Superbugger will never screw a fairy—no way, my dear—because his dream, his goal, his sole burning desire, is to put it to a REAL MAN, if possible a high-ranking military officer, a famous actor, an Olympic athlete, or a high official in the Central Committee of the Communist Party. If he can't do that, he'll screw a horse or even a crocodile, but never, *ever* will he screw a fairy. The Superbugger is that man who wishes he could screw his own father-in-law or his brothers-in-law instead of his wife. Screwing a fairy would be a betrayal;

screwing a woman is the most boring thing in the world, and barely even respectable. As I said, the Superbugger is a species that is now in danger of extinction, unlike the other types, which are multiplying daily. Oh, one of the last of the Superbuggers, perhaps even *the* last, was the President of the Spanish Royal Academy, who has just passed away before the gates of this very palace. At this terrible loss, we must all weep."

And in spite of the torrent of water that was sweeping her away, SuperChelo shed a dozen or more enormous tears, which made the flooding of the auditorium all the more horrific.

A Dying Mother

Odoriferous Gunk had just struggled up the steep stairway of the apartment house where Clara Mortera lived in a tiny room with all her children. He was one of those who had been invited to the urgent meeting that Clara Mortera had called for that afternoon. But since Odoriferous Gunk had brought along her dying mother, the famous painter firmly, but with a great show of unctuous affection, refused to let her in.

"No, my dear. Your mother cannot, absolutely cannot, attend this meeting. What I have to say is of the utmost gravity, and I fear for her life. And I don't want any problems with the chairwoman of the Watchdog Committee. I'll see you later."

And so Odoriferous Gunk had to struggle down the steep, broad stairway once again, carrying not only her mother but also her mother's collapsible pup tent and all the medications and appurtenances that a pathetic, sick old lady entails.

In Havana Park, not far from Clara's house, Odie set up the tent, hung a hammock, and helped her mother into it—as her mother began softly whimpering and moaning in pain.

The queen sat at the door of the tent waiting for her mother to fall asleep so she could go back to Clara's room. There was no way she was going to miss that meeting.

The story of Odoriferous Gunk and her dying mother (whom Odoriferous Gunk carried around on her back) is long and, of course, despicable.

I'll just summarize it for you.

As a young (though hideous) queen, Odoriferous Gunk lived in the city of Trinidad in a large residence dating from colonial times; the house had been in her family for generations. When Odie's father realized that his son was such an in-your-face fairy that he was the laughingstock of all of Trinidad (which for the father was the center of the world), he fled the country in a motorboat that he launched from the southern Cuba port of Casilda. After much struggle, and having had to sail around the entire Island ringed with sharks, he at last reached the United States, and the first thing he saw in the Miami *Herald* (which Fifo edited long-distance from Cuba) was a huge photograph of his son alongside an article in which Odoriferous Gunk was talking about the progress the Anglican Church had made in Cuba. That terrible photo was exhibited in almost every church in Miami, and even at guarapo stands and smaller shopping centers. Unable to bear such a stigma any longer (he had already been telephoned by a radio station, La Cubanísima, and asked to do an interview on his son), Odie's father grabbed a butcher knife and stood in front of the biggest Episcopal church in southern Florida and stabbed himself in the chest seventeen times.

At that, Odoriferous Gunk swathed herself in black from head to toe and became the leading light in the Anglican Church in his hometown. Fifo had already catapulted him onto the first page of the Miami *Herald,* where he'd appeared in a lovely photo, and this photo, alongside one of Queen Elizabeth of England at her coronation, hung in the great dining room of the colonial mansion in the house in Trinidad. Under those photos, Odie, surrounded by the most flaming queens in Trinidad, served tea every afternoon at five.

Odie's mother, stricken with grief at her husband's abandonment of her, his violent death, and the constant racket in that house that was always full of fairies dressed in black, caught cancer.

The poor woman was sent to the public hospital in Trinidad. While she underwent terrible chemotherapy treatments, Odie sold almost everything in the house. The truth was, he never expected his mother to come out of the hospital alive. But in two months or so his mother was released, and she returned, gravely ill, to an empty house that contained only a tea set, a little tea table, several chairs, and (but my dear, how could you doubt it?) the photos of Queen Elizabeth and Odoriferous Gunk. The old lady couldn't even have a drink of ice water, because her son had sold the refrigerator. The poor soul, in constant pain, went every afternoon to the Catholic Church and made her confession to the priest. Her words always ended with muted weeping.

"My son has deprived me of cold water, father, just when my soul was bound for the other side."

People were outraged at Odie's heartless attitude, and many complained loudly; the priest even called him to account. Odie, wearing black gloves and a long jacket with black bellows-gored pockets over which she threw a lovely black cape, promised to somehow solve the problem of ice water. Within a few weeks she arrived home to the unfurnished mansion with a stone water jug and water filter, the kind people used to use out in the country. But this water jug made no improvement in her mother's health; in fact, her mother had to be taken to the hospital again. Now, said the doctors, the poor lady's days were truly numbered.

While the mother lay dying in the hospital, Odoriferous Gunk, whose nickname was now famous for miles around because of the English toilet waters she sprinkled over her filthy, black, heavy clothes, moved into the See of the Episcopal Church in Havana as a seminary student. There she met a very professional and well-known hoodlum who claimed descent from the family of Isabel de Bobadilla, and he convinced Odie to sell her mother's house and go off with him to live in Varadero. And within minutes, the illegal sale was done and almost all the money squandered.

In a few weeks, when the dying mother returned to her house, there was no house to return to. Odie was still in Varadero with the descendant of Isabel de Bobadilla and the large portrait of Queen Elizabeth. The life she was living in Varadero was so scandalous and extravagant that soon, through the good offices of Coco Salas, the news reached Trinidad. As the mother breathed her last, she called the entire city of Trinidad to a meeting at the Iznaga Tower. With terrible pain and effort she climbed to the top of the tower and from that height addressed the multitude. She told them of the terrible trick that had been played on her, the way she'd been swindled of her own house, and said her son was *possessed by the devil.* As irrefutable proof, the mother showed them the photo of her son. That was enough to convince the crowd that all this was, indeed, the work of Satan. Then and there, a crusade was organized against the apostate. Waving clubs and sticks all the Trinidadians, even the queens who used to have tea with Odie, marched to Varadero, intending to bring the renegade queen to reason and make him accept his responsibilities as a son. This crusade has been immortalized as "the Cuban struggle against the devil," in a book written by Fernando Ortiz. . . . As their pursuers pursued them, Odie and the descendant of Isabel de Bobadilla fled across the province of Matanzas and flung themselves into the ocean on a frail little single-masted sailboat, hoping to sail to the island of Grand Cayman, which was under the British crown. All the treasure that remained to them was the water jug full of drinking water and the portrait of Queen Elizabeth. Their pursuers, however, hotly pursuing the fugitives, at last in fact caught up with them, and the fugitives were forced to surrender. Soaked to the skin and starving, they were towed to shore by their intrepid pursuers and a platoon of enraged sharks that Odie kept at bay by showing them the portrait of the queen. . . . When they reached the coast, the dying mother was waiting for them, lying on a stretcher. That bald, cadaverous, suffering figure was the first thing the son saw as he leaped onto land. And he realized that it was impossible for him ever to be separated from her again, that that dying mother (who never seemed to just get it over with and die) was his own fate, his own long bout of dying, and that wherever he went from that day forward, he would have to carry her with him and take care of her. And besides—there was the entire bellicose population of Trinidad, the most bloodthirsty queens in Cuba, and the entire army of Occidente province to see that Odoriferous Gunk met his responsibilities as a son.

But just the same, even though Odie signed all the maternal IOUs and got a tent for the two of them, he could not remain in Trinidad, because the people there were calling for his head. And so with her dying mother she set out for Havana, stopping every two miles to set up the pup tent and attend the poor lady *in extremis.* In Havana, the Party Committee of the province (who knew there was a housing shortage all over the Island) gave Odoriferous Gunk special permission to set up his tent in any vacant lot or park or on any flat roof in Havana. He was even allowed to go out into the country, where the pure air might mitigate his mother's suffering. But Odie flatly rejected that possibility—he'd rejoined the Episcopal Church in Havana, and besides, he wanted to get his hands on that descendant of Isabel de Bobadilla.

And now, waiting for his mother's pain to lessen so he can go off to Clara Mortera's room, Odie is thinking with great pleasure of the great liturgy, with organ music, that is to take place in the Episcopal church, where she herself, in a *wonderful* purple robe, will be carrying one of the holy palliums.

Crucifuckingfixion

The party in Fifo's great underground palace was coming now to its climax. The state dinner was over, at which the resurrection of Julián del Casal, José María Heredia, Gertrudis Gómez de Avellaneda, José Lezama Lima, and other celebrities had taken place (the same method that the Holy Father had used to revive Aurélico Cortés had been employed now by Oscar Horcayés to resurrect these glories of Cuban culture, and to the same effect); three hundred dancers from all over the world had danced three hundred native dances of their respective countries; five hundred pesky Rodents had been strangled by five hundred muscular midgets; Skunk in a Funk had read her Thirty Truculent Tongue Twisters; and PornoPop, The Only Remaining Go-Go Fairy Queen in Cuba, who couldn't wait for the big conference to start, had recited her brilliant PornoPop Poetry. Halisia had danced *Giselle,* and then, tireless, offered to dance it again. And now, in the midst of the most exquisite liqueurs and the most diligently attentive midgets, Fifo announced that the Crucifuckingfixion was about to begin.

He called for a volunteer to be crucifuckingfied. Hundred of guests raised their hands. They knew that being crucifuckingfied was a pleasure beyond all other pleasures, for it meant being impaled on thousands of enormous, glistening, hard, erect phalluses, all at once. Men, women, fairies, and queens jumped up and down deliriously at the idea, madly waving their hands in the air, in hopes that Fifo would choose them. Above the clamor of voices one could clearly hear the shrieks of the cunning Mahoma, the King of Syria, Macumeco, Bibi the Bimbo, the latest Miss Universe, Arthur Lumska, and Monsignor Sacchi, who was trying to get Fifo to look his way by blowing a cornet that he'd tied to his enormous rosary (from which there was also hanging a hammer and sickle and a Nazi swastika). At last, Fifo (who was not going to play favorites in *this* particular event) announced that the honor of being crucifuckingfied was to go to Yasir Arafat. And to moans of disappointment from everyone in the room, the head of the Panamanian Liberation Movement moved triumphantly toward the wall where he was to be crucifuckingfied, the midgets stripping his clothes from him as he advanced. Soon, naked, he stood with his back to the room, against the Wall of Crucifuckingfixion.

He was asked to spread his arms and legs as far apart as he could; then his wrists and ankles were bound to strong rings attached to the wall. Immediately, two hundred midgets carrying brushes and cans of red paint approached the soon-to-be-victim's body and began painting bull's-eyes on his asscheeks, legs, ankle, throat, triple chin, ass, ears. . . . There was not a single part of that voluminous body that some scurrying midget didn't get to and cover with red bull's-eyes. When this important preliminary had been accomplished, the midgets retired and the ceremony *per se* began.

From one end of the hall, more than a hundred men drawn from every known race on earth stepped forward. They were totally naked, and their enormous members were fully erect. A unanimous sigh resounded throughout the palace as those magnificent ephebes strode forward, masculinities at the ready, for their encounter with Arafat. A Congolese Negro, arriving before his fellow attackers, penetrated the Leader's anus; the phallus belonging to an immense Mongol inserted itself into a hand; an American lad from Ohio buried his vigorous rosy member in one buttock; a potent Dominican shoved his lusty lance into one foot while a Russian buried his member in one knee and an Israeli penetrated his neck. Amidst sighs of envy from the entire audience, the brawny young men went on penetrating Arafat's body, while the captive himself received those thorns of flesh with all the fervor of a Christian of the catacombs, and at each penetration sent forth a howl of glory.

Oh, the crucifuckingfixion was going exceptionally well. None of the well-turned ephebes had missed his mark. Each time a phallus penetrated the leader's deformed body, Fifo applauded and the audience panted. The crucifuckingfixion was just about to reach its climactic moment when one of the most diligent of all the midgets climbed up on Fifo's body and whispered the following news in his ear: The Condesa de Merlín had just arrived from Paris and was singing an opera in the city's great public urinal.

"Jesus fucking Christ!" exclaimed Fifo, so furiously that Arafat stopped moaning and even the upstanding phalluses of the young men flagged a bit. "I gave specific orders for somebody to be waiting on the dock for the Condesa so we could blow her to bits with a cannonball, like SuperChelo suggested. But it's too late for that now, I suppose. We'll have to show her the full honors. Run! Go get her! Apologize the best you can and bring her to the palace! And now—on with the crucifuckingfixion!"

But even though the delicious ephebes grew hot once more, and continued to drill their members into the Leader, this interruption had taken some of the luster from the celebration. *What the hell,* Fifo told himself, *when Halisia dances* Giselle *again, and Albert Jünger explains the seven great categories of queenliness, this little incident will be totally forgotten.*

The Anglo-Campesina

The Anglo-Campesina was a horrid-looking queen who'd sprung from a strange crossbreeding of Taino, Chinese, black, and Spanish bloodlines (like all Cubans today, come to think of it). But this conglomeration had not resulted in a lovely hothouse hybrid—a velvety Chinese, a muscular mulatto, a dark-skinned blue-eyed hunk with sensual lips, a monumentally endowed black man. . . . Forget that. This queen—you must have run into her someplace, my dear, no matter how much of a stay-at-home you are, because she's a bigger self-promoter than a movie star—this queen, as I say, had the shape of a scared bullfrog or a big-bellied penguin. Like all mediocre persons, she was terribly, terribly vain, and possessed of an ego that even he himself couldn't be sure where he got, because he (or *she,* take your pick) had neither talent nor grace nor beauty—but rather (in a word) the opposite: his body was round, though squashed-in at the poles, and her head was like some piece of cosmic fruit dented by asteroids. Everything about him (we summarize yet once more, again—just for the record) had the look of an owl sentenced to a thousand years of insomnia.

Given that quadruply Cuban nature of his, he was very attached to his little clod of earth, from which everybody, *but everybody,* upon seeing that freak of nature, had fled (so that in his hometown all that remained was an abandoned weaving mill belonging to H. P. Lovecraft). So of course he (or she) began to want to bury that background that she considered a stigma and become a man (or woman) of the world, a cosmopolite. At last, the praise of Fifo that she publicly and unceasingly sang, plus the secret reports *against* Fifo that he supplied to the Chinese embassy, plus the counterinformation that she sent to the Chilean embassy in order to offset those other reports, brought in enough money to allow her to set herself up in London—perhaps in the hopes that the London fog would camouflage her repugnant appearance. In London, this queen-turned-minor-local-color-scrivener married a rhumba-dancing mulatto with a fright wig who dressed in drag for all their social occasions so he could pass as the writer's wife. Naturally, this particular writer, like all Cuban writers of his/her generation, was extremely cowardly, and since s/he'd not had the courage to accompany Fifo on his trek into the mountains all those many years ago, s/he lived now but to praise and adore him. Like all the writers of his/her generation, s/he (I think this technique works, don't you?) imitated Fifo and had secret sexual fantasies about the great leader. (H. Puntilla, for example, had been *enthralled* when Fifo once slapped him.

Eee-u-u-ugh Desnoës said she'd been *impaled* upon Fifo's revolutionary rhetoric, and the Anglo-Campesina recalled with honeyed enchantment the way Fifo walked: *In two paces, he can cross an entire room,* she would muse aloud, her myopic eyes going all trembly and bleary.)

Naturally, Fifo had been informed (as he was about almost everything) of the Anglo-Campesina's mad passion for his person.

And so, after consigning him/her to oblivion for upwards of thirty years, Fifo allowed that horrific unresolved conglomeration of races to join the official delegation sent by Great Britain to help commemorate the fiftieth anniversary of the Triumphant, indeed Thriving, Revolution. Leading the delegation, as we have said (or maybe we haven't), was Princess Dinorah (naked), and behind her came the great ladies of the court, ambassadors, ministers, marquises, makeup men, pimps, directors of protocol, and all the other hangers-on that surround a great whore in all her glory. Farther back, almost blind, and leaning on the arm of his/her transvestite wife, came the Anglo-Campesina. His/her faded memory still managed to hang on to a little joke that s/he planned to use to bring a laugh to the Comandante. But just as s/he and his/her faithful walking stick were about to cross the threshold into the great hall, the door was slammed in her face, leaving her outside with (but surely we've already mentioned *this*) a pack of paparazzi. In the midst of the confusion and the noise, and while she was being photographed almost to death, the Anglo-Campesina lost his/her glasses. Now truly blind, and therefore desperate, s/he clutched his/her drag-queen seeing-eye hag in the hope that sooner or later they'd let her in. But that never happened. Every time a delegation of latecomers was admitted, burly gatekeepers would kick the Anglo-Campesina away from the door. *I should be kicked by Fifo himself,* the Anglo-Campesina would complain to herself, *not these underlings.* And then she would add: *I will remain here for the rest of my life—even if it kills me.* "Fifo doesn't like vaudeville literature," Paula Amanda (a.k.a. Luisa Fernanda) would scream at her from inside—a slight falsehood, if the Anglo-Campesina only knew, because Fifo didn't like *any* kind of literature, except the literature that he produced himself.

The pain and grief experienced by the Anglo-Campesina soon affected her body, and so while she waited on the threshold of the palace she suffered several heart attacks and succumbed to a sort of senile dementia that led her to babble no end of nonsense. Fearing for her life, the drag queen-husband dragged her over to the group of Dissed & Pissed who were milling about alongside the palace hoping to be recognized as official guests. But considering him/herself superior to all those Dissed & Pissed, she refused to sign any of their protests.

It was no doubt resentment, and not patriotism, that induced her, upon her return to London, to lend her support to the flight of Avellaneda and to publish in *El País* an article titled "*Ave,* Avellaneda!" The article was immediately plagiarized in New York by Miguel Correderas, who published it under his own byline in the Magazine *Noticias de Marte.*

THE KEY TO THE GULF

One day, walking along the golden sands of the beach at Marianao after praying a heartfelt prayer to the nonexistent though powerful gods, Skunk in a Funk bumped into the most gorgeous teenager he'd ever seen—and he'd seen a lot of them. This was a kid with a svelte, supple body, blackblack*black* curly hair, café au lait skin, and eyes the color of honey. Skunk in a Funk stood so transfixed before that barefoot, bare-chested love god that he couldn't say a word. It was the love god, in fact, who came over to him and asked if he had a cigarette. *A cigarette! A cigarette!* Skunk in a Funk slapped desperately at his pockets. No, he didn't have a single cigarette on him, but if the youngman would come home with him, he could give him a whole pack. Skunk in a Funk and the stunning barefooted teenager started walking together along the beach. While he walked, Skunk in a Funk told the younggod that his name was Gabriel. The love god, in proof of his honesty, first stated his name and both surnames, father's and mother's, and then showed the enchanted Skunk in a Funk his ID—Lázaro González Carriles, his name was, and he lived in Old Havana. They came to the Skunk's room in Aunt Orfelina's house. Naturally, because of the Watchdog Committee's constant surveillance and his own (treacherous) aunt, Skunk in a Funk couldn't go in the front door with any man, much less with this *gorgeous* barefooted and half-naked adolescent. So they went around to the back of the house and the fairy flew over the wall into the back yard, telling the youngman to jump over behind him—and not to make a sound. The delicious teenager jumped over the wall all right, but he landed on top of one of Orfelina's she-cats, which let out a bloodcurdling wail. Orfelina was washing clothes at a washtub over in a corner of the back yard, and when she turned around and saw this stunning bare-chested teenaged kid she stood speechless for a few seconds. Then she yelled: "What are you doing in my back yard?" The teenager replied that he was going to visit a gentleman named Gabriel who lived there. "There's no Gabriel living here—Skunk in a Funk lives here, and he's not allowed to have visitors," shot back Orfelina, more furiously yet, thinking that there was no *way* her nephew was going to take that jewel to bed—ay!—in *her* house (is nothing sacred?), which it had taken her umpteen jillion denunciations of her neighbors to get and which she shared with her decrepit husband, a militant member of the Communist Party. The teenager, somewhat taken aback, apologized and jumped back over the back-yard wall. But Skunk in a Funk vaulted over the wall, too, and caught up with Lázaro. Together they wandered the beach for more than twelve hours, and around dawn, when the aunt, her husband, her son Tony, and all the she-cats were asleep, they silently slipped over the wall again and went up to the maid's room which Skunk in a Funk lived in (and for which he had to pay his aunt an exorbitant rent and also give her all the products that he was allowed on his ration card). . . . Skunk in a Funk unbuttoned the formidable teenager's pants, and he discovered that in addition to his formidable beauty, he possessed, oh most beautiful of all, the largest phallus that the gods (and his constant cruising) would ever, in his entire hard-bitten life, permit the Skunk to lay his (ahem) eyes upon. And now Skunk in a Funk, having removed the young man's pants, once more contemplated that unique, and fleeting, jewel. The teenager was a lily in underwear, with a magnificent lilac-colored stalk. By the time (before the sun was fully up) that Lázaro releaped the wall, Skunk in a Funk had been absolutely transfigured, transformed, transverberated (which is the perfect word for it, thank you). A happiness which she had never before known filled out her skin, made her hair once more full and silky, brought an unwonted sparkle to her eyes, filled in all those nasty wrinkles, and turned her face into something fine and smooth. At last he had found the love god he'd always yearned for, the last to fit his shoe, the Key to the Gulf—because what she had was a gulf, and only such a monumental key could fit such a gigantic lock.

The next night, when the beautiful teenager sat (naked) in the broken-down (but only) chair in Skunk in a Funk's room, the Skunk, kneeling before him, confessed in all sincerity that he, Lázaro, was the only man that had ever fully satisfied him and that all day he'd done nothing but think about him—and that he'd decided that he loved him. "For the first time," he said, and it was true, "I've fallen in love. You have fulfilled all my dreams, have plumbed the depths of my sensuality. And when we're alone, I'm not going to call you Lázaro, but rather the Key to the Gulf." And as Skunk in a Funk was speaking these words, he gazed entranced at, and gently caressed, that monumental key that would soon open the gates to his immense gulf. Then, as he possessed him, the Key to the Gulf confessed that he had never done this with anybody, "even with a real woman," he said. And that confession almost made the fairy die from happiness.

For more than three months the Key to the Gulf leaped over the wall every night and frenziedly transverberated Skunk in a Funk, who gave thanks to St. Nelly that his Aunt Orfelina hadn't discovered the teenager's nightly visits.

One morning before dawn, after having been possessed in the most convincing way by the Key to the Gulf (who was smiling as he crept downstairs), the entranced fairy went out onto the balcony to watch how lightly and gracefully the marvelously conditioned young man jumped over the wall after more than three hours of lovemaking. But Skunk in a Funk did not see the young man vault the wall. *He's so athletic,* he thought, *he probably jumped over before I even got out onto the balcony.* The next night, Lázaro couldn't possibly have gotten all the way down the stairs before Skunk in a Funk, wrapped in his only sheet, stepped out onto the balcony so he could watch his love god leap the wall. He did see the marvelous adolescent carefully close the door to the back stairway and make his way across the yard. *Now he'll jump,* the fairy said to himself, even more entranced. *And that leap is a leap that he will make in my honor.* But instead of going toward the garden wall, the teenager crossed the back yard toward the door of Orfelina's room. The Key to the Gulf didn't have to knock; Orfelina opened the door—which showed that it had all been planned beforehand! The fairy, unable to control himself, and still wrapped in his only sheet, tiptoed swiftly down the stairs, tiptoed over to Orfelina's room, and peeked through the window. His beloved teenager was frenziedly possessing Orfelina, who was moaning with pleasure at the immense key. The fairy, mute with horror, ran up to his room. So that, he said to himself, was why he hadn't been discovered and denounced—his aunt was taking kickbacks! The whole day, Skunk in a Funk meditated, and at last he reached the conclusion that he loved the young man too much to give him up because of another woman. *If he likes women,* he said to himself, *all the better; that shows he's a real man, and that he was telling me the truth when he said I was his first fairy. But I don't care, I'll have my revenge anyway—I'll send an anonymous note to my uncle, who as an upstanding member of the Party is always trying to figure out a way to catch his wife with another man so he can throw the whore out and keep the house for himself.*

That very day, Skunk in a Funk wrote out the note and with the help of the Divinely Malign (dressed as a lieutenant) sent it to his Uncle Chucho, who worked in the regional Party headquarters. That night the fairy and the Key to the Gulf made love as passionately as always. But the second the Key to the Gulf started down the stairs, Skunk, wrapped in the sheet that she'd now dyed black (thanks to a packet of dye given him by Mahoma), went out onto the balcony. This time the teenager didn't go toward the door of Orfelina's room; he knocked on the door of the dining room. Instantly the door opened and behind it, Skunk saw his Uncle Chucho, who invited Lázaro in. *Jesus!* thought the fairy, *I never should have sent that note—now my uncle, as a member of the Party, will surely kill my beloved Key to the Gulf. How could I ever have been so perverse?* And wrapped in his black sheet, the fairy ran down the stairs so fast that he slipped and broke his kneecap and cracked his forehead wide open. Bloodied but unbowed, however, he continued on. There was no way he was going to let his Uncle Chucho, that disgusting Party slimeball, kill the Key to the Gulf. When he came to the door of the dining room, Skunk in a Funk stood aghast. On top of the huge dining table, the beautiful teenager was violently and rhythmically screwing Uncle Chucho, who had stuffed a napkin in his mouth to muffle his shrieks of pleasure. *So he's never done anything with another fairy!* Skunk in a Funk sneered to himself. *I'm going to stand right here and wait for him and get to the bottom of this.* And Skunk in a Funk waited in fury for the Key to the Gulf to finish his business with Uncle Chucho. But when he'd finished, instead of coming out of the house, he went into Tony's room. Tony, Skunk in a Funk's cousin, was famous for the number of girlfriends that he had—yet there he was in bed, on all fours, ready for the arrival of that teenager who started banging the son with even more violence than he'd screwed the father. So loud and aroused were Tony and the beautiful teenager's cries and moans of pleasure that Skunk in a Funk, tears in his eyes, had no alternative but to go back up to his room and masturbate.

While he was getting himself off, the fairy heard a terrifying wailing sound. Wrapping himself in the black sheet again, he went out onto the balcony. In the middle of the back yard, the beautiful teenager was now impaling one of Aunt Orfelina's she-cats, who though she'd begged for that magnificent member couldn't take it all, and died. Skunk in a Funk, furious (and unable to finish himself off), stomped back into his room. But the next day he woke up in a more reasonable frame of mind. What if the gorgeous teenager had been entrapped? Maybe—almost certainly—he'd been blackmailed by Orfelina and forced to screw the whole family (and the cat) in order to keep her, Skunk in a Funk, from being reported to the police. *Uh-huh, I'm sure of it—the Key to the Gulf made all those sacrifices in order to save my life. Poor thing, what a terrible sacrifice to have to make for me.* And with that fantasy of love, the enamored (and therefore blind) fairy made her way, singing and whistling happily to herself, toward the beach on Calle 16, where all the young men in Havana were supposed to meet that day—because according to the Three Weird Sisters and the Clandestine Clairvoyant, there was not going to be the usual roundup of queens and fairies. It was Tomasito the Goya-Girl who upon seeing Skunk in a Funk singing and whistling to himself asked him what might be the cause of such euphoria.

"So tell me, girl, who's been sticking it in up to the elbows to make you look so fully filled, I mean fulfilled, and cause you to go around chirping like that?"

"That's right, tell us, tell us who the owner is of the phallus that's been giving you such pleasure," leaped in Le Seigneur aux Camélias.

"It's a secret," replied Skunk in a Funk, playing enigmatic. "And besides, there's no sense in telling you nasty things his name, because you don't even know him. He's only slept with *me,* and he barely even knows my family."

"Oh, come on, tell us his name. Anyway, if we don't know him, there's no way any harm'll come to you from *us,*" argued the Dowager Duchess de Valero.

Lowering his voice, and with shyness unusual for her, Skunk in a Funk pronounced the name Lázaro González Carriles.

The fairies exploded in laughter.

"My goodness, you mean the Key to the Gulf?" said Le Seigneur aux Camélias. "The most famous, best-endowed bugger in all Havana? Why, child, the first time he gave it to me—must have been about two months ago—I thought I'd died and gone to heaven."

"You took the words right out of my mouth," nodded La Reine des Araignées. "I think that of all the hunks I'm planning to take to Fifo's party, he'll win the prize. Over a year ago I bestowed upon him my award as the Best Bugger in Arroyo Arenas," she went on, "and I have never regretted it."

"Not a bad piece of meat," commented Mahoma with some indifference, "but I'm getting tired of him coming in through my balcony door every night."

"I had a piece of that, too, and I can assure you that he is the best-endowed man in Havana," said Coco Salas, removing his glasses. And Coco, the most horrific queen in all the world, whom nobody but *nobody* would screw, even on a dare, opened a little purse woven from silver threads and took out a snapshot of the Key to the Gulf completely naked and with his immense Key standing up like a lighthouse. "I made this portrait just a few weeks ago when we were in Varadero," Coco explained, as he passed the photo around.

"You've got to hand it to whatever fairy it was that gave him that nickname he always introduces himself with," piped up Tiki Tiki, "because it fits him like a glove. Imagine me, with this Biscayne Bay of mine, he filled me up *completely,* and at least for a few hours poured oil on my erotic waters."

"Ay! what can I tell you?" exclaimed Hiram, La Reine des Araignées, throwing her arms open. "Why, only last night the Key to the Gulf showed me heaven on Monte Barreto!"

And the queen, swishing, hands and feet aflutter, gave a leap of pleasure up onto the rocks and began to describe in full detail the divine young man's phallic prowess.

"I can assure you," said Mayra the Mare as Delfín continued with his skipping about, "that if that boy would promise to screw me even once a month, I'd give up my husband and my eleven children and follow him to the ends of the earth."

Suddenly Skunk in a Funk realized that from the moment he'd met him (about three months ago), his lover had slept with almost every fairy and every queen in Havana—and almost all the women, too, including even Clara Mortera, who'd already painted his portrait—and that on top of that, he was now recognized as Número Uno among all the hustlers in El Vedado and acclaimed as the Prize Bugger of Arroyo Arenas, a title aspired to by the most famous buggers in the country. The beautiful adolescent introduced himself to all his conquests, and to all those who *aspired* to be conquered (which meant almost every inhabitant of the Island), by the nickname Key to the Gulf, the name that Skunk in a Funk had so lovingly bestowed upon him.

The Electric Venus

Although almost all the guests who filled the immense catacomb of the Fifingian Palace were unquestionably "originals"—Selecto Macumerco and Papayi Taloka come immediately to mind—about whom any number of fascinating volumes might easily have been written, there was one whose fame was so widespread and whose importance was so great that it is simply impossible for us to allow her to pass in review before Fifo without first a few brief observations.

Her name, first of all, was The Electric Venus.

The Electric Venus was an Italian queen into whose backside the Oslo Academy of Science had implanted high-voltage wires that the fairy was able to control with a locket that she wore around her neck, dangling between her silicon breasts. When someone was having his way with the queen and she wanted (or had orders) to kill him, all she had to do was turn up the voltage. Instantly, the backside-stuffer would be electrocuted.

The Electric Venus specialized in assassinating the world's political leaders. On her impressive *curriculum vitae* appeared the names of the Ayatollah Khomeini, Mae Pse-tung, Leon Trosvki, Breshnev, the dictator of the Filippines, Marshall Tito, Ché Guevara, Aristotle Onassis, Olaf Palmer, Martin Luther King, both kings of Egypt, Golda Meir (who everyone knows was a man), John F. Kennedy, and some fifteen other constitutional presidents and several secretaries-general of the United Nations.... Radiant, the Electric Venus greeted Fifo (who surreptitiously gave her a few affectionate pats on the rear) and made her way into the circle of the world's most prominent heads of state.

Coco Salas' Secret

A truly regal queen dressed head to toe in linen and lace and shod in a gloriously clunky pair of platforms (tailor-made for her by Mahoma) swept in through the magnificent doors of the García Lorca Theater, which had recently been declared a national monument and moved intact to Fifo's palace. Another fairy, dressed in an impeccable smoking jacket made out of polyethylene bags (and also wearing platforms by Mahoma), made an entrance through the doors. Ten fairies, each dressed in a *smashing* ensemble and wearing brightly polished earrings, crushed through the door of the García Lorca Theater and with their noses preceding them entered the lobby. A thousand fairies, wearing the most *striking* costumes imaginable (all designed by the peerless Clara Mortera), poured swiftly into the García Lorca Theater. An extraordinary event was about to take place in this grand hall tucked inside the very palace in which Fifo's Grand Fiesta was being held. Halisia was dancing tonight!

"What do you mean *dance,* you brazen hussy! Why on earth would you tell people, you Communist faggot, that Halisia, who's eighty years old if she's a day, was going to dance? I mean, really! I've been watching you work for quite some time now, and I haven't interrupted you because what you say is more or less right, even if every once in a while you throw in one of those snide remarks of yours or drip a little venom. But now to come along and say that *Halisia was going to dance,* when the last time I saw her she was in a wheelchair and could only take a few steps on a pair of crutches. . . . Dance! You try to tell *me,* Daniel Sakuntala la Mala (uh-huh, *la Mala* because I always tell the truth), that Halisia was going to *dance*—that's really going too far. . . ."

Oh, my lord, will this faggot never let me write my novel in peace? What dreadful fate is mine—to have this fairy on my back day and night, supervising me, tromping all over every word I write. Because she doesn't miss a word or a chance to tromp on it. Of course since she's never written a thing and I'm recognized as a *marvelous* writer, she's sick with envy, which is why she's always interrupting me, trying to rattle me and make me lose my inspiration, especially when everybody knows I might kick the bucket any minute. . . . Well, you'd better listen to me, Miss Thing, I'm not going to lose my inspiration or anything else, because I'm of perfectly sound mind and furthermore, everything I say is the truth. Yes—*Halisia was going to dance,* whether you like it or not, and if you'd let me finish what I was saying you might find out *why* that eighty-one-year-old witch (not eighty) was still able to dance. So hush, and just listen for once.

In this city there lives the most horrid of all fairies.

"Coco Salas!"

That's right, Coco Salas. All right, then—What is the mystery behind that fairy? Where does he get the wherewithal to live the way he lives? How can such an *ugly* queen get her hands on so many nice things—all those fabrics and jewelry and trinkets . . . ?

"I've always wondered about that myself. The number of frocks that queen can put on. . . . But since everybody says that she's in State Security. . . ."

Oh, child, don't be silly. *Everybody's* in State Security, even the political prisoners, and nobody else dresses in French silks or has a house full of Bulgarian roses or wears luminescent belts the way Coco Salas does. And all those things, my dear, are gifts, gifts from her intimate friend Halisia Jalonzo. Now then, knowing—as we all do—who Halisia is, think: Is that witch a friend of anybody? Has she not destroyed even the people who thought they were her closest friends? Has she not gotten rid of all the ballerinas with any talent so that she could always be the star? So—a person so monstrously perverse—does it make any sense for that person to be a friend of Coco Salas'? No way. What, then, is Coco Salas' secret? Well I'm going to tell you, you none-too-intelligent queer: It is through the offices of Coco Salas that Halisia Jalonzo dances.

"I can't believe it. I mean I'm speechless. On top of the fact that you won't just die of AIDS and get it over with, now we're going to have to take you to the mental ward."

Hush, you silly bitch, and listen. Listen to the secret of Coco Salas that only I am privy to, because I am a great observer. As you know, for many years now all Halisia has been doing is tripping all over herself on the stage, falling on her head, and smashing that big beaky nose of hers into the wall. Famous for its hilarity is the true story of the time she danced with her back to the audience and when she started to take her bows she fell on top of the conductor down in the pit and killed him. People would go to the ballet just to count the times that Halisia fell down. But five years ago, at the International Ballet Festival they hold every year in the water amphitheater in Lenin Park, Halisia, on that floating stage, surprised the world by executing a grand jeté and then doing forty-four consecutive pirouettes. The entire amphitheater broke into cheers, although no one could fathom how that old bag could suddenly have brought back her old dancing from the dead. But Coco Salas, who was in the first row with a huge pair of opera glasses, saw the cause of the octogenarian's leaps and turns. A ferocious mosquito, one of those that are spawned only in the reservoir in Lenin Park, was biting Halisia on the thighs. The old woman, feeling those stings, hadn't been able to control herself, so she *leaped*. The ballet was a success and Halisia won the Silver Slipper International Prize for Dance. The next day Coco Salas showed up in her dressing room with a cardboard box.

"*Who,*" Halisia asked him imperiously, "*are you?*" And she looked him up and down through her immense *pince-nez*. "And how dare you enter my private dressing room! Only Fifo is allowed that honor. . . ."

Coco's only reply was to pull back one corner of his cardboard box and let a mosquito out. The mosquito flew straight for one of Halisia's naked legs, bit it, and the ballerina gave a leap so high she almost hit the roof of the theater.

"You're hired," said Halisia, daubing rubbing alcohol on the bite. "Get a good supply of mosquitoes. I'm dancing tomorrow and I don't want to disappoint my fans."

"Leave it to me," said Coco. And that very night he went to Lenin Park and for hours hunted down the fiercest mosquitoes. The next day Halisia came on stage looking radiant and began to dance the first act of *Swan Lake*. From behind the curtains, Coco Salas turned loose his mosquitoes one by one. Halisia danced *Swan Lake* as she hadn't danced it in sixty years. There was no ballet critic in the world—they'd all been invited to this event—who failed to sing the praises of Halisia Jalonzo. Under mosquito attack, Halisia danced in Rome, Monte Carlo, Moscow, Madrid (where Coco Salas herself wrote an article entitled "The Privilege of Seeing Halisia Jalonzo Dance"), Paris, Buenos Aires, Mexico City, Algiers, New York, and, not to put too fine a point on it, all over the world. Coco, his box of mosquitoes always at the ready, restored her fame, and therefore her life. And that is his great secret: Halisia Jalonzo is still alive, professionally and literally, thanks to Coco Salas. It should come as no surprise, then, that Coco dresses the way she does, and that she enjoys absolute impunity. She's Halisia's fair-haired boy. (Get it now, Mary?)

And now, in the theater set inside the gigantic catacombs of the Fiferonian Palace, Halisia was dancing the second act of *Giselle,* and dancing it magnificently. Knowing that Fifo was in the theater with all his important guests, Coco tripled the number of mosquitoes that he freed. The audience sat spellbound at Halisia's performance. Even the Argentine cows were entranced. A tear fell from the eye of the Hangman of Iran. María Tosca Almendros' eyes—and this really *does* say a lot—grew teary. Fifo, sitting very near the Key to the Gulf, was doubly moved, first by the dance and then by the glow of success that this performance lent his celebration. Who would now dare deny that he was the world's greatest patron of the arts and that the world's prima ballerina was one of his most faithful subjects? Came the climactic moment, and Halisia, accompanied by a monumental orchestra and in the midst of a hushed silence on the part of the audience, began her forty-four pirouettes. At that, Coco Salas turned loose the remaining half of his imprisoned mosquitoes and Halisia whirled like a top. But suddenly, in the midst of that miraculous dancing, there was a terrifying scream that echoed throughout the theater. Coco, thinking that Halisia had been murdered by an infected mosquito, closed up his precious cardboard box. Halisia fell to the floor. But the terrifying scream echoed once more throughout the theater, which meant that nobody paid any attention to Halisia's fall—all anyone could hear was that howling that seemed to come from the official woods that bordered the theater.

"What the fuck is it *this* time? I can't believe this!" said Fifo, rising to his feet in the presidential box.

And followed by his entire escort, most of the guests, Halisia herself, and Coco Salas, Fifo went out to the official woods to find out what it was that had inspired the terrible screaming that had interrupted one of the most sublime moments of this special evening.

A Tongue Twister (11)

When ectomorphic Macumeco the sexual eclectic felt his rectal cavity concussed by the crash of the quasi-volcanic eruption that echoed clear up to his epiglottis, he was ecstatic, exclaiming, "Oh, what delectable rectal cavitation, but I pray the impregnation is not ectopic. Actually, I'd have opted for active ingurgitation."

For Aristóteles Pumariego,
a.k.a. Macumeco

THE SEVEN WONDERS OF CUBAN SOCIALISM

First Wonder: The newspaper Granma

Because it's the only newspaper in the world in which the events that the newspaper reports on have nothing whatsoever to do with reality. It is the most optimistic newspaper in the world, and among the most frequent verbs you will find in its headlines are *inspire, conquer, overthrow, achieve, optimize*. . . . It's also the newspaper with the largest potato and sugar harvests in all the world, although we ourselves never see those products anywhere. It has no obituaries, and when somebody is shot by the firing squad the newspaper says that the person died in a state of grace, proclaiming the virtues of the newspaper editor who had the person shot.

Second Wonder: Plastic shoes

These are the only shoes in the world that you don't have to actually wear, and if you do wear them you have to always be running or at least skipping, which makes for a wonderfully active populace. When these shoes get hot, your feet shrink so much that you could pass for a geisha, who, as everybody knows, gets around with little hops. With these shoes there's no need for socks. You can walk under water with them and nothing happens. Although they're generally worn on the head.

Third Wonder: "Roof croquettes"

Also known as "miracle croquettes." No one knows how these mysterious croquettes are manufactured (it's a miracle) or what their ingredients are. But they have one exceptional quality that everyone does know *all* about: they stick to the roof of your mouth and there's no way to get them off.

Fourth Wonder: The bus

This is the only vehicle in the world which once you get in, you can't get out of, and which doesn't stop anywhere, ever, although it usually doesn't come by at all. It forestalls any worry or concern on the part of its users, since there's no need to bother yourself about where it's going. It is a mythological creature, and its adventures are beyond human imagination. Once you're in one, anything can happen, because no matter how many laws have been passed to control what goes on inside, there is no regulation that can stop the vehicle itself or anything that takes place inside it.

Fifth Wonder: The ICAIC Newsreel

This, the newsreel of the Instituto Cubano para las Artes e Industrias del Cine, is the only newsreel in the world in which you can close your eyes, fall asleep, dream through it, and when you wake up give it a round of applause, secure in the knowledge that although you haven't seen a thing, you've see it all.

Sixth Wonder: The films of the former German Democratic Republic

The merit of these movies is that you never have to see them.

Seventh Wonder: Copelia ice cream

This is the only ice cream in the world sold out of a specially built cathedral, and day and night, all around its nave, which is of course a *vaulted* nave, there congregate thousands of the faithful, prepared to suffer all manner of persecution for their steadfastness. The run-of-the-mill consumer has to stand in three lines before coming at last to the yearned-for ice cream: the *pre-line,* in which one waits to be given a ticket; the *line,* in which one stands with the ticket that enables one to enter the cathedral; and the *post-line,* in which one stands, ticket in hand, once one has managed to enter the sacred area in which the ice cream is served up. Several manuals have also been written on how to go about obtaining this ice cream, among them Nikitín's famous work entitled "Instructions for Breaking into Line at Copelia." It is very likely that by the time one finally arrives at the yearned-for delicacy, it will have melted or evaporated. But who can take away the joy of having spent one entire night, like some strange Knight-Templar in constant sleepless watch, at a cathedral in which the officiant is a frozen god?

In the Library

When Skunk in a Funk entered the reading room of the National Library, everything would be suddenly transformed, herself included. There, surrounded by books, a magical halo would envelop Reinaldo. Gabriel, almost completely alone in the library, would look down the long row of books and from every book would see a unique splendor shining forth. To walk over to those bookshelves, take down a book at random—What world would it reveal to us? What distant place would it transport us to? What music would bear us off to places, beauties, ideas that we never dared to dream of, yet have always sensed? But the most extraordinary moment would be that moment when, cradling the book, he had not yet opened it. At that moment Skunk in a Funk, Gabriel, Reinaldo would hold in their hands not one book but all the books in the world, and therefore all possible and impossible mysteries. Then, a sense of utter plentitude would come upon Skunk in a Funk, Gabriel, and Reinaldo, and they would become one single being. And then, radiant, that being would take the book and turn toward the reading table and sit down and begin to read.

A CLARIFICATION BY THE THREE WEIRD SISTERS

We wish to make it clear that if we have sentenced Reinaldo Arenas (b. Perronales, Cuba, 1943) to a nasty end, it is not, as the author claims, because we were so terribly angered by the buffeting we received from that Negro whose fly was touched by Delfín Proust (b. Guajanales, Cuba, 1944). All of that—the touching of the fly, the blows we received, even our anger—is true. But it had nothing to do with our verdict. What did decide it was that Arenas (a.k.a. Gabriel, a.k.a. Skunk in a Funk) doubted our word, and therefore doubted our power. When the subject was locked in Castillo el Morro, he sent his mother to us (which exposed us to a search at the hands of Fifo's agents) to try to find out what had happened to his novel. We informed the subject's mother that the novel had been found by the subject's Aunt Orfelina, who had turned it over to State Security. But he didn't believe us. If he did, why when he got out of prison would he climb up on the roof of Orfelina's house with the intention of recovering his novel? That lack of trust in us, the Three Weird Sisters, is not to be forgiven.

[Signed:]
Clotho
Lachesis
Atropos

A SCREAM IN THE NIGHT (THOUGH IT WAS BRIGHT AS DAY)

Carlitos Olivares, the Most In-Your-Face Queen in Cuba, had finally managed to persuade a stunning recruit who was standing guard at the Castillo de la Fuerza to come home with him. The truth was, Olivares (poor thing) had been obsessively hanging around the castle for months. She would stop outside the walls, stick her black, Indian-featured face through the thick iron bars, and stand in ecstasy, contemplating the young specimen of manhood who, feet slightly apart at present-arms (the butt of the rifle gently caressing his fly), stood guard before that historic edifice constructed by Isabel de Bobadilla in 1530 so that she could live at the seaside and await her long-absent husband, who unbeknownst to her had been swallowed *years* ago by the waters of the Mississippi. . . . The crazy queen, possessed perhaps by Bobadilla's spirit of despairing hope, stood every day, hours on end (her kinky curls sometimes twining inextricably around the bars), in contemplation of that magnificent hunk of man. Sad indeed is the story of this queen—black, queer, and Taino, alas, in a country in which even Fifo himself crows about his white Spanish ancestors and his purportedly unimpeachable masculinity. I tell you, girl, it was *pathetic*. . . . And as though all this were not bad enough, that lanky, bug-eyed, big-assed queen with that wide mouth of hers that drooled like a waterfall at the sight of any masculine figure was no less than the son of the Cuban ambassador to Soviet Nippon.

"My god, maricón! What words escape those false teeth of yours!"

"False, perhaps, but of the very finest quality, my dear, for they were designed by St. Nelly herself and made from ivory and silver—unlike yours, which are made out of plastic and all you have to do is laugh, or even open your vulgar mouth, and they fall out. . . . But let me just continue with this story, if that's all right with you."

Carlitos the swishful-thinking black tinkerbell was the son of a daddy who was a big government muckety-muck and a mother that was a *santera,* so you can imagine—the poor thing couldn't sprinkle so much as a *drop* of fairy-dust at home. And yet once a force of nature—the force of fairydom—decided to set up shop in that dusky body, who could keep it from manifesting itself in a thousand ways? The way she moved her hands, for instance, or the way he batted his ears, the way she pursed her thick lips or the way he blinked his wandering eyes, the swinging of his backside and the staring into space. . . . Nothing, *nothing* could keep the fairy queen from showing herself for what he was, which was why, despite her being a high-ranking mucketymuck sort of queen, she'd been given the title of "the Most In-Your-Face Queen in Cuba."

Anyway, the Most In-Your-Face Queen in Cuba had spent the livelong day on one side of the bars at the Castillo de la Fuerza looking longingly at the round and firm and fully packed specimen of military manhood on the other side—who just happened to come, oh, my heavens, from Palma Soriano. The queen's drool had been running down the bars outside the Castillo de la Fuerza all day and was now beginning to flood the moats that surrounded the fortress. The delicious hunk thought the tide had come pretty far in.

And the tide of drool continued to rise, until it reached almost to the magnificent medieval drawbridge from whose catwalk the soldierly hunk kept watch—ears pricked, face as stern as one of the masters of the world—on the drooling queen, who apparently was spying on him. His lieutenant had given him strict orders: Contact was forbidden with any persons who might be discovered wandering about the grounds of the military fortress in which the remains of José Antonio Portuonto lie; they might be spies or imperialist agents sent to obtain strategic secrets that Portuonto had carried to his grave. All photographs were forbidden; no one could enter the castle; and no replies were to be given to any questions that might be asked the guard. And in addition, his lieutenant had ordered him to report to headquarters any strange movement in the area of the castle, and to investigate the snooper as much as he could. That was why the wondrous hunk-thunk-thunk (*thunk thunk* because his boots made that delicious sound on the wooden catwalk of the fortress; *hunk thunk* because he was solid as a treetrunk himself) ignored the black fairy tinkerbell and didn't arrest him on the spot—he just kept a careful, discreet eye on him from behind the dark glasses that gave him an even more martial, more commanding, more *manly* look. Though of course he was ready to drop the pretense the second the spy reached for a pencil or a camera. But the fact is, the drooling queen didn't reach for anything; she just stood there, drooling, hour after hour.

By the time the drool had risen all the way to the soldier's boots, his turn on guard duty was over, so he checked in his weapon and left the fortress. There beside the great picket of iron bars stood the black tinkerbell, still drooling. Drooling and quivering. As the hunk-thunk-thunk passed beside her, the black fairy queen could not contain a short death cry, a sort of muffled *ay-y-y* that came from her profoundest depths, her deepest bowels, her small intestine, her large intestine, her ardent rectum, her very heart. The hunk, upon hearing those strange rectal sounds, deduced that the fairy was a superspy equipped with supermodern equipment, so he slowed down. The fairy continued to follow him, and was putting out such a quantity of drool that thousands of housewives started following *him,* carrying every sort of container imaginable so as to make up for the water shortage that all of Old Havana suffers under. Finally Carlitos Olivares, the Most In-Your-Face Queen in Cuba, approached the hunky recruit and respectfully asked if he could tell her the time. The recruit, always on the alert, half-smiled at the supposed spy and very respectfully told him that he didn't have a watch but when he left the castle (*the unit,* he called it) it was one o'clock, so it couldn't be later than one-fifteen. It's early, moaned Olivares. Uh-huh, replied the hunk-thunk-thunk, but I've been standing guard since midnight, so what I really need is a rest. Olivares swallowed hard and somehow found the strength to whisper: *Come to my house for a rest; my mother will make you some coffee.* Oh, so this is a whole *family* of conspirators, eh? the recruit said to himself, and in the interest of national security accepted the invitation.

When the Most In-Your-Face Queen in Cuba arrived at his house with that incredible specimen of manhood, a fierce though silent battle broke out between the mother, the son, and his two sisters. The three women waged a battle of smirks and affectations, backside-waggings, giggles, smiles, and honeyed words—and they even flashed the recruit from time to time, all very subtly of course. The mother brought in the coffee and served it with the greatest of attentiveness, being sure the recruit got a good look at her enticing bosom. The daughters brought him dark Cuban sugar that the old ambassador had sent them from New Stalingrad. And as they deposited lumps of dark sweetness in his cup, both daughters ran their tongues over the hunk's ears. At which Carlitos, desperate, invited the young man up to his room to see his books. The first thing the fairy did to win the soldier's confidence (politically speaking) was show him the complete works of Karl Marx; then, to win his friendship, he opened a drawer and gave him a Rolex watch, a pair of nylon socks, a curtain made out of matchbooks, a badge from the Young Communist League, an image of the Virgin of Loreto, a ring, and a bag containing 120 pesos that he'd planned to spend at the Carnival. Then immediately he told the young soldier, who serenely accepted those gifts, that he needed something nice to put that money away in, and he ran over to a gigantic wardrobe closet and produced a silky-soft leather wallet made from the hide of one of Fifo's crocodiles, and he gave him that, too. The soldier took the wallet without a word and tucked it into one of his big military pockets. The bulge of the wallet in that military pocket so excited the queen that she *flew* over to the big wardrobe closet and came back with a tuxedo, a fez with gold braid, and some marvelous Italian shoes. Kneeling before the love god, she removed his rough boots and slipped on those luxurious pointed-toed masterworks of footware. Ay, but just then—the fairy on her knees before the hunk-thunk-thunk, adjusting the fit of the Italian shoes—the mother barged into the room with a big pot full of nice vegetable soup just like the soup that people made in the province of Oriente (where the soldier was from, you see), and right behind came the sisters with plates, silverware, a linen tablecloth and a folding table that they set up in front of the soldier boy. The hunk soon found himself at the center of the attentions of three women who never ceased cooing and swinging their backsides as they served him his favorite dish. But Carlitos was not about to be upstaged by his sisters, and so he presented the hunk-thunk-thunk with the big Medal of Lenin that had been awarded his father, the ambassador, for his sixty years of work for the Party Central Committee. He also gave him Thomas Mann's *Death in Venice,* which he'd stolen from the National Library—a theft, reported by María Teresa Freyre de Andrade, that had cost him six months of hard labor on the park project, and hadn't cost him more only because he was the son of the ambassador to Soviet Nippon; otherwise, the fairy would've been shot by firing squad. . . . My heavens, but the high muckety-muck fairy was acting more like the tooth fairy, and he continued to pile gifts upon the hunk-thunk-thunk. Around his neck he hung a medal of St. Nelly (pure gold, and struck by Mahoma herself), then he gave him eighteen lengths of fabric, the oilcloth off the coffee table, a floor lamp, a pair of maracas, several areca palms, some wax fruit (grapes, pears, and apples), a rain cape, and a pair of Spanish flip-flops. All this, the gift-fairy piled upon him while his mother and his sisters wriggled about, waggling tits and asses. And the hunk-thunk-thunk accepted all the gifts, thinking they might serve as evidence—heck, prima facie *proof*—against the spy and his family.

Obviously, thought the nonwax fruit, I'm never going to be able to sink my teeth into this delicacy here at home—so he suggested to the recruit that they take a walk through the city and later maybe go to the woods in Havana, where it would be nice and cool. The fairy crammed all the presents into an immense burlap bag and left with the soldier boy, mother and sisters still furiously wriggling.

The Most In-Your-Face Queen in Cuba (dragging the huge burlap bag) and the hunk-thunk-thunk walked all the way across Old Havana, strolled almost the entire length of the Malecón (where the fairy got the burlap bag tangled up in the wheels of a carnival float), came to Copelia, and stood in line for three hours to buy a melted ice-cream cone. On foot (the fairy never turning loose of this huge burlap *thing*) they traversed all of El Vedado, the hunk in front, the staggering fairy behind with her tongue hanging out (and drooling). And they crossed the bridge over the Almendares River and began to make their way into the Havana woods. They had come to the residential sector called New Vedado Heights, which was adjacent to a wooded area that was a more or less official park grounds surrounding the presidential palace. If they were able to enter the grounds, it was because the Most In-Your-Face Queen in Cuba was the daughter of the ambassador to Soviet Nippon and the recruit was one of Ramiro Valdés's fair-haired boys.

"Mary! *What* has gone and got through those false teeth of yours again?"

I'm telling you, Ramiro Valdés. What do you think, a hunk-thunk-thunk of that (shall we say) caliber is going to go unnoticed by Miss Ramiro Valdés? Oh yes-s-s, Miss-s-s Valdés-s-s they call her. So, now that *that's* out of the way . . .

The recruit kept strolling among the trees in the shady woods. The fairy tagged along behind, struggling with the immense bag with all the presents in it. By now she knew the recruit's whole rural-family history (which he'd of course been narrating during the course of the walk), knew the names of his sisters, his mothers, his grandmothers, but when the recruit started talking about his great-grandmother on his mother's side the queen interrupted by asking him if he had a girlfriend. The hunk-thunk-thunk told him he was single and unengaged. At that, the queen threw the giant burlap bag to the ground and feel to her knees before the manly soldier, stationing herself directly in front of his fly. The soldier boy, thinking that he wasn't the appropriate person to kill a spy, and especially a spy who hadn't confessed to anything, proudly and firmly (though not violently) rejected the fairy's advances. The fairy, still on his knees, then confessed to the soldier that for more than a year he'd been gazing longingly at him day and night from the iron bars of the Castillo de la Fuerza, that he loved him, that he couldn't live without him. Then the soldier quite calmly (thinking always of the tape recorders that were surely hidden among the trees, recording every word of their conversation) told him no way, he didn't like men, if he'd gone home with him and accepted his gifts it was out of pure military courtesy, but he abominated sexual relations between men, he thought they were absolutely immoral. The queen then dropped his pants and showed the hunk his immense black ass and said: *You screw me or I scream.* The soldier, recoiling before that immense ass thrust virtually in his face, lied and said: *Listen, I told you—I've never had sex with anybody, but the day I do, it'll be with a woman.* The desperate queen replied: *But I am a woman!* The soldier, at that, and never for a second losing his composure, pulled out a pistol he had hidden practically in his groin, pointed it at the queen's head, and spoke the following words: *If you're a woman, then show me your cunt. . . .—Uh-huh, uh-huh, right away, I'll show it to you right away,* promised the fairy, and he began to pat himself all over the body, trying to find a sudden cunt. But no luck—all he had was a cock, a pair of balls, and a desperate ass. On the verge of an epileptic fit, the fairy tucked his prick between his legs, closed them tight so all you could see anymore were her pubic hairs, and showed the recruit what she was pleased to call her cunt. But the recruit was too sharp for that—on the contrary, suspecting that an international spy and a screaming queen to boot was trying to trick him, he said: *Open your legs or I'll kill you.* The queen had to open her legs, what choice did a poor girl have, and the recruit gazed upon a pair of dried-up balls and a droopy dick. *A cunt! A cunt,* demanded the recruit, suddenly unable to control himself. *Uh-huh, uh-huh, I've got one right here,* said the fairy queen, patting herself under the arms, on the tip of her toes. My dear, what desperation, as that fairy tried to find a cunt. Finally she stood atop the sack filled with all those priceless objects, raised her arms to the heavens, and set up a silent prayer to merciful St. Nelly—*Please, send me a cunt,* right now! Ay, but since St. Nelly was almost totally blind, she missed the mark and the cunt landed on the queen's forehead, where it instantly stuck. *What in the world is that?* said the recruit, looking at the cunt that covered the queen's entire forehead—*you're not just a faggot, you're a monster.* And turning away (first picking up his presents), he began to walk off through the proud, towering trees. The truth was, there was nothing more repugnant to that hunk-thunk-thunk than a cunt. *I don't want cunt, and I don't want ass—meat is what I crave, too. And to think that in the interest of na-*

tional security I've lost a whole day on a fairy and three whores, when I planned to suck dick like a madman in the urinals at Carnival—You fuck me or I scream! You fuck me, I tell you, or I scream! screamed Carlitos, running after him. The queen's supplication was so desperate that the recruit turned and, ignoring the possibility of tape recorders, looked the fairy queen in the eye. *I've never liked cunt,* he said, *much less on a faggot's forehead.* And at that instant the queen's hands went to her head where—horrors!—her fingers found a drippy patch of hair, and a cunt. That was *it!* That was the last straw! The poor queen, doubly mocked (by men and by the gods), stood in the middle of the woods and gave out a scream so loud, so loud, that no fairy has ever equaled it. And then she did it again, but this time even louder.

So those were the cries that echoed through the theater in which Halisia was dancing *Giselle,* the cries that caused Fifo and almost his entire entourage to rush outside.

Suddenly, queer and soldierboy found themselves surrounded by Fifo's troops, Fifo himself, and a multitude of personalities.

"Oh, it's Carlitos Olivares Baloyra, the son of my friend Carlos Olivares Manet, with a cunt in the middle of his forehead," said Fifo, taking all this in as though it were the most natural thing in the world. "Come inside, come in, come to the party. You look so weird you're bound to entertain my marvelous guests. And as for your companion," and here Fifo ran his eyes over the hunk-thunk-thunk from top to bottom, "bring him along, too! Let's go—come on into the palace. Let the party continue!"

Before entering the palace, Skunk in a Funk took off the long Egyptian scarf that Margarita Camacho had given him and wrapped it around Carlitos Olivares' forehead.

"It wasn't María Teresa Freyre de Andrade who turned you in to the police for stealing *Death in Venice,*" Skunk in a Funk confessed to Olivares; "it was me. It's one of my favorite books and I used to go the library to read it almost every week. What you did, neither God nor St. Nelly can ever forgive. And I don't hold out much hope for your getting rid of that stigma on your forehead, either. For the rest of your life, you'll be a queen with a cunt. Yech . . . But let's go on in, because after I list the seven wonders of Cuban socialism (which I'm sure will cost me my life sooner or later) and recite my Thirty Truculent Tongue Twisters, Lezama is going to read something."

"Lezama," sniffed Halisia. "I've never understood a word of what that crazy old man wrote—even if one of the texts he wrote was about *me.* Didn't make a bit of sense; there was no way in the world to make head or tail of it. Fifo even banned it. But if he's been resuscitated and he's going to read, I suppose it's because Fifo has authorized it, so let's go in and listen to him. Though I suppose we'll have to applaud him, too."

Then Halisia gave a great jeté, thinking she'd be able to leap all the way through the door of the grand palace. But since she was almost completely blind her head hit the trunk of one of the trees in the park and she plummeted, headfirst, into the crowd.

"Heavens!" shrieked Coco Salas, jumping up and down hysterically. "I think she's dead!"

"Yeah, right," spat Fifo, standing before the still-rigid ballerina. "Old bitch is too mean to die. Throw a bucket of cold water on her, she'll be up in no time."

"No! No water!" screamed Halisia, sitting up. "This makeup is three inches thick and it costs a fortune! I'm perfectly fine."

And the great ballerina started walking, bumping her head into one tree after another until at last her faithful Coco took her by the hand and they followed the grand procession that was now reentering the grand catacomb of the palace.

A TONGUE TWISTER (12)

Alejo, why the long sojourn on foreign soil? Why the prolonged aloha? Your Havana Viejo loas long for you, Alejo. *Où est l'Alejo d'antan?* Return, Alejo, old boy; we're spoiling for you, old goil, to rejoin us on our soil. Loyalty to Fidel, hell no. Loyalty to the roisterers and roilers of old! Merrily we'll once more roll along, Alejo, so, hey—why not, Alejo, merrily say "Havana Viejo, ho!"?

For Alejo Sholekhov

Stool Pigeons

So poor Virgilio thought that if he burned all the originals of his poems and didn't leave any copies he'd be safe from Fifo's wrath? How very touching. But it was not to be, my dear, because while the Queen of Cárdenas (which is what Miss Queta Pando called Virgilio) was reading his poems—which were truly inspired, truly brilliant, as I said before—two of the most sinister queens on earth, strategically fitted with tape recorders in their respective anuses, recorded the entire reading. Which means that at the same time those screaming queens were following their police orders to the letter, they were also enjoying the immortal words of the above-mentioned traitor *and* enjoying those huge tape recorders up their ass. Who knows how many of the oohs and aahs and moans emitted by those vile bitches were due not to the pleasure of the reading and their grief at the burning of the poems, but rather to the way they were being *pleasured* by those tape recorders up their asses whenever they wiggled around on the floor like two orgasmic marmosets?

So who were those horrid faggots with the elephant-like bodies? Who were those vile double-cross-dressers who'd managed to infiltrate Olga Andreu's little *hommage* to the great poet? It's time their names were revealed. They were—and you should remember their names—Paula Amanda (a.k.a. Luisa Fernanda) and Miss Miguel Barniz, two of Fifo's most trusted (and most faithful) confidant(e)s, and they worshiped Fifo not only politically but physically as well.

So—the minute that Virgilio ended his brilliant reading of his poems, the faggot informants gave him a big hug, tearfully congratulated him, and hauled ass (literally and metaphorically), each in a different direction (because these were supersecret informers), for the special door high up on the side of the Fifalian Palace. And there, at the official door, the two pansies, tape recorders now in hand, met face to face. Their jaws dropped. Their faces turned red with fury. To *think* that the other one might turn in his/her report first! And so as the two faggots banged desperately on the official door with the hand that clutched the tape recorder, with the other hand they were scratching each other's eyes out and twisting each other's ears. (They were also sticking their tongues out at each other and kicking each other in their big bellies.) At one point Paula Amanda's fury reached such a pitch that she grabbed Barniz by his long hair and in one yank snatched him bald—which he remained to the end of his days (and any other version of that creature's hairlessness is a bald-faced lie). But Barniz, howling in pain at the loss of his scalp (but never ceasing to bang on the official door), wielded his free grappling hook with such fury that he pulled Paula Amanda's whole chin off (which is why since that day Miss Amanda has sported all that long straggly white hair—supposedly in honor of Fifo, but in actuality to cover up the terrible defacement done him by Barniz). The bloody queens' catfight was causing such a ruckus that at last the special door opened and Fifo himself was standing in it, surrounded by his gorgeous escorts. Both queens fell to their knees before Fifo and started licking his boots, while at the same time (still kicking at each other) they raised their hands and presented him with the tape recorders. Fifo ordered his escort to separate them while he went off to listen to the contents of the tapes. Almost immediately he returned.

"The two reports are identical," he declared, "and they have been turned in to me at the same time. Therefore only one of them will be entered into the computers. But I have magnanimously decided that both your names will be set down in the secret record book, as though the report had been handed in by you both. As for the Grand Medal of Patriotism, don't worry—you'll each be receiving one the day of the Grand Pre-Carnival Fiesta in honor of my fifty years in power." Then he turned to his gorgeous escorts. "And by the way, men—that night I want Virgilio terminated. But—and this is important—I want it to be a nice, clean, quiet job, no machine guns or ruckus like in Miami when you goons took out my enemies there. We've got to be more cautious here in Cuba—there are fewer people on our side. I want it to look as though that son of a bitch died a nice quiet natural death—a heart attack, or maybe a suicide. In all the hullabaloo of the Carnival, at which I shall be the heart and soul, nobody will notice if an old poet kicks the bucket. And as for you two—" and here he turned once more to the bloody but rapturous queens, "beat it—and keep working like the true little heroes and little ants that you are. And don't forget, girls—mum's the word!"

Foreword

Mary! Get your filthy cum-stinking hands off this book because the authoress, the queenliest queen of them all, is about to sit down and write the foreword to it. Yes, my dear, now, at this late date, more than halfway through the novel, the pansy loca has got it into her head that the book needs a foreword, and so without further ado (like every other crazy queen—no self-control, just rushes right into it) she's going to do it now, right this minute, and it has to be *now*. So beat it, you nelly queen, till the foreword is done and you can come back and read it.

First of all, about that faggot who said it's taken forty years to write this book—*fuck you!* I'm not Cirilo Villaverde, I'll have you know! It's true that many years ago, while I was still in Cuba, I conceived part of the novel. I even wrote a few chapters of it. But suffering persecution and prisons as I did, and being kept under tight surveillance, not to mention being reduced to utter penury, I wasn't able to finish it. Plus the fact that almost all my friends and some of my closest family, not to mention most of my lovers (such as Norberto Fuentes, for example), were working for the police. I'd write a page and the next day it would be gone.

I memorized a chapter or two (such as the one entitled "Clara's Hole") and the Thirty Truculent Tongue Twisters (which didn't yet number thirty), so I managed to preserve some of my writing that way. But generally I dedicated myself to survival, like all ex-jailbirds. And of course I was living on an island that was a prison. But through it all, I never forgot that if my life was to have meaning—because my life is lived more than anywhere else in the sphere of literature—I had to write this novel, *The Color of Summer,* the fourth in a Cuban pentagony of which the fifth volume, *The Assault,* had already been written there in Cuba, in a fit of fury, and sent, with all the risks that that implied, out of the country, where I hoped I would later be able to decipher it—because the manuscript was virtually unintelligible.

In New York I have become involved in a number of political activities, because I will never be able to forget the hell I left behind (the hell that in some way I still carry with me); and then of course I have had to engage in the thousand stupid, time-consuming activities required by daily life in this country where the only thing that counts is money. If to all that one adds the number of manuscripts that I had managed to get out of Cuba, and that I had to make a fair copy of for publication, plus the unending wars that I've been carrying on for ten years with the agents (official and otherwise) of Stalinist Cuba, who live in absolute ease in the United States, then one can understand that I have not had a great deal of spare time.

In this country, as in every country that I have ever visited or lived in, I have known humiliation, poverty, and hypocrisy, but here I have also had the privilege to cry out. Perhaps that cry will not meet oblivion. The hope of humanity lies precisely in those who have suffered the most. Thus, the hope of the next century obviously lies in the victims of Communism; thanks to the apprenticeship of suffering that they have served, those victims will (or should) be those in charge of constructing a world that it is possible to live in.

In the United States today there are no intellectuals; there are only third-class penlickers who think about nothing but the state of their bank accounts. It's impossible to tell whether they are progressives or reactionaries—they're quite simply fools, and therefore tools of the most sinister of forces. And as for *Cuban* literature, it has virtually ceased to exist in any palpable way either inside Cuba or in exile. Inside Cuba, it has been exterminated or silenced by propaganda, fear, the need to survive, the desire for power, and social vanities. Outside Cuba, it has been stifled by lack of communication, rootlessness, solitude, implacable materialism, and, above all, envy—that microbe that always produces a suffocating stench.

When I arrived in Miami in 1980, I discovered that there were more than three thousand people in the city who called themselves "poetesses." I fled in terror. The great writers of the Cuban diaspora (Lino Novás Calvo, Carlos Montenegro, Lydia Cabrera, Enrique Labrador Ruiz, Gastón Baquero, Leví Marrero, and certain others) by now have died—or are dying—in ostracism, oblivion, and poverty. Other writers of a certain degree of relevancy not only hardly write but are considered sacred cows. (Let's get rid of the adjective and call it even.)

My generation (those who now are, or ought to be, between forty and fifty) has not produced a single noteworthy writer, with the possible exception of myself. And it's not that there never were any; it's that one way or another they have been annihilated, destroyed, done away with. I am completely alone, I have lived alone, I have suffered not only my own horror but also the horror of all those who have not even been able to publish their horror. Not to mention that I myself will soon be dying.

But no one should think that before Castro, life in Cuba was a bed of roses, either—not at all. Most Cubans have shown an interest in beauty only in order to destroy it. A man such as José Lezama Lima was violently attacked by both his own early generation and the generation that succeeded it. During the Batista years, Virgilio Piñera was insulted by Raúl Roa, who sneeringly called him "a writer of the epicene gender"; afterward, during the Castro years, Roa became a government minister and Piñera went to jail—dying, as a matter of fact, under very suspicious circumstances. Great Cuban literature has been conceived under the sign of scorn, denunciation, suicide, and murder. Cuban exiles made José Martí's life so miserable in New York that he had to go off to fight in Cuba so that he could be killed once and for all and have done with it. Then and now, the story of the culture of our country has been a sordid one. José Lezama Lima used to say that our country is a country "frustrated in its political essence." The local color, the exuberance, the light breeze at nightfall, the rhythm of its mulatto women, these are the trappings behind which hides, and continues, our implacable tradition—I like to call it Sinistrism.

For the moment, the apotheosis of Sinistrism is Fidel Castro (that second Caligula with a desire to be a killer nun). But who is this Fidel Castro? A being fallen from another planet upon our unfortunate isle? A foreign product? No, Fidel Castro is the *summa* of that Cuba that has always been: he simply typifies the worst of our tradition. And in our case "the worst" is, apparently, that which has always prevailed, and always will. Fidel Castro *is,* to a certain degree, ourselves. Soon, perhaps, in Cuba there will be no more Fidel Castro, but the seed of evil, vulgarity, envy, ambition, abuse, injustice, betrayal, treachery, treason, and intrigue will still be there, waiting to sprout and grow. In Miami there is no dictatorship only because the peninsula has not yet been able to secede from the rest of the United States.

Cubans have never been able to gain their independence—the only thing they have ever managed to gain is *pendence.*

That perhaps explains why the word *pendejo* (meaning spineless, twit, coward, jerk) is an epithet used constantly among us. As a Spanish colony, we never freed ourselves from the Spaniards; for that, the Americans had to intervene, and then we became a colony of the United States; then, attempting to free ourselves from a fairly conventional sort of dictatorship in the colonial vein, we became a colony of the Soviets. Now that the Soviet Union is apparently on the verge of extinction, no one knows what new horror lies ahead for us, but unquestionably what we deserve, collectively, is the worst. The same people who oppose this line of thought are generally loyal exponents of an infinite vileness. . . . I feel an endless desolation, an inconsolable grief for all that evil, and yet a furious tenderness when I think of my past and present.

That desolation and that love have in some way compelled me to write this pentagony, which in addition to being the history of my fury and my love is also a metaphor for my country. The pentagony begins with *Singing From the Well,* a novel that details the vicissitudes of a sensitive boy in a brutal, primitive setting. The work takes place in what we might call the political prehistory of our Island. The pentagony then continues with *The Palace of the White Skunks,* which centers on the life of a teenage writer-to-be; it gives us a vision of a family and an entire town during the years of the Batista tyranny. The cycle then continues with *Farewell to the Sea,* which records the frustration of a man who fought for the Revolution but then, once inside the Revolution, realizes that it has degenerated into a tyranny more perfect and implacable than the one that he had fought against; the novel details the process of the Cuban Revolution from 1958 to 1969, the Stalinization of it, and the end of all hope for creativity.

Then comes *The Color of Summer,* a grotesque and satirical (and therefore realistic) portrait of an aging tyranny and the tyrant himself, the apotheosis of horror; it details the struggles and intrigues that go on around the tyrant (who is aided and abetted by the hypocrisy, cowardice, frivolity, and opportunism of the powerful of the world), the attitude of not taking anything seriously in order to go on surviving, and sex as the immediate means of escape. In some way this novel is an attempt to reflect, without idealizing or investing the story with high-sounding principles, the half-picaresque, half-heartbreaking life of a large percentage of Cuban youth, their desire to be young, to live the life of young people. This novel presents a vision of an underground homosexual world that will surely never appear in any newspaper or journal in the world, much less in Cuba. It is deeply rooted in one of the most vital periods of my life and the life of most of us who were young during the sixties and seventies. *The Color of Summer* is a world which, if I do not put it down on paper, will be lost, fragmented and dispersed as it is in the memories of those who knew it. I leave to the sagacity of critics the deciphering of the structure of this novel, but I would like to note that it is not a linear work, but circular, and therefore cyclonic, with a vortex or eye—the Carnival—toward which all the vectors whirl. So, given its cyclical nature, the novel never really begins or ends at any particular place; readers can begin it anywhere and read until they come back to their starting point. Yes, dear reader, you hold in your hand what is perhaps the first round novel to date. But please don't take that as either a merit or a defect—just a necessity that is intrinsic to the structure of the work.

The pentagony culminates in *The Assault,* an arid fable about the utter dehumanization of humanity under an implacable system.

In all these novels, the central character is an author, a witness, who dies (in the first four works) but in the next novel is reborn under a different name yet with the same angry, rebellious goal: to chant or recount the horror and the life of the people, including his own. There thus remains, in the midst of a terrible, tempestuous time (which in these novels covers more than a hundred years), a life raft, a ship of hope, the intransigence of man the creator, the poet, the rebel—standing firm before all those repressive principles which, if they could, would destroy him utterly—one of those principles being the horror that he himself exudes. Although the poet dies, the writing that he leaves behind is witness to his triumph over repression, violence, and murder, a triumph which ennobles him and at the same time is the patrimony of the entire species—which in one way or another (as we see once again) will carry on its war against that barbarism often disguised as humanism.

Writing this pentagony, which I'm still not sure I'll ever finish, has, I confess, taken me many years, but it has also given a fundamental meaning to my life that is now coming to a close.

A Tongue Twister (13)

Delfín, a femme and a nonlesbian thespian defined by his finicky fussing—for instance, his dentures are fixed with Fixodent, not Fasteeth—was desirous of finishing himself off theatrically but found it difficult to fix on the most fashionable method, and he refused to finish himself off before finalizing every detail of his grand finale. Finally, frenetically gathering information for his decision and frantic at the prospect of finagling Ford Foundation financing for his project, he fixed upon defenestration. But Delfín's defenestration plan fell flat.

For Delfín Proust

The Condesa de Merlín

In the person and estate of María de las Mercedes de Santa Cruz Mopox Jaruco y Montalvo, Condesa de Merlín, were joined all the qualities needful for happiness, and indeed she was one of the most fortunate creatures on the island of Cuba in the nineteenth century. Her wealthy family possessed an enormous sugarcane plantation and sugar processing establishment—and (very important) a large company of slaves.

Even when she was but a girl, with that tenderness that is innate in children, María de las Mercedes de Santa Cruz Mopox Jaruco y Montalvo would arouse the sexual fires of all the male Negro slaves and compel them to possess her in the middle of the sugarcane fields. *J'aime fort les jeux innocents avec ceux qui ne le sont pas.* The erotic activities of the young girl not only became the stuff of scandal throughout the province of Matanzas, in which her family's estate lay, but also caused a decline in the family's sugar production. Throughout the length and breadth of those cane fields, one heard nothing but the child-Condesa's moans of pleasure and the cries (in Mandingo, Lucumí, and Carabalí) of the aroused black slaves who, machete in hand, fought for the possession of that still-child's body. There was not a single able-bodied black man in the entire slave population of the estate who had not possessed the young Condesa in the middle of the fields, their bed the soft young cane shoots and dry leaves. And pity the black man who refused to couple with the insatiable child. The aristocratic creature would intrigue against him so cleverly and so ably that the Conde and Condesa de Montalvo y Jaruco would soon clap him in the stocks and then hang him.

Yes, the Condesa's entrance into the cane fields wreaked terrible havoc. So much havoc, in fact, that her grandparents decided to send the child off to the famous convent in Santa Clara while her parents, their reputation in tatters, fled to Spain, their faces covered by a visorlike mask of black rock crystal.

Once shut away in the convent, the Condesa set about arousing the other girls, the nuns, and even the abbess. Such was the brazen lechery that the budding young lady unleashed among those cloistered women that at any hour of the night or day, all one heard in the convent were earsplitting shrieks and wails of pleasure, the product of their unprecedented—and unnatural—couplings. For not only did the Condesa practice the sin of Sappho with all the nuns and other females of the convent and couple with the farmhands in the surrounding countryside, she also had her way with the draft animals, the fowls, and not a few well-proportioned instruments of labor, even including holy staves and a cannonball that a mad nun escaped from a French community house for lay sisters had brought to the Santa Clara nunnery. All of these unholy partners and devices would inspire erotic shrieks from the Condesa and her crew, and at last led to such cackling and carrying-on that the Bishop of Havana, one Espada, sent an army to carry out a sacred, secret investigation, which he personally directed.

Within days the Condesa, who by now was a strikingly beautiful teenage woman, had corrupted the bishop. His army, meanwhile, sired children upon all the nuns, who immediately turned the convent into an orphanage. But soon the Condesa was denounced by the spiteful mother superior, Sor Inés, who could not bear to witness (without being invited to join) the Condesa's fevered lovemaking with the bishop in the middle of the baptistry. And so the Condesa was forced to flee the convent. (First, however, she had her revenge on the mother superior by setting fire not only to the convent but also to the entire barrio of Jesús María de Santa Clara, in which the religious house was located.)

From the convent the Condesa made her way on foot across the province of Las Villas and then Matanzas, coupling whenever she could with the campesinos and farm animals. And finally, as she masturbated with the walking stick belonging to a vagabond whom she had forcibly possessed beside the very walls of the patriarchal castle in Havana, she entered her family home exclaiming that she had decided to return—since the truth was, she experienced total pleasure only when she was being possessed by her great-grandfather, an aged nobleman shaped like a rat who (one must withhold nothing) had been sodomized by one of the Condesa's little feet when she was no more than five years old. The young woman's family held a council and decided that she had to be sent away, banished, expatriated—that is, sent to the house of her mother, the Condesa Leonora. In the years since she had last seen her daughter, the mother had been widowed; she was now living in Madrid, where she kept a literary salon that was at the same time one of the most famous whorehouses in all of Europe. She numbered the entire Spanish nobility among her clientele; even Louis XVI had once spent several nights of pleasure there, in the company of Charles III of Spain. But untitled hoi polloi also passed in procession through the whorehouse—and all, to a man, contracted a strain of galloping syphilis that so infected and degraded the population of the Peninsula that most Spaniards today are deformed, insolent, mongoloidal, stunted, thin-haired, big-assed and, in a word, sculpted with a sledgehammer. The noble Montalvo family, of our own beloved Cuba, have therefore left their inexpungible mark upon the entire race.

On her arrival at the Cortes in Madrid, the Condesa, who was but sixteen years old yet already skilled in exhibiting the splendors of her fair features, immediately overshadowed her mother, so that María Mercedes soon became the center of attraction of those *soirées* attended especially by the literary, religious, and high military crowd. Sometimes while someone was reading a sonnet by Garcilaso, a shot would be fired that would do away with a bishop or some dauphin from a distant kingdom, but the reading would go on imperturbably, for everyone knew that at the end of the artistic evening the naked Condesa would interpret the most difficult passages from *La Donna del Lago*. But just as the Negroes on the Conde's sugarcane plantation had been worn to almost nothing by the fiery young Condesa, so the entire population of Spain began to suffer from the young woman's erotic insistence—the men became indolent, effeminate, and weak, while the women fled to the coast of the Mediterranean, created another jargon even more horrid than Spanish, and began to dance the *sardana,* a dance which was no more than a pretext for leaning upon one another and not falling dead to the floor.

The Montalvo women, now lacking both men and women to service them in the many ways that they required servicing, began to conspire to induce the French to invade the Peninsula. The night that Napoleon's brother Pepe entered Madrid, he slept (where else?) at the Montalvos' house. The Condesa's fire spread through the entire French army, which, touched by that flame, burned Spain to the ground. Of course one must admit that many of the massacres committed by the army were due also to the incessant acts of treason committed by Francisco de Goya, who, brush in hand, would point to the nest in which the members of the nation's armed forces had taken refuge and then, when the bloodshed that he himself had inspired was sufficiently horrendous, would pack up his colors, go to where the events were taking place, and paint the catastrophes of war. In that sense, *Los fusilados del dos de mayo* is one of his most *original* works, in every sense of the word.

But let us return, my dear astonished fairies, to the adventures of our own Cuban Condesa. After having her way with virtually the entire armed forces of France, María de las Mercedes became even more seductive, and in her face glowed even brighter the light of chastity that made her so irresistible. One night her mother, leaving Napoleon's bed, sent for her daughter.

"María, the King wishes to see you married."

"Married? Impossible. It is the King that I wish to marry."

"Mercedes, he is not the man for you. Look." And with no further ado, the elder Condesa de Montalvo pulled back the spread that covered José Bonaparte's good parts and he lay naked before María Mercedes, who was shocked at the insignificant size of his member.

"So that's why they call him the *Little* Napoleon," she said, disillusioned. "All right, then, I'll agree to marry another man, under the condition, of course, that he give me his consent to sleep around on him. Who is he?"

"General Merlín, a cold, severe count, who only sleeps with his private guards. You shall meet him soon."

"First I want to meet his private guards. I refuse to make a bad marriage."

"My dear daughter, one sees that you are the fruit of my womb. I knew that you were going to make that request."

And instantly Leonora Montalvo (whose *nom de guerre* was Teresa) clapped her hands together several times in the Andalusian manner and a hundred stunning, well-built men in jerkins and tights appeared in the room where King Joseph lay sleeping.

"I'll marry Merlín tonight," exclaimed the Condesa as her mother extinguished the lamps, the candles, and the candelabra.

That very night María Mercedes married General Merlín, and by the men of his guard she had a baby girl to whom, in homage to her mother, she gave the name Leonor. And with that union, María de las Mercedes de Santa Cruz became the Condesa de Merlín.

In early 1812 the Spaniards awoke from their syphilitic stupor and instantly tried to boot us out, my dear Leonor, raping women, men, and children who had been destined for myself. We were forced to flee Spain, for as the wife of General Merlín I was part of the court of King Joseph, who could not bear to live apart from us. And so, in the midst of a terrible fog of gunpowder, the thunder of cannons, and the unbearable heat of that summer of 1812 we crossed the Peninsula. And as though that were not sufficiently frightful, the Spaniards were shooting to kill. In addition, I had to nurse my own daughter, your sister Teresita, while being ogled lasciviously by the soldiers, clerics, and counselors of state whom at such a critical pass I could not satisfy. In Aranjuez, my mother died and we buried her in the dust produced by our coaches and horses as we continued on. This was not so much a caravan as an entire city, heaped with scorn and opprobrium, cast out by merciless fate and fleeing to foreign lands. The soldiers were burning with thirst, although I would sometimes console them by allowing them to nurse at my breast. The journey lasted so long that in the course of it I became with child and at last gave birth. This child was a boy, the son of several Breton halberdiers. With my two small children under my arm I marched onward through the smoke and fire, bullets whistling over my head. I thought that I should die, and sometimes had to exercise great control in order not to throw myself before the grapeshot and end my life once and for all. But there are two selves within me, constantly at war—one weak and the other strong. I try always to stimulate the stronger, not because it is the stronger but rather because it is the most wretched, the self which manages to obtain nothing. . . . And so we came, after a year of wandering, to *la belle* Valencia. In that city I experienced one of the greatest disappointments of my life. My confessor, after violating me from behind, ran off with Casimira, my maid, and they took with them my jewels. I shall never forgive this outrage, for I have ever been an honest woman. While my husband was in camp with the King and his escort, I set about working the streets of Valencia, which teem with the cleverest whores on earth. And yet I made a small fortune and could at last flee from Valencia in the custody of twenty-five soldiers (and what soldiers!) under the command of Captain Dupuis, Lieutenant Diógenes, and Sergeant Albert, always at present-arms. We came to Zaragoza, where the war was at its fiercest. Anywhere one turned, there were shells and shot flying through the air, and the army was bombarding the city.

And so we had to flee that city also. But before leaving, I decided to visit the tomb of the famous lovers. And so, somewhat calmed, in the midst of that incessant bombardment, and with my two children under my arm, I escaped to Paris. This was the spring of 1814.

No sooner had I come to Paris than my beauty, my literary talent, and my voice earned me great fame. Neither Cuban nor Spaniard nor Frenchwoman, though mastering all those cultures and their horrors, I had that air of worldliness, of *savoir faire* and scornfulness, that is the property only of one who belongs not to this world and therefore cares little about any of the things it holds. With some of my own capital and a loan given me personally by the Emperor, I opened an elegant salon at number 40, rue de Bondy. My salon was visited by Rossini, the Persianis, Alfred de Musset, the Countess de Villani, Mlle Malibran, Goya, George Sand, Balzac, the Viscount Chateaubriand, Mme Récamier, Fray Servando Teresa de Mier, Simón Bolívar, the Empress Joséphine, Martínez de la Rosa, Chopin, Liszt, and other personalities, for whom I sang. We had more than a hundred fifty years of artistic successes. I sang in the Théâtre de l'Opéra de Paris; accompanied by Strauss I sang on the Champs Elysées; I sang with Malibran in Florence's grand Piazza della Signoria, where even the statues of the gods were so moved that they became sexually aroused by my person; I sang Bellini's *Norma* in 1840 in Havana in the grand hall of my paternal palace, where the lamps showed me to such advantage that I was more enchanting than ever and the Negroes once again were fired to stimulate me with lascivious caresses. . . . Each time there was a grand disaster, I would sing, and so my nobility rose ever higher. I sang for the Greeks after the great earthquake; I sang for the Poles after the insurrection; I sang for the benefit of the inhabitants of Lyons at the flooding of the Rhône; in 1931 I sang for the people of Martinique when that terrible earthquake devastated their poor country. . . . *Partout où il avait une grande infortune, je travaillais à la soulager. . . . Et oui,* sometimes my husband, with the aid of his troops in Europe, would turn a river from its course and bring on terrible flooding, or cause an earthquake, or collapse a bridge or burn an entire city so that I might sing for the benefit of the victims of the catastrophe. The methods might be thought to be somewhat harsh, but the consolation of my voice would assuage every calamity suffered by the survivors. Such an expression of transport would come upon the faces of the victims when I sang the famous duets from *Semiramis* or some passage from *Norma* that all the disasters caused by us were justified by their ecstasy.

With her acceptable voice; some literary fame (though it must be said that almost all her books were written by Prosper Mérimée); a rich husband; a powerful and well-educated lover to whom the Condesa gave a fortune that did not belong to her; her own army, which she deployed in her bedchamber; wonder-working physicians who performed unending operations on her—with all these things (plus beauty) María de la Mercedes de Santa Cruz had been welcome in the salons of Paris for a century and a half. In Spain, she'd been awarded the medal of Isabel la Católica, undoubtedly for all the havoc she had wreaked there; she had been given the French Croix d'Honneur, undoubtedly for having introduced syphilis into every Parisian *palais;* during this century, she had received the Nobel Peace Prize, undoubtedly for having been one of the staunchest promoters of World War I; she had also received the Nobel Prize for Literature, specifically for those novels she'd never written. No shadow seemed to cloud the present brilliance that the Condesa was enjoying, or the shining future that Madame Cassiopeia (escaping for ten minutes from the snares of Inaca Echo) had foretold for her on the Ile de la Cité. . . .

Oh, my dear Leonor, but in 1959, beside Lac Léman, as I danced a cavatina before more than a hundred sexually aroused Turks (with the Shah of Iran at the piano, my dear), there erupted in my native land a Communist revolution, and like a bolt of lightning, there descended upon Paris one of the most fearsome faggots on the face of the earth. The name, my dear Leonor, of this fairy sprung from the Negro race and of mendicant origins was Zebro Sardoya, though all the world knew him as Miss Chelo. This satanic being who had done me such great harm was born on the flatlands of Camagüey in the midst of green cane fields. From the time he was a young man, his passion was for the black cane cutters, but since he possessed not a single silver *real,* which was the price for every Negro whether Haitian, Cuban, or Jamaican, the above-mentioned Zebro (now Miss Chelo) would set about masturbating himself with the stalks of sugarcane. Oh, my adored daughter, it pains me to say this, *mais je dois toujours dire la verité*—so powerful was the anal fire of this creature that the sugarcane stalks, entering his backside, would instantly melt, becoming sweet cane juice. And in this way he razed a number of sugarcane plantations. Sometimes the juice from an entire carload would be squeezed out by Miss Chelo before the ox-driver could lash him with his whip. So widespread did this depraved creature's fame become that soon the king of sugar of the entire island of Cuba at the time, the fabulously wealthy Señor Lobo, hired him as a one-man processing plant for one of his largest stands of cane. My god, daughter! I still have a letter (one of many) from the Dowager Duchess de Valero in which, in that wealth of detail that is hers alone, she recounts one such bout of processing in one of Señor Lobo's fields. Miss Chelo (whom as I said above was in fact Zebro Sardoya) got down upon all fours atop the platform under which the carts and wagons piled high with stalks of sugarcane would be unloaded, and as the stalks were taken from the carts they would be introduced into Miss Chelo's anus by wonderfully dexterous Negroes. The yield, she reports, was enormous; in a single day Miss Chelo would process two hundred acres of sugarcane. Señor Lobo's fortune grew even greater, he bought even more land, and he multiplied the number of his sugarcane-processing operations—in which the portable cane press was none other than Miss Chelo. Señor Lobo was one of the most important figures during the years of the Republic, and Zebro became his right arm (or, more precisely, his anus). But when the Revolution triumphed, the first thing the victors did was expropriate the ill-gotten properties of Señor Lobo, who had been denounced by the Anglo-Campesina in her newspaper *Agitación*. There was also a desire on the part of some to imprison Miss Chelo for agricultural corruption, but he flew away (tinkerbell that he was) and landed here—*ay!*—to my eternal misfortune. Now, my adored one, I shall let the narrator take over this account, for I, as the Princess Clavijo said, cannot go on. Not even the knowledge that one day long ago I was the true queen of Versailles can any longer console me. Nor the knowledge that once the castles of Dissais, Chamblois, and Charenton belonged to me; that once I owned a calash, a coupé, and a carriage with wheels of silver; that mine was the most refined pimp in all of Europe, and charged the most for our services of any man in France; that I danced with Napoleon on the day of his coronation; that my portrait was painted by Mme Paulinier (a painting which won the prize at the Grande Exposition de Paris in 1836); that I was raped by six engineers on a train bound for Baden-Baden; that I have been awarded all manner of titles, honors, and medals; that Eva Perón asked me for political advice on the running of her national bordello; that on a sailboat I spent forty-five unforgettable nights in the company of Fanny Esler—nothing, nothing of that, my daughter, can raise my spirits now. *Je suis effrayée comme un oiseau dans la plaine pendant l'orage. Car je n'ai pas d'abri.* I leave this dance that is my life and all that it contains of futility, brilliance, delight, and hope—but first I wish to express to you my thanks for having listened to me and for your letter of the thirtieth. And I leave you with the story of my tragedy in the hands of my rustic chronicler. Adieu, my beloved one. . . .

All right, then, returning to the caprices of that crazy old nymphomaniac, let's pick up the thread of her story: Yes, in 1959 Zebro Sardoya arrived in Paris—a dreadful, conceited, willful, scheming faggot with an urge to triumph in the City of Lights. Naturally, seeing that he had no talent and that his only weapon was his cane-squeezing backside, he found himself a place as a maid and also started working the streets. While he was sucking off Arabs he would steal their wallets and then pay them five francs for the blow job, usually clearing fifty francs or so; while he was sweeping the floors of the Camachos' *palais* and Princess Hasson's castle with his tongue, he would steal the drapes and à la Scarlett O'Hara make himself gorgeous frocks that he'd wear to the Place Pigalle, dressed as a rumba-dancing negress, to cruise the Japanese diplomats and Bushman ambassadors.

One Sunday while she was fornicating under the Pont Neuf in exchange for a rotten fish, a decrepit old man of Malaysian origins passed by. Though it's hard to believe, the old man (perhaps because he was almost blind) fell head over heels for the ex-sugarcane-squeezer and invited her to the Café Flora (the intellectual center of Paris) for a drink. The Camagüey roué(e)'s eyes (and every other part) lighted up. The fearsome Malay, known throughout Paris as the Mummy (at the time he was about ninety years old), had made a fortune during the Hitler years by turning in Jews, thousands of them; he would be sent the skins of his victims and would use them to manufacture the shades of table lamps that he sold wholesale to Herr Kurt von Heim. When Hitler was destroyed and World War II ended, the Mummy decided to adopt French citizenship, and of course also take on a hundred-percent French name. As for Zebro, that very night in the Café Flora the genocidal Malay, intimate friend of Jean-Paul Sartre, bestowed upon him the name Miss Chelo.

Miss Chelo, an irrepressible exhibitionist, was passionate about *bel canto* and (as a literary hack) about literature. The Mummy just *happened* to be the owner of a large publishing house in Paris, which meant that Chelo, with a quantity of flattery, affectation, humiliation of some, gratification of others, and cocktail parties that must have cost a fortune, had soon put the Condesa de Merlín in the shade, at least in the literary department. Through sophisticated international networking (conspiracy) she soon grew famous, and even won a number of prizes. As for *bel canto,* her singing teachers were Mario of Monaco, Marcelo Quillèvere, Tebaldi, Maria Callas, and Luciano Pavarotti, and although her voice was still that of a cricket and her body that of a hippopotamus struck in the head by lightning, when she was fitted with a complex mechanical apparatus that extended her register she sang at the Théâtre de l'Opéra in Paris, at La Scala in Milan, and at the Metropolitan Opera in New York. Her quavering notes were even to be heard at Chiesa di Dante. And as though *that* mechanical enhancement were not enough, the Queen of Camagüey got herself a ruinously expensive plastic cunt with which she seduced the most refined ladies of French politics and culture. This cunt had the advantage of being portable and easy to disconnect, so when she wanted to seduce a prominent man, the faggot undid the cunt and with a good deal of grudging willfulness made use of her natural member, which, her being Negro and all, was not small. On other occasions, of course, as with the ambassador from Yugoslavia, the Vatican press secretary, and the King of Equatorial Africa, she used her ass, which, as we have previously noted, was incalculably powerful. China, India, and the Arab world were seduced by her tongue. Through the French Jews she controlled all French radio; through the Muslims, television; and since she was an intimate of Khaddafi she gained control of the press through terror. For just as when faced with a woman she would become a woman to seduce her, and with a man he would become a man and screw him, so, depending upon the circumstances, s/he would be Muslim, Jew, Christian, Tibetan, pagan, Spiritist, animist, Brahman, Buddhist, Yoruba, Shi'ite, or atheist. . . . I tell you, Mary, that fairy was *amazing*—singer, orator, writer, Benedictine, schemer, lecher, and agent of any country that would stoop to flatter her hypertrophied ego. All-fucking-powerful and more—at last Zebro Sardoya, the horrid creature, once an impoverished and illiterate country girl, came to control the smoke-filled rooms and most prestigious salons of France, and of the entire terraqueous globe.

The poor Condesa de Merlín woke up one day and found that she was being increasingly overshadowed, forgotten, vilified, erased from the map (there was even a rumor that she had contracted AIDS), reduced to *nothing* by that shameless fairy who one day would be courting the head of the CIA and the next jerking off the Cuban ambassador to France. It was at this point that the Condesa de Merlín determined to over-overshadow that horrid Miss Chelo. To do so, she enlisted the aid of the great-granddaughter of Mary Shelley to fabricate two wise and *wonderful* queens, Miss AntiChelo and Miss SuperChelo, who would outshine the arriviste interloper. These lovely creatures would also have the power of ubiquity, so that they could be in both Singapore and Fifo's palace, or a men's room in Tanzania, simultaneously. But precisely because she was so wonderfully mediocre in every respect, it was Chelo who was currently in vogue, and therefore she continued to sail from one triumph to the next.

When Chelo heard the reports about the Condesa's pirated editions of her mediocre self, she sued her in the French courts. As punishment for the Condesa's crimes, the nation of France confiscated all her castles and turned them over to Chelo, who in addition had poisoned the Mummy and taken over his gigantic publishing house. My lord! That devil (or *she*-devil) Chelo's realm now extended from one bank of the Seine to the other. The Condesa, who had neither the stomach nor the power to counteract the evil fairy's twinkledust, at last gave up the fight, and in a single day her two hundred ten years (exactly) of life came crashing down upon her. *Qui peut calculer combien d'amers douleurs, combien d'immense desolation peut supporter le coeur humain.* And suddenly a terrible homesickness for her native land, as strong as her hatred for her adoptive land, came over her. *No!* she said to herself, looking at her skeletal figure in the mirror. *Not here! I shall not be buried here! That Chelo creature is capable of organizing my funeral and even singing naked at my mass. I'll die as far as I can from that faggot—I'll die in my own palace, singing within the walls of the mansion I was born in. Yes, it may be my swan song, but I'll sing it in the place that is my own, surrounded by loved ones, or at least by accomplices.* And without further ado, the Condesa sold the few pieces of jewelry she still owned; liquidated her fake Picassos, her portrait painted by Paulinier, and her former house on the rue de Bondy; bought a sailboat and a gig (which she loaded on board the sailboat); put on the same gown she had worn for her visit to her native land in 1840; and, entrusting herself to the waves and winds, set off for Havana with a little orchestra that would accompany her during her last soirée. She'd already sent a telegram to Fifo, announcing her imminent arrival.

And so in midsummer of 1999, the Condesa de Merlín sailed for a second time into Havana harbor. There was so much hullabaloo and confusion in the city on the occasion of the official festivities that everyone thought this old woman in nineteenth-century dress who sailed into the harbor on a sailboat accompanied by an orchestra had to be a special guest (some wise woman from the Orient, some glorious transvestite, perhaps Miss Chelo himself) invited by

Fifo to take part in the Carnival parade. And so it was that the Condesa de Merlín rode through Havana in her smart gig, accompanied by her escort of Versailles-esque musicians, arriving, to the ovations of Negro lowlifes and screaming queens, at the home she had been born in. She entered, followed by her French orchestra, and found herself in her former palace, now converted to a gigantic men's room. At the spectacle of this monster urinal, she had but two options: die on the spot or sing. Never less than resolute, she chose to sing, and since she knew that this was to be her last concert, from her throat there emerged the highest, sweetest notes that she had ever sung. Her voice was that of an angel, and, accompanied by the orchestra (which rose to the occasion by playing as brilliantly as the singer sang), it echoed and re-echoed in the gigantic men's room. The men, cocks in hand as they peed at the urinal troughs, stood entranced by that *grande dame* whose singing moved even the walls and ceiling of the decaying mansion to tears. And thus when the Condesa, with one of her aristocratic gestures, asked the peeing audience to join her in her song, every one of those glorious men, still peeing, joined in, producing the most extraordinary musical event in the history of *bel canto.* A thousand men, as they urinated, accompanied the old Condesa's high, crystalline voice, as did the orchestra, which produced never-before-heard arpeggios and theretofore-unsuspected harmonies. No other *Norma* will ever achieve the heights of perfection, harmonic complexity, and dramatic depths breathed into it that night by María de las Mercedes de Santa Cruz in that monster men's room. The magic flooded every inch of the palace; the Condesa de Merlín had triumphed yet again.

There was, however, one person unmoved by her singing, one person who, furious, outraged, stalked out of the building—for she'd lost the phallic prey that had been about to touch her lips. And that person was Eachurbod, who, Volume XXV of the *Complete Works of Lenin* in hand, flew like greased lightning past the Condesa and emerged, a fiery ball of rage, into the bustling street.

Impossible Dreams

I dreamed of an enormous castle that I lived in with my whole family, and in every room loved ones did trivial, familiar things.

I dreamed of a pair of comfortable shoes.

I dreamed of a cataclysm.

I dreamed of a big, sweet, manly black man, just for me.

I dreamed of a field of cape jasmines.

I dreamed of a bench alongside the ocean where I'd go in the evenings and just sit.

I dreamed that the bus I was waiting for always came on time.

I dreamed of being a teacher.

I dreamed that I had a sculptural (or at least acceptable) body, not these shriveled, fallen breasts.

I dreamed of an enormous balloon pulled by all the grackles in Lenin Park, and I would ride inside the balloon and travel far, far away, so far away . . .

I dreamed of having the same husband for a long time.

I dreamed of having a son who wasn't gay, but a big strong carpenter or bricklayer.

I dreamed of a typewriter with an Ñ.

I dreamed I wasn't bald.

I dreamed I had a nightmare—I lived in a janitor's closet in the Hotel Monserrate, and while people kept their eye on me and watched me, I kept them under surveillance too. And when I woke up I saw that the nightmare was true, so I tried to dream that I was dreaming.

I dreamed of reams and reams of white paper that I could write a novel on.

I dreamed of an almond tree growing in front of my house.

I dreamed that a naked angel came and carried me away.

I dreamed that you didn't have to have a ration book to buy salt.

I dreamed that I was young and healthy and that there was an overgrown lot across the street from my house where horny recruits hung out waiting for me.

I dreamed that I turned on the faucet and there was water.

I dreamed of a city like the one I lost, but free.

I dreamed of avenues and broad tree-shaded promenades.

I dreamed of a huge country sort of house with a palm-thatch roof and a zinc-roofed breezeway that the rain made a loud noise on.

I dreamed of a Chinese-made electric fan.

I dreamed that Lezama and María Luisa were in a big room and they called me and when I went over to them Lezama was saying to María Luisa, *Look how good he looks.*

I dreamed of a pair of comfortable false teeth.

I dreamed that somebody was knocking on the door. I opened it, and there stood a smiling young man, all hot and ready.

I dreamed of a pressure cooker.

I dreamed of a river with green water that said to me, *Come, come, here lies the end of your desires.*

I dreamed that I was going far, far away, and when I got far, far away I could still keep going far, far away . . .

I dreamed that a plague as terrible as AIDS could not be true, and that pleasure did not entail disaster.

I dreamed of the smell of the sea.

I dreamed that all the horror of the world was a dream.

At the Exit to El Morro Castle

When, after serving his two years' sentence in the prison at El Morro, Skunk in a Funk took his first steps into freedom, he found his mother waiting for him with an even more pained and grief-stricken expression on her face than usual and a new shirt and a sack full of gofio in her hands. (He hated gofio, and always had—it was nothing but sweetened cornmeal, it tasted like sugar-laced sawdust, and it turned to mud and stuck to the inside of your mouth.) A wave of indescribable pity came over Skunk in a Funk when she saw her mother standing there with that faded, heavy sack.

His mother, weeping, said: "I came to get you so you'd come home with me to Holguín. Sooner or later you're going to have to do it, so I think you should get it over with. It's the only way out that's left for you."

Suddenly all the pity that Skunk in a Funk (and Reinaldo and Gabriel) had felt for the mother turned to fury—fury at life, at El Morro Castle, at himself, and at his mother. And so, turning to her, he replied:

"Mother, after I've lived for two years in a castle, don't think I'm going to live in a hovel in Holguín. As long as I can remember, the only thing I ever wanted to do—and finally actually did—was get out of that town, get out of that awful house, get away from you, and now my plans are to get out of the country. I'm not going to live forever, and the time I have to live, I want to live somewhere besides here. So I'll be seeing you."

And Skunk in a Funk turned her back on his mother and started walking away as fast as he could. When he'd got more than a kilometer away, he turned and saw the figure of his mother standing on the esplanade before El Morro Castle, sack in hand. That's the way I'll remember you for the rest of my life, Skunk in a Funk said to himself, moved, and he even thought for a second about going back and embracing her, but then he took off running toward East Havana, where some enormous black men were tossing a ball into the air across the street from an improvised basketball court.

That night, Skunk in a Funk slept in the open, on the boulders in East Havana. The next morning, starving, he got in touch with the Brontë Sisters and found some shelter in Lenin Park. Lenin Park was an enormous craggy stretch of sandy ground turned suddenly, on a whim of Celia Sánchez, into a park. Unbelievably, at a word from Celia (with Fifo's backing, of course), that wasteland to the south of Calabazar became an oasis, with enormous trees, a dam that made a lake in which they'd installed a floating stage before an amphitheater (where day and night Joan Manuel Serrat sang), and even eight or ten plywood vendors' stands where you could buy, in unlimited quantities (a thing unheard of anywhere else in Cuba), anything from a glass of milk to a slice of cream cheese and some soda crackers. Lenin Park became a mecca for all the queens in Havana and for any recruits who wanted to screw a fairy out in the stands of reeds—all that without counting the high muckety-mucks in their Alfa Romeos who came to dine at Las Ruinas, a restaurant designed by Coco Salas herself, under the aegis of Celia. There you could also see all sorts of foreign tourists and the most sophisticated hookers (dressed head to foot in white) who would come to the park to pick up Greek sailors and carry them to the tearoom. In other words, my dear (by the way, have *you* been to Lenin Park yet?), that hot spot with its lake and its dam that had to be fed by a whole system of pipes and turbines—thereby depriving all of Havana of water—had become the coolest spot in all of Cuba.

It was there, then, that Skunk in a Funk took refuge, knowing that he'd not lack a place to sleep, trees to stroll under, and even a lake to bathe in, not to mention soldiers to devour and food that the Brontë Sisters would religiously bring him in exchange for the Skunk's listening enthusiastically to their latest works of literature. He also pretended to be "rehabilitated," and to prove it, he started pulling weeds up with his hands.

Naturally, after several weeks of Leninary life, Skunk in a Funk, accompanied by the Brontë Sisters (who were careful to walk at a distance of fifty yards from him), showed up at his Aunt Orfelina's house, but all his aunt had to do was open the door to the ex-jailbird fairy (whom she herself had reported as a counterrevolutionary queer) and she turned fiery red with patriotic outrage and threatened to call the police if he ever so much as walked down her street again. The diabolic aunt, covering her face with one hand in a sign of shame, slammed the door with the other hand while Chucho, her husband (being sodomized by the Key to the Gulf at the time), fired several shots into the air with the pistol that the Party had authorized him to carry, just in case of a national emergency.

Accompanied by the ever more nervous Brontë Sisters, Skunk in a Funk returned once more to Lenin Park. *These trees are apparently going to be my grave,* he said to himself on entering Celia Sánchez' woods once more. The Brontë Sisters opened their huge sacks and took out a number of huge notebooks, and they began to read aloud—novels, short stories, poems, plays, songs, autobiographies, and long essays. . . . *No, I was wrong. This wood is not my grave,* Skunk in a Funk said to himself as one of the Brontës read a thousand-page poem, *it's my hell, the hell that awaits us before and after death.* Yet the Skunk had to listen to those infinitely monotonous compositions because it was the Brontës who kept him supplied with cream cheese, chocolate, and soda crackers, not to mention other more humdrum sorts of victuals. Plus, where was a nonperson stamped for the rest of her life as an ex-criminal going to find bread and shelter? Ay, the poor fairy stretched out on the Leninist grass and listened to the droning of that infinite reading. One of the Brontë Sisters

(Simón) was working (tirelessly) on a novel titled *La perlana,* and although he'd already gotten to page 5237, that number was absolutely provisional, since on any given night it might be swollen by more than two hundred pages more. He wandered Havana with the immense novel under his arm and whenever he bumped into a friend (or distant acquaintance) he would greet the person with this question: "Want me to read you a chapter from *La perlana?*" And although Simón would start reading, he'd never come to a stopping place, so his detainee would finally have to flee. In time, the youngest Brontë's need to read people a chapter of *La perlana* became so pressing that he started stopping absolute strangers in the middle of the street or going up to passengers on the Number 69 bus to read them a chapter of his novel. But so dreadful was this unpublished text that soon it became famous throughout Havana, and its fame even spread to the provinces. All it took was for the youngest of the Brontë girls to appear in a park somewhere or stand in line at a movie or get on a bus, and a stampede (in the opposite direction, of course) would follow. Before the innocent-sounding yet desperate question "Want me to read you a chapter from *La perlana?*" there would be mass exoduses, clandestine escapes in boats or by swimming (with pursuit by Bloodthirsty Shark). There had even been a number of suicides. Why, even the Brontë Sisters' poor mother had hanged herself one night when there was a full moon and a chapter from *La perlana* was echoing and re-echoing through her wooden house, while the father, his eardrums burst, went off to become a charcoal-maker in the Zapata swamps. But totally oblivious to the disasters that they set off (it wasn't *just* poor Simón's fault), the Brontë Sisters kept on determinedly writing. And even more so now that they finally had a real reader, a captive reader, the sort of reader who, as in the cigar factories or prisons of the old days, was forced to sit quietly and listen to the voice that read the yawn-inducing text. Nor was it just a *chapter* from *La perlana* that Skunk in a Funk had to listen to every day—it was hundreds of big unending notebooks full. Pedro (the oldest of the girls, and the leader of the family group) would come to Lenin Park, settle his enormous backside onto a rock (which would disappear under his buttocks), and in a voice that seemed to issue from an amphora, would announce: "I am going to read from *The Boy and the Sea Horse.*" And he would wander off into lord knows what sinister labyrinths of lyricism in which a beautiful rosy child (Pedro himself, idealized) was pursued by an evil sea horse than never, unfortunately, managed to put an end to him. After that inconclusive reading, the remaining Brontë (Pablo) would rummage in her bag and produce a poem of only ten thousand lines of rhymed couplets in homage to Cassandra. *Cassandra Forever*—that was the title of the still-unfinished poem. And apparently it *was* forever that Skunk in a Funk was going to have to sit and listen to the cracked voices reading Cassandra, the sea horse, or the infinite chapters of *La perlana.* In the face of those cathartic outpourings, Skunk in a Funk opted for escape. (Always escape.) And he began to wander through El Vedado—discreetly, of course, since everyone knew that Fifo didn't allow vagrants in the city. Oh, except for the Cavalier de Paris, and only then because the Cavalier de Paris went around distributing leaflets titled *God, Peace, and Fidel*. . . . Ay, how many times, in order to survive, had the poor fairy Skunk in a Funk had to take shelter under the cape of the Cavalier de Paris (who, by the way, was Alejo Carpentier) and suck his member in order to put something in his stomach, even if only a few drops of semen.

And so it was that one day the fairy found himself trying to squeeze a few drops of semen out of that aged, noble writer who wandered the street incognito—when suddenly a neutered she-cat, also a lover of the male milk, slithered under the Cavalier's enormous cassock. She-cat and fairy fought a brief but furious battle, a violent exchange of meows, wails, howls, screams, scratches, and kicks—all of this between the legs of the poor old writer who, with those two wild beasts hanging on his testicles, began to run wildly up and down La Rampa shrieking curses in French. Finally, Skunk in a Funk, whose fury was greater than the she-cat's, took the animal by the scruff of the neck and threw her into the air. The she-cat, giving a death howl, fell at the feet of her owner, Helia del Calvo, who had been looking for her all over the city.

"No one has *ever* treated one of my cats this way," Helia del Calvo said to Skunk in a Funk.

"Lady," replied Skunk in a Funk, "I'd tear a *panther* to pieces, much less a cat, if it tried to steal my food."

And before the astonished eyes of Helia del Calvo, Skunk in an Funk picked up the moribund she-cat, disemboweled it with his bare hands, and devoured it.

"You're just the person I need!" Helia del Calvo exclaimed. "If you can do that to this cat, who's so fierce she's been making my life miserable for fifteen years, then you'll probably be able to cat-sit *all* my cats and find fish to feed them with. I have twenty-seven. Do whatever you have to do—I'll give you a place to stay and all the fish you can eat."

And so it was that Skunk in a Funk found himself living in Helia del Calvo's house on Calle Jovellar in central Havana. Helia was a dotty old woman who'd been the lover of Pichilingo, one of the comandantes who had been with Fifo in the Sierra Maestra. But since Pichilingo hadn't died in combat, he'd later been killed by Fifo himself, who's *never* been able to tolerate competition. Helia's grief at the terrible death of her lover (Fifo buried him alive) drove her mad, and she started picking up all the stray she-cats in the neighborhood and bringing them home with her. She also started picking up all the teenagers in the neighborhood and trying to bring them into her bed with her, too, but since all of them politely turned down her invitation, Helia finally gave herself over, body and soul, to her she-cats, which, lacking he-cats, would either try to screw anything they could find or simply writhe in crazed lust on the floor. To try to curb their sexual appetite, Helia had had all her she-cats neutered, and yet, alas, the neutering hadn't ended the animals' sexual hunger, and that made her very sad. Helia adored her she-cats because secretly, she herself was one. Feline, voracious, never satisfied, self-centered, vengeful, and diabolic, she had made up her mind to outlive Fifo, and had sworn to throw a dead she-cat into his grave. Her hatred and, of course, her cats were what was keeping her alive. The tyranny with which she ruled over the animals was terrible—she wouldn't even let them go out onto the balcony. Once when Helia opened the door to the balcony, two cats leaped out the door, jumped over the railing, and committed suicide. From that time on, the house was kept hermetically sealed, and since it was illuminated by powerful lightbulbs that added *kilowatts* of heat, the temperature inside hovered at somewhere around 123 degrees.

So it was to that house inhabited by twenty-seven lady-cats and one insane cat-lady that Skunk in a Funk went to live. Naturally enough, under those conditions the Skunk couldn't so much as *think* about taking out his notebook and writing his so-many-times-lost novel. All day long he had to stand in line at the fish shops to find food for those raving animals. When he would come back home, half dead, Helia would be waiting for him in her rocking chair beside the bed, on top of which twenty-seven cat bowls would be laid out.

The fairy would have to cook the fish for all those writhing, mewling, rubbing-up-against-him animals that made his life miserable. If Skunk in a Funk opened a drawer looking for a towel, with an earsplitting shriek a she-cat would jump out. If he opened the refrigerator to get a sip of cold water, a she-cat who'd climbed inside to cool off a little would scratch at his face. If he sat down in a chair he would squash a she-cat who'd "accidentally" rip the only pair of pants he owned and infect his hemorrhoids with her claws. When he went into the bathroom, the bathtub would be a writhing mass of lesbian she-cats making wild lesbian love. If he tried to walk around the house a little, the cats would get under his feet, roll over, and start writhing lasciviously, producing such moans and rowrs of cat misery that Skunk would have to stoop down and stick a finger in their cunts. At that, the she-cats, momentarily satisfied, would squeal in pleasure. "*What are you doing to my little cats?*" Helia would then cry from her rocking chair beside her bed. "Nothing," Skunk in a Funk would answer as he continued masturbating another bunch of she-cats slithering and writhing around him desperately.

Finally, unable to do everything he felt he had to do for the cats with his bare fingers (which were about worn to nubs), one day Skunk in a Funk swiped Helia del Calvo's toothbrush (which she never used), and began to deploy it on the desperate she-cats. Soon, the toothbrush became a sexual fetish for those poor animals—and *such* a fetish that when Skunk in a Funk was trying to brush his teeth one day a she-cat leaped, snatched it out of his hand, and ran with it to Helia del Calvo, presenting it to her and spreading her hind legs. Helia, nasty creature that she was, instantly figured out what was going on, and she went to Skunk in a Funk and said: "I'm so happy that you're being nice to my kitties and trying to satisfy them this way. From now on, while you masturbate them I'll read you little snatches from my autobiography. It's a text I've never read to anyone, but you—you're like a son to me. I give you permission to live in this house forever—under one condition. I won't allow you to bring men in here. Men *or* women. Just me and my kitties." And without further ado, Helia opened a thick notebook and began to read passages from her life story.

And that was the way that Skunk in a Funk's nights went from that time on. After standing in line all day for fish, at night he would sit on the bed and while Helia del Calvo read him her memoirs, Skunk in a Funk would grasp the toothbrush and masturbate all the she-cats.

One night, however, after reading Skunk in a Funk a long chapter about her sexual relations with Pichilingo, Helia, surrounded by she-cats and plates of fish, her feet propped up on the bed, fell asleep in her rocking chair. Skunk in a Funk, who couldn't take this anymore, sneaked out and went looking for a man. Fortunately, right around the corner in Maceo Park, just a few blocks from Calle Jovellar, he came across a young thug with huge boots (laces untied) and his shirt unbuttoned. Skunk in a Funk swiftly picked up the delicious hustler and with the cunning that is second nature to a queen, sneaked him into Helia del Calvo's house. In the living room, the lip-smacking-good young thug seized the chance (while Skunk in a Funk was peeking into Helia's bedroom) to cram into his open boot-tops several plaster figurines, a silver ashtray, and two porcelain teacups. Not for nothing did the Skunk's young friend wear such big butch boots. Fairy Skunk, unaware of this thievery (which didn't concern him anyway), meditated over how to get the young man into the maid's room that was back behind the kitchen. It wasn't easy, since to get to the kitchen they'd first have to go through Helia's room, and since the old biddy slept sitting up in the rocking chair with her feet propped up on the bed (which had been given over to the she-cats), there was no way (1) to get over her or (2) to slip between her and the bed. There was just one route left them—*over the bed.*

But Skunk in a Funk couldn't wait—she grabbed at the thug's fly (not noticing that now he was sticking all kinds of things into his pockets), unbuttoned it, and silently, frenziedly sucked for upwards of three minutes. Then, leaving the final mouthful (or assful) for when they were alone in the room behind the kitchen, she pulled away. "We've got to be really, really quiet," the fairy, trembling with delight, said to the thug, and taking him by the hand (while the kid tried to button up his pants) she began to lead him, very gingerly, across Helia del Calvo's bed. Top and bottom, holding hands, terrified and in silence, were crossing that bed as though through the straits of Thermopylae. The fairy jetéed like a ballerina freed from the bonds of gravity over to the other side of the bed. A few feet more, and she would be with her beloved. But just then the mouthwatering butch, also eager to screw the fairy queen (and steal all the dishes out of the kitchen), lost his footing and stepped on one of those damned she-cats (there was always a she-cat interfering in a fairy's love life!) that were sleeping alongside Helia's feet. The she-cat gave her standard ear-piercing cat-howl; Helia, who hadn't slept for at least ten years, woke up to find a thug wearing gigantic boots (and with his pants down around his ankles) on top of her bed attacking one of her adored kittens. The old biddy, enraged, gave a shrill scream (comparable only to the scream given by José María when Helio Trigoura hit him in the face with a bottle of maltine) and all the she-cats leaped as one at the butch young hunk—who, staggering, pants around his ankles, rolled down the stairs and out of the house, stolen goods scattering everywhere.

Skunk in a Funk, who knew what she was in for, pulled a sheet (reeking of cat piss) over her head and shot like a bolt of lightning over Helia del Calvo's bed, grabbed up all her things, (including the toothbrush he'd masturbated the she-cats with), and took off for Maceo Park. Even when she'd gained the relative safety of the park, Skunk in a Funk, never releasing her grip on that toothbrush (which of course did not belong to her), had to be afraid that Helia had called the police, so she sought refuge under the huge statue of that bronze titan Maceo who, machete in hand, forever bestrides his likewise bronze horse. But Jesus! What spectacle should meet the astonished fairy farmboy's eyes when he'd reached the shadow of the titanic horse but Hiram Prats, naked and on all fours, humping and writhing in frenzy under Maceo's horse's huge bronze cock! At one point the queen reared back against the bronze horsecock with such force that not only did he plunge the whole thing up inside him—he even managed to get the horse's balls into that gigantic Holguín ass. At that, the queen gave a shriek of pleasure and shot a long arc of cum. At the same time, another jet of cum issued from the statue of Maceo and hit Skunk in a Funk in the face. Naturally, she thought Maceo had just jerked himself off. *Maybe in my honor,* she thought proudly; she had a thing for Negroes.

"Don't flatter yourself, honey," Hiram, La Reine des Araignées, told her, pulling his ass off the horse's bronze phallus. "That cum isn't from Maceo, it's from Rubén Valentín Díaz Marzo, the Areopagite, a confirmed jerk-off who, by the way, is a great admirer of your work. While I was taking this horse dick, I had Rubén up there on lookout, in exchange for watching me get off. Rubén! Get down off that horse—Reinaldo Arenas is here!"

Farewell to the Sea

It was about that time (or was it before? or after?) that Skunk in a Funk had certain other adventures, but those belong to another novel.

José Lezama Lima's Lecture

Among the many events that had taken place in Fifo's palace, undoubtedly one of the most remarkable (and newsworthy!) was the Russian-roulette duel between Tomasito the Goya-Girl and the governor of Boston. Both men comported themselves like true heroes. Finally it was the governor of Boston who blew his head off, so it was Tomasito the Goya-Girl who received from Fifo personally the Fiftieth Anniversary Medal.

To the strains of "The Star-Spangled Banner," the governor of Boston's body was removed from the stage, and then several midgets bleated several cornets and Fifo stepped onto the stage once more to announce that the great writer José Lezama Lima, who had died in 1976 and been resuscitated especially for the Carnival by the magical hands of Oscar R. Horcayés, was going to give his last lecture—a lecture which, owing to its length and the prestige of the speaker, had been made a separate event from the Grand Oneirical Theological Political Philosophical Satirical Conference that was to take place later in the Grand Hall of International Conferences.

An expectant silence fell over the theater, as was only fitting for such a momentous event. After a dramatic pause, Oscar, using his gigantic wings, opened the curtains and onto the stage came, with slow, careful steps, José Lezama Lima, the revered author of *Paradiso.* He sat at the small table that had been placed there for him, drank down at one gulp the pitcher of water that a diligent midget had set out, pulled a handful of papers from his black bag, and, nodding in greeting to his audience, began to speak. These are the words he spoke:

My dear friends. Before I begin this lecture I wish to inform you that if I have decided to take my leave for a few hours from the realm of Proserpine where I have the good fortune not only to taste pleasures both Luciferian and Christian but also to enjoy the company of my mother and my wife, María Luisa Bautista—a woman whose life, like mine, was snuffed out by Fifo—Oh yes, I know that this denunciation might cost me my life, but since I have none, I don't give a fig whether I lose it or not—the reason for my decision is not that I dare not disobey the order of a fifth-rate dictator and his velvety intrigues or defy his Coryphaei with their membranous wings and sinister designs. No, I have come here, first, because I did not wish to miss the opportunity to witness this night on which so many heretofore unimagined things were to take place; second, because I wished to know in person

Madame Gertrudis Gómez de Avellaneda and Messieurs Juan Clemente Zenea and André Bréton, all reborn from the dead—as have been others—for this celebration; and third, because my lecture for you tonight is worthy of the raising of a dead man. I am that dead man, eager to see the friends who have not yet descended into the shadowy Moira . . . and now, *vade retro* to all those official devils, sprites, and demons who, filling the hall, writhe now in their seats or hide behind the faux-Japanese vases—I shall begin my reading.

For many years, an enigma as mysterious as the oracle at Delphi and the visage of the Sphynx, and as tempting as a Roman bath, has been for me an obsession during my most lucid moments. That enigma, which I have been able to unravel only in the calm of Hecate's mansion, can be summed up in the following phrase: HAD THAT YOUNG FLORENTINE GIOVANOTTO WHO POSED FOR MICHELANGELO'S DAVID JUST EJACULATED, OR HAD HE NOT? This question has obsessed scholars, specialists, and simple dilettantes of the *dolce stile nuovo* for hundreds of years.

To answer it, let us turn first to the Egyptians, whose prehistoric imagery was invariably phallic, and therefore germinative. In Egypt, the god of creation is portrayed in profile and wearing a purse; were he not, his potent phallus would dominate the entire fresco, and therefore it would no longer be so fresh a *fresco*, strictly speaking, but would become a hot-blooded *relief*. And then let us journey to the age of the harmonious Greeks, who venerated the triumphant phallus so inordinately, and yet so fittingly, that the erect male member was a god, the god Priapus, who rules our destinies to this day. Finally, employing as a springboard those ever-throbbing phalluses, let us leap into the heart of Christianity, to examine the era with none of the small-town piety that is customary in this case—that is, we shall put aside the sanctimoniousness of the Council of Trent and the histories of that Isabel the Catholic who was led by a lack of the fruit of Adam (we all know that Ferdinand was impotent) to commit atrocities against all those who worshiped the penetrant stalk whose nectar sweetens all things. *Cock*, ladies and gentlemen, to say it with Xenophontian clarity, or, if you prefer, the clarity of midday, as González de la Solana might put it.—Our theme shall be *cock*.

Because, dear friends, I would ask you to consider: What is Christianity and its greatest symbol, Christ our Lord, but the secret and therefore sacred worship of that corpus, ne'er infused by the grace of God, which is the phallus Nikē? We are moved by Christ because he has a phallus, and His body, human by reason of that phallus, hangs naked on the Cross, covered with an improvised wrapping which points to, rather than covers, the divine prepuce. The fragrance of that towel (a gift no doubt from the Magdalene), the fragrance of Christian balls and buttwipe, has Proustian reverberation. Here, the fragrance of that towel has the same power as that other *madeleine* (for it is Magdalenes of all types that we are discussing) exercised upon the young Proust when it brought back his entire erotic past, so that in the shadow of its savor and odor he might erect his *magnum opus*, *A la recherche du temps perdu*. The same power, yet different—for that brief Christian girdle, that towel which is the annunciation of that which is, so to speak, beneath the belt, yields up to us not some mere *novel*, but all of Western culture. The slender, naked body encircled by a severe band of cloth—that image which has obsessed so many, which has reigned on beaches, at swimming holes, at thermal baths, in films, and upon crucifixes is, without a doubt, the *summa* of the Christian tradition. Every young man with a towel laid across his groin, hiding yet promising the Adamic fruit, is a replica of Christ. The *imago phallico*, which has dominated virtually all pre- and post-Hellenic civilizations, is also the index, indicator, and *pointer* of our own. A young man thirty-three years old preaches love to the ecstatic apostles with a passion that makes his loincloth tremble. That is why—doubt it not, my friends—St. John, at the *Last Supper*, knowing that his Lord was about to leave him, could bear it no longer, and in the presence of the rest of the disciples fell to his knees before his Master's legs and under the tablecloth ingurgitated the serpent divine. Meanwhile, the Master was delivering a holy, venerable sermon—a double explosion of life to a single rhythm. That is why we, the devout, bow down to every young man (in allusion to Christ Himself) who modestly but irresistibly hides under a small knotted towel his pink, or bronze, or sable balls. . . . Hosanna! Hosanna! The divine dart, the shaft of life, shall always be there, before out emotion-stirred eyes. Now we know that the Gordian knot of our lives (that compulsive tragedy) can be cut if we but stretch out our arms and unwrap that towel under which lies the sweet, divine—yet human—Lestrigon. No matter who it is that wears the towel, he is part of the harmony of the spheres. In the delectation of that Lestrigon, in the arrow wounds it gives us, lie our redemption and our peace. To be penetrated by that dart—it burns us, and in burning heals us. That penetration may be a *metaphoric* hypostasis, yet it must be deep. The delight of believing oneself, *feeling* oneself, my friends, nailed by that arrow, penetrated, transverberated—that delight is the secret correlative of the holy act. Arrow, spear, pallium, candle, musket—all are priapic symbols which, as factotums, make the skin and backside tingle and bring on spasms of Christian faith and devotion. And so the spear that pricks the side of Our Lord, *qua* penetrant spear, imago of the great and yearned-for dart of flesh, brings on, under the towel He wore, a slight final temblor. At the exultation inspired by the imago, there springs forth the *toconema*. And with thanksgiving we receive the final arrow wounds that bring on the final shudder.

Let us enter the Scuola Grande di San Rocco (a place which the orders of that wretch Fifo have prevented me from ever entering) and observe, with the blossoming-forth of a night-slug and the voracity of a Tibetan daisy, the portrait of St. Sebastian painted by Tintoretto. As with every true St. Sebastian, the young body of the saint (like some pre-Attic discus-thrower) is naked, his formidable groin covered by a peremptory loincloth. But look how that cloth rises as the arrows penetrate the flesh. Two concurrent events make the Tuscan-fleshed and therefore irresistible saint (or the model for him), as he is pierced by the arrows, become aroused. First wonder, to a Rimbaudian thrumming of the dice upon the drumhead: the penetrant arrows (from the Latin *penis erectum*) produce in the man who receives them a sweet, voluptuous stinging sensation like that felt by the white mouse upon being bitten by a bear cub on the islands of Terranova. Second drumroll: we must not forget that the lad who poses for the arrow-pierced saint was a beautiful naked *giovanotto* standing under the voracious gaze of his Master. The fact of knowing oneself chosen and painted by Tintoretto—summa Gloria, my dear friends! Do not these things, then, justify in that naked youth the proud homage of the glorious erection of his phallus? I am certain that on more than one occasion Tintoretto had to interrupt his work at the easel, as all the Greek and Roman masters did, to deliver a veritable tongue-lashing on account of the undiplomatic interruptions of that capitoline promontory. Although the *giovanotto* no doubt was often pacified by the painter, we can see in the finished work the remnants of a Tower of Pisa swaddled in rags and protruding from the groin of the arrow-riddled youth. The realism of Life (that supreme delectation of unreality) emerges, as always, even at the very moment of our Death. St. Augustine erred, then, in complaining of the tragedy (the temptation) experienced by the Florentine masters when their models, upon being looked upon by the masters, were pricked by the angel of antsiness—for none of those dominics of wisdom tossed their inkstands, or their brushes, or a tubful of paint at the model (who might be a fisherman on the Arno), but, on the contrary, they went on, delighting in their pictorial occupations, despite (or inspired by) the sprouting of the holy bulrushes. Thus it was that Andrea del Sarto painted his San Giovanni Battista naked from the waist up, but camouflaged from navel to knees with all sorts of cooking pots, mantles, rocks, crosses, and even a gigantic ferret which, while it sat upon a rock and covered the lad's groin, nursed at the member of life. That opportunity, not scorned by the ferret, magnetized Andrea del Sarto's San Giovanni with that imperative, imperious modesty typical of a naked adolescent who while someone is sucking him looks at us with his big naughty innocent eyes as though supplicating us, and also commanding us, to participate in the feast.

That unique canvas, which has brought on spasms in not a few prominent marquises and even in Pope Pius XII, can fortunately still be admired in the gallery of the Palazzo Pitti, in Florence. . . . And what say you of that adolescent Bacchus by Caravaggio? This Bacchus—that is, this delicious Florentine rogue—had a prick so high-strung that even being one of the favorites of the Vergamasco family, his pyramid never found repose, not even with the good offices of Caravaggio. Finally, bags under his eyes, eyelids drooping, swaddled in layers of rags that hardly left a single victorious nipple exposed, the adolescent played a Bacchus with his legs pinned behind a table and with an enormous bowl of fruit before him, so that the marvelous *fata morgana* which opens all the communicating vessels would not arise, or at least would not be seen. Those models' erections, in a time when (like today) things could not be painted as they truly are, caused no Augustinian tragedies, but they did cause neuroses both aesthetic and emotional among the Florentine masters who, like all true artists, were lovers of the truth.

The problem, however, seemed to have been solved under the bloody Florentine dynasty of the Medici, who, devotees of the most *straightforward* realism, ordered that all statues and paintings be painted or sculpted totally nude, and with all the burgeoning splendor of their models. Thus the Piazza della Signoria of Florence contains a huge Neptune carved with great erotic genius, in which the glory of Orphism extends from the magnificent creases in the buttocks to the filigreed pubic hairs from which there emerges the Delphic mace that held sway over the entire rapt city. And let us not forget that thanks to those erect, pulsating, and naked maces that made the very wind of the Apennines moan, Florence had its Dante, Giotto, Leonardo, Michelangelo, and Botticelli, among other singular masters whose genius, and anus, were flooded by inspiration and inseminated with creativity.

When the skirmishes between the Guelphs and Ghibellines were ended, the potent families who held all power in their hands (the Pitti, the Frescobaldi, the Strozzi, the Albizi, and of course the Medici-Riccardi), claiming their independence from Rome, raised upon every bridge along the Arno statues of vigorous, virile, naked gods (who defied and struck fear in the old popes), their vital parts proudly lifted to the skies. The enemy, faced with those manifestations of magnetic power, would immediately surrender and fall to its knees. And so, where before had stood Urbino's Venus, who covered her sex with a modest hand, or Sandro Botticelli's other Venus, who tugged at her peplum so as to hide her cunt—though unable to hide an expression of sadness in her eyes—were erected a series of Moseses with rampant phalluses, Achilleses with imposing bulges, Apollos that stood upon a piazza and ruled the city with their formidable mandrels—warriors with defiant bulges, naked fishermen, their eyes closed, hunched over a rock and as they held aloft a golden fish revealing between their thighs the succulent treasure of their own delicious catch.

Amor and Psyche, sculpted by Canova, brought luster to Villa Carlotta—Amor with wings and quiver, but an erect arrow between his legs, aimed at Psyche. A naked Leda, legs upraised, openly copulating with the swan in the gardens of Florence and later in the Museo Nazionale. A naked Adam at the instant of his expulsion from the garden, and therefore still sporting an enormous erection, standing petrified upon the Florentine portico.

And thus the city was filled with handsome youths in marble, stony youths whose models still wandered through the piazzi—easy, delicious prey for all the city's painters. Famous in the history of sculpture is the Boy with a Sliver (whose first model must now be twenty-five centuries old), a servant lad who sits nude upon a rock and crosses one leg over the other in order to pull a sliver out of his foot while he shows those who are fortunate enough to have eyes to see that greater splinter that rests, though alert, upon two magical stones. . . . Worthy of all contemplation, praise, and enjoyment are the balls of the centaur by Botticelli, who came into fashion and after copulating with his own centaur, the Condotta family's draft horse, began to paint, as he had always wished, scenes of damsels and blooming adolescents with long ringleted hair who while they saluted their ladies peeked at each other out of the corners of their longing eyes. We should look for this same feature in the Madonna del Magnificat, painted in about 1510. But the matter, of course, did not end with languid looks. The portico of the Palazzo dei Lasquenete was teeming with phallic Hermeses and crouching thieves desperately gazing upon those rods, not knowing whether to grab them and make a run for it or swallow them down in one gulp. The fountains became filled with Neptunes with imposing dongs, surrounded in turn by dribbling and most graciously endowed demigods. The piazzi, palazzi, porticos, triumphal arches, woods, bridges, and even churches became filled with stunning Patrocluses, hyperaroused Achilleses, athletes tensed into penetrating poses, forever-naked gods with their all-consoling staffs on high.

A glistening erotic boar's tooth was certain to emerge from each of those monumental statues. Even one of Cellini's Perseuses, lance at the ready, waited, and still waits, for us before the doors of the Bargello, and a black Bacchus with a deliciously domesticated serpent awaits us when we cross the Ponte Vecchio, while panting Antinouses beg for our kisses in galleries and museums. The Salone dei Cinquecento in the Palazzo della Signoria, or Palazzo Vecchio as it is often called, where the nobility of Florence met to rule the city, was (and still is) surrounded by men with naked balls, some displaying irresistible erotic intentions, others engaged in daring sexual combat, such as Hercules and Diomedes—as Hercules holds a spread-legged Diomedes, his testicles and prick inflamed, Diomedes still more daringly grabs Hercules' twin manly orbs and phallus, while an Alcibiades with clenched ass and magnificent Etruscan pontoon observes the scene.

We should not be surprised that in such a city, in which the most beautiful young men had been reproduced in the nude and much larger than life-size, a virulent fever, a veritable epidemic, of male and female nymphomarmoreals should break out. At night, and sometimes in broad daylight, men and women would copulate for hours on end with the statues. Catherine dei' Medici was excommunicated several times by the pope for having been discovered on numerous occasions in the Piazza della Signoria impaling herself on Neptune's erotic trident. It is said that on more than one occasion Dante was hung by his servants from the enormous breasts of Giambologna's Sabine. And as for Lorenzo the Magnificent, he had such a desire to be possessed by the god Apollo that he stripped naked and backed into the statue located on the Ponte Victoria, thereby introducing into himself the divine attribute which drove Juana la Loca loca, yet toppling the statue from its pedestal, both man and god tumbling, still as it were *engaged*, into the depths of the Arno. Lorenzo was saved thanks to the skillful maneuvers of some fishermen, but the statue of Apollo remained at the bottom of the river, inflaming it to such a degree that its aroused waters overflowed their banks, flooded the city, and rose all the way to the tomb of Beatrice de Portinari. But the eros aroused by those naked men with their magical, enchanted wands not only impregnated the entire city (and the river), but also inflamed the very pigeons with lust. In flocks these birds would fly all over Florence and, desperate (the poet Zenea, present here with us tonight, will be able to confirm the case), bill and coo among the gigantic germinative orbs and peck at the magic flute. So overwhelming was the invasion of Florence by these winged creatures that since that day, in the language of the Tuscans every fairy is a pigeon, and Signora Medici-Riccardi, who found that there were so many birds that she was barely able to fornicate with the statues any longer, issued an edict which sentenced to death any *golondrina* that lighted upon those marmoreal ephebes. And since then, the pigeons, driven mad by their inability to peck the fruit of Adam, fly, shrieking, up into the sky and then dive headfirst into Giotto's campanile. Yes, they, like so many others, prefer death to a life in which they are forbidden to experience the dart of Eros. This suicidal event is the reason the Duomo is visited every spring by millions of tourists, who know that there will be plenty of fresh meat in both senses of the word. The flesh of the *pigeon* (pun intended, my dear friends) is, of course, a delicacy. And once more I turn for confirmation to the great bard Zenea.

Thus we see that the pinnacle of Florentine culture (or its *vita nuova*) was a *true* pinnacle, for it was a *phallic* pinnacle, a tribute to the god Priapus and a recognition of those who incorporated the serpent of the outside world into their own. Peace reigned in the Piazza della Signoria, and in the city as a whole, for more than two hundred years. Imagine an entire people being possessed by the most glorious gods, the strongest and most muscular athletes. Do you suppose they had time or motive for vain complaints against their neighbors? When una madonna or a country girl was not absolutely fulfilled by her husband or her lover (or by both), there, among the trunks of a little glade, she could find a magnificent Apollo waiting for her, his glistening boa always erect. And as for the country boy, the priest, the poet, and the melancholy prince, they might easily make their afflictions fly—all they had to do was wander into the woods a bit, and they could screw or be screwed by Hercules, or lift that purse they wore to cover their groin and back into a sword-wielding Perseus. The people laughed and sang thanksgivings to the staff that measures all and consoles all. Only the pigeons went on committing suicide, as did the crabs and turtles who, of course, were unable to climb the phallus Nikē. And who was that city screwing and being screwed by if not the city itself? Because who *were*, after all, those pagan gods, those heroes, those magnificent Biblical figures, if not the youths of the *popolo* who for a thousand lires would allow themselves to be painted *au naturel*? We can safely say that the great period of Florentine culture was an age of unparalleled equality because everyone lived in a democracy of the phallus.

In the midst of that erotic riot, Michelangelo, who had already decorated the Sistine Chapel for the pope, was hired by the rulers of the city to make a statue of David for the city, larger than life-size. The artist went to the Ponte Vecchio, and there he hired a *giovanotto* of slender build who might pass for the Biblical hero.

When they arrived at the studio, Michelangelo ordered the young man to remove his clothes while he himself unveiled a huge piece of marble brought down from the mountains of Siena. When the master turned around again, hammer and chisel in hand, he saw that his model had a veritable flamboyán tree, and that it was the season of flower. But as he was accustomed to seeing splendid bodies, he went on with his work. Nevertheless, as the great master, for purely professional reasons, continued to lay eyes—though nothing else—upon the young man, the young man gave signs of a tremendous length of phallus, which in fact grew longer with every chisel blow, as though the sound of the chisel on the stone were the pealing of some magical bell. The great sculptor gazed at that impressive show and discovered that the part between the shaft and the glans looked extraordinarily *dimesticable* (if I may be pardoned the Italian, but after all, we *are* in Florence) and that the length that extended in almost a straight line from the glans to the place where two cannonballs lay (as polished and rosy as strawberries from a Rabelaisian garden) was indeed considerable, even to the eye of a Florentine sculptor. The priapic rod, which perfectly reproduced the corporeal leptosomia of its owner, made the great master's eyelids flutter several times, but since he had a Biblical hero to carve, he went on with his chiseling. But the Florentine's python continued to uncoil. It was impossible to stop looking at it; it was also impossible to carve it, because a true Biblical hero, who in addition had just killed a man with his slingshot, was hardly the sort of person to exhibit that prodigious altar candle striving to butt its head into some dark humid grotto. In the first place, the master could not carve the figure of the *giovanotto* if the *giovanotto* could not find a more (let us say) relaxed pose; in the second place, one would have to possess the cruelty of an Ottoman to dismiss one model with that gigantic erect Aaron's rod and find another, less (shall we say) eager one. And so, leaning back against the virgin marble, the master looked once more, apart from any value judgment, at the Alexandrian lighthouse. The unquiet beauty of the youth was comparable only to that of a Greek warrior, spear raised, suddenly lost among the ranks of the Dalmatae and their cruel tumults. The master, across the room, fell to his knees. Then the *giovanotto's* penetrant tool began to oscillate, rising and slapping against his breast, with each blow producing the vibration of a glorious *campanum* pealing out the *Te Deum Laudamus*. With the epicurean calculation of a Pascal (though Pascal had not yet given any signs of life), the master advanced toward the deity in the manner of the Chinese or the Tibetan monks; that is, contrite and on all fours. When the master arrived at the enormous tree of life, a bituminous whirlwind issued from his mouth.

But he remained immobile in the shadow of the umbravit, the creator of infinite possibilities. The umbravit—that is, the rounded, angelic presence of that virgin adolescent—flooded over him. And it was an *invading* shadow. Umbravit: a Florentine pontoon which *blotted out the sun not with a finger but rather with its rosy glans. That shadow, like the apparition of a Potens, plus the circular, solar shadow of the adolescent balls, fell upon the face of Michelangelo, darkening it yet at the same time bathing it in celestial light. A wondrous relationship was silently forged between umbravit and the laboradit; that is, between that form delineated by the triumphal arc of balls and erect phallus (umbravit) and the titanic crepitations (laboradit) which emerged from the throat and tongue of the unexcelled fairy. The genius queen, now turned whimpering lamb, took shelter in the shadow of the phallic god, and as he leaped upward toward that monumental branch his chisel, his hammer, and a feather fell from him. This feather is part of the grand stew of Pythagorean cosmology, for in Aztec mythology the umbravit also acts by means of a white feather. That is, as Quetzalcoátl stood guard at the temple, grace was shown him in the form of a feather; he flew to it, picked it up, and with royal motions of his hands began to caress his sex and toucan's balls until he came, in a powerful ejaculation which was the cause of the great lake of the City of Mexico, today the dunghill for that great city. The Olympian orgasm complete, Quetzalcoátl placed the feather under his great serpent, now in repose. "Feathered Serpent"—such was the god's name. Feathered serpent there, and also here. Here, the playful pigeon feather, fairy feather, fluttering down upon the sweet dome of the Florentine prick; there, a reigning feather between the balls and serpent phallus of that Mexican god who, thanks to that feather, passed into the eternity of myth, and through the fragrance of the feather which came from the West foretold a great invasion, a terrible, destructive war, sensed the defeat, and spurred on the combat. And these theological and historical deeds were produced by the magnificent Achilles' heel of all fairies, the phallus. . . . At that instant the delicious giovanotto stepped forward, one hand on his hip, and, showing the same indifference as we see in a certain painting by Velázquez when the key to a city is presented upon a red pillow, deposited his phallus upon the red, cushiony tongue of Michelangelo, who in the presence of the literally palatable Priapic daemon became faint, as though struck inwardly by a tempest from Oceania, and at one gulp swallowed the magic cue with its enormous billiard balls.*

The master stuffed those gigantic balls into his mouth and then sat back on his heels and nipped and bit at them as methodically and swiftly as a squirrel in New York's Central Park plays with a walnut before leaping with it up into its dark lair. And that was precisely what the great sculptor did—with the agility of a trapeze artist in the Great Theater of Shanghai, he leaped up onto the Florentine lad's prick and straddled it with his two skinny legs. Then he who was David took the master by the waist, deposited him on the culminative tip of his manhood and began to penetrate the master with his serpent, which butted and nosed its way forward with the sureness of the jungle mole, spreading open the countless rings of that dark anal grot. While the young man's awl worked with impassioned artistry, Michelangelo bit one hand and with the other caressed the reproductive orbs that were battering his buttocks like the furious twin clappers of a bell calling the faithful to their unction. Many years later, as he was joyously dying, Michelangelo was to recall those caresses he had given the formidable germinative lobules, associating them with a Japanese history lesson in which an emperor, after losing his final battle, caresses the polished filigree of the handle of the sword with which he is about to commit hara-kiri. But suddenly, and with no warning or battle cry, the giovanotto introduced the full length of his rod of life into the backside of the great sculptor, who, giving a bellow of glory, opened his arms and was upheld only by the phallus of the youth, who was inching his way with ever greater perseverance along la via angosta. The master, as though possessed by some Titanic wind, began to rise through the air. And as he floated, he seemed to be ridden by a young hippogryph. Finally the master, perhaps under the weight of the still-drilling youth, fell to the floor, where the giovanotto began to pump his member in and out of the master's body with such swiftness that it surpassed even his own sighs. And so that penetration became supersonic. At that, Michelangelo burst forth with a terrible shrieking, which alarmed (and brought into the studio) the entire population of Florence, while the gladiators continued with their unparalleled combat. And then, in a final coup de grâce, the entire length of the imposing young Tuscan's horn of flesh passed into the master's cavern. Yet still not content with this advance, the young man grasped the master by the girdle of his loins and also plunged his two gigantic testicular onions into his channel. When the great sculptor felt not only the umbravit's tree of life but also the seeds of the tree possess him, a pain (which was ineffable pleasure) came over him, and he tried to dislodge that enormous stalk and its two enormous bulbs from himself. But just as dogs when they couple in the street cannot separate themselves until the bout is done, just so Michelangelo could not unsheathe that magnificent virility from its scabbard and, unable to escape that transpiercing potency of life, the master began to bite, with all the voracity of a shark of the Caribbean Sea, the masses of marble that awaited his magical hands. His teeth now atomic drill bits (thereby stealing a march on Einstein by some four hundred years), and chiseling with the velocity of a Malayan typhoon, he carved a good number of the statues which, like the Pietà and other masterworks, are the glory of the Florentine Academy today. A cloud of dust arose from those marmoreal masses upon which it appeared that some beaver had attempted to carve out unending tunnels. Under that cloud of dust, the two gladiators (the younger one completely naked, the other with his sweaty cloak twisted up about his waist) continued their combat. The young man went on growing inside the master, and the master went on chewing up boulders and slabs of marble from Murano and Siena, carving out extraordinary works of art. The entranced Florentines gathered at windows and doors could also watch the colossal battle, like some silent film, on the walls of the great studio, where the gigantic shadows of the umbravit and the laboradit were projected in an extraordinary dance, creating a cinematographic precedent that would be followed centuries later by the brothers Lumière.

At last the giovanotto, unable any longer to contain his passion, exploded with the power of a volcanic fumarole (this was his first orgasm in his life), bathing with his fiery liquor the entire intestinal tract of the master, who, feeling himself filled with that lava (which issued even from his mouth), sprinkled his own well-aged liquor on the half-finished statues. And just as the gladiators produced their seminal eruptions both at once, they emitted, in unison, a titanic howl of pleasure. That sound, like the sound of Armenian earthquakes, not only made the Arno once more overflow its banks, but crumbled the tower of the Cathedral of San Marcos in Venice, dangerously tilted the Tower of Pisa, and devastated Pompeii.

The sweet giovanotto pulled his sword from the recumbent body and stood up, proudly contemplating the conquered master. The master, lying upon the floor, looked up at the young man—his spread and firmly planted legs, serene and at the same time in an attitude of glorious advance; his thighs like solid, indestructible columns; the phallus, with its typi-

cal Italian shape like a bobbin or a country boy's tipcat-peg (with a slight bulge in the middle and pointed at the ends), resting upon a pair of satisfied and recently discharged balls; the half-clutched hands, their throbbing veins still half-engorged; the full, virile face and the curls stuck to the forehead; the ears still alert; the eyes possessed by a look like none other. Everything about the young man displayed—exhaled!—the strength and harmonious serenity of a man who had just tasted victory. . . . Don't move! *Michelangelo ordered him, gazing up at the* giovanotto *from under the triumphal arc of the balls. And taking up hammer and chisel, in less time than it took Cleopatra to squash a mosquito bred upon the Nile with her golden flyswatter, he had reproduced on a colossal scale every heroic feature of the Florentine youth who had just slain him.*

Quadruple adventure, that: phallic, anal, holy, and glorious, for in bringing Michelangelo to the petit mort *the young man had laid him at the gates of paradise, and at the gates of glory.*

Observe, then, my friends, the reposeful and yet tense features of the sculpture; observe the circulation of the blood under the skin of the hands. Observe those feet planted with the assurance of a lord of columns, the legs, the thighs, which proudly rise with the plentitude of a king who, victorious, has just passed unscathed through a tempest; observe those buttocks, the backside of a demigod, clenched in the rectal contraction that impelled the phallic thrusts, observe the pubes, still moist with sweat from the backside of Michelangelo. Observe the ensemble, *and especially the sweet glans now in repose, and above all, observe the magnificent balls drained of their unquiet semen (the right one hanging somewhat lower than the left), observe the fingernails, the ears, the still-tense muscle in the throat, the arms that still show the mark of one who has just indulged in vigorous exercise; observe the belly still contracted, the erect nipples, the tousled hair. Observe yet again, after the ejaculation, the sweet triumphant member, so recently refurled, immobile yet as though ready once more to advance, and you will see that the model who posed for the* David, *that anonymous Florentine youth who hung out on the old bridge, had just ejaculated, gloriously, within his master, just moments before the master's genius (which visits us only at the most exceptional moments) transfigured him to the immortality of stone.*

A Tongue Twister (14)

That false, forged information she feeds Fifo—disinformation feebly feigning faithfulness to the facts, but in fact faked—so fully and unfairly deforms the prima facies of the case that it should be flatly dismissed as fictional flights of fancy. Furthermore, the false facts she feeds Fifo—falsehoods vilely betraying fellow poets and patriots—are the unpublishable fictions of a fibbing informant frustrated in publishing fictions legitimately. Phooey on all fibbing informants feeding Fifo fiction!

For Paula Amanda

A LETTER

Miami, May 9, 1998

Dearest Reinaldo,

I suspect you haven't gotten the other letters I've been sending you from Paris, New York, and even Timbuktu. I'll write more another day, but for now I just wanted to drop you this note to tell you that I've never felt such a cosmic, suffocating, and implacable loneliness as I've been feeling on these beaches in Miami. Everything is so dehumanized, so alien, so plastic, so monumental, so soulless. The mystery of a little grove of palm trees, a sheltered place in the sand, a hill (even a tiny little hill) on which you can stand and look out over a palm grove and feel the wind in your face, a dusty path winding down to the water's edge, a wild jasmine plant, the water so clear that you can see the bottom—a place where there's the chance of a chance meeting, and where there's a high sky, and a street with sidewalks and doorways—all of that, all of it lost. I put up a Christmas tree this year, decorated it, painted the apartment, read some of my texts aloud—to help me remember you. But nothing works. I reach out to touch and I can't touch myself. I don't exist and yet I suffer from my existence. I don't belong to this world, yet I know, of course, that the world I yearn for no longer exists.

Don't think for a second that this climate is like Havana's. The city is an oven. I say city, but it really isn't a city; it's more like a conglomeration of short, squat, spread-out housing projects—a cowboy town where the automobile has elbowed out the horses.

I'm dying of loneliness, dying of love. I'm dying because of all the things I don't have, because of all the things I wanted to do and never got to do. Because of all that I did do, and all the things I had but didn't know I had, and therefore lost. Because of all that I didn't have the sense to enjoy while I had it. Because of all that I enjoyed and that doesn't belong to me anymore. Because of all the things that I'll never do now. Where to find a place in which to live out this horror?—And as though all these other horrors were not enough, I also have to work so I can keep on being horrified. I've washed cars, I've washed floors, I've washed dishes in hotels. Sometimes I get lucky and I make off with a whole set of china and sell it in Southwest Miami—with the help of Pedro Ramona Lépera, let me add, a petty criminal who's famous here (where there's so much competition that achieving that kind of fame is not easy). But other people may have had it even worse. SuperChelo, for instance, was stabbed and died instantly, covered in oil; if you see her down there, it's her spirit that you're seeing. Some people said it was drugs, but the _real_ gossips—who unfortunately almost always get it right—say that it was a murder planned by Chelo. Then there's Miguel Correderas—with that huge hairy body of his, I hear somebody thought he was a bear and tried to stick him in the zoo. Fortunately he was saved by the fact that he now has his American citizenship, which he managed to get because he'd spent more than a year in jail accused of the perfect homicide. I saw the old thing yesterday—she looked like a plucked rooster, as the song says (or said). He told me he's going through a terrible time financially because besides the fact that his parents came from Cuba he's got a lover. He went to an employment agency to get a job as a licensed cocksucker; he figured he'd do home delivery, if you know what I mean, for the most respectable gentlemen of the city. So poor Correderas, after filling out _reams_ of forms and I don't know what—they gave him an aptitude test. I mean they had him give this old guy a blow job in front of the licensing board—and you won't believe this, but the fairy flunked! Is it a tough field here or what? Can you imagine, that poor old queen who'd spent her whole life sucking cock in vacant lots and undergrowth, and now they won't give her her license? I mean, how humiliating! But it just goes to show you—here in Miami, our calvary is unending. . . .

But there _is_ one ray of hope—people are saying that Fifo's fall may come any day now—though you don't see anybody doing anything to help him along. I hope it's true. But I wouldn't want to live to see 2000, and if

I've hung on this long (I'm sure you know I have AIDS) it's in the distant hope that someday, somehow, we may be able to meet again and be just one person, the way we used to be. That may happen only after death; I don't know. Of course I'm not so sure of the existence of the Beyond, either. In fact I'll tell you the truth, I frankly don't think there's any there there—no Beyond, and no Here, either. I remember Cuba and I feel like screaming. I look at myself here, and I am screaming. How can I go on living like this—nowhere—with one piece of my soul here and another piece there, with my life split in two (or maybe a million) pieces? I am just a shell of myself, the old dried-out rind of myself. That is my tragedy. This might sound tacky, or even incredible, to you, but it's worse than a tragedy—it's my life. This rind will never be able to fill the void within its rindness. I will never be able to join myself to myself again. I will never again be myself, or you—which is the same thing. This ocean, this beach, this sun—they have nothing to do with that man I once was; no complicity links us, none of these places recognizes me, or ever will. If I live another hundred years here, I will still be a stranger, a foreigner, an alien.

Now I'm going to take my horror out for a walk along the beach—which at least has less surveillance than it had down there. After I come back, I may write a few pages—the last. Glory and martyrdom, my dear—it's all that keeps me going. It's late. Everybody around me is asleep. I'm still awake.

Think of me as an infinite but always present absence, and know that I send you the tenderest, most eternal affection.

Yours,
Reinaldo

The Areopagite

Rubén Valentín Díaz Marzo, the Areopagite, had a two-room apartment in the Hotel Monserrate, one of the most appalling dives in all of Old Havana. The variety of tenants sheltered by this rundown flophouse was *amazing*—retired hookers; obese marchionesses such as Mahoma; clandestine clairvoyants such as Sakuntala la Mala; insanely fiendish ballet lovers such as Coco Salas; queens with unquenchable rectal fires such as Eachurbod; murderous bull dykes such as Beba Carriles, who had a female slave, a husband, and several children, bragged about her knowledge of the law, and passed herself off as a witch; well-plowed dancers such as Miss Mayoya, who passed herself off as a virgin field; slam-bam-thank-you-ma'am fairies such as SuperSatanic; refined bull macho butt-stuffers such as the Flower Boys, who never screwed a queen without first wringing her neck; well-mannered, superendowed, and super-*super*-sought-after hustlers like the Key to the Gulf; triple agents for State Security, the KGB, and the CIA such as Kilo Alberto Montamier, who stayed in that fleabag hotel on his supposedly clandestine visits so he'd "fit in"; traffickers in yard goods, black beans, refrigerators, and works of art such as Ramón Sernada (a.k.a. the Ogress); former chairwomen of the Comités para la Defensa de la Revolución, those nefarious Watchdog Committees, who would drag themselves and their huge tits along the hotel's ancient marble halls and up and down its stairways; poètes manqués; women like Teresa Rabijo, who'd been abandoned with her three kids; pimps with long eyelashes and immeasurable meat; drug dealers; pianists without pianos; transvestites that still owned twenty-seven wigs, such as Alderete; former lovers of former captains and former Party members; gorgeous bisexual teenagers and male sluts such as Pepe, Beba Carriles' son; judokas, santeros, karatecas, sailors. . . . That was the congeries of people who lived in the Hotel Monserrate; that was the explanation for the deafening, boiling vibration that came from the hotel. These were the people doing all that shrieking and yelling.

Day and night, all you could hear was doors being kicked down, the screams of hookers being stabbed to death, the throbbing of drums, jealous dykes slapping each other, political speeches, glasses being smashed against walls and floors, exorcisms in Lucumí, Chopin's *Swan Lake* (to which Coco Salas and Mayoya would dance), a crazy old woman constantly calling out to some guy named Jesús who never answered her, the unbelievable goings-on of a family of incestuous pygmies—seven brothers who were constantly fighting over their only sister. When the "domestic disturbance" would start, everybody would say "There go Snow White and the Seven Pygmies!" . . . But in all that racket, it was almost impossible to discern any *specific* noise. The noises of that hellish concert all ran together so, that you couldn't pick out any scream in particular. Gigantic black men in shorts would prowl the halls of that seven-story wreck armed not only with pricks that would open any door, but also with crowbars that would pry open the vaults of the Banco Nacional before you knew what was happening. And if there was no peace in the hotel rooms, there was even less of it, honey, in the halls, where a constant stream of whores, tops, bottoms, dealers in anything you could imagine, unpublished writers—you name it—would be going up and down the stairs yelling and knocking on doors. It wasn't unusual to come across a member of the Communist Youth Organization on the stairway, being screwed by an old drunk; one daily spectacle was provided by several Chinese sisters who were forever having their catfights in the halls. . . . Greek sailors, mulattoes from Coco Solo, Asian recruits, and screaming Lawton queens would stand in line in front of the door to Skunk in a Funk's room. While she was being taken from behind (once again) by the Key to the Gulf, she'd be looking out the peepholes to see the procession that awaited her.

And as though all that were not enough, hundreds of homeless men and women and former fugitives from justice had taken up residence on the roof, setting up their tents and even building fires to keep warm and do their cooking—which meant that several times the Holy City they had built up there had been invaded by firemen who, seeing all those people, would run back down the stairs in terror. Among the people who set up their tents on the roof of the Hotel Monserrate was Odoriferous Gunk, with his dying mother.

Naturally the Hotel Monserrate had only one entrance. And before the door to the hotel there would gather a huge crowd of pickpockets, murderers who murdered for the fun of it, fairies cruising, and guys selling foreign jeans that were "wrapped up in this newspaper here," though the package contained nothing but a bunch of rags. (The only pair of pants the con man owned was the pair he had on.) Also at the hotel entrance was a bus stop, at which every bus headed for Old Havana, Marianao, El Vedado, and Guanabo supposedly had to stop—which meant that at the door of the Hotel Monserrate there were not only the persons mentioned just above but also, like a throng of the faithful before the gates of Jerusalem, a crowd of people, all carrying shopping bags, who would rain curses on the mother of God and the bus driver when—as was almost invariably the case—the bus would howl by without stopping, leaving in its wake a cloud of pestilential exhaust.

One day, at precisely three o'clock in the afternoon, a really strange thing happened at that bus stop. A bus shrieked to a stop before the door of the Hotel Monserrate and before you could blink—it disappeared! It, my dear, and all its passengers, who were mugged, stripped of their belongings, carved up, and sold as cuts of beef all over Old Havana. As for the bus itself, Mahoma, Coco Salas, SuperSatanic, and Mayra the Mare (who also lived in the hotel) instantly turned it into earrings, combs, pots and pans, table knives, and even metal sandals that made a hellish racket you could hear all over the building. The inhabitants of the Hotel Monserrate lived for days and days in terror as Fifo's police searched the building from top to bottom and inside out. Finally, the police found one of the wheels off the carved-up bus under Alderete's bed. So as to avoid being carved up himself, Alderete made a run for it, changing wigs at every corner. All the inhabitants of the building were charged as accomplices to a political crime, since the fact of wanting to keep, or conspiring to keep, the wheel off a bus was proof—according to the prosecutor—that every one of them was about to try to escape the Island.

In order to jail all the tenants until a trial could be held—which of course might take years—Fifo ordered a gigantic iron prison gate installed across the Hotel Monserrate's only door. But with criminals like these, my dear, there was no security measure that anybody could take that would *ever* work. Within hours, Snow White and the Seven Pygmies, aided by Beba Carriles, the Clandestine Clairvoyant, and Mayoya, had dug a tunnel that came out in a big seven-door refrigerator in the bar on the first floor. Thousands of half-frozen criminals poured through the bar to freedom. Other stratagems were also employed by the whores and fairies so they could get out and fornicate even while the gate remained locked tighter than a drum. To give just one quick example, Beba Carriles' slave, known as Dimwit, a countrywoman from Pinar del Río and purportedly a virgin, would dangle from the window in a huge sack tied to a rope attached to a pulley that Pepe, Beba's son, would operate. Pepe would lower the sack with Beba's slave inside down to the street level; the slave's current boyfriend would climb into the sack with her (coining a phrase in use in Cuba to this day), screw her eyes out, and then take off; and the Dimwit would have herself, much relieved, pulled back up again by Pepe. Then the Dimwit, who as always had picked the pocket of her boyfriend of the moment, would turn over to Pepe the fortune that she'd reaped: a tin matchbox, a pack of cigarettes, a linen handkerchief . . .

It looked as though the building were sentenced to quarantine for life. So the tenants started throwing down onto Calle Monserrate (the street on which the eponymous hotel stood) every imaginable object and all manner of filth, especially urinals full of piss and plastic bags filled with excrement. They also rained down dead rats, dishes, gigantic platform shoes (made by Mahoma) that would cause the immediate death of anyone struck by one, bloody Kotex, aborted fetuses. Once a poor old lady who had been waiting patiently for over a year for a Number 98 bus was hit by a bloody hand thrown from the roof by a drugged-out satan-worshiping homeless man who had been celebrating a religious ritual (in which Odoriferous Gunk took part) involving human body parts. A lead mannequin once fell off the balcony of Coco Salas' room and made a huge hole in the middle of Calle Monserrate, not to mention taking the lives of several militia boys. Another day, a big sinister bull dyke—a sculptor who'd been given both a Guggenheim and a Wilson Center Fellowship for work which consisted of runny-looking splayed-out turds—was thrown from the balcony by her husband (Sr. Marsopo Antoni), instantly becoming what she had always sculptured: a huge splat of shit.

In addition to flicking lice and ticks down into the street, the itinerants up on the roof would spend their days throwing rocks (which Pepe would haul up with his pulley) at pigeons, trying to kill them for dinner. These hungry vagrants seldom had much luck hitting the pigeons, but they often (perhaps accidentally) hit the students at a high school across the street. Several students died from brain injuries after being hit in the head with rocks. Because of these killings and several other, more minor casualties, a new wave of police officers stormed the building, to do another search. But this time they didn't leave. For several days, little packages of ground meat would be tossed from the building to homemakers on the street below, who would tussle and elbow each other for the prize—and generally catch the packages before they hit the ground. All this despite a rain of foul-smelling, bloody water that also fell on the furiously shoving housewives.

The truth was, by now Fifo's Secret Police were seriously considering taking down the prison gate at the entrance to the Hotel Monserrate and letting the people inside get on with their lives; the internment was more expensive than the danger to public safety if they were all set free. The last straw—the event that brought down the iron bars at last—was laid by Coco Salas. For months, Coco had been using a telescope to watch a teenager at the high school across the street. One day, Coco threw the teenager a note inviting him up to his room. He wrapped the note, a twenty-peso bill, and a little Tiffany lamp to give the package some weight, in a page from the Revolution's (and Cuba's only) newspaper, *Granma,* and he lobbed it across the street. The gorgeous twink picked up the note and read it; it contained the secret of the entrance to the hotel through the refrigerator in the bar next door. All he had to do, the note said, was bribe the manager with the twenty pesos. The young man, who was nothing if not quick-witted—it was Davidcito, one of the most sinister faggots on earth in spite of the fact that nobody would ever have suspected he was "that way"—crawled through the refrigerator and came up to Coco's room. He was sporting an irresistible hard-on as he came through the door, and he instantly started stripping off his clothes. Coco wasn't far behind. But then Davidcito pushed Coco out onto the balcony and locked the door from the inside! That left the old queen naked and imprisoned on his own balcony, which as luck would have it was directly over Calle Monserrate (oh, I forgot—it was also called Avenida de Bélgica). While Coco, standing naked on the balcony, pleaded with David to open the door, David took the queen's enormous suitcases and a big portmanteau he found in the back of the closet and packed up all the queen's belongings—including some old ballet slippers, a box of mosquitoes, and some fresh surveillance reports that Coco hadn't even had time to turn in to Fifo's computers. Giving the manager of the bar a handsome tip (a mosquito bigger than a turtle), the teenage hustler strutted out of the building.

From the balcony, the naked queen saw David emerge from the building and make his way down the street, dragging all her belongings behind him. At that, Coco began to scream like an air-raid siren. For more than a week that horrid old thing ran from one end of the balcony to the other, screaming. All Havana was put on alert; everyone was nervous; there was even talk of a curfew. Not only did Coco's screaming interrupt Halisia's sleep, and Fifo's; his naked body, running from one end of the balcony to the other on the busiest street in Havana—a block from Central Park—made a visual as well as aural impact that drove away tourists, counterspies, and important journalists. Finally, some two hundred midgets from Fifo's crack Secret Police took down the iron gate at the entrance to the hotel and released the howling banshee from the balcony.

And that was the building, as I said, that Skunk in a Funk had wound up living in. More specifically, he lived in one of the two rooms belonging to Rubén Valentín Díaz Marzo, the Areopagite. After paying Rubén the royal sum of one thousand pesos, Skunk in a Funk had been inscribed in the Areopagite's ration book and, with that, had become mistress of a room in that brilliant flea trap—a *historic* room, from which the marchioness Cristina Guzmán was one day to steal a floor tile and in which Skunk in a Funk was visited by countless other figures of renown, such as Delfín Proust, who read some really marvelous poems there. . . . Well. The question is, then, How did Skunk in a Funk ever manage to lay her hands on a thousand pesos? Quite easily, Mary, you old snoop. And thank you for asking.

It seems that Skunk in a Funk, Rubén Valentín Díaz Marzo, Beba Carriles, el Negro Cuquejo (who had temporarily moved into the Hotel Monserrate), Clara Mortera, Teodoro Tampon, Odoriferous Gunk with his dying mother, and the cunning Mahoma, among others, all showed up one day at the house where Gabriel's despicable Aunt Orfelina lived, and Beba Carriles produced a document (falsified by a lieutenant who was screwing her at the time and who was also one of her slave's husbands) and waved it in Orfelina's face. This document stated that it was the inalienable right of Reinaldo Arenas to reside in the maid's quarters of that residence, currently occupied by Orfelina and family, from which Skunk in a Funk had been violently and rudely expelled when he was released from jail. Beba shoved Orfelina aside and broke the lock on the door to the room in which Skunk had formerly lived, and in a trice the entire royal procession had occupied that maid's room in Miramar. (By this time, Orfelina had sold the room to her son Tony so he'd have a place to screw the big black bucks that were his type.) Orfelina was dumbstruck—what was going on here? And to top it all off, the chairwoman of the block's Watchdog Committee (who had quickly been lesbianized by Beba) agreed that the room belonged to Skunk in a Funk. . . . *Let's do an inventory,* said Clara Mortera, *and see if all the victim's belongings are in order.* A search was conducted on the instant and a list was made of everything that remained—not just in the room but in the rest of the house as well. The Brontë Sisters showed Skunk in a Funk the resulting inventory.

"My swim fins, the typewriter, all my clothes, an ashtray, four wooden testicles, a beetle-case with a cornucopia, a Globe lock, and Günter Grass's *The Tin Drum* are missing," Skunk in a Funk said.

"Girl, if it was Günter Grass's it wasn't *yours,*" said Teodoro Tampon reasonably.

"At any rate, madam," Beba Carriles intoned before the openmouthed Orfelina, "in accordance with all these wherefores and therefores here, you must make restoration to your nephew for the losses you have occasioned him, either by finding all his belongings and returning them to him or by compensating him for their value, and you must also return to him the key to the room—a room which by law, I remind you, belongs to him."

Orfelina promptly faked a fainting spell and crumpled to the floor, her eyes squeezed tight. At the point Odoriferous Gunk said a few words in Latin, which terrified Orfelina so much that her eyes popped open. But upon seeing that queen dressed in black from head to foot, and accompanied by her dying mother, Orfelina *really* fainted dead away.

When the chairwoman of the Watchdog Committee marched away on the arm of Beba Carriles, the others—Clara Mortera, Rubén Valentín Díaz Marzo (the Areopagite), Cuquejo, and the Brontë Sisters—slapped Orfelina until she regained consciousness and then they began to hammer out an agreement between her and Skunk in a Funk (who'd managed to pick up a good-looking kid from the National Institute of Sports and Recreation and even as we speak was getting his eyes screwed out in the maid's room). The negotiating team told Orfelina that Reinaldo would agree to give up his room and all his belongings except the swim fins (which, by the way, Tatica, not his aunt, had stolen from him) on the condition that Orfelina immediately pay him two thousand pesos. The old whore threw herself to the floor howling—where, oh where, would she ever be able to find that much money? "Well then, Reinaldo will keep his room and *you* will go to prison." Those were the words of Clara Mortera, seconded immediately by Rubén Valentín Díaz Marzo, the Areopagite. Seeing in the faces of that menacing delegation that she had no real choice (and given that the Dowager Duchess de Valero, SuperSatanic, Sanjuro la Dame sans Camélias, Snow White and the Seven Pygmies, Chug-a-Lug, and the Divinely Malign were just now arriving on a Number 132 bus), Orfelina begged for mercy—she pleaded with them to give her twenty-four hours to come up with the two thousand pesos. At that, the entire troupe moved into the Skunk's room to await developments—including the yummy teenager from Sports and Recreation, who that night screwed the entire group, bringing on such resounding sighs and moans that Orfelina's husband, condemned to washing up the dishes, almost died of envy.

That night, as (we repeat) the athletic young twink screwed Skunk in a Funk and her entire entourage, Orfelina, two of her offspring, and her obedient husband made a sweep of Miramar and sacked all the mansions abandoned by their owners. They then held an auction, at which they sold off mattresses, sets of china, statues, windows, doors, mirrors, toilets, and other bath accessories to the highest bidder. People say that even Fifo attended the auction, and that he bought a marble bathtub and a huge mirror that would be *perfect* for his orgies.

And so, my dear, the next day Orfelina was back with a pair of shiny swim fins and the two thousand pesos in a brand-new (stolen) purse. On an Underwood typewriter which Orfelina had also stolen (and which of course went to Skunk in a Funk), the negotiating team drew up a document stating that "in return for the permanent transfer of one of his rooms in the Hotel Monserrate to Sr. Gabriel Fuentes, a.k.a. Reinaldo Arenas, a.k.a. Skunk in a Funk, Sr. Rubén Valentín Díaz Marzo receives the amount of two thousand pesos, in liquid assets." And "to that effect," everyone present, including Orfelina herself and the Dying Mother, affixed his or her or his/her signature as witness. As for Skunk in a Funk and Rubén Valentín Díaz Marzo, the Areopagite, they signed in the spaces marked for the "in acceptance of" and "duly agreed." And at that, the entourage, with the swim fins and the Underwood, and the money tucked in the warm bosom of Beba Carriles, set off for the Hotel Monserrate, where lived the great majority of those persons who for many years or several hours had been the friends or acquaintances of Skunk in a Funk.

Once Skunk had moved in, Beba gave the Areopagite a thousand pesos.

"There's a thousand missing," said the little thug.

"No there's not," said Beba. "Read the document you signed."

"It says right here that I'm supposed to receive 'two thousand pesos in liquid assets.' "

"Oh, right," said Beba. "I gave you a thousand, and I'll give you the rest right now." And she went to her room and came back with a bucket full of slops that she threw in the Areopagite's face.

"A thousand pesos in bills. And another thousand in liquid assets. Count it, you'll see it's all there."

Rubén could hardly protest, since he'd signed the document himself.

That night almost all the tenants of the Hotel Monserrate were invited by Beba Carriles and the Areopagite to dinner at the Peking Restaurant. Mahoma gave a speech welcoming Skunk in a Funk "to our unique residential property, the Hotel Monserrate." And the next day Padre Gastaluz brought his silver aspergillum to Gabriel's room and sprinkled holy water in all the corners.

As we said—or maybe we didn't, so we'll say it now— Rubén Valentín Díaz Marzo, the Areopagite, was a well-known miscreant who, after his parents had fled to the United States, had sold their apartment under the ruse of a "permuta"—that peculiarly Cuban tradition of trading property that one doesn't own (the State owns everything) in order to be able to move out of one place and into another—and wound up living in a two-room suite in the Hotel Monserrate. Rubén lived in one of the rooms and he methodically sold the other one. By the time of our story he'd already sold it at least fifteen times to the poor people in Cuba who have no place to live—which is practically everybody. The Areopagite would charge the "buyers" one, two, or three thousand pesos and then legally throw them out of the room—because in Cuba, my dear, nobody can buy a house, or an apartment, or practically *anything,* because everything is in the hands of Fifo the almighty. So after Rubén Valentín Díaz Marzo had bilked the buyer and spent the money, he'd throw 'im out in the street. Since it was illegal to buy a place to live, and Fifo punished that crime with all the severity he was capable of—which was plenty—the person who'd been conned had only two alternatives: give up the room or go to jail.

So not surprisingly, after a month in his room Skunk in a Funk was visited one afternoon by the Areopagite, who knocked very politely on the interconnecting door.

The Skunk invited him in, and the Areopagite informed him very courteously that he was to vacate the premises immediately, since *he* was the legitimate owner of same. "You," he whispered confidentially to Skunk in a Funk, "have no title to this room."

"What do you mean I have no title to this room?" replied Skunk in a Funk. "I most certainly do!"

"Then perhaps you would be so kind as to show it to me," said the Areopagite with the most ex*cru*ciating politeness.

"But of course. Right away," replied the steaming queen, who opened a drawer in the kitchenette, pulled out a very well sharpened butcher knife about a foot and a half long, and showed it to the Areopagite, saying at the same time in the suavest and most delicate of voices, "My dear, *here* is the title to my room. The next time you ask to see it, you can be sure I'll give it to you and you'll never mislay it again."

Skunk in a Funk's eyes were so icy-cold, so filled with rage, and the look that gazed upon the Areopagite was so clearly that of a man who has seen every hell and therefore no longer fears any, that their gleam—and the gleam of the knife blade—persuaded Rubén Valentín Díaz Marzo, a.k.a. the Areopagite, that he'd sold his room for the last time.

And from that moment on, the Areopagite became an unconditional admirer of Skunk in a Funk. And also his confidant.

A TONGUE TWISTER (15)

Smack-dab in the middle of the synagogue, undercover cop Gogo, going incognito as Chug-a-Lug the unglamorous, glommed on the long glabrous organ of a Galápagos tortoise, gobbled it down hungrily, smacked his lips, licked his chops, and subsequently stepped into the toilet, where he gargled noisily.

"Gonococcus," he gurgled, grinning girlishly.

For Miss Chug-a-Lug

Forbidden Costumes

The success of the exhibit of Clara Mortera's paintings was so overwhelming that although she had refused to sell the pictures in her hole, she did take in substantial entrance fees. With that money, Clara applied herself with great dedication to the design and production of a vast and extraordinary collection of costumes—gowns, masks, shoes, and getups of all kinds that she planned to exhibit during Carnival at the Gala Forbidden Costumes Contest. Fifo, in honor of the great night, had given special permission for the contest—which otherwise would, naturally, have been forbidden. I mean, duh. Of course there was always the possibility that the contest really *was* forbidden and was just a snare for the unwary, in which case Clara might very well wind up in jail. Her costumes would be so irreverent, so *crushing,* so real, that should the contest be a trap, for her there would almost certainly be neither clemency nor mercy. (Even Fifo himself was going to be caricatured!) But even so, Clara felt that she couldn't *not* make the costumes. This work was the complement, the other face, of her great exhibit of paintings. And so Clara Mortera, confident of victory in the contest, began to confect the most astonishing gowns and suits and headware and masks—which she herself would don the night of the Grand Carnival.

THE AREOPAGITE'S STORY

The story of Rubén Valentín Díaz Marzo, the Areopagite, like the story of every petty criminal, is a pathetic one. When he was a little boy, if his parents wanted to screw without him around they would just throw him out of the house, so the poor little thing would have to sit out on the porch and listen to his parents' moaning—or more often, the racket they made as they slapped and yelled terrible insults at each other. As a teenager, while his mother was in bed with one of the neighbors (his father would be away on militia duty), Rubén was raped on the porch by a vagrant, then by a black man, and then—horrors!—by an old hag with huge tits who practically suffocated him not only with her tits but with her cunt as well, since she sat on Rubén's face and made the poor thing eat beaver-pie. Then when he was a young man his parents fled to the United States, leaving him behind; since he was of military age, it was against the law for him to leave the country. And it was that same law that forced him into Obligatory Military Service, where in less than a month he'd been passed from hand to hand (i.e., raped) by his entire platoon, including the lieutenant and the head of the Political Section. Terrified and half dead, reeling from this dreadful experience, Rubén escaped from the camp and negotiated the *permuta* that we mentioned earlier, which left him not only swindled (because he never received the money that was coming to him) but thrown into the world to suffer even further outrages in his two-room "suite" in the Hotel Monserrate—for there, Mahoma, SuperSatanic, Coco Salas, Mayra the Mare, and all the other aging whores in the building immediately forced Rubén Valentín Díaz Marzo to screw them. Even one of Fifo's foreign spies, who came into Cuba on a diplomatic passport and had an *unbelievable* potbelly, commanded the young man to "take her." And to top off the humiliation, the spy, who signed her name "Anastasia Filipovna," turned out to be a military officer in drag.

It was only to be expected, then, that the young man should develop an incurable sexual block. He would have liked to make love, he knew he would enjoy the act of sex, but he couldn't do it. The only way he could enjoy sex was by watching other couples screw—and from a certain distance even then, since Fifo had handed down a law that punished peeping toms severely.

Thus, Rubén Valentín Díaz Marzo would go off to the parks in Havana, climb up in the leafiest tree he could find, and peek through the foliage at the benches on which lovers would be frenziedly making love. Then, protected by the foliage, Rubén would masturbate. It was only thus, sitting amidst the shady branches of a tree, that he could reach orgasm. And by now there wasn't a tree in the entire city of Havana that the Areopagite hadn't climbed up and jerked off in. Yes, the *Areopagite,* because so famous were his aerial masturbations as he looked down upon any sort of couple at all—men with women, tops with bottoms, German shepherds with midgets, vagrants with police chaplains—that Rubén Valentín Díaz Marzo had at last acquired that nickname—which was really more an honorific, or a title, than some tacky *nickname.* But the Areopagite would never be capable of making love to any of those bodies that writhed in pleasure as he secretly gazed upon them. He had to content himself—for such was the nature of his block—to watching, and to cumming all alone, among the leaves. He was, then, condemned to be the Areopagite for the remainder of his poor complex-ridden life!—Jesus! St. Nelly! Could anything be sadder than a poor man who can taste sexual pleasure only by spying on the pleasures of others?

Yes, sad indeed, my dear, is the Areopagite's story. Sometimes he had to sit on a tree limb for hours on end, waiting for a lukewarm couple to heat up enough for the boyfriend to lift his girlfriend's skirt and the girlfriend to grab her boyfriend's member. No matter that rain soaked him to the skin, that sometimes lightning hit the very tree he was perched in, that the wind buffeted him in his nest—the Areopagite would cling to his branches with the stubbornness of a lizard. . . . My tears flood the page as I write the Areopagite's tale, which I have heard his very lips, terrified and trembling, tell in a wrenching voice of loneliness, despair, and forever-unsatisfied longing. His is a sadness born of the horror and baseness of the present age. The poor Areopagite would madly hump the trunk of a spruce tree, a bully tree, a haya tree, a bay laurel tree, a thorny ceiba, or a swaying pine tree, and to muffled sighs and weeping he would at last ejaculate, while the impassioned lovers down below would actually, deliciously, couple.

Dear lord, and if to this we add the dire risks and near-fatal pratfalls that his erotic adventures sometimes entailed, then surely the reader will see how truly and terribly wretched the Areopagite's life was. For instance, sometimes the uncontainable arc of his semen would fall from the heights down onto the face of a lover, who would indignantly discover the peeping tom above, grab rocks and sticks and anything else he could find, and hurl them furiously at the Areopagite, who would make his escape (by leaping from tree to tree) only at the risk of a fall that could easily break his leg, or even his very neck. But at other times, the Areopagite would actually be the cause of other people's pleasure. Once, for instance, after a young lady had spent hours futilely sucking an impotent soldier's cock, the Areopagite solved the problem when his stream of warm cum fell into the young woman's face, naturally leading her to think that it was the soldier's and that she had at last succeeded. She embraced her soldier in an ecstasy of pleasure, and from then on the couple always went to the same bench, where the Areopagite could generously bathe the young woman's face with his love liquor. But mishaps occurred more often than successes. Many times as he came he would almost swoon, and he would lose his balance. At that, he would crash down out of the tree onto the impassioned lovers, who, enraged, would usually give him a double beating—for the physical damage he'd caused by falling on them and for the coitus interruptus. . . . Once the Areopagite made such a racket up in the tree that he was discovered by an army lieutenant whose meaty member was being deep-throated at the time by Carlitos Olivares, the Most In-Your-Face Queen in Cuba. The lieutenant, thinking that the Areopagite was a spy who'd report him to that jealous bitch Raúl Kastro, pulled out his pistol and, to the desperate shrieks of Carlitos, who thought she was about to be murdered, blasted away at the treetop. It was a miracle that Rubén got out of that one alive, I'll tell you. And another time, when a bunch of students were having a little circle-jerk under a tree in Central Park, the Areopagite came crashing down on them and smashed several of their erect members flat; they almost kicked him to death. Another time, in Lenin Park, the Areopagite lost his grip on a huge rubber tree under which a hundred scouts in the Camilo Cienfuego troop of the Followers of Ché Guevara had formed a delicious daisy chain. The ensuing fall broke not only the daisy chain but the bones of the poor Areopagite as well, who in spite of his injuries had to make his escape before the scouts could pull up their shorts and stone him to death.

Over time, the Areopagite conceived a special voyeuristic fantasy—he dreamed of climbing up into the rafters of the García Lorca Theater and jerking off while Azari Plizeski or Jorge Esquivel made love to Halisia Jalonzo, naked, in her dressing room. To fulfill this fantasy, he sought Coco Salas' help, and at last, after making all manner of promises to Coco (even going so far as pledging to make the Key to the Gulf Coco's own personal and exclusive sex slave), he was allowed to climb up into the heights of the theater, from where he could look down into Halisia's dressing room. That night, like almost every night, Halisia hobbled out on her crutches to the middle of the stage (this was just an ordinary performance—no mosquitoes) and danced *Giselle.* At one of the ballet's most romantic moments, when Giselle was dancing with that gorgeous prince with the big basket, Halisia whirled offstage for a moment, stuck her hand into her cunt, pulled out a bloody Kotex, and then did a marvelous (and most uncommon) jeté into the arms of the prince—to deafening applause. Oh, but the desperate Areopagite, who was hoping for something a bit more erotically inspiring, was so disappointed that he lost his grip on the rope he was hanging on and fell onto the stage—at the precise moment the entire corps de ballet had encircled the lovers in a beautifully choreographed scene. Leaping off the stage, the Areopagite tried to escape, but Fifo's implacable police, tipped off by the all-knowing midgets, grabbed him before he could get away.

So now the Areopagite is awaiting trial for contempt, sabotage, and personal damages—crimes punishable by up to eleven years in prison and a thousand rations of five pesos each. And Skunk in a Funk, the Areopagite's friend and confessoress, has promised to intervene for him. This very afternoon, in fact, Skunk has an appointment with Blas Roka at the Palace of Justice. Oh, yes, she was going to speak to Blas, whose prick the Skunk had sucked once in an elevator when she was on her way to the courtroom to be tried for corrupting the morals of a minor. Once again she would get on her knees before the old militant in the Communist Party Central Committee, kiss his shriveled balls—all that and *much more* the poor Skunk would do to save that poor, long-suffering Areopagite from prison. For once in prison, what tree or statue was the poor voyeur ever going to be able to climb in order to get his rocks off? Yes—she, Skunk in a Funk, was willing to perform the most *appalling* sacrifices, even go so far as to suck Blas Roka's cock, or Felipe Carnedehado's, even to screw Alfredo (Güé) Güevavara—anything, everything—she would do it all if it would free the poor lonely Areopagite, *son frère, son semblable,* from the claws of justice. . . . Yes, but first I've got to go over to Clara Mortera's house—she gave me an ultimatum, and I've *got* to run over to her room on Wall Street in time for that meeting. My heavens, what's gotten into that creature? And the worst part of it is that I can't say I'm not going because in addition to being such a horrid sinister old woman she's a genius, and *mon semblable,* too—plus she'd done me no end of favors. So I'll go. Then we'll see about Blas.

A Tongue Twister (16)

Ah, the jolly Goya-Girl, all curls and gurgles. Her tastes, god-awful, run to gaudy jewelry, gewgaws, gadgets, gimcracks, gentry, country junkets, jocks in jeweled jockstraps she can chew on, and youngish hunks with monikers such as Yeyo, Yayo, Gugo, Lastayo, and Tellez. The Goya-Girl lures the yummy gullible youngish hunks she goes for with gifts of yo-yos, pogo sticks, boomerangs, bronze gongs from Hong Kong, glass balls, rolls of foil, oil, doilies, go-go-girl thongs, and funky old g-strings; then when they're gaga over the goodies, she gulps down their lingams and engulfs them in cunning Goya-Girl tonguings or, gurgling, humps them.

For Tomasito the Goya-Girl

A Fugitive's Toccata and Fugue

Eachurbod shot like lightning out of the gigantic men's room.

She was *so* furious at missing out on that wonderful phallus—which she was *just* about to pop into her mouth—that for an hour she could hardly see.

Meanwhile, back in the gigantic men's room, in the cloud of dust she left when she made her exit, all the men were still pissing and singing along with the Condesa in *Norma,* while Eachurbod, momentarily blind, pushed her way through the crowd, lashing out right and left with Volume XXIX of the *Complete Works of Lenin.* . . .

Now just hold on right there! I'd like to get this straight if you don't mind. Is it Volume XXV, XXVI, or XXVII, or XXIX? Make up your mind, sweetie, because you really seem to be jumping from one volume to the next.

Good lord, girl, will you *ever* get down off that academic high horse of yours? I mean, what *difference* does it make for chrissake whether it's Volume One or Volume Two Jillion of the Complete Fucking Works of Lenin, if nobody in her right mind but Eachurbod is ever going to stick her nose in the goddamn thing? So, please, do you *mind?* Let me just see where I was now. . . . Oh, yeah—

Eachurbod was pushing her way through the crowd, elbowing people right and left and waving around Volume XXXIX of the *Complete Works of Lenin,* with an Introduction by Juan Marinello. It was a huge red book, as I've said a hundred times already, whose cover bore not only the fearsome name of Lenin but also that of the publisher. Which just *happened* to be the Soviet Academy of Science. And which just *happened* to be enough to make the entire crowd, which was on its way to the Carnival, part like the Red Sea before the blind queen, who finally, bumping into the wall of the military fortress called El Catillo del Príncipe (the Prince's Castle, for those of you who haven't taken Spanish 101), magically recovered her sight. This enormous former prison, now converted into a military barracks, was an *extremely* dangerous place for Eachurbod. If the lieutenant of the guard so much as caught *sight* of her he'd have her arrested, and who knows—maybe even locked up in a cell right there in the Prince's Castle. *A black prince is not the same thing as a black girl in Prince's,* said the devouress to herself. *Although I myself, of course, being black from all the sun I've been exposed to from cruising all the time, am a black princess, not a prince . . . though unfortunately I don't live in a castle. . . .* And without further ado she turned down Avenida de Rancho Boyeros and took a bus that was packed full of people, hoping to continue her cruising in Central Park and the Paseo del Prado, where the Carnival was already beginning to show some signs of life.

The minute she climbed onto that Number 67, which had seen more than forty years of hard service, our heroine's nostrils were set quivering by the scent of a beloved perfume. It was the exquisite fragrance given off by round, firm, fully packed black hunks crammed together inside that oven, and ready to make some carnival. The sniffing queen, wielding her ubiquitous red tome, pushed her way to the back of the bus at the precise instant that someone was vacating one of the rear seats, so into it the queen gratefully plopped, heaving a sigh. Eachurbod was, then, sitting on that long rear seat in the bus, and to her left were some truly impressive specimens, a couple of mulattoes with their shirts open and some black men (*oh, those scrumptious black men who on the burning plains of my homeland . . .*) who looked as if they'd been sculpted by Cárdenas himself; there was also a pregnant woman on that side. But on the right, between the window and the faggot, there sat a hunk every bit as striking as those black men. He was white, with the look of an innocent country boy—athletic-looking, with full, straight hair—and the minute the fairy sat down beside him he spread his magnificent legs.

Eachurbod stole a quick furtive glance at the hunk, who just then spread his muscular legs even wider and—oh, Mary, can you believe it!—drew one of his powerful hands up his thigh to touch his crotch. At that, Eachurbod opened the immense Volume XXV of the *Complete Works of Lenin* that he always carried, wherever he went, and he began to pretend to read, all the while looking out of the corner of his eye at the delectable hunk of man who was sitting there squeezing his crotch. Then, as though accidentally, Eachurbod let one of the flaps of the book flop onto the thigh of the magnificent male. The magnificent male made not a motion, not a peep. Which led Eachurbod, still apparently engrossed in Leninism, to let the whole volume brush the delightful passenger's thigh. The delightful passenger, drawing his hand once again up to his crotch, adjusted his pants leg so as more comfortably to accommodate what he needed to accommodate—for under the cloth of the pants leg, the hunk showed Eachurbod a very impressive-looking nightstick. Once more Volume XXXOOO (silly me, I mean XXXIII) of the *Complete Works of Lenin* fell, softly, upon the horny traveler's thigh. And this time the fairy, her delicate hand shielded by the thick tome, actually touched the divine phallus of the athletic love god. And the phallus gave a leap that lifted the red volume with its Introduction by Juan Marinello. Such was the joy felt by the fairy at touching that bulge that in order to prolong her ecstasy, like the cat before she leaps upon her prey, she read a paragraph from that Volume XXXI of the *Complete Works of Lenin.* It was a boring, complicated diatribe against Bakunin and the anarchists. When she had done her religious duty, the fairy turned her attention (and her bug-eyes) once more upon the magic torpedo. She picked up the red tome and let it brush, softly, softly, against the traveler's leg. And yes, there it was—the magnificent one-eyed serpent, practically drooling, and ready to breathe fire. But just then the fairy, suddenly seized with caution, looked around and saw that the muscular Negroes and the woman with the big belly had seen her maneuvers, or some of them. And an old man who was standing in the aisle seemed to be aware of Eachurbod's legwork. So naturally the fairy, though almost on the verge of swooning, had no choice but to return, prudently, to her Lenin, and so she swan-dived once more into the book. Now Lenin was calling for the death of Bakunin and all of his followers, including Trosky, Malenkov, and Rosa Luxemburg. At least that was what Eachurbod, in his desperation, thought it said—the truth was, she really could *not* concentrate on her reading. I mean, how could she, my dear, with that incredible piece of man sitting next to her with his legs spread wide and his prick about to burst out of his pants? Could *you,* Miss Thing? But there sat those big black bucks and that big-bellied sow, and there stood the old man over her, and everybody in the whole bus, including the bus driver, no doubt, peeking in his rearview mirror (but of course pretending absolute insouciance, you realize), just *dying* to see whether the fairy was going to make a dive at that monster cock. But given the risk she'd be running, the fairy returned to her deadly-dull Lenin—and knowing that a horny hunk was sitting beside her, she allowed her face to take on the radiance of devotion as she read.

And so, in that state of ecstasy, Eachurbod continued her journey. An observer might easily have thought that the author of "Imperialism, A Superior Phase of Capitalism" was imparting mystical lashes to the impassioned soul of the young faggot. Oh, but wait—out of the mist of her contemplation she begins to discern that the turned on traveler sitting next to her has stretched one of his legs out, touching the queen's beside it, and in a hoarse voice has said: "Touch my dick again." It was not simply a supplication by an aroused male, it was a divine commandment, given by Lenin himself: *Touch it again,* Lenin commanded. Clearly, reasoned the devouress, the hunk wants me to touch him so he can cum once and for all, and in peace. She had to keep that commandment of the gods; not to do so would be heresy. What did she care about the envious crowd that was observing it all? Besides, with that immense red tome protecting her nobody would be able to see a thing, and if people had a dirty imagination, that was *their* problem. Yes, clearly the queen should make her move. So with one hand she let Volume XLVII of the *Complete Works of Lenin* fall gently across the thighs of the muscular hunk and with the other she grasped the serpent, which gave such a leap that it sent the red-bound volume flying. And suddenly everyone on the bus could see the fairy queen grasping the delectable hunk's member. The delectable hunk, meanwhile, seeing himself exposed, his delectable dick grasped firmly in the hand of the fairy queen, and also seeing himself seen by everyone on the bus—he did what anybody *would* do, he tried to salvage his morals (and especially his freedom) by swelling with pretended, and thus obviously sincere, wrath. *You faggot!* he yelled at the faggot so that everybody on the bus could hear, *how dare you touch my cock? I'm a man, goddammit!* . . . And he picked up the sacred text with an

Introduction by Juan Marinello and started beating Eachurbod over the head with it. Eachurbod tried to protect herself from the Leninist onslaught—she even crawled under the seat—but the muscular hunk, apparently now even more enraged, stood up and started *kicking* the poor fairy (who by now was bleeding profusely) in the head. I tell you, hon, it was hit the lights and let's make a run for it! And now the formerly delectable piece of meat was grabbing the handrail at the top of the bus and swinging back to get a good start and kicking with both feet at the poor fairy huddled under the seat. The big-bellied woman started screaming and threatening to have a miscarriage, the black guys tried to step in to save Eachurbod, and one of them even tried to hold back the big raging bull, who was still kicking as he yelled, "This faggot touched my dick, and *no* faggot touches my dick!" It was the rage of a deity profaned that was roaring and kicking there; it was as though that phallus, only seconds ago erect and drooling for Eachurbod's caresses, had suddenly been transformed into a silver chalice or the face of Moctezuma, which no man can look upon and live. A basilisk that kills the man who gazes upon it, that phallus was.

Meanwhile, the bus was going crazy—the big-bellied woman was still shrieking, the black men were trying to save Eachurbod's life, and other people were yelling that the faggot deserved to die, preferably on the spot.

Eachurbod somehow recovered the red-bound tome and shielded his head with it, trying to protect herself from the enraged hunk, who was still kicking and hurling insults while all the passengers were loudly giving their opinions or verdicts. And to make matters worse, it was five o'clock in the afternoon and the bus was traveling through the José Martí Revolutionary Plaza. The pregnant woman gave an earsplitting scream of desperation. And just at the moment, the bus driver stopped the bus and threw all the doors wide open. A police officer was walking toward Eachurbod, pistol drawn. But Eachurbod, Volume XXV of the *Complete Works of Lenin* held aloft, pushed through the crowd, snatched up off the floor a wallet that she thought belonged to her, and took off running across the Plaza de la Revolución. Off the bus leaped the pistol-packing policeman, the supposedly offended well-packed hunk, several rehabilitated hookers, a park guard, and three resentful closet homos who also wanted to see Eachurbod done away with so they could win a medal for being Workers in the Vanguard. Eachurbod ran—or *flew,* if the truth be told, my dear—across the plaza. So great was her desperation that in almost no time she had put a good English mile between herself and her pursuers—none of that metric stuff for her. And yet her feet never slowed until she came to the locked gates of the grounds of UNEAC—the Cuban National Union of Writers and Artists—where she screamed for political asylum, as on a previous occasion Tomasito the Goya-Girl and Reinaldo Arenas had also done (though fruitlessly, it must be noted). So piercing and so terrifying were the shrieks of the poor pursued and persecuted queen that the president of UNEAC, Nicolás Guillotina, that great bulldog-looking creature, came down the marble steps himself and opened the gate to Eachurbod. Of course he had to, didn't he? After all, Eachurbod—a.k.a. José Martínez Matus—was the only creature on the entire Island who knew *Sóngoro Cosongo* by heart and who would, on the arm of Nancy Mojón, recite it in its entirety while dancing on Nicolás's glass coffee table.

Once inside the offices of UNEAC, Eachurbod explained to the bulldog what had happened and he put the red-bound volume and what was purportedly his wallet down on that same glass table.

"What's this!?" asked Nicolás in utter terror.

"Not to fear," said Eachurbod. "It's just Volume XXVII of the *Complete Works of Lenin.* Don't you remember that you gave it to me yourself? It has that introduction by Juan Marinello."

"The hell with Marinello and that whole fucking book! What terrifies me is that wallet with the initials of the Communist Party on it."

"I picked it up when I was trying to get away. I thought it was mine; I figured it fell out of my pocket when that guy was trying to kick me to death, but now I realize that it was the guy that was kicking me that lost it."

"Idiot!" said Nicolás Guillotina, opening the wallet. "You were playing with the dick of no less than Juantormenta, the world champion runner. This is *his* wallet. I don't know why he didn't catch you. My God, I think he's outside now!"

Terrified again, Eachurbod peeked through the blinds. "Yep, that's him, that's the guy I was fooling with, but he can't be Juantormenta. He's white."

"He's black and he's queer," said Nicolás Guillotina. "Haven't you heard that he puts on white makeup when he goes out cruising, so nobody'll recognize him? As always, my dear, you fucked up."

"Ay!" shrieked Eachurbod, falling to his knees before Nicolás (but not before putting Volume XXVIII of the *Complete Works of Lenin* down as a prayer stool). "Protect me! Cover me with your flag! Take me in as a phallicopolitical refugee. If I leave this building that son of a bitch will cut off my head just to win some more points with Fifo! I'll recite *Sóngoro Cosongo* for you!"

"I can't! I can't!" Nicolás was saying as he paced back and forth across his luxurious office. "Sooner or later Juantormenta will get in here and kill you, and if I try to help you you'll take me down with you. Look at what happened to me when I tried to defend José Mario—Carlos Franqui almost refused to make me Cultural Attaché to the Soviet Union. . . . No, hon. There's nothing I can do for you. Run, try to save yourself the best you can. I can't even stay here with you another minute. I've got to leave—I've got to leave right now. Today that son of a bitch Fifo is celebrating his fiftieth anniversary in power and I've been officially invited to preside over H. Puntilla's second retractation. The first time I got out of it by checking myself into the hospital, but this time there's no way, because I was resuscitated especially for this event and Fifo personally invited me. Ay, there's the limousine they sent to drive me to the celebration, straight to the Hall of Retractations. So long, Eachurbod, and may Lenin and Sensemayá the serpent help you. After all, it was a serpent that got you into this, wasn't it? And by the way, I think it's best if you don't try to go out the back way. Oh, but you can't stay inside. I'll tell you what—if I were you, I'd go up on the roof and wait for Halley's Comet to pass by and grab a ride on its tail."

Nicolás made his deliberate, bulldog way down the enormous marble steps, opened the outside gate and closed it again behind him, gave a contemptuous look at Juantormenta, and got into the hearse that was to drive him to Fifo's palace.

A Journey to the Moon

No one, not even Skunk in a Funk herself, knew the name of that particular prisoner, or what his sentence was (though it seemed eternal), or what his crime had been—though once again, people said it was monstrous: strangling his mother, wife, and children or something along that line. Two passions ruled the deranged murderer, and that was all anybody knew about him: one was his desperate love for or attraction toward the moon; the other was his obsession to fill a huge tank with water that he brought from the bathroom with an eyedropper.

So irresistible was the loco's attraction toward the moon that at night, when the moon came out, he would jump up and down, howl in apparent agony, and fall to his knees in contemplation of the heavenly body, and then moan, bellow, and beat his breast as he stretched his arms out toward it, almost as though trying to embrace it. Sometimes he would throw it kisses and break out in some weird language, prayer, or supplication to the moon—the immense moon whose light streamed through the thick iron bars of the prison in Castillo del Morro. When the great orb would rise out of the sea, looking as though one could reach out and touch it, the madman's paroxysm would reach its peak. He would writhe in convulsions, froth at the mouth, change color, and be shaken by unspeakable trembling; finally, bathed in moonlight, he would fall as though struck by lightning, whimpering amorously until he lost consciousness.

Several times over the years, on nights when there was a full moon, the other prisoners and the cruelest of the guards had tied the madman up and locked him away in a dark cell, but so pathetic, so eerie, was the moaning of the poor man that no one had been able to sleep and he was taken out and returned to the common cells. The most uncanny thing about the man was that when he was locked up in that tiny cell of his, cut off from the world, there was no way he could know when the moon was full, and yet he did know—because when the moon was full his moaning and howling were much louder and more unsettling than on other nights. Once when the prisoners had tied him up to keep him from seeing the moon, the madman somehow freed himself from the ropes, killed several inmates, and ran out into the prison courtyard, howling in lunatic despair.

All of which meant that the murderer, now resentenced (hospitals would have nothing to do with him—he was *way* too crazy for them), had been returned to the common cells, where no one ever bothered him again.

By the time Skunk in a Funk was sent to the prison, the madman was very close to achieving his goal of filling the tank. Ten years he had been at it, and he had only inches to go—though of course since he was filling it with an eyedropper, it would still take him a few months longer. Day and night the madman would make his way through the clumps of prisoners fighting and bickering among themselves, but he never seemed to see or hear them—all he did was scurry with his eyedropper from the tank to the bathroom and the bathroom back to the tank, trying monomaniacally to fill it. His job was made even harder by the frequent lack of water; sometimes, too, he would have to stand in line to fill his eyedropper. But despite all the shortages and outages, no one even *thought* of using the water in the loco's tank. Several years earlier, when one of the prisoners had tried to, he paid for it with his life. Even talking to the loco was risky—the *least* you'd get for your trouble was a kick and a barrage of unintelligible insults. Skunk in a Funk decided not to speak to the madman, just watch him.

Clearly, filling the tank with the eyedropper was a task of vital importance to the man. After some time watching him, Skunk in a Funk, thinking to help the poor fellow, cupped some water in his hands and started toward the tank. The madman, moaning, shrieking, and making terrible threatening sounds and gestures, stopped Skunk in a Funk in her tracks. Obviously, this was a personal mission that he alone could fulfill. Skunk in a Funk understood, and he never again interrupted the madman's labor. She did, however, help make a way for the madman as he hurried back and forth from bathroom to tank cradling his eyedropper in his hand. But one night while the others slept and the madman was scurrying back and forth with the eyedropper, Skunk in a Funk, unable to control herself, asked him in the friendliest yet most respectful way what the purpose of all this work was. The madman, in a voice which was not much more than a confused and hurried moan, or bellow, and which Skunk in a Funk alone was able to decipher, said he was going to the moon.

Skunk in a Funk never interrupted the madman again; day and night the loco continued on his inalterable track, pausing briefly only to shout, moan, howl, in desperate, piteous ritual. At last, one night the tank was completely filled. The next day the madman spent in constant scurrying back and forth, bringing out (whenever he could—the prisoners were allowed out of their cells only for breakfast, or to go out into the courtyard or to the dining room) pieces of chairs, the legs off benches, sticks, stakes, planks, and any other kind of wood (which the prisoners carved into clubs and daggers to kill each other with). He piled all the wood around the tank and that night, as the moon rose, he lighted it. And when the fire was raging, the madman jumped into the water-tank-turned-cauldron and pulled a metal cover over it.

The prisoners could hear the madman's convulsions inside the tank of boiling water, and some tried to get close enough to tip the tank over with sticks and iron bars. But Skunk in a Funk, armed with an even longer bar, kept them all at bay. In the light from an enormous moon suspended before the prison gates, the tank would shake and shiver as the steaming water bubbled, threatening to boil over and flood the gallery. Toward dawn, the sounds inside grew still and the fire flickered out. Skunk in a Funk raised the metal cover from the tank and saw the prisoner, in a fetal position, drowned, boiled, and suffocated. On his face was the placid expression of a child who, cradled by his mother, had just fallen off to sleep. At that, Skunk in a Funk realized that the man had flown off to the moon, for his smile was not of *this* world.

A Tongue Twister (17)

On a remote pastoral tract of agricultural grazing land, a plot abutting a cattle pond whose brackish undrinkable waters were kept in check by a dike, a gaunt and gaga gaggle of ogresses—a pack of particularly ugly hags—delightedly greeted, i.e., applauded, the miraculous copulative contraption concocted by their chocolate-skinned compatriot, an ogre named Otto—a sexual prosthesis affixed to his previously stiff-standing, now pooped-out, prick.

Otto's copulative contraption kept the gaggle of ogresses, that pack of ugly hags, contentedly plugged even while Otto was recuperating his powers or complying with other contractual obligations—so plugged they practically purred.

For the fairies imprisoned in a forced-labor camp

MONKEYSHINES

In the immense Hall of Retractations, all was in readiness. The guests, especially invited for this event, had taken their seats before the stage. Fifo was wearing an impressive dress uniform spangled with stars, with a fatigue cap on his head and an Übercap on top of that one, and on top of the supercap he had pinned an olive branch so long that it reached almost to the floor. He also had on a long red cape and knee boots. H. Puntilla climbed the steps onto the stage; his face was covered with white makeup onto which had been painted the marks and bruises of a recent beating. Then came Nicolás Guillotina, with a solemn, mournful expression and flapping his enormous ears. Guillotina produced a sheaf of papers from a burlap bag and began to read the introduction he had prepared for this precedent-setting event, H. Puntilla's second public self-retractation.

"Dear friends," began the famous poet and rumba dancer, "we are gathered together here today for an event that fills us all with enormous pleasure . . ."

But suddenly he was interrupted by a sound like an exploding submarine, which shook the Hall of Retractations to its foundations. Terrified, Guillotina dropped his papers, scattering them all over the stage, and froze—his enormous ears even stopped flapping. H. Puntilla grew whiter than his white makeup.

"What the *hell* was that?" demanded Fifo.

Several diligent midgets climbed up into the dictator's box and explained what was happening. It seems that Bloodthirsty Shark was doing his underwater performance behind the glass wall of the huge aquarium. No doubt the magnificent creature had gotten the time mixed up, because his performance was scheduled for later—or maybe earlier (I'm not very good at this shark business). Anyway, giving pride of place to his favorite, Fifo ordered the midgets to conduct all the guests in the Hall of Retractations over to the Aquarium Theater. Instantly Nicolás Guillotina, H. Puntilla, the *grandes dames* with their magnificent gowns, the kings, the ministers and foreign dignitaries, the presidents, the henchmen and -women, and all the other VIPs were led by the diligent midgets over to the gigantic underwater grotto, at the very rear of which, before a huge plate-glass window, they gathered to watch Bloodthirsty Shark do his pirouettes. The midgets quickly distributed bottles of champagne and various aphrodisiac delicacies among the guests. *Cocaine,* girl—following the advice of Dulce María Leynaz—was passed around on silver trays.

The act that took place before the guests had no parallel in the history of water ballet. Behind the huge plate-glass wall that opened into the Caribbean, Bloodthirsty Shark was dancing a dance of such singular beauty that it made even Halisia fume with envy. The magnificent creature of the depths rose up like a firebird, hung suspended in the water, waved its fins to fill the aquarium with bubbles of every color, and swam toward the glass, its enormous member fully erect. Each time Bloodthirsty Shark executed one of those magnificent moves, a sigh of almost sexual pleasure escaped the lips of the generals, heads of state, queens, *grandes dames,* and secret agents—indeed, everyone who was honored to view the glorious spectacle.

Fifo ordered his midgets to drop a naked prisoner, hands tied, into the underwater grotto. The first thing Bloodthirsty Shark did was cut through the prisoner's bonds with its teeth and watch for a moment as the victim desperately swam away, trying to escape. But Bloodthirsty Shark easily overtook the man, wrapped him a cloud of bubbles, and dragged him to the bottom of the sea. There, holding the prisoner tight between its monstrous fins, it swam straight up to the surface and with him danced, before a spellbound audience, a dizzying, circular dance—while its erect member created a sea of froth. Finally, crushing the prisoner against the plate-glass wall, it began to devour him, its throbbing member growing larger and larger and swinging about more and more wildly, creating patterns of gorgeous bloody bubbles. This indescribable scene—you just had to be there to see with your own eyes how elegantly the shark swallowed down the pieces of the prisoner's body—aroused the entire audience, who began frenziedly to masturbate (themselves and each other).

"Release the monkeys!" shouted Fifo from his royal box, pushing away the Marquesa de Macondo, who was on her knees madly trying to suck his cock.

Instantly the diligent midgets opened cages at each side of the aquarium, and thousands of sexually aroused simians poured out and began to mate with the crowd, women and men alike. I tell you, Mary, I couldn't *believe* how those big hairy animals with their enormous sex organs would just as soon screw a general as a first lady, an oil magnate or an Oriental henchman as a Miss Universe. I never knew that about gorillas!

But anyway—Meanwhile Bloodthirsty Shark, who by now had gulped down his prisoner, was still lecherously bumping and grinding before Fifo (who was being screwed by a giant monkey) and, of course, all the honored guests, who were also being screwed by the magnificent simians. But even through the racket of that *amazing* bacchanal you could hear the piercing shrieks of pleasure from the Condesa de Merlín, who had been rescued from the gigantic men's room by Fifo's troops. Hearing those screams, Bloodthirsty Shark, at the peak of arousal and abandon, turned toward the crowd and exhibited not only his gleaming and now even more swollen member, but also his testicles, which were as round and glorious as a centaur's.

Seeing those divine stones bobbing almost before her very eyes but out of reach behind the plate-glass wall, Mayoya, unable to control the passion he felt for the shark, violently rejected the advances of an insistent (and magnificent) orangutan and took off running through the audience (who were having their own fun, thank you). Mayoya fled the Aquarium Theater and headed for the sea.

No one saw the little dancing-fairy escape, since everyone, including the soldiers on guard and the diligent midgets, was being *had* by the wondrously endowed, and ever so lecherous, monkeys, who by now were scattering throughout the palace.

IN EL MORRO CASTLE

When Skunk in a Funk walked into the medieval tunnel that connected the outside world to El Morro Castle, she realized that once more she was descending into the depths of hell, and as always, given her sixth sense for horror, she was not mistaken. Nor was this a metaphoric hell, because the castle was an exact replica of the original Stygian stronghold—maybe it even *was* the original. The heat of the walled prison was unbearable, but the noise made by the prisoners was even worse. Day and night, the immense gallery that Gabriel had been sent to was a cacophony of banging cans and sticks, screams, shouts, clapping hands, and the dull sounds of beatings and bellowings. Reinaldo took up residence on a cot that no else would occupy because it was so high up—it was directly under the barred open-air skylight in the roof, so at night the dew would fall on whoever slept in it and the light from the castle's watchtower keep him awake. There, Skunk thought, at least she could stay out of people's way. But prisoners have their ways of finding out everything there is to know about newcomers, so in almost no time they had learned, perhaps from the guards, perhaps from the warden himself (a thug named Torres), that Skunk in a Funk was a writer. "The writer," then, became the name the inmates hung on her, and they took it literally. They would carry their paper and pencils to wherever Reinaldo happened to be and ask him to write a letter for them—to reconcile with a disenchanted girlfriend or a wife who wanted a divorce, or to encourage a faithful, co-conspiring friend or saddened mother. Gabriel, therefore, soon became the official "writer" for the entire gallery, and then for the entire prison. Reinaldo had never written so much in his life. Sometimes he had to find an epistolary solution to really difficult problems. For example, one of the prisoners received a terrible surprise visit one day from his girlfriend, his mistress, and his wife, all at the same time; Reinaldo wrote three letters—pleas with three different pitches. The next visit, he saw how the prisoner was embraced by all three women, who had also brought him a bag filled with his favorite things to eat. (Grateful prisoners would usually invite Skunk in a Funk to these feasts of reconciliation.) Often when Reinaldo saw an inmate kiss his girlfriend or wife, he would think with pleasure that it was *his* skilled letter-writing that had brought about this happy outcome. Other times, his loving letters (written at the behest of a murderer) would lead to a prisoner's conquest of a woman who'd come to visit her brother or her husband.

Given these triumphs, Skunk in a Funk's fame as a writer spread like wildfire through the prison. From the seventeen galleries in El Morro came an unending stream of requests for his services, sent him via balls of soap tied to a long cord that the prisoners lobbed with uncanny skill from their galleries into the writer's. (This clever means of communication was called, with elegant simplicity, "the mail.") The correspondence that Reinaldo sent out (hundreds of balls of soap whizzing through the air, day and night) was almost infinite. But naturally Skunk did not perform these labors free of charge; for each letter, she charged from two to five cigarettes, which were also remitted to her via aerial soap balls. Soon Gabriel had amassed a small fortune—inside the prison, cigarettes, which were severely rationed all over the Island, were as valuable as gold itself.

Because of his role as writer-in-residence, Reinaldo was a sacred personage within the prison; he was a magician, a wizard, a sorcerer, able with a wave of his magic pencil to send messages and images and emotions into the outside world, calm stormy emotional waters, resolve intrigues, foster reconciliations, mend betrayals. This amazing skill assured him a certain degree of impunity within the walls and, as one would expect, the unconditional admiration of all the men, even those Don Juans who had been jailed for "woman problems" and the most renowned and muscular tops, who wasted no time in propositioning her or showing her (with a certain amount of gentility) their erect members and gorgeous balls. Every day the cook and the cook's assistant risked their necks to snitch a plate of food from the dining hall and bring it to Skunk in a Funk.

"Oh, I had plenty of offers, my dear, offers I had aplenty, but I accepted none. I put a cork in my ass is what I did. I had seen that when two machos had a fight over a faggot, it was always the faggot who wound up mincemeat while the two machos kissed and made up, and sometimes did more than kiss. Not to mention all the fucked-up fairies with their *own* complexes to deal with—some of them so jealous that they'd kill a guy they thought was poaching on their territory, while the guy slept; they'd run a long thin iron blade up through the guy's cot or skin him alive with razor blades glued to a stick. And all that on account of 'platonic' friendships, as they called them."

No, Skunk in a Funk wanted nothing to do with sex between men so long as she was in prison—and not just because of the risk that sexual activity entailed in and of itself. In prison, you see, *everybody* did it, which made it practically *de rigueur,* or at least the conventional thing to do—"And, girl, you know I've never been conventional."

For Skunk in a Funk, sex had been an act almost of rebellion, certainly of freedom and *fun*. For Gabriel, picking up a man was a heroic act, and it made him proud. Coming on to a black man at a bus stop, going off into the undergrowth or darkness somewhere with him, facing the whole spectrum of dangers that a homosexual man faced—including the risk that while Skunk in a Funk sucked the black man off, the guy might stomp her, mug her, even slice up her face—that was an act of freedom because it was a risk one *chose*. For

Reinaldo, glory lay in free, spontaneous cruising, the unexpected pickup, the pickup free of second thoughts, free of double-crosses, free of complications. If he had cruised men on the outside it was because they were hard to pick up, they were mysterious and free—at least free to choose whether to have sex or not. Now, in jail, where everybody was desperate for a piece of ass, having sex with a man was an act that was neither heroic nor even really pleasuring. It was insulting to Reinaldo to *have* to have sex with a prisoner—a slave—who was doing it with a fairy only because there were no women. "If there's no bread, let 'em eat cake"—that was the rule among the prisoners. . . . So Skunk in a Funk, who had spent her entire life chasing after men—in fact had wound up in jail because of a man—and who now could have them by the dozen, flatly refused to have anything to do with them. *I'll never have sex with a prisoner,* she swore to herself. A prick dressed up in a prison uniform was a physical and metaphysical fraud, in her view. After witnessing more than a few suicides (by slitting their throats) by fairies desperate for sex with prisoners but never satisfied, Skunk in a Funk decided to dedicate herself to what we might call professional writing (*letter*-writing), and to setting down the fifth version of her novel *The Color of Summer.* After she'd written the day's love letters or pleas to women she'd never met, the fairy would climb up to his cot and work on his book. And so it was to the racket of banging cans and sentimental ballads sung by inmates, the screams of men being stabbed and the moans of pleasure of men screwing or being screwed, that Reinaldo finally reached the end of his thick novel, a work he considered central to his *oeuvre.* He knew that he *had* to rewrite it—because he'd sent his mother to consult the Three Weird Sisters about the fate of the manuscript he'd hidden under the roof tiles of the house in Miramar, and the Weird Sisters had told him in no uncertain terms (by way of his sorely afflicted mother) that the manuscript of Gabriel's novel had been turned over to the police by his Aunt Orfelina and her fag son Tony. Now with the novel completed, all that was left to take care of was one terribly difficult task, the semi-demi-culmination of his labors: smuggle the manuscript out of prison. And I call it the semi-demi-culmination because the semi-culmination would be to smuggle it off the Island and the culmination of culminations, to get it published. . . . But for the moment, the most important thing for Gabriel was the semi-demi-culmination. He had to get the manuscript outside the walls of El Morro Castle.

But that was *not* an easy thing to do. Although inside the galleries the prisoners had a certain degree of freedom (they could screw or suck each other's pricks practically whenever they got the urge), when they left their gallery for visiting hours (which were allowed every two weeks) they were subjected to implacable searches. The prisoners had to strip naked and walk the length of a long table at which dozens of officers were sitting "inspecting" them. Every article of clothing was minutely inspected. Then each inmate had to stand in front of the officers ("combatants," as the Revolution called them) and spread his legs, pull up his balls and prick, open his mouth, and then open his asshole to show that he wasn't trying to smuggle anything out. Skunk in a Funk noticed that during these searches many officers and soldiers became visibly aroused; these were the ones who wore dark glasses so they could ogle the naked prisoners all they wanted to without being called peeping toms or voyeurs—or worse yet, fags.

Through that tunnel with all those inspectors and oglers it was very difficult to smuggle out a sheet of paper, let alone a whole thick novel. And yet Gabriel discovered that under the noses of those guards who watched the prisoners' every move, one of the most intense smuggling operations of any prison anywhere was going on. The prisoners would smuggle out knives, jewelry stolen from other inmates, hundreds of letters that for one reason or another couldn't be submitted to the prison censors, and whatever else they wanted to send back home with the family members that came to visit them. And they also smuggled practically anything they wanted *into* the prison—even revolvers and spare clips. How did they manage to carry on such an operation under the very noses of the officers? Well might you ask, you swishy snoop. . . . It was easy—they hired a mule queen.

The mule queens were fairies who had been screwed by so many men that the carrying capacity of their assholes was almost infinite. In the depths of those asses, apparently all tight and puckered-up (even when they had to spread their cheeks for the searches), they could transport just about anything. For instance, there was the famous mule queen who had brought in two bags of candy, ten cartons of cigarettes, a bar of La Caridad guava paste, six pounds of sugar, and a tube of deodorant—all, of course, in the depths of his ass. Then there was also the famous fairy who died of acute peritonitis when she tried to smuggle out the long, sharp iron bar—known in the prison as a "skewer"—that she had killed her lover with. There were literally hundreds of mule queens, and they would all rush off to the toilet when they came out into the visiting area or back into the gallery. In the toilet, they would look like female fish or insects depositing their eggs as they shat out the goods, wrapped in black plastic bags.

But it wasn't easy to hire a mule queen. All the ones that Skunk in a Funk approached (cautiously hinting at her intentions) absolutely refused to help, saying they'd never been and would never be a mule—though after a little persuading they would confess that they were booked up for months or even years. But since the best coin the mule queens could be paid in was cigarettes (everybody smoked like a chimney), Reinaldo finally managed to hire a famous mule queen who in three trips, for the sum of a thousand cigarettes, smuggled out the manuscript and delivered it, in the standard black plastic wrapping, to Skunk in a Funk's mother, who whined and protested and complained no end about the shit-covered bundles but finally carried them home. When Skunk in a Funk was sure that his entire novel had been smuggled out of the prison, he breathed a sigh almost of relief.

But the relief was short-lived, because before two weeks were out (one day, exactly, before the next visit) a soldier came for Skunk in a Funk and led him to the warden's offices. Gabriel was put into a small room with a vaulted ceiling—like all the rooms in El Morro, including the prison galleries, the hospital and the room they did the searches in. In this small room a young officer was awaiting him, the lieutenant who was in charge of Skunk in a Funk's case, who had interrogated her at State Security, and who was, my dear, a *very* good-looking young man. After furiously pacing back and forth several times while he tugged at his obviously well-stocked basket as though his uniform were more than a little tight, the young lieutenant turned to the little desk in the little room and took from a drawer the latest manuscript of *The Color of Summer,* slamming it over and over again on the little desk, which shivered and shook under the thick stack of papers that assaulted it. Then the officer squeezed his crotch again and, staring at Skunk in a Funk, said:

"There's just no way to rehabilitate you faggots, is there? How many times have we confiscated this counterrevolutionary novel of yours, and you persist in writing it again! Don't you know this could get you ten years more prison time, or even cost you your life? All I'd have to do is send this manuscript to Fifo and in two seconds he'd have some common prisoner strangle you—and make it look like one prisoner with a grudge against another. Don't ever forget that you are in our hands, Reinaldo. We can do away with you right now, or we can set you free tomorrow. It all depends on you. It all depends on how you conduct yourself. And if you persist in this obsession of yours to write these novels, you won't last very long, I can assure you. I'll give you five minutes to reconsider."

But the fairy could hardly reconsider her entire life in five minutes. How could she, with this gorgeous lieutenant pacing back and forth in front of her squeezing his basket, which seemed to have an eel in it that needed some extra space? Obviously the uniform was a little tight in the crotch for the lieutenant, who, being from State Security, was more accustomed to wearing civilian clothes.

"Well, what do you have to say?" the lieutenant, still adjusting his sausage casing, suddenly demanded of Skunk in a Funk.

"I think you're fabulous," said the fairy, staring at the lieutenant's bulging bulge.

"What?" asked the lieutenant in surprise, though still hanging on to his billy club.

"I said I think it's really fabulous that the Revolution has sent a person as kindhearted and generous as you to speak to me and that you've given me time to think, and even given me the opportunity—I hope—to rectify my actions and offer a retractation of all my crimes and misdemeanors. Please—give me some paper and a pencil."

The lieutenant, releasing his instrument of torture at last, held out a sheaf of paper and a pen.

Skunk in a Funk immediately and at remarkable speed composed a lo-o-ong retractation in which she accused herself of treason, counterrevolutionary thoughts and deeds, perversion, and uncleanness and praised the nobility, magnanimity, and greatness of the lieutenant who was in charge of her case—and with respect to the lieutenant's greatness, Reinaldo was not exaggerating, at least in the physical department; then she went into minute detail over the goodness and genius of Fifo. "Everything I have written before this day," the retractation closed, "is garbage, and should be consigned to the garbage heap. From this day forward I shall be a man, and I shall become a worthy child of this marvelous Revolution."

"Very nice," said the lieutenant, nodding, as he read the confession. "Here's your manuscript." And standing, he held out the manuscript to Skunk in a Funk.

"Could you lend me a match?" asked Reinaldo softly.

"You can't smoke in here," answered the delectable lieutenant, once more squeezing his magic wand and divining balls.

"I don't smoke," said the fairy.

The lieutenant handed Gabriel a box of Chispa matches.

Reinaldo struck one and set fire to the manuscript.

"That's the way a man does it!" the lieutenant beamed, and embraced Skunk in a Funk, who, feeling the young officer's stiffie against his crotch, almost fainted dead away. "Now," continued the officer, stepping away (the fairy shuddered with pleasure), "you can go back to your gallery, and you don't need to worry anymore. I promise that nothing will happen to you."

The lieutenant held out his hand to Skunk in a Funk, who squeezed it tight and kissed it (here the lieutenant gave a little shudder of repugnance), and then hurried off to his gallery. As soon as he could, he traded all the cigarettes he had left for blank paper, and once more began the story of his novel.

The Story

This is the story of an island that once had the most beautiful beaches in the world, the most fertile land in the world, the most enchanting capital in the world. This is the story of an island that once had one of the world's most remarkable ballerinas, one of the world's most distinguished poets, and unquestionably the world's best music. This is the story of an island that was once called the loveliest place on earth by a sailor who washed up desperate on its shore, thereby saving himself from a crew that had been threatening to cut off his head for signing them on to a voyage that was, to all appearances, unending.

But little by little, all the inhabitants of this island decided, individually, that they alone should enjoy these beauties. They all began scheming to possess the entire island for themselves, to take over the best land for themselves, to live in the most luxurious house even if everyone else had to live on the street. In their colossal egotism, the prima ballerina refused to allow anyone else to become a prima ballerina, the great poet silenced all the other good poets, and the musicians wouldn't let anybody sing or dance to any music that they themselves didn't make. And as if all that were not enough, they all used every trick they had up their respective sleeves to corner for themselves or their families or their close friends all the public buildings in the city and all the most important positions. The city became a sea of inaccessible towers and walled mansions. Among the most prominent citizens—who all had remarkable criminal minds—so fierce was the struggle to take over the island that soon from among their ranks there emerged a sort of supercriminal, the offspring of generations of criminals, and with his own band of criminals he shut out (or wiped out) the other criminals, so that after a while he was able to proclaim himself the *only* criminal. He quickly moved to take over all the beaches, all the land, and all the cities, and he forced the great ballerina, the great poet, the great singers and orchestras to dance, play, and sing only for him.

A Tongue Twister (18)

Me!—*I'm* no kin to Guillén, that hyena whose tendencies to malfeasance and heinous treason are so fiendish, so deep-seated that I feel they're in the genes. Oh, Guillén, a queen who would be king, unlike others, for instance Arenas, is seen as a winner and his treason and malfeasance have remained secret, but if I were he—or is it him?—I'd seek quarantine in China or even Indonesia, somewhere Asian, because if Fifo gets wind of his evil machinations, there'll be revenge—Guillén will wind up in a hyena roundup and be eased under the guillotine.

For Nicolás Guillotina

The Confession of H. Puntilla

In the immense Hall of Retractations, all was in readiness. The guests had once again taken their seats. Fifo was still wearing his impressive dress uniform spangled with stars, with a fatigue cap on his head and an Übercap on top of that one, and on top of the supercap the olive branch so long that it reached almost to the floor. He also still had on the long red cape and knee boots. H. Puntilla was onstage. Nicolás Guillotina took out his papers again and began to read what might be taken to be an introduction of the alleged traitor.

"Dear friends," began the famous poet and rumba dancer, "we are gathered together here today . . ."

But he got no further because just then, at a signal from the master of ceremonies, the diligent midgets produced enormous trumpets and played a fanfare and Paula Amanda stepped forward to announce that the president of the Spanish Senate wished to bestow upon Fifo the highest distinction awarded by the Spanish government. The president of the Spanish Senate advanced across the stage with the careful movements and pained expression of a man who for many years has been suffering the most terrible hemorrhoids. And he came to the imposing figure of Fifo and awarded him the medal. But so nervous was the poor devil that as he bestowed the medal he stuck Fifo with the pin. "Fascist asshole jackanapes" were the words of thanks that Fifo spoke to the hemorrhoid sufferer.

The diligent midgets blew their trumpets again and Paula Amanda announced that Avellaneda would now come up on the stage to read a sonnet to Fifo.

Avellaneda's immense figure, dressed head to toe in black, slowly began to climb the steps to the stage; she was followed by her literary agent, Miss Karment Valcete. So slowly did these ladies ascend the steps that while we wait for them to take their places we can break away for a couple of minutes to comment on the state of euphoria that Fifo was now in. And for good reason, we might add, because everything about this celebration was going swimmingly, not only with respect to the arts and letters but also financially and politically. The Prime Minister of Canada had signed a pledge to Fifo for a loan of more than a hundred million dollars. An even bigger loan had been promised by the Viceroy of Santo Domingo, and the President of Venezuela had given a speech in which he maintained that every country in the world should annex Fifo's republic. "We might as well," concluded this little tropical Machiavelli, "since soon the world will be but a single monolithic state—Fifoland. And I believe that it is better to sign a peace accord with ink than with our own blood. . . ." When the president of Venezuela finished his speech, Fifo presented him with a package containing a million dollars in hundred-dollar bills. Unbeknownst to the president, however, the package also contained an almost invisible but extremely powerful time bomb set to explode as the president's plane was flying over the Gulf of Mexico, because Fifo's secret informants (among them, the unspeakable E. Manetta) had informed him that the president had also received a check from the United States. . . . But that's all the time we have now, since Avellaneda is just stepping up on the stage with her literary agent. Let's go back to the auditorium and see what happens next. . . .

When those two enormous women mounted the stage where Fifo was awaiting them, many people in the audience feared they would trigger an earthquake. If we include the two women and Fifo, there were more than four thousand pounds of flesh on the stage, and if to that we add the considerable bulk of Nicolás Guillotina and H. Puntilla, who were also on stage, one can see that the fears of the audience were not altogether unfounded. But unaware of the ripples of anxiety she was causing, Avellaneda advanced toward the center of the proscenium and announced that she would read a sonnet dedicated to a man of truly *heroic* proportions. Fifo of course thought the sonnet was dedicated to him, and he bowed his head in grateful appreciation. But when Avellaneda, who was wearing a laurel crown that Raúl Kastro had lent her for a few minutes, began to read her sonnet, it turned out to be about George Washington the very antithesis of Fifo! I mean, Washington was an honest-to-goodness hero! When she came to the end of the sonnet, Fifo, to all appearances unfazed, presented Avellaneda with a red rose and gave her and her literary agent a kiss on the cheek. The midgets played their cornets or clarinets or whatever the hell they were, and Paula Amanda, in yet another long formal gown (this one with a lovely bell-shaped skirt), announced that *now* H. Puntilla would begin his long-awaited second retractation. Avellaneda and Karment Valcete returned to their seats beside H. Puntilla's wife, Miss Baká Kozá Malá, who was holding a machine gun in her lap. Fifo retired to his presidential box, and the spectacle commenced.

Nicolás Guillotina directed a look of disgust at H. Puntilla (who murmured "Thank you, professor") and began to read from his sheaf of papers. It was a *totally* boring speech, full of praise for Fifo, but in the last paragraph all ears pricked up, because Guillotina said that Fifo was aware of everything that was to take place there tonight. Since H. Puntilla's confession was supposed to be "spontaneous," those words had to be taken as a snide poke at the entire event. And that was, in fact, how Fifo took them; he ordered his most loyal midgets to cut off both of Nicolás Guillotina's legs ("Guillotine him! Guillotine him!" were the exact words he used) and leave him to die of double galloping gangrene. The great bulldog finished his speech without looking at H. Puntilla (who once again said, "Thank you, professor") and left the stage to go sit beside Avellaneda. Then Baká Kozá Malá, brandishing her machine gun, called out to her husband—"Talk!"—and H. Puntilla began his "spontaneous" retractation. This statement followed the guidelines set forth in a document entitled "First-Degree Retractation," a model which had with great foresight been drafted more than thirty years earlier by E. Manetta and Edith García Bachaca; it was long, typically bureaucratic statement in which the retractor was to confess to having committed all possible crimes of *lèse-patria* and treason against Fifo and plead that as an act of contrition he or she be executed by firing squad. The document ended with a cry of "¡Patria o muerte! ¡Venceremos!"

But to that Manichean/Manettian document, H. Puntilla added certain touches of his own. For instance, while he was denouncing himself as a traitor and counterrevolutionary he also denounced most of his friends, among them Paula Amanda and César Lapa (the fiery queen of the mulattoes) and even his own wife, who, hearing her name, quickly whipped out the machine gun and fired off a wild barrage that hit a gigantic statue of Karl Marx that stood to the right of the stage and blew it to smithereens. Thinking (as who wouldn't?) that he was actually being executed by the firing squad from which this time not even a retractation would save him, H. Puntilla began to scream uncontrollably and, as proof of his loyalty to the regime, recite the three poems to Spring that he had composed (or so he said) while he was confined in the cells at State Security. At that, Baká Kosá Malá fired off another barrage that brought down the monumental statue of Lenin that stood stage left. H. Puntilla gave a bloodcurdling shriek and screamed "Don't kill me! Don't kill me! I'm sorry, I'm really, really, sorry for all my crimes. I love and revere Fifo—desperately! And if the Comandante of the Dawn of Revolution will come up on the stage, I'll get down on my knees and beg his forgiveness. Please, Comandante, come up here with me!"[1]

Still wearing his long red cape, Fifo bounded up onto the stage with his three famous bounds. H. Puntilla shuffled over to him on his knees, bowed low, and begged the Maximum Leader to spit on him and kick him—which the Maximum Leader, one hand grasping the cape and the other steadying the monumental Übercap, immediately did. The hall exploded with deafening applause. Then H. Puntilla asked the Leader to urinate on him, and instantly a stream of urine so powerful that it seemed to issue from a fire hose bathed the genuflecting body. And again the hall erupted, but this time the applause was even more deafening than before. H. Puntilla then lowered his pants and begged Fifo to give his naked buttocks a kick, and immediately Fifo violently kicked the poet's ass, inspiring a round of applause so thunderous that it threatened to bring the roof down. But H. Puntilla was still weeping, and now

[1] What H. Puntilla really wanted to happen, of course, was for Baká Kosá Malá to kill the Commander in Chief with some of her wild shooting, thereby eliminating *two* of his worst enemies—Fifo and his wife. But his plan was foiled when several diligent midgets disarmed the distraught poetess before Fifo went up on the stage.—Author.

he was pleading with Fifo to please, please, ram his foot, boot and all, up his ass—and getting down on all-fours, H. Puntilla presented his black and apparently bottomless asshole. The Maximum Leader seemed to like that idea. He walked over to the far side of the stage and (aided by the diligent midgets) removed all his clothes, leaving on only his boots, the long red cape, and the magnificent hood with its olive branch. Then, rocking back and forth for a good start, he leaped—all the way from one side of the stage to the other—and planted one of his booted feet square up H. Puntilla's ass. Puntilla gave a piercing scream of pleasure, louder even than the renewed applause that rocked the hall. "What a *fabulous* evening," purred Sr. Torquesada.

The problem came when Fifo tried to pull his boot out of the poet's ass. He couldn't seem to free it from that sphincter that was squeezing the boot like the suckers on an octopus's tentacle or the pincer of a giant crab. More than sixty-nine midgets clambered up onto the stage and started pulling on H. Puntilla, but they couldn't extricate the Leader's foot. Finally, one of the midgets (the supervisor midget, apparently) untied the boot, which left the boot in the backside quicksand and Fifo with a bootless foot, but free. And the boot *remained* inside H. Puntilla's bowels. Folding his long red cape around him, Fifo descended from the stage to wild applause. The smell of shit that came from his foot was dreadful, but the diligent midgets immediately set about licking it clean. (In this they were aided by Mario Bendetta, Eduardo Alano, Juana Bosch, and the Marquesa de Macondo.)

Now H. Puntilla was standing in the very center of the stage. He stripped off all his clothes and with great pride showed the audience his bulging belly with the outline of the Commander in Chief's size-thirteen boot. I'll tell you, my dear, the man's face had never displayed such an expression of joy—at last he had been impregnated by the Maximum Leader's hated yet infinitely beloved boot. But H. Puntilla was always an *extremely* ambitious man, as you know, so once again he begged the Maximum Leader to come up on stage, and this time bury his *second* boot in his ass. That way he would bear within his womb the impress of the greatest man of this century—those were the very words he spoke, and he was instantly echoed by Bosch, still licking the Leader's shit-covered foot. The Comandante, beet-red with rage at the stench of shit, rose from his seat and reached the stage in only two large bounds—and that was with one foot missing a shoe! "Now I'm *really* going to screw this faggot," he murmured to himself as, rocking back and forth to get up a good head of steam, he flew through the air—cape flying, body naked, booted foot extended—and landed, his boot sinking not just up to the knee but all the way up to the thigh. H. Puntilla gave an indescribable shriek. The audience gave a standing ovation. But this time it was *really* hard for the Commander in Chief to extricate himself from that anal bog. Even though H. Puntilla could hardly breathe, his sphincter maintained a death grip on that foot. The diligent midgets tugged desperately on the poet, but all their efforts were in vain. Finally they called on Avellaneda and Karment Valcete to lend a hand. The two women lumbered up onto the stage again, and Avellaneda took H. Puntilla,

Valcete took Fifo, and they each began to pull. H. Puntilla was still howling in pleasure, Fifo was muttering curses, and the audience was going wild. The two gigantic sweaty women huffed and puffed and tugged and pulled, but they could not separate the two bodies. They were almost ready to give up when a sound without parallel in the history of terraqueous sounds (and there have been plenty of them) split the rear curtains in the theater and shattered windowpanes and chandeliers. The sound was louder than fifteen torpedoed submarines, the detonation of a gigantic mine in the Bartlett Trench, the suicidal self-detonation of a whale in the Antarctic Ocean, and an atomic explosion in the Japan Sea, all at once. And it seemed to be coming from the Aquarium Theater!

In a single tremendous tug, Fifo pulled his half-body from the poet's ass (causing the poet to swoon into the arms of Avellaneda) and, followed by a crowd of guests and the ubiquitous diligent midgets, ran to the aquarium. There, he was halted in his tracks at a spectacle like none any human had ever seen before. Behind the plate-glass wall of the aquarium, and before an audience stretched out in the comfort of their seats, Bloodthirsty Shark and Miss Mayoya were writhing in the throes of passionate, violent copulation.

SKUNK IN A FUNK

Throughout Fifo's party, Skunk in a Funk had taken part in the festivities with real abandon, though also with wisdom and cunning. She intrigued, entertained, enchanted; her conversation ranged from the most trivial (a play on words, for example) to the most transcendental (a proof of the existence of the Devil). But which one was it that was there that night? Which one was it that now, shimmying and shaking and dancing through the delirious Carnival, was looking for Tatica so she could kill him? Was it Skunk in a Funk, the screaming queen? Was it Gabriel, the farm boy, the country bumpkin from the hills of Holguín? Was it Reinaldo, the ill-fated and forever luckless writer? We cannot be sure which of the three was there that night representing the other doubles who, inspired by the example of Ñica, had fled the country years earlier across the Strait of Florida. But whichever one it was, s/he embodied all the absent ones to perfection. So well, in fact, that however long, however deeply we have investigated, we have not been able to discover which one it was who attended the Carnival festivities in representation of his/her *true and authentic* doubles. Who was Skunk in a Funk actually representing? Who was she being represented by?

A Tongue Twister (19)

Lulled by Liberace's "Clair de lune," Lala, Lapique's loyal ally, a lusty lollapalooza of a lass, was lolling languorously on her chaise longue in a long lovelorn lethargy when, looking up, she saw Lilliputian libertine Lulu, whose licorice lollipop she began to lustily lick.

How long did Lala lustily lick Lilliputian Lulu's licorice lollipop?

And did the Lilliputian libertine Lulu like having her lollipop licked by Lala the lecherous lollapalooza? Loved it!

For Lala the lollapalooza

That Earthshaking Coupling

For many years, all the queens on the Island, including those who were apparently on Fifo's side (or even his informants), had gleefully whispered among themselves that Bloodthirsty Shark, like all sharks, was a top. Many of the queens who had dived down and gnawed away at the Island's undermooring had seen how the male gnawers who were caught by Bloodthirsty Shark or the other, smaller sharks would not only be torn to pieces by those creatures but also cruelly raped.

One day, a group of imprisoned ogresses sitting on the side of a dam in a concentration camp formed a committee and decided that the only way to eliminate Bloodthirsty Shark was through love. Yes, one of the most beautiful queens on the Island had to be trained in the art of seduction so he could seduce Bloodthirsty Shark. The choice fell on Miss Mayoya. This mulatto-skinned beauty seemed to have discovered the secret of eternal youth; his neck was long and perfect, her mouth was ripe and sensual, his eyes were green, and her hair fell in ringlets as gleaming as her eyes. And so the wisest queens on Fifo's staff—queens such as Ho' Guerra, Capitán Pachuca, Miss Güé Güevavara—spent hours, days, weeks instructing the beautiful fairy in the art of seducing sharks. And because they were all high officials in the regime, these queens could bring back from Paris all the perfume, sex oils, makeup, shampoo, and hair spray imaginable to make Mayoya even more irresistible to the carnivorous sea creature. Mayoya, perfectly oiled, perfumed, and dressed in nothing but a sequined bikini (which concealed a silver dagger), would spend long hours on a rock beside the ocean, dancing, swaying his hips, and generally enticing Bloodthirsty Shark, who would swim back and forth, snorting, before the glistening beauty on the beach. It was not long before Bloodthirsty Shark began to court, or at least strut his stuff for, Mayoya, who went on dancing on her rock beside the sea, the long silver dagger at his waist. Bloodthirsty Shark would emerge from the bottom of the sea and begin to frolic about on the surface. At that, the queen would swing his hips even more seductively, toss her ringleted hair, and neigh as beguilingly as she could. The great ocean creature would swim on its back, shoot up out of the water like a jet-propelled missile, touch the clouds, and in a tumult of spray dive straight down into the water again, directly before the dancing queen. Clearly, Bloodthirsty Shark had fallen in love with Mayoya. Oh, but something unplanned had happened—the dishy Mayoya had fallen in love with the great shark, too. . . . And yet, being a family-values kind of queen, she always set principles before passion. The shark, however, had been trained by Fifo, who had *no* principles, and within the most rigid antifaggot upbringing, and though it would often screw a male victim (who would die a double death, of pleasure and shark bite simultaneously), its first obligation, as we have seen, was *to kill the traitor.* A bloodthirsty shark can never forgive a traitor, much less a faggot whose very nature it was to be a *double* traitor. That was the implacable law in which the shark had been brought up—not only by Fifo but also by Isabel Monal and all the other distinguished professors of dialectical materialism. Clearly, then, between the love the shark felt for Mayoya and its conscience, there yawned an unbridgeable chasm. And above that yawning chasm the desperate shark, member erect, would dance. . . .

And as for Miss Mayoya, he had always demanded the biggest piece of meat in existence—indeed a unique piece of meat (which was why the silly thing was actually still a virgin)—and so he believed that in the bearing, grace, and proportions (!) of Bloodthirsty Shark he had at last discovered the object of his unfulfilled rectal longings. And yet that same shark was the symbol of the repression that had prevented her and everyone else on the Island from ever finding fulfillment. And so between Mayoya and Bloodthirsty Shark there *also* lay a gulf of grave moral principle. . . . Still, to be swept off her feet by that marine *beast,* to feel—ohmigod—that monstrous carnivore wrap her in its fins, carry her to the bottom of the sea, penetrate her in one swift terrible thrust, and then in a transport of ecstasy and glory, crowned with seashells, sea urchins, and jellyfish, fly with her up to the very clouds—it would be *heaven*. . . . And so, torn between principle and love, the queen would weep as she danced upon her seaside boulder, and Bloodthirsty Shark, its face unmistakably macho-tough yet suddenly tragic, perhaps even filled with remorse, would dance in lustful pirouettes before the forbidden faggot.

This romance had been contained, controlled, and kept virtually in secret until the day that Mayoya saw, up close—up *very* close, separated by only the plate-glass wall of the aquarium—the unbelievable dimensions of Bloodthirsty Shark's tool. The poor fairy could bear it no longer—he gave a cry that nobody heard (since everyone was being raped by the primates) and ran madly from the catacomb palace. He traversed the broad lawns, crossed the Malecón, vaulted the crowd of Pissed Disinvitees, ripped off all her gorgeous clothes (except for the sequin-spangled bikini), and, dagger at her waist, plunged into the sea. He was going to meet his lover, who meantime was soaring through the waters near the Presidential Palace.

"Now, at last, divine justice shall be done," intoned Padre Gastaluz, seeing the faggot madly run into the sea, dagger at his waist. And the entire group of Disappointees fell to their knees upon the rocks.

"Now, my dear, what is going to happen is that that shark creature is going to rip her to shreds, unless of course a miracle should occur," said the King of Romania, kissing an image of the Black Virgin of Kraków and watching Bloodthirsty Shark swim toward Miss Mayoya.

"She's going to kill Bloodthirsty Shark," were the words of Sakuntala la Mala and the head of the Italian Communist Party, in unison.

Alongside the palace, near the shore, and in full sight of the Nobodies, the long-awaited meeting at last occurred. Mayoya, opening her arms, embraced the potent phallus of Bloodthirsty Shark—a phallus which emerged from the shark's sleek body like a black periscope—as the sea creature beat its fins in pleasure. In a fit of ecstasy, Mayoya planted kisses along the whole splendid length of it. The shark, propelling itself with its powerful tail, sailed with the queen high into the air as it kissed her and with its magnificent teeth ripped off her sequined bikini. In the air, the queen hurled away the silver dagger, which fell into the sea, and lifting her arms high, fell backside-first upon the shark's gigantic member. The shark, at that, performed a violent contraction and penetrated her to the hilt. Smoke issued from the queen's mouth—boiling-hot steam produced by the shark's sleek piston in Miss Mayoya's ignition chamber. Mayoya, like some lascivious buoy, bobbed and floated on the surface of the waves, spitted deliriously upon the shark's stiff member. The pleasure that the two bodies were giving and receiving was so great that powerful electrical charges flashed from them like lightning bolts or huge sputtering arrows launched toward the heavens, and these electrical discharges set off a terrible storm, which the Uninvitees on the shore, in their anxiety over the outcome of the sexual combat, faced with uncommon bravery as they clung to the rocks along the beach. When the storm clouds cleared, they could once more watch the lustful sport that was still going on out at sea—and, disappointed and dejected by this new disillusionment, plot a new route to vengeance. But shark and fairy, oblivious to all dangers (which were considerable), were intent only upon their savagely licentious encounter—which, by the way, was now taking place under serene and cloudless skies. Mayoya walked, arms spread, upon the water and then suddenly, opening her sensual mouth, dived onto and deep-throated Bloodthirsty Shark's black rod. Bloodthirsty Shark, rising higher and higher out of the blue ocean with Mayoya in its jaws, began to tickle him with its many rows of sparkling teeth. And so, never touching the waves, and before the terrified eyes of Deaconess Marina and Bishop O'Condom, fairy and shark performed a coupling so high in the air that it seemed to be freed from the laws of gravity. Mayoya then took the shark's pole with a tremendous howl of laughter and stuck her head in the beast's jaws—the beast, still more aroused, and without withdrawing its member from the little fairy, leapt from wave to wave, giving off a smell of male sex hormone so strong that it polluted those waters for all eternity (which is why you always see so many maricones having sex on that beach—it's the pheromaricones, I mean pheromoans, I mean pheromones) and even stimulated the sea cucumbers, who awoke from their thousand-year sleep. . . . That unparalleled member even temporarily blocked the path of the Gulf Stream, which, breaking loose at last, gave an enormous heave and threw Ernest Hemingway (who'd been resuscitated to attend Fifo's party) all the way to Greenland, where, seeing himself naked and with such a little tiny dick, he hanged himself with one of his fairy feathers. And for several minutes more the priapic sleek black shark and fiery fairy writhed in one ultimate sexual spasm, emitting shrieks, fish scales, streams of hot and cold semen, muffled giggles, and stunning flutters of the fins. Then, meshed into one great whirlpool of lust, they spiraled downward into the depths of the waters, setting off a waterspout that even today is the bane of sailors around the world. Then, like an erotic meteor scuttling across the ocean floor and setting off undersea earthquakes, shark and fairy, still carnally coupled, came at last to the plate-glass wall of the underwater Aquarium Theater in Fifo's palace. There the copulation was in full flower when Fifo and his entourage burst into the hall.

We should note here, I think, that never in the entire long history of screwing had such a screw been seen—or would ever be seen again. There in the great underground fishbowl, the shark and the fairy writhed, leaped, twined, twisted, embraced, nibbled, bubbled with pleasure, and unleashed deafening underwater thunder. . . . Fifo was red with rage. This was not only an emotional blow, but a moral blow as well—emotional because he had always secretly been in love with that shark (as he had once been with a very special cow); moral, because the sex he was seeing was an act of high treason, an act of ideological betrayal committed, to make matters worse, before his VIP guests—first ladies, ministers, attorneys general, kings, drug traffickers, magnates, henchmen and flunkies, poetesses, and other well-educated whores.

And what, in the meantime, were those VIP guests doing as they contemplated the spectacle from their velvet seats? The only thing one *can* do, my dear—they were all sitting there jerking off.

Fifo, who never once gave any sign of losing his composure, first gave secret orders that Bloodthirsty Shark was to be annihilated by any means necessary and then, in a loud voice, ordered his midgets to release the monkeys again. But after the titanic bout of lovemaking that they had just gone through with all the guests, the monkeys acted more like zombies than lecherous simians, and were able to do little more than drape themselves over the aroused bodies of the guests. The only person who managed to stimulate her primate partner was Mother Teresa, who finally worked up an erection in a gigantic orangutan by whispering a stream of Latin in its ear. The other guests had to make out the best they could. The Prime Minister of India, for example, unwound the wrappings from the mummy of his mother (whom he himself had killed) and began to mount her while he was being mounted by several of his muscular escorts, each wearing a costume of his home province.

Suddenly, a sleek frogman (dispatched by the diligent midgets) swam into the waters of the aquarium and fired off a harpoon at Bloodthirsty Shark. Seeing the deadly lance, Mayoya made a desperate effort—the effort that can be inspired only by love—and pulled Bloodthirsty Shark, still harpooning *her,* out of the way just in the nick of time. But the hail of deadly harpoons continued, and then there came a depth charge so powerful that Bloodthirsty Shark (taking care that nothing happen to his beloved Mayoya, whom he never ceased embracing) was thrown against the glass wall of the Aquarium Theater. So hard did Bloodthirsty Shark crash into the glass that it shattered into a million pieces—and a wall of water exploded into the auditorium. Terrified, the audience, their clothes soaked through, began to flee the mini-tsunami, with the monkeys right behind (though many of them were so exhausted that they drowned). Water flooded not only the Aquarium Theater but the whole catacomb palace, despite the most diligent efforts of the diligent midgets, who were desperately stopping up cracks and closing air locks.

Just then, from outside the palace, a metallic roar, a clanking clamor, was heard.

"Oh, my god, the Garden of Computers!" cried Fifo, now paddling one of the rafts that the diligent midgets had distributed among the guests. "I forgot! It's feeding time! Come on! You've gotta see this!"

And plucking up their courage, the entire floating entourage followed Fifo to the Garden of Computers.

Meanwhile, Mayoya and Bloodthirsty Shark were swimming out of the palace into open water. They were pursued by the harpooners, several planes, and a fleet of enormous attack helicopters presented to Cuba by the former dictator of Romania so Fifo could "contain the rebellious hordes"—it was clear that Fifo had no intention of allowing those two traitors to live. Bloodthirsty Shark, fearing for its life, gave Mayoya a lingering farewell kiss, dropped him off near the shore, and then dived into the waves and began to gnaw at the Island's foundation—much to the surprise of the other rodents. And even more surprising, Bloodthirsty Shark ordered all the other sharks (with depth charges still going off all around them) to start gnawing at the foundation, too. And all the sharks began to gnaw. They were joined by throngs of octopuses, squid, crabs, sea urchins, sea turtles, and other sea creatures whose family members had been wounded or killed by the depth charges and harpoons. And as though that were not amazing enough, several bishops in full bishopric regalia, nuns in their wimples, the head of Soviet counterespionage, some of Fifo's most trusted generals, a Miss Universe, a Nobel Prize winner, and even a high official in the Chinese Empire (among others), taking advantage of the momentary confusion, dived into the water to help.

Meanwhile, Miss Mayoya, with the triumphant air of a queen who's just had the screw of his life, had reached the shore and collapsed, exhausted with pleasure, near the milling crowd of Dissed and Pissed. Immediately this group, egged on relentlessly by Deaconess Marina, King Miguel I of Portugal, the head of the Zambian Armed Forces, Clara Mortera, and the Prince of Batavia, decided that the fairy should be tried by court-martial for high treason. The tribunal was composed of, among other celebrities, the queen of the Carnival in Rio de Janeiro, the president of Amnesty Intercontinental, Padre Gastaluz, Sakuntala la Mala, Odoriferous Gunk and his dying mother, and the head of the Italian Communist Party; also seated on the panel were the cunning Mahoma, Delfín Proust, SuperSatanic, and Skunk in a Funk, who, under cover of the confusion caused by the flood, had escaped the palace to confront Mayoya. The court's sentence (unanimous) was handed down within five minutes: Mayoya was to be burned alive on the seashore before the anguished eyes of Bloodthirsty Shark, who was constantly poking its head up out of the water to see what the fate of its beloved little fairy queen was to be.

Mayoya was bound to a sharp rock and dry sticks were piled all around her. Hiram, la Reine des Araignées, lit the pyre. Padre Gastaluz and Bishop O'Condom began to pray for the salvation of the fairy's soul. The queen of the Carnival in Rio de Janeiro, in all her regal splendor, approached the flames, waving a huge cross she had made out of two planks. "Abjure! Abjure as Joan did!" the queen of Carnival was shouting as she waved her cross around like a magic wand.

"Yeah, like crazy Joan," said Sakuntala la Mala loudly as she threw more kindling on the fire.

But instead of abjuring, Mayoya hawked a wad of smoking spit straight at the queen of the Carnival in Rio, putting out her eye.

While the queen burned, the Disappointees, including the head of the Third Independence Party of Puerto Rico, Corazon Aquino, Uglíssima, and even the Anglo-Campesina and Odoriferous Gunk's dying mother, formed a huge circle around her, clasped hands, and began to dance around the gigantic pyre. This ritual continued for a long time, since although the queen was burning on the outside from the flames, inside he was just *hot,* remembering the incredible pleasure she had experienced during the world's greatest screw with Bloodthirsty Shark. And as she recalled the ecstasy of those moments, the queen came in a flood of cum, extinguishing part of the fire, which had to be started again.

Meanwhile, in a delirium of rage and impassioned grief, Bloodthirsty Shark rose into the sky, its horrid teeth crushing Fifo's planes—which could never have destroyed the fearsome fish anyway.

At last, the once sexy, once dancing fairy was fried to a crisp. *Requiescat in pace,* said Padre Gastaluz, sprinkling the ashes with water from his silver aspergillum (the same aspergillum he had used to bless a steam engine more than a hundred and fifty years earlier). And then the ashes were thrown into the sea, where Bloodthirsty Shark was once again gnawing at the Island's foundation.

A Tongue Twister (20)

I, Meme, mummified male mammal, hum as I munch the yummy male member of Momo, the Mameluke mime. My mommy, muse of all member-munchers and sometimes memo-minder for Mumo the Minister of Mammal Morals, always gave me mameys to munch as a mimetic mimicry of male-member munching. Mommy herself makes music on Mumo the minister's much-munched male member by mimicking *me* humming munching on Momo's yummy male member.

Which male members does Meme's mommy munch and which members are munched by Meme? Who munches the member of Momo the Mameluke mime, and who munches the member of Mumo the Minister of Mammal Morals? Who merely mimics munching? And what is the exact meaning of mimetic?

For Meme Solas, a.k.a. the Mummy

A Letter

Havana, July 25, 1999

My dearest Reinaldo, Gabriel, and Skunk in a Funk,

I just want to answer—once and for all—those letters from the three of you that have managed to get through. (And since the ones I've gotten all say more or less the same thing, I don't think I'll be failing to address anything important.) I assure you that I can imagine how much you've all suffered—and will go on suffering—and how lonely you must be up there, far from this country that is and always will be ours, no matter where we live. But get real. Nothing that you suffer can compare with the horror of life down here. Up there, even if all you get is kicks in the ass, at least you can yell about it—here, we have to applaud when we get kicked, and applaud enthusiastically. How can the three of you have the nerve to tell me I should stay here? Have you forgotten so soon that living under a tyranny is not just a shame and a curse, but an abject act that fills us with self-disgust because if we want to live, we have to play the game by the tyrant's rules, whether we want to or not?

I'm really tired of all your moaning and carrying-on, and of hearing how alone you are, and about the plagues that are killing you. We're all alone here, too, and I have the plague, too, but I don't get the medical attention I need—there's no way for me to get it—and I can't make the slightest whimper.

You might ask, then, how I dare to write so openly. The answer is very simple: Tomorrow, at the height of Carnival, I plan to throw myself into the sea with my latest (my last) novel—which I haven't been able to smuggle out of the country—and my swim fins. Into the sea! With a little luck the coast guard and the sharks will be drunk celebrating the triumph of Fifo's reign, and I'll be able to escape. Although most likely I'll just die trying.

You haven't said anything about my books. I hope all the ones I've sent you arrived safely. You know, I think, that everything I've done comprises a single enormous work. Sometimes, as in the case of the Pentagony, it follows a single line, with the same characters and the same desperations and calamities; in other cases, the characters, in other guises, travel through time—they're friars, black slaves, pathetic mad condesas. But all the things I've done—poems, stories, novels, plays, and essays—are linked; they form a series of historical, autobiographical, and agonic cycles, a series of anguished transmutations. Even in the book of poems I titled The Will to Live Manifesting Itself, there is a sonnet inspired by Skunk in a Funk. So I ask of you—please, if all this is published, tell people that my books constitute a single enormous whole in which the characters die, are reborn, appear, disappear, travel through time—always mocking, always suffering as we ourselves have mocked and suffered. All of my characters form a single mocking, despairing spirit, the spirit of my work, which is also, perhaps, the spirit of our country. As for my play Abdala, don't publish it, for heaven's sake—I really don't like it; it's a sin of my youth.

Well, that's about it—I've got to go get my novel into a bottle. And tomorrow, into the sea. There's no way for me to tell you how I feel, so I'll resist the temptation to put into words things that can't be put into words. . . . As I finish writing this letter, I feel that I am holding each of your hands in mine—this may be the last time we ever do that.

It's terrible to say good-bye when almost certainly we'll never see each other again yet we are all, still, part of a single scattered person, and when in addition we say good-bye across a distance, in absentia, without being able to see one another, and through a letter that may well never reach you. Really, the horror we've experienced not even the worst kind of criminal deserves. Maybe when I get to Hell I'll be able to smash the Devil in the face and ask him what we've done to deserve this. But no—I'm sure I'll never have that consolation. Not even the consolation of Hell. Before me, the ocean, just the ocean. . . . Beyond that, oblivion. Period. Maybe that's the best thing. Maybe. . . .

Farewell—
Skunk in a Funk

The Death of Virgilio Piñera

Just five minutes to go before the official inauguration of the Grand Carnival (although it had, of course, actually started several hours ago), which meant that Fifo's orders to assassinate Virgilio Piñera were coming down to the wire. The agents had to work fast.

Virgilio's closest friends—José Rodríguez Pío, for one—had provided Fifo's security forces with detailed reports on his routine: the old poet went to bed early and got up at sunrise, had a cup of coffee that he'd bought on the black market, and immediately sat down to write. Later, he went out with his burlap sack to stand in line for yogurt.

Virgilio lived alone on the tenth floor of a small apartment house in El Vedado. It was ten P.M. and he was already in bed, deaf to the noise of Carnival that filled the street below. The poet's eyes were closed, but the memory of Humberto Arenal's latest novel was keeping him awake. How, wondered the poet, can a person write so badly and at the same time be my friend? These literary and ethical questions prevented the poet from falling asleep even though the law of the household (set down by himself) said that he should have been in dreamland long ago in his absolutely darkened bedroom.

Virgilio thought he heard the door to his apartment open and someone come in.

"Is that you, Arrufada?" he asked fearfully, for Arrufada had a key to his apartment and would often stop in to read him his latest play.

But the old poet got no reply. In the darkness he thought he heard someone come through his little living room, bump into a chair, and enter his bedroom. From the heaviness of the footfalls, Virgilio deduced that it couldn't be Antoni Arrufada—in fact, that it couldn't be a single person.

The reader will remember that when Fifo gave the order for the hit, he had given strict instructions that it be carried out in silence and that it appear to be not murder but rather suicide or heart attack, something along that line.

Suddenly, the bedroom light came on and the poet saw four muscular men jump at him. They grabbed him by the neck and started strangling him. That was one of the alternatives Fifo had suggested to his stooges—Barniz and Paula Amanda had told Fifo that Virgilio had mentioned several times that he wanted to hang himself, and strangling was a lot like hanging. Plus, once Virgilio was dead they could string him up with a rope that one of the killers had brought along. "Wring that chicken neck good for me"—those had been

Fifo's very words. So the agents had their hands around Virgilio's neck as the poet's big frightened eyes stared back at them. But the old poet's neck was so long, so skinny, and so flexible that there was no way to wring it. So the eight murderous hands began to pull on it, intending to at least rip the poet's head off. But this, too, was not to be, because the poet's long, narrow head was no bigger around than his neck, which meant that the murderers' hands slipped up his neck and right off the top of his head, and the agents found themselves clutching air. In fact, to the chagrin of the four agents, not only Virgilio's neck but his entire body was so slippery and so virtually ungraspable that it was more like the body of a snake or an eel than a man's—which made it impossible to strangle him, pull his head off, or draw and quarter him, especially since everything had to be done in silence. (Don't forget that Fifo wanted this done discreetly.) Exhausted after tugging for more than an hour on the poet's untuggable neck, the gorillas turned out the lights in the apartment and went outside to regroup. They decided to have a couple of beers, which they drank from their cardboard cartons to the sound of the Carnival bacchanalia.

"What a nightmare I had!" Virgilio said to himself when he was alone once more in his darkened room. "I dreamed that four men came in and tried to strangle me. I *have* to stop reading Humberto Arenal."

And making a tremendous effort—because outside, the Carnival was in full swing, the noise was unbelievable, and the memory of the novel continued to haunt him—the poet fell asleep. But in a few minutes the front door of his apartment creaked open again, and Virgilio awoke.

"Is that you, Arrufada?" the poet asked, sitting up in his bed.

But there was no reply.

The four agents, now about half drunk, entered Virgilio's bedroom and turned on the light. While one of them put his hand over the poet's mouth, the others carried the playwright's fragile body out to the balcony. If what Fifo wanted was for Virgilio's assassination to look like suicide, then what better way to do it than by throwing him over the balcony? What proof would people have—people who didn't dare speak out openly, anyway—that the poet hadn't leaped to his death intentionally? And without further ado the four muscular agents threw Virgilio's body (dressed in lilac-, black-, and white-striped pajamas) over the balcony railing.

And that seemed to be that, thought the exhausted assassins, who peeped over the edge to see the mess the poet made when he splattered on the sidewalk down below. But to their amazement and consternation, the body of Virgilio hadn't splattered; it was floating in the air. And then, to make matters worse, it was picked up by a passing breeze and blown back onto the balcony. Clearly the man was so skinny that he was weightless, or at least lighter than air—which made it hard to throw him off the balcony. Virgilio grabbed the railing and pulled himself back into his apartment.

"Pepe! Pepe!" the desperate poet called out to his putative friend. "There's four blackguards in here who're trying to kill me! Guillotina sent them!"

But Rodríguez Pío, watching through the peephole in the front door of his apartment across the hall, didn't make a peep.

Fifo's stooges picked up Virgilio's body and threw it over the balcony three more times, but the body would always float up again and waft into the apartment.

"Try this arsenic!" said a voice (Rodríguez Pío's) behind the murderers manqués, and a hypodermic needle filled with arsenic clattered across the hall and into the apartment.

The four stooges grabbed the body that had just floated into the apartment again and held Virgilio down for the lethal injection. But the poet's skin had been so toughened by his diet of wheat-based products and Bulgarian yogurt, plus the sun he was exposed to when he stood in the infinite lines, that it was more like a turtle shell than human skin. So the injection was useless—it was like trying to stick a straight pin into a crocodile. Enraged, the murderers threw the poet *and* the hypodermic needle over the balcony and decided to go down and have a few more beers and think up some way to finish this off.

"What a nightmare I had!" Virgilio told Rodríguez Pío, who had crept into the apartment to see if the murderers had left so he could steal the presumably dead poet's copy of *Larousse*. "I dreamed that four muscular men—the kind you don't see much in Havana anymore—had thrown me over the balcony!"

"An old man's bad dreams," Pepe tried to calm him. "Muscle-men don't even know you exist anymore. Go to bed—tomorrow you won't remember a thing."

And he left.

It took Virgilio, who was still a bit nervous from all the excitement, a long time to get back to sleep. Besides, the noise from the Carnival down below was deafening. But he made a great effort and fell asleep at last. He had hardly closed his eyes, though, when the four persistent stooges came back.

"Is that you, Arrufada?" Virgilio asked for the third time, now convinced that he was going to get no sleep that night.

But the poet got no response. All he heard was the muffled sound of footsteps coming toward him in the otherwise silent darkness. The sound stopped beside the big bed in which Virgilio was lying. And then one of Fifo's secret police agents turned on the light. Standing before Virgilio were the four thugs out of his nightmare, now realer than ever, carrying a huge easel on which stood a large painting covered with a black cloth. The men swooped the cloth away, and Virgilio's eyes opened wider than they had ever opened in his life, despite all the horrors he had seen. The only thing on the canvas (whose paint, by the way, was still fresh) was a gigantic cunt surrounded by glistening pubic hair, the cunt lips open wide to reveal the pink bud inside, which was painted with such realism that it seemed to leap out at the poet. In fact, it seemed to be writhing on the canvas, oozing sexual juices, and gurgling lasciviously. Piñera, unable to bear such a sight, died instantly of cardiac arrest.

The four stooges checked to make sure the poet was really dead; then they dressed him and began arrangements for his funeral, which would be held that very morning. As they left, they picked up the gigantic painting—which Fifo had already sold to Anastasia Filipovna, who was waiting impatiently in a yacht just off the coast—and carried it away with them.

Today, dear readers, the murder weapon that was used in the assassination of Virgilio Piñera, a canvas three feet wide by six feet high, can be seen in Gallery 21 (Fetishes and Religious Objects) in the Tyrant's museum, thanks to a generous donation from Peggy Guggenheim. It is Clara Mortera's masterpiece, a painting entitled *Portrait of Karilda Olivar Lubricious,* an oil on canvas which she had done earlier that day.

A Tongue Twister (21)

Ñica, in a soignée gown of brown vicuña, growled "Coño, Geño," at his friend Geño Ñañez when Geño, the meany, went "Nyah nyah, nyah nyah nyah" at Ñica's soignée vicuña gown. Ñica had just asked Geño if he liked vicuña, and thought if he didn't he should have just said Nyet, not nyah nyah, nyah nyah nyah.

For Ñica

The Trials and Tribulations of Young Teodoro Tampon

In the midst of all the complications that Skunk in a Funk was involved in—denunciations, persecutions, threats of blackmail, unconfessable diseases, the unavoidable visit to Blas Roka to seek clemency for the Areopagite—and above all at the most complex and difficult moment of his novel *The Color of Summer,* the part in which Fifo was finally leading his guests out to the Garden of Computers—at precisely *that* climactic and terribly complex moment in the plot, Reinaldo had to put down his pen and run off as fast as he could to the house, or room, or *dump* that Clara Mortera lived in. Where, it turned out, he found Teodoro Tampon, round and out of breath, waiting for him. And in Teodoro's pained expression Skunk in a Funk read a desperate plea for aid for Teodoro and his wife.

The trouble, however, as Skunk in a Funk knew, was that things were not that simple. There was no way it would all end there, with him magically solving whatever the problem was between Teodoro and Clara and then just going back to what he'd been doing. No, Skunk in a Funk knew that problems between a husband and wife (whether she was a whore and he a fairy, or she was a nun and he a Knight of Malta) were *never* really solved.

And there stood Teodoro Tampon with that pained look on his face.

For years now, Skunk in a Funk had had to put up with the clandestine visits of Teodoro Tampon, who would slink into Skunk in a Funk's room in the Hotel Monserrate and in a gasping voice (and flapping his short little arms) exclaim:

"Please, Reinaldo, lend me your swim fins! Tonight I'm jumping in the ocean! I can't stand it anymore—I've got to get out of this country!"

And with a sigh of resignation Gabriel would crawl under the bed, pull out his beloved swim fins (which were not even a *shadow* of those wonderful swim finds that Tatica had stolen from him), and hand them to Teodoro. *What the heck,* thought Reinaldo, taking it all philosophically, *I'll probably never get to use them anyway. And besides, Teodoro Tampon will give them back, like he always does. This dork will never jump in the ocean.*

And sure enough, just like always, once he was cradling the swim fins in his arms Teodoro Tampon would grow calmer. He would slide his little cylindrical body into one of Skunk in a Funk's few armchairs, caress the swim fins (his last life raft), sigh, and begin to intone to poor Skunk in a Funk the infinite rosary of insults and offenses that Clara had inflicted upon him. But his whining voice would sound so resigned to the horror of his life that Skunk in a Funk would soon stop worrying about his swim fins and his mind would wander to the manuscript of his novel, which, if he didn't finish it quickly, Fifo would surely destroy yet again. So Teodoro would rattle on while Reinaldo would try to mentally compose the chapter titled "In the Garden of Computers."

Among the terrible humiliations which Teodoro Tampon's wife had inflicted on him (and which he never failed to mention) was that terrible one the night that he, encouraged by some friends from his native province, first met her. It happened to be a night when Clara had invited a group of sailors to take part in a superskewer in which she (naturally) would be the recipient of the tribute paid by the chain of hunky kabobers to her seductive charms—but Clara had refused to allow Teodoro to take part in that unparalleled coupling. Instead, when it was all over she had ordered him (her voice like a cross between a little girl's and a high-ranking witch's) to clean up her room, which looked as though a hurricane had swept through it, and also to stay and live with her. He would be her pimp and protector. Ten years had passed since that night, and the list of humiliations to which Clara had subjected (and was still subjecting) Teodoro was endless.

Every night, when Clara came in from her tour of the docks or the secret swamps of Lenin Park where she'd been playing her dangerous love games, Teodoro would have to take a kitchen knife and scrape off the dried mud that clung to Clara's legs. And it was a herculean task to get the crust of mud off those knobby knees of hers. Not to mention that before she came in, he would have to go out looking for water all over Old Havana—which was like going out and prospecting for gold.

"One of my worst humiliations," Teodoro would confess bitterly, clutching the swim fins, "is having to carry a bucket of water across Central Park." And to top it off, sometimes after he'd climbed the monumental staircase to the room that he and Clara lived in, carrying the bucket that was falling apart and had to be soldered together and plugged up with pieces of soap, Clara would refuse to open the door. Teodoro would have to sit out in the hall and listen to the sounds of orgy inside while he tried to keep the water from leaking out altogether. "And how can I forgive her for not inviting me to her orgies?" he would (not unnaturally) complain. "If you could hear the moaning that *I* hear behind that door. . . ." And Teodoro, his voice slow and hoarse, would attempt to mimic those moans and shrieks of lust—moans and shrieks that Skunk in a Funk would finally halt with a gesture of one of his claws, to indicate that he got the idea.

Clara had also made Teodoro Tampon carve a wooden dildo, and she would order him to use it on her as she screamed "impotent pervert!" at him. Of course Teodoro Tampon, as the legal (yes, legal) spouse of the brilliant painter, was obliged to escort her on all her visits to other painters, where he would keep their host occupied while Clara stuffed tubes of paint, rolled-up canvases, and brushes into the huge pockets of her smock (which she herself had made). When they weren't paying visits (many painters wouldn't allow Clara into their houses or studios), Teodoro, risking years of imprisonment for armed robbery and theft, would be sent out to steal the sheets off the clotheslines in Old Havana. It was on those stolen sheets and canvases that Clara painted the masterpieces that Teodoro admired almost ashamedly.

Clara would oblige her husband to invite some friend of his up to her room, and there she would steal his ration card, which she'd then sell on the black market. "Why, she stole my ration card from *me,*" Skunk in a Funk exclaimed when Teodoro reached this point of his tale of woe—"and I had planned to buy myself a knit polo shirt that Clara promised to paint for me for the big Carnival!" Then he turned back to his novel.

Clara also forced Teodoro Tampon to eat anything he could get his hands on, including grass and sawdust, so that he'd be so fat that alongside him, Clara would look svelte and beautiful. It was truly pathetic to see those two walking along the Malecón—Clara tall, straight, and thin with her long dress made of flour sacks embroidered by hand (by Clara herself) and her long neck encircled by an artsy necklace made by Poncito, and Teodoro waddling along like a ball that from time to time the grand Clara would help to roll along with the tip of one of her elegant Greek sandals. Sometimes when they went out, Clara would dress Teodoro up as a woman, piling humiliation upon humiliation so that all the men would be sure to look at her. The pathetic round ball, in drag, would also have to carry all of Clara's accoutrements—the makeup, parasols, perfumes, condoms, sexual lubricants, and other paraphernalia that she, as the *grande dame,* refused to carry. "What hurts me more than anything is that she's made me get so fat and look so much *older,*" Teodoro would complain. "You know I'm just twenty-three, and she's fifty-seven." Skunk in a Funk knew that Teodoro was older than that, and Clara younger, but he kept his mouth shut. He was just there to *listen* to Teodoro—ay, and the chapter on the Garden of the Computers hanging fire—as Teodoro told how his wife had forced him to legally recognize all the children that she'd had by men from the most distant corners of the world. Teodoro Tampon was the only man in the world who, with the same wife, had had three Chinese children, one Yugoslav, four Arab, two African, one Swedish, one Russian, several Greek, one Basque, one Indian, and one Syrian. The house was a maddening babble of tongues. And Clara would make Teodoro go out in the street with that gaggle of children of every race and age and beg for food and money while she made love to some sailor in a doorway down on the docks. Then Teodoro would have to turn over the take from their begging to his wife's lover and in addition take on the responsibility for the fruit of that furtive coupling, since the sailor would invariably leave Clara pregnant—this was a woman who, in spite of her age (or Teodoro's count of it), seemed never to lose her fertility.

From time to time Teodoro Tampon would also have to write the reports that Clara, an "underground" artist, had to file not only on other underground artists but also on those who had gone public. Clara (and therefore Teodoro) also had to turn in all the freelance hookers who didn't have their licenses from State Security.

Every week Teodoro would have to turn in these reports to Fifo's Counter-Information Headquarters—i.e., *the Garden of Computers,* which Skunk in a Funk had still not been able to finish. . . . "I even have to turn in a report on you," Teodoro had confessed to Skunk in a Funk as, like a child, he caressed the swim fins in his lap.

But this confession, no doubt sincere, neither irritated Skunk in a Funk nor alarmed her in the slightest. She knew she was under constant surveillance, wherever she went. And especially by her most faithful friends—friends such as Teodoro Tampon. . . . "I *have* to make those reports!" Teodoro would whimper. "If I don't, I'll be picked up under the vagrant law, because Clara has contacts. Why, not long ago she committed murder and got away with it." Skunk in a Funk, like everyone else in Old Havana, knew about this, but he had to listen resignedly as Teodoro Tampon once again recited the tale of his mother's murder. Yes, my dear, his *mother.* What happened was that Clara Mortera had invited her mother-in-law, a countrywoman from Holguín, to spend a few days with her. After the old lady had moved in, Clara poisoned her so she could steal a pair of the old lady's rubber shoes and some costume-jewelry earrings. Teodoro could not allow himself to flinch or say a word as he watched that murder-robbery. But his exasperation reached the breaking point when he told (and here he raised the swim fins and then put them down on his lap again) how Clara had made him enter the College of Philosophy and Letters at the University of Havana—an unbearable place where Teodoro was forced not only to write literary compositions of his own but also to read his classmates', and in addition join the university militia (in which, to his chagrin, he had already been promoted to corporal and squad leader).

So Skunk in a Funk had to sit resignedly and hear the harrowing trials and tribulations, and pathetic confessions, of Teodoro Tampon—and more than that (even when she put her hands over her ears), his final, oft-repeated, exclamation, "But I can't take it anymore! Tonight I'm putting on your swim fins and jumping into the ocean! I don't care if the sharks *do* eat me! It's better than this!"

"The only favor I ask of you is that if you're captured you don't tell them that the swim fins belong to me."

"Not to worry," replied Teodoro. And perhaps because this was the friends' last farewell, he invited himself to a cup of Russian tea that Skunk in a Funk had bought on the black market from a dealer from over in Regla.

Still, it would be unfair to leave the impression that Teodoro Tampon was under Clara Mortera's thumb this way simply because of cowardice or greed or fear or some other ignoble emotion. The truth was, Tampon also had immense admiration for Clara's artistic talent, and he loved her. Clara often encouraged Teodoro to develop his own creative potential. Clara, in fact, had been the spark that lighted the fire in the somewhat ditzy but infinitely inventive mind of Teodoro Tampon.

Of all Teodoro's confessions, those that most interested Skunk in a Funk (and so of course Gabriel and Reinaldo, too) were the ones that dealt with the inventions that Teodoro, under Clara's inspiration, had made or attempted to make. Often these were inventions or ideas for things to be used around the house or for a specific occasion, albeit for the delight and enjoyment of everyone—such as the time Teodoro hooked up the entire apartment building to a lightbulb outlet in the park. The whole thing exploded, but fortunately Teodoro had time to retrieve the hookup before the police arrived. Some of Teodoro's ideas also allowed him to live a few hours of hope, happiness, and mockery—because like all such ideas, they stemmed from irreverence for the status quo.

What would you say, my dear, if I told you that Teodoro Tampon had invented a fruit milkshake that contained no fruit or milk? It was this strange mixture of egg white, seawater, and ashes that some people claimed was what *really* killed Teodoro's mother. . . . Then there was the time that Teodoro (obviously under the influence of Clara) made fake coins out of bottle caps off Son soft drinks. These bottle caps, hammered into shape, would sometimes fool the coin-counter on the bus so you could ride for free. Of course if one of them happened not to, and the trick was discovered ("robbery of the People"), you had to run for your life. . . . The famous bounce-back glass display window had also been Teodoro's invention. This was a special piece of plate glass installed in a store window, and when a thief would throw a rock at it to break in, the rock would bounce back, hit the thief in the head, and knock him out. That way, the criminal would be brought to justice by the same instrument with which he'd committed the crime. (Teodoro *loved* poetic justice.) The invention was not a bad one, but it was expensive—not to mention that there was nothing worth protecting in any store window in Havana. Finally Clara pressured Teodoro to sign over the patent to Fifo, who sold it to a French jeweler. Today this jeweler is one of the wealthiest men in the world, has an enormous castle, and rides around on horseback while his wife, a very refined lady, makes love to the domestic staff and the eye-popping black doormen. They say that the sale of the patent brought Fifo a huge fortune (*another* huge fortune) and that he became known throughout the world as not only a shrewd businessman but also an inventor.

Another of Teodoro's inventions was plastic litter bags (so to speak) for the backsides of the blackbirds in Central Park in Havana. The idea was that by using the bags, these birds, whose singing Teodoro loved, wouldn't always be shitting on the passersby at nightfall when the birds congregated to sing awhile and then settle in to sleep in the park's wonderful old bay laurel trees. But this invention was also too expensive for the government to use—and the government, of course, was the only possible purchaser. Thousands of tiny black polyethylene bags would be needed, and when any were to be found they were immediately requisitioned, at Fifo's behest, for use with the coffee plant seedlings that were transported from nurseries to be planted all around Havana. Finally those singing blackbirds, the only consolation in Teodoro's entire life, were exterminated one by one by the soldiers of the Territorial Militia. (That was the other blow from which Teodoro could never recover.)

Perhaps in order to entertain himself with something and not go out of his mind, Teodoro was currently working very hard on a portable smoke-generating machine. When it was completed, Teodoro would be able to throw a switch and fill the entire Payrot Theater with clouds of billowing black smoke. For ten straight years, you see, the Payrot had been showing *King Kong,* but the film drew such crowds that neither Teodoro nor Clara nor Skunk in a Funk could bear to even *think* about standing in the lines. So with the smoke machine and its clouds of smoke, Teodoro, Clara, all their children, and Skunk in a Funk (or so she was promised) would be able to sneak in without standing in line or paying. And once they were inside, with the lights out, who would ever catch them? That was Teodoro's newest dream, his newest plan, and it was this dream that was currently keeping him from throwing himself into the ocean. But by now Skunk in a Funk knew this plan down to the tiniest detail, because every time Teodoro came to visit her and tell his story of woe (and borrow the swim fins), he would bring Skunk in a Funk up to date on his new invention, which he intended to keep working on no matter where he finally wound up.

But tonight Teodoro Tampon had not run to Gabriel's room in the Hotel Monserrate to borrow his swim fins and tell her his troubles. Tonight—breathless, panting, beating his short arms and wiggling his short neck, and in a voice of desperation—he had come to tell Reinaldo an urgent piece of news:

"Clara's called an emergency meeting. . . . Apparently it's really serious this time. Says we're *lost.* . . . Told me t'tell you that you *had* to come. . . . She's waiting."

And without any other explanation, Teodoro Tampon rolled downstairs so swiftly and so arrow-straight that Skunk in a Funk realized that obviously she *had* to attend that meeting.

A Tongue Twister (22)

To the echoing tick of the tacky cuckoo clock, the cop, a prick in mock crocodile moccasins with checked socks, dropped the ocarina he liked to suck, coughed, hacked, hawked up a wad, spat, slicked back his locks, kicked a rock, ducked a mock rocket attack, and, stoking up a rock of crack coke, cried, "Fuck! What luck! I asked for smack!"

For Dulce María Leynaz

A PORTRAIT OF LUISA PÉREZ DE ZAMBRANA

Although Skunk in a Funk (who *loved* this cloak-and-dagger stuff) took off like lightning for Clara Mortera's room, by the time he got there many of the others that Clara had invited had already arrived. Amazingly, even Teodoro Tampon (who must have *flown*) was back already—though when he opened the door to the Skunk his droopy, sluggish movements were the very picture of dejection.

In the middle of the room, sitting in a big armchair, Clara Mortera held court in a long white dress that covered her from ankles to throat. She was surrounded by her guests, an extraordinary spectrum of people, who were sitting cross-legged on the floor, perched on any surface they could find, or standing about the best they could.

Among those present were Clara's great-grandparents from the country, several Cuban and foreign sailors, and Misses Reinaldo Slam-bam-thank-you-man and Dario Mala, two queens lugging shopping bags containing hard-boiled eggs and some kind of black crackers and escorted by two hoodlums of the worst sort—since, as the two fairies were fond of saying, they liked to travel with provisions for both the mouth and the backside. Naturally Odoriferous Gunk was there, though without his dying mother. There was also a Buddhist bonze wearing a full-length robe made of the finest silk and with his head totally shaved except for a long braid that sprouted from the crown of his head and fell to below his shoulders. The bonze had been on the Island for several months now, and he was hoping that after he'd filled out endless forms and trekked endlessly from one office to another, he'd be invited by Fifo to the Grand Fiesta. He was also trying to win proselytes to Buddha, so he was planning a meditation-march on the night of the Carnival. Clara, who naturally intended to get her hands on the magnificent robe the bonze was wearing, had built up his hopes for converting her, though the truth was, she planned to denounce him to Fifo once she had mugged and stripped him.

Also present was Clara's mother, with a tragic expression on her face.

Suddenly someone was banging furiously at the room's only door. Teodoro, at a sharp nod from Clara, opened it, though his fear was evident.

"Oh, it's *her* . . ." Sakuntala la Mala sneered to Coco Salas.

And we must confess that the diabolic horse-faced fairy was right in calling the potbellied, dewlapped man who had just made his entrance "her." Yes, *her,* because—despite the tall leather boots with iron spurs, cowboy blue jeans, khaki work shirt, and wide-brimmed hat; and despite the affectedly baritone voice, the gold bracelet, and the heavy gold chain across the hairy chest—everyone recognized in that chubby, not-quite-human-looking rotundity the person of Miguel Barniz. . . . I mean, really, girl, *anybody* could see that this was a faggot of the *worst* kind—plus, who was with her but that mean-looking dyke Nancy Mojón.

"And now that the Holy Father is here . . ." whispered Skunk in a Funk to Tomasito the Goya-Girl and Renecito Cifuentes.

Sitting next to them, and wrapped in a heavy shawl (though the heat was terrible), was Ramón Sernada (a.k.a. the Ogress). The Ogress was shivering and hugging himself, and every pustule on her body was suppurating—and when Miguel Barniz came in, she almost *popped.* But with the royal welcome extended to the inquisitor by Clara, the guests returned to what they'd been doing and even Sernada sank into a sort of shivering flutter. Overshadowing Sernada in every sense of the word was a swarm of art dealers, special-forces police agents unknown to the other police officers who were present, working-class hunks, straights who made a living as gigolos to faggots, licensed hookers, members of Fifo's inner circle, conspirators, fishermen, neighborhood kids, and a dozen or so representatives of sinister and/or patriotic organizations.

But one must in all honesty say that putting all of *those* personages in the shade, in terms of brilliance and evil, goodness and cunning, grandeur, sensitivity, and naiveté, was (in addition, of course, to Skunk in a Funk) the SuperWeird Sister or Big Weird (as he himself sometimes referred to himself)—Delfín Proust, a.k.a. la Reine des Araignées, who was back at the back of the room, tied hand and foot to an iron bar attached to the wall. Delfin was there as a hostage to himself (or rather to his work), and as prisoner perhaps for life. And for good reason . . .

For several months now, Delfín Proust had been at work on his autobiography, snatches of which he would read to people when he went to their houses to visit. But these autobiographical memoirs were of a *very* shifting and changeable nature. For instance—when Delfín Proust was invited by Paula Amanda (a.k.a. Luisa Fernanda) to read an excerpt from his work-in-progress at her place, he would suppress all the offensive (and therefore objective) pages that he'd written about that particular witch and replace them with pages that portrayed Paula Amanda as the goddess of poetry, goodness, and political genius. Then, the reading done, he would put the real pages back in and go off to read in other *salons.* He had written the heads and tails, the pros and cons, the pluses and minuses of every person mentioned in his autobiography. And when he read, he would read the version best suited to the circumstances.

If, for example, he was at the home of one of Skunk in a Funk's enemies (Coco Salas, for instance), Delfín would read the most virulent diatribes against Reinaldo. If he was doing a reading at Reinaldo's house, he would read in great detail how Coco Salas had been beaten almost to death by some fag-rollers in Old Havana who'd mugged him for the camera that Halisia brought him from Monte Carlo. The beating they'd given Coco was so terrible (Delfín read) that the doctors had had to give him a platinum throat, and now he couldn't suck cock any more. "The worst misfortune that could befall her," La Reine des Araignées concluded the chapter against Coco. And also in Skunk in a Funk's house Delfín had read a long apologia for Reinaldo, which compared him to José Martí, the greatest of Cuban patriot-poets. "He is without question the foremost genius of our generation, our Apostle, the only man capable of destroying himself through passion, our defining figure." That was the last line of the apologia. And Skunk in a Funk, filled with sadness, saw that it was all true. But the truth was, if La Reine des Araignées had read the pages that insulted and mocked Reinaldo, Reinaldo would have seen that *that* was all true, as well.

So anyway, to make a long story short, what had happened was that when Clara found out that Delfín had these chameleon-like memoirs which one day said terrible things about her and another day praised her to the skies, she invited Delfín Proust over for a cup of Russian tea. And when he came, she enlisted Teodoro, her numerous children, and the bodega man down on the corner to help her tie Delfín up, and she told him that he'd stay there until he revealed where he'd hidden his memoirs. . . .

Some of the guests tonight, taking pity on him, went over to Delfín Proust and slipped a moist cracker into his mouth, or even gave him a sip of watery coffee and a caramel.

According to Clara, who was constantly consulting a long list, a number of personages had still not arrived, among them Urania Bicha, Poncito, the cultural attaché of the Jamaican embassy, the Divine Malign, a dealer in primitive paintings from Alturas de Chabón in the Dominican Republic. . . . And at that point, who should arrive but the cunning Mahoma, Chug-a-Lug, a political refugee from Panama, a graduate from Columbia University in New York on the arm of Casandra Levinson, and a dozen or so hunky tops and VIP fairies.

As the guests finished arriving, Skunk in a Funk, tightrope-walking through the wall-to-wall sea of people, decided to have another look at some of Clara's paintings. The one she loved most was of an enchanted forest, filled with immense lianas and violent jungle leaves.

That particular painting radiated a vitality and a power that were almost otherworldly. Every flower blossomed into a strange pair of scissors endlessly opening and closing. The background of the painting was an infinite world of hallucinatory perspectives and barking birds. Filled with wonder at its skill, Skunk in a Funk minutely studied the masterpiece, but she was careful not to touch the canvas or even get too close to it; many of those who did had injured themselves on the leaves and flowers. Ramón Sernada, who had once been director of a museum and a dealer in fakes, confessed to his intimates (so we can't reproduce his exact words here) that he had gotten AIDS from a prick from one of Clara's paintings. And although that is *extremely* doubtful, it was true that Clara received a small commission or a government pardon every time she transmitted AIDS to someone in the general population.

Skunk in a Funk continued exploring that fantastic picture gallery. Naturally she stopped to marvel at the *Portrait of Karilda Olivar Lubricious,* an unfinished masterwork that we will be mentioning in a short while, in the chapter titled "The Death of Virgilio Piñera." But her moment of true ecstasy came when she was standing before the immense canvas entitled *Homage to Luisa Pérez de Zambrana.* This painting, like all extraordinary things in this world, had the wondrous ability to hint at depths of mystery, at facet after facet of significance. Once one had seen that painting, it was simply impossible not to return to it again.

Like all great works of art, it beggared explanation, and it also, of course, eluded all attempts to grasp it whole; nor did it allow of rational, or any single, interpretation. Superficially, it was the portrait of a poet, a woman who had actually lived—a woman who was young, olive-skinned, sitting under a tree with her hair pulled back, and with a white flower (or perhaps a butterfly) in her hair. This lovely young poet was holding a book, though she was not reading it—she was looking outward at the spectator of the painting. To Skunk in a Funk, this meant that all the terrible truth the book contained was useless, that there was something more terrible still that lay beneath the first discovery, and beneath that, things still more terrible.

The problem was that from that woman—her eyes, her hands, her hair, her entire figure, and the painting that surrounded her—there emanated a mystery so total, so desolate, and yet so resigned, that it was outside time. That face was the outward symbol of the heart of a woman who had seen her children, still in childhood, die, and then seen her husband die as well. The work was touched with an infinite grief, as terrible as the resignation that also filled it. Its subject was a woman who came from the Night and had known its minute terror. One could say that it was the sum of all misfortunes, all calamities, concentrated in one horrific, stoic act of wisdom.

That woman, that painting, was not a painting; it was a spell, an awesome and irrepeatable force that could have been born only out of an ecstasy of genius and madness. It was enigma and consolation; it was faith in the belief that come what may, life does still have meaning; and it was absolute despair. It was concentrated diabolism and goodness that struck the person who looked upon it dumb—and then made him weep.

Perhaps no painting but the *Mona Lisa* itself could compare with that portrait hanging in a dim corner of Clara's stifling hovel. The portrait, in this room that *breathed* defeat, was a triumphant, pathetic, and terrifying cry of defiance.

The amazing thing was that the brilliant painter's room was crammed *full* of wonderful paintings—they covered the walls and even the high colonial ceiling. But Skunk in a Funk, entranced, and temporarily oblivious to all the world's horrors—especially the horror of being alive—could not tear himself from the portrait of Luisa Pérez de Zambrana. To look upon that painting was a privilege that transformed any pain, any grief, any calamity.

But then Clara told Teodoro to lock the door and slide the crossbar into place—everyone had finally arrived. And she began to speak to the gathered guests.

"My children," she said, although among her guests were several of her former fathers- and mothers-in-law and even her great-grandfather, "you know that all my life I have been a whore. You know the dangers I have had to face in the practice of my profession. But thanks to that profession I have survived in every sense of the word—I have helped you all, I have supported an enormous family, and I have been able to work on my paintings. But above all, I have lived independently and freely, practicing the only profession that has still not been prostituted: i.e., prostitution. This wonderful calling has allowed me to be the captain of this household and, even more importantly perhaps, the captain of my own life. But now, something terrible has happened to me. My breasts have fallen. Look!"

And Clara stood up and ripped open the bodice of her long white dress, showing the entire room her dry, shriveled, discolored tits, which hung like worms or leeches down below her waist.

An *Oh!* of horror swept the gathered guests, including even Miguel Barniz. This was a truly devastating development.

All of Clara's children ran to her, clutched at her skirts, and wept, while Clara, still standing erect before the world, exposed her fallen tits. Her great-grandfather, her former fathers- and mothers-in-law, and even her mother (for whom Clara had always done so much) fell to their knees and kissed her long, ripped-open dress. The bonze pronounced a few strange yet obviously pain-filled words in his native tongue. The monumental sailors and hunky stevedores wept like babies. The most stoic queens buried their heads in their arms. Coco Salas turned aside and removed his spectacles. Even Delfín Proust, bound to his iron bar, looked on in emotion, and Sakuntala la Mala had to clear her throat. But perhaps the most moving thing about the moment was those hoarse, despairing moans that came from Teodoro Tampon as he rolled around the figure of Clara Mortera.

Then Skunk in a Funk, stepping over the sorrowful heads, walked up to the tall, tragic figure and looked at her fixedly. And seeing her standing there—svelte, her gown ripped open, her breasts shriveled, her eyes vacant and staring into space—Reinaldo realized that for a long time Clara had known that her tits had fallen and had suffered because of that, and realized too that this moment of confession was the most painful moment in her life, because she was making her defeat public. And Skunk in a Funk realized something else: she realized that the portrait of the mourning, afflicted, maternal, despairing, patient, enigmatic, and brilliant poetess Luisa Pérez de Zambrana was the self-portrait of Clara Mortera.

A Tongue Twister (23)

After the botched boycott of the Coptic optician's shop, inept Calypso, black-market operative, opted to boycott an agricultural cooperative trafficking in captured raptors and eucalyptus concocted into cough drops. This cockamamie boycott cooked up by inept Calypso also flopped.

What boycott cooked up by Calypso *could* succeed? Hah! Calypso's boycotts suck.

For Mayra the Mare

Clara's Hole

It would be unfair not to chronicle, as best we can, the proofs of solidarity that almost all of Clara's guests immediately showed her. Even Odoriferous Gunk, in an unprecedented gesture, promised to sell all his dying mother's medicine on the black market and turn over the proceeds of the sale to Clara. Sakuntala la Mala pulled off one of the gold earrings that had been left to her by her slave-trading great-grandmother and in the most respectable way deposited it, like a votive offering, at the painter's feet. Urania Bicha slipped off her imported brassiere (which she had battled so fiercely to get her hands on!) and laid it before Clara. Mahoma took off her amazing platform shoes (more than a food and a half high) and put them down beside Clara. The bonze cut off the braid that grew from the crown of his shaved head and with a bow of reverence dropped it at Clara's feet. Even Coco Salas swore an oath to sell Maya Plisezcaya the secret of his mosquitoes and with the two sacks full of rubles he made on the sale, accompany Clara to the Black Sea, the waters of which would surely, Coco said, restore Clara's fallen breasts. . . . The offerings, the promises, the gestures of encouragement and compassion went on and on—until finally Clara, pushing aside the mound of objects that were accumulating before her long body, spoke as follows:

"No more . . . no more. Don't you people understand that none of these things is going to lift my tits? I am no longer myself. I am no longer what I was. I am no longer I."

At that irrefutable statement, silence fell. But it was a brief silence, because almost immediately a violent tropical shower began pouring down on Old Havana—so violent that some of Clara's guests thought the Apocalypse had come.

Suddenly the room was like a sauna, and Clara, pulling herself together and laboriously making her way through her friends as she fanned herself with a tin plate that Teodoro had stolen from a pizzeria, exclaimed:

"This heat is killing me! I can't breathe! This room needs a window! Quick, a window, or we'll all suffocate!"

And she began passing out objects for making a hole in the wall—a long wood-handled kitchen knife, a hundred-year-old machete, a flagpole, two forks, a crowbar, and the long, pointed wooden dildo carved by Teodoro. Several people proceeded to clear a space on the wall on which hung one of Clara's masterpieces, *Birds Mourning the Caonao Massacre,* and set to work digging at the wall. With the thunderstorm still pounding outside, the heat in Clara's room really *was* suffocating, especially if you consider the number of people who were crammed into that miserable hovel. Hacking out a window was, in a word, a matter of life or death.

Almost everyone took a turn at the job, attacking the wall with those outlandish picks and drills—which, by the way, had to be muffled so the noise of hammering and chipping wouldn't draw the attention of the block chairman of the Watchdog Committee. As sailors pounded their fists against that wall which seemed to be forty feet thick, the Jamaican cultural attaché wielded the crowbar with surprising expertise and Casandra Levinson stabbed frenziedly at the hole—which by now was more than six feet deep. Clara's children used their bare little hands to extract the rubble produced by the excavations. Mahoma hammered at the tunnel with her enormous platform shoes. Some of the neighborhood hunks addressed the hole, emitted intimidating whoops and grunts, and gave the wall karate chops.

With her long fingers and long, tough fingernails, Skunk in a Funk clawed at the grout and cement.

The heat was getting more and more unbearable, and although by now they had dug through more than nine feet of wall and the room was filled with rubble, there was no sign that they were coming to the other side. One of the brick masons who happened to be there, Lutgardito from the town of Regla across the bay, explained that this wall had been built in colonial times—back then, he said, the walls might be built as much as fifteen or sixteen feet thick. But instead of discouraging the tunnelers, this information spurred them on to even greater fury.

And so with the desperation of moles pursued by wildfire—and fire was what the room felt like—they continued to burrow.

They unanimously agreed to free Delfín Proust, who was now asleep, so they could use the iron bar he was bound to.

Delfín rubbed his hands, wrists, feet, and ankles, swung his arms and stamped his legs to return feeling to his numb extremities, then he opened his little snakelike eyes and registered a serious protest.

"Why have you people waked me up?" he whined. "I was dreaming that I was fucking Stalin. I was riding the old man's enormous prick while I pulled at the ends of his moustache. We were speaking Russian, of course, since as you all know I speak Russian perfectly. Just as you woke me up, Stalin and I were about to have our third orgasm. What a magnificent fuck! The only other time I've ever enjoyed a fuck that much was back in the days when I used to screw my great-grandfather. My love affairs have always been fleeting, doomed, it seems, almost from the start. . . ."

"A sad fate, indeed," replied Skunk in a Funk sympathetically. "And we're sorry to have interrupted your wet dream, but right now what we need is that iron bar you were tied to. Either we finish this hole or we all die of asphyxiation."

"Yes! Yes! But my screw with Stalin has been interrupted, probably for all time. Now I shall never find solace or satisfaction—never!"

But very few people were paying any attention to Delfín's complaints anymore; practically everybody was holding the iron bar (wrapped in one of Clara's sheets) using it like a ramrod on the wall. But the weight and the blunt nose of the bar prevented any great progress.

When it began to seem as though no one's strength could hold out any longer, and chubby Teodoro, tunneling through the wall, looked like some poor little rat in a hole that apparently went on and on and finally led nowhere, the cunning Mahoma, aided by Skunk in a Funk and Lutgardito, smashed her platform shoe so violently against the wall that the three of them, with a thunderous far-off crash, were hurled right through to the other side. Everyone thought the poor things (now including Teodoro Tampon, who had tumbled through behind them) had plunged headlong into Calle Muralla (which was where the tunnel was supposedly going to come out), where they would now be no more than broken and twisted bodies. But no! Suddenly Teodoro, Mahoma, Skunk in a Funk, and Lutgardito found themselves not on the street—not on *any* street—but rather in a cavernous colonial-looking building that lay, unbeknownst to either Clara or any of her guests, on the other side of the wall. Yes, the four friends now stood in (or rather sprawled on the floor of) the central convent of the Sisters of Santa Clara, a vast colonial edifice that those nineteenth-century nuns from Santa Clara had fled to when the Condesa de Merlín had torched their provincial nunnery, and then that their twentieth-century sisters had abandoned when Fifo's Revolution had come to power. The doubly ill-starred nuns had left the impressive building absolutely intact, and since that time, the convent had been sealed by Urban Reform and forgotten. It was one of many buildings that Fifo had locked and shuttered and on whose massive door there had been placed, like the medieval mark of the plague, a sign that read

RECOVERY OF MISAPPROPRIATED PROPERTY
NATIONAL INSTITUTE OF URBAN REFORM

—a notice that was capable of scaring off even the most intrepid of burglars.

Lutgardito, Skunk in a Funk, Mahoma, and Teodoro Tampon picked themselves up and wandered through the immense shell of what had been the religious center, their eyes filled with the vision of enormous round-backed trunks, huge chests, slabs of marble, pieces of statuary, lovely tapestries and rugs, crosses, grandfather clocks and wall clocks, cedar benches, confessionals, wicker chairs, and literally thousands of other objects, artifacts, and pieces of furniture. What they found most awesome, though, was the high, caissoned ceiling, which was so massive and so high that it muffled the sound of the thunderstorm that still raged outside. The four of them stood in wide-eyed amazement, huddled together, breathing a peace and grandeur that no longer existed in their world. Clearly, the hole in Clara's room had given them not only a huge fortune but another universe.

And it was a *monumental* universe. It had been frozen in a time when one did not have to ask permission to take off running—a universe in which at last Mahoma, breaking out of her spell, began to tap-dance in her platform shoes over the medieval floor tiles and glazed enamels that covered the remains of the first Mother Superior, who had been laid to rest there more than three hundred years ago. "The acoustics are perfect," said Mahoma, her tap dancing coming to an end. Then, looking up toward the high opening through which they'd tumbled, she yelled for the others to throw down a rope so they could come down and see this.

"Not a rope, a scaling ladder," said Skunk in a Funk, suddenly feeling medieval.

The guests tied together sheets (on which Clara had planned to paint her future paintings) and began to rappel down the wall. By the time the descent was completed, it had stopped raining and the guests, wandering in astonishment through the convent, were bathed in a watery, wavering, many-colored light that filtered down through the high stained-glass windows.

"This is a *gold mine,*" said the cunning Mahoma—though with the astounding variety and luxury of things that the nuns had patiently accumulated through the centuries and then been forced to abandon in less than twenty-four hours, no one person, not even the brilliant entrepreneuse Mahoma, could, in such a short time, take it all in. Each person, therefore, went his or her (or his/her) own way, exploring to inspect the place—down the corridors, into the large halls, the chapels, the cells, the collective sleeping quarters, the enormous library, the refectory, the sacristy, the toilets, and the thousand and one other compartments that the building contained. They stood in awe before a tapestry, a lamp, a cushion, a length of copper tubing, a religious painting, a metal fan, a stone drip water filter in its cabinet, a marble table, a monumental crucifix, a wooden *santo*. . . . In one immense chest the nuns had piled strange cylindrical objects about a foot long carved from precious woods. At first no one could figure out what these objects were, but at last Clara offhandedly (as she continued her exploration) told them.

"They used to call them 'the nun's solace'—they're dildos, you dildos!"

The altar stood majestically under a stained-glass vault.

Then they all began to appropriate what most struck their fancy—an urn, a sconce, a lamp, a piece of antique furniture, a beautifully glazed tile, a reliquary, an icon, a water filter, a book of religious music, a set of dishes, a dildo, a missal. . . . But Clara Mortera, as owner of the hole, took charge of the situation. First, they needed to build a ladder to reach the opening into her room. Then they'd see how to get the stuff out of the convent.

"Remember," said Clara, foreseeing the legal troubles that might face them, "all this stuff has been claimed by the Commission on Misappropriated Property. We've got to do everything with the greatest caution, so as not to call attention to ourselves. And, of course, nothing will be done without my express permission."

Stacking trunks, marbles, benches, cots, and chairs into a sort of ramp, Clara and her cohort soon made a stairway up to the opening high in the wall. Of course there was no way that everything in the convent—some of the things, such as the mother superior's bed, trunks, confessionals, and tables, were immense—would fit through that little hole. Almost everyone pitched in, though, to expand it.

At some point Odoriferous Gunk had seized a gigantic musket, one of the many in the convent (who knows why), and now, dressed from head to foot in black and standing on the huge pile of stuff that made up the jumbled stairway, he began to hack away at the hole.

As all this bustling back and forth was going on, Skunk in a Funk was off on her own, wandering through the scores of apartments, halls, caves, crypts, and oratories in the convent. She even found a reading room tucked away in a corner of the immense nave.... As she entered what had once been the kitchen, an army of rats scurried away in terror. Pushing aside barrels, demijohns, and pots of every size, at last she came to a cupboard, made of the finest woods, that rose from the floor all the way to the high ceiling. She opened its doors and suddenly, as she realized what was inside, her face grew young again and glowed as though all the light that entered the convent were trained directly upon her.

She had discovered a cupboard filled with empty bottles. There were *hundreds* of bottles, my dear—thick, heavy, bottle-green bottles that looked as though they'd withstand anything. Skunk in a Funk fell to her knees before those empty bottles with such devotion (never before expressed) that even the walls of the antique convent seemed to gently throb—for the first time, an act of true religious fervor had been performed within its walls.

The peace of the place, and the evening light, created a new dimension in time in that immense kitchen—on whose floor Reinaldo knelt before a cupboard full of empty bottles.

That same evening, the pillaging began. Each person carried off what he, she, or s/he could, promising to pay Clara half the real value of the merchandise. Through the front (and only) door of Clara's little room, there began to emerge the most incongruous stream of objects—from frills and fringes to Venetian ceramics, from gigantic crosses to iceboxes filled with chapter records, from portable hermitages to trunks full of leather whips and smocks for altar boys, from tapestries more than nine feet long to strange dried flowers and gigantic coffers with silver handles.... At midnight, when the pillaging was at its frenzied peak, the chairwoman of the block's Watchdog Committee appeared at Clara's door. Quickly, Clara (who was keeping a notebook with a record of everything that came through the tunnel) covered the hole with the painting (*Birds Mourning the Caonao Massacre,* remember?) and invited Madame Chairwoman Snoop in. The old snoop came right to the point.

"Listen, Clara, I'm not going to ask you who owns the things that've been coming out of your room. But what I do want you to tell me right now is how such huge stuff can come out of such a tiny place."

Clara knew that there was no way she could carry on her new trade without the consent of the chairwoman of the Watchdog Committee, so she took down the famous painting and showed the investigator the hole.

"You can go down and take whatever you want."

The chairwoman of the Watchdog Committee peeked through the hole and stood in shock for a few seconds as her eyes took in that mob of fairies, queens, hustlers, hunks, hookers, and wheezing old men and women who, in the light of gigantic oil lamps and rusty sconces, were trying to move, push, lift, or dismantle the (to her) *most* unsuspected things. Shaking off her astonishment, the chairwoman of the Watchdog Committee rushed down the stairway-ramp, picked up a huge hemp hammock, stuffed several copper pots and kettles, a chamber pot, fourteen screws, and four or five of what looked like railway spikes (nobody could figure out what *they* were doing there) in it, and throwing that huge bundle over her shoulder, she clambered back up the improvised stairway and headed for Clara's front door. As she left, she lifted her hand in farewell and said:

"I haven't seen a thing, I want that clear. Do you hear me?"

"I haven't seen a thing, either," replied Clara as she stared fixedly at the huge bundle over the chairwoman's back. "But if you need anything, come back anytime."

And so, with the tacit permission of the chairwoman of the Watchdog Committee, Clara and her troops began to dismantle the convent with the freedom of sinners given dispensation by a papal bull and with the speed of squirrels who've just heard that a blizzard is on the way. . . .

In the streets and alleys of Old Havana there began to be seen the most *amazing* variety of objects bumping and rattling along atop draft vehicles manufactured inside the convent itself—in most cases consisting of no more than five or six planks sitting on wooden wheels. A dozen husky queens would be pulling a cart on which a pipe organ was precariously balanced; Mahoma would be pushing a gigantic upholstered armchair; Clara's children would be pulling a weird-looking makeshift cart piled high with globes of the world; round and red, Miguel Barniz would be huffing and puffing as he tugged at a monstrous coffin-looking box filled with porcelain toilets and washbasins; behind him, Casandra Levinson would be pulling a little red wagon full of religious books that she planned to sell ("for their weight in gold!") at a New York cultural center. And while these two sinister personages were staggering along with their shit pots and religious books (which they would never pay Clara for), they were already planning the report that they would be turning in to Fifo's computers. . . . A black man was dragging a marble bathtub filled with copper wire, oil lamps, missals, and wooden dildos. . . . A fairy was pulling a covered wagon full of portable cookstoves and plaster virgins. Several sailors were rolling a huge tapestry down the street, toward the ocean. Sets of dishes; sections of brass and clay pipe; cushions, pillows, and bolsters of all kinds; decanters; floor tiles and wall tiles and ceiling tiles; pendulum clocks, pilasters, marble tables, armchairs and thrones, confessionals, portable hermitages, and cameos were *pouring* out of that little room, headed for still-unknown but undoubtedly avid recipients. Almost everything could be taken (or ripped) out and sold—but when Tomasito the Goya-Girl emerged from the tunnel with two big metal cans filled with kerosene, Clara's face turned very serious and she told him that *that* was not for sale.

Finally, knowing that she couldn't possibly control the sale of all these objects, Clara decided to charge her clients, or "associates," a toll fee. She began to charge by the minute for a visit to the convent. If you wanted to go inside the convent, you had to pay cash on the barrelhead, although you could bring out almost anything you wanted if time (and in this, Clara was implacable) allowed.

Since the demand grew by leaps and bounds, an almost unsustainable spirit of competition emerged among the scavengers. Sometimes a skinny, tottering, malnourished old woman would have to wrestle fifty clay water filters out of the tunnel in less than fifteen minutes if she was going to cover the price of her admission. Sometimes in five minutes Odoriferous Gunk would have to carry out ninety iron penitential shirts studded with nails—which, wrapped in mosquito netting, would make an infernal racket as he dragged them down the building's stairway into the street. But be all that as it might, within a very few weeks all the even remotely transportable furniture, utensils, and other objects that had once filled the convent had been sold off. Naturally, the chairwoman of the Watchdog Committee came in almost every afternoon to pay a terrified visit to Clara's hole; she would grab up the first thing that came to hand (a piece of tile, the leg of a chair, the hinge off a trunk, a rush chair seat, the springs from a mattress, a carpenter's plane, or a scapular) and leave again, her brows knit in tribulation.

During this time, Skunk in a Funk, aided by the Key to the Gulf and even sometimes Teodoro Tampon, was helping enormously to make Old Havana a better place to live, for he was filling the old city with *wonderful* artifacts which, by both the dictionary definition and Fifo's repressive laws, would be classified as "extravagances." The drunks at the pilot breweries now quaffed their beer from silver chalices; housewives stood in line for vinegar ladled out of huge violet-colored demijohns; the children of Old Havana would play ball in the street with copper candy dishes that made a tremendous clanging sound when the kids hit them with their bats, which themselves had begun life as enormous crucifixes.

All over the city, altars to San Lázaro and Santa Barbara were lighted by enormous medieval wax candles. Many bathrooms in even the most distant parts of the city were tiled with glazed Islamic tiles, and in the darkest hovels, Flemish tapestries adorned the walls.

Out of the finest wood, Skunk in a Funk and his trusty assistant the Key to the Gulf constructed a really marvelous loft—what the citizens of Old Havana, in honor of the loft's design, called a "barbecue grill"—and they furnished it with the most exquisite religious tapestries, and then they built a spiral staircase by which to reach it. The Skunk's room, multiplying from within, acquired a bathroom with copper tubing, a living room with a marble table, furniture carved from a single block of wood, and (of course) a magnificent long cameo. Chandeliers with crystal teardrops hung both above and below. Then, Skunk in a Funk transformed the window (which opened onto a black void) in her room (which was no longer *one* room but rather a two-story apartment) into a door, and out from that door, using steel bars and pieces of wood that she brought in through the building next door, she constructed a cantilevered terrace that she adorned with brass rails and mosaics with fleurs-de-lis and huge rosettes. On that improvised terrace, which spanned the building's air shaft and was therefore always much cooler than anywhere else in the neighborhood, the queen set wicker chairs, wrought-iron tables, flowerpots with plants stolen from Lenin Park, lovely stained-glass panels, and lanterns which on nights when there was no electricity (i.e., almost every night) produced a soft yellow glow that was the envy even of Coco Salas, although *her* room, girl, was practically a medieval stained-glass birdcage!

Even Odoriferous Gunk had decked his pup tent with brass rings, rugs, tapestries, mats, mother-of-pearl flowers, velvet runners, and convent record books. His dying mother said she was going to be suffocated by all that bric-a-brac that Stinky had crammed into the tent—among which *objets d'art* were a long-barreled musket and a strange-looking mandolin, set like offerings before a portrait of Elizabeth II of England. But no matter how wonderful the objects were, the Dying Mother (now swathed in a black shroud that had also been lifted from the convent) still complained.

From that most unusual tent Odoriferous Gunk would sometimes emerge attired in vestments taken from Clara's cave-convent: a billowing chasuble, an alb, a cope, black sandals, a gold miter, a mantle, a maniple. He now walked with the aid of a three-hundred-year-old crosier.

But even *this* apparition caused no particular surprise among the inhabitants of Old Havana, since they were all caught up in the hallucinatory frenzy over Clara's things—clothing, furniture, ceiling fans, mantles, table runners, psalters, missals, whips, rosaries—and in figuring out a way to get some of the loot, even if they then gave it away or auctioned it off. And speaking of auctions, my dear, the auction of leather-bound Bibles conducted by the Areopagite from a tree in Central Park became world-famous.

Skunk in a Funk even gave José Lezama Lima—who was alive at the time (or maybe resurrected, I don't remember which) and kept up-to-date on everything that happened in the hole—a huge silver cross and a long gold watch chain to wear it on. One day Lezama showed up at a meeting of the Cuban Writers and Artists Union with that immense cross hanging from his waistcoat down over one of his Pantagruelian legs, putting to flight Nicolás

Guillotina, who locked himself in his office and begged Eachurbod to dance while singing *Sóngoro Cosongo.* Lezama said the cross would exorcise even Lucifer himself, given that it had a stored *potens* of more than five hundred years. With María Luisa Bautista on his arm, Lezama would walk into the Bella Napoli pizzeria on Calle Trocadero and not even have to stand in line, even if there were (which there *always* were) thousands of people waiting. The cross would part the crowds.

"María Luisa," Lezama would say to her in his asthmatic voice before they stepped into the street, "get the *potens;* we're going to the pizzeria."

It was also rumored that Mahoma (that cunning creature) had made a fortune selling the platform shoes that she'd manufactured with the fine woods and calfskin she hauled out of Clara's hole.

Despite the fact that the traffic through Clara's hole went on day and night, and that the convent appeared to be plundered to the last nail, every once in a while, amid the rubble, someone would find some unsuspected object—a metal hairnet of some kind, a leather whip, even a strange sacred jewel that sparkled with an otherworldly gleam. In a shadowy cell, somebody discovered a pillory, which reawakened in Clara the idea of punishing Delfín Proust, who'd used the excitement of the discovery of the convent to avoid turning over his autobiography. At that new threat, La Reine des Araignées made her escape dressed in a mantle of fine batiste and with her huge head covered by a bishop's wide-brimmed hat that had perhaps been left, forgotten, in the convent for hundreds of years. As Delfín Proust was making his escape from the building (which was humming like an anthill), Odoriferous Gunk was slowly and ceremoniously ascending the stairway in his pontifical vestments. The two queens stopped, made the sign of the cross over one another, and continued on their respective ways. . . . In a huge portmanteau, someone discovered more than a hundred men's suits, several masks, yards of black lace, some cowboy costumes, a little cannonball, a number of evening gowns, a dozen mantillas, and other exquisite confections.

Clara Mortera, who was not only a painter of genius but also one of the world's finest *haute couture* seamstresses, altered the most extravagant pieces of clothing for herself, while storing away other pieces for the now-famous but then-future exhibit of forbidden costumes which, with Fifo's permission, would take place on the day of the Grand Carnival. It was not, then, strange, as we have *almost* said several times, to see people strolling through Old Havana dressed in the most *outrageous* costumes, but since Fifo had decided to encourage tourism just then, and precisely in Old Havana, not even the most diligent of the diligent midgets could take action against this extravagant behavior, since to tell the truth, nobody could tell the natives from the tourists. And besides, even though there was lots of time before the Grand Carnival, rehearsals for it had already started. So it seemed normal to bump into figures decked out in the most bizarre ways. Not even Sakuntala la Mala caused a stir when she walked down Calle Muralla dressed in a costume made out of medieval wood—a painted altarpiece that s/he had turned into a triptych and that opened and closed as she walked along, revealing his horrible naked body.

But the market in wood was one aspect of Clara's merchandising that had been cornered by Skunk in a Funk and the Key to the Gulf from the beginning. Knowing that one of the most pressing problems of Old Havana (and the Island as a whole) was housing, Skunk in a Funk realized that with the wood that paneled the caissoned and coffered ceilings of the convent, she could fashion barbecue grills—the wonderful loftlike structures that she had constructed for herself and, of course, Clara—for custom home installation in *other* people's rooms. I mean, is there anyone who lives in a tiny room in a dilapidated building who *doesn't* want to expand? And if you consider the height of the ceilings in the buildings in Old Havana, you can see how easy it would be to build barbecue grills—and the tenants wouldn't even have to give themselves a concussion every time they stood up.

And so, under the leadership genius of Skunk in a Funk, and with the invaluable aid of the Key to the Gulf and a small team of helpers (such as Teodoro Tampon and Lutgardito), Old Havana became the only city in the world that grew *inward.* The barbecue grill, designed by Skunk in a Funk, was soon the absolute rage, an inspired solution to the problem of urban housing. At any hour of the night, Skunk in a Funk and the Key to the Gulf (who was now sleeping at Skunk's place) might be awakened by some desperate housewife who wanted to separate from her husband and so needed a barbecue grill. New mothers urgently needed barbecue grills. Queens who wanted to move out of the family home (or even to have a good screw above their families' heads) practically screamed for their barbecue grills.

Construction of the barbecue grill was undertaken on the basis of an oral contract, with payment of one-half the total cost required up front; when the grill was finished, the client had to pay the other half or the barbecue grill would be dismantled and whisked away on the instant. The barbecue grills had to be put up at night and in complete silence, of course, since otherwise Fifo would root them out and punish them as "clandestine constructions." And yet almost the entire population of Old Havana, including Fifo's secret police, turned a blind eye on the proliferation of these constructions (with which so many of those very secret police solved the problem of a place to live), or even collaborated in the feverish work. In a single night, almost all the rooms in the Hotel Monserrate doubled in size, and although the din of hammering was terrible, nobody seemed to hear a thing. . . . For people of limited means, Skunk in a Funk designed a half-grill, which was a sort of interior balcony or mezzanine cantilevered from one wall of a little room.

Every piece of wood in the convent—the columns, brackets and supports, uprights, coffered ceilings, and the pine laths and sheathing that the coffering had been attached to—all of it was stripped from the building.

At any hour of the day or night, Skunk in a Funk or the Key to the Gulf might be seen up on the distant ceiling of the nave—saw, hammer, or crowbar in hand—pulling down the glorious paneling, which would boom and creak like the rigging of a ship. Then they would cross the city with their cargo and that very night put up two (or twenty) barbecue grills.

As the demand for the improvised housing grew more and more insistent—three comandantes in Fifo's army requisitioned six barbecue grills—there came a moment when the wood simply ran out. Then, at Clara's suggestion, Skunk in a Funk's associates set out to pull down the interior walls of the convent and dismantle all the tilework. That way, if a person couldn't have a barbecue grill he could at least build a wall and enjoy a degree of privacy. Other people used the tiles to build dovecote-like sheds up on their roofs. Teodoro Tampon would patiently scrape the tiles and bricks before they were sent off to their buyers.

One day, as they were pulling down one of the thick interior walls, the demolition team discovered a sealed chamber containing five enormous iron safes. "The nuns' treasure!" exclaimed Lutgardito. While Clara, Coco, and SuperChelo sang at the top of their lungs to drown out the noise, Lutgardito, Skunk in a Funk, and Teodoro took sledgehammers to the strongboxes. But they were all empty. The only thing they found was the last will and testament of one of the first nuns in the convent—before it was even officially the Convent of Santa Clara—who had left all her worldly goods to the pirate William Morgan "for his constant loyalty to my person." But Lutgardito argued that if the nuns barely had time to flee with the shirts or habits or whatever they had on their backs, they couldn't possibly have carried their fortune back to Spain, which meant that they had buried it—and it was still somewhere in the convent!

So they bought picks, shovels, and crowbars on the black market and began the excavation. The entire building suddenly became pockmarked with deep holes, and they even dug under the main altar, which Clara had refused to sell. But the treasure was not to be found.

They did unearth a cemetery for newborn babies—a common grave full of tiny bones. Apparently that was the way the nuns had covered up their forbidden love affairs, or the fruits of them. With great solemnity the treasure hunters reburied the bones, and all further excavations were suspended.

"Why, we might have come across the bones of Christopher Columbus if we'd gone on with this," said Clara.

When the last shovelful of earth had been spread over the grave, Lutgardito, furious and discouraged, rammed his crowbar into the ground. And suddenly, there spurted forth a liquid so precious in Old Havana, and the entire Island, that it was probably worth *more* than the fabled nuns' treasure. It was water—*water!* Unwittingly they had broken into an underground cistern. The water pressure in Old Havana was so low, and there was so little water to begin with, that it seldom reached the faucets of the old city, but the cistern had been dug at such a low point that rainwater would accumulate in it. Everyone, Clara herself included, decided to bathe in those miraculous waters. Then they all agreed on a plan to sell water wholesale and retail throughout Old Havana. They would sell it in cans, in buckets, by the gallon, by the liter, or even by the glass.

The lines outside Clara's room sometimes stretched down the stairs and around the block.

Lutgardito, Teodoro Tampon, Skunk in a Funk, and the Key to the Gulf would spend the entire day climbing down into the convent and hauling up containers filled with water, which Clara would sell at the door. Then, thanks to Clara's contacts with the chairwoman of the Watchdog Committee (who by now was practically her best friend), they got a pump and a hose, and the water could be pumped right to the front door and the infinitely snaking line.

Late at night, Skunk in a Funk and the Key to the Gulf would go back to the Hotel Monserrate and make the barbecue grill shake and shiver. Sometimes there would be so much friction as the wooden boards rubbed together that the grill would give off the wonderful fragrance of freshly cut cedar. Night after night, the two carpenters made passionate love, but one thing kept it all from being perfect: the creaking of the wood and the rattling of the empty bottles that Skunk in a Funk was jealously hiding under the bed (which was also made of aromatic cedar) drove the Key to the Gulf crazy. Several times he tried to throw them out the window, but Skunk in a Funk would have none of it. Finally, the Key to the Gulf resigned himself to the noise, perhaps because Skunk in a Funk built free barbecue grills for his mother, his girlfriend of the moment, and several of his country cousins in the little town of Guane, in Pinar del Rio.

"Almost everybody has a barbecue grill now," Skunk in a Funk would say whenever she had a visitor. "But mine is unique, because it is made of the cedars of Lebanon. I chose the wood myself. When I make love, I can almost hear the Song of Songs."

For weeks the convent had been completely denuded of wood, and now, with the removal of the bricks and tiles, there were no more halls, or columns, or interior walls, or coffered ceiling. The only thing, really, that remained of the convent was the immense shell of the building with its thick outer walls, the high altar, and a roof that consisted only of transparent sheets of plastic. Of course the huge studded front door was still closed and barred and locked with a huge padlock and sealed with the official Urban Reform seal. But inside, what had once been a beautiful convent looked like a slave barracks, or a bullring, or a gothic cathedral after an earthquake. The floor was nothing but earth tamped down with infinite patience by Teodoro Tampon. There was nothing left to sell except water. Realizing that something had to be done, and fast, or she'd be forced to close up shop, Clara used the hose to wet down the entire plot, and then she planted tomatoes. The tomato farm kept all of Old Havana supplied with tomatoes for several months, but weeds at last choked out the tomato plants. Undaunted, Clara planted aloe, rosemary, basil, and all sorts of other aromatic and medicinal plants among the weeds—even a bed of impressive cape jasmine that perfumed the whole building. People said that

Clara, who knew not only herbal medicine but also magic, planned to plant a clandestine herbarium in the convent and offer private consultations. But probably that was just a rumor.

Thus, that hole dug through the wall in Clara's room provided the group with several months of comfort. Friends, acquaintances, and sometimes strangers would gather in the convent to bask in the sun that filtered through the sheets of plastic that now made up the roof. Their financial problems were temporarily solved. Clara would lie in the sun, naked, on top of the altar that she refused to sell, while throughout the building people would go about their own concerns. PornoPop (the Only Remaining Go-Go Queen in Cuba) would loudly declaim the PornoPop poems that she had chosen for presentation at Fifo's party, while Coco Salas and SuperChelo would emit operatic trills and whinnies. The Three Weird Sisters blithely knitted people's fates. Delfín Proust would hop around and wave his arms (often covering his hands with thorns from the prickly pears that Clara had planted). Clara's children would swim in the cistern from which everyone drank. Skunk in a Funk would be sitting on a rock writing while the Key to the Gulf would be jogging around the convent and doing exercise to maintain his graceful physique—he knew that in the next (and last) Carnival he was to be the officiant/sacrificial victim/love god in the ceremony of the Elevation of the Holy Hammer. Throughout the weeds and undergrowth, which had grown up with all the exuberance of things repressed for over four hundred years, jetéing queens would hop and skip, interrupting readings, literary compositions, recitations, and even the meditations of scholarly faggots and disgraced government officials.

The convent teemed with retired actresses, sailors weary of the sea, and teenagers who just wanted to *be there*—all sensing (or knowing) that this paradise, like all paradises, would be fleeting. Fugitive prostitutes, vagrants, deserters from obligatory military service, children abandoned by their parents, and housewives who were tired of cooking, dishwashing, and all the other tribulations occasioned by housekeeping—all sought refuge in the convent. Even the director of the national library, a woman now blind and in political disgrace, found shelter in the nave in the company of Maria las Tallo. One day they paid homage to a certain gentleman from Paris (none other than Alejo Carpentier) who had also in desperation taken refuge there, because he thought his literary identity was about to be discovered and he knew that if it was, Fifo would send him off as cultural attaché to Martinique. *J'ai toujours deteste le tropique mais une petite île tropical, c'est trop. . . .* Suddenly, among the patches of weeds there arose the tall, imposing figure of Ramón Sernada (a.k.a. the Ogress), who was searching in the convent's garden (which he considered sacred), for the magical plant, leaf, root, or vine that would turn out to be the cure for AIDS. The Ogress, making her dolorous way through the building, would go to the altar on which Clara was sunning herself and show her a new branch or leaf. Clara would smell it and regretfully shake her head. But everyone tried to give the sick queen hope.

"The day you discover that weed, we'll all be millionaires," they would say.

"But even if you don't discover it, don't worry—we're all in the same boat, and there's no way out for any of us. We all love life too much to live very long—and besides, what's the use? . . . But go on over to the cistern and have a swim; that water will cure anything."

Then Clara would signal the conversation was over by closing her eyes and lying back once more on the altar, while the soft filtered sunlight bathed her naked body.

One day, Clara emerged from her sun-bathed lethargy. She climbed up to her barbecue grill; unrolled all the canvases, tapestries, mosquito netting, linen sheets, and shawls that she had pulled through the hole or bought (with her earnings from the hole) on the black market; and started painting. Shut up in that immense nave, oblivious to everything that was happening around her, in less than a month she had created over three hundred incredible paintings. Never before had such creative energy, or genius, or explosive vitality been seen before. In five minutes she would overpaint a centuries-old canvas white, and then on that surface Clara's hands, moving so fast they were practically invisible, would create a masterpiece.

In a matter of weeks, the convent was *filled* with masterpieces. Clara also brought down into the building all the paintings that she'd been keeping in her room, even those that she hadn't finished yet, such as the *Portrait of Karilda Olivar Lubricious.* Aided by her friends, the entire *oeuvre* was mounted and hung as though for an exhibition; almost overnight, the convent became a gallery. Even on the high altar they erected great easels upon which reposed such inimitable masterworks as *The Color of Summer, or the New Garden of Earthly Delights,* with its thunderous explosion and collapse in the last panel of the triptych. Skunk in a Funk didn't mind Clara's using the name of his novel for this painting. She knew that Clara and she were a single person and that their works therefore complemented one another. . . . When the exhibit was totally installed, Clara decided to have a party to celebrate the opening of her show.

The immense shell of the old convent was lighted by all the lanterns, oil lamps, wall sconces, torches, votives, and tapers that Clara had managed to collect and store in her room. Even before the exhibition was opened to a clandestine yet knowledgeable public (and to the curious of every stripe), the news of that event unique in the history of Cuban (and world) painting had spread through Havana. Some three hundred masterpieces by a single painter, gathered in a single place, painted in a single fit of creative inspiration, and exhibited for only a short time—that was something that doesn't happen very often (perhaps it happens but once) in the history of art.

The exhibit opened.

In addition to Clara's friends and enemies, an enormous number of people managed to jostle their way inside. They all wandered among the canvases, so struck with their brilliance that they couldn't open their mouths, or couldn't close them. It was impossible, standing among those paintings, to make a single comment—nor was it expected. *Seeing* them was what counted, not commenting on them. Some people wept silently. The entire universe—or at least the entire universe to Clara Mortera—with all its visions, myths, terrors, and ecstasies, had come to this final birth. Clara had never been able to visit the Prado Museum, or the Uffizi, or the Louvre—in fact, she had never been off the Island—and yet that night, in that badly lighted hole, paintings were shown that were far superior to some works that hang permanently in the world's most famous museums.

The exhibit lasted for three days. It closed on the third night, when the candles guttered out.

Before the last lights were extinguished, Clara invited everyone to have a bit of dinner. Hard-boiled eggs and water from the cistern were passed around.

Women, men, and fairies attired in amazing costumes, in addition to the entire Cuban intelligentsia, foreign cultural advisers, and ambassadors, filed past the paintings, each holding a hard-boiled egg that gleamed like some strange fruit. Finally, they all put their hard-boiled eggs in their pocket or purse as a souvenir of a magical night (perhaps the only magical night of their lives).

A cosmos in the palm of one's hand. All who emerge from it emerge bewitched, enchanted. In this convent I have heard the trumpets of the Epiphany. So thought José Lezama Lima (without speaking) when, even though he'd been carried on a litter by Skunk in a Funk, Mahoma, Sakuntala la Mala, and Delfín Proust, he arrived home panting and almost at the verge of exhaustion.

"I saw the All, and because it was the All, nothing of it can be spoken," Virgilio Piñera said in Olga Andreu's house.

But in all honesty it must be said that Virgilio saw only two of the hundreds of paintings that were shown: *The Portrait of Luisa Pérez de Zambrana* and *The New Garden of Earthly Delights.* Virgilio spent the entire evening standing in front of those two paintings, as though he had realized that there was no reason to go any farther, and that besides, it was impossible to take in over three hundred masterworks in a single night.

The next day, Clara Mortera closed the exhibition and sealed up the entrance to the convent with a piece of cardboard. Until the day of the Carnival, no one except Clara herself would enter the building again.

What the neighbors lamented most was that with the sealing off of the convent, the sale of water came to an end forever.

A Tongue Twister (24)

In a fit of sybaritic ecstasy inspired by Horatian verses and Samothracian statues, two sisters, incestuous lesbians, Anastasia of Russia and Anisia of Prussia, seated on a sealskin-upholstered sofa, spent several leisure hours in vice and dissipation, spurning Boethian consolations and seesawing, instead, first Anastasia up and Anisia down, then vice versa, in bouts of licentious caresses.

For Nancy Mojón and Urania Bicha

The Grand Oneirical Theological Political Philosophical Satirical Conference

Following Fifo, the audience rushed to flee the Aquarium Theater, in which the water was rapidly rising.

Fifo was on a large motorized raft. Bobbing along behind him came his guests, who were on not only rafts but also inner tubes, motorboats, dinghies, sloops with bellied sails, and even gondolas quickly improvised by the diligent midgets, who poled them with uncanny dexterity.

Fifo was *very* excited; he couldn't *wait* to get to the Garden of Computers, whose denizens were roaring desperately—clearly, it was feeding time. But as he was putt-putting down a long flooded passageway, he caught a glimpse of the International Conference Hall, a huge auditorium with a high vaulted ceiling and perfect acoustics—although the water was beginning to rise in this theater, too. Fifo pulled up his huge raft (on which his intimates and favorites were also riding) and abruptly decided that then, at that very instant, before the auditorium was completely inundated by the rising waters, the Grand Oneirical Theological Political Philosophical Satirical Conference, a fundamental part of the Carnival program, would be held. And instantly orders were given to that effect.

While everyone was sailing, rowing, paddling, and poling into the auditorium, in which an enormous dais had been set up with a long table and chairs of various sizes, the President of the PEN Club of Germany, Herr Günter Greasy, thought he'd take advantage of the lull in the activities to present Fifo with the Grand Medal of Honor, an award given only on very special occasions by the German PEN Club to the most distinguished Western intellectual of the past twenty-five years. Ruddy, smiling from ear to ear, and dressed in a black jacket, Greasy leapt onto Fifo's raft and pinned the medal on him. Everything was done very quickly and without ceremony, but when the famous author pinned the medal on Fifo's chest, Fifo was filled with such pride that his prominent potbelly swelled to *tremendous* proportions, and it pushed the author of *The Ten-Cent Drum* right off the raft. Instantly, Greasy's hefty body sank into the depths of the auditorium waters, along (oh, dear!) with the medal, which he'd grabbed to try to steady himself.

Several Vietnamese guests dived into the water to try to save it (yes, the medal, silly), as did other important personages, such as the President of Mexico, the head of the Syrian Institute of Sports, the Chancellor of World University in Santo Domingo, and the writer Carlos Puentes. But they all came up empty-handed.

Accompanied by notables from the worlds of science, culture, religion, politics, and philosophy, Fifo turned his prow toward the dais at the front of the auditorium, where any minute now the Grand Oneirical Theological Political Philosophical Satirical Conference would be beginning. As the procession of water vehicles t . . .

"All right! Hold it right there, miss! This time I have *definitely* caught you. You have just committed a serious literary omission!"

"And precisely what might that be, my *dear* Sakuntala la Mala, if I might ask?"

"Elementary. Elementary, my *dear* Reinaldo. If there are going to be all those important scientists—'notables from the world of science,' as you yourself just said—then the conference has to be called the Oneirical *Scientifical* Theological Political Philosophical Satirical Conference. You forgot *scientific,* which is *basic.*"

"You know something, you old queen? You're absolutely right. *This* time. Sometimes I'm so absentminded . . ."

"Absentminded when it's convenient, because every time you write my name in that book of yours you manage to remember to add the epithet *la Mala.* So I wonder if you would be so kind as to just call me Sakuntala, period. Or Daniel Sakuntala, which is the name that appears on my birth certificate in Nuevitas."

"Yes, well, I'll try to remember, dear. . . . Now if you'll just let me get back to my salt mine . . ."

As the audience made itself (themselves?—I never know about these plurals and singulars) comfortable on its (their) flotation devices, the midgets used enormous hoses to siphon out the water and keep it at an acceptable level.

There is *no way* to list all the famous people who took part in this conference, but let me give you some idea . . .

Among the notables were Maltheatus, Macumeco, the queen of Holland, Skunk in a Funk, Fray Bettino, Tomasito the Goya-Girl, the Condesa de Merlín, Joseph Pappo, the president of the Tierra del Fuego Liberation Organization (the TLO), the Bishop of Santa Marta, Alderete (in a red wig), the mayor of Venice, Coco Salas, the director of the National Ballet of Chile, SuperSatanic, the inventor of AIDS, the president of the World Federation of Women, the head of the Medellín Cartel, the inventor of the neutron bomb, Miss Papayi Toloka, Jimmy Karter, Delfín Proust, the AntiChelo, the premier of the Communist International, Miss Tiki-Tiki, Robert Roquefort, the SuperChelo, and many, many famous writers (some brought back to life especially for this occasion and even over their own objections, as in the case of André Breton) and prince regents, dictators, and celebrated murderers. The head of the Swedish Academy presided over the conference; as noted by the mayor of Pretoria, he was there because he came from a neutral country.

Milling about the head table there were also many scholars, reporters, listeners, and observers, all of whom did everything they could to get close enough to Fifo to speak to him. But Fifo, surrounded by his personal corps of guards and his brother, allowed only two persons to sit next to him and speak to him: the Marquesa de Macondo and Carlos Puentes, the two most perfect expressions of a race of headless, stunted, ambitious, arrogant, lawless, and unctuously greasy pygmies, whom Fifo had personally chosen to be his intellectual escorts, since he knew that next to those two dim bulbs he'd look like an Einstein.

Before the conference began, the lights in the auditorium went down and for a few seconds the only sound heard was the gurgling of the water and the muffled rumbling of the pumps and hoses. But then suddenly a huge screen lit up, and the world première of the full-length feature *Adios to Maritza Paván* flickered to life on the screen. This film had been shot forty years ago by Alfredo Güevavara in the woods around Havana. It was introduced by the Marquise del Pinar del Río, director of the Florida International Film Festival and creator of the New York New Film Makers Festival and president of the Cartagena Film Institute. The movie ended to deafening applause. Then, to the surprise of almost everyone, Maritza Paván herself appeared. This personage was a faggot something over a hundred years old who had fled the Island forty years earlier; his farewell party had been held in the Havana Woods (and was the subject of the movie they'd all just seen). Now she was included among the guests of honor whom Fifo wanted to introduce that night so as to win over the world's public opinion and get some international financial aid. The audience applauded Maritza Paván for over ten minutes—although it was impossible to give her the usual standing ovation, considering how tricky it was to stand up on a raft, or a gondola, or any other small craft.

When the applause finally died down, the president of the Swedish Academy opened the conference.

The theological section was amazing. A statement read by the Bishop of Santa Marta and, he claimed, approved by the leaders of every world religion concluded that there was only one God, and that God was Fifo. The moment was a solemn one. Fifo, who had already been invested by the president of Venezuela as one of the Caesars, now was to be worshiped as a god. Unfortunately for Fifo, however, and without appearing on the program *anywhere,* just then Salman Rishidie raised his hand and said it was impossible to talk about the existence of God without also mentioning the existence and potency of the devil and the irrefutable *proofs* of his existence.

At that, the imposing figure of Tomasito the Goya-Girl rose to her full height behind the table and waved a huge notebook at the audience.

"Here," she said, "I *have* those irrefutable proofs of the existence of the devil, which I will now proceed to read."

And standing atop a stunning new pair of platform shoes that she had bought from Mahoma, Tomasito the Goya-Girl began to read (from a document drafted by Skunk in a Funk, by the way). By the time Tomasito reached the end of the document, the evidence of the existence of the devil was clearly overwhelming, but the *most* overwhelming proof had been saved for last—the existence of Fifo himself. At that, Fifo instantly decided that Tomasito the Goya-Girl had to be put to death, but he couldn't give the order at that particular moment, so publicly and all, and *certainly* couldn't have the execution carried out there in front of everybody. "I want you to slit her throat and cut out her tongue during the Carnival," Fifo whispered to one of his most conscientious midgets, who transmitted the order to Raúl Kastro.

Naturally, the accusation that Fifo was the devil incarnate raised an angry protest, most conspicuously and vociferously on the part of Carlos Puentes and Elena Polainatosca. For minutes on end the uproar was deafening. The head of the Swedish Academy, perhaps because of his country's neutrality, didn't know what to do. But Dulce María Leynaz, loudly banging the gavel (which was supposedly the Swedish scholar's prerogative), said that this was a panel in which people could say whatever they wanted, and that there would be a discussion period after they all had given their papers.

"And if you people don't settle down, I'm not going to donate to the state the manuscript of Federico García Lorca's *Blood Wedding,* which is, I warn you, the only thing that pleases the palate of my precious rats. . . ."

And since it was not to be *conceived* that the Island let that manuscript get away (especially since Fifo had already sold it to the University of Halifax in Nova Scotia for a fortune—and pocketed the money for it), the conference had to be allowed to continue.

Now it was Skunk in a Funk's turn to speak; she had chosen a theological topic.

"Since we are talking about God and the Devil," she began, "which in the long run are the same sinister thing, we should delve a little deeper into Hell, or Paradise—which of course are *also* the same thing.

"In every life, in every work of art, in every book—i.e., in every hell—there is a descent into the absolute inferno. I invite my listeners to descend with me. Our journey will be brief, for I will show you only the Seven Wonders of Cuban Socialism."

And in a dizzyingly brief voyage which lasted only fifteen minutes but summarized forty years of horror, Skunk in a Funk descended into the most recent Cuban inferno.

Other papers were longer than Skunk in a Funk's, but we must remember that Skunk had also pre-presented a paper at the Satirical session, her Thirty Truculent Tongue Twisters, so she couldn't really take too long for this one. Some of the most memorable presentations at the Conference were André Breton's on "Impossible Dreams" (during, naturally, the Oneirical session) and the AntiChelo's on "The Seven Major Categories of Queenhood," which combined the Scientifical and the Philosophical—although it was read during the Theological session, perhaps because it dealt at length with "Sublime" and therefore *divine* queenhood. Of the Theological and Philosophical sessions perhaps the most memorable paper was entitled *"Nouveaux Pensées de Pascal, ou Pensées de l'Enfer,"* an apocryphal work read by SuperSatanic, who explained that Pascal was unable to be resuscitated for the Conference because no one was absolutely sure where he was buried. . . . During the Scientifical session, of extra-special interest to all was the Condesa de Merlín's paper on "Clocks and Steam Engines," which made a substantial critique of the steam engine ("the cause of so much destruction, so much slavery") and clocks ("which only serve to remind us of our mortality"); during the Political session, the brilliant Fray Bettino, with his text titled "Grand Captains of the Morning Sun," read an apologia for Hitler, Stalin, and Fifo and attacked democracy as "ephemeral and vulgar, a state which results from a scarcity of great men able to bridle human passions." This paper caused considerable controversy among the audience, and *that* in turn again caused the head of the Swedish Academy some distress, and *that* led Dulce María Leynaz to gavel the proceedings once more to order.

The schedule for the Philosophical and Theological sessions indicated that at this point in the proceedings, Odoriferous Gunk would speak. However, thanks to intrigues on the part of Skunk in a Funk, Coco Salas, and La Reine des Araignées, Odoriferous Gunk had been refused entrance to the Palace. But Odie had cleverly made arrangements to send his text to the chair of the panel, who couldn't refuse to accept it, since it clearly fell within the subject of the conference. In fact, it virtually capped it. They had spoken of God and the Devil, they had descended into the jaws of Hell, and so now clearly they needed to speak of the pleasures of Paradise, of the mission of those who dwell in Paradise and all its avatars, and of their struggles to bring about a world in which one could live happily and at peace. In an introductory aside, Odoriferous Gunk requested that since he, the author, was not to be allowed to read his text, it be read by the Archbishop of Canterbury, but all the bishop had to do was take a quick glance at those pages and he changed color—from red to the blackest of blacks. And so he remained to the end of his days—black, black, black—which made him the object of the most *exquisite* erotic attentions on the part of Tomasito the Goya-Girl, Delfín Proust, Skunk in a Funk, the Dowager Duchess of Valero, and the Condesa de Merlín, all of whom found Negroes *fascinating*. . . . But anyway—Odoriferous Gunk's paper was tabled for lack of a person willing to read it, and the grand hall continued to fill with water.

It was finally the queen of Holland who (perhaps because she lived in the Low Countries and was used to all this flooding) picked up Odoriferous Gunk's text (written in Latin) and read it without batting an eye, translating it on the fly into almost perfect Spanish—although sometimes she did skip words like "espingole," "archivolt," and "repéchage" and phrases such as "Sursum corda" and "ut supra." Odie's thesis was simple yet profound:

We have lost all meaning in life because we have lost paradise, and we have lost paradise because pleasure has been condemned. But pleasure—persecuted, execrated, condemned, exploited to exhaustion, and almost vanished from the world—still had its armies: clandestine, silent armies, always in imminent danger of defeat but utterly unwilling to renounce life, which is defined by giving pleasure to others. "These armies," boomed the voice of the queen of Holland throughout the flooded auditorium, "are made up of queers, faggots, fairies, and other species of homosexuals all over the world. These are the greatest heroes of all time, those who truly have the dream of paradise and hold to it unflinchingly, those who at all costs attempt to recover their—and our—paradises lost." And here Odoriferous Gunk took his argument into Egypt and the great male love affairs of Thutmose I, Thutmose II, and Thutmose III; jumped over into Mesopotamia, where he offered a detailed list of all the youths who had brought enchantment to the nights of King Asurbanipal; leaped down to the Greeks, "whose exaltation of the love of one man for another has bequeathed to us that greatest literary work of all times, the *Iliad*"; hopped over to Rome, where he cited all the geniuses and Caesars who had lived basically to make love to men. And then he came to Christ, "that thirty-three-year-old man who wandered about the countryside preaching, and making love, to his twelve apostles." And with a wave of her hand the queen of Holland called up onto the screen an ancient painting in which Jesus Christ was portrayed with his legs spread and John, the beloved apostle, a *gorgeous* teenage hunk, sleeping placidly with his hand on his master's lap, the Christ himself and the other disciples glowing with beatitude. Then the paper discussed pagan feasts with their invincible armies of pleasure, the coming of Catholicism, and the widespread use of the bonfire. "Beautiful naked bodies were mutilated. People covered statues' nakedness with cloaks or fig leaves, cruelly smashed and broke off their sexes. Caped and uncaped, masked and unmasked, the Middle Ages unleashed, and today somehow still unleash, the wrath of their sordid splendor. But the battle to recover Paradise has never ceased being fought, and the army of pleasure, the true angels expelled from life, continue to practice, however and whenever they can, what inquisitors and cowards call 'the sin against nature.'"

There followed a detailed history of the horrors to which queer men of all stripes—both queens and tops—had been subjected from the time of Constantine to the implementation of bourgeois morality and militant Communism. The list invoked the names of Heliogabalus, Julius Caesar, William Shakespeare, Louis XIII of France, Percy Bysshe Shelley, George Gordon (Lord Byron), Edward II of England, Michelangelo, Walt Whitman, Louis of Bavaria, Petronius, James I of Scotland, Pyotr Ilych Tchaikovsky, Marcel Proust, Pier Paolo Pasolini, André Gide, Julio Cortázar, Yukio Mishima, Vincent Van Gogh, Oscar Wilde, Jean Genet, Federico García Lorca, Tennessee Williams, Witold Gombrowicz, Jacinto Benavente, Virgilio Piñera, José Lezama Lima, and a thousand other famous men. There was a history of the sufferings to which almost every queen and faggot in the world had always been subjected. There was mention of the thousands of Indians exterminated, according to statements by the chronicler and soldier López de Gómora, for practicing sodomy. . . . "And yet, despite persecution," the queen of Holland's voice rose in righteousness, "those natives continued to gather together in groups of more than three thousand men to practice that 'forbidden love.'" There was also a list of the names of Spanish-colonial queens and independent-republican queens who had been persecuted in Cuba and throughout Latin America, the names of queens massacred elsewhere under Communism and Fascism. The screen lit up to show the spellbound audience Russian queens frozen in remote gulags, queens burned to cinders in Nazi concentration camps. Photographs were shown of the Cuban queens confined in Fifo's own concentration camps. There was even a documentary in which one could see how the queer men of Havana had been rounded up in Central Park, on the beaches, on the Paseo del Prado, at the Copelia Ice Cream Parlor and the García Lorca Theater, and even on the Hill of the Cross in Holguín and on Gran Piedra. There were pictures of confinement camps for victims of AIDS. The audience was shown prisons, keys, towers—and tunnels filled with sexual prisoners. In pictures that flashed across the screen almost too fast for the eye to catch, the audience was presented with queens planting coffee in the Havana Cordon, queens cutting brush in Camagüey, queens weeding fields with their bare hands in Pinar del Río, queens crushing rocks in flooded quarries. They were shown the famous driver Pistolprick, the man who was credited with the arrest of César Lapa (that hot-hot-hot mulatto queen) in London. Pistolprick was a *stunning* specimen of manhood who worked in Fifo's Ministry of the Interior and kept a .45 in his shorts. His secret mission was detecting which Cuban diplomat was a swish. The driver would sit at the wheel of the car with the pistol bulging in his crotch, and when the poor queen, in a moment of rapture, madness, or *life,* threw herself onto that bulge, she'd find herself clutching a pistol. "If you turn it loose, it fires," the driver would say as he took out a camera and photographed the queen with her hand in the cookie jar. And so the good work of Pistolprick had ruined the diplomatic careers of not only César Lapa but also Paula Amanda, Retamarina, Miss Harolda Gramatges, the Anglo-Campesina, Rogelio Martínez Furiosa, Miss Pereyra, and hundreds more, who now wandered in madness or degradation through the world and Fifo's Island—cowed or threatened (blackmailed!) by that fateful photo, locked away in Fifo's secret files, that showed them with their hand on Pistolprick's fly. "The documentation, as you see," the text went on, "is overwhelming and irrefutable, so let's move on to the conclusions."

The queen of Holland took a sip from the bottle of water which, to guard against poisoning, she always carried in her purse (you wondered what queens carried in their purses, didn't you, dear?), and went on reading:

—Just a few weeks ago in the García Lorca Theater, while I was watching (who else?) Halisia dance, I was struck by a remark made by one queen to another in the seats behind me. _I left this morning and I haven't returned since._ That was the remark I overheard, and it struck me that it somehow illuminates all our lives. Who, what, is it that returns? Migratory birds—_birds_—in their eternal quest for the clime, the nest, the tree, the branch to which their memories are forever turning. A homosexual is an aerial, untethered being, with no fixed place, no place to call his own, who yearns to return to . . .—but, my friends, he knows not where. We are always seeking that apparently nonexistent place. We are always in the air, keeping our eyes peeled. Our aerial nature is perfect, and so it should not be strange that we have been called _fairies._ We are fairies because we are always in the air, in an air that is not ours because it is unpossessable—though at least it is not bounded by the walls and fences of _this_ world.

And even when we are on terra firma, such as now, we are always somehow ready to take flight—that is why we always have that alert expression on our faces, why we always seem to be flitting along on tiptoe or, as our great poet Lezama Lima put it, like some _crucified swallow,_ always expectant, always unmoored, always clasping the fairy dream of an almost impossible return—a return that would unquestionably be a return to _pleasure._ And pleasure, as we all know, is the essence of Paradise. We have been expelled from Paradise, and Paradise has been wiped off the map. And who gets the blame for the sin that caused Paradise to be closed and locked up? _We_ do, my friends, for we are, in fact, the true birds of paradise—sparkling, twinkling, multicolored beings of light. We are not ashamed to sprinkle a little fairy dust, a feather from our feather boa, in public. One of our missions as former denizens of Eden is to fill the world with fairy dust and feathers of all colors and sizes, so that no one will forget, first, that we have descended into the world from Paradise and, second, that we intend to recover that Paradise from which we were expelled. And expelled, I must insist, not because we were the classical biblical couple who were commanded to love each other "chastely" and then broke the rule, but rather because we were _different_—because the real Adam and Eve were two men (one, apparently, in drag) or two queens, or two women who broke the celestial rule because they sought their <u>own</u> heaven. Yet there is no heaven, my friends, but the heaven of pleasure. That has been clear since the beginning of life. We have before us, then, a sacred task: To create the army of pleasure, or, better said, to continue to be soldiers in that army, its eternal reinforcements. It is a divine mission because it exalts (and for a moment makes us forget) the human. Our object is to create (or, if you prefer, preserve) a mythology and metaphysics of pleasure. A dangerous, difficult mission, yet disinterested—because what we want is for <u>everybody</u> to have a little fun! What man doesn't like his dick sucked by a fairy? A fairy who suddenly appears and then flies away, with no complications of any kind. Let's be honest, here, girls—the pleasure that that man feels is <u>wonderful.</u> And not only do we give that pleasure free of charge—sometimes we even pay for it! And when we give someone pleasure, we feel pleasure too. The good thing about us fairies is that when we look back, we can always say, What a life I've lived! <u>How much</u> life I've lived! Because in addition to our own lives, we have helped other people live. . . . That, then, explains my firm decision to create, or make better known, the mythology and metaphysics of pleasure. I say metaphysics because it is a general, Aristotelian theory of great and devout fervor. We queens are the members of a religious, and therefore fanatical and holy, body whose purpose is to give and receive pleasure. Over against all the horrors of the world, and even within them, we set the only thing we possess—our enslaved bodies—as the source, fount, and vessel of grace. It is this aspect of our worship that is the justification for our beloved St. Nelly, patron saint of our aerial altars (so often vilified and smashed)—for all religious bodies must have their holy virgins (and, in our case, martyrs), who in one way or another stand for, symbolize, our unending <u>via crucis.</u> For we have experienced, and continue to experience, all the sufferings that strike the human species—domestic strife, illness, old age, abandonment, loneliness—yet in addition to those sufferings common to all we are made to live through yet more terrible calamities. We have suffered derision and extermination. We have been buried alive, walled up, burned, hanged, shot by firing squads, discriminated against, blackmailed, and imprisoned. There have been, and still are, attempts to destroy our kind completely. Science, politics, and religion have taken up arms against us. The creation of the AIDS virus, manufactured with the clear intention of annihilating us and all those who, like us, seek after adventure (for all adventure is the expression of a disquiet, a yearning, and holds out erotic possibilities), is but the most recent attempt to bring our history to an end—and yet ours is a history that cannot have an end, because it is the history of life itself in its most rebellious, authentic manifestation. What has been sought by every means possible is a world that is chaste, practical, and sober. We oppose that horror with all our hearts and souls, we assume all possible risks, and we wield against it that infinitely powerful weapon the only weapon that we possess—pleasure.

It is quite possible that Odoriferous Gunk's paper, read by the queen of Holland, would have ended at this point, but we shall never know, for at this last word, "pleasure," there leaped up, like a frog seeing a snake, La Reine des Araignées—none other than Delfín Proust—who spoke as follows:

"What I don't understand about this paper is why there's such a fuss to make a distinction between a man and a faggot, when there is no doubt that every faggot is a man and no man is anything but a faggot. There are, ladies and gentlemen, four major categories into which all fairies or faggots or whatever you want to call them can be divided, and those four categories include all men. Listen, then, I beg you, to the Four Major Categories into Which All Fags Can Be Divided. And don't forget, sir, that *you* are in one of these categories. Yes, *you,* whether you admit it or not. Reality is more compelling than your silly sanctimoniousness or your craven cowardice. So open your ears, and listen:

"**First Category:** The Ringed Queen, also known as the Screaming Queen and the Menace to Society. This pansy scurries like a desperate mole, a blind spider snuffling about for a fly—a fly to unzip, my dear. Her most elemental concern is to find a phallus, and she is invariably about to faint or die—or go berserk from desperation. She does not sleep, and hardly eats. She leaves no corner, nook, vacant lot, beach, patch of underbrush, stairwell, or men's room unexplored. She never encounters the object of her desire—or when she thinks she's actually, finally found it she becomes even more desperate and rushes off in a new search.

"This type of queen is so outrageous, and so disruptive, that the system installs a metal ring around her neck. The ring may be visible or invisible. Whenever politics, morality, or the economy leads the powers that be to feel that the Ringed Queen should be locked up in a work camp, the only thing the system's security forces have to do is latch onto the ring with a hook. So this type of queen is easily rounded up and carted off. Once she's in the concentration camp and she and her sister queens are all kabobbed together on a long metal skewer that passes through their rings, they're made to plant potatoes, taro roots, and tomatoes; or to cut sugar cane, weeds, or hemp; or to do whatever other nasty work needs to be done.

"Although they are constantly persecuted, their numbers continue to grow—to the extent that sometimes you can hear the sound of rings clanking as you walk down the street. A typical example of this type of queen is EACHURBOD. Here she is, although not in person as I would have wished:"

(The huge movie screen behind the speakers' table flickered to life, and on it the audience saw the image of Eachurbod, who indeed exhibited all the features that La Reine des Araignées [it takes one to know one!] had just listed.

The screen then flickered dark again, and Delfín Proust [a.k.a. La Reine des Araignées] continued his enumeration:)

"**Second Category:** The Common, or Simple, Queen. This type of faggot is committed to another common queen—his 'partner,' or 'associate,' or 'friend,' and sometimes even 'significant other'—and they are often seen strolling through a pine grove chatting about their plans, or buying a pair of plastic flipflops, or taking a trip to Varadero. The common queen generally lives with her mother and goes to the movies every Friday to see *The Umbrellas of Cherbourg.* A clerk, a translator, a petty bureaucrat, this queen wears long-sleeved white shirts, sometimes with a tie. She does not dream about being screwed by some well-muscled hunk who might possibly, just possibly, be bi. Let us look at a typical specimen: this one's name is Reynaldo Filippe, but it might just as well be Juan Pérez or Jesús Briel:"

(The screen lighted up, and on it there appeared a black-and-white photograph of a queen about forty years old, her hair combed neatly and parted on one side, with thin lips and regular, rather impersonal features somewhat reminiscent of T. S. Eliot's. But Delfín Proust made it clear that because she was so common, the name of this queen was unknown, and that what the audience was seeing was an example that might be seen almost anywhere. "It's as though you were looking at a blank page," La Reine des Araignées said, and the screen went black.)

"In the **Third Category** we find The Closet Queen. This queen may be a lawyer, a professor of Marxism-Leninism, a militant in the Communist Youth, the director of a government office, a member of the Communist Party, or a regular attendee at masses in the Catholic Church. She might occasionally be the editor of a literary journal and make trips to Bulgaria or Mongolia. Of course the closet queen is a queen who absolutely denies *being* a queen. She's a *dying* queen, because she can almost never *live,* almost never be herself to her fullest measure. She lives in terror, fearing that she'll fall into some phallic trap. She wants nothing to do with other queens. She vegetates; she lives in a state of denial. But sometimes, unable to bear it any longer, she steps into the men's room of a pilot brewery. There, back at the back, a black man with a beckoning prick pretends to be urinating. The closet queen can't stand it. She has lived in abstinence for years, going to Lenin Park to stroll hand-in-hand with her daughters or meeting with the block Watchdog Committee, in which she's an activist. The closet queen, all aquiver, approaches the gigantic phallus and puts out her index finger, right there next to where she's wearing the wedding ring her wife gave her, that overpoweringly heavy bundle of sticks that she must carry throughout life—which is perhaps why she's often called a *faggot.* The terrified closet queen touches the gleaming phallus, then grasps it in her hand, gives it a little squeeze, looks desperately all around, especially toward the door. Then, frantically, she kneels and sucks—but only for a few seconds, for she thinks she hears a noise, or footsteps. The closet queen quickly gets to her feet and takes off running through the pilot brewery, terrified that the black man will pull out a pistol and arrest her on the spot. She flees across the entire city and takes refuge in her house, with her wife and their daughters. That night she'll ask her mother-in-law out for a pizza. . . . I beg you, my friends, look with pity and understanding upon the image of this poor, suffering—*miserably* suffering—queen:"

(The screen lit up, and on it appeared the figure of Luis Marrano, director of the literary journal *La Maceta de Cuba.* This pitiful specimen was dressed in a coat and tie and wearing a green beret. Her appearance on the screen caused a certain amount of muttering and rustling among the audience, because clearly the editor of *La Maceta* was in the room. But this middle-level functionary quickly removed his olive-green beret and slipped off his jacket and tie and sat quietly in his shirtsleeves. The screen, fortunately, went dark immediately, and La Reine des Araignées went on talking:)

"The **Fourth and Last Major Category of Queens** is the Queenly Queen. This is the *only* queen who lives the life of a queen, doesn't hide the fact from anybody, holds prominent political posts, travels to capitalist countries, and has several cars and several drivers—whose well-oiled steering mechanisms she handles with real expertise! The queenly queen has something on *everybody,* and she is filled with unbounded malignity and an immense talent for opportunism. She has a past with ties to the most sordid and permanent powers. Immune to all setbacks, to all changes in the political winds, to all political and moral manipulation, she is, in and of herself, a state secret—or at least an enigma. Perhaps when she was young she had compromising relations with a head of state, the secretary-general of the United Nations, a king, or a dictator-for-life. Here is an example of the queenly queen."

The screen flickered to life once more, and on it there appeared one of Fifo's ministers, Sr. Alfred Güevavara, who in real life just happened to be sitting on the official raft, right beside Fifo. This personage was a flabby, almost transparent-skinned, slant-eyed, big-cheeked, fat-jowled queen with a big double chin and an undisguisably bald head, so of course it was impossible for the audience not to recognize her. That explained the deafening whispers that ran from one side of the auditorium to the other.

And to top it off, when the screen went dark, Delfín Proust, advancing across the platform toward the floating audience, began to point out the queenly queens who were present for the Carnival, along with all the other types of queens who caught his eye.

Oh, my god, Fifo couldn't believe the tone that his own personal Oneirical Scientifical Theological Political Philosophical Satirical Conference was taking. If so far he had (grudgingly) tolerated it, it was to demonstrate to his guests his magnanimity and liberalism (although may of those attending the conference had been secretly sentenced to death by Fifo that very night), but when Delfín Proust, with that unparalleled cool of hers (and that unmitigated gall), started to point out virtually the entirety of Fifo's General Staff and most of his bodyguards as queenly queens, he could stand it no longer, and he ordered his diligent midgets to take out the faggot before she could go any further.

There was just one condition he put on the assassins: The faggot had to be stabbed, whether with a knife or other sharp object he didn't care, but definitely stabbed, since using a pistol or other firearm in the middle of the conference would surely be considered an insult to the VIPs and heads of state, and might even wound somebody. And so, while the fairy hopped deliriously from raft to raft calling out the category of the queen that was aboard—queenly, ringed, common, closet—the midgets, clutching knives or other sharp-pointed weapons, pursued him, thrusting and jabbing at him and sometimes even *throwing* knives at him, though Delfín was hopping about so much that they never touched him. Of course, some of the knives and other sharp instruments did puncture the *rafts,* sinking them and their passengers on the instant. Meanwhile, the pursued queen, leaping like a frog princess, continued to elude the menacing blades of the diligent midgets by hopping from flotation device to flotation device (never failing to point out the fairy who was sitting in it). But just as she *was* about to be overtaken, just as the knives and other sharp instruments were flying through the air like a rain of arrows, Delfín Proust lifted the skin of his face (which turned out to be a mask) to reveal to the audience what seemed to be her true visage: that of none other than Miss Chelo. The revelation was astounding. An ally of that importance could not just be *killed* (although we should make it clear that under Chelo's face there was the true face of the AntiChelo, who, on orders from the Condesa de Merlín, was revenging herself on Chelo). Fifo turned livid with fury, while his mind was assailed with questions. Was it right to murder a person who had always been a faithful Mata Hari for him? Should the life of that ridiculous faggot be spared? And just at that crucial moment, throughout the auditorium there boomed the even more stentorian roaring of the computers, which were bellowing like bulls in the Garden of Computers, demanding their reports. The visit to them could no longer be postponed. There was a blast of cornets, trumpets, bullhorns, alarms, sirens, or whatever it is that people blow moments before an atomic blast begins. And then, as the floodwaters continued to inundate his Palace, Fifo gave the order to depart immediately for the Garden of Computers.

A Prayer

And here again is the color of summer, with its repetitive, terrible hues . . . desperate bodies in this blinding light seeking solace, consolation . . . bodies that exhibit themselves, writhe and squirm, yearn for each other, and stretch out to bake in this endless, hopeless summer. Here again is the color of summer—the summer glare that blurs our outlines and drives us mad, in this country—run aground on its own deterioration, its own terrible weather, its own madness—that is Hell incarnate: a lethal, glaring, colorful eternity. And out there beyond this horrible watery prison—what, if anything, awaits us? Who, if anyone, cares about our summer, or our watery prison, or this weather that simultaneously isolates us within ourselves and fulminates against us? Outside this summer, what do we have? . . . Here again is the threat of the teenagers that the sun first, like a spotlight, turns its light on and then, as they pass before it, plunges into darkness. And one must walk on, as though that street corner down there held some compelling reason for us to walk toward it; one must walk on, as though this sidewalk of fire were itself the promised land. The plants' exhalations produce hallucinatory mirages. The smell of cut grass rises in waves; the fragrance of tiny white flowers greets us as we pass, and carries us up and away. *To be, to be, we want to* ***be***. . . . And the color of summer has taken over every nook and corner. Our wet bodies thrill to a boundless prickling. And still, sometimes, as we grow old, we dream. And still, sometimes, we feel that in this blinding light—in a *vision of blinding light*—a naked angel with lovely wings will come down to visit us. And still, sometimes, like withering old maids, we are ready (mistakenly) to grow tender. And so we walk on through this thick, steamy, fiery air, which from time to time turns reddish. Our wet, razor-sharp bodies slice through this frightening quietness, which echoes, silently, in our every fiber—and we defy the heavens to fall upon us as we try to find a response out there in the glowing splendor of the sea. But all there is is bodies—writhing, squirming, coiling about one another, hooking to one another in the midst of a Carnival without shadows, in which every person wears the mask he feels like wearing, in which betrayal and ass-wiggling are part of the official system, part of our most fundamental tradition. . . . Later, the rains will come, great downpours, and a desperation beyond time will begin to germinate within us all. New waves of light and humidity will come, and there will be no rock, or doorway, or tree, or shrub that will not be fuel for our desolation and despair. We will be that pile of bones, abandoned, rotting in the sun in a patch of weeds, a pile of bones calcined by tedium and the merciless certainty that there is no escape. Because it is not possible to escape the color of summer. Because that color, that sadness, that petrified flight, that sparkling, gleaming, glaring tragedy—that knowledge—is *us*.

O Lord, don't let me just melt away in these interminable summers. Let me be a meteor-like flash of horror that comes and is gone forever. Don't let the new year, the new summer—the same summer as always—continue to beat me down, wear me away, erode me, and once more command me to throw myself into the light, ridiculous, wrinkled, pathetic, wet to my skin, and searching. By next summer, Lord, grant that I'll have ceased to exist. Let me be that pile of bones abandoned in a patch of weeds, calcined by the sun.

A Tongue Twister (25)

Rodrigo de Triana, tireless tamer of Tainos, was initially distressed when a Taino trickster sneaked into his cot and, hitching Triana's britches, with his thick tricky-stick quickly trespassed upon the delectable conquistadorial bubble butt. Triana kicked but couldn't unstick himself from the Taino trickster's thick tricky-stick. "Shit!" Triana then snickered, his prick distinctly piqued, "What sick tricks these Taino tricksters think of!"

For Rodrigo de Triana

The Garden of Computers

Fifo and all his guests scrambled up out of the subterranean catacomb of the Palace (into which the floodwaters continued to pour) and made their way to the hill on which the Garden of Computers had been installed—a high, walled garden planted with hundreds of computers of all shapes and sizes. All the computers had been painted shades of green, and each one was set within a fenced circular enclosure topped with barbed wire, like some precious exotic plant. The guests marveled at the enormous garden planted with green computers roaring furiously, demanding reports to process. All the machines had opened their metallic maws and were shaking and jerking so much that it looked as though at any moment they might jiggle themselves off their bases—and they were clamoring for denunciations, backstabbings, and betrayals of friendship for their insatiable iron stomachs. These denunciations, backstabbings, and betrayals of friendship were the nourishment the machines lived on. And in the bowels of those voracious, implacable machines lay Fifo's true power. The only thing the machines asked in return for that power was food—and there was plenty of it. Over on one side of the garden, on a broad expanse of lawn, and restrained from entering the garden proper by an enormous barbed-wire fence, was a shouting, raving mob of people. And every member of that crowd of people had a sheet of paper, a letter, a document that betrayed or denounced or ruined someone, and that this person wanted desperately to feed to the computers. Usually the computers were fed every day, but Fifo wanted to be sure to make an impression on his guests, to show them his power, so he hadn't allowed the computers to be fed anything for a *week*. And he had invited his guests here today to see the crowd of people who had been gathering around his palace in that time—the usual number of informants had septupled, and the computers were *ravenous*.

Fifo, enraptured, stood with his guests on the highest point of the hill and ordered his midgets to open the gates. In a howling, fevered mob, the informants stormed the garden, running in mad panic toward the computers. They knew they had to turn in their reports as fast as possible, before other people turned in other reports against *them*. The pushing and shoving to get to the computers made hand-to-hand combat look tame. Desperate women turned in reports against their husbands; husbands brought accusations against their children and their wives and their wives' lovers and even their *own* lovers. Hundreds of professors turned in reports on their students; thousands of students inculpated their professors. A throng of workers filed a grievance against the chairwoman of a union delegation, but the chairwoman of the union brought in a huge text (in code) that leveled irrefutable charges against the workers. A little boy ran up panting to a computer and tossed it a monstrously long report against his great-grandmother—the same great-grandmother who had carried him in her own arms from Artemisa and now was smiling as she lodged a complaint against her elderly husband, who in turn was ratting on her and the rest of her family, not to mention the driver of an interprovince bus who was engaged in the black-market trafficking of root vegetables. From the most distant points of the Island, people had made the pilgrimage to the Garden of Computers with their reports. And no one escaped. Charges would be lodged against the people who lived on her block by the chairwoman of the Watchdog Committee; imputations would be made against the chairwoman of the Watchdog Committee by the head of the zone; the head of the zone would be impeached by a member of the Party; grave accusations would be filed against the Party member by the provincial committee; the provincial committee would be reported by the national committee; the national committee, by an agent from State Security; and this agent would be burned by a superagent. There was not a single person in that crowd of stool pigeons, rats, songbirds, and other assorted denunciatory vermin who was not, in turn, denounced. They all robbed, conspired, and lied; they all wished Fifo in hell; they were all rodents.

The computers opened their huge maws and stuck out their metallic tongues, their teeth clamped down on the fresh reports, and in a millisecond the reports were processed. A sense of happiness (almost of security and peace) came over the people in the crowd once their reports were safely in the gullets of the computers. Respectful whispers were directed to certain selected machines. *This is one of the best. . . . Thanks to this one, I can get rid of my nephew and my husband. . . . That was the one that on the basis of a single report from me did away with every faggot on my block. . . . This one helped me get that beach in my neighborhood closed down, thank goodness, and sent my brother to the firing squad. . . .* And the words of praise, of quiet thanks, went on—but in whispers, so as not to irritate the other computers, all of which were chewing away.

The garden was one huge roiling sea of papers thrown over the tops of the barbed-wire fences to the computers, which, hopping and jiggling inside, would snatch them in their jaws on the fly and swallow them with a sound like a six-gun shoot-out. Among those turning in reports were Clara Mortera, tossing in a report on Teodoro, and Teodoro, with his report on Clara. A group of sailors were lodging charges against a group of bull macho tops, and a priest was bringing a complaint against a beggar—a whole *book* of charges, and written in just a week. Accusations were brought against a bridge and an almond tree. Hundreds of poets turned in manuscripts of self-denunciatory verses. Housewives accused themselves of wasting imported butter. Teenagers, hiding their long hair under enormous caps, denounced longhairs. Officially licensed whores brought complaints against freelancers. Millions of reports were filed on people who listened to the Voice of America, Radio Martí, and Radio Tinguaro and those who read Moscow gossip magazines. A huge report was turned over to one enormously fat computer, listing all the people who would probably be committing suicide during the next month.

In the midst of that mob of informants, Skunk in a Funk thought she spied her mother. Quickly she grabbed the Dowager Duchess of Valero's binoculars (as the old dame drafted a report against her great-great-grandmother—dead these two hundred years) and looked to see. Sure enough, Skunk in a Funk's mother, waving a report madly in the air, was there among the crowd. Skunk in a Funk focused the excellent binoculars (which the Dowager Duchess used to find black men up in the tops of coconut trees) and was able to read the report. It was on *her,* Skunk in a Funk, and his mother had brought it here from Holguín, with lord only knew what adventures and stumbling blocks on the way. Skunk in a Funk quickly scanned the report that his mother was so determined to toss into the jaws of the computers. It was addressed directly to Fifo, and it accused Gabriel of corrupting the morals of a minor and being a lazy good-for-nothing bum, a degenerate, and a pervert; of being a lost sheep who wanted to leave the country; of being the leader of a band of wild faggots; and of being in the process of writing a book against Fifo and the whole country—an atheistic, accursed, and counterrevolutionary book. It also said that on his last visit to Holguín, her son had stolen a bottle of rendered pork fat and a special two-horned anvil from her. "The only two-horned anvil there was in the whole neighborhood, perfect for fixing our shoes with—I used to lend it to all the neighbors. I've come all the way from Holguín with my soles flapping in the wind." Last, she told Fifo that she was writing all this in the knowledge of his, Fifo's, kindness and high principles and that she hoped that he would rehabilitate her son and set him on the right path. "He never had a good father (good *or* bad); you could be one. I give him to you with all my trust and all my love. Rehabilitate him, reeducate him for me, so that he will be a moral, unblemished man. So I can walk through the town I live in with my head held high. He is my son, and he is the thing I love best in all the world, but he is also my shame. He is not a bad person, but he has lost his way on account of all the bad influences in Havana. Take him away from all that—set him on the right track for me! Make him work hard—hard work never hurt anybody. I suggest that you send him to the Isle of Pines to break rocks. As I write this, the paper is covered with my tears." And then Skunk in a Funk saw his weeping mother throw the report to a computer, which swallowed it in one gulp. Stumbling and tottering (no doubt because of her tattered shoes) Reinaldo's mother disappeared into the crowd. Skunk in a Funk tried to follow her with the Dowager Duchess's binoculars; he knew this was the last time he would ever see her. But just then another human tide washed into the Garden of Computers, with another sea of reports, and he lost her. A second hail of denunciations and complaints pelted the voracious computers. Skunk in a Funk, perhaps in an attempt to forget her horror, perhaps simply to amuse herself, used the binoculars to read a report presented by the commissioner of the Municipality of Arroyo Apollo claiming that the terrible heat waves that had been sweeping over Havana recently were caused when all the inhabitants of the city got up early in the morning to stand in line for bread that they didn't intend to eat, but rather to stop up their ears with so they wouldn't have to listen to another chapter of *La perlana,* an underground novel that a slum-dwelling novelist was reading all over the city. While Skunk in a Funk hung the binoculars around the neck of the Dowager Duchess of Valero, who had meantime finished her report, the reports continued to pour in—complaints against people for disturbing the peace, for contempt, for precriminality, for theft, for corruption, for abuse of power, for negligence, for ideological softness, for bestiality, for sodomy, for cronyism—in a word, for conspiring against the Powers of the State and, therefore, committing High Treason. The garden was flooded with paper. . . . There was also a detailed report in which Fifo was accused of being a perfidious murder, a drug trafficker, and an international gangster. But the person who filed *this* report (an old major general, now retired and in disgrace) was garrotted instantly by the computer that received the complaint. The man disappeared along with all the aides who had accompanied him.

Fifo, who had witnessed this summary execution, was extremely pleased with the effectiveness of his machines, and he ordered the crowd of informants to leave the garden now, even those who had not yet been able to turn in their reports.

"You can do it tomorrow," he said. "Right now, it's our turn."

And while the diligent midgets violently removed all the informants from the premises, Fifo asked his guests to file *their* reports. Followed by the members of the audience, Fifo (first in all things) strode forward and stood before an immense computer, the Fifarian Computer, and dropped in his report.

"It's my examination of conscience," he smiled. "Now come on—it's your turn."

Immediately the guests, in their gala attire, began filing toward the computers and dropping in their reports.

Someone presented a complaint against the emotional and ideological weaknesses of Bloodthirsty Shark. The Condesa de Merlín took the opportunity to file charges of high treason against her rival, Miss Chelo. Two Eskimos turned in a denunciation of Federico Fellini. The Queen of Castile lodged a complaint against her husband, stating that the King was the leader of the ETA, the Basque Separatists; the Empress of Yugoslavia reported that her mother was the head of the largest whorehouse in Brazil and had entered into a conspiracy against Mao's daughter to take power and turn South America into one huge neo-Nazi state. There was a report on the Pope which claimed that in addition to being a woman she was the head of the KGB. The "Antonio Maceo Freedom Front" (with headquarters in Miami) delivered a videocassette which showed the President of the United States making love to a rabbit. There was also an accusation against Mother Teresa; it seems she had spread AIDS throughout India. And Marlon Brandy was accused of having infected all of Africa and Oceania. A color photograph was turned in that showed Agostino Neto jacking off a rhinoceros.

It is simply impossible to chronicle here all the reports which, with great elegance, Fifo's guests delivered to the computers. The only thing we might add is that the reports, which the machines deciphered for him on the instant, made Fifo feel more elated by the minute. *If this keeps up,* he thought, *I may actually start looking good.* But just as the VIPs' denunciations of other VIPs or world-famous personalities were reaching epic proportions, one of the midgets came up to Fifo and gave him a staggering piece of news. In all the confusion Gertrudis Gómez de Avellaneda had escaped! She'd stolen one of the motorboats from the Fifaronian Palace, but before she'd launched it, she had tossed a report into the computer compound calling Fifo a "bloodthirsty old hawk with its talons gone."

"It can't be! It can't be!" roared Fifo. "That ruins my public image. Stop that whore! Stop her! Or at least perform an act of repudiation against her! I want her *smeared* when she gets back to Spain. And if *El País* interviews her, I'll withdraw my financial support from that rag! Send Raúl and one of my doubles to preside over the act of repudiation. A *big* act of repudiation! And let the Carnival begin!"

And immediately the delegation of guests prepared to follow Fifo to the Carnival's assembly point for the Carnival parade, while the diligent midgets organized the act of repudiation against Avellaneda and made secret plans to kill her. The guests mounted armored cars, floats, horse-drawn carriages, a nineteenth-century gig, trains with rubber tires, Alfa Romeos, trucks covered with flags, and every other kind of vehicle imaginable and set off for the Grand Fiesta. At the head of the procession was Fifo, riding inside a gigantic lighted transparent balloon with a red neon sign on top with huge blinking red letters that spelled out a single word—***FIFO.***

But before Fifo climbed into this huge whatchamacallit, the chief of protocol (none other than Raúl Kastro), who had to get going for the Carnival, approached him and handed him a dress uniform and a pair of new boots, reminding him that before the kickoff of the Carnival there was another activity scheduled.

"What?" roared Fifo, one foot inside the balloon.

"A tour of Old Havana with Alejo Sholekhov," said the second-in-command (who still harbored some hopes of becoming Number One).

"Well, then, Old Havana it is! Let's get going! Tell Sholekhov to start getting his talk ready. And tell him to keep it short—we've got to get this goddamned Carnival on the road!"

A Tongue Twister (26)

The Adventures of Toto and the Hottentot Tootsie

"Oh, Tito, look, a Hottentot," commented Toto. "And to top it off, she's quite a tootsie!" And at the sight of the Hottentot tootsie's titanic tattooed tits, Toto was totally smitten. "Will you be my t-t-tootsie?" Toto stuttered. "If you'll be my totem pole," tittered the Hottentot trollop. And they trotted off to try some thitherto taboo totem-pole tupping.

That was Thursday. On Tuesday Toto felt terribly fatigued, so he attempted to teach himself some new tricks. To his torrid Hottentot tootsie he sighed, "Say—totting up my tepid existence till today, I'd venture an attempt at something new, not *too* difficult, a task at which I could tickle the black-and-whites of this electric typewriter."

"Toto, you're a total trip!" trilled the tattoo-titted Hottentot. "You could typewrite about tons of things—tepees, Thebes, tautologies, cataracts, catheters, tarantulas, tetanus, tigers in Tibet, or tortoises in Lake Titicaca. You could type texts about extinct turtles, tom-toms in Tanzania, Tartuffe, steroids such as testosterone, tops, bottoms, bottles, stoppers, storm troopers, tanks, gigantic testicles, or tens of thousands—tons and tons—of terribly trite subjects such as these. You can't be too trite, in fact, because if you turn out treacly stupidities on your trusty typewriter, they'll sell like hotcakes."

"Oh, my Hottentot, is that true?" Toto asked timidly.

"Totally," the Hottentot tootsie hooted happily. "And I'll just take twenty percent!"

And so in a trice Toto started typewriting, and today, Toto has triumphed, taking to his pup tent (or tepee or tenement) a Nobel Prize for typewriting.

For the Marquesa de Macondo and Karmen Valcete

Ass-Wiggling and Backside-Swinging

A bald, fish-shaped creature (Julio Gámez) stre-e-etched its gelatinous body; a round, squat queen (Miss Lois Suardiaz) began to whirl like a top; a gray owl (the Anglo-Campesina) opened its round, watery eyes, shook the sleepiness out of its wings, and began to flutter; one particular plump, spiny fairy (Mendivito, they called her) pulled from her bag some *hideous* pieces of cloth painted all over (by her) with Picasso-like parrots and impossible pricks, and waving them about as her *hideous* banner, began to move. The body of that bearded fairy who was spilling out of her costume (Miss Emilio Bedell) left a wake like an eighteen-wheeler's as it moved down the street. A squiggle dressed all in black (Odoriferous Gunk) was dragging the tent in which his mother lay eternally dying. . . . SuperSatantic (shooting out of the Palace like a bottle rocket) grabbed a hypodermic syringe, filled it with her own AIDS-contaminated blood, and waved it around in the air as she joined the Dissed & Pissed. A queen ran, arms and legs going every which way, along the coastline, brandishing a huge pair of scissors. Where was that silly queer going with those enormous scissors?

Where, you ask, Miss Thing? To cut off Coco Salas' false eyelashes in the middle of the Carnival so everybody would see her, of course—because I'm *not* going to let that ugly little gnome prance around in Carnival and bat eyelashes that don't belong to her. Eyelashes *which,* I'll have you know, she got by cruelly snitching on her friends and family members, one of whom being her father, who's now been executed. That's why she put the whip to her sleigh dogs like that, to get away . . ."

"*Sleigh* dogs?"

"Yes, *sleigh* dogs, my dear. Do you think a sleigh won't work on sand? . . . I'm off! Out of the way, Sakuntala, or you're roadkill!"

The queen was whipping at the dogs harnessed to her sleigh (which she'd just climbed up on), insulting them verbally, calling them Vicentina Antuna, Vilma Espina, Clementina Cirea, María Roca Almendros. . . . The dogs (bitches, all of them, as you can see from the names Coco was calling them), stung by the fury of being so terribly insulted, ran faster and faster.

Following the queen in her sleigh (which was now moving at quite a clip) marched the members of the group of Snubbed and Seething, who had been heroically waiting at a spot near Fifo's subterranean castle. They marched (or rather trotted) hard on the heels of Fifo and his splendid entourage in order to have their revenge and, if possible, prevent both Fifo *and* his famous guests from making it to the Carnival alive.

But one of the queens in Fifo's court—to wit, the cunning and satanic Delfín Proust—took in the entire surroundings with one sweep of his country-boy, milk-fed gaze, calculated the fury of the attackers, and quickly concocted an invincible plan of defense, consisting of assigning Halisia Jalonzo, walking backward and performing the mad scene from *Giselle,* as the rear guard. If seeing that old hyena-toothed, big-nosed hag with her hair standing up all over her head and waving a sword at them didn't freeze the enraged attackers in their tracks, then nothing would. The seconds gained by the paralysis (the shock!) of the attackers would give Fifo and his entourage plenty of time to get to the Carnival, and even to take a detour first through Old Havana with Alejo Sholekhov. Only one person was not stunned into immobility by the horrific sight of the classical ballerina—the husband of Karilda Olivar Lubricious, who just kept coming, saber aloft, making death-dealing slashes at the air (which whistled at every stroke), and determined to hack the poetess to pieces. Karilda Olivar Lubricious, seeing her husband gaining on her, broke from the official group and (with her faithful cats) *ran*—trying to lose herself in the hurly-burly of the Carnival.

Karilda's husband zoomed like a meteorite through the procession, trying to catch the poetess and put her out of his misery. *What do we do?* Fifo asked the thoughtful (though bald) head of Güevavara, using the microphone installed in his balloon. (Fifo often sought Güevavara's advice at critical moments.)

"Give orders to start the ass-wiggling and backside-shaking while we do our duty with Sholekhov," replied the queenly queen. "Don't forget that UNASCO's people are here, and they brought their checkbooks."

Instantly, all the Fifaronian orchestras, including the Aragon Symphony and a hundred others even worse, began to play as loudly as they could. Ears were assailed by the simultaneous rhythms of a salsa, a merengue, a dengue, a guaracha, a mambo, a pachanga, a cha-cha-cha, a rumba, a lambada, a fox-trot, and one rhythm even catchier than these, a rhythm that made anyone who heard it feel the irresistible need to shake his ass (or hers). All those in the procession were suddenly shaking their backsides, wiggling their asses, moving their legs and thighs, shimmying their shoulders, bobbing and weaving their necks. The hunkiest hunks shook their little bubble-butts and rubbed them up against the bubble-butts of other hunks who, had it not been for that music and that party, would have pulled out their switchblades and sliced and diced them. . . . Oh, honey, you just can't imagine—this tickling, I've just got to scratch it. It's like a thrumbling in the blood, it's like something's nipping at you and you gotta shake it out, even if you disenjoint your whole body. *Go, girl! Go!* The engine backfires. *Weed! Grass! Shake yo' ass!* Go *awn,* man, step right on! Shake it, but don't break it! Let that rhythm get you, girl! Go with it, flow with it, let it *do* you, hon! I'm gonna shake till I come undone, I'm gonna shake myself till my legs fall off, shake myself till my arms fall off—why, honey, I'm gonna shake myself till my *ass* falls off!

Listen, now that the music's started let's go have some real *fun over in Bartolo's plantain field.* Oh, that plantain field has got a plantain for you all right, honey, the biggest plantain you ever saw, bigger than the one Rapet Diego shoves up his ass. Oh, grandma, what a big *plantain* you have! The better to *mmmm* you with, my dear! Ay, ay, ay-y-y-y-y!

Shake it, shake it! I don't think I can take it!

And while I'm shaking my ass and wiggling my backside, I think—though I can't imagine why—about the word *rumpityhumpity.* And I keep wiggling and shaking—I can't control myself—to the rhythm of this music. Such music, my lord! Such music! I can't control myself! Can*not!* Shake it, shake it! It's our national rhythm, our national song, our national *anthem!* It's our national movement—our very own ass-shaking and backside-wiggling!

The orchestras, bands, and marching musicians go on playing. The unanimous, spontaneous ass-wiggling and backside-shaking goes on wiggling and shaking. All of which gives Fifo time to put on that *huge* olive-green uniform of his and take the official swing through Old Havana and then, though his entourage is a bit perplexed (having just witnessed the burial of Alejo), put on a big smile and join the Carnival. To the sound of snare drums and with a preliminary throb and shudder, out of Fifo's balloon shoot fireworks the likes of which the world has never seen, while the participants in the act of repudiation take their places. . . . The music goes on playing and everyone is dancing—and as people dance and swig their beer out of cardboard cups, they all grow more and more excited. (I mean *aroused,* you know?) And not caring who they're next to, or who's watching, everybody in the crowd starts touching, rubbing, humping, feeling up neighbors, and dancing close. And right there in the middle of the crowd, people started taking it up the backside, or at least giving and getting a good blow job. . . . And up in the gigantic illuminated ball that looks like some shining Popemobile on steroids, Fifo, floating some three feet off the ground, waves to the millions of ass-shakers and backside-wigglers—and even *he* begins to wiggle a little. But then he becomes very serious—and then he starts shaking his ass again—and then he recovers his composure and puts on his bad-guy expression. Oh, but then he can't control himself, and starts shaking like he'll throw his joints out. . . .

That duality is his tragedy, thought a Uruguayan essayist (and medalist of the Casa de las Americas) who, temporarily pausing in his ass-wagging, began to write an essay which he provisionally titled "The Dual Nature of the Genius." The despicable essayist thought that if things went badly for Fifo he could always replace the word "genius" with "tyrant" and submit it for consideration for the Mikhail Gorbachev prize given by the PEN Club of New York.

A Tongue Twister (27)

Despite tight precautions, that tireless tractor-trailer inspector in his astrakhan caftan kicked the bucket when he tried to tap his rear intake onto the trailer jack of an intractable tractor-trailer driver known for his operatic thrills as the Truckin' Troubador. Because the tragic bucket-kicking triggered the total destruction of the tractor-trailer driver's trailer jack, the trailer inspector, despite his tireless tractor-trailer inspections during his tragically short lifetime, is being tried by State Security, at the instigation of his truculent detractors, as a traitor. Why would a deceased tractor-trailer inspector be tried as a traitor by State Security? Did his trailer inspections tick off too many detractors? How many detractors does it take to trigger the trial for treason of a deceased tractor-trailer inspector, anyway?

For Nene Saragoitía, a.k.a. Sakuntala la Mala

The Dual Nature of the [Genius, Tyrant]

And yet, the monster's childhood was a sad one. . . .

"Hey! José Manuel Poveda wrote that line over eighty years ago."

"You nasty *thing!* Do you dare to deny that the culture of socialist Cuba is the heritage of the entire country, the heritage of the masses, and therefore that anyone and everyone has a right to it? Huh? . . . Gotcha there, don't I? So just hush up, because I've got the floor, and I'm exercising my rights."

Yes, terribly sad was the childhood of the angel—I mean devil—I mean madman—I mean child—I mean *monster,* though they're all the same thing. On the one hand, the influence of his mother—a countrywoman, former housemaid, and former whore, a Catholic and one of the suffering and afflicted—left in Fifo a deep and compelling desire to be feminine. Oh, how he was drawn to the beckoning crotches of those field laborers who worked under the whips and bayonets on his father's enormous plantation. Yes, the influence of his mother was decisive in his formation as a faggot. But what, then, of the influence of his father, a Spaniard to the bone—and to make matters worse, from Galicia? Once, the father took aim and with one shot brought a worker down out of a coconut tree that the poor man had climbed to quench his thirst. I mean, this feudal lord manqué would not even give coconut water to *les misérables* who worked for him. The machista example set by Fifo's father—who would rape mares, hens, female turtles, and his own mother (who had started off as the cook)—awoke in Fifo an irresistible desire to be a *real man,* a *heterosexual,* although the author of this novel (a screaming queen if ever there was one) would deny that. But Fifo had known many women (in the biblical sense of the word), just as he had been bedded down by many men. . . . But oh, then there was the example of Fifo's great-great-grandfather, whose greatest sexual pleasure had been derived from screwing a horse (a *male* horse), though actually he wasn't that particular—he'd screw anything from a male boa constrictor in Santa María to a fighting cock. This great-great-grandfather awoke in the young boy's heart the wish to be a surly bull macho and screw *other* machos. But if to all this we add that in the Jesuit school he attended, the priests were constantly buggering the students and that Fifo, with his broad yet flat backside, was a roomy harbor that all the holy vessels sought to drop their anchors in after a hard day at the blackboard and the altar, then honey, you can see for yourself that Fifo (who also, don't forget, had had the promiscuous example of his mother) turned out to be a *queen,* the very queenliest of queens. . . . In his little heart there stirred three stirrings—he hearkened to the call of the ass (Faggotry), the call of the phallus (Butt-Fucking), and the call of the balls (Womanizing), and this last tendency led him to want to impregnate every woman he met so as to leave a human trace of his passage through this vale of tears.

And so our little man had no peace upon this earth. When he saw a good-looking woman he would grow impassioned, when he saw a man he would become almost faint, and when he spotted a fairy he would grow inflamed with thoughts of buggering. And the worst thing was that when he was screwing a man he wanted to be screwing the mother of that glorious ephebe, and when he was screwing a woman he wanted to be taken by the woman's brother, and when he finally was being screwed by the woman's brother he wanted to screw the father of the hunk who was screwing him. Nothing satisfied him; nothing fulfilled him. Sometimes, on the advice of Paula Amanda, he would host multiorgies. That way, as he sat (so to speak) in the center of the action (as Paula Amanda had recommended), as he took his place at the midpoint of the daisy chain, he could enjoy screwing and being screwed at the same time. But not even that worked—when he was at the center of the daisy chain he'd want to be the first one in it, or sometimes the last. So the chain would come apart (and not so easily, either, sugar) and the poor man would find no solace.

And now, up there in his transparent balloon lighted from the inside, he looked out upon that constant ass-wiggling and backside-shaking, those shimmies and shakes given by men, women, and fairy queens alike, and as his eyes caressed that ass, that piece of meat, that pair of tits, Fifo, despite his age (about ninety, although the author of this novel has portrayed him as considerably younger), saw that he was getting an uncontrollable erection, so he turned off the light inside his balloon, unzipped his trousers, and began to masturbate. Ay, but as he approached his climax, as he reached the moment of orgasm, there was no one body part (cunt, ass, or prick) to concentrate his imagination on, no one thing to get him off. Fifo could not cum! *No, there is no peace to be had for me on earth,* shouted Fifo, dressed in that huge, shapeless, olive-green uniform-thing that Raúl had given him to wear. So once more he turned on the overhead light in his floating balloon and—shining-bright, martial, "mechanical and ecumenical" (as the author of this novel put it in a previous one)—he smiled and lifted one arm and saluted the crowd that was applauding him as he led the grand parade, the Big Float at the head of all the little floats. But the truth is that while he was raising his arm and saluting, apparently with enthusiasm and joy, inside he was weeping tears of frustration and despair. Oh, if only he could be that black man who twisted and wiggled and showed off his basket; or that whore dressed as a militia recruit dancing on top of the wall; or that fairy clandestinely, passionately, squeezing a patriotic soldier's crotch; or that old guy with his hand on that cheering boy's butt. But no-o-o-o—he was everything at once, and he was therefore nothing. He was all of them and none of them. And therefore, being no definite human being, he was able to find fulfillment (or even solace) only in the destruction of every life-affirming instinct, every trace of authenticity and integrity. And so, as the ass-shaking and backside-wiggling went on, Fifo was almost howling (inside, of course) in grief and loneliness. The only thing he had was power. But power could not be possessed—power was solitude, loneliness, and death.

It was then that the voice of Raúl, dressed in a smashing red outfit and parading along atop a tank, came through to him on the intercom:

"Fifo, don't forget that I've had all your noblest friends taken out, just as you asked me to, including Arnaldo. I hope that when you give your speech tonight you'll name me as your heir."

Just look at Raúl in that red getup of hers! thought Fifo. *She at least knows what she wants and goes after it. She's had every man in my army up her ass.*

"No!" screamed Fifo into the intercom. "I will name no heir! The person who replaces me will be the man or woman who's amassed the most brownie points when it's all over. And besides, I plan never to die."

And not waiting for a reply, Fifo turned off the intercom and with his tragic eyes followed the enormous waves of ass-shaking and backside-wiggling as they rippled through the crowd.

In the Monster Men's Room

Now, Mary dear, I don't want you think that Eachurbod had resigned herself to staying back there at the UNEAC headquarters while those drums at Carnival were beating so insistently that every fold in his virginal asshole was throbbing. (Yes, sadly, despite all her efforts, *virginal . . .*) No *way,* sugar. Once the Carnival had been officially kicked off and was going strong, the queen (in spite of the memory of almost being murdered back there a few pages ago for having tried to take the handoff of the famous long-distance runner's baton) grabbed up the *Collected Works of Nicolás Guillotina* and made a monumental staircase out of them. And without more ado, though still clutching Volume XXVII of the *Complete Works of Lenin,* she scaled the fence at the UNEAC headquarters and leaped to the other side. Of course on the other side Juantormenta was waiting to wring her pretty neck, but Eachurbod threw Volume XLVI of the *Complete Works of Lenin* at his head, her tormentor Juantormenta was knocked unconscious, and the queen ran off, elbows and knees flying. After, of course, picking up Volume XXX of the Complete Works of Vladimir what's-his-name.

Desperately Eachurbod searched through bars and sewers, on bridges, and in every kind of nook and crevice imaginable. Finding nothing *(nothing!)* yet still seeking, she darted down the Paseo del Prado, where she saw a queen with a huge pair of scissors leap out of her sleigh, jump Coco Salas, and trim the poor thing's eyelashes. On tippy-toe, and still undicked, Eachurbod saw Skunk in a Funk being screwed by an *unbelievable* black man up in one of the laurel trees on the promenade. Tripping on a crack in the sidewalk and sprawling on the ground, she saw Karilda Olivar Lubricious' husband run right over her fetching body, saber raised. And Eachurbod shouted at him: "Oh, *stab* me! I'm Karilda!" But no, that saber was not meant for her. The offended spouse turned a look of fury upon her, kicked her, and ran on after his senile but still hormone-driven wife. Then heavens, in the midst of that debacle, those drums drumming, thrumming, commanding, clamoring, making magical danceable lecherous lickerous musical *demands* on a poor girl, the queen saw SuperSatanic with her hypodermic needle infecting hundreds of people with her AIDS-infected blood, and she begged her, for heaven's sake, to prick her with that mosquito-prick, but SuperSatanic, throwing needle-stabs left and right, said, "Don't even *think* about it, hon, you're fated to live a thousand years—if you haven't already—and to die of chronic virginitis!"

"No! *No!* cried Eachurbod madly, and she ran to join the ass-shaking and backside-wiggling in a conga line of glorious mulatto hunks shaking maracas and banging rhythm sticks together with their expert hands, and opening their legs to show off their *own personal* (and even more hypnotic) maracas and rhythm sticks, which Eachurbod would've dearly *loved* to get her hands on. And so Eachurbod danced, shook her ass, and danced some more, but the Regla rhythm boys didn't ask her to join their band. In the midst of the noise and celebration she saw Skunk in a Funk again, now wielding a machete and running after Tatica to revenge the theft of her first swim fins—but even that spectacle couldn't distract Eachurbod from his itch. Then he was run over and knocked to the ground by the Lady of the Veil, who was running madly toward a gigantic float belonging to the Ministry of Construction—but that blow (to more than her dignity) was also unable to shake some sense back into her—not that she ever had any, but you know what I mean. Her goal was to find a man, so she had no scruples about gazing at a policeman in his green uniform, his big gloves, boots, helmet, visor—and *nightstick!* This magnificent cop looked like a centaur in the flesh as he sat astride his equally magnificent steed. Eachurbod, taking a quick glance at the testicles on the horse, took a better look at the crotch on the cop, who sat like a stern statue in the center of the crowd that swirled around him. Eachurbod offered a pint of beer to the officer, who politely declined, saying that since he was on duty he couldn't drink. Encouraged by the cop's courtesy, Eachurbod took a step closer to the centaur and as she made sure he saw the red cover of Lenin's book (sure to gain his trust, she reasoned), she told him she had taken part in forty-nine People's Harvests and won every medal it was possible to win. The centaur looked down on her approvingly. Eachurbod then caressed the horse's back legs, its magnificent testicles, and from the horse moved on to the rider—she touched his military boot, touched a leg, and then, with one foot in the stirrup (like some fairy Cervantes) she swung up astride the horse's withers, and right there, hands together as though in silent prayer, she began to worship at the police officer's waist, and to touch with the tip of her tongue the tip of the saddle on which the man-part of the centaur sat. The drums beat faster, more insistently. Eachurbod couldn't wait any longer, and tucking the volume of Lenin under her arm, she plunged her shaved and numbered head into the cop's lap. The agent of Authority then raised the visor (revealing only stunning eyes), removed the helmet, and began to smash Eachurbod's head with it—Eachurbod was beaten until she fell off the horse, which then began to trample her. From between the magnificent steed's legs, Eachurbod raised his anguished eyes and saw that the policeman was no *man* at all—she was a police*woman,* and she even had long blond hair. Eachurbod had been thrown off by all that damned police drag. The queen took off running (limping) through the crowd.

"Criminal!" the policewoman screamed at him, charging after him on her fearsome mount. "How dare you attempt to corrupt the morals of a revolutionary woman? Criminal! You'll be punished by the Law!"

The fearsome police officer (who had twice been awarded the Lydia and Clodomira Medal) spurred her horse directly at poor Eachurbod, who used Volume XXVII of the *Complete Works of Lenin* to shield herself from the attack. But the terrifying policewoman just kept spurring her mount, which was now rearing and kicking furiously at the red-covered volume under which Eachurbod, in fear of her very life, was cowering. And then, just as she was about to give up the ghost, she cried out in pain to St. Nelly once more, and St. Nelly—despite the pains in her joints and despite the fact that she had retired from sainthood *ages* ago—descended from the clouds illuminated by the huge klieg lights of Carnival, and with one puff from her hideous lips detoured the syringe filled with arsenic that Fifo's thugs had just thrown from the balcony of Virgilio Piñera's apartment, directing it instead at the hideous, murderous horse, which it punctured in the croup (which is horse talk for "butt"). The horse, hit with the poison, dropped dead on the spot.

"Stop, you son of a bitch, you've killed my horse!" shouted the policewomen, drawing her revolver. Then, firing several times in the air, she took off after Eachurbod on foot. But the fairy queen, taking advantage of the confusion and hullabaloo, ran like crazy, bumping into Karilda Olivar Lubricious' indignant husband, who took out his fury on poor Eachurbod by swiping at her with his saber, which barely missed her but did split Volume XXXIX of the *Complete Works of Lenin* right down the middle. Eachurbod, tossing away the book at last, ran on through the crowd. She flew like a rocket through the mob and came to the Avenida del Puerto, leaped clean over the Condesa de Merlín's gig (snatching off the poor lady's wig in the process), and took refuge in one of the dark corners of the docks, while in the distance she heard the shots of the angry policewoman and, much closer, the beating of the Carnival drums.

Thousands of fairies and thousands of hunks paraded past, as did thousands of women shaking their gigantic tits so hard they squeaked, thousands of midgets frisking people, hundreds of high-ranking military types, dozens of glorious athletes, and all the high-wire acts and dancers that were scheduled to do their routines around and under Fifo's balloon. And now parading past were thousands of enlisted men beating their drums and flashing their radiant cymbals. And all that was just too much for the sensitive eyes of any human being, much less a human being as supersensitive as Eachurbod. She left her hiding place and once more abandoned herself to the abandonment of the celebrating throng.

How many men, in the midst of all that ass-wiggling and backside-shaking, were rubbing up against other men and so being semibuttfucked by the ones who were coming up from behind? Oh, in the midst of that conga line, in the midst of all that music, how many fairies were unzipping flies and jerking off the respectable young hunks who were kissing (up there above street level) their official girlfriends before the approving eyes of their future mothers-in-law, who were being taken from behind by off-duty midgets? But *she,* Eachurbod the Devouress, could find nothing. Half-dead, she leaned up against an aspen tree (yes, an aspen tree—this is *my* novel, Mary) in whose branches a group of sailors were screwing—oh, my God!—Coco Salas, while higher in the treetop the Areopagite was jerking off. Eachurbod looked, and in every tree, on every branch, there perched a midget, masturbating like the Areopagite or screwing to the rhythm of the moaning of Coco Salas, who appeared to be the queen of this arborescent orgy. Lord, to think that Coco Salas, one of the most hideous faggots in creation, was the queen of the prom! Was there no justice? Eachurbod considered slitting her own throat, even thought about that little bottle of kerosene that she'd slipped past Clara. *Yes, that's it—I'll incinerate myself right here in the middle of the crowd; I'll immolate myself like a despairing monk who can't find his God.* But a strong smell of urine brought Eachurbod back to her senses and set her back on track.

Yes, on track, because that smell of man-urine was coming from *somewhere,* and Eachurbod set out to find that spot. She sniffed at trees, walls, people, and stairways, following the scent. And at last she came to a huge wooden outhouse, a portable toilet—a john for johns!—that had been set up especially for use during the Carnival, and right in the center of El Prado. Man after man, beer in hand and face lit up by the music, was entering that holy place, and none were coming out. Like a shot off a shovel, Eachurbod whisked into that men's room, in quest of his deepest, dearest desire. . . .

And now she's in another monster men's room. There is no light, because some cunning queer has removed the bulb. In the darkness Eachurbod can make out crouching forms, magnificent forms erect and standing, hunks with their pants wide open. She can hear the wet slurping sound of tongues, the moans of pleasure, the sucking sound of lips like vacuum-cleaner heads. She hears (because she can hardly see a *thing*) the puffing and grunting of pleasure from several men being violently taken by their buddies, their pals, or their drunken first cousins. Glug-glugs, slurps, smacks, gulps, ingurgitations, clucks and clicks—mouths and throats like caverns, deep-throating pricks and making sounds so glorious, so irresistible, that they would electrify, energize, and eroticize even men who'd just stepped in to pee. Oh, that irresistibly sexy sound of frenetic fucking. And men keep filing in. . . .

And the fairies and the queens and the faggots who don't look like faggots keep on suckin'. Policemen with helmets and nightsticks put aside their duties as officers of repression for a moment and kneel before a heroic black man who's just come home from fighting in some international conflict and hasn't had any for ten years. All, in that dense darkness, recover their ultimate identities. Eachurbod feels himself caressed, squeezed, rubbed, palpated, touched from head to foot—and it's not one hand, it's *several* hands that are touching and rubbing her. Something hard yet inexplicably soft, slick, and wonderful-feeling is being rubbed on her; something arousing yet unclassifiable is passing over his face. And as he is stroked, someone pulls down her pants. Oh, is this a dream? No, no . . . in the midst of the smell of urine and cum, in the darkness, while the Carnival is booming out there outside, here inside Eachurbod feels powerful hands rubbing him—they reach his head, come down across his throat and neck, squeeze his nipples, drop to his thighs, squeeze and massage his legs, then rise to search for his asshole. They scrub him, rub him, rub-a-dub him, and spread her pink virginal cheeks. Something that feels like a clenched fist covered in heavy goo penetrates Eachurbod's behind, opening a passageway for itself almost up into his belly. Eachurbod's howl of pleasure is so piercing that only the drums beating thunderously outside can drown it out. And while she's drilled and thrilled, Eachurbod pushes back against the whatever-it-is, which (fleshy, slick) goes on pumping her body—in and out, in and out—at the same time as dozens of hands (which felt more like suction cups) caress her. Unable to contain her excitement, as the hands caress her and the *thing* penetrates her, Eachurbod cums, over and over.

In pure ecstasy, almost on the verge of fainting, Eachurbod leaves the men's room. And it is then, as she smells herself and looks at herself, that she discovers that she has been smeared from head to foot with shit. Someone, out of pure spite or getting his perverse rocks off, has covered her entire body with excrement—she looks like a walking *turd!* She hasn't been screwed, she's been covered with shit, even up her ass and in her mouth. *Shit, shit, shit!* she says. She's even got shit in her eyebrows. She's been slathered in a layer of shit that now, out in the glaring light of Carnival, gleams like some horribly sinister *something.* —*Ee-e-eek!* Eachurbod screams, slaps out insanely all around her (killing PornoPop, the Only Remaining Go-Go Queen in Cuba) and like some pestilential lightning bolt bolts down Paseo del Prado, the crowd on the avenue parting before her like the Red Sea—*holy Moses!,* you can hear people say. She comes to the Malecón, strips off all her shit-caked clothes, dives into the waves, and swims out to sea, trying to get rid of that smell of shit even as she prays for some hungry shark to come and screw her, or at least eat her. But when they smell the smell of this stinking queen, the sharks turn tail and run. And so the beshat fairy, floating on the surface of the sea, dives, over and over, into the waves, trying to wash off that smell which somehow only grows more smelly. And as she floats (and she's now been in the water for *hours*) she thinks that the Malecón (but how can this be?) seems to be getting farther and farther away. . . . Eachurbod tries to swim to the coast, but the coast keeps getting farther away. . . . And now the city is a distant point on the horizon, though Eachurbod can hear the drums and see the lights of Carnival.

A Tongue Twister (28)

To the tune of his boom box, vain Valero, once a boxer but his varicose veins now veiled by a fringe of violet voile, dances a fandango and sings a bolero at the bowling alley, where, misshapen, he is mistaken for a bowling pin and forced to dodge a barrage of bowling balls bowled by violent bowlers. Besieged, bleating, his vanity in tatters, Valero belatedly and bad-humoredly beats it, and to cover his bitter retreat he turns up the volume on his boom box, which blasts out a ballad. How did vain Valero the fey balladeer with varicose veins escape the barrage of bowling balls bowled by violent bowlers irate at the volume of the bolero played by the boom box? By beating it, behind a bulwark of blasting ballad, before being bowled over.

For the Dowager Duchess de Valero

THE LADY OF THE VEIL

Naturally, the diligent midgets had not forgotten Fifo's orders that the Lady of the Veil be killed during the height of Carnival by a stab wound to the honey-pot, so that it would appear to be a crime of passion. Killing her was easy, but stabbing her in the cunt was another thing—first because she was wearing so many veils that it was hard to tell exactly where her cunt *was,* and second because despite the veiled lady's social class and political importance she had gotten out of her carriage and mixed into the Carnival throng, and she was moving with uncanny speed through the crowd.

The diligent midgets ran after the Lady of the Veil clutching their knives and daggers, but there were *so many* people, honey, that it was worth your *life* to squat down and stab somebody in the cunt. If the order had been to stab her in the neck, or in the tits, or even in the stomach, the poor midgets wouldn't have been so hard put, but to duck down and find a honey-pot was just not *possible* in this crowd—not to mention the space needed for a hand to grip the knife and draw back enough to make the stab wound fatal. Besides, the Lady of the Veil was moving faster and faster, perhaps helped along by all her veils, which were now *sails,* girl—she was scudding along, slithering through the crowd like a snake on a wind-surfer. The diligent midgets had *no* idea where this ditzy dame was headed for in that getup of hers—although since it was Carnival, and the last night of Carnival to boot, she could *almost* pass unnoticed among all the outlandish costumes.

"Where in the world was that lady of the seven thousand veils going?"

"Sakuntala, dear, there weren't seven thousand veils, even if it looked like it."

"OK, but where was she *going?*"

"That, my dear, only she and I, in all the world, know. But if you promise not to tell, *this* is the cause of all her secret avatars and her personal pandemonium—"

In her country, where she was the Boss, the supposedly Omnicuntpotent Leader, she had heard the news of Fifo's Carnival, and specifically of the existence of a very special float that was to appear—the Lovin' Spoonful, it was called—sponsored by the Ministry of Construction. Atop this marvelous contraption, fifteen whores were to ride, and they would be wiggling their asses and shaking their tits around a mechanical bulldozer shovel shaped like a spoon that would rise and fall as it dipped into something that resembled a tub of cement. In the bowl of the bulldozer shovel, or "spoon" as they insisted on calling it, rode a magnificent half-naked rumba-dancing "chorus girl," the undisputed queen of Fifo's proletarian (and delirious) Carnival. On the bed of the float there was to be a gigantic illuminated fish tank, inside which there were to be hundreds of tropical fishes, thereby attracting the attention of the entire populace to that float and therefore to its queen, who was (as I believe I have mentioned) to be dancing frenziedly in the spoon. From the moment the Lady of the Veils had seen a documentary on Fifo's previous Carnival (a film made by Manuel Octavo Gómez which had won first prize at the Fez Film Festival, where the award was presented by President Omar Cavafy himself), it had been her dream to take the place of the working girl and shake her *own* ass in that spoon. And so, holding tight to that *idée fixe* (to be a working-class mambo dancer, the queen of ass-shaking, while tropical fishes performed aquatic maneuvers at her feet and the drunken crowd applauded), she had traveled incognito to Cuba and found lodging (thanks to her impeccable credentials as a terrorist and Arab multimillionairess) in Fifo's palace. Which was why now, hotly pursued by the indefatigable midgets who could not seem to manage to kill her, she was running toward that very Ministry of Construction float, her racing feet flattening she-cats, cat and horse turds, empty cans, suckling babes abandoned by their mothers, and thousands of other objects. Panting, she reached the float and took out a flask that contained a curious liquor prepared from a formula in an unpublished passage in *The Arabian Nights* (a passage, actually, that for certain legal reasons no publisher had ever dared to print). The Lady of the Veil invited all the whores in the corps de ballet to take a drink, and no sooner had they sniffed at the potion than they fell, profoundly sleeping, into the arms of the murderous midgets, who took advantage of the occasion to rape them. Then, as the monumental spoon made one of its descents, the Lady of the Veil offered her flask to the magnificent rumba dancer, who took a sip and instantly toppled off the float into the arms of the dancing crowd. Leaping aboard the spoon, the Lady of the Veil began to dance. The spoon rose almost into the clouds, then fell again, down into a gray, frothy semiliquid substance which looked like fresh-mixed cement and underneath which swam the schools of brilliantly colored tropical fish. The spoon rose, the spoon fell, and the Lady of the Veil, moving her hips and thighs more and more hypnotically, more and more frenetically, swayed her veils, her ass, her neck, her long-fingered hands, and astounded the applauding crowd—who were doing some dancing themselves, I tell you, honey. And while all this was going on, Fifo (still inside his globe) was once more issuing the secret, urgent order to the midgets—"In the cunt! In the cunt! Stab her in the cunt!"

So urgent, so insistent was that order that the midgets decided to make a human pyramid and boost one of their number up onto the spoon. Soon, the agent chosen for this mission had sneaked under the madly dancing veils, his murderous knife drawn and ready to stab her in the cunt. But it was not a cunt the midget found; it was a pair of balls and a prick—a pair of balls and a prick so irresistible that the midget instantly dropped to his knees and starting sucking. The Lady of the Veil, enraged, picked up the midget by the neck, strangled him, and tossed him to the crowd, which bellowed in delirium. Once more, the human pyramid. And once more, a midget under the Lady of the Veil's veils. This one made the same discovery, and fell to the same temptation, and so he, too, was tossed into the crowd, which suddenly began to chant: "She gives birth while she's dancing!" One after another, the Lady of the Veil tossed dead midgets into the hysterical crowd, which roared its approval, while Fifo, growing more infuriated by the second, was yelling "In the cunt, I tell you! In the cunt!"

Finally, one of the midgets (who, being a woman, was totally uninterested in men) got through to Fifo on her walkie-talkie: "No cunt here, just prick."

"Well give it to her in the ass, then!" screamed the Maximum Leader.

With the knife in her teeth, the midget climbed up on the float once more and gave a powerful dagger-thrust straight in the asshole of the Lady of the Veil, who, feeling that mortal wound to her ass, danced even more frenetically. It was her swan song, and knowing that it was, she drew it out as long as she could. And so the Lady of the Veil was gyrating madly if mortally-woundedly upon the spoon when she was glimpsed by Karilda Olivar Lubricious' husband, who thought that that whore up there with a mask on and dancing the dance of the jillion veils had to be his wife, who just didn't want to be discovered. So, weapon at the ready, the wronged husband climbed onto the float, leaped into the spoon with a tae kwon do move he'd learned from one of the kids in the neighborhood, and with a single swipe of the saber ripped off the lady's veils, revealing to all the world the naked body of Omar Cavafy, who, dagger up his ass, promptly expired. Well, maybe not so promptly, because first he gave several gyrations. His naked body, whirling like some weird lawn sprinkler, bathed the crowd in blood—and the crowd, thinking this was just another part of the dancer's show, applauded even more hysterically.

Ass-Wiggling

Oooh, what sweet ass-wiggling! whispered (and sometimes even screamed) the ass-waggling, hip-wiggling crowd, clutching paper cups filled with beer. And yet from time to time the dancers would set their cups filled with the precious liquid down on the Malecón and in groups of three, or twenty, or sometimes a hundred, dive into the water, gnaw awhile on the Island's foundation, and then return to the Carnival, where they would go on dancing and drinking. Policemen, too, would leave their helmets on the seawall and dive down to gnaw at the Island's foundation. Rumba-dancing black women would disappear from their floats for a few moments, dive in, gnaw awhile, and return to join the dance; army cadets, sailors off the Gulf Fleet (who were therefore expert in aquatic maneuvers), brigade leaders, army officers, and members of the Party would dive down, gnaw, come up again, and then even more enthusiastically applaud the glorious parade. Fabulous trapeze artists would make their way along the center of the avenue that ran beside the Malecón, do an incredible somersault, plunge into the sea, gnaw at the Island's moorings, and somersault back up into the center of the parade, making deep bows to the globe in which Fifo was riding. Behind the acrobats came Halisia Jalonzo, who was dancing the Black Swan while Coco Salas filled the air with mosquitoes; some of the supporting dancers, in a single jeté, would dive into the water, gnaw, and return to the corps de ballet. (One can't say that Halisia turned a blind eye to this behavior because the truth is, she didn't have any choice which eye to turn—they were both blind, and besides, she was *exhausted,* my dear, from having taken part in the act of repudiation that had been held not far from where she was now dancing.)

Behind Halisia came Pablito Malés and Salvia Rodríguez, who were singing (or howling, really) "They're even killing themselves for love"—and weaving in and out between their legs were the terrified she-cats belonging to Karilda Olivar Lubricious, who had disappeared into the crowd. Now thousands of painters were making their way past; perched on a gigantic easel, or dangling from ropes, they were wielding their brushes on a canvas as big as a billboard—and on the canvas there began to emerge a gigantic portrait of Fifo. Then came hundreds of musical groups of every kind—symphony orchestras, bands, conga players—and then all the official limousines with Fifo's VIP guests. (Fifo himself, of course, in his red balloon, was up front leading the parade.) Among the guests, we might make special mention of the Condesa de Merlín in her elegant gig, with her huge fake hairdress and her incredible fan and a midget in blackface sitting on her lap (and sometimes under it). The Condesa was tossing colored streamers into the crowd. So thrilled was the Condesa with the spectacle, and especially with the streamers (the reverse side of which bore a long diatribe against Fifo), that she didn't realize when SuperSatanic, sitting beside her in the gig, jabbed her with the fatal needle (following orders from Miss Chelo). The Condesa, thinking it was an affectionate pinch, thanked SuperSatanic and expelled her from her carriage with a soft kick. . . . As the parade continued, Skunk in a Funk was now searching ever more frantically for Tatica, who had stolen her first pair of swim fins. Although Tatica had disappeared into the crowd of thugs from Arroyo Arenas, Skunk in a Funk continued with her search, for the quest had become a question of honor. Clara Mortera was exhibiting her collection of forbidden costumes—a work that was truly unique and that was the *dernieríssimo cri* in both Carnival and street attire. And yet . . . somehow, she was outdone by Evattt, the Black Widow (which was the name she'd been known by for many, many years), who won the People's Palm for her monumental mourning gown crocheted from black silk and spangled with crosses confected of barbed wire. Hundreds of poets paraded by, reciting a hymn composed in honor of Fifo. And now the journalists were passing, an army of them, taking photos right and left and especially trying to get a picture of Fifo's balloon. Suddenly—breaking up the parade, the wild throng of drums, the ass-swinging and backside-shaking—from out of the crowd rose Raúl Kastro, swathed in a huge mosquito net and wearing a ponytail and a crown of laurel. Sighing piteous and mournful sighs, he pushed his way through the crowd, stood for a moment on the Malecón, and in a final act of protest against Fifo, who had refused to transfer absolute power to him, leaped into the ocean. When the old soldier swathed in mosquito netting fell into the sea like some weird interplanetary parachutist, Fifo, up in his balloon, gave a huge howl of laughter that was echoed by the crowd, who continued dancing wildly. And in the midst of all this hurly-burly, hubbub, and hullabaloo, Delfín Proust announced that the moment had come for the Elevation of the Holy Hammer.

A Tongue Twister (29)

In the midst of the mellifluous melée, Ye-Ye, Yeyo's once-male man-child, now the only remaining go-go queen in Cuba, mooned a marvelously endowed camel, who mistook her manifest meaning and, it makes me grimace to say, martyred her.

To Ye-Ye, a.k.a. Pornopop,
the Only Remaining Go-Go Fairy Queen in Cuba

The Elevation of the Holy Hammer

Several years ago, or maybe it was several hours—with all these drums banging all over the place my poor queer brain has lost all track of time—Fifo, under the alias De Chico, commissioned Delfín Proust, a.k.a. La Reine des Araignées, to pick out the select group of young stud-muffins who would be invited to his grand Fifofest. From among these, Hiram (or La Reine des Araignées) (or Delfín Proust) also was charged with selecting the twink with the biggest, longest, plumpest, sweetest twinkie and the hunkiest physique, who would be, at the head of all the ephebes and other manly youths (and as their very essence), the He-Male whose presence would illuminate the entire vast catacomb in which the Fifiesta was to take place. After countless measurements, taste-tests, trial runs, and computations, the choice fell upon Lázaro González Carriles, a.k.a. the Key to the Gulf. The Key to the Gulf was selected to be, like Juan Arocha one thousand seven years earlier, the escort and "special friend" to all—and I mean *all*—the guests at the Fifofest, and to arouse all the prime ministers, presidents, kings, *grandes dames,* and magnates so that as they were shivered by their orgasmic shudder they would sign not only a trade agreement (favorable to Fifo, of course) but also, if necessary, their own death sentence. The Key to the Gulf, with discretion, gallantry, and great charm, and despite the daggers stared at him by Miss Possessive (Skunk in a Funk to you), carried out his duties with extraordinary ability and success, persuading the president of Argentina to cede to Fifo all of Patagonia and the Prime Ministeress of Canada to sign over the Peninsula of Labrador. . . . And now, with the Carnival in full swing, the divine proportions of the Key to the Gulf's body—his peerless legs, his muscular arms, his narrow waist, his broad chest, the ringlets of his gleaming hair, and (more than anything) that UNBELIEVABLE horse-cock of his—made him the unanimous choice as the love god who would preside over the ceremony of the Elevation of the Holy Hammer. This ceremony could be held only at a moment such as this—this *sacred* moment at which Fifo was celebrating the triumphant apotheosis of his fifty years in power.

The naked youth (or eternal adolescent) was tied to a wooden cross, and since those who were crucifying him could not restrain themselves from caressing his extraordinary member, that rosy phallus grew and GREW and GREW, until it reached truly unparalleled dimensions. Thus, a double erection took place—the young man's erection, and the erection of the gigantic cross that was raised in the center of the Carnival.

"The great gods have been reborn!" cried the cunning Mahoma as she gazed upon the beautiful youth in all his arousal (I mean *glory*) upon the cross.

Instantly, every person knelt before the theophany.

That naked, aroused young man tied up there on that cross was *so* amazing! The crowd could simply not take their *eyes* off him. Or rather, off *it.* For there it hovered, vibrating in the air, like the sword of Damocles, victorious and unconquerable—the most extraordinary phallus that had ever been. And the longer the crowd looked at it, the bigger it got. Hundreds of the faithful bore the cross along, holding it (the cross) aloft. But sometimes they would stop and allow some uncontrollable worshiper to climb up the wooden shaft and before the eyes of the multitude suck that other, fleshy, yet still more glorious shaft—a *living* shaft which, when it received these worshipful attentions, would throb and grow yet longer and thicker and bestow a slap of affection upon the cheek of the desperate shaft-swallower. The beating of the drums grew more and more feverish. Suddenly it was not a solitary faggot or macho man or even woman who wanted to worship the Holy Hammer, but the entire *nation,* my dear. Despite her years, Karilda climbed up on the cross and sucked, and she was followed by her she-cats, who sucked as they clawed in fury at Karilda—with this morsel in front of them, they couldn't bear the *sight* of her anymore. Even the diligent midgets responsible for keeping order climbed the cross like starving squirrels and sucked. . . . Oh, my dear, remarkable things have happened, and will continue to happen, in this world, but the sight of that cross making its way through the multitude with a fully aroused naked man on it, getting his dick sucked by kings, bishops, workingmen, soldiers, Young Communists, young terrorists, cloistered nuns, virginal young ladies, midgets, housewives, and screaming queens—*that,* darling, is a thing unparalleled in the history of things that have stirred, or will stir, this globe. Neither the execution of Marie Antoinette nor the orgies of Catherine the Great nor the apparition of the Virgin Mary to Pope Pius XII nor the sinking of the *Titanic* nor the sudden and most unexpected pregnancy of the King of Sweden nor the death by firing squad of Elena Ceauşescu nor the discovery (which will take place in fifteen years) that the Chief Rabbi of Israel is a woman nor the strange and inexplicable fall of a live whale into the Plaza de España in Madrid (an event which will occur six months from now) nor the fact that the island of Jamaica woke up one morning covered with snow (as happened just last year) nor the electrocution of Ethel Rosenberg nor the storming of the Bastille (which will take place in about ten years) nor the fall of the Berlin Wall nor the revelation (in 1998) that Greta Garbo was a man nor the mysterious disappearance of Australia nor the news (in 1996) that all of Dalí's paintings were painted by José Gómez Sicre nor the fall of the Austro-Hungarian Empire (which will take place three months from now) nor the fall of Fifo (which will take place thirty-five minutes from now) nor the marriage of Prince Pan Carlos to Miss Chelo (which will take place next year) nor the terrible explosion of the Asteria volcano in the Place de Concorde in Paris caused—or will cause, as the case may be—as much amazement and confusion or as much international tail-wagging as the Procession of the Erection. And as the cross-bearers continued to bear the Key to the Gulf through the transfixed and desperate crowd, and as the Key to the Gulf's member was licked or sucked by the licker or sucker of the moment, that member grew ever pinker, ever rosier, and ever more delectably engorged—it was *so* gorgeous that it even made the Three Weird Sisters shiver with delight.

Meanwhile, inside his balloon, Fifo had turned out the light again and was jerking off. The Condesa de Merlín had ordered her black-painted midget to get underneath her skirt and ravish her while she, apparently impassively, went on waving to the crowd.

Despite his obesity, Teodoro Tampon climbed up onto the cross and attached himself to the Key to the Gulf's phallus with such suction that it took two hundred jealous miscreants and a platoon of militiamen to pry him away from that Divine Lollipop. Expert trapeze artists, ballet stars, and members of the clergy would launch themselves into the air, do an airborne pirouette, drop their trousers, and fall ass-first onto the Holy Hammer, which after hammering them would throb so lustily that they would be tossed like flecks of foam into the crowd that was waiting below to climb the cross and enjoy the next Flying Fuck.

Suddenly, out of the midst of the hammering and thumping, a figure emerged—Skunk in a Funk, possessed by jealousy (because she loved the Key to the Gulf) and carrying a step stool, with which she ascended the cross. But instead of falling upon the magnificent stud-sword like everybody else, the evil, resentful creature placed her lips to one of the Key to the Gulf's ears and whispered the following words: "They just opened the Bulgarian embassy. Anybody who can get there can seek asylum. Fifo withdrew his guards."

Hearing those words (which, needless to say, were false), the Key to the Gulf did what almost anybody who lived on the Island would do—he determined to get there any way he could. So he untied himself from the cross and leaped through the crowd from head to head until he could reach the ground and run as hard as he could toward the Bulgarian embassy, in search of political asylum. And immediately the worshipers of the Holy Hammer (who included almost everybody at the Carnival) took off after the young man—who, now leaping along on his prick like some superhung kangaroo or bright pink pogo stick, continued on toward the embassy.

Girl, you had to see it to believe it! I mean *pandemonium* broke out. Everybody took off in hot pursuit of the holy prepuce—even flies. The musicians tootled, the midgets scootled, the policemen-centaurs on their horses stampeded (and their pricks stood stiff) on the trail of the sacrificial young love god. Why, even Halisia was groping her way after him—but maybe she was following the scent with that big nose of hers. So then Skunk in a Funk, knowing that *this* trick hadn't worked to pry her man loose from the raving, screaming crowd, used her stepladder to climb up on the shoulders of the cunning Mahoma and with big tears in her eyes make the following pronouncement:

"I just heard the news! A procession's on the way to the cemetery to bury Virgilio Piñera!"

The Burial of Virgilio Piñera

Quicker than you could say Jack Robin, or is it Jack Rabbit?—I've never been very good at zoology—the crowd froze.

"Yes!" cried Skunk in a Funk, "Virgilio has been murdered and they're taking the body off to bury it. And there's not a single fairy riding on top of the coffin to sprinkle fairy dust . . ."

"Now *that* is inconceivable!" bellowed Mahoma, raising his voice till it cracked, as though she were Skunk in a Funk (who now was only doing lip-synch). "The greatest man—I mean queen—in Cuba has been murdered and they're carrying her off to bury her in the middle of the night so nobody will attend the funeral, and us standing here dancing and chasing a disgusting AC-DC! It's our duty to get over to Virgilio's burial as quick as we can and pay him our last respects—show our gratitude to the man, I mean queen, who sacrificed everything for us girls. Come on, you ingrates! Let's get a wiggle on!"

The news of Virgilio's murder and clandestine burial ran like wildfire through the crowd. The whole country did an about-face and began making its way by any means it could find toward Colón Cemetery—the same cemetery toward which a black hearse was even now racing at full speed with the mortal remains of the author of Electra Garrigó. Soon the crowd caught sight of the funeral car—which was not so much racing as *flying,* girl, down Calle Línea—and the chase was on! Thousands of people started running as fast as they could. Hundreds of queens hopped into cabs at Fifo's taxi stands, while others commandeered buses and some were reduced to scooters (you know, those kids' scooters you haven't seen since the fifties). Teenagers hopped on their bicycles.

The most alert members of Fifo's political police force joined the procession bearing large wreaths and sprays of roses among which they'd concealed tape recorders with supersensitive microphones that could pick up the slightest remark, complaint, weeping, lament, sigh, sniffle, or other expression of emotion. Also swelling the procession were thousands of people who knew Virgilio Piñera only by name, or not even that, but who considered it their duty (or an act of protest against Fifo) to accompany him on his last journey. There were also, of course, thousands of midgets and other agents of public order. In a word, for whatever reason, the Carnival crowd swung around and headed at full speed for the Colón Cemetery, where the burial of the great poet was to take place.

Since he couldn't control the crowd, Fifo decided to join it, so he ordered his diligent midgets to blow his balloon as hard as they could toward the cemetery. Immediately he got on his walkie-talkie and told Paula Amanda to prepare a eulogy. Behind Fifo streamed all of his VIP guests. The Condesa de Merlín hung a mourning ribbon on her gig and began to pray a prayer in French—doubtless something from Bossuet. The fact was, virtually everyone was sincerely moved. Even Karilda Olivar Lubricious, once more hotly pursued by her indefatigable husband, stopped in the middle of the crowd, turned to him, and held her arms skyward and cried: "Go ahead, kill me if you must, but let's not go on with this scene at such a tragic moment!" The wannabe murderer dropped his saber, lowered his eyes, and took Karilda by the hand, while the she-cats, softened by grief, mewled in mourning at the couple's feet.

The Key to the Gulf lowered his flag to half-staff, picked some leaves off a banana tree growing in a yard in El Vedado, covered his nakedness, and joined the funeral procession. Evattt, the Black Widow, accompanied the cortège on skates, her enormous gown (most remarkably suited for a state funeral) flying out behind her.

Meanwhile, learning of Fifo's latest murder, the rodents wept as they gnawed ever more furiously at the Island's foundation. Even the sharks, like reincarnated steeds of Patroclus, wept as they gnawed, for they too were moved by the death of the brilliant faggot. (Of course, since they were underwater, no one—save I—was aware of those tears that swelled the ocean.)

But Skunk in a Funk, bowed with grief, and Clara Mortera, defeated in the costume contest by Evattt, declined to join the funeral stampede. Instead, they returned to their respective hovels. As they were entering Old Havana, now deserted, they saw Padre Gastaluz riding toward the cemetery on a wagon pulled by Cynthio Metier.

"Faster! Faster!" Padre Gastaluz was shouting at Cynthio as he whacked him with his enormous scapular. "Faster, or I'll never get there in time to give Virgilio a last blessing!"

The Departure

So fierce and compelling (to say the least) were the blows rained down on Cynthio Metier by Padre Gastaluz that soon they had overtaken the hearse that was racing toward the cemetery at full speed—because, as the reader will recall, Fifo wanted Virgilio's burial, which could no longer be kept secret, to be performed before the whole Island got there. But all the hearse driver's efforts were in vain, because by the time the vehicle arrived at the cemetery, the whole city, in Carnival clothes and mourning faces, was awaiting the remains of the poet, to bid him one last farewell.

"Get it over with as fast as possible," Fifo had ordered Paula Amanda, who in order not to compromise herself, and also be *very* brief, had composed a farewell eulogy of only eight words. The text read by Paula Amanda was as follows:

"Virgilio Piñera was born and died in Cuba."

The coffin was borne to the graveside, Padre Gastaluz sprinkled it with holy water from his silver holy-watering can, and it was launched with great dispatch (under the supervisory eye of Marcia Leseca) into the open grave. But the sound that was heard as the coffin slipped into the grave was not that of wood on earth, but rather the splash of something falling into water—water that in fact splashed all those who had gathered at the edge of the grave for the farewell. Clearly, this wasn't a proper *interment* because the body hadn't been consigned to a resting place on *terra firma,* but rather dumped into the water. Hearing the soft rippling of the water that was running two or three yards underground, everyone realized that the Island had at last been freed from its moorings, and that the funeral splash was the first notice of total liberation.

The Island, gnawed off its foundation, was drifting off into the unknown.

A Tongue Twister (The Last One)

Let us march, then, militarily, down to an emaciated sea where a marmoreal marmot murmurs myriads of mistreatments. . . . And yet we find that we have come, finally, to the finest fuckup of them all, the great floating flophouse where a phonograph forever flutes its philanthropic fluff and an unphotogenic, fetid, syphilitic, aphonic mephitic proffers us, frothing at the mouth, his furious physiognomy. *Ay-y-y-e-e-e.*

To all of us . . .

Clara in Flames

When Clara Mortera entered her room, she was overwhelmed by a sense of defeat. The glorious costumes that she had worked on with such love, such commitment, such devotion had not won the prize. And the worst part about it was that she had been beaten by Evattt, a frivolous woman who knew not the first thing (according to Clara) about the art of true dissipation or the profundity of exhibitionism. And she had lost Teodoro Tampon at the Carnival. Yet even more serious was the fact that her husband had climbed up on the cross on which the Key to the Gulf's engorged cock was on display for all to see and, dressed in the regal robes that Clara had created for him, publicly sucked it for much longer than the prescribed time—so long, in fact, that he had had to be pulled from it, like a leech, by the crowd. Despite the kicks and blows he had received (including some that Clara herself had given him), Teodoro had disappeared in a renewed search for the Key to the Gulf's peerless and impeccable phallus. Teodoro had never shown such devotion for Clara. And as though all *that* weren't enough, Clara's children had abandoned her after her defeat at the costume exhibit because they realized that she was finished—no one would ever again buy one of her forbidden costumes. "I have been defeated, but I shall not be destroyed," thought Clara, taking a deep breath and assuming a Hemingwayesque air (which tended to happen at her age and with her self-destructive inclinations). "No, I am not destroyed. I have my work, I have my paintings."

And Clara Mortera opened the hole that led to the convent, thinking to console herself by gazing upon her lifework. But the lifework no longer existed. When Fifo's thugs had entered the convent to take the portrait of Karilda Olivar Lubricious to give Virgilio Piñera a heart attack with, they had (perhaps on Fifo's orders, perhaps out of sheer pleasure) destroyed all the rest of Clara's paintings. The tapestries, the sheets, and the mosquito netting that had borne the brilliant work lay now in shreds and tatters. Nothing remained of the painter's marvelous paintings.

For several minutes Clara stood and contemplated the disaster. Then she went to where she'd hidden the two cans of kerosene, poured the liquid all over her body, took out a box of Chispa-brand matches, and struck a match. But it was not exactly a spark that was produced—it was more like the lighting of a gigantic torch, or the eruption of a volcano. The entire convent went up in flames, and a giant ball of fire engulfed the entire block. In seconds, the sparks and ashes had risen into the clouds.

Pandemonium

It was drifting, drifting, drifting away. The Island was drifting away. This was not just some faggoty queen who'd thrown herself into the ocean and turned into a red snapper (like Ñica and company) and swum off for Key West, not just some army recruit who'd gotten tired of the humiliations and abuses of the military and thrown himself into the sea on an inner tube, not just some big muscular black man who had been doubly discriminated against (first as a man and then as a black man) and built himself a raft, not just some family that had hammered together a raft out of the dining table and launched themselves into the gulf, nor was it even just *thousands* of people fleeing on anything that floated in search of a future that was uncertain but at least gave them *some* hope. No, this time it was the whole country—and it was floating away, in geographical, geological flight. This was an exodus unlike any other in the history of exoduses—the Island of Cuba, unmoored from its foundations, was sailing out of the Gulf like some huge ocean liner, leaving a wake of choppy, foaming waves and making its way toward the open sea. It was leaving behind the great catacomb-palace as it sank into the ocean, computers howling, to the sound of muffled explosions of fury, leaving behind the immense underground arsenals of weapons, the atomic warehouses, the tunnels built by Fifo where he could take refuge in case of an emergency, the treasures which he'd buried (like the typical campesino he was) in deep holes out in the backyard. All of that was now covered with ocean.

And as the Island floated away, the people of the Island, seized by the euphoria of flight and therefore of freedom, began to shout with joy, and with their hands, like oars, they tried to steer the Island . . . each one to a different place.

Meanwhile, Fifo, inside his balloon, ordered his midgets to machine-gun all the conspirators, knife all the traitors, hang all the leaders of the rebellion *pour encourager les autres,* use any and all means necessary to wipe out anyone who applauded, sweep Havana and all rebel cities for guerrillas, and if necessary drop the atomic bomb. "Let their blood bathe the world all the way to Poland!" he screamed in fury (from inside his balloon). But the midgets weren't listening. They were desperately throwing themselves into the water, because they knew that if they remained on the Island they'd be torn to pieces by enraged mobs. And besides—what weapons were they supposed to use to defend themselves with, if all the arsenals had been lost to the waves? And so, one by one or sometimes in groups of a hundred or as many as a thousand, the midgets were throwing themselves into the water and, as they did so, being devoured by patrolling sharks, vast numbers of which had become sworn enemies of Fifo after the immolation of Mayoya. The sharks figured, logically, that at this point, anybody who jumped into the water was a Fifonian agent trying to get away. Inside his balloon, Fifo was jumping up and down and stamping his feet, but the midgets just went on throwing themselves into the ocean, as did any number of military types and high officials—although others, more calculating, went over to the side of the rodents and in fact became those who most loudly applauded the triumph of this departure and most furiously called for Fifo's head. "Kill him, kill him, kill him now—for years he's showed us how!" was the chant that everyone was chanting, including Fray Bettino, Miss Miguel Barniz, Miss Paula Amanda, and even Vilma Spinar (that was her new last name). Many foreign VIPs made their getaway on anything that flew or floated, but others stayed and organized anti-Fifo committees and movements. The Condesa de Merlín, who had raised the French tricolor on her gig, was shouting for Fifo to be guillotined. Güé Güevavara wanted to make an example of the execution. Even the Marquesa de Macondo was now declaring that what was happening was "marvelous," and she confessed that on several occasions she had tried to kill Fifo but had just never quite managed. So now the base marquesa was a heroine. . . . Good lord, the clamor of this crowd—which up until a few minutes ago had been applauding Fifo but now was calling for his head—grew louder and louder, more and more insistent. And Fifo, inside his balloon, was still floating less than three feet above the crowd—although he was unable to control the device, since by now the midgets who had been blowing on it to move it along had all perished in the jaws of the sharks. And so, Fifo thought he was going to die of asphyxiation inside that transparent balloon of his—he tore at his clothes, screamed hysterically, whirled about like a snake on hot coals, clenched his fists, shouted, made threatening gestures that for all those down in the streets looking up at him were no more than strange, silent mimicry, because when the midgets and government officials and military men who were in charge of the microphones had disappeared or died, Fifo's voice could no longer be heard outside his illuminated globe—and now, through the curse of technology, the light couldn't be turned off, either. Seeing Fifo's mad contortions, the crowd gave a unanimous howl of laughter. Then out of the crowd there emerged a queen—Mahoma? Sanjurjo? Uglíssima? La Reine des Araignées? The SuperChelo? Miss Coco Salas?—who, removing a hatpin from somewhere about her person, punctured the balloon in which Fifo was riding. Instantly, the balloon shot off like a comet, sputtering and farting. Then, like some gigantic condom tossed into the toilet bowl, it plummeted (with Fifo still aboard) into the sea, where Bloodthirsty Shark awaited it, jaws open.

All across the floating Island, a shout of joy was heard.

And now, some people proposed that they head for the United States as quickly as possible, since they needed economic aid. But another group, led by Odoriferous Gunk, insisted that they turn the Island toward England and become a member of the British Commonwealth. But no sooner had this group been heard than another insisted even more determinedly that they should turn the bow toward Spain, "because that's where we all came from, and this is no time to be learning a foreign language." Then a leader of the black population said in a powerful voice that if they were going to sail to any continent it ought to be to the continent of *Africa,* because the Carnival itself, whose drumbeats had freed them from their chains, was living proof of the African roots of the Cuban people—and turning theory into practice, he dipped his hands into the sea and began to turn the Island toward the Cape of Good Hope. "Now is no time to turn *backward,* my friends!" shouted the followers of the Condesa de Merlín. "Why return to Africa, the past, when there is a more civilized destination available—the destination of the future: *France!*" And the Condesa de Merlín and her group attempted to turn the Island toward France. But another committee, calling itself the SuperIndependent Party, was in favor of political neutrality and therefore had reached the conclusion—the *emphatic* conclusion—that if the Island was going anywhere it ought to go to Switzerland. . . . "To die of cold and even let our gods freeze over?" sarcastically asked a patriarchal, bearded figure. "No! No! *No!* We are Latin Americans! Let us sail southward, and anchor near the Malvinas—what the British arrogantly call the Falklands—or the coast of Brazil!"

"Enough of this stupid nationalism!" cried the leader of a group called the Centro-Democratic Party. "We should moor our Island near longitude 40, latitude 37, which is a location that all the ships and planes of the civilized world pass by."

"I propose that we head for the Black Sea and join the new political movement in the Caucasus," suggested Lois Suradíaz, who had once been buttfucked by a swimmer on the Black Sea.

"To India!" cried a queen who had seen *Pather Panchali* about a thousand times.

"To Sumatra, where we can live in peace, far from all political dirty tricks!" cried a creature of wilderness tendencies, who then added convincingly—"I mean, *nobody* talks about Sumatra!"

"I ask you, my friends, my sons and daughters, to imagine what it would mean to sail into Venice and be only a few kilometers from Rome. I believe that with the help of God, we could drop anchor in the Adriatic," proposed Padre Gastaluz solemnly.

"To Japan!" commanded an electrical engineer.

"To New Guinea!" shouted a lady who could have an orgasm only when she was screwed by a crocodile.

While this discussion was going on, the midgets who had stayed on the Island, hiding among the trees, felt compelled to throw themselves into the sea, and those who didn't do so of their own accord were launched seaward by the crowd, which also tossed overboard all those who (in their opinion) were suspected of having collaborated with Fifo—which meant that the number of sharks that now prowled the waters just offshore grew greater by the minute. And meanwhile, the Island, with Clara in flames, continued drifting away.

Message in a Bottle

Heedless of all that, because wrapped in her own tragedy (the death of Virgilio, her public betrayal by the Key to the Gulf, the impossibility of making Tatica pay), Skunk in a Funk slunk to her room in the Hotel Monserrate. To raise to even greater heights her sense of the tragedy of life, like some new Unamula . . .

"Pu-*leeze,* Mary! It's not Unamula, it's Una*muno.*"

"Are you *never* going to stop pestering me with that idiotic pedantry of yours, Sakuntala? *Unamula!* Do you hear? It's *Unamula* because I *say* it's Unamula! And that's that! I've had it with you, girl—from now on, I'm wiping you off the map! *Forever!*"

To raise to even greater heights her sense of the tragedy of life, like some new Unamula, she looked at herself in the mirror. What a horror. No doubt about it, she was finally an old queen. An old queen with wrinkles and those awful bags under her eyes—look what one bad night had done. "Well, the time has come for your departure, too, honey," Gabriel said to himself as he looked at himself in the mirror. "And besides," added Reinaldo, "yesterday you wrote that letter to your doubles telling them that you were leaving the country today."

And without further ado, the queen climbed up to her barbecue grill, took out the bottles that she'd stashed under the bed, and started filling them with the manuscript pages of her novel *The Color of Summer*—seizing the opportunity to put the finishing touches on it as she stuffed the bottles. When every page of the novel had been rolled up and safely slipped into the bottles, she sealed them, put them in a sack, tossed in the swim fins that her Aunt Orfelina had found for her, and with her precious cargo she started for the beach. Arriving there, Skunk in a Funk pulled on the swim fins and with the huge sack over her shoulder she dived into the water.

At the same instant he hit the water, Reinaldo could see that the Island was quickly drifting away, with the entire population jumping for joy on it. Yes, the Island was drifting away, while Gabriel remained in the same place the Island had been only seconds earlier. So it wasn't exactly that he was *escaping*—it was the Island that was escaping from him. He was bobbing in the center of a swirl of water that not only didn't allow him to swim away but also threatened at every moment to drag him and his bottles under.

Skunk in a Funk looked around her, and she saw Raúl Kastro with a mosquito net, a ponytail, and a crown of laurel floating in the whirlpool as several sharks fought over him. A little farther away she could see Eachurbod, covered with excrement, and floating almost alongside her she saw hundreds of midgets bobbing in the waves, trying to stay afloat, and the Key to the Gulf swimming furiously, trying to escape the voracious sharks. Knowing that at any moment she could be eaten or pulled down in the whirlpool and drowned, Skunk in a Funk began to lob the bottles outside the whirlpool's vortex. Even if she should perish—and that was a real possibility—her work would survive, she thought, opening the sack and hurling bottles. But the moment a bottle would hit the water it would be swallowed up by the sharks. The last one didn't even hit the water; a sexually aroused and very expert shark (it was Bloodthirsty Shark itself) leaped from the sea and caught it in the air. And then the animal, its fearsome eyes looking deep into Gabriel's, dived and headed for Reinaldo, its terrifying teeth gleaming. As the shark devoured her, Skunk in a Funk realized that she was losing her life, but before she did so, she was determined to start her novel again.

The Story

This is the story of an island whose people were never allowed to live in peace, an island that seemed not so much an island as a constant battleground, a vipers' nest of intrigue, abuse, mistreatment, and unending horror—not to mention betrayals, double-crosses, dirty tricks, and backstabbings without number. No one ever forgave anyone for anything, much less greatness. When someone had a brilliant idea, no one would help the person develop the idea; instead, everyone would try to steal it. This is the story of an island that emerged from one war only to get into another, even crueler one, that marched off a battleground into a concentration camp. This is the story of an island on which wrangling, intrigue, bad faith, ulterior motives, and ambitiousness knew no bounds, and where those who didn't shake their ass to that sinister national dance were sooner or later destroyed by the island's curse. Thus the island's inhabitants, unable to stand the island yet equally unable to escape it, decided to rip the island from its foundation and sail away, free, in search of other seas in which to drop anchor and form an independent state. But as they drifted, they could not agree on which sea to drop their anchor in and thereby survive—much less agree on what kind of government to establish. Every single person had a different idea. Every single person wanted, that is, to govern the island the way *they* wanted to, and to steer it in the direction *they* wanted it to go in, no matter what the next person thought. The farther the island floated, the more heated the protests and wrangling grew, and soon people were screaming at each other, insulting one another, throwing tantrums. Finally, the yelling and carrying-on became so violent that the island, which had no foundation, sank into the sea, to the sound of protests, insults, curses, glug-glugs, and muffled whispering.

Afterword

It is 1991, the year *The Color of Summer* was originally written; New Year's Day, 1999, the day that will mark the fortieth anniversary of Fidel Castro's Revolution in Cuba, still lies somewhere in the hazy future. You pick up this recently published book and you begin to read of the great celebration, the Fiesta, the Carnival, that a character named Fifo, a Latin American dictator, is holding to mark his fiftieth year in power (some scoff that it's really only his fortieth but that Fifo says it's fifty because he likes big round numbers). You read on a bit and you learn that the waters surrounding the Island ruled over by Fifo are patrolled by trained sharks with interesting sexual proclivities, that the streets of the Island's cities are policed by an army of "diligent midgets." (The sharks, of course, are not there to keep invaders out, but to keep potential escapees in.) *Ah,* you perhaps think, *this is like Swift, or Voltaire, or maybe even Thomas Pynchon—real life, a real moment in history, rendered grotesque and hilarious through the lens of satire.* And you would be right. This novel would be about to take you on a Swiftean, Voltairean, Pynchonian, and especially Rabelaisian voyage to Fifonian Carnival 1999 and the many Lords (and "Ladies") of Misrule who, in the form of that most disempowered and disenfranchised and downtrodden of citizens, the "sexual pervert," the queer, the queen, invert Order and send up the pretensions (and consequent absurdities) of inevitably macho-associated Power.

It is unfortunate for readers in English that the vagaries of publishing (and, it must be confessed, in part the vagrancies of the translator) have caused this powerful, funny, wrenching novel to be published *after* the future that it foresees, that January 1, 1999, when the Island, unmoored from the seafloor, was supposedly going to drift off into the sunset with a new gaggle of would-be tyrants disputing over the course it should be guided on. Because it would be interesting for us to be able to wait around to find out whether the fate predicted by Reinaldo Arenas for his Island were going to happen also to that other island that his Island is modeled on. But there is still a future in our future, so we may see this outcome yet. . . .

To understand what has brought Arenas' fictive Island to this pass in the first place, consider the novels that comprise his "pentagony" (a punning portmanteau-word he coined for a first novel cycle). There are, as the name implies, five of them; this one, *The Color of Summer,* though the last novel that Arenas ever wrote and here, in English, published last, is the fourth in the series. All the novels take place on this same Island, which it would surely be overly naive of us not to see as Cuba. Read serially, they take readers chronologically, though with certain skips, through the life of a single central character, who may be the "hero" of the pentagony but is almost always beleaguered terribly by the circumstances of his life.

The first novel chronicles the character's miserable childhood on a hard-scrabble farm in pre-Revolutionary Cuba (*Singing From the Well*); the second (*The Palace of the White Skunks*) follows his young manhood in the heady months of the anti-Batista struggle when he is searching for his place in the Army of Revolution and (less successfully) in the New Social Order. The third novel (*Farewell to the Sea*) is set in the first years under the Castro regime, when the hero, conforming to society's and the political order's expectations, is now married and working in an office in the Revolution. This novel, *The Color of Summer,* set fifty (forty) years later, portrays the protagonist as a writer and a queer and a son who's deep in the closet, and the last novel, *The Assault,* takes place in a dystopian future when all the men and women of the Island have been reduced under the emotionally and physically crushing Regime to animals, "vermin," and the hero is a furious, raging nameless Avenger-Son out to get the Mother of all Tyrants. (Arenas himself addresses the shape of the pentagony, and some of his intentions for it, in his "Foreword" on page 225—yes, page 225—of this novel.) From one book to the next, the hero's name changes—it is first Celestino (unless Celestino is an imaginary playmate for the unnamed *real* main character), then Fortunato, then Hector, then Gabriel/Reinaldo/Skunk in a Funk (depending upon whether he is in his role as Dutifully Masculine Son or Long-Suffering Writer or Flaming Queer), then that anonymous no-longer-victim of the fifth novel. But through the changes of name there are two constants that tell us that the character is always the same—first, the character is always a writer, and second, the character is always a homosexual.

Indeed, for the purposes of the themes that run throughout the pentagony, those two identity-tags, "writer" and "homosexual," are one and the same. Arenas makes this clear in *Singing From the Well,* when the boy-hero wants to write, to "tell his story," "sing his song," but no one will give him paper. (In fact, the whole family is illiterate, so there's no paper around.) He steals his grandfather's account books to "scribble" in and is thrashed within an inch of his life, perhaps even killed (there is much ominous talk of "burying the hatchet"), and so as a last recourse he takes a knife and begins to carve poems ("gobbledygook," his grandfather calls them) on the trunks of the trees. Unable to bear this assault on "nature"—one might ask which is worse, though: carving on trees or carving *poetry* on trees—the boy's grandfather takes up that ever-present hatchet and chops down every tree for miles around, while the grandmother has this to say about the boy's writing, or perhaps about writing in general: "That's what girls do." Thus, in the Cuba that Arenas portrays, writing and non-machista malehood, separately and together, are "unnatural," and represent the terrible threat to the Order of Things that arises when a person fails to conform, or questions the status quo, or quests after transcendent beauty (often evoked very movingly by Arenas). It is a threat that the harsh, glaring, hellishly hot reality of this particular society, perhaps all societies, cannot admit or allow. And when Society, the Status Quo, the Family, Social and Sexual Normalcy—all those Institutions with a capital *I*—feel themselves under threat, they defend themselves with violence, fury, rage, and even, sometimes, murderous destruction.

Put the other way around, Arenas' subject is always the crushingly asymmetrical relationship between Power (whether political, social, religious, family, or, in the New Social Order, all of those at once) and the Individual, that person who does not want to live the way his society or his religion or his family says he should live until he's experimented with living the way he's drawn to live. Arenas writes about the buried life of Possibility, the life that is portrayed to us in our dreams and imaginings, the life of sweetness and beauty that our depressing surroundings deny us, the life that is so often taken from us (especially if we live in a "traditional society," and who, in a way, does not?) by those who say they know what's best for us, what's best for *us all.* Arenas' constant question is why differentness must be a curse, why any attempt at freedom of self must finally lead not just to our imprisonment (whether real or self-inflicted: the prison of the closet) but ultimately to our destruction.

Each of the books addresses this question in its own way. *The Color of Summer* does so with wicked satiric humor. This, as we indicated above, is the most Rabelaisian of Arenas' novels; the Carnival planned by Fifo for his fiftieth (fortieth) anniversary allows the oppressed citizens of the Island, and more especially the outcast and persecuted queers among them, to take part in that transgression/inversion of the power structure that Mikhail Bakhtin has discussed in relation to François Rabelais—and they take part in it with, as the saying goes, a vengeance. "No dogma, no authoritarianism, no narrow-minded seriousness can coexist with Rabelaisian images," Bakhtin says; precisely the same is true of the images of Reinaldo Arenas.

With its many different faces and voices, the vengeance portrayed in *The Color of Summer* is embedded in an aesthetic that Bakhtin called grotesque realism. A reflection of the folk idiom of the Middle Ages, its essential components are powerful forces: laughter, mockery/parody/degradation ("the lowering of all that is high"), and behavior transgressive of official norms and dogma, expressed especially in frank talk of sexual acts, body parts, and bodily functions. (This same behavior, this same type of humor characterizes the Cuban *choteo,* which Jorge Mañach, in a famous study, has defined as "taking seriously nothing that ought to be taken seriously.") During Carnival, these forces are allowed out, they are allowed to rule the society; free rein (and free reign) is given to all those aspects associated with the "lower bodily stratum," which during the rest of the year the Establishment, as we used to call it, has done everything it can to suppress. But authorities are clever; they know that they must not *totally* suppress them, for these "lower" instincts can become explosive if they are corked too long; the authorities know that they must allow at least one day during the year when these impulses can be expressed, for they are, as Bakhtin insists (though we already knew it), tied to the universe's powerful forces of regeneration. The earthy folk humor of the Middle Ages and the Renaissance recognized this, Rabelais recognized this, and it is easy to see why Bakhtin, writing at a time when an utterly different (and entirely humorless) aesthetic—Socialist Realism—was being imposed from above, would find so appealing the combination of laughter, degradation, and regeneration that he saw in Rabelais. It is also easy to see why Arenas, in a situation much like Bakhtin's, would also feel the appeal of the forbidden, the appeal of Carnival.

The major reason for this appeal, even more than its elementary "fun," its release of the "wickedness" of laughter, is that the Carnival aesthetic has the capacity to redirect the course of events in positive ways. In this novel, for instance, the Carnival is the final straw that breaks the Island's platform off the seafloor and sends it sailing off toward new and so far undefined, unsocialized horizons. Although the ensuing struggle on the high seas for power and authority makes it difficult to sort through those regenerating elements that Bakhtin viewed as indisputably present in Carnival, Arena's grand Fiesta certainly creates a linguistic, geographic, and social momentum that pushes hard against the stasis of official culture.

The two principles that both Arenas and Bakhtin viewed as absolutely alien to the humorlessness and petrification of dogma are beauty and pleasure. The homosexuals in *The Color of Summer,* like the folk of the Middle Ages, take on the role of defenders of those "pleasure principles"; camping, dressing up, acting out, and fornicating like rabbits, they rub the Establishment's nose in them and, seen now as subversives, try to overthrow the (olive-)drab and petrified official canon. Using laughter, exaggeration, and common, even foul language; converting insulting epithets into powerful signifiers; and recognizing, even embracing, the supreme importance of the lower instincts and their geography in the body, *The Color of Summer*'s Carnival counters the official hierarchy—and a "feast of the fools" is the result, in which the low confront the high with the high's essential absurdity.

One example from the dozens that are possible: At a public and official conference whose hilarious adjectivally burdened name pokes fun at the sobriety of all that comes from above, especially rational thought and categorization, the homosexuals of Fifo's Island, the usual outcasts, get their chance to speak out against the ruling class—and speak out they do. Not only do they denounce the abuses enacted by the regime, but also, in typical carnivalesque spirit, they "out" a number of officials, some of whom are present. This rebellion, this pulling down of the idols that occurs in their act of outing, is pervasive throughout Arenas' work; in the carnivalization of the world that is enacted in this particular novel, the most sacred moments in history are the most likely to be targeted. In one instance, satirizing the central scene of Christianity, crucifixion transforms into crucifuckingfixion as all the orifices of a Great Teacher and Leader (Yasir Arafat in his role as social messiah) are nailed by random phalluses. In another instance, this one clearly tied to "pagan" fertility celebrations, a naked man—a virtual god, and with, of course, an erect phallus—is nailed to a cross and carried dionysiacally, orgiastically through the streets to commemorate the Revolution's fifty fertile, plentiful years. Even Fifo himself, by the fact of his having arisen out of the people, possesses a duality that is similar to Carnival's: at one and the same time, he acts with great seriousness and pisses. Fifo is, at once, all the sexuality and erotics of the people (not a spectator) and nothing but power. His, however, is a *great* power, through which he sanctions but finally unsuccessfully controls a ceremony whose official purpose is to keep tabs on that power and the canon that he prescribes by reining in, temporally and spatially, the queer vagrancies of his people.

Fifo's control is unsuccessful; in the end the rodents, skunks, and fairies win the day. And their corrosive attack on the rock-hard immutability of a tradition-transformed-into-tyranny, their "gnawing at the foundations," finds allies in the novel's nonlinear form (Arenas calls it "cyclonic") and its heteroglossia, which Bakhtin defines as the presence in a "high" literary work of a wide variety of linguistic registers. Linearity and fixed meanings, such as the solemnity with which History treats leaders or the piety with which Christianity faces its Messiah's nailing to the cross, are present in *The Color of Summer* only to be skewered, only to act as the "straight man" for the warping or perverting or "queering" double entendres and tongue twisters of the carnivalesque text. Unlike the official system, which dictates and packages (petrified) truth in neat prose statements, Arenas' novel—containing in addition to narrative prose a rhymed playlet, letters, parodies of literary works, the discourse of both learned disquisitions and fable, tongue twisters, styles ranging from the elegiac to the apoplectic—corresponds to a desire to make manifest the collisions of fields of meaning often suppressed by systems of authority. And so, as in the folk festivals of the Middle Ages, the Arenian Carnival takes on an idiom of its own, which parallels and parodies the official canon. And as we see in the end of the novel, this idiom has the capacity to engender not only linguistic but also geographic shifts. In addition, the entire novel is endowed, like a couple of its characters, with the capacity for temporal and spatial simultaneity, allowing for uncanny encounters between personages representative of the nation's greatness and between those same national treasures and the supreme dung of Carnival. In obedience to this defiant structure, no space in the city, no linguistic signifier representing that space, remains faithful to its proposed function: a urinal is not only a urinal, a convent is not only a convent. Men's rooms may be raised to the "sacred space" of transformative and redemptive (homo)sexual encounter; convents may be plundered for wood with which to make sleeping lofts and platform shoes. In Carnival, these inversions become the new norm against which the authoritarian Norm is measured, and with whose pointed humor the high, inhuman seriousness of that Norm is punctured.

Another inversion central to Arenas' novel, as it is to the Rabelaisian aesthetic, is the inversion of forbidden/permitted in language. Taking his lead, perhaps, from the civil rights struggles of women and blacks and gays in the United States over the last thirty (forty) years, in *The Color of Summer* Arenas turns the insulting epithets of the bigoted Establishment into proud statements of identity. In a society or a time in which politeness is a form of suppression, of exclusion, in which "Negroes" and "homosexuals" and "ladies" are patronized in public with those supposedly respectful terms while behind their backs they are called all those hate- and contempt-filled names that we can surely still remember, and they are *never* fully integrated members of the Establishment, then a clever strategy, as "blacks" and "niggers" (in certain limited contexts, still) and "queers" have seen, is to co-opt the hate-filled name and endow it with pride of identity, pride of self. To call yourself a black or a nigger or a queer in a society that uses those words pejoratively is to say to that society *Yes, I am that hard, strong, defiant person that the name makes you think of, a person as filled with pride and anger as* you *may be by hate.* In the Spanish original of *The Color of Summer,* Arenas used none of the polite and all of the taboo, pejorative words of Cuban homosexuality: *maricón, pájaro, marica, mariquita, loca. . . .* He was never "nice," never "polite," never "well behaved," never "considerate of other people's feelings." He knew that one of the ways a society can work its violence on you is by calling you names—*both* sticks and stones *and* names can, in fact, hurt you—but that at the same time, you can deflect those names by turning them into cries of defiance. Arenas will allow none of his queer characters to be "gay" in that assimilationist meaning of the word which applies to homosexuals in the United States, who may be queer and yet an integral and accepted part of the social fabric, for all of Arenas' queer characters are persecuted, oppressed, under siege, under the constant threat of social and physical nonbeing. And so they are, in this English version, *faggots, fairies, queers, queens. . . .* In English, or in the United States, and in the late nineties, Arenas' strategy surely will not seem terribly shocking (though sometimes he is emphatically *not* politically correct), but just as Spanish-language letters had not for a long time, perhaps never, seen a book as open and unapologetic and homosexually graphic as Arenas' autobiography *Before Night Falls (Antes que anochezca),* so *The Color of Summer (El color del verano)* was something of a *succès de scandale* when it came out. Arenas knew that one way of getting the (Spanish-speaking) bourgeoisie's attention was (*pace* Nelson Algren) by slapping it in the face with a mackerel. Arenas' novel does not portray a world in which "gay pride" is possible, and so it must be "queer pride," or even "faggot pride"—harder, more in-your-face, more defiant, more dangerous and revolutionary (at least as seen from the perspective of the Revolution).

We must also remember that Cuba—indeed, Latin America in general—has not experienced "coming-out" in the same way the United States has. "Gay"-ness, as that social construct is defined and lived in the U.S., is not native to those countries, and even though there is a great deal of U.S. cultural influence in Latin America, the naturalization of the construct "gay" is far from complete. As Ian Lumsden tells us in his book *Machos, Maricones, and Gays: Cuba and Homosexuality,* it means a different thing to be a homosexual in the U.S. than in the various countries of Latin America and the Caribbean. That cultural difference has, then, also influenced the choice of epithets to be used in the translation for the homosexuals of Arenas' novel; they do not inhabit the U.S., and so they are *never* "gay."

Yet another transgressive strategy used by Arenas is what we might call multigendering. In one paragraph, one sentence of the original Spanish, a character may be *el,* "he," and *ella,* "she," and then *el* again. The translation has respected those shifting gender-attributions caused by Arenas' switching back and forth of pronoun gender for a single character—readers should not think that someone forgot to proofread the manuscript. Arenas also frequently transgenders his characters, calling a male character "*La* Something"—the Spanish equivalent of saying "*Miss* Something"—when the person referred to is male but queer or, at times, uppity. The translation generally renders this as "Miss X," though sometimes it uses some other clearly "bitchy," "queenly" locution. In this regard, Arenas' camping is thoroughgoing, and used the way even straight audiences of *La Cage aux Folles* or *Torch Song Trilogy* have been made aware it is used—for "attitude."

But we must be clear about campiness and queerness: being scandalous was not only Arenas' way of saying "I am" but also his way of making two broadly human points, applicable to all, gay or straight: first, all persons deserve the freedom to live as they want to live, without the oppressions and constraints that are imposed from somewhere above; and second, the imagination must be given free rein, for only thus can beauty be brought into the world. Arenas' novella *The Brightest Star* (*Arturo, la estrella más brillante*) is a working-out in fiction of that last postulate.

Seen in this way, homosexuality, or queerness, is but one of a number of *metaphors,* as much as *issues,* that Arenas uses to portray the larger, overarching struggle of Power versus Freedom. The political system of Cuba is another of those metaphors—an obvious one—but so is the family, and especially the mother-son relationship; so is religion; so is salaried work; and so, amazingly enough, is the weather, which in Arenas' novels batters the characters into submission. The artfulness of Arenas was, as it is of any great writer, to make *literature* out of the stuff of life—and not only out of the stuff of life, but out of all the rest of literature as well. All of these novels are shot through with, even based on, literary allusions and parallels and references. In *Farewell to the Sea,* the seven days of Creation form one of the scaffoldings upon which the "plot" is hung; in *The Assault,* there are explicit parallels with Aeschylus' *The Libation-Bearers.* This novel, *The Color of Summer,* might be seen on one level as a rewriting, in fiction, of Bakhtin's ideas on Carnival and on political and social satire; its subtitle makes explicit its debt to the ideas and figures of Hieronymus Bosch. Many of Arenas' novels borrow their shapes and approaches and styles from other genres and a range of techniques: science fiction, Greek drama, other sorts of theatrical presentation, the dramatic monologue, magic realism, Swiftean satire (one thinks inevitably of Gulliver throughout Arenas), fable, the tongue twister, the ballad, the operetta, nursery rhymes. . . . (The list goes on and on.) Thus, while there is much that is autobiographical in this and the other novels (and this one in particular asks to be seen as a roman à clef), Arenas' work is also, and we believe more importantly, a dense literary fabric that has an integrity and an aesthetic of its own; its debts to life, while great, are nothing in comparison with its debts to the world of literature that Reinaldo Arenas so desperately wanted to inhabit yet was for so many years cruelly prevented even from visiting. (His novels were banned in Cuba, and his reading privileges at the National Library were revoked.)

Now that we have brought up the question of *The Color of Summer* as a roman à clef, a word no doubt needs to be said about the playlet that begins the novel and about some of the characters that are seen within the novel per se. As though he wanted to erase the "fourth wall" that stands between the reader of fiction and the book just as it is felt to stand between the playgoer and the play, Arenas begins this novel with a closet-drama, inviting the reader to imagine the two locales, Key West and Havana, standing off ninety miles from one another, and the characters that tread the boards there—this is not a novel in the realist vein, a "slice of life," he is saying, but very clearly a *literary* work. (To make the point all the clearer, he makes the first fifty or so pages of his novel, the pages of the playlet, rhyme—though more on the order of Ogden Nash than Shakespeare.) The situation is this: To celebrate his anniversary, Fifo has decided to stage a grand cultural gala, using (co-opting) the biggest stars of Cuban literature to give luster to the event. To make the gala even more awe-inspiring, he has decided to bring the very greatest lights of Cuban culture back from the dead—namely, the poets José Martí and Gertrudis Gómez de Avellaneda and the novelist José Lezama Lima. (Martí and Avellaneda are poets whose verses Cuban schoolchildren learn by heart, as American schoolchildren learn, or used to learn, Longfellow and Poe and Frost; Lezama Lima is as legendary a novelist in Spanish-language letters as Joyce or Faulkner is in English.) Trouble is, Avellaneda will have nothing to do with Cuba or with allowing herself to be used to legitimate Fifo, and so she makes a run for it (in a matter of speaking), over the sea, trying to get to Key West and safety. At that, Fifo stages an act of repudiation, and this is where the curtain rises.

As the characters come on stage, many of the lines they speak, especially in the case of the poets and novelists, are famous lines taken from their works, and in the Spanish original Arenas italicizes those lines. Here they have been translated to fit into the context Arenas builds for them, this hilarious doggerel he weaves their grand poetry into, and likewise italicized so that the reader can at least know that they are instances of Arenas' intertextualizing. English-language readers may miss some of the references, some of the allusions, some of the fun of Arenas' spoofing, but by imagining that all the lights of Cuban literature (whether in Cuba or abroad) and the entirety of Fifo's entourage are being skewered on the sharp pen of Arenas, the play will be *almost* perfectly comprehensible.

What is supremely clear, in the playlet and in the novel as a whole, is that even in the worst of times, the human spirit of the oppressed and abused allows them to find humor in their situation. The "facts" that Arenas narrates are appalling, the conditions of life that he portrays are often subhuman, and yet through creativity and ingenuity, the characters of his novel, and of his real-life Havana, draw pleasure, even hilarity, out of their Fifo-constricted lives. The Cuban *choteo*—irreverent humor, black humor, gallows humor which takes seriously nothing that "ought" to be taken seriously—is, like Rabelaisian humor, redemptive; it springs from the indomitable spirit of the folk. This novel, and the pentagony as a whole, is a tribute to that indomitable human spirit, which in Arenas' case is not a cliché, but the central fact of his tragic life and all his writing.

Andrew Hurley
Jacqueline Loss
San Juan, Puerto Rico
Austin, Texas
September 1999

A Note on the Translation

The one-act playlet that begins this novel is a farce, written in a kind of doggerel. Taking my cue from the high comedy and irreverent tone of that text, I have produced a playful and some would say "irreverent" translation that is, I think, faithful to it in spirit. Just as servility and sobriety are anathema in those pages, servility and sobriety in the translation would have betrayed them.

Andrew Hurley